FOUCAULT'S PENDULUM

Umberto Eco is internationally renowned as a novelist, philosopher, historian and literary critic. *The Name of the Rose* was his first novel and became a bestseller throughout the world. He has written another novel, *The Island of the Day Before*, and published collections of essays, including *Faith in Fakes*, and *How to Travel with a Salmon*. A professor of semiotics at the University of Bologna, he lives in Milan.

Umberto Eco

FOUCAULT'S PENDULUM

VINTAGE BOOKS
London

Published by Vintage 2001

13 15 17 19 20 18 16 14

Copyright © 1988 Gruppo Editoriale Fabbri Bompiani,
Sonzogno Eta S.p.A., Milano
English translation copyright © 1989
Harcourt Brace Jovanovich, Inc.

Vintage
Random House, 20 Vauxhall Bridge Road,
London SW1V 2SA

www.vintage-books.co.uk

Addresses for companies within The Random House Group
Limited can be found at: www.randomhouse.co.uk/offices.htm

The Random House Group Limited Reg. No. 954009

A CIP catalogue record for this book
is available from the British Library

ISBN 9780099287155

The Random House Group Limited supports The Forest
Stewardship Council (FSC), the leading international forest
certification organisation. All our titles that are printed on
Greenpeace approved FSC certified paper carry the FSC logo.
Our paper procurement policy can be found at
www.rbooks.co.uk/environment.

Printed in the UK by CPI Bookmarque, Croydon, CR0 4TD

Only for you, children of doctrine and learning, have we written this work. Examine this book, ponder the meaning we have dispersed in various places and gathered again; what we have concealed in one place we have disclosed in another, that it may be understood by your wisdom.
    —Heinrich Cornelius Agrippa von Nettesheim, *De occulta philosophia*, 3, 65

Superstition brings bad luck.
    —Raymond Smullyan, *5000 B.C.*, 1.3.8

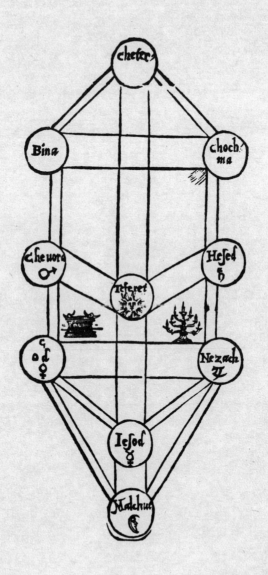

Table of Contents

NEZAH

HOD

YESOD

MALKHUT

KETER

I

ב) והנה בהיות אור הא״ס נמשך,
בבחינת (ה) קו ישר תוך החלל
הנ״ל, לא נמשך ונתפשט (ו) תיכף
עד למטה, אמנם היה מתפשט לאט
לאט, רצוני לומר, כי בתחילה הת־
חיל קו האור להתפשט, ושם תיכף
(ז) בתחילת התפשטותו בסוד קו,
נתפשט ונמשך ונעשה, כעין (ח)
גלגל אחד עגול מסביב.

That was when I saw the Pendulum.

The sphere, hanging from a long wire set into the ceiling of the choir, swayed back and forth with isochronal majesty.

I knew—but anyone could have sensed it in the magic of that serene breathing—that the period was governed by the square root of the length of the wire and by π, that number which, however irrational to sublunar minds, through a higher rationality binds the circumference and diameter of all possible circles. The time it took the sphere to swing from end to end was determined by an arcane conspiracy between the most timeless of measures: the singularity of the point of suspension, the duality of the plane's dimensions, the triadic beginning of π, the secret quadratic nature of the root, and the unnumbered perfection of the circle itself.

I also knew that a magnetic device centered in the floor beneath issued its command to a cylinder hidden in the heart of the sphere, thus assuring continual motion. This device, far from interfering with the law of the Pendulum, in fact permitted its manifestation, for in a vacuum any object hanging from a weightless and unstretchable wire free of air resistance and friction will oscillate for eternity.

The copper sphere gave off pale, shifting glints as it was struck by the last rays of the sun that came through the great stained-glass windows. Were its tip to graze, as it had in the past, a layer of damp sand spread on the floor of the choir, each swing would make a light furrow, and the furrows, changing direction imperceptibly, would widen to form a breach, a groove with radial symmetry— like the outline of a mandala or pentaculum, a star, a mystic rose. No, more a tale recorded on an expanse of desert, in tracks left by countless caravans of nomads, a story of slow, millennial migrations, like those of the people of Atlantis when they left the continent of Mu and roamed, stubbornly, compactly, from Tasmania to Greenland, from Capricorn to Cancer, from Prince Edward Island to the Svalbards. The tip retraced, narrated anew in compressed time what they had done between one ice age and another, and perhaps were doing still, those couriers of the Masters. Perhaps the tip grazed Agarttha, the center of the world, as it journeyed from Samoa to Novaya Zemlya. And I sensed that a single pattern united Avalon, beyond the north wind, to the southern desert where lies the enigma of Ayers Rock.

At that moment of four in the afternoon of June 23, the Pendulum was slowing at one end of its swing, then falling back lazily toward the center, regaining speed along the way, slashing confidently through the hidden parallelogram of forces that were its destiny.

Had I remained there despite the passage of the hours, to stare at that bird's head, that spear's tip, that obverse helmet, as it traced its diagonals in the void, grazing the opposing points of its astigmatic circumference, I would have fallen victim to an illusion: that the Pendulum's plane of oscillation had gone full circle, had returned to its starting point in thirty-two hours, describing an ellipse that rotated around its center at a speed proportional to the sine of its latitude. What would its rotation have been had it hung instead from the dome of Solomon's Temple? Perhaps the Knights had tried it there, too. Perhaps the solution, the final meaning, would have been no different. Perhaps the abbey church of Saint-Martin-des-Champs was the true Temple. In any case, the experiment would work perfectly only at the Pole, the one place where the Pendulum, on the earth's extended axis, would complete its cycle in twenty-four hours.

But this deviation from the Law, which the Law took into account, this violation of the rule did not make the marvel any less marvelous. I knew the earth was rotating, and I with it, and Saint-Martin-des-Champs and all Paris with me, and that together we were rotating beneath the Pendulum, whose own plane never changed direction, because up there, along the infinite extrapolation of its wire beyond the choir ceiling, up toward the most distant galaxies, lay the Only Fixed Point in the universe, eternally unmoving.

So it was not so much the earth to which I addressed my gaze but the heavens, where the mystery of absolute immobility was celebrated. The Pendulum told me that, as everything moved—earth, solar system, nebulae and black holes, all the children of the great cosmic expansion—one single point stood still: a pivot, bolt, or hook around which the universe could move. And I was now taking part in that supreme experience. I, too, moved with the all, but I could see the One, the Rock, the Guarantee, the luminous mist that is not body, that has no shape, weight, quantity, or quality, that does not see or hear, that cannot be sensed, that is in no place, in no time, and is not soul, intelligence, imagination, opinion, number, order, or measure. Neither darkness nor light, neither error nor truth.

I was roused by a listless exchange between a boy who wore glasses and a girl who unfortunately did not.

"It's Foucault's Pendulum," he was saying. "First tried out in a cellar in 1851, then shown at the Observatoire, and later under the dome of the Panthéon with a wire sixty-seven meters long and a sphere weighing twenty-eight kilos. Since 1855 it's been here, in a smaller version, hanging from that hole in the middle of the rib."

"What does it do? Just hang there?"

"It proves the rotation of the earth. Since the point of suspension doesn't move . . ."

"Why doesn't it move?"

"Well, because a point . . . the central point, I mean, the one right in the middle of all the points you see . . . it's a geometric point; you can't see it because it has no dimension, and if something has no dimension, it can't move, not right or left, not up or down. So it doesn't rotate with the earth. You understand? It can't even rotate around itself. There is no 'itself.' "

"But the earth turns."

"The earth turns, but the point doesn't. That's how it is. Just take my word for it."

"I guess it's the Pendulum's business."

Idiot. Above her head was the only stable place in the cosmos, the only refuge from the damnation of the panta rei, and she guessed it was the Pendulum's business, not hers. A moment later the couple went off—he, trained on some textbook that had blunted his capacity for wonder, she, inert and insensitive to the thrill of the infinite, both oblivious of the awesomeness of their encounter—their first and last encounter—with the One, the Ein-Sof, the Ineffable. How could you fail to kneel down before this altar of certitude?

I watched with reverence and fear. In that instant I was convinced that Jacopo Belbo was right. What he told me about the Pendulum I had attributed to esthetic raving, to the shapeless cancer taking gradual shape in his soul, transforming the game into reality without his realizing it. But if he was right about the Pendulum, perhaps all the rest was true as well: the Plan, the Universal Plot. And in that case I had been right to come here, on the eve of the summer solstice. Jacopo Belbo was not crazy; he had simply, through his game, hit upon the truth.

But the fact is that it doesn't take long for the experience of the Numinous to unhinge the mind.

I tried then to shift my gaze. I followed the curve that rose from the capitals of the semicircle of columns and ran along the ribs of the vault toward the key, mirroring the mystery of the ogive, that supreme static hypocrisy which rests on an absence, making the columns believe that they are thrusting the great ribs upward and the ribs believe that they are holding the columns down, the vault being both all and nothing, at once cause and effect. But I realized that to neglect the Pendulum that hung from the vault while admiring the vault itself was like becoming drunk at the stream instead of drinking at the source.

The choir of Saint-Martin-des-Champs existed only so that, by virtue of the Law, the Pendulum could exist; and the Pendulum existed so that the choir could exist. You cannot escape one infinite,

I told myself, by fleeing to another; you cannot escape the revelation of the identical by taking refuge in the illusion of the multiple.

Still unable to take my eyes from the key of the vault, I retreated, step by step, for I had learned the path by heart in the few minutes I had been there. Great metal tortoises filed past me on either side, imposing enough to signal their presence at the corner of my eyes. I fell back along the nave toward the front entrance, and again those menacing prehistoric birds of wire and rotting canvas loomed over me, evil dragonflies that some secret power had hung from the ceiling of the nave. I saw them as sapiential metaphors, far more meaningful than their didactic pretext. A swarm of Jurassic insects and reptiles, allegory of the long terrestrial migrations the Pendulum was tracing, aimed at me like angry archons with their long archeopterix-beaks: the planes of Bréguet, Blériot, Esnault, and the helicopter of Dufaux.

To enter the Conservatoire des Arts et Métiers in Paris, you first cross an eighteenth-century courtyard and step into an old abbey church, now part of a later complex, but originally part of a priory. You enter and are stunned by a conspiracy in which the sublime universe of heavenly ogives and the chthonian world of gas guzzlers are juxtaposed.

On the floor stretches a line of vehicles: bicycles, horseless carriages, automobiles; from the ceiling hang planes. Some of the objects are intact, though peeling and corroded by time, and in the ambiguous mix of natural and electric light they seem covered by a patina, an old violin's varnish. Others are only skeletons or chassis, rods and cranks that threaten indescribable tortures. You picture yourself chained to a rack, something digging into your flesh until you confess.

Beyond this sequence of antique machines—once mobile, now immobile, their souls rusted, mere specimens of the technological pride that is so keen to display them to the reverence of visitors—stands the choir, guarded on the left by a scale model of the Statue of Liberty Bartholdi designed for another world, and on the right by a statue of Pascal. Here the swaying Pendulum is flanked by the nightmare of a deranged entomologist—chelae, mandibles, antennae, proglottides, and wings—a cemetery of mechanical corpses that look as if they might all start working again at any moment—magnetos, monophase transformers, turbines, converters, steam engines, dynamos. In the rear, in the ambulatory beyond the Pendulum, rest Assyrian idols, and Chaldean, Carthaginian, great Baals whose bellies, long ago, glowed red-hot, and Nuremberg Maidens whose hearts still bristle with naked nails: these were once airplane engines. Now they form a horrible garland of simulacra that lie in adoration of the Pendulum; it is as if the progeny of Reason and the Enlightenment had been condemned to stand guard forever over the ultimate symbol of Tradition and Wisdom.

The bored tourists who pay their nine francs at the desk or are admitted free on Sundays may believe that elderly nineteenth-century gentlemen—beards yellowed by nicotine, collars rumpled and greasy, black cravats and frock coats smelling of snuff, fingers stained with acid, their minds acid with professional jealousy, farcical ghosts who called one another cher maître—placed these exhibits here out of a virtuous desire to educate and amuse the bourgeois and the radical taxpayers, and to celebrate the magnificent march of progress. But no: Saint-Martin-des-Champs had been conceived first as a priory and only later as a revolutionary museum and compendium of arcane knowledge. The planes, those self-propelled machines, those electromagnetic skeletons, were carrying on a dialog whose script still escaped me.

The catalog hypocritically informed me that this worthy undertaking had been conceived by the gentlemen of the Convention, who wanted to offer the masses an accessible shrine of all the arts and trades. But how could I believe that when the words used to describe the project were the very same Francis Bacon had used to describe the House of Solomon in his *New Atlantis?*

Was it possible that only I—along with Jacopo Belbo and Diotallevi—had guessed the truth? Perhaps I would have my answer that night. I had to find a way to remain in the museum past closing, and wait here for midnight.

How would They get in? I had no idea. Some passageway in the network of the Paris sewers might connect the museum to another point in the city, perhaps near Porte St.-Denis. But I was certain

8

that if I left, I would not be able to find that route back in. I had to hide somewhere in the building.

I tried to shake off the spell of the place and look at the nave with cold eyes. It was not an epiphany now I was seeking, but information. I imagined that in the other halls it would be difficult to escape the notice of the guards, who made the rounds at closing time, checking to see that no thief was lurking somewhere. The nave, however, crammed with vehicles, was the ideal place to settle in for the night as a passenger: a live man hiding inside a lifeless vehicle. We had played too many games for me not to try this one, too.

Take heart, I said to myself: don't think of Wisdom now; ask the help of Science.

2

Wee haue divers curious *Clocks;* And other like *Motions of Return.*
. . . Wee haue also *Houses* of *Deceits* of the *Senses,* where we represent all manner of *Feats* of *Juggling, False Apparitions, Impostures,*
and *Illusions.* . . . These are (my sonne) the Riches of *Salomon's
House.*
        —Francis Bacon, *The New Atlantis,* ed. Rawley, London,
        1627, pp. 41–42

I gained control of my nerves, my imagination. I had to play this
ironically, as I had been playing it until a few days before, not letting myself become involved. I was in a museum and had to be
dramatically clever and clearheaded.

I looked at the now-familiar planes above me: I could climb into
the fuselage of a biplane, to await the night as if I were flying over
the Channel, anticipating the Legion of Honor. The names of the
automobiles on the ground had an affectionately nostalgic ring. The
1932 Hispano-Suiza was handsome, welcoming, but too close to the
front desk. I might have slipped past the attendant if I had turned
up in plus fours and Norfolk jacket, stepping aside for a lady in a
cream-colored suit, with a long scarf wound around her slender neck,
a cloche pulled over her bobbed hair. The 1931 Citroën C64 was
shown only in cross section, an excellent educational display but a
ridiculous hiding place. Cugnot's enormous steam automobile, all
boiler, or cauldron, was out of the question. I looked to the right,
where velocipedes with huge art-nouveau wheels and draisiennes with
their flat, scooterlike bars evoked gentlemen in stovepipe hats, knights
of progress pedaling through the Bois de Boulogne.

Across from the velocipedes were cars with bodies intact, ample
receptacles. Perhaps not the 1945 Panhard Dynavia, too open and
narrow in its aerodynamic sleekness; but the tall 1909 Peugeot—an
attic, a boudoir—was definitely worth considering. Once I was inside, deep in its leather divan, no one would suspect a thing. But
the car would not be easy to get into; one of the guards was sitting
on a bench directly opposite, his back to the bicycles. I pictured

myself stepping onto the running board, clumsy in my fur-collared coat, while he, calves sheathed in leather leggings, doffed his visored cap and obsequiously opened the door. . . .

I concentrated for a moment on the twelve-passenger Obeissante, 1872, the first French vehicle with gears. If the Peugeot was an apartment, this was a building. But there was no hope of boarding it without attracting everyone's attention. Difficult to hide when the hiding places are pictures at an exhibition.

I crossed the hall again, and there was the Statue of Liberty, "éclairant le monde" from a pedestal at least two meters high in the shape of a prow with a sharp beak. Inside the pedestal was a kind of sentry box, from which you could look through a porthole at a diorama of New York harbor. A good observation point at midnight, because through the darkness it would be possible to see into the choir to the left and the nave to the right, your back protected by a great stone statue of Gramme, which faced other corridors from the transept where it stood. In daylight, however, you could look into the sentry box from outside, and once the visitors were gone, a guard would probably make a routine check and peer in, just to be on the safe side.

I didn't have much time: they closed at five-thirty. I took another quick look at the ambulatory. None of the engines would serve the purpose. Nor would the great ship machinery on the right, relics of some *Lusitania* engulfed by the waves, nor Lenoir's immense gas engine with its variety of cogwheels. In fact, now that the light was fading, watery through the gray windowpanes, I felt fear again at the prospect of hiding among these animals, for I dreaded seeing them come to life in the darkness, reborn in the shadows in the glow of my flashlight. I dreaded their panting, their heavy, telluric breath, skinless bones, viscera creaking and fetid with black-grease drool. How could I endure in the midst of that foul concatenation of diesel genitals and turbine-driven vaginas, the inorganic throats that once had flamed, steamed, and hissed, and might again that very night? Or maybe they would buzz like stag beetles or chirr like cicadas amid those skeletal incarnations of pure, abstract functionality, automata able to crush, saw, shift, break, slice, accelerate, ram, and gulp fuel, their cylinders sobbing. Or they would jerk like sinister marionettes, making drums turn, converting frequencies, transforming energies, spinning flywheels. How could I fight them if they came after me, instigated by the Masters of the World, who used them as proof—useless devices, idols only of the bosses of the lower universe—of the error of creation?

I had to leave, get away; this was madness. I was falling into the same trap, the same game that had driven Jacopo Belbo out of his mind, I, the doubter. . . .

I don't know if I did the right thing two nights ago, hiding in that museum. If I hadn't, I would know the beginning of the story but not the end. Nor would I be here now, alone on this hill, while dogs bark in the distance, in the valley below, as I wonder: Was that really the end, or is the end yet to come?

I decided to move on. I abandoned the chapel, turned left at the statue of Gramme, and entered a gallery. It was the railroad section, and the multicolored model locomotives and cars looked like reassuring playthings out of a Toyland, Madurodam, or Disney World. By now I had grown accustomed to alternating surges of anxiety and self-confidence, terror and skepticism (is that, perhaps, how illness starts?), and I told myself that the things seen in the church upset me because I was there under the spell of Jacopo Belbo's writings, writings I had used so many tricks to decipher, even though I knew they were all inventions.

This was a museum of technology, after all. You're in a museum of technology, I told myself, an honest place, a little dull perhaps, but the dead here are harmless. You know what museums are, no one's ever been devoured by the Mona Lisa—an androgynous Medusa only for esthetes—and you are even less likely to be devoured by Watt's engine, a bugbear only for Ossianic and Neo-Gothic gentlemen, a pathetic compromise, really, between function and Corinthian elegance, handle and capital, boiler and column, wheel and tympanum. Jacopo Belbo, though he was far away, was trying to draw me into the hallucinations that had undone him. You must behave like a scientist, I told myself. A vulcanologist does not burn like Empedocles. Frazer did not flee, hounded, into the wood of Nemi. Come, you're supposed to be Sam Spade. Exploring the mean streets—that's your job. The woman who catches you has to die in the end, and if possible by your own hand. So long, Emily, it was great while it lasted, but you were a robot, you had no heart.

The transportation section happened to be right next to the Lavoisier atrium, facing a grand stairway that led to the upper floor.

The arrangement of glass cases along the sides, the alchemical altar in the center, the liturgy of a civilized eighteenth-century macumba—this was not accidental but symbolic, a stratagem.

First, all those mirrors. Whenever you see a mirror—it's only human—you want to look at yourself. But here you can't. You look at the position in space where the mirror will say "You are here, and you are you," you look, craning, twisting, but nothing works, because Lavoisier's mirrors, whether concave or convex, disappoint you, mock you. You step back, find yourself for a moment, but move a little and you are lost. This catoptric theater was contrived to take away your identity and make you feel unsure not only of yourself but also of the very objects standing between you and the mirrors. As if to say: *You* are not the Pendulum or even near it. And you feel uncertain, not only about yourself, but also about the objects set there between you and another mirror. Granted, physics can explain how and why a concave mirror collects the light from an object—in this case, an alembic in a copper holder—then returns the rays in such a way that you see the object not within the mirror but outside it, ghostlike, upside down in midair, and if you shift even slightly, the image, evanescent, disappears.

Then suddenly I saw myself upside down in a mirror.

Intolerable.

What was Lavoisier trying to say, and what were the designers of the Conservatoire hinting at? We've known about the magic of mirrors since the Middle Ages, since Alhazen. Was it worth the trouble of going through the Encyclopédie, the Enlightenment, and the Revolution to be able to state that merely curving a mirror's surface can plunge a man into an imagined world? For that matter, a normal mirror, too, is an illusion. Consider the individual looking back at you, condemned to perpetual left-handedness, every morning when you shave. Was it worth the trouble of setting up this hall just to tell us this? Or is the message really that we should look at everything in a different way, including the glass cases and the instruments that supposedly celebrate the birth of physics and enlightened chemistry?

A copper mask for protection in calcination experiments. Hard to believe that the gentleman with the candles under the glass bell actually wore that thing that looks like a sewer rat's head or a space invader's helmet, just to avoid irritating his eyes. Quelle délicatesse, M. Lavoisier! If you really wanted to study the kinetic theory of gases, why did you reconstruct so painstakingly the eolopile—a little spouted sphere that, when heated, spins, spewing steam—a device first built by Heron in the days of the Gnostics to assist the speaking statues and other wonders of the Egyptian priests?

And what about this contraption for the study of necrotic fermentation, 1781? A fine allusion, really, to the putrid, reeking bastards of the Demiurge. A series of glass tubes that connect two ampules and lead through a bubble uterus, through spheres and conduits perched on forked pins, to transmit an essence to coils that spill into the void . . . Balneum Mariae, sublimation of hydrargyrum, mysterium conjunctionis, the Elixir!

Or this apparatus for the study of the fermentation of wine. A maze of crystal arches leading from athanor to athanor, from alembic to alembic. Those little spectacles, the tiny hourglass, the electroscope, the lens. Or the laboratory knife that looks like a cuneiform character, the spatula with the release lever, the glass blade, and the tiny, three-centimeter clay crucible for making a gnome-size homunculus—infinitesimal womb for the most minuscule clonings. Or the acajou boxes filled with little white packets like a village apothecary's cachets, wrapped in parchment covered with untranslatable ciphers, with mineral specimens that in reality are fragments of the Holy Shroud of Basilides, reliquaries containing the foreskin of Hermes Trismegistus. Or the long, thin upholsterer's hammer, a gavel for opening a brief judgment day, an auction of quintessences to be held among the Elfs of Avalon. Or the delightful little apparatus for analyzing the combustion of oil, and the glass globules arrayed like quatrefoil petals, with other quatrefoils connected by golden tubes, and quatrefoils attached to other, crystal, tubes leading first to a copper cylinder, then to the gold-and-glass cylinder below it, then to other tubes, lower still, pendulous appendages, testicles, glands, goiters, crests . . . This is modern chemistry? For this the author had to be guillotined, though truly nothing is created or destroyed? Or was he killed to silence what his fraud revealed?

The Salle Lavoisier in the Conservatoire is actually a confession, a confession in code, and an emblem of the whole museum, for it mocks the arrogance of the Age of Reason and murmurs of other mysteries. Jacopo Belbo was reasonably right; Reason was wrong.

I had to hurry; time was pressing now. I walked past the meter, the kilogram, the other measures, all false guarantees. I had learned from Agliè that the secret of the pyramids is revealed if you don't calculate in meters but in ancient cubits. Then, the counting machines that proclaimed the triumph of the quantitative but in truth pointed to the occult qualities of numbers, a return to the roots of the notarikon the rabbis carried with them as they fled through the plains of Europe. Astronomy and clocks and robots. Dangerous to linger among these new revelations. I was penetrating to the heart of a secret message in the form of a rationalist theatrum. But I had to hurry. Later, between closing time and midnight, I could explore them, objects that in the slanted light of sunset assumed their true aspect—symbols, not instruments.

I went upstairs, walked through the halls of the crafts, of energy, electricity. No place to hide here, not in these cases. I began to guess their meaning, but suddenly I was gripped by the fear that there would not be time to find a place from which I could witness the nocturnal revelation of their secret purpose. Now I moved like a man pursued—pursued by the clock, by the ghastly advance of numbers. The earth turned, inexorably, the hour was approaching. In a little while I would be kicked out.

Crossing the exhibit of electrical devices, I came to the hall of glass. By what logic had they decided that the most advanced and expensive gadgetry of the modern mind should be followed by a section devoted to an art known to the Phoenicians thousands of years ago? A jumble of a room, Chinese porcelain alongside androgynous vases of Lalique, poteries, majolica, faïence, and Murano, and in an enormous case in the rear, life-size and three-dimensional, a lion attacked by a serpent. The apparent reason for this piece was its medium, that it was made entirely of glass; but there had to be a deeper reason. Where had I seen this figure before? Then I remembered that the Demiurge, Yaldabaoth, the first Archon, odious creation of Sophia, who was responsible for the world and its fatal flaw, had the form of a serpent and of a lion, and that his eyes cast fire. Perhaps the whole Conservatoire was an image of the vile process by which, through the eons, the fullness of the first principle, the Pendulum, and the splendor of the Plerome give way, by which the Ogdoades crumbles and Evil rules in the cosmic realm. If so, then the serpent and lion were telling me that my initiatory journey—à rebours, alas—was already over, and that soon I would see the world anew, not as it should be, but as it is.

Near a window in the right-hand corner, I noticed the sentry box of the periscope. I entered it and found myself facing a glass plate, as on the bridge of a ship, and through it I saw shifting images of a film, blurred; a scene of a city. What I saw was projected from a screen above my head, where everything was upside down, and this second screen was the eyepiece, as it were, of a primitive periscope made of two packing cases arranged in an obtuse angle. The longer case stuck out like a pipe from the cubicle above and behind me, reaching a higher window, from which a set of wide-angle lenses gathered the light from outside. Calculating the route I had followed, coming up here, I realized that the periscope gave me a view of the outside as if I were looking through a window in the upper part of the apse of Saint-Martin—as if I were swaying there with the Pendulum, like a hanged man, taking his last look. After my eyes adjusted to the pale scene, I could make out rue Vaucanson, which the choir overlooked, and rue Conté, on a line with the nave. Rue Conté split into rue Montgolfier to the left and rue de Turbigo to the right. There were a couple of bars at the corners, Le Weekend and La Rotonde, and opposite them a façade with a sign that I could just barely discern: LES CREATIONS JACSAM.

The periscope. There was no real reason it should be in the hall of glass rather than in the hall of optical instruments, but obviously it was important for this particular view of the outside to be in this particular place. But important how? Why should this cubicle, so positivist-scientific, a thing out of Verne, stand beside the emblematic lion and serpent?

In any case, if I had the strength and the courage to stay here for another half hour or so, the night watchman might not see me.

And so I remained underwater for what seemed a very long time. I heard the footsteps of the last of the visitors, then the footsteps of the last guards. I was tempted to crouch under the bridge to elude a possible random glance inside, but decided against it. If they discovered me standing, I could pretend I was an enthusiast who had lingered to enjoy the marvel.

Later, the lights went out, and the hall was shrouded in semi-darkness. But the cubicle seemed less dark now, illuminated as it was by the screen. I stared steadily at it, my last contact with the world.

The best course was to stay on my feet—if my feet ached too much, then in a crouch, for at least two hours. Closing time for visitors was not the same as quitting time for the employees. I was seized by sudden fear: Suppose the cleaning staff started going through all the rooms, inch by inch. But then I remembered: the museum opened late in the morning, so the cleaners probably worked by daylight and not in the evening. And that must have been the case, at least in the upper rooms, because I heard no one else pass by, only distant voices and an occasional louder sound, perhaps of doors closing. I stood still. There would be plenty of time for me to get back to the church between ten and eleven, or even later. The Masters would not come until close to midnight.

A group of young people emerged from La Rotonde. A girl walked along rue Conté and turned into rue Montgolfier. Not a very busy neighborhood. Would I be able to hold out, watching the humdrum world behind my back for hours on end? Shouldn't I try to guess the secret of the periscope's location here? I felt the need to urinate. Ignore it: a nervous reaction.

So many things run through your mind when you're hiding alone inside a periscope. This must be how a stowaway feels, concealed in a ship's hold, emigrating to some far-off land. To the Statue of Liberty, in fact, with the diorama of New York. I might grow drowsy, doze; maybe that would be good. No, then I might wake up too late. . . .

The worst would be an anxiety attack. You are certain then that in a moment you will start screaming. Periscope. Submarine. Trapped on the ocean floor. Maybe the great black fish of the abyss are already circling you, unseen, and all you know is that you're running out of air. . . .

I took several deep breaths. Concentrate. The only thing you can rely on at a time like this is the laundry list. Stick to facts, causes, effects. I am here for this reason, and also for this reason and this. . . .

Memories, distinct, precise, orderly. Of the past three frantic days, of the past two years, and the forty-year-old memories I found when I broke into Jacopo Belbo's electronic brain.

I am remembering now (as I remembered then) in order to make sense out of the chaos of that misguided creation of ours. Now (as then, while I waited in the periscope) I shrink into one remote corner of my mind, to draw from it a story. Such as the Pendulum. Diotallevi told me that the first Sefirah is Keter, the Crown, the beginning, the primal void. In the beginning He created a point, which became Thought, where all the figures were drawn. He was and was not, He was encompassed in the name yet not encompassed in the name, having as yet no name other than the desire to be called by a name. . . . He traced signs in the air; a dark light leapt from His most secret depth, like a colorless mist that gives form to formlessness, and as the mist spread, a burst of flames took shape in its center, and the flames streamed down to illuminate the lower Sefirot, and down, down to the Kingdom.

But perhaps in that simsun, that diminishment, that lonely separation—Diotallevi said—there was already the promise of the return.

HOKHMAH

3

In hanc utilitatem clementes angeli saepe figuras, characteres, formas et voces invenerunt proposueruntque nobis mortalibus et ignotas et stupendas nullius rei iuxta consuetum linguae usum significativas, sed per rationis nostrae summam admirationem in assiduam intelligibilium pervestigationem, deinde in illorum ipsorum venerationem et amorem inductivas.

—Johannes Reuchlin, *De arte cabalistica*, Hagenhau, 1517, III

It had been two days earlier, a Thursday. I was lazing in bed, undecided about getting up. I had arrived the previous afternoon and had telephoned my office. Diotallevi was still in the hospital, and Gudrun sounded pessimistic: condition unchanged; in other words, getting worse. I couldn't bring myself to go and visit him.

Belbo was away. Gudrun told me he telephoned to say he had to go somewhere for family reasons. What family? The odd thing was, he took away the word processor—Abulafia, he called it—and the printer, too. Gudrun also told me he had set it up at home in order to finish some work. Why had he gone to all that trouble? Couldn't he do it in the office?

I felt like a displaced person. Lia and the baby wouldn't be back until next week. The previous evening I'd dropped by Pilade's, but found no one there.

The phone woke me. It was Belbo; his voice different, remote.

"Where the hell are you? Lost in the jungle?"

"Don't joke, Casaubon. This is serious. I'm in Paris."

"Paris? But I was the one who was supposed to go to the Conservatoire."

"Stop joking, damn it. I'm in a booth—in a bar. I may not be able to talk much longer. . . ."

"If you're running out of change, call collect. I'll wait here."

"Change isn't the problem. I'm in trouble." He was talking fast, not giving me time to interrupt. "The Plan. The Plan is real. I know, don't say it. They're after me."

"Who?" I still couldn't understand.

"The Templars, Casaubon, for God's sake. You won't want to believe this, I know, but it's all true. They think I have the map, they tricked me, made me come to Paris. At midnight Saturday they want me at the Conservatoire. Saturday—you understand—Saint John's Eve. . . ." He was talking disjointedly; and I couldn't follow him. "I don't want to go. I'm on the run, Casaubon. They'll kill me. Tell De Angelis—no, De Angelis is useless—keep the police out of it. . . ."

"Then what do you want me to do?"

"I don't know. Read the floppy disks, use Abulafia. I put everything there these last few days, including all that happened this month. You weren't around, I didn't know who to tell it to, I wrote for three days and three nights. . . . Listen, go to the office; in my desk drawer there's an envelope with two keys in it. The large one you don't need: it's the key to my house in the country. But the small one's for the Milan apartment. Go there and read everything, then decide for yourself, or maybe we'll talk. My God, I don't know what to do. . . ."

"All right. But where can I find you?"

"I don't know. I change hotels here every night. Do it today and wait at my place tomorrow morning. I'll call if I can. My God, the password—"

I heard noises. Belbo's voice came closer, moved away, as if someone was wresting the receiver from him.

"Belbo! What's going on?"

"They found me. The word—"

A sharp report, like a shot. It must have been the receiver falling, slamming against the wall or onto that little shelf they have under telephones. A scuffle. Then the click of the receiver being hung up. Certainly not by Belbo.

I took a quick shower to clear my head. I couldn't figure out what was going on. The Plan real? Absurd. We had invented it ourselves. But who had captured Belbo? The Rosicrucians? The Comte de Saint-Germain? The Okhrana? The Knights of the Temple? The Assassins? Anything was possible, if the impossible was true. But Belbo might have gone off the deep end. He had been very tense lately, whether because of Lorenza Pellegrini or because he was becoming more and more fascinated by his creature. . . . The Plan,

22

actually, was our creature, his, mine, Diotallevi's, but Belbo was the one who seemed obsessed by it now, beyond the confines of the game. It was useless to speculate further.

I went to the office. Gudrun welcomed me with the acid remark that she had to keep the business going all on her own. I found the envelope, the keys, and rushed to Belbo's apartment.

The stale, rancid smell of cigarette butts, the ashtrays all brimming. The kitchen sink piled high with dirty dishes, the garbage bin full of disemboweled cans. On a shelf in the study, three empty bottles of whiskey, and a little left—two fingers—in a fourth bottle. This was the apartment of a man who had worked nonstop for days without budging, eating only when he had to, working furiously, like an addict.

There were two rooms in all, books piled in every corner, shelves sagging under their weight. The table with the computer, printer, and boxes of disks. A few pictures in the space not occupied by shelves. Directly opposite the table, a seventeenth-century print carefully framed, an allegory I hadn't noticed last month, when I came up to have a beer before going off on my vacation.

On the table, a photograph of Lorenza Pellegrini, with an inscription in a tiny, almost childish hand. You saw only her face, but her eyes were unsettling, the look in her eyes. In a gesture of instinctive delicacy (or jealousy?) I turned the photograph facedown, not reading the inscription.

There were folders. I looked through them. Nothing of interest, only accounts, publishing cost estimates. But in the midst of these papers I found the printout of a file that, to judge by its date, must have been one of Belbo's first experiments with the word processor. It was titled "Abu." I remembered, when Abulafia made its appearance in the office, Belbo's infantile enthusiasm, Gudrun's muttering, Diotallevi's sarcasm.

Abu had been Belbo's private reply to his critics, a kind of sophomoric joke, but it said a lot about the combinatory passion with which he had used the machine. Here was a man who had said, with his wan smile, that once he realized that he would never be a protagonist, he decided to become, instead, an intelligent spectator, for there was no point in writing without serious motivation. Better to rewrite the books of others, which is what a good editor does. But

Belbo found in the machine a kind of LSD and ran his fingers over the keyboard as if inventing variations on "The Happy Farmer" on the old piano at home, without fear of being judged. Not that he thought he was being creative: terrified as he was by writing, he knew that this was not writing but only the testing of an electronic skill. A gymnastic exercise. But, forgetting the usual ghosts that haunted him, he discovered that playing with the word processor was a way of giving vent to a fifty-year-old's second adolescence. His natural pessimism, his reluctant acceptance of his own past were somehow dissolved in this dialog with a memory that was inorganic, objective, obedient, nonmoral, transistorized, and so humanly in-human that it enabled him to forget his chronic nervousness about life.

FILENAME: Abu

O what a beautiful morning at the end of November, in the beginning was the word, sing to me, goddess, the son of Peleus, Achilles, now is the winter of our discontent. Period, new para-graph. Testing testing parakalò, parakalò, with the right pro-gram you can even make anagrams, if you've written a novel with a Confederate hero named Rhett Butler and a fickle girl named Scarlett and then change your mind, all you have to do is punch a key and Abu will global replace the Rhett Butlers to Prince Andreis, the Scarletts to Natashas, Atlanta to Moscow, and lo! you've written war and peace.

Abu, do another thing now: Belbo orders Abu to change all words, make each "a" become "akka" and each "o" become "ulla," for a paragraph to look almost Finnish.

Akkabu, dulla akkanullather thing nullaw: Belbulla ullarders Akkabu tulla chakkange akkall wullards, makkake eakkach "akka" becullame "akkakkakka" akkand eakkach "ulla" becullame "ul-lakka," fullar akka pakkarakkagrakkaph tulla lullaullak akkal-mullast Finnish.

O joy, O new vertigo of difference, O my platonic reader-writer racked by a most platonic insomnia, O wake of finnegan, O animal charming and benign. He doesn't help you think but he helps you because you have to think for him. A totally spir-itual machine. If you write with a goose quill you scratch the sweaty pages and keep stopping to dip for ink. Your thoughts go too fast for your aching wrist. If you type, the letters cluster together, and again you must go at the poky pace of the mechanism, not the speed of your synapses. But with him (it? her?) your fingers dream, your mind brushes the keyboard, you are borne on golden pinions, at last you confront the light of critical reason with the happiness of a first encounter.

An loo what I doo now, I tak this pac of speling monnstrosties an I orderr the macchin to coppy them an file them in temrary memry an then brring them bak from tha limbo onto the scren, folowing itsel.

There, I was typing blindly, but now I have taken that pack of spelling monstrosities and ordered the machine to copy the mess, and on the copy I made all the corrections, so it comes out perfect on the page. From shit, thus, I extract pure Shinola. Repenting, I could have deleted the first draft. I left it to show how the "is" and the "ought," accident and necessity, can coexist on this screen. If I wanted, I could remove the offending passage from the screen but not from the memory, thereby creating an archive of my repressions while denying omnivorous Freudians and virtuosi of variant texts the pleasure of conjecture, the exercise of their occupation, their academic glory.

This is better than real memory, because real memory, at the cost of much effort, learns to remember but not to forget. Diotallevi goes Sephardically mad over those palaces with grand staircases, that statue of a warrior doing something unspeakable to a defenseless woman, the corridors with hundreds of rooms, each with the depiction of a portent, and the sudden apparitions, disturbing incidents, walking mummies. To each memorable image you attach a thought, a label, a category, a piece of the cosmic furniture, syllogisms, an enormous sorites, chains of apothegms, strings of hypallages, rosters of zeugmas, dances of hysteron proteron, apophantic logoi, hierarchic stoichea, processions of equinoxes and parallaxes, herbaria, genealogies of gymnosophists—and so on, to infinity. O Raimundo, O Camillo, you had only to cast your mind back to your visions and immediately you could reconstruct the great chain of being, in love and joy, because all that was disjointed in the universe was joined in a single volume in your mind, and Proust would have made you smile. But when Diotallevi and I tried to construct an ars oblivionalis that day, we couldn't come up with rules for forgetting. It's impossible. It's one thing to go in search of a lost time, chasing labile clues, like Hop-o'-My-Thumb in the woods, and quite another deliberately to misplace time refound. Hop-o'-My-Thumb always comes home, like an obsession. There is no discipline of forgetting; we are at the mercy of random natural processes, like stroke and amnesia, and such self-interventions as drugs, alcohol, or suicide.

Abu, however, can perform on himself precise local suicides, temporary amnesias, painless aphasias.

Where were you last night, L

There, indiscreet reader: you will never know it, but that half-line hanging in space was actually the beginning of a long sentence that I wrote but then wished I hadn't, wished I hadn't even thought let alone written it, wished that it had never happened. So I pressed a key, and a milky film spread over the fatal and inopportune lines, and I pressed DELETE and, whoosh, all gone.

But that's not all. The problem with suicide is that sometimes you jump out the window and then change your mind between the eighth floor and the seventh. "Oh, if only I could go back!" Sorry, you can't, too bad. Splat. Abu, on the other hand, is merciful, he grants you the right to change your mind: you can recover your deleted text by pressing RETRIEVE. What a relief! Once I know that I can remember whenever I like, I forget.

Never again will I go from one bar to another, disintegrating alien spacecraft with tracer bullets, until the invader monster disintegrates me. This is far more beautiful: here you disintegrate thoughts instead of aliens. The screen is a galaxy of thousands and thousands of asteroids, all in a row, white or green, and you have created them yourself. Fiat Lux, Big Bang, seven days, seven minutes, seven seconds, and a universe is born before your eyes, a universe in constant flux, where sharp lines in space and time do not exist. No numerus Clausius here, no constraining law of thermodynamics. The letters bubble indolently to the surface, they emerge from nothingness and obediently return to nothingness, dissolving like ectoplasm. It's an underwater symphony of soft linkings and unlinkings, a gelatinous dance of self-devouring moons, like the big fish in the Yellow Submarine. At a touch of your fingertip the irreparable slides backward toward a hungry word and disappears into its maw with a slurrrp, then darkness. If you don't stop, the word swallows itself as well, fattening on its own absence like a Cheshire-cat black hole.

And if you happen to write what modesty forbids, it all goes onto a floppy disk, and you can give the disk a password, and no one will be able to read you. Excellent for secret agents. You write the message, save it, then put the disk in your pocket and walk off. Not even Torquemada could find out what you've written: It's between you and it (It?). And if they torture you, you pretend to confess; you start entering the password, then press a secret key, and the message disappears forever. Oh, I'm so sorry, you say, my hand slipped, an accident, and now it's gone. What was it? I don't remember. It wasn't important. I have no Message to reveal. But later on—who knows?—I might.

4

He who attempts to penetrate into the Rose Garden of the Philosophers without the key resembles a man who would walk without feet.

—Michael Maier, *Atalanta Fugiens*, Oppenheim, De Bry, 1618, emblem XXVII

That was the only file that had been printed out. I would have to go through the disks on the computer. They were arranged by number, and I thought I might as well start with the first. But Belbo had mentioned a password. He had always been possessive with Abulafia's secrets.

When I loaded the machine, a message promptly appeared: "Do you have the password?" Not in the imperative. Belbo was a polite man.

The machine doesn't volunteer its help. It must be given the word; without the word, it won't talk. As though it were saying: "Yes, what you want to know is right here in my guts. Go ahead and dig, dig, old mole; you'll never find it." We'll see about that, I said to myself; you got such a kick out of playing with Diotallevi's permutations and combinations, and you were the Sam Spade of publishing. As Jacopo Belbo would have said: Find the falcon.

The password to get into Abulafia had to be seven letters or fewer. Letters or numbers. How many groups of seven could be made from all the letters of the alphabet, including the possibility of repetition, since there was no reason the word couldn't be "cadabra"? I knew the formula. The number was six billion and something. A giant calculator capable of running through all six billion at the rate of a million per second would still have to feed them to Abulafia one at a time. And it took Abulafia about ten seconds to ask for the password and verify it. That made sixty billion seconds. There were over thirty-one million seconds in a year. Say thirty, to have a round figure. It would take, therefore, two thousand years to go through all the possibilities. Nice work.

I would have to proceed, instead, by inductive guesswork. What word would Belbo have chosen? Was it a word he had decided on at the start, when he began using the machine, or was it one he had come up with only recently, when he realized that these disks were dangerous and that, for him at least, the game was no longer a game? This would make a big difference.

Better assume the latter, I thought. Belbo feels he is being hunted by the Plan, which he now takes seriously (as he told me on the phone). For a password, then, he would use some term connected with our story.

But maybe not: a term associated with the Tradition might also occur to Them. Then I thought: What if They had already broken into the apartment and made copies of the disks, and were now, at this very moment, trying all the combinations of letters in some remote place? Using the supreme computer, in a castle in the Carpathians.

Nonsense, I told myself. They weren't computer people. They would use the notarikon, the gematria, the temurah, treating the disks like the Torah, and therefore would require as much time as had passed since the writing of the *Sefer Yesirah*. No, if They existed, They would proceed cabalistically, and if Belbo believed that They existed, he would follow the same path.

Just to be on the safe side, I tried the ten Sefirot: Keter, Hokhmah, Binah, Hesed, Gevurah, Tiferet, Nezah, Hod, Yesod, Malkhut. They didn't work, of course: it was the first thing that would have occurred to anyone.

Still, the word had to be something obvious, something that would come to mind at once, because when you work on a text as obsessively as Belbo must have during the past few days, you can't think of anything else, of any other subject. It would not be human for him to drive himself crazy over the Plan and at the same time pick Lincoln or Mombasa for the password. The password had to be connected with the Plan. But what?

I tried to put myself inside Belbo's head. He had been chain-smoking as he wrote, and drinking. I went to the kitchen for a clean glass, found only one, poured myself the last of the whiskey, sat down at the keyboard again, leaned back in the chair, and propped my feet on the table. I sipped my drink (wasn't that how Sam Spade did it? Or was it Philip Marlowe?) and looked around. The books were too far away; I couldn't read the titles on their spines.

I finished the whiskey, shut my eyes, opened them again. Facing me was the seventeenth-century engraving, a typical Rosicrucian allegory of the period, rich in coded messages addressed to the members of the Fraternity. Obviously it depicted the Temple of the Rosy-Cross, a tower surmounted by a dome in accordance with the Renaissance iconographic model, both Christian and Jewish, of the Temple of Jerusalem, reconstructed on the pattern of the Mosque of Omar.

The landscape around the tower was incongruous, and inhabited incongruously, like one of those rebuses where you see a palace, a frog in the foreground, a mule with its pack, and a king receiving a gift from a page. In the lower left was a gentleman emerging from a well, clinging to a pulley that was attached, through ridiculous winches, to some point inside the tower, the rope passing through a circular window. In the center were a horseman and a wayfarer. On the right, a kneeling pilgrim held a heavy anchor as though it were his staff. Along the right margin, almost opposite the tower, was a precipice from which a character with a sword was falling, and on the other side, foreshortened, stood Mount Ararat, the Ark aground on its summit. In each of the upper corners was a cloud illuminated by a star that cast oblique rays along which two figures floated, a nude man in the coils of a serpent, and a swan. At the top center, a nimbus was surmounted by the word "Oriens" and bore Hebrew letters from which the hand of God emerged to hold the tower by a string.

The tower moved on wheels. Its main part was square, with windows, a door, and a drawbridge on the right. Higher up, there was a kind of gallery with four observation turrets, each turret occupied by an armed man who waved a palm branch and carried a shield decorated with Hebrew letters. Only three of these men were visible; the fourth had to be imagined, since he was behind the octagonal dome, from which rose a lantern, also octagonal, with a pair of great wings affixed. Above the winged lantern was another, smaller, cupola, with a quadrangular turret whose open arches, supported by slender columns, revealed a bell inside. To the final small four-vaulted dome at the top was tied the thread held by the hand of God. The word "Fa/ma" appeared here, and above that, a scroll that read "Collegium Fraternitatis."

There were other oddities. An enormous arm, out of all proportion to the figures, jutted from a round window in the tower on the left. It held a sword, and belonged perhaps to the winged creature shut up in the tower. From a similar window on the right jutted a great trumpet. Once again, the trumpet.

The number of openings in the tower drew my attention. There were too many of them, and the ones in the dome were too regular, whereas the ones in the base seemed random. Since only half the tower was shown in this orthogonal perspective, you could assume that symmetry was preserved and the doors, windows, and portholes on this side were repeated in the same order on the other side. That would mean, altogether, four arches in the dome of the bell tower, eight windows in the lower dome, four turrets, six openings in the east and west façades, and fourteen in the north and south façades. I added it up.

Thirty-six. For more than ten years that number had haunted me. The Rosicrucians. One hundred and twenty divided by thirty-six came to 3.333333, going to seven digits. Almost too perfect, but it was worth a try. I tried. And failed.

It occurred to me then that the same number, multiplied by two, yielded the number of the Beast: 666. That guess also proved too farfetched.

Suddenly I was struck by the nimbus in the middle, the divine throne. The Hebrew letters were large; I could see them even from my chair. But Belbo couldn't write Hebrew on Abulafia. I took a closer look: I knew them, of course, from right to left, yod, he, vav, he. The Tetragrammaton, Yahweh, the name of God.

5

The name of God . . . Of course! I remembered the first conversation between Belbo and Diotallevi, the day Abulafia was set up in
the office.

Diotallevi was at the door of his room, pointedly tolerant. Diotallevi's tolerance was always exasperating, but Belbo didn't seem to
mind it. He tolerated it.

"It won't be of any use to you, you know. You're not planning,
surely, to rewrite the manuscripts you don't read anyway."

"It's for filing, making schedules, updating lists. If I write a book
with it, it'll be my own, not someone else's."

"You swore that you'd never write anything of your own."

"That I wouldn't inflict a manuscript on the world, true. When I
concluded I wasn't cut out to be a protagonist—"

"You decided you'd be an intelligent spectator. I know all that.
And so?"

"If an intelligent spectator hums the second movement on his way
home from the concert, that doesn't mean he wants to conduct it in
Carnegie Hall."

"So you'll try humming literature to make sure you don't write
any."

"It would be an honest choice."

"You think so?"

Diotallevi and Belbo, both from Piedmont, often claimed that any
good Piedmontese had the ability to listen politely, look you in the

eye, and say "You think so?" in a tone of such apparent sincerity
that you immediately felt his profound disapproval. I was a barbarian, they used to say: such subtleties would always be lost on me.

"Barbarian?" I would protest. "I may have been born in Milan,
but my family came from Val d'Aosta."

"Nonsense," they said. "You can always tell a genuine Piedmontese immediately by his skepticism."

"I'm a skeptic."

"No, you're only incredulous, a doubter, and that's different."

I knew why Diotallevi distrusted Abulafia. He had heard that
word processors could change the order of letters. A text, thus,
might generate its opposite and result in obscure prophecies. "It's a
game of permutation," Belbo said, trying to explain. "Temurah?
Isn't that the name for it? Isn't that what the devout rabbi does to
ascend to the Gates of Splendor?"

"My dear friend," Diotallevi said, "you'll never understand anything. It's true that the Torah—the visible Torah, that is—is only
one of the possible permutations of the letters of the eternal Torah,
as God created it and delivered it to the angels. By rearranging the
letters of the book over the centuries, we may someday arrive again
at the original Torah. But the important thing is not the finding, it
is the seeking, it is the devotion with which one spins the wheel of
prayer and scripture, discovering the truth little by little. If this machine gave you the truth immediately, you would not recognize it,
because your heart would not have been purified by the long quest.
And in an office! No, the Book must be murmured day after day
in a little ghetto hovel where you learn to lean forward and keep
your arms tight against your hips so there will be as little space as
possible between the hand that holds the Book and the hand that
turns the pages. And if you moisten your fingers, you must raise
them vertically to your lips, as if nibbling unleavened bread, and
drop no crumb. The word must be eaten very slowly. It must melt
on the tongue before you can dissolve it and reorder it. And take
care not to slobber it onto your caftan. If even a single letter is lost,
the thread that is about to link you with the higher sefirot is broken.
To this Abraham Abulafia dedicated his life, while your Saint Thomas
was toiling to find God with his five paths.

"Abraham Abulafia's *Hokhmath ha-Zeruf* was at once the science
of the combination of letters and the science of the purification of

33

the heart. Mystic logic, letters whirling in infinite change, is the world of bliss, it is the music of thought, but see that you proceed slowly, and with caution, because your machine may bring you delirium instead of ecstasy. Many of Abulafia's disciples were unable to walk the fine line between contemplation of the names of God and the practice of magic. They manipulated the names in an effort to turn them into a talisman, an instrument of dominion over nature, unaware—as you are unaware, with your machine—that every letter is bound to a part of the body, and shifting a consonant without the knowledge of its power may affect a limb, its position or nature, and then you find yourself deformed, a monster. Physically, for life; spiritually, for eternity."

"Listen," Belbo said to him then. "You haven't discouraged me, you know. On the contrary. I have Abulafia—that's what I'm calling him—at my command, the way our friends used to have the golem. Only, my Abulafia will be more cautious and respectful. More modest. The problem is to find all the permutations of the name of God, isn't it? Well, this manual has a neat little program in Basic for listing all possible sequences of four letters. It seems tailormade for YHVH. Should I give it a whirl?" And he showed Diotallevi the program; Diotallevi had to agree it looked cabalistic:

```
10    REM anagrams
20    INPUT L$(1),L$(2),L$(3),L$(4)30   PRINT
40    FOR I1=1 TO 4
50    FOR I2=1 TO 4
60    IF I2=I1 THEN 130
70    FOR I3=1 TO 4
80    IF I3=I1 THEN 120
90    IF I3=I2 THEN 120
100   LET I4=10-(I1+I2+I3)
110   LPRINT L$(I1);L$(I2);L$(I3);L$(I4)
120   NEXT I3
130   NEXT I4
140   NEXT I1
150   END
```

"Try it yourself. When it asks for input, type in Y, H, V, H, and press the ENTER key. But you may be disappointed. There are only twenty-four possible permutations."

"Holy Seraphim! What can you do with twenty-four names of God? You think our wise men hadn't made that calculation? Read the *Sefer Yesirah*, Chapter Four, Section Sixteen. And they didn't have computers. 'Two Stones make two Houses. Three Stones make six Houses. Four Stones make twenty-four Houses. Five Stones make one hundred and twenty Houses. Six Stones make seven hundred and twenty Houses. Seven Stones make five thousand and forty Houses. Beyond this point, think of what the mouth cannot say and the ear cannot hear.' You know what this is called today? Factor analysis. And you know why the Tradition warns that beyond this point a man should quit? Because if there were eight letters in the name of God, there would be forty thousand three hundred and twenty permutations, and if ten, there would be three million six hundred twenty-eight thousand eight hundred, and the permutations of your own wretched little name, first name and last, would come to almost forty million. Thank God you don't have a middle initial, like so many Americans, because then there would be more than four hundred million. And if the names of God contained twenty-seven letters—in the Hebrew alphabet there are no vowels, but twenty-two consonants plus five variants—then the number of His possible names would have twenty-nine digits. Except that you have to allow for repetitions, because the name of God could be aleph repeated twenty-seven times, in which case factor analysis is of no use: with repetitions you'd have to take twenty-seven to the twenty-seventh power, which is, I believe, something like four hundred forty-four billion billion billion billion. Four times ten with thirty-nine zeros after it."

"You're cheating, trying to scare me. I've read your *Sefer Yesirah*, too. There are twenty-two fundamental letters, and with them—with them alone—God formed all creation."

"Let's not split hairs. Five, at this order of magnitude, won't help. If you say twenty-two to the twenty-second power instead of twenty-seven to the twenty-seventh, you still come up with something like three hundred and forty billion billion billion. On the human scale, it doesn't make much difference. If I counted one, two, three, and so on, one number every second, it would take me almost thirty-two years to get to one lousy little billion. And it's more complicated than that, because cabala can't be reduced to the *Sefer Yesirah* alone. Besides which, there's a good reason why any real

35

permutation of the Torah must include all twenty-seven letters. It's true that if the last five letters fall in the middle of a word, they are transformed into their normal variant. But not always. In Isaiah 9:2, for instance, there's the word "LMRBH," lemarbah—which, note the coincidence, means to multiply—but the mem in the middle is written as a final mem."

"Why is that?"

"Every letter corresponds to a number. The normal mem is forty, but the final mem is six hundred. This has nothing to do with te-murah, which teaches permutation; it involves, rather, gematria, which seeks sublime affinities between words and their numeric values. With the final mem the word "LMRBH" totals not two hundred and seventy-seven but eight hundred and thirty-seven, and thus is equiv-alent to ThThZL, or thath zal, which means 'he who gives pro-fusely.' So you can see why all twenty-seven letters have to be considered: it isn't just the sound that matters, but the number too. Which brings us to my calculation. There are more than four hundred billion billion billion billion possibilities. Have you any idea how long it would take to try them all out, using a machine? And I'm not talking about your miserable little computer. At the rate of one permutation per second, you would need seven billion billion billion billion minutes, or one hundred and twenty-three million billion billion billion hours, which is a little more than five million billion billion billion days, or fourteen thousand billion billion bil-lion years, which comes to a hundred and forty billion billion bil-lion centuries, or fourteen billion billion billion millennia. But suppose you had a machine capable of generating a million permutations per second. Just think of the time you'd save with your electronic wheel: you'd need only fourteen thousand billion billion millennia!

"The real and true name of God, the secret name, is as long as the entire Torah, and there is no machine in the world capable of exhausting all its permutations, because the Torah itself is a permu-tation with repetitions, and the art of temurah tells us to change not the twenty-seven letters of the alphabet but each and every character in the Torah, for each character is a letter unto itself, no matter how often it appears on other pages. The two hes in the name YHVH therefore count as two different letters. And if you want to calculate all the permutations of all the characters in the entire Torah, then all the zeros in the world will not be enough for you. But go ahead, do what you can with your pathetic little accountant's machine. A machine does exist, to be sure, but it wasn't manufactured in your Silicon Valley: it is the holy cabala, or Tradition, and for centuries the rabbis have been doing what no computer can do and, let us hope, will never be able to do. Because on the day all the combinations are exhausted, the result should remain secret, and in any case the universe will have completed its cycle—and we will all be consumed in the dazzling glory of the great Metacyclosynchrotron."

"Amen," Jacopo Belbo said.

Diotallevi was already driving him toward these excesses, and I should have kept that in mind. How often had I seen Belbo, after office hours, running programs to check Diotallevi's calculations, trying to show him that at least Abu could give results in a few seconds, not having to work by hand on yellowing parchment or use antediluvian number systems that did not even include zero? But Abu gave his answers in exponential notation, so Belbo was unable to daunt Diotallevi with a screen full of endless zeros: a pale visual imitation of the multiplication of combinatorial universes, of the exploding swarm of all possible worlds.

After everything that had happened, it seemed impossible to me, I thought as I stared at the Rosicrucian engraving, that Belbo would not have returned to those exercises on the name of God in selecting a password. And if, as I guessed, he was also preoccupied with numbers like thirty-six and one hundred and twenty, they would enter into it, too. He would not have simply combined the four Hebrew letters, knowing that four Stones made only twenty-four Houses.

But he might have played with the Italian transcription, which contained two vowels. With six letters—Iahveh—he had seven hundred and twenty permutations at his disposal. The repetitions didn't count, because Diotallevi had said that the two hes must be taken as two different letters. Belbo could have chosen, say, the thirty-sixth or the hundred and twentieth.

I had arrived at Belbo's at about eleven; it was now one. I would have to write a program for anagrams of six letters, and the best way to do that was to modify the program I already had written for four.

I needed some fresh air. I went out, bought myself some food, another bottle of whiskey.

I came back, left the sandwiches in a corner, and started on the whiskey as I inserted the Basic disk and went to work. I made the usual mistakes, and the debugging took me a good half hour, but by two-thirty the program was functional and the seven hundred and twenty names of God were running down the screen.

```
iahveh   iahvhe   iahevh   iahehv   iahhve   iahhev   iavheh   iavhhe
iavehh   iavehh   iavhhe   iavheh   iaehvh   iaehhv   iaevhh   iaevhh
iaehhv   iaehvh   iahhve   iahhev   iahvhe   iahveh   iahehv   iahevh
ihaveh   ihavhe   ihaevh   ihaehv   ihahve   ihahev   ihvaeh   ihvahe
ihveah   ihveha   ihvhae   ihvhea   iheavh   iheahv   ihevah   ihevha
ihehav   ihehva   ihhave   ihhaev   ihhvae   ihhvea   ihheav   ihheva
ivaheh   ivahhe   ivaehh   ivaehh   ivahhe   ivaheh   ivhaeh   ivhahe
ivheah   ivheha   ivhhae   ivhhea   iveahh   iveahh   ivehah   ivehha
ivehah   ivehha   ivhahe   ivhaeh   ivhhae   ivhhea   ievhah   ievhha
ieahvh   ieahhv   ieavhh   ieavhh   ieahhv   ieahvh   iehavh   iehahv
iehvah   iehvha   iehhav   iehhva   ievahh   ievahh   ievhah   ievhha
ievhah   ievhha   iehahv   iehavh   iehhav   iehhva   iehvah   iehvha
ihahve   ihahev   ihavhe   ihaveh   ihaehv   ihaevh   ihhave   ihhaev
ihhvae   ihhvea   ihheav   ihheva   ihvahe   ihvaeh   ihvhae   ihvhea
ihveah   ihveha   iheahv   iheavh   ihehav   ihehva   ihevah   ihevha
aihveh   aihvhe   aihevh   aihehv   aihhve   aihhev   aivheh   aivhhe
aivehh   aivehh   aivhhe   aivheh   aiehvh   aiehhv   aievhh   aievhh
aiehhv   aiehvh   aihhve   aihhev   aihvhe   aihveh   aihehv   aihevh
ahiveh   ahivhe   ahievh   ahiehv   ahihve   ahihev   ahvieh   ahvihe
ahveih   ahvehi   ahvhie   ahvhei   aheivh   aheihv   ahevih   ahevhi
ahehiv   ahehvi   ahhive   ahhiev   ahhvie   ahhvei   ahheiv   ahhevi
aviheh   avihhe   aviehh   aviehh   avihhe   aviheh   avhieh   avhihe
avheih   avhehi   avhhie   avhhei   aveihh   aveihh   avehih   avehhi
avehih   avehhi   avhihe   avhieh   avhhie   avhhei   avehih   avehhi
aeihvh   aeihhv   aeivhh   aeivhh   aeihhv   aeihvh   aehivh   aehihv
aehvih   aehvhi   aehhiv   aehhvi   aevihh   aevihh   aevhih   aevhhi
aevhih   aevhhi   aehihv   aehivh   aehhiv   aehhvi   aehvih   aehvhi
ahihve   ahihev   ahivhe   ahiveh   ahiehv   ahievh   ahhive   ahhiev
ahhvie   ahhvei   ahheiv   ahhevi   ahvihe   ahvieh   ahvhie   ahvhei
ahveih   ahvehi   aheihv   aheivh   ahehiv   ahehvi   ahevih   ahevhi
hiaveh   hiavhe   hiaevh   hiaehv   hiahve   hiahev   hivaeh   hivahe
hiveah   hiveha   hivhae   hivhea   hieavh   hieahv   hievah   hievha
hiehav   hiehva   hihave   hihaev   hihvae   hihvea   hiheav   hiheva
haiveh   haivhe   haievh   haiehv   haihve   haihev   havieh   havihe
haveih   havehi   havhie   havhei   haeivh   haeihv   haevih   haevhi
haehiv   haehvi   hahive   hahiev   hahvie   hahvei   haheiv   hahevi
```

hviaeh hviahe hvieah hvieha hvihae hvihea hvaieh hvaihe
hvaeih hvaehi hvahie hvahei hveiah hveiha hveaih hveahi
hvehia hvehai hvhiae hvhiea hvhaie hvhaei hvheia hvheai
heiavh heiahv heivah heivha heihav heihva heaivh heaihv
heavih heavhi heahiv heahvi heviah heviha hevaih hevahi
hevhia hevhai hehiav hehiva hehaiv hehavi hehvia hehvai
hhiave hhiaev hhivae hhivea hhieav hhieva hhaive hhaiev
hhavie hhavei hhaeiv hhaevi hhviae hhviea hhvaie hhvaei
hhveia hhveai hheiav hheiva hheaiv hheavi hhevia hhevai

viaheh viaheh viaehh viaehh viahhe viahhe vihaeh vihahe
viheah viheha vihhae vihhea vieahh vieahh viehah viehha
viehah viehha vihahe vihaeh vihhae vihhea viheah viheha
vaiheh vaiheh vaiehh vaiehh vaihhe vaihhe vahieh vahihe
vaheih vahehi vahhie vahhei vaeihh vaeihh vaehih vaehhi
vaehih vaehhi vahihe vahieh vahhie vahhei vaheih vahehi
vhiaeh vhiahe vhieah vhieha vhihae vhihea vhaieh vhaihe
vhaeih vhaehi vhahie vhahei vheiah vheiha vheaih vheahi
vhehia vhehai vhhiae vhhiea vhhaie vhhaei vhheia vhheai
veiahh veiahh veihah veihha veihah veihha veaihh veaihh
veahih veahhi veahih veahhi vehiah vehiha vehaih vehahi
vehhia vehhai vehiah vehiha vehaih vehahi vehhia vehhai
vhiahe vhiaeh vhihae vhihea vhieah vhieha vhaihe vhaieh
vhahie vhahei vhaeih vhaehi vhhiae vhhiea vhhaie vhhaei
vhheia vhheai vheiah vheiha vheaih vheahi vhehia vhehai

eiahvh eiahvh eiavhh eiavhh eiahhv eiahhv eihavh eihahv
eihvah eihvha eihhav eihhva eivahh eivahh eivhah eivhha
eivhah eivhha eihahv eihavh eihhav eihhva eihvah eihvha
eaihvh eaihvh eaivhh eaivhh eaihhv eaihhv eahivh eahihv
eahvih eahvhi eahhiv eahhvi eavihh eavihh eavhih eavhhi
eavhih eavhhi eahihv eahivh eahhiv eahhvi eahvih eahvhi
ehiavh ehiahv ehivah ehivha ehihav ehihva ehaivh ehaihv
ehavih ehavhi ehahiv ehahvi ehviah ehviha ehvaih ehvahi
ehvhia ehvhai ehhiav ehhiva ehhaiv ehhavi ehhvia ehhvai
eviahh eviahh evihah evihha evihah evihha evaihh evaihh
evahih evahhi evahih evahhi evhiah evhiha evhaih evhahi
evhhia evhhai evhiah evhiha evhaih evhahi evhhia evhhai
ehiahv ehiavh ehihav ehihva ehivah ehivha ehaihv ehaivh
ehahiv ehahvi ehavih ehavhi ehhiav ehhiva ehhaiv ehhavi
ehhvia ehhvai ehviah ehviha ehvaih ehvahi ehvhia ehvhai

hiahve hiahev hiavhe hiaveh hiaehv hiaevh hihave hihaev
hihvae hihvea hiheav hiheva hivahe hivaeh hivhae hivhea
hiveah hiveha hieahv hieavh hiehav hiehva hievah hievha
haihve haihev haivhe haiveh haiehv haievh hahive hahiev
hahvie hahvei haheiv hahevi havihe havieh havhie havhei
haveih havehi haeihv haeivh haehiv haehvi haevih haevhi

```
hhiave   hhiaev   hhivae   hhivea   hhieav   hhieva   hhaive   hhaiev
hhavie   hhavei   hhaeiv   hhaevi   hhviae   hhviea   hhvaie   hhvaei
hhveia   hhveai   hheiav   hheiva   hheaiv   hheavi   hhevia   hhevai
hviahe   hviaeh   hvihae   hvihea   hvieah   hvieha   hvaihe   hvaieh
hvahie   hvahei   hvaeih   hvaehi   hvhiae   hvhiea   hvhaie   hvhaei
hvheia   hvheai   hveiah   hveiha   hveaih   hveahi   hvehia   hvehai
heiahv   heiavh   heihav   heihva   heivah   heivha   heaihv   heaivh
heahiv   heahvi   heavih   heavhi   hehiav   hehiva   hehaiv   hehavi
hehvia   hehvai   heviah   heviha   hevaih   hevahi   hevhia   hevhai
```

I took the pages from the printer without separating them, as if I were consulting the scroll of the Torah. I tried name number thirty-six. And drew a blank. A last sip of whiskey, then with hesitant fingers I tried name number one hundred and twenty. Nothing.

I wanted to die. Yet I felt that by now I was Jacopo Belbo, that he had surely thought as I was thinking. So I must have made some mistake, a stupid, trivial mistake. I was getting closer. Had Belbo, for some reason that escaped me, perhaps counted from the end of the list?

Casaubon, you fool, I said to myself. Of course he started from the end. That is, he counted from right to left. Belbo had fed the computer the name of God transliterated into Latin letters, including the vowels, but the word was Hebrew, so he had written it from right to left. The input hadn't been IAHVEH, but HEVHAI. The order of the permutations had to be inverted.

I counted from the end and tried both names again.

Nothing.

This was all wrong. I was clinging stubbornly to an elegant but false hypothesis. It happens to the best scientists.

No, not to the best scientists. To everyone. Only a month ago we had remarked that in three recent novels, at least three, there was a protagonist trying to find the name of God in a computer. Belbo would have been more original. Besides which, when you choose a password, you pick something easy to remember, something that comes to mind automatically. Ihvhea, indeed! In that case he would have had to apply the notarikon to the temurah, to invent an acrostic to remember the word. Something like Imelda Has Vindicated Hiram's Evil Assassination.

But why should Belbo have thought in Diotallevi's cabalistic terms?

Belbo was obsessed by the Plan, and into the Plan we had put all sorts of other ingredients: Rosicrucians, Synarchy, Homunculi, the Pendulum, the Tower, the Druids, the Ennoia . . .

Ennoia. I thought of Lorenza Pellegrini. I reached out, picked up her censored photograph, looked at it, and an inopportune thought surfaced, the memory of that evening in Piedmont. . . . I read the inscription on the picture: "For I am the first and the last, the honored and the hated, the saint and the prostitute. Sophia."

She must have written that after Riccardo's party. Sophia. Six letters. And why would they need to be scrambled? I was the one with the devious mind. Belbo loves Lorenza, loves her precisely because she is the way she is, and she is Sophia. And at that very moment she might be . . . No, no good. Belbo was devious, too. I recalled Diotallevi's words: "In the second sefirah the dark aleph changes into the luminous aleph. From the Dark Point spring the letters of the Torah. The consonants are the body, the vowels the breath, and together they accompany the worshiper as he chants. When the chant moves, the consonants and vowels move with it, and from them rises Hokhmah—wisdom, knowledge, the primordial thought that contains, as in a box, everything, all that will unfold in creation. Hokhmah holds the essence of all that will emanate from it."

And what was Abulafia, with its secret files? The box that held everything Belbo knew, or thought he knew. His Sophia. With her secret name he would enter Abulafia, the thing—the only thing— he made love to. But, making love to Abulafia, he thinks of Lorenza. So he needs a word that will give him possession of Abulafia but also serve as a talisman to give him possession of Lorenza, to penetrate Lorenza's heart as he penetrates Abulafia's. But Abulafia should be impenetrable to others, as Lorenza is impenetrable to him. It is Belbo's hope that he can enter, know, and conquer Lorenza's secret in the same way that he possesses Abulafia.

But I was making this up. My explanation was just like the Plan: substituting wishes for reality.

Drunk, I sat down at the keyboard again and tapped out SOPHIA. Again, nothing, and again the machine asked me politely: "Do you have the password?" You stupid machine, you feel no emotion at the thought of Lorenza.

6

Judá León se dio a permutaciones
De letras y a complejas variaciones
Y alfin pronunció el Nombre que es la Clave,
La Puerta, el Eco, el Huésped y el Palacio . . .
   —Jorge Luis Borges, *El Golem*

And then, in a fit of hate, as I worked again at Abulafia's obtuse question "Do you have the password?" I typed: NO.

The screen began to fill with words, lines, codes, a flood of communication.

I had broken into Abulafia.

Thrilled by my triumph, I didn't ask myself why Belbo had chosen that, of all words. Now I know, and I know, too, that in a moment of lucidity he understood what I have come to understand only now. But last Thursday, my only thought was that I had won.

I danced, clapped my hands, sang an old army song. Then I went to the bathroom and washed my face. When I came back, I began printing out the files, last files first, what Belbo had written just before his flight to Paris. As the printer chattered implacably, I devoured some food and drank some more whiskey.

When the printer stopped and I read what Belbo had written, I was aghast, unable to decide whether this was an extraordinary revelation or the wild raving of a madman.

What did I really know about Jacopo Belbo? What had I learned about him in the two years I worked at his side, almost every day? How much faith could I put in the word of a man who, by his own admission, was writing under exceptional circumstances, in a fog of alcohol, tobacco, and terror, completely cut off from the world for three days?

It was already night, Thursday, June 21. My eyes were watering. I had been staring at the screen and then at the printer's pointillist anthill since morning. What I had read might be true or it might be false, but Belbo said he would call in the morning. I would have to wait here. My head swam.

I staggered into the bedroom and fell, still dressed, onto the unmade bed.

At around eight I awoke from a deep, sticky sleep, not realizing at first where I was. Luckily I found a can of coffee and was able to make myself a few cups. The phone didn't ring. I didn't dare go out to buy anything, because Belbo might call while I was gone.

I went back to the machine and began printing out the other disks in chronological order. I found games, exercises, and accounts of events I knew about, but told from Belbo's private point of view, so that they were reshaped and appeared to me now in a different light. I found diary fragments, confessions, outlines for works of fiction made with the bitter obstinacy of a man who knows that his efforts are doomed to failure. I found descriptions of people I remembered, but now I saw them with different faces—sinister faces, unless this was because I was seeing them as part of a horrible final mosaic.

And I found a file devoted entirely to quotations taken from Belbo's most recent reading. I recognized them immediately. Together we had pored over so many texts during those months. . . . The quotations were numbered: one hundred and twenty in all. The number was probably a deliberate choice; if not, the coincidence was disturbing. But why those passages and not others?

Today I reinterpret Belbo's files, the whole story they tell, in the light of that quotation file. I tell the passages like the beads of a heretical rosary. For Belbo some of them may have been an alarm, a hope of rescue. Or am I, too, no longer able to distinguish common sense from unmoored meaning? I try to convince myself that my reinterpretation is correct, but as recently as this morning, someone told me—me, not Belbo—that I was mad.

On the horizon, beyond the Bricco, the moon is slowly rising. This big house is filled with strange rustling sounds, termites perhaps, mice, or the ghost of Adelino Canepa. . . . I dare not walk along the hall. I stay in Uncle Carlo's study and look out the window. From time to time I step onto the terrace, to see if anyone is coming up the hill. I feel that I'm in a movie. How pathetic! "Here come the bad guys. . . ."

Yet the hill is so calm tonight, a summer night now.

Adventurous, dubious, and demented were the events I reconstructed to pass the time, and to keep up my spirits, as I stood waiting in the periscope two nights ago, between five and ten o'clock, moving my legs as if to some Afro-Brazilian beat to help the blood circulate.

I thought back over the last few years, abandoning myself to the magic rolling of the atabaques, accepting the revelation that our fantasies, begun as a mechanical ballet, were about to be transformed, in this temple of things mechanical, into rite, possession, apparition, and the dominion of Exu.

In the periscope I had no proof that what I had learned from the printout was true. I could still take refuge in doubt. At midnight, perhaps, I would discover that I had come to Paris and hidden myself like a thief in a harmless museum of technology only because I had foolishly fallen into a macumba staged for credulous tourists, letting myself be hypnotized by the perfumadores and the rhythm of the pontos.

As I recomposed the mosaic, my mood changed from disenchantment to pity to suspicion—and I wish that now I could rid myself of this present lucidity and recover that same vacillation between mystic illusion and the presentiment of a trap; recover what I thought then as I mulled over the documents I had read so frantically the day before and reread that morning at the airport and during the flight to Paris.

How irresponsibly Belbo, Diotallevi, and I had rewritten the world, or—as Diotallevi would have put it—had rediscovered what in the Book had been engraved at white heat between the black lines formed by the letters, like black insects, that supposedly made the Torah clear!

And now, two days later, having achieved, I hope, serenity and amor fati, I can tell the story I reconstructed so anxiously (hoping it was false) inside the periscope, the story I had read two days ago in Belbo's apartment, the story I had lived for twelve years between Pilade's whiskey and the dust of Garamond Press.

BINAH

7

Do not expect too much of the end of the world.
—Stanislaw J. Lec, *Aforyzmy. Fraszki,* Kraków,
    Wydawnictwo Literackie, 1977, "Myśli nieuczesane"

To enter a university a year or two after 1968 was like being admitted to the Académie de Saint-Cyr in 1793: you felt your birth date was wrong. Jacopo Belbo, who was almost fifteen years older than I, later convinced me that every generation feels this way. You are always born under the wrong sign, and to live in this world properly you have to rewrite your own horoscope day by day.

I believe that what we become depends on what our fathers teach us at odd moments, when they aren't trying to teach us. We are formed by little scraps of wisdom. When I was ten, I asked my parents to subscribe to a weekly magazine that was publishing comic-strip versions of the great classics of literature. My father, not because he was stingy, but because he was suspicious of comic strips, tried to beg off. "The purpose of this magazine," I pontificated, quoting the ad, "is to educate the reader in an entertaining way." "The purpose of your magazine," my father replied without looking up from his paper, "is the purpose of every magazine: to sell as many copies as it can."

That day, I began to be incredulous.

Or, rather, I regretted having been credulous. I regretted having allowed myself to be borne away by a passion of the mind. Such is credulity.

Not that the incredulous person doesn't believe in anything. It's just that he doesn't believe in everything. Or he believes in one thing at a time. He believes a second thing only if it somehow follows from the first thing. He is nearsighted and methodical, avoiding wide horizons. If two things don't fit, but you believe both of them, thinking that somewhere, hidden, there must be a third thing that connects them, that's credulity.

49

Incredulity doesn't kill curiosity; it encourages it. Though distrustful of logical chains of ideas, I loved the polyphony of ideas. As long as you don't believe in them, the collision of two ideas—both false—can create a pleasing interval, a kind of diabolus in musica. I had no respect for some ideas people were willing to stake their lives on, but two or three ideas that I did not respect might still make a nice melody. Or have a good beat, and if it was jazz, all the better.

"You live on the surface," Lia told me years later. "You sometimes seem profound, but it's only because you piece a lot of surfaces together to create the impression of depth, solidity. That solidity would collapse if you tried to stand it up."

"Are you saying I'm superficial?"

"No," she answered. "What others call profundity is only a tesseract, a four-dimensional cube. You walk in one side and come out another, and you're in their universe, which can't coexist with yours."

(Lia, now that They have walked into the cube and invaded our world, I don't know if I'll ever see you again. And it was all my fault: I made Them believe there was a depth, a depth that They, in their weakness, desired.)

What did I really think fifteen years ago? A nonbeliever, I felt guilty in the midst of all those believers. And since it seemed to me that they were in the right, I decided to believe, as you might decide to take an aspirin: It can't hurt, and you might get better.

So there I was, in the midst of the Revolution, or at least in the most stupendous imitation of it, seeking an honorable faith. It was honorable, for example, to take part in rallies and marches. I chanted "Fascist scum, your time has come!" with everybody else. I never threw paving stones or ball bearings, out of fear that others might do unto me as I did unto them, but I experienced a kind of moral excitement escaping along narrow downtown streets when the police charged. I would come home with the sense of having performed a duty. In the meetings I remained untouched by the disagreements that divided the various groups: I always had the feeling that if you substituted the right phrase for another phrase, you could move from group to group. I amused myself by finding the right phrases. I modulated.

At the demonstrations, I would fall in behind one banner or another, drawn by a girl who had aroused my interest, so I came to the conclusion that for many of my companions political activism was a sexual thing. But sex was a passion. I wanted only curiosity. True, in the course of my reading about the Templars and the various atrocities attributed to them, I had come across Carpocrates's assertion that to escape the tyranny of the angels, the masters of the cosmos, every possible ignominy should be perpetrated, that you should discharge all debts to the world and to your own body, for only by committing every act can the soul be freed of its passions and return to its original purity. When we were inventing the Plan, I found that many addicts of the occult pursued that path in their search for enlightenment. According to his biographers, Aleister Crowley, who has been called the most perverted man of all time and who did everything that could be done with his worshipers, both men and women, chose only the ugliest partners of either sex. I have the nagging suspicion, however, that his lovemaking was incomplete.

There must be a connection between the lust for power and impotentia coeundi. I liked Marx, I was sure that he and his Jenny had made love merrily. You can feel it in the easy pace of his prose and in his humor. On the other hand, I remember remarking one day in the corridors of the university that if you screwed Krupskaya all the time, you'd end up writing a lousy book like *Materialism and Empiriocriticism*. I was almost clubbed. A tall guy with a Tartar mustache said I was a fascist. I'll never forget him. He later shaved his head and now belongs to a commune where they weave baskets.

I evoke the mood of those days only to reconstruct my state of mind when I began to visit Garamond Press and made friends with Jacopo Belbo. I was the type who looked at discussions of What Is Truth only with a view toward correcting the manuscript. If you were to quote "I am that I am," for example, I thought that the fundamental problem was where to put the comma, inside the quotation marks or outside.

That's why I wisely chose philology. The University of Milan was the place to be in those years. Everywhere else in the country students were taking over classrooms and telling the professors they should teach only proletarian sciences, but at our university, except for a few incidents, a constitutional pact—or, rather, a territorial compromise—held. The Revolution occupied the grounds, the auditorium, and the main halls, while traditional Culture, protected, withdrew to the inner corridors and upper floors, where it went on talking as if nothing had happened.

The result was that I could spend the morning debating proletarian matters downstairs and the afternoon pursuing aristocratic knowledge upstairs. In these two parallel universes I lived comfortably and felt no contradiction. I firmly believed that an egalitarian society was dawning, but I also thought that the trains, for example, in this better society ought to run better, and the militants around me were not learning how to shovel coal into the furnace, work the switches, or draw up timetables. Somebody had to be ready to operate the trains.

I felt like a kind of Stalin laughing to himself, somewhat remorsefully, and thinking: "Go ahead, you poor Bolsheviks. I'm going to study in this seminary in Tiflis, and we'll see which one of us gets to draft the Five-Year Plan."

Perhaps because I was always surrounded by enthusiasm in the morning, in the afternoon I came to equate learning with distrust. I wanted to study something that confined itself to what could be documented, as opposed to what was merely a matter of opinion.

For no particular reason I signed up for a seminar on medieval history and chose, for my thesis subject, the trial of the Templars. It was a story that fascinated me from the moment I first glanced at the documents. At that time, when we were struggling against those in power, I was wholeheartedly outraged by the trial in which the Templars, through evidence it would be generous to call circumstantial, were sentenced to the stake. Then I quickly learned that, for centuries after their execution, countless lovers of the occult persisted in looking for them, seeking everywhere, without ever producing proof of their existence. This visionary excess offended my incredulity, and I resolved to waste no more time on these hunters of secrets. I would stick to primary sources. The Templars were monastic knights; their order was recognized by the Church. If the Church dissolved that order, as in fact it had seven centuries ago, then the Templars could no longer exist. Therefore, if they existed, they weren't Templars. I drew up a bibliography of more than a hundred books, but in the end read only about thirty of them.

It was through the Templars that I first got to know Jacopo Belbo—at Pilade's toward the end of '72, when I was at work on my thesis.

8

Having come from the light and from the gods, here I am in exile, separated from them.
— Fragment of Turfa'n M7

In those days Pilade's Bar was a free port, a galactic tavern where alien invaders from Ophiulco could rub elbows peaceably with the soldiers of the Empire patrolling the Van Allen belt. It was an old bar near one of the navigli, the Milan canals, with a zinc counter and a billiard table. Local tram drivers and artisans would drop in first thing in the morning for a glass of white wine. In '68 and in the years that followed, Pilade's became a kind of Rick's Café, where Movement activists could play cards with a reporter from the bosses' newspaper who had come in for a whiskey after putting the paper to bed, while the first trucks were already out distributing the Establishment's lies to the newsstands. But at Pilade's the reporter also felt like an exploited proletarian, a producer of surplus value chained to an ideological assembly line, and the students forgave him.

Between eleven at night and two in the morning you might see a young publisher, an architect, a crime reporter trying to work his way up to the arts page, some Brera Academy painters, a few semi-successful writers, and students like me.

A minimum of alcoholic stimulation was the rule, and old Pilade, while he still stocked his big bottles of white for the tram drivers and the most aristocratic customers, replaced root beer and cream soda with pétillant wines with the right labels for the intellectuals and Johnnie Walker for the revolutionaries. I could write the political history of those years based on how Red Label gradually gave way to twelve-year-old Ballantine and then to single malt.

At the old billiard table the painters and motormen still challenged each other to games, but with the arrival of the new clientele, Pilade also put in a pinball machine.

I was never able to make the little balls last. At first I attributed that to absent-mindedness or a lack of manual dexterity. I learned the truth years later after watching Lorenza Pellegrini play. At the beginning I hadn't noticed her, but then she came into focus one evening when I followed the direction of Belbo's gaze.

Belbo had a way of standing at the bar as if he were just passing through (he had been a regular there for at least ten years). He often took part in conversations, at the counter or at a table, but almost always he did no more than drop some short remark that would instantly freeze all enthusiasm, no matter what subject was being discussed. He had another freezing technique: asking a question. Someone would be talking about an event, the whole group would be completely absorbed, then Belbo, turning his pale, slightly absent eyes on the speaker, with his glass at hip level, as though he had long forgotten he was drinking, would ask, "Is that a fact?" Or, "Really?" At which point everyone, including the narrator, would suddenly begin to doubt the story. Maybe it was the way Belbo's Piedmont drawl made his statements interrogative and his interrogatives taunting. And he had yet another Piedmont trick: looking into his interlocutor's eyes, but as if he were avoiding them. His gaze didn't exactly shirk dialogue, but he would suddenly seem to concentrate on some distant convergence of parallel lines no one had paid attention to. He made you feel that you had been staring all this time at the one place that was unimportant.

It wasn't just his gaze. Belbo could dismiss you with the smallest gesture, a brief interjection. Suppose you were trying hard to show that it was Kant who really completed the Copernican revolution in modern philosophy, suppose you were staking your whole future on that thesis. Belbo, sitting opposite you, with his eyes half-closed, would suddenly look down at his hands or at his knee with an Etruscan smile. Or he would sit back with his mouth open, eyes on the ceiling, and mumble, "Yes, Kant . . ." Or he would commit himself more explicitly, in an assault on the whole system of transcendental idealism: "You really think Kant meant all that stuff?" Then he would look at you with solicitude, as if you, and not he, had disturbed the spell, and he would then encourage you: "Go ahead, go ahead. I mean, there must be something to it. The man had a mind, after all."

But sometimes Belbo, when he became really angry, lost his composure. Since loss of composure was the one thing he could not tolerate in others, his own was wholly internal—and regional. He would purse his lips, raise his eyes, then look down, tilt his head to the left, and say in a soft voice: "Ma gavte la nata." For anyone who didn't know that Piedmontese expression, he would occasionally explain: "Ma gavte la nata. Take out the cork." You say it to one who is full of himself, the idea being that what causes him to swell and strut is the pressure of a cork stuck in his behind. Remove it, and phsssssh, he returns to the human condition.

Belbo's remarks had a way of making you see the vanity of things, and they delighted me. But I drew the wrong conclusion from them, considering them an expression of supreme contempt for the banality of other people's truth.

Now, having breached the secret of Abulafia and, with it, Belbo's soul, I see that what I thought disenchantment and a philosophy of life was a form of melancholy. His intellectual disrespect concealed a desperate thirst for the Absolute. This was not immediately obvious, because Belbo had many moods—irresponsibility, hesitation, indifference—and there were also moments when he relaxed and enjoyed conversation, asserting absolutely contradictory ideas with lighthearted disbelief. Then he and Diotallevi would create handbooks for impossibilities, or invent upside-down worlds or bibliographical monstrosities. When you saw him so enthusiastically talkative, constructing his Rabelaisian Sorbonne, there was no way of knowing how much he suffered at his exile from the faculty of theology, the real one.

I had deliberately thrown that address away; he had mislaid it and could never resign himself to the loss.

In Abulafia's files I found many pages of a pseudo diary that Belbo had entrusted to the password, confident that he was not betraying his often-repeated vow to remain a mere spectator of the world. Some entries carried old dates; obviously he had put these on the computer out of nostalgia, or because he planned to recycle them eventually. Others were more recent, after the advent of Abu. His writing was a mechanical game, a solitary pondering on his own errors, but it was not—he thought—"creation," for creation had to be inspired by love of someone who is not ourselves.

But Belbo, without realizing it, had crossed that Rubicon; he was creating. Unfortunately. His enthusiasm for the Plan came from his ambition to write a book. No matter if the book were made entirely of errors, intentional, deadly errors. As long as you remain in your private vacuum, you can pretend you are in harmony with the One. But the moment you pick up the clay, electronic or otherwise, you become a demiurge, and he who embarks on the creation of worlds is already tainted with corruption and evil.

FILENAME: A bevy of fair women

It's like this: toutes les femmes que j'ai recontrées se dressent aux horizons—avec les gestes piteux et les regards tristes des sémaphores sous la pluie . . .

Aim high, Belbo. First love, the Most Blessed Virgin. Mama singing as she holds me on her lap as if rocking me though I'm past the age for lullabies, but I asked her to sing because I love her voice and the lavender scent of her bosom. "O Queen of Heaven fair and pure, hail, O daughter, queen demure, hail, mother of our Savior!"

Naturally, the first woman in my life was not mine. By definition she was not anyone's. I fell immediately in love with the only person capable of doing everything without me.

Then, Marilena (Marylena? Mary Lena?). Describe the lyric twilight, her golden hair, big blue bow, me standing in front of the bench with my nose upward, she tightrope-walking on the top rail of the back, swaying, arms outstretched for balance (delicious extrasystoles!), skirt flapping around her pink thighs. High above me, unattainable.

Sketch: that same evening as Mama sprinkles talcum powder on my sister's pink skin. I ask when her wee-wee will finally grow out. Mama's answer is that little girls don't grow wee-wees, they stay like that. Suddenly I see Mary Lena again, the white of her underpants visible beneath the fluttering blue skirt, and I realize that she is blond and haughty and inaccessible because she is different. No possible relationship; she belongs to another race.

My third woman, swiftly lost in the abyss, where she has plunged. She has died in her sleep, virginal Ophelia amid flowers on her bier. The priest is reciting the prayer for the dead, when suddenly she sits up on the catafalque, pale, frowning, vindictive, pointing her finger, and her voice cavernous: "Don't pray for me, Father. Before I fell asleep last night, I had an impure thought, the only one in my life, and now I am damned." Find the book of my first communion. Does it have this illustration, or did I make the whole thing up? She must have died while thinking of me; I was the impure thought, desiring the untouchable Mary Lena, she of a different species and fate. I am guilty of her damnation, I am guilty of the damnation of all women who are damned. It is right that I should not have had these three women: my punishment for wanting them.

I lose the first because she's in paradise, the second because she's in purgatory envying the penis that will never be hers, and the third because she's in hell. Theologically symmetrical. But this has already been written.

On the other hand, there's the story of Cecilia, and Cecilia is here on earth. I used to think about her before falling asleep: I would be climbing the hill on my way to the farm for milk, and when the partisans started shooting at the roadblock from the hill opposite, I pictured myself rushing to her rescue, saving her from the horde of Fascist brigands who chased her, brandishing their weapons. Blonder than Mary Lena, more disturbing than the maiden in the sarcophagus, more pure and demure than the Virgin—Cecilia, alive and accessible. I could have talked to her so easily, for I was sure she could love one of my species. And, in fact, she did. His name was Papi; he had wispy blond hair and a tiny skull, was a year older than I, and had a saxophone. I didn't even have a trumpet. I never saw the two of them together, but all the kids at Sunday School laughed, poked one another in the ribs, and whispered, giggling, that the pair made love. They were probably lying, little peasants, horny as goats, but they were probably right that she (Marylena Cecilia bride and queen) was accessible, so accessible that someone had already gained access to her. In any case—the fourth case—I was out in the cold.

Could a story like this be made into a novel? Perhaps I should write, instead, about the women I avoid because I can have them. Or could have had them. Same story.

If you can't even decide what the story is, better stick to editing books on philosophy.

<hr>

9

In his right hand he held a golden trumpet.
—Johann Valentin Andreae, *Die Chymische Hochzeit des Christian Rosencreutz*, Strassburg, Zetzner, 1616, 1

In this file, I find the mention of a trumpet. The day before yesterday, in the periscope, I wasn't aware of its importance. The file had only one reference to it, and that marginal.

During the long afternoons at the Garamond office, Belbo, tormented by a manuscript, would occasionally look up and try to distract me, too, as I sat at the desk across from his sorting through old engravings of the World Fair. Then he would drift into reminiscence, prompt to ring down the curtain if he suspected I was taking him too seriously. He would recall scenes from his past, but only to illustrate a point, to castigate some vanity.

"I wonder where all this is heading," he remarked one day.

"Do you mean the twilight of Western civilization?"

"Twilight? Let the sun handle twilight. No. I was talking about our writers. This is my third manuscript this week: one on Byzantine law, one on the Finis Austriae, and one on the poems of the Earl of Rochester. Three very different subjects, wouldn't you say?"

"I would."

"Yet in all these manuscripts, at one point or another, Desire appears, and the Object of Desire. It must be a trend. With the Earl of Rochester I can understand it, but Byzantine law?"

"Just reject them."

"I can't. All three books have been funded by the National Research Council. Actually, they're not that bad. Maybe I'll just call the three authors and ask them to delete those parts. The Desire stuff doesn't make them look good either."

"What can the Object of Desire possibly be in Byzantine law?"

"Oh, you can slip it in. If there ever was an Object of Desire in Byzantine law, of course, it wasn't what this guy says it was. It never is."

"Never is what?"

"What you think it is. Once—I was five or six—I dreamed I had a trumpet. A gold trumpet. It was one of those dreams where you can feel honey flowing in your veins; you know what I mean? A kind of prepubescent wet dream. I don't think I've ever been as happy as I was in that dream. When I woke up, I realized there was no trumpet, and I started crying. I cried all day. This was before the war—it must have been '38—a time of poverty. If I had a son today and saw him in such despair, I'd say, 'All right, I'll buy you a trumpet.' It was only a toy, after all, it wouldn't have cost a fortune. But my parents never even considered such a thing. Spending money was a serious business in those days. And they were serious, too, about teaching a child he couldn't have everything he wanted. 'I can't stand cabbage soup,' I'd tell them—and it was true, for God's sake; cabbage made me sick. But they never said: 'Skip the soup today, then, and just eat your meat.' We may have been poor, but we still had a first course, a main course, and fruit. No. It was always: 'Eat what's on the table.' Sometimes, as a compromise, my grandmother would pick the cabbage out of my bowl, stringy piece by stringy piece. Then I'd have to eat the expurgated soup, which was more disgusting than before. And even this was a concession my father disapproved of."

"But what about the trumpet?"

He looked at me, hesitant. "Why are you so interested in the trumpet?"

"I'm not. You were the one who brought it up, to show how the Object of Desire is never what others think."

"The trumpet . . . My uncle and aunt from *** arrived that evening. They had no children, and I was their favorite nephew. Well, when they saw me bawling over my dream trumpet, they said they would fix everything: tomorrow we would go to the department store where there was a whole counter of toys—wonder of wonders—and I'd have the trumpet I wanted. I didn't sleep all night, and I couldn't sit still all the next morning. In the afternoon we went to the store, and they had at least three kinds of trumpets there. Little tin things, probably, but to me they were magnificent brass worthy of the Philharmonic. There was an army bugle, a slide trombone, and a trumpet of gold with a real trumpet mouthpiece but the keys of a saxophone. I couldn't decide, and maybe I took too long. Wanting them all, I must have given the impression that I didn't want any of them. Meanwhile, I believe my uncle and aunt looked at the price tags. My uncle and aunt weren't stingy; on the other hand, a Bakelite clarinet with silver keys was much cheaper. 'Wouldn't you like this better?' they asked. I tried it, produced a reasonable honk, and told myself that it was beautiful, but actually I was rationalizing. I knew they wanted me to take the clarinet because the trumpet cost a fortune. I couldn't demand such a sacrifice from my relatives, having been taught that if a person offers you something you like, you must say, 'No, thank you,' and not just once, not 'No, thank you,' with your hand out, but 'No, thank you' until the giver insists, until he says, 'Please, take it.' A well-bred child doesn't accept until that point. So I said maybe I didn't care about the trumpet, maybe the clarinet was all right, if that's what they wanted. And I looked up at them, hoping they would insist. They didn't, God bless them, they were delighted to buy me the clarinet, since—they said—that was what I wanted. It was too late to backtrack. I got the clarinet."

Belbo looked at me out of the corner of his eyes. "You want to know if I dreamed about the trumpet again?"

"I want to know," I said, "what the Object of Desire was."

"Ah," he said, turning back to his manuscript. "You see? You're obsessed by the Object of Desire, too. But it's not all that simple. . . . Suppose I had taken the trumpet. Would I have been truly happy then? What do you think, Casaubon?"

"I think you would have dreamed about the clarinet."

"I got the clarinet," he concluded sharply, "but I never played it."

"Never played it? Or never dreamed it?"

"Played it," he said, underlining his words, and for some reason I felt like a fool.

10

And finally nothing is cabalistically inferred from *vinum* save VIS NUMerorum, upon which numbers this Magia depends.
  —Cesare della Riviera, *Il Mondo Magico degli Eroi*, Mantua, Osanna, 1603, pp. 65–66

But I was talking about my first encounter with Belbo. We knew each other by sight, had exchanged a few words at Pilade's, but I didn't know much about him, only that he worked at Garamond Press, a small but serious publisher. I had come across a few Garamond books at the university.

"And what do you do?" he asked me one evening, as we were both leaning against the far end of the zinc bar, pressed close together by a festive crowd. He used the formal pronoun. In those days we all called one another by the familiar tu, even students and professors, even the clientele at Pilade's. "Tu—buy me a drink," a student wearing a parka would say to the managing editor of an important newspaper. It was like Moscow in the days of young Shklovski. We were all Mayakovskis, not one Zhivago among us. Belbo could not avoid the required tu, but he used it with pointed scorn, suggesting that although he was responding to vulgarity with vulgarity, there was still an abyss between acting intimate and being intimate. I heard him say tu with real affection only a few times, only to a few people: Diotallevi, one or two women. He used the formal pronoun with people he respected but hadn't known long. He addressed me formally the whole time we worked together, and I valued that.

"And what do you do?" he asked, with what I now know was friendliness.

"In real life or in this theater?" I said, nodding at our surroundings.

"In real life."

"I study."

"You mean you go to the university, or you study?"

"You may not believe this, but the two need not be mutually exclusive. I'm finishing a thesis on the Templars."

"What an awful subject," he said. "I thought that was for lunatics."

"No. I'm studying the real stuff. The documents of the trial. What do you know about the Templars, anyway?"

"I work for a publishing company. We deal with both lunatics and nonlunatics. After a while an editor can pick out the lunatics right away. If somebody brings up the Templars, he's almost always a lunatic."

"Don't I know! Their name is legion. But not *all* lunatics talk about the Templars. How do you identify the others?"

"I'll explain. By the way, what's your name?"

"Casaubon."

"Casaubon. Wasn't he a character in *Middlemarch?*"

"I don't know. There was also a Renaissance philologist by that name, but we're not related."

"The next round's on me. Two more, Pilade. All right, then. There are four kinds of people in this world: cretins, fools, morons, and lunatics."

"And that covers everybody?"

"Oh, yes, including us. Or at least me. If you take a good look, everybody fits into one of these categories. Each of us is sometimes a cretin, a fool, a moron, or a lunatic. A normal person is just a reasonable mix of these components, these four ideal types."

"Idealtypen."

"Very good. You know German?"

"Enough for bibliographies."

"When I was in school, if you knew German, you never graduated. You just spent your life knowing German. Nowadays I think that happens with Chinese."

"My German's poor, so I'll graduate. But let's get back to your typology. What about geniuses? Einstein, for example?"

"A genius uses one component in a dazzling way, fueling it with the others." He took a sip of his drink. "Hi there, beautiful," he said. "Made that suicide attempt yet?"

"No," a girl answered as she walked by. "I'm in a collective now."

"Good for you," Belbo said. He turned back to me. "Of course, there's no reason one can't have collective suicides, too."

"Getting back to the lunatics."

"Look, don't take me too literally. I'm not trying to put the universe in order. I'm just saying what a lunatic is from the point of view of a publishing house. Mine is an ad-hoc definition."

"All right. My round."

"All right. Less ice, Pilade. Otherwise it gets into the bloodstream too fast. Now then: cretins. Cretins don't even talk; they sort of slobber and stumble. You know, the guy who presses the ice cream cone against his forehead, or enters a revolving door the wrong way."

"That's not possible."

"It is for a cretin. Cretins are of no interest to us: they never come to publishers' offices. So let's forget about them."

"Let's."

"Being a fool is more complicated. It's a form of social behavior. A fool is one who always talks outside his glass."

"What do you mean?"

"Like this." He pointed at the counter near his glass. "He wants to talk about what's in the glass, but somehow or other he misses. He's the guy who puts his foot in his mouth. For example, he says how's your lovely wife to someone whose wife has just left him."

"Yes, I know a few of those."

"Fools are in great demand, especially on social occasions. They embarrass everyone but provide material for conversation. In their positive form, they become diplomats. Talking outside the glass when someone else blunders helps to change the subject. But fools don't interest us, either. They're never creative, their talent is all secondhand, so they don't submit manuscripts to publishers. Fools don't claim that cats bark, but they talk about cats when everyone else is talking about dogs. They offend all the rules of conversation, and when they really offend, they're magnificent. It's a dying breed, the embodiment of all the bourgeois virtues. What they really need is a Verdurin salon or even a chez Guermantes. Do you students still read such things?"

"*I* do."

"Well, a fool is a Joachim Murat reviewing his officers. He sees one from Martinique covered with medals. 'Vous êtes nègre?' Murat asks. 'Oui, mon général!' the man answers. And Murat says: 'Bravo, bravo, continuez!' And so on. You follow me? Forgive me, but

64

tonight I'm celebrating a historic decision in my life. I've stopped drinking. Another round? Don't answer, you'll make me feel guilty. Pilade!"

"What about the morons?"

"Ah. Morons never do the wrong thing. They get their reasoning wrong. Like the fellow who says all dogs are pets and all dogs bark, and cats are pets, too, and therefore cats bark. Or that all Athenians are mortal, and all the citizens of Piraeus are mortal, so all the citizens of Piraeus are Athenians."

"Which they are."

"Yes, but only accidentally. Morons will occasionally say something that's right, but they say it for the wrong reason."

"You mean it's okay to say something that's wrong as long as the reason is right."

"Of course. Why else go to the trouble of being a rational animal?"

"All great apes evolved from lower life forms, man evolved from lower life forms, therefore man is a great ape."

"Not bad. In such statements you suspect that something's wrong, but it takes work to show what and why. Morons are tricky. You can spot the fool right away (not to mention the cretin), but the moron reasons almost the way you do; the gap is infinitesimal. A moron is a master of paralogism. For an editor, it's bad news. It can take him an eternity to identify a moron. Plenty of morons' books are published, because they're convincing at first glance. An editor is not required to weed out the morons. If the Academy of Sciences doesn't do it, why should he?"

"Philosophers don't either. Saint Anselm's ontological argument is moronic, for example. God must exist because I can conceive Him as a being perfect in all ways, including existence. The saint confuses existence in thought with existence in reality."

"True, but Gaunilon's refutation is moronic, too. I can think of an island in the sea even if the island doesn't exist. He confuses thinking of the possible with thinking of the necessary."

"A duel between morons."

"Exactly. And God loves every minute of it. He chose to be unthinkable only to prove that Anselm and Gaunilon were morons. What a sublime purpose for creation, or, rather, for that act by which God willed Himself to be: to unmask cosmic moronism."

"We're surrounded by morons."

"Everyone's a moron—save me and thee. Or, rather—I wouldn't want to offend—save thee."

"Somehow I feel that Gödel's theorem has something to do with all this."

"I wouldn't know, I'm a cretin. Pilade!"

"My round."

"We'll split it. Epimenides the Cretan says all Cretans are liars. It must be true, because he's a Cretan himself and knows his countrymen well."

"That's moronic thinking."

"Saint Paul. Epistle to Titus. On the other hand, those who call Epimenides a liar have to think all Cretans aren't, but Cretans don't trust Cretans, therefore no Cretan calls Epimenides a liar."

"Isn't that moronic thinking?"

"You decide. I told you, they are hard to identify. Morons can even win the Nobel prize."

"Hold on. Of those who don't believe God created the world in seven days, some are not fundamentalists, but of those who do believe God created the world in seven days, some are. Therefore, of those who don't believe God created the world in seven days, some are fundamentalists. How's that?"

"My God—to use the mot juste—I wouldn't know. A moronism or not?"

"It is, definitely, even if it were true. Violates one of the laws of syllogisms: universal conclusions cannot be drawn from two particulars."

"And what if you were a moron?"

"I'd be in excellent, venerable company."

"You're right. And perhaps, in a logical system different from ours, our moronism is wisdom. The whole history of logic consists of attempts to define an acceptable notion of moronism. A task too immense. Every great thinker is someone else's moron."

"Thought as the coherent expression of moronism."

"But what is moronism to one is incoherence to another."

"Profound. It's two o'clock, Pilade's about to close, and we still haven't got to the lunatics."

"I'm getting there. A lunatic is easily recognized. He is a moron who doesn't know the ropes. The moron proves his thesis; he has a logic, however twisted it may be. The lunatic, on the other hand, doesn't concern himself at all with logic; he works by short circuits. For him, everything proves everything else. The lunatic is all idée fixe, and whatever he comes across confirms his lunacy. You can tell him by the liberties he takes with common sense, by his flashes of inspiration, and by the fact that sooner or later he brings up the Templars."

"Invariably?"

"There are lunatics who don't bring up the Templars, but those who do are the most insidious. At first they seem normal, then all of a sudden . . ." He was about to order another whiskey, but changed his mind and asked for the check. "Speaking of the Templars, the other day some character left me a manuscript on the subject. A lunatic, but with a human face. The book starts reasonably enough. Would you like to see it?"

"I'd be glad to. Maybe there's something I can use."

"I doubt that very much. But drop in if you have a spare half hour. Number 1, Via Sincero Renato. The visit will be of more benefit to me than to you. You can tell me whether the book has any merit."

"What makes you trust me?"

"Who says I trust you? But if you come, I'll trust you. I trust curiosity."

A student rushed in, face twisted in anger. "Comrades! There are fascists along the canal with chains!"

"Let's get them," said the fellow with the Tartar mustache who had threatened me over Krupskaya. "Come on, comrades!" And they all left.

"What do you want to do?" I asked, feeling guilty. "Should we go along?"

"No," Belbo said. "Pilade sets these things up to clear the place out. For my first night on the wagon, I feel pretty high. Must be the cold-turkey effect. Everything I've said to you so far is false. Good night, Casaubon."

His sterility was infinite. It was part of the ecstasy.
—E. M. Cioran, *Le mauvais demiurge*, Paris, Gallimard,
    1969, "Pensées étranglées"

The conversation at Pilade's had shown me the public Belbo. But a keen observer would have been able to sense the melancholy behind the sarcasm. Not that Belbo's sarcasm was the mask. The mask, perhaps, was the private confessing he did. Or perhaps his melancholy itself was the mask, a contrivance to hide a deeper melancholy.

There is a document in which he tried to fictionalize what he told me about his job when I went to Garamond the next day. It contains all his precision and passion, the disappointment of an editor who could write only through others while yearning for creativity of his own. It also has the moral severity that led him to punish himself for desiring something to which he did not feel entitled. Though he painted his desire in pathetic and garish hues, I never knew a man who could pity himself with such contempt.

FILENAME: Seven Seas Jim

Tomorrow, see young Cinti.

1. Good monograph, scholarly, perhaps a bit *too* scholarly.

2. In the conclusion, the comparison between Catullus, the poetae novi, and today's avant-garde is the best part.

3. Why not make this the introduction?

4. Convince him. He'll say that such flights of fancy don't belong in a philological series. He's afraid of alienating his professor, who is supposed to write the authoritative preface. A brilliant idea in the last two pages might go unnoticed, but at the beginning it would be too conspicuous, it would irritate the academic powers that be.

5. If, however, it is put into italics, in a conversational form, separate from the actual scholarship, then the hypothesis remains only a hypothesis and doesn't undermine the seriousness

of the work. And readers will be captivated at once; they'll approach the book in a totally different way.

Am I urging him to an act of freedom—or am I using him to write my own book?

Transforming books with a word here, a word there. Demiurge for the work of others. Tapping at the hardened clay, at the statue someone else has already carved. Instead of taking soft clay and molding my own. Give Moses the right tap with the hammer, and he'll talk.

See William S.

"I've looked at your work. Not bad. It has tension, imagination. Is this the first piece you've written?"

"No. I wrote another tragedy. It's the story of two lovers in Verona who—"

"Let's talk about this piece first, Mr. S. I was wondering why you set it in France. May I suggest—Denmark? It wouldn't require much work. If you just change two or three names, and turn the château of Châlons-sur-Marne into, say, the castle of Elsinore . . . In a Nordic, Protestant atmosphere, in the shadow of Kierkegaard, so to speak, all these existential overtones . . ."

"Perhaps you're right."

"I think I am. The work might need a little touching up stylistically. Nothing drastic; the barber's snips before he holds up the mirror for you, so to speak. The father's ghost, for example. Why at the end? I'd put him at the beginning. That way the father's warning helps motivate the young prince's behavior, and it establishes the conflict with the mother."

"Hmm, good idea. I'd only have to move one scene."

"Exactly. Now, style. This passage here, where the prince turns to the audience and begins his monologue on action and inaction. It's a nice speech, but he doesn't sound, well, troubled enough. 'To act or not to act? This is my problem.' I would say not 'my problem' but 'the question.' 'That is the question.' You see what I mean? It's not so much his individual problem as it is the whole question of existence. The question whether to be or not to be . . ."

. . . .

If you fill the world with children who do not bear your name, no one will know they are yours. Like being God in plain clothes. You are God, you wander through the city, you hear people talking about you, God this, God that, what a wonderful universe this is, and how elegant the law of gravity, and you smile to yourself behind your fake beard (no, better to go without a beard, because in a beard God is immediately recognizable). You soliloquize (God is always soliloquizing): "Here I am, the One, and they don't know it." If a pedestrian bumps into you in the street, or even insults you, you humbly apologize and move on, even though you're God and with a snap of your fingers can turn the world to ashes. But, infinitely powerful as you are, you can afford to be long-suffering.

A novel about God incognito. No. If I thought of it, somebody else must have already done it.

. . . .

You're an author, not yet aware of your powers. The woman you loved has betrayed you, life for you no longer has meaning, so one day, to forget, you take a trip on the *Titanic* and are shipwrecked in the South Seas. You are picked up, the sole survivor, by a pirogue full of natives, and spend long years, forgotten by the outside world, on this island inhabited only by Papuans. Girls serenade you with languorous songs, their swaying breasts barely covered by necklaces of pua blossoms. They call you Jim (they call all white men Jim), and one night an amber-skinned girl slips into your hut and says: "I yours, I with you." How nice, to lie there in the evening on the veranda and look up at the Southern Cross while she fans your brow.

You live by the cycle of dawn and sunset, and know nothing else. One day a motorboat arrives with some Dutchmen aboard, you learn that ten years have passed; you could go away with these Dutchmen, but you refuse. You start a business trading coconuts, you supervise the hemp harvest, the natives work for you, you sail from island to island, and everyone calls you Seven Seas Jim. A Portuguese adventurer ruined by drink comes to work with you and redeems himself. By now you're the talk of the Sunda, you advise the maharajah of Brunei in his campaign against the Dayaks of the river, you find an old cannon from the days of Tippo Sahib and get it back in working order. You train a squad of devoted Malayans whose teeth are blackened with betel. In a skirmish near the coral reef, old Sampan, his teeth blackened with betel, shields you with his own body; I gladly die for you, Seven Seas Jim. Good old Sampan, farewell, my friend.

Now you're famous in the whole archipelago, from Sumatra to Port-au-Prince. You trade with the English, too; at the harbor master's office in Darwin you're registered as Kurtz, and now you're Kurtz to everyone—only the natives still call you Seven Seas Jim. One evening, as the girl caresses you on the veranda and the Southern Cross shines brighter than ever overhead—ah! so different from the Great Bear—you realize you want to go back. Just for a little while, to see what, if anything, is left of you there.

You take a boat to Manila, from there a prop plane to Bali, then Samoa, the Admiralty Islands, Singapore, Tenerife, Timbuktu, Aleppo, Samarkand, Basra, Malta, and you're home.

Eighteen years have passed, life has left its mark on you: your face is tanned by the trade winds, you're older, perhaps also handsomer. Arriving, you discover that all the bookshops are displaying your books, in new critical editions, and your name has been carved into the pediment of your old school, where you learned to read and write. You are the Great Vanished Poet, the conscience of a generation. Romantic maidens kill themselves at your empty grave.

And then I encounter you, my love, with those wrinkles around your eyes, your face still beautiful though worn by memory and tender remorse. I almost pass you on the sidewalk, I'm only a few feet away, and you look at me as you look at all people, as though seeking another beyond their shadow. I could speak, erase the years. But to what end? Am I not, even now, fulfilled? I am like God, as solitary as He, as vain, and as despairing, unable to be one of my creatures. They dwell in my light, while I dwell in unbearable darkness, the source of that light.

. . . .

Go in peace, then, William S.! Famous, you pass and do not recognize me. I murmur to myself: To be or not to be. And I say to myself: Good for you, Belbo, good work. Go, old William S., and reap your meed of glory. You alone created; I merely made a few changes.

We midwives, who assist at the births of what others conceive, should be refused burial in consecrated ground. Like actors. Except that actors play with the world as it is, while we play with a plurality of make-believes, with the endless possibilities of existence in an infinite universe. . . .

How can life be so bountiful, providing such sublime rewards for mediocrity?

71

12

Sub umbra alarum tuarum, Jehova.
—*Fama Fraternitatis*, in *Allgemeine und general Reformation*,
Cassel, Wessel, 1514, conclusion

The next day, I went to Garamond Press. Number 1, Via Sincero Renato, opened into a dusty passage, from which you could glimpse a courtyard and a rope-maker's shop. To the right was an elevator that looked like something out of an industrial archeology exhibit. When I tried to take it, it shuddered, jerked, as if unable to make up its mind to ascend, so prudently I got out and climbed two flights of dusty, almost circular wooden stairs. I later learned that Mr. Garamond loved this building because it reminded him of a publishing house in Paris. A metal plate on the landing said GARAMOND PRESS, and an open door led to a lobby with no switchboard or receptionist of any kind. But you couldn't go in without being seen from a little outer office, and I was immediately confronted by a person, probably female, of indeterminate age and a height that could euphemistically be called below average.

She accosted me in a foreign language that was somehow familiar; then I realized it was Italian, an Italian almost completely lacking in vowels. When I asked for Belbo, she led me down a corridor to an office in the back.

Belbo welcomed me cordially: "So, you are a serious person. Come in." He had me sit opposite his desk, which was old, like everything else, and piled high with manuscripts, as were the shelves on the walls.

"I hope Gudrun didn't frighten you," he said.

"Gudrun? That . . . signora?"

"Signorina. Her name isn't really Gudrun. We call her that because of her Nibelung look and because her speech is vaguely Teutonic. She wants to say everything quickly, so she saves time by leaving out the vowels. But she has a sense of justitia aequatrix: When she types, she skips consonants."

72

"What does she do here?"

"Everything, unfortunately. In every publishing house there is one person who is indispensable, the only one who can find things in the mess that he or she creates. At least when a manuscript is lost, you know whose fault it is."

"She loses manuscripts, too?"

"Publishers are always losing manuscripts. I think sometimes that's their main activity. But a scapegoat is always necessary, don't you agree? My only complaint is that she doesn't lose the ones I'd like to see lost. Contretemps, these, in what the good Bacon called *The Advancement of Learning.*"

"How do they get lost?"

He spread his arms. "Forgive me, but that is a stupid question. If we knew how they got lost, they wouldn't get lost."

"Logical," I said. "But look, the Garamond books I see here and there seem very carefully made, and you have an impressive catalog. Is it all done here? How many of you are there?"

"There's a room for the production staff across the hall; next door is my colleague Diotallevi. But he does the reference books, the big projects, works that take forever to produce and have a long sales life. I do the university editions. It's not really that much work. Naturally I get involved with some of the books, but as a rule we have nothing to worry about editorially, academically, or financially. Publications of an institute, or conference proceedings under the aegis of a university. If the author's a beginner, his professor writes the preface. The author corrects the proofs, checks the quotations and footnotes, and receives no royalties. The book is adopted as a textbook, a few thousand copies are sold in a few years, and our expenses are covered. No surprises, no red ink."

"What do you do, then?"

"A lot of things. For example, we publish some books at our own expense, usually translations of prestige authors, to add tone to the catalog. And then there are the manuscripts that just turn up, left at the door. Rarely publishable, but they all have to be read. You never can tell."

"Do you like it?"

"Like it? It's the only thing I know how to do well."

We were interrupted by a man in his forties wearing a jacket a

73

few sizes too big, with wispy light hair that fell over thick blond eyebrows. He spoke softly, as if he were instructing a child.

"I'm sick of this *Taxpayer's Vade Mecum*. The whole thing needs to be rewritten, and I don't feel like it. Am I intruding?"

"This is Diotallevi," Belbo said, introducing us.

"Oh, you're here to look at that Templar thing. Poor man. Listen, Jacopo, I thought of a good one: Urban Planning for Gypsies."

"Great," Belbo said admiringly. "I have one, too: Aztec Equitation."

"Excellent. But would that go with Potio-section or the Adynata?"

"We'll have to see," Belbo said. He rummaged in his drawer and took out some sheets of paper. "Potio-section . . ." He looked at me, saw my bewilderment. "Potio-section, as everybody knows, of course, is the art of slicing soup. No, no," he said to Diotallevi. "It's not a department, it's a subject, like Mechanical Avunculogratulation or Pylocatabasis. They all fall under the heading of Tetrapyloctomy."

"What's tetra . . . ?" I asked.

"The art of splitting a hair four ways. This is the department of useless techniques. Mechanical Avunculogratulation, for example, is how to build machines for greeting uncles. We're not sure, though, if Pylocatabasis belongs, since it's the art of being saved by a hair. Somehow that doesn't seem completely useless."

"All right, gentlemen," I said, "I give up. What are you two talking about?"

"Well, Diotallevi and I are planning a reform in higher education. A School of Comparative Irrelevance, where useless or impossible courses are given. The school's aim is to turn out scholars capable of endlessly increasing the number of unnecessary subjects."

"And how many departments are there?"

"Four so far, but that may be enough for the whole syllabus. The Tetrapyloctomy department has a preparatory function; its purpose is to inculcate a sense of irrelevance. Another important department is Adynata, or Impossibilia. Like Urban Planning for Gypsies. The essence of the discipline is the comprehension of the underlying reasons for a thing's absurdity. We have courses in Morse syntax, the history of antarctic agriculture, the history of Easter Island painting, contemporary Sumerian literature, Montessori grading, Assyrio-

74

Babylonian philately, the technology of the wheel in pre-Columbian empires, and the phonetics of the silent film."

"How about crowd psychology in the Sahara?"

"Wonderful," Belbo said.

Diotallevi nodded. "You should join us. The kid's got talent, eh, Jacopo?"

"Yes, I saw that right away. Last night he constructed some moronic arguments with great skill. But let's continue. What did we put in the Oxymoronics department? I can't find my notes."

Diotallevi took a slip of paper from his pocket and regarded me with friendly condescension. "In Oxymoronics, as the name implies, what matters is self-contradiction. That's why I think it's the place for Urban Planning for Gypsies."

"No," Belbo said. "Only if it were Nomadic Urban Planning. The Adynata concern empirical impossibilities; Oxymoronics deal with contradictions in terms."

"Maybe. But what courses did we put under Oxymoronics? Oh, yes, here we are: Tradition in Revolution, Democratic Oligarchy, Parmenidean Dynamics, Heraclitean Statics, Spartan Sybaritics, Tautological Dialectics, Boolean Eristic."

I couldn't resist throwing in "How about a Grammar of Solecisms?"

"Excellent!" they both said, making a note.

"One problem," I said.

"What?"

"If the public gets wind of this, people will show up with manuscripts."

"The boy's sharp, Jacopo," Diotallevi said. "Unwittingly, we've drawn up a real prospectus for scholarship. We've shown the necessity of the impossible. Therefore, mum's the word. But I have to go now."

"Where?" Belbo asked.

"It's Friday afternoon."

"Jesus Christ!" Belbo said, then turned to me. "Across the street are a few houses where Orthodox Jews live; you know, black hats, beards, earlocks. There aren't many of them in Milan. This is Friday, and the Sabbath begins at sundown, so in the afternoon they start preparing in the apartment across the way: polishing the candlesticks, cooking the food, setting everything up so they won't have to light any fires tomorrow. They even leave the TV on all night, picking a channel in advance. Anyway, Diotallevi here has a pair of binoculars; he spies on them with delight, pretending he's on the other side of the street."

"Why?" I asked.

"Our Diotallevi thinks he's Jewish."

"What do you mean, 'thinks'?" Diotallevi said, annoyed. "I *am* Jewish. Do you have anything against that, Casaubon?"

"Of course not."

"Diotallevi is not Jewish," Belbo said firmly.

"No? And what about my name? Just like Graziadio or Diosiacontè. A traditional Jewish name. A ghetto name, like Sholom Aleichem."

"Diotallevi is a good-luck name given to foundlings by city officials. Your grandfather was a foundling."

"A Jewish foundling."

"Diotallevi, you have pink skin, you're practically an albino."

"There are albino rabbits; why not albino Jews?"

"Diotallevi, a person can't just decide to be a Jew the way he might decide to be a stamp collector or a Jehovah's Witness. Jews are born. Admit it! You're a gentile like the rest of us."

"I'm circumcised."

"Come on! Lots of people are circumcised, for reasons of hygiene. All you need is a doctor with a knife. How old were you when you were circumcised?"

"Let's not nitpick."

"No, let's. Jews nitpick."

"Nobody can prove my grandfather wasn't Jewish."

"Of course not; he was a foundling. He could have been anything, the heir to the throne of Byzantium or a Hapsburg bastard."

"He was found near the Portico d'Ottavia, in the ghetto in Rome."

"But your grandmother wasn't Jewish, and Jewish descent is supposed to be matrilineal. . . ."

"And skipping registry reasons—and municipal ledgers can also be read beyond the letter—there are reasons of blood. The blood in me says that my thoughts are exquisitely Talmudic, and it would be racist for you to claim that a gentile can be as exquisitely Talmudic as I am."

76

He left. "Don't pay any attention," Belbo said. "We have this argument almost every day. The fact is, Diotallevi is a devotee of the cabala. But there were also Christian cabalists. Anyway, if Diotallevi wants to be Jewish, why should I object?"

"Why indeed. We're all liberals here."

"So we are."

He lit a cigarette. I remembered why I had come. "You mentioned a manuscript about the Templars," I said.

"That's right. . . . Let's see. It was in a fake-leather folder. . . ." He tried to pick a manuscript out of the middle of a pile without disturbing the others. A hazardous operation. Part of the pile fell to the floor. Now Belbo was holding the fake-leather folder.

I looked at the table of contents and the introduction. "It deals with the arrest of the Templars," I said. "In 1307, Philip the Fair decided to arrest all the Templars in France. There's a legend that two days before Philip issued the arrest warrant, an ox-drawn hay wain left the enclave of the Temple in Paris for an unknown destination. They say that hidden in the wain was a group of knights led by one Aumont. These knights supposedly escaped, took refuge in Scotland, and joined a Masonic lodge in Kilwinning. According to the legend, they became part of the society of Freemasons, who served as guardians of the secrets of the Temple of Solomon. Ah, here we are; I thought so. This writer, too, claims that the origins of Masonry lie in the Templars' escape to Scotland. A story that's been rehashed for a couple of centuries, with no foundation to it. I can give you at least fifty pamphlets that tell the same tale, each cribbed from the other. Here, listen to this—just a page picked at random: 'The proof of the Scottish expedition lies in the fact that even today, six hundred and fifty years later, there still exist in the world secret orders that hark back to the Temple Militia. How else is one to explain the continuity of this heritage?' You see what I mean? How can the Marquis de Carabas not exist when Puss in Boots says he's in the marquis's service?"

"All right," Belbo said, "I'll throw it out. But this Templar business interests me. For once I have an expert handy, and I don't want to let him get away. Why is there all this talk about the Templars and nothing about the Knights of Malta? No, don't tell me now. It's late. Diotallevi and I have to go to dinner with Signor

Garamond in a little while. We should be through by about ten-thirty. I'll try to persuade Diotallevi to drop by Pilade's—he goes to bed early and usually doesn't drink. Will you be there?"

"Where else? I belong to a lost generation and am comfortable only in the company of others who are lost and lonely."

13

Li frere, li mestre du Temple
Qu'estoient rempli et ample
D'or et d'argent et de richesse
Et qui menoient tel noblesse,
Où sont ils? que sont devenu?
—*Chronique à la suite du roman de Favel*

Et in Arcadia ego. That evening Pilade's was the image of the golden age. One of those evenings when you feel that not only will there definitely be a revolution, but that the Association of Manufacturers will foot the bill for it. Where but at Pilade's could you watch the bearded owner of a cotton mill, wearing a parka, play hearts with a future fugitive from justice dressed in a double-breasted jacket and tie? This was the dawn of great changes in style. Until the beginning of the sixties, beards were fascist, and you had to trim them, and shave your cheeks, in the style of Italo Balbo; but by '68 beards meant protest, and now they were becoming neutral, universal, a matter of personal preference. Beards have always been masks (you wear a fake beard to keep from being recognized), but in those years, the early seventies, a real beard was also a disguise. You could lie while telling the truth—or, rather, by making the truth elusive and enigmatic. A man's politics could no longer be guessed from his beard. That evening, beards seemed to hover on clean-shaven faces whose very lack of hair suggested defiance.

I digress. Belbo and Diotallevi arrived tense, exchanging harsh whispers about the dinner they had just come from. Only later did I learn what Signor Garamond's dinners were.

Belbo went straight to his favorite distillations; Diotallevi, after pondering at length, decided on tonic water. We found a little table in the back. Two tram drivers who had to get up early the next morning were leaving.

"Now then," Diotallevi said, "these Templars . . ."

"But, really, you can read about the Templars anywhere. . . ."

"We prefer the oral tradition," Belbo said.

"It's more mystical," Diotallevi said. "God created the world by speaking, He didn't send a telegram."

"Fiat lux, stop," Belbo said.

"Epistle follows," I said.

"The Templars, then?" Belbo asked.

"Very well," I said. "To begin with . . ."

"You should never begin with 'To begin with,' " Diotallevi objected.

"To begin with, there's the First Crusade. Godefroy worships at the Holy Sepulcher and fulfills his vow. Baudouin becomes the first king of Jerusalem. A Christian kingdom in the Holy Land. But holding Jerusalem is one thing; quite another, to conquer the rest of Palestine. The Saracens are down but not out. Life's not easy for the new occupiers, and not easy for the pilgrims either. And then in 1118, during the reign of Baudouin II, nine young men led by a fellow named Hugues de Payns arrive and set up the nucleus of an order of the Poor Fellow-Soldiers of Jesus Christ: a monastic order, but with sword and shield. The three classic vows of poverty, chastity, and obedience, plus a fourth: defense of pilgrims. The king, the bishop, everyone in Jerusalem contributes money, offers the knights lodging, and finally sets them up in the cloister of the old Temple of Solomon. From then on they are known as the Knights of the Temple."

"But what were they really?"

"Hugues and the original eight others were probably idealists caught up in the mystique of the Crusade. But later recruits were most likely younger sons seeking adventure. Remember, the new kingdom of Jerusalem was sort of the California of the day, the place you went to make your fortune. Prospects at home were not great, and some of the knights may have been on the run for one reason or another. I think of it as a kind of Foreign Legion. What do you do if you're in trouble? You join the Templars, see the world, have some fun, do a little fighting. They feed you and clothe you, and in the end, as a bonus, you save your soul. Of course, you had to be pretty desperate, because it meant going out into the desert, sleeping in a tent, spending days and days without seeing a living soul except other Templars, and maybe a Turk now and then. In the meantime, you ride under the sun, dying of thirst, and cut the guts out of other poor bastards."

I stopped for a moment. "Maybe I'm making it sound too much like a Western. There was probably a third phase. Once the order became powerful, people may have wanted to join even if they were well off at home. By that time, though, you could be a Templar without having to go to the Holy Land; you could be a Templar at home, too. It gets complicated. Sometimes they sound like tough soldiers, and sometimes they show sensitivity. For example, you can't call them racists. Yes, they fought the Moslems—that was the whole point—but they fought in a spirit of chivalry and with mutual respect. Once, when the ambassador of the emir of Damascus was visiting Jerusalem, the Templars let him say his prayers in a little mosque that had been turned into a Christian church. One day a Frank came in, was outraged to see a Moslem in a holy place, and started to rough him up. But the Templars threw the intolerant Frank out and apologized to the Moslem. Later on, this fraternization with the enemy helped lead to their ruin: one of the charges against them at their trial was that they had dealings with esoteric Moslem sects. Which may have been true. They were a little like the nineteenth-century adventurers who went native and caught the mal d'Afrique. The Templars, lacking the usual monastic education, were slow to grasp the fine points of theology. Think of them as Lawrences of Arabia, who after a while start dressing like sheiks. . . . But it's difficult to get an objective picture of their behavior because contemporary Christian historiographers, William of Tyre, for example, take every opportunity to vilify them."

"Why?"

"The Templars became too powerful too fast. It all goes back to Saint Bernard. You're familiar with Saint Bernard, of course. A great organizer. He reformed the Benedictine order and eliminated decorations from churches. If a colleague got on his nerves, as Abelard did, he attacked him McCarthy-style and tried to get him burned at the stake. If he couldn't manage that, he'd burn the offender's books instead. And of course he preached the Crusade: Let us take up arms and *you* go forth. . . ."

"You don't care for him," Belbo remarked.

"If I had my way, Saint Bernard would end up in one of the nastier circles of the inferno. Saint, hell! But he was good at self-promotion. Look how Dante treats him: making him the Madonna's right-hand man. He got to be a saint because he buttered up all the right people. But to get back to the Templars. Bernard realized right away that this idea had possibilities. He supported the nine original adventurers, transformed them into a Militia of Christ. You could even say that the heroic view of the Templars was his invention. In 1128 he held a council in Troyes for the express purpose of defining the role of those new soldier-monks, and a few years later he wrote an elogium on them and drew up their rule, seventy-two articles. The articles are fun to read; there's a little of everything in them. Daily Mass, no contact with excommunicated knights, though if one of them applies for admission to the Temple, he must be received in a Christian spirit. You see what I mean about the Foreign Legion. They're supposed to wear simple white cloaks, no furs, at most a lambskin or a ram's pelt. They're forbidden to wear the curved shoes so fashionable at the time, and must sleep in their underwear, with one pallet, one sheet, and one blanket. . . ."

"With the heat there, I can imagine the stink," Belbo said.

"We'll come to the stink in a minute. There were other tough measures in the rule: one bowl for each two men; eat in silence; meat three times a week; penance on Fridays; up at dawn every day. If the work has been especially heavy, they can sleep an extra hour, but in return they must recite thirteen Paters in bed. There is a master and a whole series of lower ranks, down to sergeants, squires, attendants, and servants. Every knight will have three horses and one squire, no decorations are allowed on bridles, saddles, or spurs. Simple but well-made weapons. Hunting forbidden, except for lions. In short, a life of penance and battle. And don't forget chastity. The rule is particularly insistent about that. Remember, these are men who are not living in a monastery. They're fighting a war, living in the world, if you can use that word for the rat's nest the Holy Land must have been in those days. The rule says in no uncertain terms that a woman's company is perilous and that the men are allowed to kiss only their mothers, sisters, and aunts."

"Aunts, eh?" Belbo grumbled. "I'd have been more careful there. . . . But if memory serves, weren't the Templars accused of sodomy? There's that book by Klossowski, *The Baphomet*. Baphomet was one of their satanic divinities, wasn't he?"

"I'll get to that, too. But think about it for a moment. You live for months and months in the desert, out in the middle of nowhere, and at night you share a tent with the guy who's been eating out of the same bowl as you. You're tired and cold and thirsty and afraid. You want your mama. So what do you do?"

"Manly love, the Theban legion," Belbo suggested.

"The other soldiers haven't taken the Templar vow. When a city is sacked, they get to rape the dusky Moorish maids with amber bellies and velvet eyes. And what is the Templar supposed to do amid the scent of the cedars of Lebanon? You can see why there was the popular saying: 'To drink and blaspheme like a Templar.' It's like a chaplain in the trenches who drinks brandy and curses with his illiterate soldiers. The Templar seal depicts the knights always in pairs, one riding behind the other on the same horse. Now why should that be? The rule allows them three horses each. It must have been one of Bernard's ideas, an attempt to symbolize poverty or perhaps their double role as monks and knights. But you can imagine what people must have said about it, two men galloping, one with his ass pressed against the other's belly. But they may have been slandered. . . ."

"They certainly were asking for it," Belbo interrupted. "That Saint Bernard wasn't stupid, was he?"

"Stupid, no. But he was a monk himself, and in those days monks had their own strange ideas about the body. . . . I said before that maybe I was making this sound too much like a Western, but now that I think about it . . . Listen to what Bernard has to say about his beloved knights. I brought this quotation with me, because it's worth hearing: 'They shun and abhor mimes, magicians, and jugglers, lewd songs and buffoonery; they cut their hair short, for the apostle says it is shameful for a man to groom his hair. Never are they seen coiffed, and rarely washed. Their beards are unkempt, caked with dust and sweat from their armor and the heat.' "

"I would hate to sleep in their quarters," Belbo said.

"It's always been characteristic of the hermit," Diotallevi declared, "to cultivate a healthy filth, to humiliate his body. Wasn't it Saint Macarius who lived on a column and picked up the worms that dropped from him and put them back on his body so that they, who were also God's creatures, might enjoy their banquet?"

"The stylite was Saint Simeon," Belbo said, "and I think he stayed on that column so he could spit on the people who walked below."

"How I detest the cynicism of the Enlightenment," Diotallevi said. "In any case, whether Macarius or Simeon, I'm sure there was a stylite with worms, but of course I'm no authority on the subject, since the follies of the gentiles don't interest me."

"Whereas your Gerona rabbis were spick and span," Belbo said.

"They lived in squalor because you gentiles kept them in the ghetto. The Templars, on the other hand, chose to be squalid."

"Let's not go overboard," I said. "Have you ever seen a platoon of recruits after a day's march? The reason I'm telling you all this is to help you understand the dilemma of the Templar. He had to be mystic, ascetic, no eating, drinking, or screwing, but at the same time he roamed the desert cutting off the heads of Christ's enemies; the more heads he cut off, the more points he earned for paradise. He stank, got hairier every day, and then Bernard insisted that after conquering a city he couldn't jump on top of some young girl—or old hag, for that matter. And on moonless nights, when the simoom blew over the desert, he couldn't seek any favors from his favorite fellow-soldier. How can you be a monk and a swordsman at the same time, disemboweling people one minute and reciting Ave Marias the next? They tell you not to look even your female cousin in the eye, but when you enter a city, after days of siege, the other Crusaders hump the caliph's wife before your very eyes, and marvelous Shulammite women undo their bodices and say, Take me, Take me, but spare my life. . . . No, the Templar had to stay hard, reciting compline, hairy and stinking, as Saint Bernard wanted him to. For that matter, if you just read the retraits . . ."

"The what?"

"The statutes of the order, drawn up rather late, after the order had put on its robe and slippers, so to speak. There's nothing worse than an army when the war is over. At one point, for instance, brawling is forbidden, it's forbidden to wound a Christian for revenge, forbidden to have commerce with women, forbidden to slander a brother. A Templar could not allow a slave to escape, lose his temper and threaten to defect to the Saracens, let a horse wander off, give away any animal except a dog or cat, be absent without leave, break the master's seal, go out of the barracks at night, lend the order's money without authorization, or throw his habit on the ground in anger."

"From prohibitions you can tell what people normally do," Belbo said. "It's a way of drawing a picture of daily life."

"Let's see," Diotallevi said. "A Templar, annoyed at something the brothers said or did that evening, rides out at night without leave, accompanied by a little Saracen boy and with three capons hanging from his saddle. He goes to a girl of loose morals and, bestowing the capons upon her, engages in illicit intercourse. During this debauchery, the Saracen boy rides off with the horse, and our Templar, even more sweat-covered and dirty than usual, crawls home with his tail between his legs. In an attempt to pass unnoticed, he slips some of the Temple's money to the Jewish usurer, who is waiting like a vulture on its perch. . . ."

"Thou hast said it, Caiaphas," Belbo remarked.

"We're talking in stereotypes here. With the money the Templar tries to recover, if not the Saracen boy, at least a semblance of a horse. But a fellow Templar hears about the misadventure, and one night—we know that envy is endemic in such communities—he drops some heavy hints at supper, when the meat is served. The captain grows suspicious, the suspect stammers, flushes, then draws his dagger and flings himself on his brother. . . ."

"On the treacherous sycophant," Belbo corrected him.

"On the treacherous sycophant, good. He flings himself on the wretch, slashing his face. The wretch draws his sword, an unseemly brawl ensues, the captain with the flat of his sword tries to restore order, the other brothers snigger . . ."

"Drinking and blaspheming like Templars," Belbo said.

"God's bodkin, in God's name, 'swounds, God's blood," I said.

"Our hero is enraged, and what does a Templar do when he's enraged?"

"He turns purple," Belbo suggested.

"Right. He turns purple, tears off his habit, and throws it on the ground."

"How about: 'You can shove this tunic, you can shove your goddamn temple!' " I suggested. "And then he breaks the seal with his sword and announces that he's joining the Saracens."

"Violating at least eight precepts at one blow."

"Anyway," I said, driving home my point, "imagine a man like that, who says he's joining the Saracens. And one day the king's bailiff arrests him, shows him the white-hot irons, and says: 'Confess, knave! Admit you stuck it up your brother's behind!' 'Who,

85

me? Your irons make me laugh. I'll show you what a Templar is! I'll stick it up your behind, and the pope's. And King Philip's, too, if he comes within reach!' "

"A confession! That must be how it happened," Belbo said. "Then it's off to the dungeon with him, and a coat of oil every day so he'll burn better when the time comes."

"They were just a bunch of children," Diotallevi concluded.

We were interrupted by a girl with a strawberry birthmark on her nose; she had some papers in her hand and asked if we had signed the petition for the imprisoned Argentinean comrades. Belbo signed without reading it. "They're even worse off than I am," he said to Diotallevi, who was regarding him with a bemused expression. "He can't sign," Belbo said to the girl. "He belongs to a small Indian sect that forbids its members to write their own names. Many of them are in jail because of government persecution." The girl looked sympathetically at Diotallevi and passed the petition to me.

"And who are they?" I asked.

"What do you mean, who are they? Argentinean comrades."

"But what group do they belong to?"

"The Tacuaras, I think."

"The Tacuaras are fascists," I said. As if I knew one group from the other.

"Fascist pig," the girl hissed at me. She left.

"What you are saying, then," Diotallevi asked, "is that the Templars were just poor bastards?"

"No," I said. "Perhaps I shouldn't have tried to liven up the story. We were talking about the rank and file, but from the beginning the order received huge donations and little by little set up commanderies throughout Europe. Alfonso of Aragon, for example, gave them a whole region. In fact, in his will he wanted to leave the kingdom to them in the event that he died without issue. The Templars didn't trust him, so they made a deal—took the money and ran, more or less. Except that instead of money it was half a dozen strongholds in Spain. The king of Portugal gave them a forest. Since the forest happened to be occupied by the Saracens, the Templars organized an attack, drove out the Moors, and in the process founded Coimbra. And these are just a few episodes. The point is this: Part of the order was fighting in Palestine, but the bulk of it stayed home. Then what happened? Let's say someone has to go to Palestine. He needs money, and he's afraid to travel with jewels and gold, so he leaves his fortune with the Templars in France, or in Spain, or in Italy. They give him a receipt, and he gets cash for it in the East."

"A letter of credit," Belbo said.

"That's right. They invented the checking account long before the bankers of Florence. What with donations, armed conquests, and a percentage from their financial operations, the Templars became a multinational. Running an operation like that took men who knew what they were doing. Men who could convince Innocent II to grant them exceptional privileges. The order was allowed to keep its booty, and wherever they owned property, they were answerable not to the king, not to the bishops or to the patriarch of Jerusalem, but only to the pope. They were exempted from all tithes, but they had the right to impose their own tithes on the lands under their control. . . . In short, the organization was always in the black, and nobody had the right to pry into it. You can see why the bishops and monarchs didn't like them, though they couldn't do without them. The Crusaders were terrible screwups. They marched off without any idea of where they were going or what they would find when they got there. But the Templars knew their way around. They knew how to deal with the enemy, they were familiar with the terrain and the art of fighting. The Order of the Temple had become a serious business, even though its reputation was based on the boasting of its assault troops."

"And the boasting was empty?" Diotallevi asked.

"Often. Here again, what's amazing is the gulf between their political and administrative skill on the one hand and their Green Beret style on the other: all guts and no brains. Let's take the story of Ascalon—"

"Yes, let's," Belbo said, after a moment's distraction as he greeted, with a great show of lust, a girl named Dolores.

She joined us, saying, "I must hear the story of Ascalon!"

"All right. One fine day the king of France, the Holy Roman emperor, King Baudouin III of Jerusalem, and the grand masters of the Templars and the Hospitalers all decided to lay siege to Ascalon. They set out together: king, court, patriarch, priests carrying crosses and banners, and the archbishops of Tyre, Nazareth, Caesarea. It was like a big party, oriflammes and standards flying, tents pitched around the enemy city, drums beating. Ascalon was defended by one hundred and fifty towers, and the inhabitants had long been preparing for a siege: all the houses had slits made in the walls; they were like fortresses within the fortress. I mean, the Templars were smart fighters, they should have known these things. But no, everybody got excited, and they built battering rams and wooden towers: you know, those constructions on wheels that you push up to the enemy walls so you can hurl stones or firebrands or shoot arrows while the catapults sling rocks from a distance. The Ascalonites tried to set fire to the towers, but the wind was against them, and they burned their own walls instead, until in one place a wall collapsed. The attackers all charged the breach.

"And then a strange thing happened. The grand master of the Templars had a cordon set up so that only his men could enter the city. Cynics say he was trying to make sure that only the Templars would get the booty. A kinder explanation is that he feared a trap and wanted to send his own brave men in first. Either way, I wouldn't make him head of a military academy. Forty Templars ran full steam straight through the city, came to a screeching halt in a great cloud of dust at the wall on the other side, looked at one another, and wondered what in hell they were doing there. Then they about-faced and ran back, racing past the Saracens, who pelted them with rocks and darts, slaughtering the lot of them, grand master included. Then they closed the breach, hung the corpses from the walls, and jeered at the Christians, with obscene gestures and horrid laughter."

"The Moor is cruel," Belbo said.

"Like children," Diotallevi added.

"These Templars of yours were really crazy!" Dolores said with admiration.

"They remind me of Tom and Jerry," Belbo said.

I felt a little guilty. After all, I had been living with the Templars for two years, and I loved them. Yet now, catering to the snobbery of my audience, I had made them sound like characters out of a cartoon. Maybe it was William of Tyre's fault, treacherous histo-riographer that he was. I could almost see my Knights of the Temple, bearded and blazing, the bright red crosses on their snow-white cloaks, their mounts wheeling in the shadow of the Beauceant, their black-and-white banner. They had been so dazzlingly intent on their feast of death and daring. Perhaps the sweat Saint Bernard talked about was a bronze glow that lent a sarcastic nobility to their fearsome smiles as they celebrated their farewell to life. . . . Lions in war, Jacques de Vitry called them, but sweet lambs in times of peace; harsh in battle, devout in prayer; ferocious to their enemies, but full of kindness toward their brothers. The white and the black of their banner were so apposite: to the friends of Christ they were pure; to His adversaries they were grim and terrible.

Pathetic champions of the faith, last glimmer of chivalry's twilight. Why play any old Ariosto to them when I could be their Joinville? The author of the *Histoire de Saint Louis* had accompanied the sainted king to the Holy Land, acting as both scribe and soldier. I recalled now what he had written about the Templars. This was more than a hundred and eighty years after the order was founded, and it had been through enough crusades to undermine anyone's ideals. The heroic figures of Queen Melisande and Baudouin the leper-king had vanished like ghosts; factional fighting in Lebanon—blood-soaked even then—had drawn to a close; Jerusalem had already fallen once; Barbarossa had drowned in Cilicia; Richard the Lion-Heart, defeated and humiliated, had gone home disguised as, of all things, a Templar; Christianity had lost the battle. The Moors' view of the confederation of autonomous potentates united in the defense of their civilization was very different. They had read Avicenna, and they were not ignorant, like the Europeans. How could you live alongside a tolerant, mystical, libertine culture for two centuries without succumbing to its allure, particularly when you compared it to Western culture, which was crude, vulgar, barbaric, and Germanic? Then, in 1244, came the final, definitive fall of Jerusalem. The war, begun a hundred and fifty years earlier, was lost. The Christians had to lay down their arms in a land now devoted to peace and the scent of the cedars of Lebanon. Poor Templars. Your epic, all in vain.

Little wonder that in the tender melancholy of their faded, aging glory they lent an ear to the secret doctrines of Moslem mystics, hieratic guardians of hidden treasures. Perhaps that was how the legend of the Knights of the Temple was born, the legend with which some frustrated and yearning minds are still obsessed, the myth of a boundless power lying unused, unharnessed. . . .

Even in Joinville's day, the saint-king Louis, at whose table Aquinas dined, persisted in his belief in the crusade, despite two centuries of dreams ruined by the victors' stupidity. Was it worth one more try? Yes, Louis said. And the Templars were ready and willing; they followed him into defeat, because that was their job. Without a crusade, how could they justify the Temple?

Louis attacks Damietta from the sea. The enemy shore glitters with pikes, halberds, oriflammes, shields, and scimitars. Fine-looking men, Joinville says chivalrously, who carry arms of gold struck by the sun. Louis could wait, but he decides to land at any cost. "My faithful followers, we will be invincible if we are inseparable in our charity. If we are defeated, we will be martyrs. If we triumph, the glory of God will be the greater." The Templars don't believe it, but they have been trained to be knights of the ideal, and this is the image of themselves they must confirm. They will follow the king in his mystical madness.

Incredibly, the landing is a success; equally incredibly, the Saracens abandon Damietta. But the king hesitates to enter the city, fearing treachery. But there is no treachery: the city is his for the taking, along with its treasures and its hundred mosques, which Louis immediately converts into churches of the Lord. Now he has a decision to make: Should he march on Alexandria or on Cairo? The wise choice would be Alexandria, thus depriving Egypt of a vital port. But the expedition has its evil genius, the king's brother, Robert d'Artois, a megalomaniac hungry for glory. A typical younger son. He advises Louis to head for Cairo, the heart of Egypt. The Templars, cautious at first, are now champing at the bit. The king issues orders to avoid isolated skirmishes, but the marshal of the Temple takes it upon himself to violate that prohibition. Seeing a squadron of the sultan's Mamelukes, he cries out: "Now have at them, in the name of God, for a shame like this I cannot bear!"

The Saracens dig in beyond the river near Mansura. The French try to build a dam and create a ford, protecting it with their mobile towers, but the Saracens have learned the art of Greek fire from the Byzantines. Greek fire is a barrel-like container with a kind of big spear as a tail. It is hurled like a lightning bolt, a flying dragon. It burns so brightly that in the Christian camp at night one can see as clearly as if it were day.

While the camp burns, a Bedouin traitor leads the king and his men to a ford in exchange for a payment of three hundred bezants. The king decides to attack. The crossing is not easy; many are drowned and swept away by the current, while three hundred mounted Saracens wait on the other side. When the main body of the attack force finally comes ashore, the Templars, as planned, are in the vanguard, followed by the Comte d'Artois. The Moslem horsemen flee, and the Templars wait for the rest of the Christian army. But Artois and his men dash off in pursuit of the enemy.

The Templars, anxious to avoid dishonor, then join in the assault, but catch up with Artois only after he has penetrated the enemy camp and begun a massacre. The Moslems fall back toward Mansura, which is just what Artois has been hoping for. He sets out after them. The Templars try to stop him; Brother Gilles, supreme commander of the Temple, tries flattery, telling Artois that he has performed a wondrous feat, perhaps the greatest ever achieved overseas. But Artois, eager for glory, accuses the Templars of treachery, claiming that the Templars and Hospitalers could have conquered this territory long ago if they had really wanted to. He has shown them what a man with blood in his veins can do. This is too much. The Templars must prove that they are second to none. They charge into the city and chase the enemy all the way to the wall on the opposite side. Then suddenly the Templars realize that they have repeated the mistake of Ascalon. While the Christians are busy sacking the sultan's palace, the infidels reassemble and fall upon the now unorganized group of jackals.

Have the Templars allowed themselves to be blinded once again by greed? Some say that before accompanying Artois into the city, Brother Gilles spoke to him with stoic lucidity: "My Lord, my brothers and I are not afraid. We follow you. But great is our doubt that any of us will return." And indeed, Artois was killed, and many good knights died with him, including two hundred and eighty Templars.

It was more than a defeat; it was a disgrace. Yet not even Joinville recorded it as such. It happened and that is the beauty of war.

Joinville's pen turns many of these battles and skirmishes into charming ballets. Heads roll here and there, implorations to the good

Lord abound, and the king sheds tears over a loyal follower's death. But the whole thing is Technicolor, complete with crimson saddle-cloths, gilded trappings, the flash of helmets and swords under the yellow desert sun, and an azure sea in the background. And who knows? Perhaps the Templars really lived their daily butchery that way.

Joinville's perspective shifts vertically, depending on whether he has fallen from his horse or just remounted. Isolated scenes are sharply focused, but the larger picture eludes him. We see individual duels, whose outcome is often random. Joinville sets off to help the lord of Wanon. A Turk strikes him with his lance, Joinville's horse sinks to its knees, Joinville falls over the animal's head, he stands up, sword in hand, and Chevalier Erard de Siverey ("may God grant him grace") points to a ruined house where they can take refuge. They are trampled by Turks on horseback. Chevalier Frédéric de Loupey is struck from behind, "which made so large a wound that the blood poured from his body as if from the bunghole of a barrel." Siverey receives a slashing blow in the face, so that "his nose was left dangling over his lips." And so on, until help arrives. They leave the house and move to another part of the battlefield, where there are more deaths and last-minute rescues, and loud prayers to Saint James. In the meantime, the good Comte de Soissons, wielding his sword, cries, "Seneschal, let these dogs howl as they will. By God's bonnet, we shall talk of this day yet, you and I, sitting at home with our ladies!" The king asks for news of his brother, the wretched Comte d'Artois, and Brother Henri de Ronnay, provost of the Hospitalers, answers that he "has good news, for certainly the count is now in Paradise." "God be praised for everything He gives," says the king, big tears falling from his eyes.

But it isn't always a ballet, angelic and bloodstained. Grand Master Guillaume de Sonnac dies, burned alive by Greek fire. With the great stink of corpses and the shortage of provisions, the Christian army is stricken with scurvy. Saint Louis's men are finally routed. The king is so badly racked by dysentery that he cuts out the seat of his pants to save time in battle. Damietta is lost, and the queen has to negotiate with the Saracens, paying five hundred thousand livres tournois to ransom the king.

The crusades were carried out in virtuous bad faith. On his return to Saint-Jean-d'Acre, Louis is hailed as a victor; the whole city comes out in procession to greet him, including the clergy, ladies, and children. The Templars, seeing which way the wind is blowing, try to open negotiations with Damascus. Louis finds out and, furious at being bypassed, repudiates the new grand master in the presence of the Moslem ambassadors. The grand master has to retract the promises he made to the enemy, has to kneel before the king and beg his pardon. No one can say the Knights haven't fought well—and selflessly—but the king of France still humiliates them, to reassert his power. And, half a century later, Louis's successor, Philip, to reassert *his* power, will send the Knights to the stake.

In 1291 Saint-Jean-d'Acre is conquered by the Moors, and all its inhabitants are put to the sword. The Christian kingdom of Jerusalem is gone for good. The Templars are richer, more numerous, more powerful than ever, but they were born to fight in the Holy Land, and in the Holy Land there are none left.

They live in splendor, isolated in their commanderies throughout Europe and in the Temple in Paris, but they dream still of the plateau of the Temple in Jerusalem in their days of glory, dream of the handsome church of Saint Mary Lateran spangled with votive chapels, dream of their bouquets of trophies, and all the rest: the forges, the saddlery, the granaries, the stables of two thousand horses, the cantering troops of squires, aides, and turcopoles, the red crosses on white cloaks, the dark surplices of the attendants, the sultan's envoys with their great turbans and gilded helmets, the pilgrims, a crossroads filled with dapper patrols and outriders, and the delights of rich coffers, the port from which instructions and cargoes were dispatched for the castles on the mainland, or on the islands, or on the shores of Asia Minor. . . .

All gone now, my poor Templars.

That evening, at Pilade's, by then on my fifth whiskey, for which Belbo was paying, insisted on paying, I realized that I had been dreaming aloud and—the shame of it—with feeling. But I must have told a beautiful story, full of compassion, because Dolores's eyes were glistening, and Diotallevi, having taken the mad plunge and ordered a second tonic water, was seraphically gazing toward heaven—or, rather, toward the bar's decidedly noncabalistic ceiling. "Perhaps," he murmured, "they were all those things: lost souls and saints, horsemen and grooms, bankers and heroes. . . ."

"They were remarkable, no doubt about it" was Belbo's summation. "But tell me, Casaubon, do you love them?"

"I'm doing my thesis on them. If you do your thesis on syphilis, you end up loving even the Spirochaeta pallida."

"It was lovely," Dolores said. "Like a movie. But I have to go now. I have to mimeograph the leaflets for tomorrow morning. There's picketing at the Marelli factory."

"Lucky you. You can afford it," Belbo said. He raised a weary hand and stroked her hair. Then he ordered what he said was his last whiskey. "It's almost midnight. I say that not for normal people, I say it for Diotallevi's benefit. But let's go on. I want to hear about the trial. Who, what, when, and why."

"Cur, quomodo, quando," Diotallevi agreed. "Yes, yes."

14

> He declares that he saw, the day before, five hundred and four brothers of the order led to the stake because they would not confess the above-mentioned errors, and he heard it said that they were burned. But he fears that he himself would not resist if he were to be burned, that he would confess in the presence of the lord magistrates and anyone else, if questioned, and say that all the errors with which the order has been charged are true; that he, if asked, would also confess to killing Our Lord.
> —Testimony of Aimery de Villiers-le-Duc, May 13, 1310

A trial full of silences, contradictions, enigmas, and acts of stupidity. The acts of stupidity were the most obvious, and, because they were inexplicable, they generally coincided with the enigmas. In those halcyon days I believed that the source of enigma was stupidity. Then the other evening in the periscope I decided that the most terrible enigmas are those that mask themselves as madness. But now I have come to believe that the whole world is an enigma, a harmless enigma that is made terrible by our own mad attempt to interpret it as though it had an underlying truth.

With the collapse of the Christian kingdoms of the Holy Land, the Templars were left without a purpose. Or, rather, they soon turned their means into an end; they spent their time managing their immense wealth. Philip the Fair, a monarch intent on building a centralized state, naturally disliked them. They were a sovereign order, beyond any royal control. The grand master ranked as a prince of the blood; he commanded an army, administered vast landholdings, was elected like the emperor, and had absolute authority. The French treasury was located in the Temple in Paris, outside the king's control. The Templars were the trustees, proxies, and administrators of an account that was the king's only in name. They paid funds in and out and manipulated the interest; they acted like a great private bank but enjoyed all the privileges and exemptions of a state institution. The king's treasurer was a Templar. How could a ruler rule under such conditions?

If you can't lick 'em, join 'em. Philip asked to be made an honorary Templar. Request denied. An insult no king could swallow. He suggested that the pope merge Templars and Hospitalers and place the new order under the control of one of his sons. Jacques de Molay, grand master of the Temple, arrived with great pomp from Cyprus, where he lived like a monarch in exile. He handed the pope a memorandum that supposedly assessed the advantages of the merger but actually emphasized its disadvantages. Molay brazenly argued that, among other things, the Templars were far wealthier than the Hospitalers, that the merger would enrich the latter at the expense of the former, thus putting the souls of his knights in jeopardy. Molay won this first round: the plan was shelved.

The only recourse left was slander, and here the king held good cards. Rumors about the Templars had been circulating for a long time. Imagine how these "colonials" must have looked to right-thinking Frenchmen, these people who collected tithes everywhere while giving nothing in return, not even—anymore—their own blood as guardians of the Holy Sepulcher. True, they were Frenchmen. But not completely. People saw them as pieds noirs; at the time, the term was poulains. The Templars flaunted their exotic ways; it was said that among themselves they even spoke the language of the Moors, with which they were familiar. Though they were monks, their savage nature was common knowledge: some years before, Pope Innocent III had issued a bull entitled *De insolentia Templariorum*. They had taken a vow of poverty, but they lived with the pomp of aristocrats, with the greed of the new merchant classes, and with the effrontery of a corps of musketeers.

The whispering campaign was not long in coming: the Templars were homosexuals, heretics, idolaters worshiping a bearded head of unknown provenance. Perhaps they shared the secrets of the Isma'ilis, for they had had dealings with the Assassins of the Old Man of the Mountain. Philip and his advisers put these rumors to good use.

Philip was assisted by his two evil geniuses, Marigny and Nogaret. It was Marigny who ultimately got control of the Templar treasury, administering it on the king's behalf until it was transferred to the Hospitalers. It is not clear who got the interest. Nogaret, the king's lord chancellor, in 1303 had been the strategist behind the incident in Anagni, when Sciarra Colonna slapped Boniface VIII and the pope died of humiliation less than a month later.

Then a man by the name of Esquin de Floyran appeared on the scene. Apparently, while imprisoned for unspecified crimes and on the verge of being executed, Floyran encountered a renegade Templar in his cell and from him heard a terrible confession. In exchange for his life and a tidy sum, Floyran told everything. Which turned out to be exactly what everybody was already rumoring. Now the rumors became formal depositions before a magistrate. The king transmitted Floyran's sensational revelations to the pope, Clement V, who later moved the papal seat to Avignon. Clement believed some of the charges, but knew it would not be easy to interfere in the Temple's affairs. In 1307, however, he agreed to open an official inquiry. Molay, the grand master, was informed, but declared that his conscience was clear. At the king's side, he continued to take part in official ceremonies, a prince among princes. Clement V seemed to be stalling, and the king began to suspect that the pope wanted to give the Templars time to disappear. But no, the Templars went on drinking and blaspheming in their commanderies, seemingly unaware of the danger. And this is the first enigma.

On September 14, 1307, the king sent sealed messages to all the bailiffs and seneschals of the realm, ordering the mass arrest of the Templars and the confiscation of their property. A month went by between the issuing of this order and the arrest on October 13. But the Templars suspected nothing. On that October morning they all fell into the trap and—another enigma—gave themselves up without a fight. In fact, in the days before the arrests, using the most feeble excuses, the king's men, wanting to make sure that nothing would escape confiscation, had conducted a kind of inventory of the Temple's possessions throughout the country. And still the Templars did nothing. Come right in, my dear bailiff, take a look around, make yourself at home.

When he learned what had happened, the pope hazarded a protest, but it was too late. The royal investigators had already brought out their irons and ropes, and many Knights had begun to confess under torture. When they confessed, they were handed over to inquisitors, who had methods of their own, even though they were not yet burning people at the stake. The Knights confirmed their confessions.

This is the third mystery. Granted, there was torture, and it must have been vigorous, since thirty-six Knights died in the course of it. But not a single one of these men of iron, seasoned by their battles with the cruel Turk, resisted arrest. In Paris only four Knights out of a hundred and thirty-eight refused to confess. All the others did, including Jacques de Molay.

"What did they confess?" Belbo asked.

"They confessed exactly what was charged in the arrest warrant. There was hardly any variation in the testimony, at least not in France and Italy. In England, where nobody really wanted to go through with the trial, the usual accusations appeared in the depositions, but they were attributed to witnesses outside the order, whose testimony was hearsay. In other words, the Templars confessed only when asked to, and then only to what was charged."

"Same old inquisitional stuff. We've seen it often," Belbo remarked.

"Yet the behavior of the accused was odd. The charges were that during their initiation rites the Templars denied Christ three times, spat on the crucifix, and were stripped and kissed in posteriori parte spine dorsi, in other words, on the behind, then on the navel and the mouth, in humane dignitatis opprobrium. That they then engaged in mutual fornication. That they were then shown the head of a bearded idol, which they had to worship. Now, how did the accused respond to these charges? Geoffroy de Charnay, who was later burned at the stake with Molay, said that, yes, it had happened to him; he had denied Christ, but with his mouth, not his heart; he didn't recall whether he spat on the crucifix, because they had been in such a hurry that night. As for the kiss on the behind, that also had happened to him, and he had heard the preceptor of Auvergne say that, after all, it was better to couple with brothers than to be befouled by a woman, but he personally had not committed carnal sins with other knights. In other words: Yes, it's all true, but it was only a game, nobody really believed in it, and anyway it was the others who did it, I just went along to be polite. Jacques de Molay—the grand master himself—said that when they gave him the crucifix, he only pretended to spit on it and spat on the ground instead. He admitted that the initiation ceremonies were more or less as described, but—to tell the truth—he couldn't say for sure, because he had initiated very few brothers in the course of his career. Another Knight said that he had kissed the master, but only on the mouth, not the behind; it was the master who kissed him on the behind. Some did confess to more than was necessary, saying that they had not only denied Christ but also called Him a criminal, and they had denied the virginity of Mary, and they had urinated on the crucifix, not only on the day of their initiation, but during Holy Week as well. They didn't believe in the sacraments, they said, and they worshiped not only Baphomet but also the Devil in the form of a cat. . . ."

Equally grotesque, though not as incredible, is the pas de deux that now begins between the king and the pope. The pope wants to take charge of the case; the king insists on seeing the trial through to its conclusion. The pope suggests a temporary suspension of the order: the guilty will be sentenced, then the Temple will be revived in its original purity. The king wants the scandal to spread, wants it to involve the entire order. This will lead to the order's complete dissolution—politically, religiously, and, most of all, financially.

At one point a document is produced that's a pure masterpiece. Some doctors of theology argue that in order to prevent them from retracting their confessions, the accused should be denied any defense. Since they have already confessed, there is no need for a trial. A trial is required only if some doubt about the case exists, and here there is no doubt. "Why allow them a defense, whose only purpose would be to shield them from the consequences of their admitted errors? The evidence renders their punishment inescapable."

But there is still a risk that the pope might take control of the trial, so the king and Nogaret set up a sensational case involving the bishop of Troyes, who is accused of witchcraft by the secret testimony of a mysterious conspirator named Noffo Dei. It will be discovered later that Dei lied—and he will be hanged for his trouble—but in the meantime the poor bishop is publicly accused of sodomy, sacrilege, and usury; the same crimes as the Templars. Perhaps the king is trying to show the sons of France that the Church has no right to sit in judgment on the Templars, since it is itself not untouched by their sins; or perhaps he is simply giving the pope a warning to stay away. It's all very murky, a crisscrossing of various police forces and secret services, mutual infiltrations and anonymous accusations. The pope is now cornered, and he agrees to interrogate seventy-two Templars, who repeat the confessions they made under torture. But the pope observes that they have repented, and uses their abjuration—a trump card—as an excuse to pardon them.

And here something else happens—it was a problem I had to resolve in my thesis, but I was torn between contradictory sources. Just when the pope has finally won jurisdiction over the knights, he suddenly hands them back to the king. Why does this happen? Molay retracts his confession; Clement allows him a defense, and three cardinals are summoned to interrogate him. On November 26, 1309, Molay proudly defends the order and its purity; he even goes so far as to threaten its accusers. But then he is visited by an envoy from the king, Guillaume de Plaisans, whom Molay considers a friend. He is given some obscure advice, and two days later, on November 28, he issues a meek and vague deposition, in which he claims to be a poor, uneducated knight, and he confines himself to listing the (now remote) merits of the Temple, its acts of charity, the blood the Templars shed in the Holy Land, and so on. To make matters worse, Nogaret suddenly arrives and reminds everyone that the Temple once had dubious contacts with Saladin. Now the implied crime is high treason. Molay's excuses are pathetic. He has endured two years in prison, and in this deposition he seems a broken man, but he seemed a broken man immediately after his arrest, too. In March of the following year Molay adopts a new strategy in a third deposition. Now he refuses to speak at all, saying that he will address the pope himself but no one else.

A dramatic twist, and here the epic theater begins. In April of 1310, five hundred and fifty Templars ask to be allowed to speak in defense of the order. They denounce the torture to which they have been subjected and deny the charges against them. They demonstrate that all the accusations are implausible. But the king and Nogaret know what to do. Some Templars have retracted their confessions? Fine. Their retraction only makes them recidivists and perjurers—relapsi—a terrible charge in those days. He who confesses and repents may be pardoned, but he who not only does not repent but also retracts his confession, forswears himself, and stubbornly denies that he has anything to repent, he must die. Fifty such perjurers are condemned to death.

It is easy to predict the response of the other prisoners. If you confess, you stay alive, though locked up, and you can wait and see what happens. If you do not confess, or, worse, if you retract your confession, you go to the stake. The five hundred surviving retractors retract their retraction.

As it turns out, the ones who repented chose wisely. In 1312 those who have not confessed are sentenced to life imprisonment, whereas those who confessed are pardoned. Philip is not looking for a massacre; he just wants to dissolve the order. The freed knights, broken in mind and body by four or five years in prison, quietly drift into other orders. All they want is to be forgotten, and this silent disappearance will fuel the legend of the order's underground survival.

Molay was still asking to be heard by the pope. Clement had convened a council in Vienne in 1311, but Molay had not been invited. The suppression of the order is ratified and its property turned over to the Hospitalers, though temporarily it is to be administered by the king.

Another three years go by, and finally an agreement is reached with the pope. On March 19, 1314, in front of Notre-Dame, Molay is sentenced to life imprisonment. He reacts with a surge of dignity. He had expected the pope to allow him to exculpate himself; he now feels betrayed. He knows that if he retracts yet again he will be condemned as a recidivist and perjurer. What does he feel in his heart as he stands there after almost seven years awaiting judgment? Does he regain the courage of his forebears? Or does he simply decide that, ruined as he now is, condemned to end his days in dishonor, buried alive, he might as well die a decent death? Because he protests in a loud voice that he and his brothers are innocent. The Templars, he says, committed one crime and one crime only: out of cowardice they betrayed the Temple. He will do so no longer.

Nogaret is overjoyed. A public crime requires public condemnation, definitive, immediate. Geoffroy de Charnay, the Templar preceptor of Normandy, follows Molay's example. The king makes his decision that very day: a pyre is erected at the tip of the Ile de la Cité. At sundown, Molay and Charnay are burned at the stake.

Tradition has it that before his death the grand master prophesied the ruin of his persecutors. And, indeed, the pope, the king, and Nogaret all die before the year is out. Once the king is gone, Marigny comes under suspicion of embezzlement. His enemies accuse him of witchcraft and have him hanged. Many begin to think of

Molay as a martyr. Dante himself voices widespread indignation at the persecution of the Templars.

And that is where history ends and legend begins. One part of the legend insists that when Louis XVI was guillotined, an unknown man climbed onto the block and shouted: "Jacques de Molay, you are avenged!"

That was more or less the story I told that night at Pilade's, with constant interruptions.

Belbo, for instance, would ask: "Are you sure you didn't read this in Orwell or Koestler?" Or: "Wait a minute, this is just what happened to what's-his-name, that guy in the Cultural Revolution." And Diotallevi kept interjecting, sententiously: "Historia magistra vitae." To which Belbo responded: "Come on, cabalists don't believe in history." And Diotallevi invariably answered: "That's just the point. Everything is repeated, in a circle. History is a master because it teaches us that it doesn't exist. It's the permutations that matter."

"We still haven't answered the real question," Belbo finally said. "Who were the Templars? At first you made them sound like sergeants in a John Ford movie, then like a bunch of bums, then like knights in an illuminated miniature, then like bankers of God carrying on their dirty deals, then like a routed army, then like devotees of a satanic sect, and finally like martyrs to free thought. What were they in the end?"

"Probably they were all those things. 'What was the Catholic Church?' a Martian historian in the year 3000 might ask. 'The people who got themselves thrown to the lions or the ones who killed heretics?' All of the above."

"But did they do those horrible things or didn't they?"

"The funny thing is that their followers—the neo-Templars of various epochs—say they did. And they offer justifications. For instance, it was like fraternity hazing. You want to be a Templar? Okay, prove you have balls, spit on the crucifix, and let's see if God strikes you dead. If you join this militia, you have to give yourself to your brothers heart and soul, so let them kiss your ass. An alternative thesis is that they were asked to deny Christ in order to see how they would behave if the Saracens got them. Which seems idiotic, because you don't train someone to resist torture by making him do—even if only symbolically—what the torturer will ask of him. A third thesis: In the East the Templars had come into contact with Manichean heretics who despised the Cross, regarding it as the instrument of the Lord's torture. The Manicheans also preached renunciation of the world and discouraged marriage and procreation. An old idea, common to many heresies in the early centuries of Christianity. It was later taken up by the Cathars—and in fact there's a whole tradition claiming that the Templars were steeped in Catharism. And this would explain the sodomy—also only symbolic. Let's assume the knights came into contact with Manichean heretics. Well, they weren't exactly intellectuals, so perhaps—partly out of naïveté, partly out of snobbery and esprit de corps—they invented a personal ceremony to distinguish themselves from the other Crusaders. They performed various ritual acts of recognition, without bothering about their significance."

"And that Baphomet business?"

"Many of the depositions do mention a figura Baffometi, but this may have been an error made by the first scribe, an error copied into all subsequent documents. Or the records may have been tampered with. In some cases there was talk of Mahomet (istud caput vester deus est, et vester Mahumet), which would suggest that the Templars had created a syncretic liturgy of their own. Some depositions say that they were also urged to call out 'Yalla,' which could be Allah. But the Moslems didn't worship images of Mahomet, so where does the object come from? The depositions say that many people saw carved heads, but sometimes it was not just a head but a whole idol—wooden, with kinky hair, covered with gold, and always with a beard. It seems that investigators did find such heads and confronted the accused with them, but no trace of them remains. Everyone saw the heads, and no one saw them. Like the cat: some saw a gray cat, others a red cat, others still a black cat. Imagine being interrogated with a red-hot iron: Did you see a cat during the initiation? Well, why not a cat? A Templar farm, where stored grain had to be protected against mice, would be full of cats. The cat was not a common domestic animal in Europe back then. But in Egypt it was. Maybe the Templars kept cats in the house, though right-minded folk looked upon such animals with suspicion. Same thing with the heads of Baphomet. Maybe they were reliquaries in the shape of a head; not unknown at the time. Of course, some say Baphomet was an alchemic figure."

"Alchemy always comes up," Diotallevi said, nodding. "The Templars probably knew the secret of making gold."

"Of course they did," Belbo said. "It was simple enough. Attack a Saracen city, cut the throats of the women and children, and grab everything that's not nailed down. The truth is that this whole story is a great big mess."

"Maybe the mess was in their heads. What did they care about doctrinal debates? History is full of little sects that make up their own style, part swagger, part mysticism. The Templars themselves didn't really understand what they were doing. On the other hand, there's always the esoteric explanation: They knew exactly what they were doing, they were adepts of Oriental mysteries, and even the kiss on the ass had a ritual meaning."

"Do explain to me, briefly, the ritual meaning of the kiss on the ass," Diotallevi said.

"All right. Some modern esotericists maintain that the Templars were reviving certain Indian doctrines. The kiss on the ass serves to wake the serpent Kundalini, a cosmic force that dwells at the base of the spinal column, in the sexual glands. Once wakened, Kundalini rises to the pineal gland . . ."

"Descartes's pineal gland?"

"I think it's the same one. A third eye is then supposed to open up in the brow, the eye that lets you see directly into time and space. This is why people are still seeking the secret of the Templars."

"Philip the Fair should have burned the modern esotericists instead of those poor bastards."

"Yes, except that the modern esotericists don't have two pennies to rub together."

"Now you see the kind of stories we have to listen to!" Belbo concluded. "At least I understand why so many of my lunatics are obsessed with these Templars."

"It's a little like what you were saying the other day. The whole thing is a twisted syllogism. Act like a lunatic and you will be inscrutable forever. Abracadabra, Manel Tekel Phares, Pape Satan Pape Satan Aleppe, le vièrge le vivace et le bel aujourd'hui. Whenever a

104

poet or preacher, chief or wizard spouts gibberish, the human race spends centuries deciphering the message. The Templars' mental confusion makes them indecipherable. That's why so many people venerate them."

"A positivist explanation," Diotallevi said.

"Yes," I agreed, "maybe I am a positivist. A little surgery on the pineal gland might have turned the Templars into Hospitalers; normal people, in other words. War somehow damages the cerebral circuitry. Maybe it's the sound of the cannon, or the Greek fire. Look at our generals."

It was one o'clock. Diotallevi, drunk on tonic water, was clearly unsteady. We all said good night. I had enjoyed myself. So had they. We didn't yet know that we had begun to play with fire—Greek fire, the kind that burns and destroys.

15

Erard de Siverey said to me: "My lord, if you think that neither I nor my heirs will incur reproach for it, I will go and fetch you help from the Comte d'Anjou, whom I see in the fields over there." I said to him: "My dear man, it seems to me you would win great honor for yourself if you went for help to save our lives. Your own, by the way, is also in great danger."

—Joinville, *Histoire de Saint Louis*, 46, 226

After that evening of the Templars, I had only fleeting conversations with Belbo at Pilade's, where I went less and less often because I was working on my thesis.

One day there was a big march against fascist conspiracies. It was to start at the university, and all the left-wing intellectuals had been invited to take part. Magnificent police presence, but apparently the tacit understanding was to let things take their course. Typical of those days: the demonstration had no permit, but if nothing serious happened, the police would just watch, making sure the marchers didn't transgress any of the unwritten boundaries drawn through downtown Milan (there were a lot of territorial compromises back then). The protesters operated in an area beyond Largo Augusto; the fascists were entrenched in Piazza San Babila and its neighboring streets. If anybody crossed the line, there were incidents; otherwise nothing happened. It was like a lion and a lion tamer. We usually believe that the tamer is attacked by the lion and that the tamer stops the attack by raising his whip or firing a blank. Wrong: the lion was fed and sedated before it entered the cage and doesn't feel like attacking anybody. Like all animals, it has its own space; if you don't invade that space, the lion remains calm. When the tamer steps forward, invading it, the lion roars; the tamer then raises his whip, but also takes a step backward (as if in expectation of a charge), whereupon the lion calms down. A simulated revolution must also have its rules.

I went to the demonstration but didn't march with any of the groups. Instead, I stood at the edge of Piazza Santo Stefano, where reporters, editors, and artists who had come to show their solidarity were milling around. The whole clientele of Pilade's.

I found myself standing next to Belbo and a woman I had often seen him with at the bar, who I thought was his companion. (She later disappeared—and now I know why, having read about it in the file on Dr. Wagner.)

"What are you doing here?" I asked.

"You know how it is," he said, smiling, embarrassed. "We have to save our souls somehow. Crede firmiter et pecca fortiter. Doesn't this scene remind you of something?"

I looked around. It was a sunny afternoon, one of those days when Milan is beautiful: yellow façades and a softly metallic sky. The police, across the square, were armored with helmets and plastic shields that gave off glints like steel. A plainclothes officer girded with a gaudy tricolor sash strutted up and down in front of his men. I turned and looked at the head of the march. People weren't moving; they were marking time. They were lined up in ranks, but the rows were irregular, almost serpentine, and the crowd seemed to bristle with pikes, standards, banners, sticks. Impatient groups chanted rhythmic slogans. Along the flanks of the procession, activists darted back and forth, wearing red kerchiefs over their faces, motley shirts, studded belts, and jeans that had known much rain and sun. Even the rolled-up flags that concealed the incongruous weapons looked like dabs of color on a palette. I thought of Dufy, his gaiety. Freely associating, I went from Dufy to Guillaume Dufay. I had the impression of being in a Flemish miniature. In the little crowds gathered on either side of the marchers, I glimpsed some androgynous women waiting for the great display of daring they had been promised. But all this went through my mind in a flash, as if I were reliving some other experience without recognizing it.

"It's the taking of Ascalon, isn't it?" Belbo said.

"By the lord Saint James, my good sir," I replied, "this is truly a Crusaders' combat! I do believe that this night some of these men will be in paradise!"

"No doubt," Belbo said. "But can you tell me where the Saracens are?"

"Well, the police are definitely Teutonic," I observed, "which would make us the hordes of Aleksandr Nevski. But I'm getting my texts mixed up. Look at that group over there. They must be the companions of the Comte d'Artois, eager to enter the fray, for they will brook no offense, and already they head for the enemy lines, shouting threats to provoke the infidel!"

That was when it happened. I don't remember it that clearly. The marchers had started moving, and a group of activists with chains and ski masks began to force their way through the police lines toward Piazza San Babila, yelling. The lion was on the move. The front line of police parted and the fire hoses appeared. The first ball bearings, then the first stones, came hurtling from the forward positions of the demonstration. A cordon of police advanced, swinging clubs, and the procession recoiled. At that moment, in the distance, from the far end of Via Laghetto, a shot was heard. Maybe it was only a tire exploding, or a firecracker; maybe it was a popgun shot from one of those groups that in a few years would regularly be using P-38s.

Panic. The police drew their weapons, trumpet blasts for a charge were heard, the march split into two groups: one, militants, who were ready to fight, and one, all the others, who considered their duty done. I found myself running along Via Larga, with the mad fear of being hit by some blunt object, such as a club. Suddenly Belbo and his companion were beside me, running fast but without panic.

At the corner of Via Rastrelli, Belbo grabbed me by the arm. "This way, kid," he said. I wanted to ask why; Via Larga seemed much more spacious and peopled, and claustrophobia overcame me in the maze of alleys between Via Pecorari and the Archbishop's Palace. It seemed to me that where Belbo was going there were fewer places to hide or blend in if the police intercepted us. But he signaled me to be quiet, turned two or three corners, and gradually slowed down. We found ourselves walking unhurriedly, right behind the cathedral, where traffic was normal and no echoes came from the battle taking place less than two hundred meters away. Still silent, we walked around the cathedral and finally came to the side facing the Galleria. Belbo bought a bag of corn and began feeding the pigeons with seraphic pleasure. We blended into the Saturday crowd completely; Belbo and I were in jackets and ties, and the girl had on the uniform of a Milanese lady: a gray turtleneck with a strand of pearls—cultured, or maybe not.

Belbo introduced us. "This is Sandra. You two know each other?"

"By sight. Hi."

"You see, Casaubon," Belbo said to me then, "you must never flee in a straight line. Napoleon III, following the example of the Savoys in Turin, had Paris disemboweled, then turned it into the network of boulevards we all admire today. A masterpiece of intelligent city planning. Except that those broad, straight streets are also ideal for controlling angry crowds. Where possible, even the side streets were made broad and straight, like the Champs-Elysées. Where it wasn't possible, in the little streets of the Latin Quarter, for example, that's where May '68 was seen to its best advantage. When you flee, head for alleys. No police force can guard them all, and even the police are afraid to enter them in small numbers. If you run into a few on their own, they're more frightened than you are, and both parties take off, in opposite directions. Anytime you're going to a mass rally in an area you don't know well, reconnoiter the neighborhood the day before, and stand at the corner where the little streets start."

"Did you take a course in Bolivia, or what?"

"Survival techniques are learned only in childhood, unless as an adult you enlist in the Green Berets. I had some bad experiences during the war, when the partisans were active around ***," he said, naming a town between Monferrato and the Langhe. "We had been evacuated from the city in '43, a great idea, exactly the time and place to savor everything: mass arrests, the SS, gunfire in the streets. . . . One evening I was going up the hill to get some fresh milk from a farm, and I heard a sound up in the trees: frr, frr. I realized that some men on a distant hill were machine-gunning the railroad line in the valley behind me. My instinct was to run, or just dive to the ground. I made a mistake: I ran toward the valley, and suddenly I heard a chack-chack-chack in the field around me. Some of the shots were falling short of the railroad. That's when I learned that if they're shooting from a high hill down at a valley, then you should run uphill. The higher you go, the higher the bullets will be over your head. Once, my grandmother was caught in a shoot-out between Fascists and partisans deployed on opposite sides of a cornfield. Wherever she ran, she risked stopping a bullet. So she just flung herself down in the middle of the field, right in the line of fire, and lay there for ten minutes, her face in the dirt, hoping that neither side would advance very far. She was lucky. When you learn these things as a child, they are hard-wired in your nervous system."

"So you were in the Resistance."

"As a spectator," he said. I sensed a slight embarrassment in his voice. "In 1943 I was eleven, and at the end of the war, barely thirteen. Too young to take part, but old enough to follow everything with—how shall I put it?—photographic attention. What else could I do? I watched. And ran. Like today."

"You should write about it, instead of editing other people's books."

"It's all been told, Casaubon. If I had been twenty back then, in the fifties I'd have written a poetic memoir. Luckily I was born too late for that. By the time I was old enough to write, all I could do was read the books that were already written. On the other hand, I could also have ended up on that hill with a bullet in my head."

"From which side?" I asked, then immediately regretted the question. "Sorry, I was just kidding."

"No you weren't. Sure, today I know, but what did I know then? You can be obsessed by remorse all your life, not because you chose the wrong thing—you can always repent, atone—but because you never had the chance to prove to yourself that you would have chosen the right thing. I was a potential traitor. What truth does that entitle me now to teach to others?"

"Excuse me," I said, "but potentially you were also a Jack the Ripper. This is neurotic—unless your remorse is based on something specific."

"What does that mean? But, speaking of neurosis, this evening there's a dinner party for Dr. Wagner. Let's take a taxi at Piazza della Scala. Coming, Sandra?"

"Dr. Wagner?" I asked, about to take my leave of them. "In person?"

"Yes. He's in Milan for a few days, and maybe I'll be able to persuade him to give us some of his unpublished essays for a little volume. It would be a real coup."

So Belbo was in contact with Dr. Wagner even then. I wonder if that was the evening Wagner (pronounced Vagnère) psychoanalyzed Belbo free of charge, without either of them knowing it. But perhaps this happened later.

In any case, that was the first time I heard Belbo talk about his childhood in ***. Strange, he talked about running away, investing it with a kind of heroism, in the glorious light of memory, but the memory had come back to him only after—with me as accomplice but also as witness—he had unheroically, if wisely, run away again.

16

After which, brother Etienne de Provins, brought into the presence of the aforesaid officials and asked by them to defend the order, said he did not wish to. If the masters wished to defend it, they could, but before his arrest, he had been in the order only nine months.

—Deposition, November 27, 1309

In Abulafia I found other tales of Belbo's running away. And I thought about them that evening as I stood in the darkness in the periscope listening to a sequence of rustling sounds, squeaks, creaks and telling myself not to panic, because that was how museums, libraries, and antique palaces talked to themselves at night. It is only old cupboards settling, window frames reacting to the evening's humidity, plaster crumbling at a miserly millimeter-per-century rate, walls yawning. You can't run away, I told myself. You're here to learn what happened to a man who, in a mad (or desperate) act of courage, tried once and for all to stop running away—perhaps in order to hasten his encounter, so many times postponed, with the truth.

FILENAME: Canal

Was it from a police charge or, once again, from history that I ran away? Does it make any difference? Did I go to the march because of a moral choice or to subject myself to yet another test of Opportunity? Granted, I was either too early or too late for all the great Opportunities, but that was the fault of my birth date. I would have liked to be in that field of bullets, shooting, even at the price of hitting Granny. But I was absent because of age, not because of cowardice. All right. And what about the march? Again I ran away for a generational reason: it was not my conflict. But I could have taken the risk even so, without enthusiasm, to prove that if I had been in the field of bullets, I would have known how to choose. Does it make sense to choose the wrong Opportunity just to convince yourself that you would have chosen the right one—had you had the Opportunity? I wonder how many of those who opt for fighting today do it for that reason. But a contrived Opportunity is not the right Opportunity.

Can you call yourself a coward simply because the courage of others seems to you out of proportion to the triviality of the occasion? Thus wisdom creates cowards. And thus you miss Opportunity while spending your life on the lookout for it. You have to seize Opportunity instinctively, without knowing at the time that it *is* the Opportunity. Is it possible that I really did seize it once, without knowing? How can you feel like a coward because you were born in the wrong decade? The answer: You feel like a coward because once you were a coward.

But suppose you passed up the Opportunity because you felt it was inadequate?

....

Describe the house in ***, isolated on the hill among the vineyards—don't they call those breast-shaped hills?—and then the road that led to the edge of town, to the last row of houses (or the first, depending on the direction you come from). The little evacuee who abandons the protection of his family and ventures into the tentacular town, walking the broad avenue, skirting the Alley he so enviously fears.

The Alley was the gathering place of the Alley gang. Country boys, dirty, loud. I was too citified: better to stay away from them. But to reach the square, and the newspaper kiosk and the stationery store, unless I essayed a circumnavigation almost equatorial and quite undignified, the only course was to go along the Canal. And the boys of the Alley gang were little gentlemen compared to the Canal gang, named after a former stream, now a drainage ditch, that ran through the poorest part of town. The Canal kids were filthy subproletarians, and violent.

The Alley kids couldn't cross the Canal area without being attacked and beaten up. At first I didn't know that I was an Alley kid. I had just arrived, but already the Canal gang had identified me as an enemy. I walked through their area with a children's magazine open before my face, reading as I went. They saw me. I ran. They chased me, throwing stones. One stone went right through a page of the magazine, which I was still holding in front of me as I ran, trying to retain a little dignity. I got away but lost the magazine. The next day I decided to join the Alley gang.

I presented myself at their Sanhedrin and was greeted with cackles. My hair was very thick at the time, and it tended to stand up on my head a bit like Struwwelpeter's. The style in those days, as shown in movies and ads, or on Sunday strolls after Mass, featured young men with broad-shouldered, double-breasted jackets, greased mustaches, and gleaming hair combed straight back and stuck to their skulls. And that's what I wanted, sleek hair like that. In the market square, on a Monday, I spent what for me was an enormous sum on some boxes of brilliantine thick as beanflower honey. Then I spent hours smearing it on until my hair was laminated, a leaden cap, a camauro. Then I put on a net, to keep the hair tightly compressed. The Alley gang had seen me go by wearing the net, and had shouted taunts in that harsh dialect of theirs, which I understood but couldn't speak. That particular day, after staying two hours in the house with the net on, I took it off, checked the splendid result in the mirror, and set out to meet the gang to which I hoped to swear allegiance. I approached them just as the brilliantine was losing its glutinous power and my hair was again assuming, in slow motion, its vertical position. Delight among the Alley kids, in a circle around me, nudging one another. I asked to be admitted.

Unfortunately, I spoke in Italian. An outsider. Their leader, Martinetti, who seemed a giant to me then, came forward, splendid, barefoot. He decided I should undergo one hundred kicks in the behind. Perhaps the kicks were meant to reawaken the serpent Kundalini. I agreed and stood against the wall. Two sergeants held my arms, and I received one hundred barefoot kicks. Martinetti applied himself to his task with vigor and skill, striking sideways so he wouldn't hurt his toes. The gang served as chorus for the ritual, keeping count in their dialect. Then they shut me up in a rabbit hutch for half an hour, while they passed the time in guttural conversation. They let me out when I complained that my legs were numb. I was proud because I had been able to stand up to the liturgy of a savage tribe. I was a man called Horse.

In *** in those days were stationed latter-day Teutonic Knights, who were not particularly alert, because the partisans hadn't yet made themselves felt—this was toward the end of '43, the beginning of '44. One of our first exploits was to slip into a shed, while some of us flattered the soldier on guard duty, a great Langobard eating an enormous sandwich of—we thought, and were horrified—salami and jam. The decoys distracted the German, praising his weapons, while the rest of us crept through some loose planks in the back of the shed and stole a few sticks of TNT. I don't believe the explosive was ever used subsequently, but the idea was, according to Martinetti's plan, to set it off in the countryside, for purely pyrotechnical purposes and by methods I now know were very crude and would not have worked. Later, the Germans were replaced by the Fascist marines of the Decima Mas, who set up a roadblock near the river, right at the crossroads where the girls from the school of Santa Maria Ausiliatrice came down the avenue at six in the evening. Martinetti convinced the Decima marines (who couldn't have been over eighteen) to tie together a bunch of hand grenades left by the Germans, the ones with a long pin, and remove the safeties so they could explode at the water's edge at the exact moment the girls arrived. Martinetti knew how to calculate the timing. He explained it to the Fascists, and the effect was prodigious: a sheet of water rose up along the bank in a thunderous din just as the girls were turning the corner. General flight, much squeaking, and we and the Fascists split our sides laughing. The survivors of Allied imprisonment would remember that day of glory, second only to the burning of Molay.

The chief amusement of the Alley kids was collecting shell cases and other war residue, which after September 8 and the German occupation of Italy were plentiful: old helmets, cartridge pouches, knapsacks, sometimes live bullets. This is what you did with a good bullet: holding the shell case in one hand, you stuck the projectile into a keyhole, twisted it, and pulled out the case, adding it to your collection. The gunpowder was emptied out (sometimes there were thin strips of ballistite) and deposited in serpentine trails that were set alight. The casings, especially prized if the caps were intact, went to enrich one's army. A good collector would have a lot of them, arranged in rows by make, color, shape, and origin. There were squads of foot soldiers, which were submachine-gun and Sten casings, then squires and knights, which were 1891 rifle shells (we saw Garands only after the Americans came), and finally, a boy's supreme ambition, towering grand masters, which were empty machine-gun shells.

One evening, as we were absorbed in these peaceful pursuits, Martinetti informed us that the moment had come. A challenge had been sent to the Canal gang, and they had accepted. The battle was to take place on neutral ground, behind the station. That night, at nine.

It was late afternoon, on a summer day, enervating but charged with excitement. We decked ourselves out in the most terrifying paraphernalia, looking for pieces of wood that could be easily gripped, filling pouches and knapsacks with stones of various sizes. Some of us made whips out of rifle slings, awesome if wielded with decision. During those twilight hours we all felt like heroes, me most of all. It was the excitement before the attack: bitter, painful, splendid. So long, Mama, I'm off to Yokohama; send the word over there. We were sacrificing our youth to the Fatherland, just as they had taught us in school before September 8.

Martinetti's plan was shrewd. We would cross the railroad embankment farther to the north and come at them from behind, take them by surprise, and thus would be victors from the start. Then no quarter would be granted.

At dusk we crossed the embankment, scrambling up ramps and across gullies, loaded down with stones and clubs. From the crest of the embankment we saw them lying in ambush behind the station latrines. But they saw us, too, because they were watching their backs, suspecting we would arrive from that direction. The only thing for us to do was to move in without giving them time for astonishment at the obviousness of our ploy.

Nobody had passed around any grappa before we went over the top, but we flung ourselves into battle anyway, yelling. Then came the turning point, when we were about a hundred meters from the station. There stood the first houses of the town, and though they were few, they created a web of narrow paths. There, the boldest group dashed forward, fearless, while I and (luckily for me) a few others slowed down and ducked behind the corners of the houses, to watch from a distance.

If Martinetti had organized us into vanguard and rear guard, we would have done our duty, but this was a spontaneous deployment: those with guts in front, and the cowards behind. So from our refuges—mine was farther back than the others—we observed the conflict. Which never took place.

The two groups came within a few meters of each other, and stood in confrontation, snarling. Then the leaders stepped forward to confer. Yalta. They decided to divide their territories into zones and agreed to allow an occasional safe-conduct pass, like Christians and Moslems in the Holy Land. Solidarity between groups of knights had prevailed over the ineluctability of battle. Each side had proved itself. The opposing camps withdrew in harmony, still opponents, in opposite directions.

Now I tell myself that I didn't rush into the attack because I found it laughable. But that's not what I told myself then. Then, I felt like a coward, and that was that.

Today, even more cowardly, I tell myself that as it turned out I would have risked nothing had I charged with the others, and my life afterward would have been better. I missed Opportunity at the age of twelve. If you fail to have an erection the first time, you're impotent for the rest of your life.

A month later, some random trespass brought the Alley and Canal gangs face to face in a field, and clods of earth began to fly. I don't know whether it was because the outcome of the earlier conflict had reassured me or because I desired martyrdom, but one way or another, this time I stood in the front line. A clod, which concealed a stone, struck my lip and split it. I ran home crying, and my mother had to use the tweezers from her toilet case to pick pieces of earth out of the wound on the inside of my lip. In fact I was left with a lump next to the lower right canine, and even now, when I run my tongue over it, I feel a vibration, a shudder.

But this lump does not absolve me, because I got it through heedlessness, not through courage. I run my tongue over my lip and what do I do? I write. But bad literature brings no redemption.

After the day of the march I didn't see Belbo again for about a year. I fell in love with Amparo and stopped going to Pilade's—or, at least, the few times I did drop in with Amparo, Belbo wasn't there. Amparo didn't like the place anyway. In her moral and political severity—equaled only by her grace, her magnificent pride—she considered Pilade's a clubhouse for liberal dandies, and liberal dandysme, as far as she was concerned, was a subtle thread in the fabric of the capitalist plot. For me this was a year of great commitment, seriousness, and enchantment. I worked joyfully but serenely on my thesis.

Then one day I ran into Belbo along the navigli, not far from the Garamond office. "Well, look who's here," he said cheerfully. "My favorite Templar! Listen, I've just been presented with a bottle of ineffably ancient nectar. Why don't you come up to the office? I have paper cups and a free afternoon."

"A zeugma," I said.

"No. Bourbon. And bottled, I believe, before the fall of the Alamo."

I followed him. We had just taken the first sip when Gudrun came in and said there was a gentleman to see Belbo. He slapped his forehead. He had forgotten the appointment. But chance has a taste for conspiracy, he said to me. From what he had gathered, this individual wanted to show him a book that concerned the Templars. "I'll get rid of him quickly," he said, "but you must lend me a hand with some keen objections."

It had surely been chance. And so I was caught in the net.

17

And thus did the knights of the Temple vanish with their secret, in whose shadow breathed a lofty yearning for the earthly city. But the Abstract to which their efforts aspired lived on, unattainable, in unknown regions . . . and its inspiration, more than once in the course of time, has filled those spirits capable of receiving it.
—Victor Emile Michelet, *Le secret de la Chevalerie*, 1930, 2

He had a 1940s face. Judging by the old magazines I had found in the basement at home, everybody had a face like that in the forties. It must have been wartime hunger that hollowed the cheeks and made the eyes vaguely feverish. This was a face I knew from photographs of firing squads—on both sides. In those days men with the same face shot one another.

Our visitor was wearing a blue suit, a white shirt, and a pearl-gray tie, and instinctively I asked myself why he was in civilian clothes. His hair, unnaturally black, was combed back from the temples in two bands, brilliantined, though with discretion, showing a bald, shiny crown traversed by fine strands, regular as telegraph wires, that formed a centered V on his forehead. His face was tanned, marked—marked not only by the explicitly colonial wrinkles. A pale scar ran across his left cheek from lip to ear, slicing imperceptibly through the left half of his black Adolphe Menjou mustache. The skin must have been opened less than a millimeter and stitched up. Mensur? Or a grazing bullet's wound?

He introduced himself—Colonel Ardenti—offering Belbo his hand and merely nodding at me when Belbo presented me as an assistant. He sat down, crossed his legs, drew up his trousers from the knee, revealing a pair of maroon socks, ankle-length.

"Colonel . . . on active service?" Belbo asked.

Ardenti bared some high-quality dentures. "Retired, you could say. Or, if you prefer, in the reserves. I may not look old, but I am."

"You don't look at all old," Belbo said.

"I've fought in four wars."

"You must have begun with Garibaldi."

"No. I was a volunteer lieutenant in Ethiopia. Then a captain, again a volunteer, in Spain. Then a major back in Africa, until we abandoned our colonies. Silver Medal. In '43—well, let's just say I chose the losing side, and indeed I lost everything, save honor. I had the courage to start all over again, in the ranks. Foreign Legion. School of hard knocks. Sergeant in '46, colonel in '58, with Massu. Apparently I always choose the losing side. When De Gaulle's leftists took over, I retired and went to live in France. I had made some good friends in Algiers, so I set up an import-export firm in Marseilles. This time I chose the winning side, apparently, since I now enjoy an independent income and can devote myself to my hobby. These past few years, I've written down the results of my research. Here . . ." From a leather briefcase he produced a voluminous file, which at the time seemed red to me.

"So," Belbo said, "a book on the Templars?"

"The Templars," the colonel acknowledged. "A passion of mine almost from my youth. They, too, were soldiers of fortune who crossed the Mediterranean in search of glory."

"Signor Casaubon has also been studying the Templars," Belbo said. "He knows the subject better than I do. But tell us about your book."

"The Templars have always interested me. A handful of generous souls who bore the light of Europe among the savages of the two Tripolis . . ."

"The Templars' adversaries weren't exactly savages," I remarked.

"Have you ever been captured by rebels in the Magreb?" he asked me with heavy sarcasm.

"Not that I recall," I said.

He glared at me, and I was glad I had never served in one of his platoons. "Excuse me," he said, speaking to Belbo. "I belong to another generation." He looked back at me defiantly. "Is this some kind of trial, or—"

"We're here to talk about your work, Colonel," Belbo said. "Tell us about it, please."

"I want to make one thing clear immediately," the colonel said, putting his hands on the file. "I am prepared to assume the production costs. You won't lose money on this. If you want scholarly references, I'll provide them. Just two hours ago I met an expert in the field, a man who came here from Paris expressly to see me. He could contribute an authoritative preface. . . ." He anticipated Belbo's question and made a gesture, as if to say that for the moment it was best to leave the name unsaid, that it was a delicate matter.

"Dr. Belbo," he said, "these pages contain all the elements of a story. A true story, and a most unusual story. Better than any American thriller. I've discovered something—something very important—but it's only the beginning. I want to tell the world what I know, hoping that there may be somebody out there who can fit the rest of the puzzle together—somebody who might read the book and come forward. In other words, this is a fishing expedition of sorts. And time is of the essence. The one man who knew what I know now has probably been killed, precisely to keep him from divulging it. But if I can reach perhaps two thousand readers with what I know, there will be no further point in doing away with me." He paused. "The two of you know something about the arrest of the Templars?"

"Signor Casaubon told me about it recently, and I was struck by the fact that there was no resistance to the arrest, and the knights were caught by surprise."

The colonel smiled condescendingly. "True. But it's absurd to think that men powerful enough to frighten the king of France would have been unable to find out that a few rogues were stirring up the king and that the king was stirring up the pope. Quite absurd! Which suggests that there had to be a plan. A sublime plan. Suppose the Templars had a plan to conquer the world, and they knew the secret of an immense source of power, a secret whose preservation was worth the sacrifice of the whole Temple quarter in Paris, and of the commanderies scattered throughout the kingdom, also in Spain, Portugal, England, and Italy, the castles in the Holy Land, the monetary wealth—everything. Philip the Fair suspected this. Why else would he have unleashed a persecution that discredited the fair flower of French chivalry? The Temple realized that the king suspected and that he would attempt its destruction. Direct resistance was futile; the plan required time: either the treasure (or whatever it was) had to be found, or it had to be exploited slowly. And the Temple's secret directorate, whose existence everyone now recognizes . . ."

"Everyone?"

"Of course. It's inconceivable that such a powerful order could have survived so long without having a secret directorate."

"Your reasoning is flawless," Belbo said, giving me a sidelong glance.

The colonel went on. "The grand master belonged to the secret directorate, but he must have served only as its cover, to deceive outsiders. In *La Chevalerie et les aspects secrets de l'histoire,* Gaulthier Walther says that the Templar plan for world conquest was to be finally realized only in the year 2000. The Temple decided to go underground, and that meant that it had to look as if the order were dead. They sacrificed themselves, that's what they did! The grand master included. Some let themselves be killed; they were probably chosen by lot. Others submitted, blending into the civilian landscape. What became of the minor officials, the lay brothers, the carpenters, the glaziers? That was how the Freemasons were born, later spreading throughout the world, as everyone knows. But in England things happened differently. The king resisted the pope's pressure and pensioned the Templars off. They lived out their days meekly, in the order's great houses. Meekly—do you believe that? I don't. In Spain the order changed its name to the order of Montesa. Gentlemen, these were men who could bring a king to heel; they held so many of his promissory notes that they could have bankrupted him in a week. The king of Portugal, for instance, came to terms. Let us handle it like this, dear friends, he said: don't call yourselves Knights of the Temple anymore; change the name to Knights of Christ, and I'll be happy. In Germany there were very few trials. The abolition of the order was purely formal, and in any case there was a brother order, the Teutonic Knights, who at the time were not merely a state within the state: they *were* the state, having acquired a territory as big as those countries now under the Russian heel, and they kept expanding until the end of the fifteenth century, when the Mongols arrived. But that's another story, because the Mongols are at our gates even now. But I mustn't digress."

"Yes, let us not digress," Belbo said.

"Well then. As everyone knows, two days before Philip issued the arrest warrant, and a month before it was carried out, a hay wain drawn by oxen left the precincts of the Temple for an unknown destination. Nostradamus himself alludes to it in one of his

Centuries. . . ." He looked through his manuscript for the quotation:

> *Souz la pasture d'animaux ruminant*
> *par eux conduits au ventre herbipolique*
> *soldats cachés, les armes bruit menant . . .*

"The hay wain is a legend," I said. "And I would hardly consider Nostradamus an authority in matters of historical fact."

"People older than you, Signor Casaubon, have had faith in many of Nostradamus's prophecies. Not that I am so ingenuous as to take the story of the hay wain literally. It's a symbol—a symbol of the obvious, established fact that Jacques de Molay, anticipating his arrest, turned over command of the order, as well as its secret instructions, to a nephew, Comte de Beaujeu, who became the head of the now clandestine Temple."

"Are there documents that bear this out?"

"Official history," the colonel said with a bitter smile, "is written by the victors. According to official history, men like me don't exist. No, behind the story of the hay wain lies something else. The Temple's secret nucleus moved to a quiet spot, and from there they began to extend their underground network. This obvious fact was my starting point. For years—even before the war—I kept asking myself where these brothers in heroism might have gone. When I retired to private life, I finally decided to look for a trail. Since the flight of the hay wain had occurred in France, France was where I should find the original gathering of the secret nucleus. But where in France?"

He had a sense of theater. Belbo and I were all ears. We could find nothing better to say than "Well, where?"

"I'll tell you. Where would the Templars have hidden? Where did Hugues de Payns come from? Champagne, near Troyes. And at the time the Templars were founded, Champagne was ruled by Hugues de Champagne, who joined them in Jerusalem just a few years later. When he came back home, he apparently got in touch with the abbot of Cîteaux and helped him initiate the study and translation of certain Hebrew texts in his monastery. Think about it: the White Benedictines—Saint Bernard's Benedictines—also invited the rabbis of upper Burgundy to come to Cîteaux, to study whatever texts

Hugues had found in Palestine. Hugues even gave Saint Bernard's monks a forest at Bar-sur-Aube, where Clairvaux was later built. And what did Saint Bernard do?"

"He became the champion of the Templars," I said.

"But why? Did you know he made the Templars even more powerful than the Benedictines? That he prohibited the Benedictines from receiving gifts of lands and houses, and had them give lands and houses to the Templars instead? Have you ever seen the Forêt d'Orient near Troyes? It's immense, one commandery after the other. And in the meantime, you know, the knights in Palestine weren't fighting. They were settled in the Temple, making friends with the Moslems instead of killing them. They communicated with Moslem mystics. In other words, Saint Bernard, with the economic support of the counts of Champagne, built an order in the Holy Land that was in contact with Arab and Jewish secret sects. An unknown directorate ran the Crusades in an effort to keep the order going, and not the other way around. And it set up a network of power that was outside royal jurisdiction. I am a man of action, not a man of science. Instead of spinning empty conjectures, I did what all the long-winded scholars have never done: I went to the place the Templars came from, the place that had been their base for two centuries, their home, where they could live like fish in water. . . ."

"Chairman Mao says that revolutionaries must live among the people like fish in water," I said.

"Good for your chairman. But the Templars were preparing a revolution far greater than the revolution of your pigtailed communists."

"They don't wear pigtails anymore."

"No? Well, so much the worse for them. As I was saying, the Templars must have sought refuge in Champagne. Payns? Troyes? The Eastern Forest? No. Payns was—and still is—a tiny village. At the time, it had a castle at most. Troyes was a city: too many of the king's men around. The forest, which the Templars owned, was the first place the royal guards would look. Which they did, by the way. No, I said to myself, the only place that made sense was Provins."

18

If our eye could penetrate the earth and see its interior from pole to pole, from where we stand to the antipodes, we would glimpse with horror a mass terrifyingly riddled with fissures and caverns.
—Thomas Burnet, *Telluris Theoria Sacra*, Amsterdam, Wolters, 1694, p. 38

"Why Provins?"

"Have you ever been to Provins? A magic place: you can feel it even today. Go there. A magic place, still redolent of secrets. In the eleventh century it was the seat of the Comte de Champagne, a free zone, where the central government couldn't come snooping. The Templars were at home there; even today a street is named after them. There were churches, palaces, a castle overlooking the whole plain. And a lot of money, merchants doing business, fairs, confusion, where it was easy to pass unnoticed. But most important, something that has been there since prehistoric times: tunnels. A network of tunnels—real catacombs—extends beneath the hill. Some tunnels are open to the public today. They were places where people could meet in secret, and if their enemies got in, the conspirators could disperse in a matter of seconds, disappearing into nowhere. And if they were really familiar with the passages, they could exit in one direction and reappear in the opposite, on padded feet, like cats. They could sneak up behind the intruders and cut them down in the dark. As God is my witness, gentlemen, those tunnels are tailor-made for commandos. Quick and invisible, you slip in at night, knife between your teeth, a couple of grenades in hand, and your enemies die like rats!"

His eyes were shining. "Do you realize what a fabulous hiding place Provins must have been? A secret nucleus could meet underground, and the locals, even if they did see something, wouldn't say a word. The king's men, of course, did come to Provins. They arrested the Templars who were visible on the surface and took them to Paris. Reynaud de Provins was tortured, but didn't talk. Clearly,

125

the secret plan called for him to be arrested to make the king believe that Provins had been swept clean. But at the same time he was to give a signal, by refusing to talk: Provins will not yield—not Provins, where the new, underground Templars live on. Some tunnels lead from building to building. You can enter a granary or a warehouse and come out in a church. Some tunnels are constructed with columns and vaulted ceilings. Even today, every house in the upper city still has a cellar with ogival vaults—there must be more than a hundred of them. And every cellar has an entrance to a tunnel."

"Conjecture," I said.

"No, young man, fact. You haven't seen the tunnels of Provins. Room after room, deep in the earth, covered with ancient graffiti. The graffiti are found mostly in what speleologists call lateral cells. Hieratic drawings of druidic origin, scratched into the wall before the Romans came. Caesar passed overhead, while down below men plotted resistance, ambushes, spells. There are Catharist symbols, too. Yes, gentlemen, the Cathars in Provence were wiped out, but there were Cathars in Champagne also, and they survived, meeting secretly in these catacombs of heresy. One hundred and eighty-three of them were burned aboveground, but the others hid below. The chronicles call them bougres et manichéens. Now, mind you, the bougres were simply Bogomils, Cathars of Bulgarian origin. Does the French word bougres tell you anything? Originally it meant sodomite, because the Bulgarian Cathars were said to have that little failing. . . ." He gave a nervous laugh. "And who else was accused of that same failing? The Templars. Curious, isn't it?"

"Up to a point," I said. "In those days the easiest way to get rid of a heretic was to accuse him of sodomy. . . ."

"True, and you mustn't think that I believe the Templars actually . . . They were fighting men, and we fighting men like beautiful women. Vows or not, a man is a man. I mention this only because I don't believe it's a coincidence that Cathar heretics found refuge where the Templars were. But in any case the Templars learned from them the use of caves and tunnels."

"But all this, really, is guesswork," Belbo said.

"It started with guesswork, yes. I'm just explaining why I set out to explore Provins. But now we come to the actual story. In the center of Provins is a big Gothic building, the Grange-aux-Dîmes, or tithe granary. As you may know, one of the sources of the Templars' strength was that they collected tithes directly and didn't have to pay anything to the state. Under the building, as everywhere else, there's a network of passages, today in very bad condition. Well, as I was going through archives in Provins I came across a local newspaper from 1894. In it was an article about two dragoons, Chevalier Camille Laforge of Tours and Chevalier Edouard Ingolf of Petersburg—yes, Petersburg!—who had visited the Grange a few days earlier. Accompanied by the caretaker, they went down into one of the subterranean rooms, on the second level belowground. When the caretaker, trying to show that there were other levels even farther down, stamped on the earth, they heard echoes and reverberations. The reporter praised the bold dragoons, who promptly fetched lanterns and ropes and went into the unknown tunnels like boys down a mine, pulling themselves forward on their elbows, crawling through mysterious passages. And the paper says they came to a great hall with a fine fireplace and a dry well in the center. They tied a stone to a rope, lowered it, and found that the well was eleven meters deep. They went back a week later with stronger ropes, and two companions lowered Ingolf into the well, where he discovered a big room with stone walls, ten meters square and five meters high. The others then followed him down. They realized that they were at the third level, thirty meters beneath the surface. We don't know what the men saw and did in that room. The reporter admits that when he went to the scene to investigate, he lacked the courage to go down into the well. I was excited by the story and felt a desire to visit the place. But many of the tunnels had collapsed since the end of the last century, and even if such a well did exist at that time, there was no way of telling where it was now.

"It suddenly occurred to me that the dragoons might have found something down there. I had recently read a book about the secret of Rennes-le-Château, another story in which the Templars figure. A penniless and obscure parish priest was restoring an old church in a little village of some two hundred souls. A stone in the choir floor was lifted, revealing a box said to contain some very old manuscripts. Only manuscripts? We don't know exactly what happened next, but in later years the priest became immensely rich, threw money around, led a life of dissipation, and was finally brought before an ecclesiastical court. What if something similar had happened to one of the dragoons? Or to both? Ingolf went down first;

let's say he found some precious object small enough to be hidden in his tunic. He came back up and said nothing to his companions. Well, I am a stubborn man; otherwise I wouldn't have lived the life I have."

The colonel ran his fingers over his scar, then raised his hands to his temples and brushed his hair toward his nape, making sure it was in place.

"I went to the central telephone office in Paris and checked the directories of the entire country, looking for a family named Ingolf. I found only one, in Auxerre, and wrote a letter introducing myself as an amateur archeologist. Two weeks later I received a reply from an elderly midwife, the daughter of the Ingolf I had read about. She was curious to know why I was interested in him. In fact, she asked: For God's sake, could I tell her anything? I realized there was a mystery here, so I hurried to Auxerre. Mademoiselle Ingolf lives in a little ivy-covered cottage, its wooden gate held shut by a string looped around a nail. An old maid—tidy, kind, and uneducated. She asked me right away what I knew about her father, and I told her I knew only that one day he had gone down into a tunnel in Provins. I said I was writing a historical monograph on the region. She was dumbfounded; she had no idea her father had ever been to Provins. Yes, he had been a dragoon, but he resigned from the service in 1895, before she was born. He bought this cottage in Auxerre, and in 1898 he married a local girl with some money of her own. Mademoiselle Ingolf was five when her mother died, in 1915. Her father disappeared in 1935. Literally disappeared. He left for Paris, which he regularly visited at least twice a year, but was never heard from again. The local gendarmerie telephoned Paris: the man had vanished into thin air. Presumed dead. And so our mademoiselle, left alone with only a meager inheritance, had to go to work. Apparently she never found a husband, and judging by the way she sighed, thereby also hangs a tale—probably the only tale in her life, and it must have ended badly. 'Monsieur Ardenti,' she said, 'I suffer constant anguish and remorse, having learned nothing of poor Papa's fate, not even the site of his grave, if indeed there is one.' She was eager to talk about him, describing him as very gentle and calm, a methodical, cultured man who spent his days reading and writing in a little attic study. He puttered in the garden now and then, and exchanged a few words with the pharmacist—also dead now. From time to time he traveled to Paris—on business, he said—and always came home with packages of books. The study was still full of them; she wanted to show them to me. We went upstairs.

"It was a clean and tidy little room, which Mademoiselle Ingolf dusted once a week: she could take flowers to her mother's grave, but all she could do for poor Papa was this. She kept it just as he left it; she wished she had gone to school so she could read those books of his, but they were in languages like Old French, Latin, German, and even Russian. Papa had been born and spent his childhood in Russia; his father had been a French Embassy official. There were about a hundred volumes in the library, most of them—I was delighted to see—on the trial of the Templars. For example, he had Raynouard's *Monuments historiques relatifs à la condamnation des chevaliers du Temple*, published in 1813, a great rarity. There were many volumes on secret writing systems, a whole collection on cryptography, and some works on paleography and diplomatic history. As I was leafing through an old account ledger, I found an annotation that made me start: it concerned the sale of a case, with no further description and no mention of the buyer's name. Nor was any price given, but the date was 1895, and the entries immediately below were quite meticulous. This was the ledger of a judicious gentleman shrewdly managing his nest egg. There were some notes on the purchase of items from antiquarian booksellers in Paris. I was beginning to understand.

"In the crypt in Provins, Ingolf must have found a gold case studded with precious stones. Without a moment's thought, he slipped it into his tunic and went back up, not saying a word to the others. At home, he found a parchment in the case. That much seems obvious. He went to Paris and contacted a collector of antiques—probably some bloodsucking pawnbroker—but the sale of the case, even so, left Ingolf comfortably off, if not rich. Then he went further, left the service, retired to the country, and started buying books and studying the parchment. Perhaps he was something of a treasure hunter to start with; otherwise he wouldn't have been exploring tunnels in Provins. He was probably educated enough to believe that he would eventually be able to decipher the parchment on his own. So he worked calmly, unruffled, for more than thirty years, a true monomaniac. Did he ever tell anyone about his discoveries? Who knows? One way or another, by 1935 he must have felt either that he had made considerable progress or that he had come to a dead end, because he then apparently decided to turn to someone, either to tell that person what he knew or to find out what he needed to know. And what he knew must have been so secret and awesome that the person he turned to did away with him.

"But let us return to his attic. I wanted to see whether Ingolf had left any clues, so I told the good mademoiselle that if I examined her father's books, I might perhaps find some trace of the discovery he had made in Provins. If so, I would give him full credit in my essay. She was enthusiastic. Anything for poor Papa. She invited me to stay the whole afternoon and to come back the next morning if necessary. She brought me coffee, turned on the lights, and went back to her garden, leaving me in full charge. The room had smooth, white walls, no cupboards, nooks, or crannies where I could rummage, but I neglected nothing. I looked above, below, and inside the few pieces of furniture; I searched through an almost empty wardrobe containing a few suits filled with mothballs; I looked behind the three or four framed engravings of landscapes. I'll spare you the details, but, take it from me, I did a thorough job. It's not enough, for instance, to feel the stuffing of a sofa; you have to stick needles in to make sure you don't miss any foreign object. . . ."

The colonel's experience, I realized, was not limited to battlefields.

"That left the books. I made a list of the titles and checked for underlinings and notes in the margins, for any hint at all. After a long while, I clumsily picked up an old volume with a heavy binding; I dropped it, and a handwritten sheet of paper fell out. It was notebook paper, and the texture and ink suggested that it wasn't very old: it could have been written in the last years of Ingolf's life. I barely glanced at it, but suddenly noticed something written in the margin: 'Provins 1894.' Well, you can imagine my excitement, the wave of emotion that swept over me. . . . I realized that Ingolf had taken the original parchment to Paris, and that this was a copy. I felt no compunction. Mademoiselle Ingolf had dusted those books for years and had never come across that paper, otherwise she would have told me. Very well, let her continue to be unaware of it. The world is made up of winners and losers. I had had my share of defeat; it was time now to grasp victory. I folded the paper and put it in my pocket. I bade Mademoiselle Ingolf good-bye, telling her that, though I had found nothing of interest, I would nevertheless mention her father if I wrote anything. Bless you, she said. A man of action, gentlemen, especially one burning with the passion that blazed within me, can't have scruples when dealing with a dismal woman already sentenced by fate."

"No need to apologize," Belbo said. "You did it. Just tell us the rest."

"Gentlemen, I will now show you this text. Forgive me for using a photocopy. It's not distrust. I don't want to subject the original to further wear."

"But Ingolf's copy wasn't the original," I said. "The parchment was the original."

"Casaubon, when originals no longer exist, the last copy is the original."

"But Ingolf may have made errors in transcription."

"You don't know that he did. Whereas I know Ingolf's transcription is true, because I see no way the truth could be otherwise. Therefore Ingolf's copy is the original. Do we agree on this point, or do we sit and split hairs?"

"No," Belbo said. "I hate that. Let's see your original copy."

19

After Beaujeu, the Order has never ceased to exist, not for a moment, and after Aumont we find an uninterrupted sequence of Grand
Masters of the Order down to our own time, and if the name and
seat of the true Grand Master and the true Seneschals who rule the
Order and guide its sublime labors remain a mystery today, an impenetrable secret known only to the truly enlightened, it is because
the hour of the Order has not struck and the time is not ripe. . . .

—Manuscript of 1760, in G. A. Schiffmann, *Die Entstehung
der Rittergrade in der Freimauerei um die Mitte des XVIII
Jahrhunderts*, Leipzig, Zechel, 1882, pp. 178-190

This was our first, remote contact with the Plan. I could easily be
somewhere else now if I hadn't been in Belbo's office that day. I
could be—who knows?—selling sesame seeds in Samarkand, or editing a series of books in Braille, or heading the First National Bank
of Franz Josef Land. Counterfactual conditionals are always true,
because the premise is false. But I was there that day, so now I am
where I am.

The colonel handed us the page with a flourish. I still have it here
among my papers, in a little plastic folder. Printed on that thermal
paper photocopies used in those days, it is more yellowed and faded
now. Actually there were two texts on the page: the first, densely
written, took up half the space; the second was divided into fragments of verses. . . .

The first text was a kind of demoniacal litany, a parody of a Semitic language:

Kuabris Defrabax Rexulon Ukkazaal Ukzaab Urpaefel Taculbain
Habrak Hacoruin Maquafel Tebrain Hmcatuin Rokasor Himesor
Argaabil Kaquaan Docrabax Reisaz Reisabrax Decaiquan
Oiquaquil Zaitabor Qaxaop Dugraq Xaelobran Disaeda Magisuan
Raitak Huidal Uscolda Arabaom Zipreus Mecrim Cosmae
Duquifas Rocarbis.

"Not exactly clear," Belbo remarked.

"No, it isn't," the colonel agreed slyly. "And I might have spent my life trying to make sense of it, if one day, almost by chance, I hadn't found a book about Trithemius on a bookstall and noticed one of his coded messages: 'Pamersiel Oshurmy Delmuson Thafloyn. . . .' I had uncovered a clue, and I pursued it relentlessly. I knew nothing at all about Trithemius, but in Paris I found an edition of his *Steganographia, hoc est ars per occultam scripturam animi sui voluntatem absentibus aperiendi certa*, published in Frankfurt in 1606. The art of using secret writing in order to bare your soul to distant persons. A fascinating man, this Trithemius. A Benedictine abbot of Spannheim, late fifteenth–early sixteenth centuries, a scholar who knew Hebrew and Chaldean, Oriental languages like Tartar. He corresponded with theologians, cabalists, alchemists, most certainly with the great Cornelius Agrippa of Nettesheim and perhaps with Paracelsus. . . . Trithemius masked his revelations about secret writings behind magical smoke screens. For instance, he recommended sending coded messages like the one you're looking at now. The recipient was then supposed to call upon angels like Pamersiel, Padiel, Dorothiel, and so on, to help him decipher the real message. But many of his examples are actually military dispatches, and his book—dedicated to Philip, Count Palatine and Duke of Bavaria—represents one of the first serious studies of cryptography."

"Correct me if I'm wrong," I said, "but didn't you say that Trithemius lived at least a hundred years after the manuscript we're talking about was written?"

"Trithemius was associated with a Sodalitas Celtica that was concerned with philosophy, astrology, Pythagorean mathematics. You see the connection? The Templars were an order whose initiates were also inspired by the wisdom of the ancient Celts; that has been widely demonstrated. Somehow Trithemius also learned the cryptographic systems used by the Templars."

"Amazing," Belbo said. "And the transcription of the secret message? What does it say?"

"All in good time, gentlemen. Trithemius presents forty major and ten minor cryptosystems. Here I was lucky—either that or the Templars of Provins simply didn't make any great effort, since they were sure nobody would ever crack their code. I tried the first of the forty major systems and assumed that only the first letter of each word counted."

Belbo asked to see the page and glanced over it. "You still get nonsense: kdruuuth . . ."

"Naturally," the colonel said condescendingly. "The Templars may not have made a great effort, but they weren't altogether lazy either. This first sequence of letters is itself a coded message, and I wondered whether the second series of ten minor coding systems might not give an answer. For this second series, you see, Trithemius used some wheels. Here is the wheel for the first system."

He took another photocopy from his file, drew his chair up to the desk, and, asking us to pay careful attention, touched the letters with his closed fountain pen.

"It's the simplest possible system. Consider only the outer circle. To code something, you replace each letter of your original message with the letter that precedes it: for A you write Z, for B you write A, and so on. Child's play for a secret agent nowadays, but back then it was considered witchcraft. To decode, of course, you go in the opposite direction, replacing each letter of the coded message with the letter that follows it. I tried it, and I was lucky again; it worked the very first time. Here's what it says." He recited: " 'Les 36 inuisibles separez en six bandes.' That is: the thirty-six invisibles divided into six groups."

"Which means what?"

"Apparently nothing, at first glance. It's a kind of headline announcing the establishment of a group. It was written in secret language for ritualistic reasons. Our Templars, satisfied that they were putting their message in an inviolable inner sanctum, were content to use their fourteenth-century French. But let's look at the second text."

> a la . . . Saint Jean
> 36 p charrete de fein
> 6 . . . entiers avec saiel
> p . . . les blancs mantiax
> r . . . s . . . chevaliers de Pruins pour la . . . j.nc.
> 6 foiz 6 en 6 places
> chascune foiz 20 a . . . 120 a . . .
> iceste est l'ordonation
> al donjon li premiers
> it li secunz joste iceus qui . . . pans
> it al refuge
> it a Nostre Dame de l'altre part de l'iau
> it a l'ostel des popelicans
> it a la pierre
> 3 foiz 6 avant la feste . . . la Grant Pute.

"This is the decoded message?" Belbo asked, disappointed and amused.

"Obviously the dots in Ingolf's transcription stand for words that were illegible. Perhaps the parchment was damaged in places. But I've made a final transcription and translation, based on surmises that are, if I do say so myself, unassailable. I've restored the text to its ancient splendor—as the saying goes."

With a magician's gesture, he flipped over the photocopy and showed us his notes, printed in capitals.

THE (NIGHT OF) SAINT JOHN
36 (YEARS) P(OST) HAY WAIN
6 (MESSAGES) INTACT WITH SEAL
F(OR THE KNIGHTS WITH) THE WHITE CLOAKS [TEMPLARS]
R(ELAP)S(I) OF PROVINS FOR (VAIN)JANCE [REVENGE]
6 TIMES 6 IN SIX PLACES
EACH TIME 20 Y(EARS MAKES) 120 Y(EARS)

THIS IS THE PLAN
THE FIRST GO TO THE CASTLE
IT(ERUM) [AGAIN AFTER 120 YEARS] THE SECOND JOIN THOSE
   (OF THE) BREAD
AGAIN TO THE REFUGE
AGAIN TO OUR LADY BEYOND THE RIVER
AGAIN TO THE HOSTEL OF THE POPELICANS
AGAIN TO THE STONE
3 TIMES 6 [666] BEFORE THE FEAST (OF THE) GREAT WHORE.

"Clear as mud," Belbo said.

"Of course, it still needs interpretation. But Ingolf surely must have done that, as I have. If you know the history of the order, it's less obscure than it seems."

A pause. He asked for a glass of water and went over the text with us again, word by word.

"Now then. The night of Saint John's Eve, thirty-six years after the hay wain. The Templars charged with keeping the order alive escaped capture in September 1307 in a hay wain. At that time the year was calculated from Easter to Easter. So 1307 would end at what we would consider Easter of 1308. Count thirty-six years after Easter 1308 and you arrive at Easter 1344. The message was placed in the crypt inside a precious case, as a seal, a kind of deed attesting to some event that took place there on Saint John's Eve after the establishment of the secret order. In other words, on June 23, 1344."

"Why 1344?"

"I believe that between 1307 and 1344 the secret order was reorganized in preparation for the project proclaimed in the parchment. They had to wait till the dust had settled, till links could be forged again among Templars in five or six countries. Now if the Templars waited thirty-six years—not thirty-five or thirty-seven—clearly it was because the number 36 had mystical properties for them, as the coded message confirms. The sum of the digits of thirty-six is nine, and I don't have to remind you of the profound significance of this number."

"Am I disturbing you?" It was Diotallevi, who had slipped in behind us, on padded feet like a Templar of Provins.

"Right up your alley," Belbo said. He introduced him to the colonel, who didn't seem particularly disturbed. On the contrary, he was happy to have a larger, and keen, audience. He continued his exegesis, Diotallevi salivating at those numerological delicacies. Pure gematria.

"We come now to the seals: six things intact with seals. Ingolf had found a case closed with a seal. For whom was this case sealed? For the White Cloaks, for the Templars. Next comes an *r*, several missing letters, and an *s*. I read it as 'relapsi.' Why? Because, as we all know, relapsi were confessed defendants who later retracted, and relapsi played a crucial role in the trial of the Templars. The Templars of Provins bore their identity as relapsi proudly. They were the ones who disassociated themselves from that wicked farce of a trial. So the message refers to the knights of Provins, relapsi, who are preparing—what? The few letters we have suggest 'vainjance,' revenge."

"Revenge for what?"

"Gentlemen! The whole Templar mystique, from the trial on, was focused on the plan to avenge Jacques de Molay. I don't think much of the Masonic rite—a mere bourgeois caricature of Templar knighthood—but nevertheless it's a reflection, however pale, of Templar practices. And one of the degrees of Scottish Masonry was kadosch knight, the knight of revenge."

"All right, the Templars were preparing for revenge. What next?"

"How much time would it take to carry out the plan of revenge? In the coded message there is mention of six knights appearing six times in six places; thirty-six divided into six groups. Then it says 'Each time twenty.' What follows is unclear, but in Ingolf's transcription it looks like an *a*, for 'ans,' or years. Every twenty years, I conclude; six times or one hundred and twenty years in all. Later on in the message we find a list of six places, or six tasks to be performed. There is mention of an 'ordonation,' a plan, project, or procedure to be followed. And it says the first group must go to a donjon or castle while the second goes somewhere else, and so on down to the sixth. Then the document tells us there should be another six documents, still sealed, scattered in different places. It is obvious to me that the seals are supposed to be opened in sequence, at intervals of a hundred and twenty years."

"But what does twenty years each time mean?" Diotallevi asked.

"These knights of revenge are to carry out missions in particular places every hundred and twenty years. It's a kind of relay race.

Clearly, six Templars set out on that night in 1344, each one going to one of the six places included in the plan. But the keeper of the first seal surely can't remain alive for a hundred and twenty years. Instead, each keeper of each seal is to hold his post for twenty years and then pass the command on to a successor. Twenty years seems a reasonable term. There would be six keepers per seal, each one serving twenty years. When the hundred and twenty years had gone by, the last keeper of the seal could read an instruction, for example, and then pass it on to the chief keeper of the second seal. That's why the verbs in the message are in the plural: the first are to go here, the second there. Each location is, so to speak, under surveillance for a hundred and twenty years by six knights who serve terms of twenty years each. If you add it up, you'll see that there are five spaces of one hundred and twenty years between the first location and the sixth. Five times one hundred and twenty is six hundred. Add six hundred to 1344 and you get 1944. Which, by the way, is confirmed in the last line. Perfectly clear."

"Clear how?"

"The last line says, 'Three times six before the feast (of the) Great Whore.' This is another numerological game, because the digits of 1944 add up to eighteen. Eighteen is three times six. This further miraculous numerical coincidence suggested another, very subtle, enigma to the Templars. The year 1944 is the terminal date of the plan. But with a view to another target: the year 2000! The Templars believed that the second millennium would see the advent of their Jerusalem, an earthly Jerusalem, the Anti-Jerusalem. They were persecuted as heretics, and in their hatred of the Church they came to identify with the Antichrist. They knew that throughout the occult tradition 666 was the number of the Beast, and the six hundred and sixty-sixth year was the year of the Beast. Well, the six hundred and sixty-sixth year after 1344 is the year 2000, when the Templars' revenge will triumph. The Anti-Jerusalem is the New Babylon, and this is why 1944 is the year of the triumph of La Grande Pute, the great whore of Babylon mentioned in the Apocalypse. The reference to 666 was a provocation, a bit of bravado from those fighting men. A gesture of defiance from outsiders, as they would be called today. Great story, don't you think?"

His eyes were moist as he looked at us, and so were his lips and mustache. He stroked his briefcase.

"All right," Belbo said. "Let's assume that the message outlines the timing of a plan. But what plan?"

"Now you're asking too much. If I knew that, I wouldn't need to cast this bait. But one thing I do know. Somewhere along the line something went wrong, and the plan was not carried out. Otherwise, if I may say so, we'd know it. And I can understand the reason: 1944 wasn't an easy year. Back in 1344, the Templars had no way of predicting a disruptive world war."

"Excuse me for butting in," Diotallevi said, "but if I understood correctly, when the first seal is opened, the succession of keepers of that seal doesn't end; it lives on until the breaking of the last seal, when all the representatives of the order are to be present. In every century, then—or, strictly speaking, every hundred and twenty years—there would always be six keepers for each place, or thirty-six in all."

"Right," Ardenti said.

"Thirty-six knights for each of the six places makes two hundred and sixteen, the digits of which add up to nine. And since there are six centuries, we can multiply two hundred and sixteen by six, which gives us one thousand two hundred and ninety-six, whose digits add up to eighteen, or three times six, or 666." Diotallevi would perhaps have gone on to a numerological reconstruction of the history of the world if Belbo hadn't stopped him with one of those looks mothers give children when they are acting up. But the colonel immediately recognized Diotallevi as an enlightened mind.

"Splendid, Professor. It's a revelation! By the way, did you know that nine was the number of the knights who founded the Temple in Jerusalem?"

"And the Great Name of God, as expressed in the Tetragrammaton," Diotallevi said, "has seventy-two letters—and seven plus two makes nine. But that's not all, if you'll allow me. The Pythagorean tradition, which cabala preserves—or perhaps inspired—notes that the sum of the odd numbers from one to seven is sixteen, and the sum of the even numbers from two to eight is twenty, and twenty plus sixteen makes thirty-six."

"My God, Professor!" The colonel was beside himself. "I knew it, I knew it! You've given me the courage to go on. Now I know that I'm close to the truth."

Had Diotallevi turned arithmetic into a religion, or religion into arithmetic? Perhaps both. Or maybe he was just an atheist flirting with the rapture of some superior heaven. He could have become a fanatic of roulette (and that would have been better); instead, he thought of himself as an unbelieving rabbi.

I don't remember exactly how it happened, but Belbo intervened and broke the spell with his Piedmont-style good sense. More lines of the message remained for the colonel to interpret, and we were all eager to hear. It was now six o'clock. Six P.M., I thought: eighteen hours.

"All right," Belbo said. "Thirty-six per century; step by step the knights prepare to converge on the Stone. But what is this Stone?"

"Really, gentlemen! The Stone is, of course, the Grail."

20

The Middle Ages awaited the hero of the Graal and expected that the head of the Holy Roman Empire would become an image and a manifestation of that "King of the World." . . . The invisible Emperor was to become also the visible one, and the Middle Ages would be "middle" in the sense of "central" . . . the invisible, inviolable center, the sovereign who must reawaken, the same hero, avenging and restoring. These are not fantasies of a dead, romantic past, but, rather, the simple truth for those who, today, alone can legitimately call themselves alive.

—Julius Evola, *Il mistero del Graal*, Rome, Edizioni
   Mediterranee, 1983, chapter 23 and epilogue

"You mean the Grail also comes into this?" Belbo asked.

"Naturally. And I'm not the only one who says so. You are educated men; there is no need for me to go into the legend of the Grail. The Knights of the Round Table, the mystical quest for this miraculous object, which some believe was the chalice in which the blood of Jesus was collected. The Grail taken to France by Joseph of Arimathea. Others say it is a stone that possesses mysterious powers. The Grail is often depicted as a dazzling light. It's a symbol representing power, a source of immense energy. It nourishes, heals wounds, blinds, strikes down. . . . Some have thought of it as the philosopher's stone of the alchemists, but even if that's so, what was the philosopher's stone if not a symbol of some cosmic energy? The literature on the subject is endless, but you can easily distinguish signs that are irrefutable. In Wolfram von Eschenbach's *Parzival* the Grail is said to be kept in a Templar castle! Was Eschenbach an initiate? A foolhardy writer who revealed too much? But there is more. This Grail kept by the Templars is described as a stone fallen from the heavens: lapis exillis. It's not clear whether the expression means 'stone from heaven' (ex coelis) or 'stone from exile.' But in either case, it is something that comes from far away, and some suggest that it could have been a meteorite. As far as we're concerned, however, it is definitely a stone. Whatever the Grail may have been, for the Templars it was the symbol of the objective, or end of the plan."

"Excuse me," I said, "but the document indicates that the knights' sixth meeting would be held near or above a stone. It doesn't tell them to find the stone."

"Another subtle ambiguity, another luminous mystical analogy! Yes, indeed: the sixth meeting is to be held near a stone, and we shall soon see where; but at that stone, where the transmission of the plan is fulfilled and the six seals opened, the knights will learn where to find the Stone! It's like the pun in the New Testament: Thou art Peter and upon this rock . . . On the stone you shall find the Stone."

"It's all quite obvious," Belbo said. "Please go on. Casaubon, stop interrupting. We're all eager to hear the rest."

"Well then," the colonel said, "the reference to the Grail made me think for a long time that the treasure was a huge deposit of radioactive material, perhaps of extraterrestrial origin. Consider, for example, the mysterious wound in the legend of King Amfortas. The account makes him sound like a radiologist who has been dangerously exposed. He is not to be touched. Why not? Imagine how excited the Templars must have been when they reached the shores of the Dead Sea, whose waters, as you gentlemen surely know, are so dense that on them you float like a cork. It is a sea with curative powers. They could have discovered a deposit of radium or uranium in Palestine, a deposit they weren't in a position to exploit then and there.

"The relationship between the Grail, the Templars, and the Cathars was investigated scientifically by a valiant German officer. I'm referring to Otto Rahn, an SS Obersturmbannführer who devoted his life to rigorous, scholarly study of the European and Aryan nature of the Grail. I won't go into why and how he lost his life in 1939, but some insist that . . . Well, how can I forget what happened to Ingolf? In any case, Rahn demonstrated a link between the Golden Fleece of the Argonauts and the Grail. It's obvious that there's a connection between the Grail, the philosopher's stone, and the enormous power source that Hitler's followers were seeking on the eve of the war and pursued to their last breath. In one version of the Argonauts' story, remember, they see a cup—a cup, mind you—floating over the Mountain of the World with the Tree of Light. When the Argonauts find the Golden Fleece, their ship is magically borne into the Milky Way, in the austral sky, where the luminous nature of God eternal is made manifest by the Southern Cross, the Triangle, and the Altar. The triangle symbolizes the Holy Trinity, the cross the divine Sacrifice of love, and the altar is the Table of the Supper, on which stood the Cup of the Resurrection. The Celtic and Aryan origin of all these symbols is obvious."

The colonel seemed caught in the same heroic ecstasy that had impelled his Obersturmunddrang, or whatever the hell that German was, to the supreme sacrifice. Someone had to bring him down to earth.

"Where is all this leading?" I asked.

"Signor Casaubon, can't you see it for yourself? The Grail has been called the Luciferian Stone, which points to the figure of Baphomet. The Grail is a power source, the Templars were the guardians of an energy secret, and they drew up their plan accordingly. Where would the unknown commanderies be established? Where, gentlemen?" And the colonel looked at us with a conspiratorial air, as if we were all in the plot together. "I had a trail to follow, erroneous but useful. In 1797, Charles Louis Cadet de Gassicourt, an author who must have overheard some secrets, wrote a book entitled *Le tombeau de Jacques Molay ou le secret des conspirateurs à ceux qui veulent tout savoir*. By an interesting coincidence, his work turned up in Ingolf's little library. He claims that Molay, before his death, set up four secret lodges: in Paris, Scotland, Stockholm, and Naples. These four lodges were to exterminate all monarchs and destroy the power of the pope. Gassicourt was an eccentric, of course, but I used his idea as a starting point from which to determine where the Templars might have located their secret centers. I wouldn't have been able to understand the enigmas of the message if I hadn't had some guiding idea. But I did have such an idea. It was my conviction, based on abundant evidence, that the Templar spirit was of Celtic, druidic origin; it was the spirit of Nordic Arianism, traditionally associated with the island of Avalon, seat of the legendary civilization of the far north. As you surely know, various authors have identified Avalon as the Garden of the Hesperides or as Ultima Thule, or as the Colchis of the Golden Fleece. It's hardly an accident that history's greatest chivalric order was la Toison d'Or, the Order of the Golden Fleece. Which makes it clear what the word 'castle' in the message really means: it refers to the hyperboreal, the northernmost castle, where the Templars kept the Grail, probably the mythical Monsalvat."

He paused, wanting us to hang on his every word. We hung.

"Now let's go back to the second command in the message: The guardians of the seal are to go to a place associated with bread. This instruction is completely clear: the Grail is the chalice that contained Christ's blood, the bread is Christ's body, the place where the bread was eaten is the place of the Last Supper, Jerusalem. It seems impossible that the Templars wouldn't have maintained a secret base there, even after the Saracen reconquest. I must admit that at first I was troubled by this Jewish element in a plan so deeply imbued with Aryan mythology. But then I realized: we are the ones who continue to regard Jesus as deriving from the Judaic religion, because that's what the Church of Rome has always taught us. But the Templars knew that Jesus was actually a Celtic myth. The whole gospel story is a hermetic allegory: resurrection after dissolution in the bowels of the earth, and all that. Christ is simply the elixir of the alchemists. For that matter, everyone knows that the Trinity is an Aryan concept anyway, and that's why the whole rule of the Templars, drawn up by the Druid Saint Bernard, is riddled with the number 3."

The colonel took another sip of water. He was hoarse. "And now we come to the third stage: the refuge. It's Tibet."

"Why Tibet?"

"Because, in the first place, Eschenbach tells us the Templars left Europe and took the Grail to India. Cradle of the Aryan race. The refuge is Agarttha. You gentlemen must have heard talk of Agarttha, seat of the King of the World, the underground city from which the Masters of the World control and direct the developments of human history. The Templars established one of their secret centers there, at the very source of their spirituality. You must be aware of the connection between the realm of Agarttha and the Synarchy . . ."

"Frankly, no."

"All the better. There are secrets that kill. But let's not digress. In any case, you know that Agarttha was founded six thousand years ago, at the beginning of the Kali Yuga era, in which we are still living. The task of the knightly orders has always been to maintain contact with Agarttha, the active link between the wisdom of the East and the wisdom of the West. And now it's clear where the fourth meeting is to take place, in another druidic sanctuary, in a city of the Virgin: the cathedral of Chartres. From Provins, Chartres lies across the chief river of the Ile-de-France, the Seine."

We were completely lost. "Wait a minute," I said. "What does Chartres have to do with your Celts and Druids?"

"Where do you think the idea of the Virgin came from? The first virgins mentioned in Europe were the black virgins of the Celts. Once, as a young man, Saint Bernard was in the church of Saint Voirles, kneeling before the black virgin there, and she squeezed from her breast three drops of milk, which fell on the lips of the future founder of the Templars. That was why the romances of the Grail arose: to create a cover for the Crusades, which were meant to find the Grail. The Benedictines are the heirs of the Druids. Everybody knows that."

"And where are these black virgins now?"

"They were destroyed by forces who wanted to corrupt the Nordic and Celtic traditions and transform them into a Mediterranean religion by inventing the myth of Mary of Nazareth. Or else those virgins were disguised, distorted, like so many other black madonnas still displayed to the fanaticism of the masses. But if you examine the images in the cathedrals as carefully as the great Fulcanelli did, you will find that this story is told quite clearly, and the ties between the Celtic virgins and the alchemist tradition, Templar in origin, are equally clear. The black virgin symbolizes the prime matter that seekers employ in their quest for the philosopher's stone, which, as we have seen, is simply the Grail. Where do you think Mahomet, another great Druid initiate, got the inspiration for the Black Stone of Mecca? Someone walled up the crypt in Chartres that leads to the underground site where the original pagan statue still stands, but if you look carefully, you can still make out a black virgin, Notre-Dame-du-Pilier, carved by an Odinian canon. In her right hand she holds the magic cylinder of the high priestesses of Odin, in her left the magic calendar that once depicted—I say 'once,' because these sculptures unfortunately were vandalized by orthodox canons—the sacred animals of Odinism: the dog, the eagle, the lion, the white bear, and the werewolf. At the same time, none of the scholars of Gothic esoterica has overlooked in Chartres a statue of a woman holding the chalice, the Grail. Ah, gentlemen, if only it were possible not just to read Chartres cathedral according to the tourist guides—Roman, Catholic, and Apostolic—but to see it, really see it, with the eyes of Tradition! Then the true story told by that rock of Erik at Avalon would be known."

"Which brings us to the Popelicans. Who were they?"

"The Cathars. 'Popelican'—or 'Popelicant'—was one of the names given to heretics. The Cathars of Provence had been destroyed, and I am not so naïve as to imagine a meeting in the ruins of Montségur, but the sect itself didn't die. There's a whole geography of hidden Catharism, which produced Dante as well as the dolce stil nuovo poets and the Fedeli d'Amore sect. The fifth meeting place is therefore somewhere in northern Italy or southern France."

"And the last?"

"Ah, what is the most ancient, the most sacred, the most enduring of Celtic stones, the sanctuary of the sun-god, most favored observation point from which finally the reunited descendants of the Templars of Provins, having reached the end of their plan, can look upon the secrets hidden till then by the seven seals and at last discover how to exploit the immense power granted by their possession of the Holy Grail? Why, it's in England! The magic circle of Stonehenge! Where else?"

"O basta là," Belbo said. Only another child of Piedmont could have understood the spirit in which this expression of polite amazement was uttered. No equivalent in any other language or dialect (dis donc, are you kidding?) can convey the apathy, the fatalism with which it expresses the firm conviction that the person to whom it is addressed is, irreparably, the product of a bumbling creator.

But the colonel wasn't from Piedmont, and he seemed flattered by Belbo's reaction.

"Yes indeed. Such is the plan, the ordonation, in its marvelous simplicity and coherence. And there's something else. If you take a map of Europe and Asia and trace the development of the plan beginning with the castle in the north and moving from there to Jerusalem, from Jerusalem to Agarttha, from Agarttha to Chartres, from Chartres to the shores of the Mediterranean, and from there to Stonehenge, you will find that you have drawn a rune that looks more or less like this."

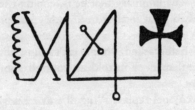

"And?" Belbo asked.

"And the same rune, ideally, would connect the main centers of Templar esotericism: Amiens, Troyes—Saint Bernard's domain at the edge of the Forêt d'Orient—Reims, Chartres, Rennes-le-Château, and Mont-Saint-Michel, a place of ancient druidic worship. The rune also recalls the constellation of the Virgin."

"I dabble in astronomy," Diotallevi said shyly. "The Virgin has a different shape, and I believe it contains eleven stars. . . ."

The colonel smiled indulgently. "Gentlemen, gentlemen, you know as well as I do that everything depends on how you draw the lines. You can make a wain or a bear, whatever you like, and it's hard to decide whether a given star is part of a given constellation or not. Take another look at the Virgin, make Spica the lowermost point corresponding to the Provençal coast, use only five stars, and you'll see a striking resemblance between the two outlines."

"You just have to decide which stars to omit," Belbo said.

"Precisely," the colonel agreed.

"Listen," Belbo said, "how can you rule out the possibility that the meetings did take place as scheduled and that the knights are now hard at work?"

"Because I perceive no symptoms, and allow me to add, 'unfortunately.' No, the plan was definitely interrupted. And perhaps those who were to carry it to its conclusion no longer exist. The groups of the thirty-six may have been broken up by some worldwide catastrophe. But some other group of men with spirit, men with the right information, could perhaps pick up the thread of the plot. Whatever it is, that something is still there. I'm looking for the right men. That's why I want to publish the book: to encourage reactions. And at the same time, I'm trying to make contact with people who can help me look for the answer in the labyrinth of traditional learning. Just today I managed to meet the greatest expert on the subject. But he, alas, luminary that he is, couldn't tell me anything, though he expressed great interest in my story and promised to write a preface. . . ."

"Excuse me," Belbo asked, "but wasn't it unwise to confide your secret to this gentleman? You told us yourself about Ingolf's misstep. . . ."

"Please," the colonel replied. "Ingolf was a bungler. The person I'm in contact with is a scholar above suspicion, a man who doesn't venture hasty conclusions. Today, for instance, he asked me to wait a little longer before showing my work to a publisher, until I had resolved all the controversial points. I didn't want to antagonize him, so I didn't tell him I was coming here. But I'm sure you can understand how impatient I am, having come this far in my task. The gentleman . . . oh, to hell with discretion! I don't want you to think I'm bragging idly. He is Rakosky."

He paused for our reaction.

Belbo disappointed him. "Who?"

"Rakosky. *The* Rakosky! The authority on traditional studies, the former editor of *Les Cahiers du Mystère!*"

"Oh, *that* Rakosky," Belbo said. "Yes, yes, of course . . ."

"Before writing the final version of my book, I'll wait to hear this gentleman's advice. But I wanted to move as quickly as possible, and if I could come to an agreement with your firm in the meantime . . . As I said, I am eager to stir up reactions, to collect new information. . . . There are people who surely know but won't speak. . . . Around 1944, gentlemen, though he knew the war was lost, Hitler began talking about a secret weapon that would allow him to turn the situation around. He was crazy, people said. But what if he wasn't crazy? You follow me?" His forehead was bathed in sweat, and his mustache bristled like a feline's whiskers. "In any event," he said, "I'm casting the bait. We'll see if anyone bites."

From what I knew and thought of Belbo then, I expected him to show the colonel out with some polite words. But he didn't. "Listen, Colonel," he said, "this is enormously interesting, regardless of whether you sign a contract with us or with someone else. Do you think you could spare another ten minutes or so?" He turned to me. "It's late, Casaubon, and I've kept you too long already. Can we meet tomorrow?"

I was being dismissed. Diotallevi took my arm and said he was leaving, too. We said good-bye. The colonel shook Diotallevi's hand warmly and gave me a nod accompanied by a chilly smile.

As we were going down the stairs, Diotallevi said to me: "You're probably wondering why Belbo asked you to leave. Don't think he was being rude. He's going to make the colonel an offer. It's a delicate matter. Delicate, by order of Signor Garamond. Our presence would be an embarrassment."

As I learned later, Belbo meant to cast the colonel into the maw of Manutius.

I dragged Diotallevi to Pilade's, where I had a Campari and he a root beer. Root beer, he said, had a monkish, archaic taste, almost Templar.

I asked him what he thought of the colonel.

"All the world's follies," he replied, "turn up in publishing houses sooner or later. But the world's follies may also contain flashes of the wisdom of the Most High, so the wise man observes folly with humility." Then he excused himself; he had to go. "This evening, a feast awaits me," he said.

"A party?"

He seemed dismayed by my frivolity. "The Zohar," he explained. "Lekh Lekha. Passages still completely misunderstood."

The Graal . . . is a weight so heavy that creatures in the bondage
of sin are unable to move it from its place.
                                   —Wolfram von Eschenbach, *Parzival*, IX, 477

I hadn't taken to the colonel, yet he had piqued my interest. You
can be fascinated even by a tree frog if you watch it long enough. I
was savoring the first drops of the poison that would carry us all to
perdition.

I went back to see Belbo the following afternoon, and we talked
a little about our visitor. Belbo said the man had seemed a mytho-
maniac to him. "Did you notice how he quoted that Rakosky, or
Rostropovich, as if the man were Kant?"

"But these are typical old tales," I said. "Ingolf was a lunatic who
believed them, and the colonel is a lunatic who believes Ingolf."

"Maybe he believed him yesterday and today he believes something else. Before he left, I arranged an appointment for him with—
well, with another publisher, a firm that's not choosy and brings
out books financed by the authors themselves. He seemed enthusiastic. But I just learned that he didn't show up. And—imagine—
he even left the photocopy of that message here. Look. He leaves
the secret of the Templars around as if it were of no importance.
That's how these characters are."

At this moment the phone rang. Belbo answered: "Good morn-
ing, Garamond Press, Belbo speaking. What can I do for you? . . .
Yes, he was here yesterday afternoon, offering me a book. . . .
Sorry, that's rather confidential. If you could tell me . . ."

He listened for a few seconds, then, suddenly pale, looked at me
and said: "The colonel's been murdered, or something of the sort."
He spoke into the phone again: "Excuse me. I was talking to Signor
Casaubon, a consultant of mine who was also present at yesterday's
conversation. . . . Well, Colonel Ardenti came to talk to us about
a project of his, a story I consider largely fabrication, about a supposed treasure of the Templars. They were medieval knights . . ."

Instinctively, he put his hand around the mouthpiece as if to talk privately, then took his hand away when he saw I was watching. He spoke with some hesitation: "No, Inspector De Angelis, the colonel discussed a book he wanted to write, but only in vague terms. . . . What, both of us? Now? All right, give me the address."

He hung up and was silent for a while, drumming his fingers on the desk. "Sorry, Casaubon," he said. "I'm afraid I've dragged you into this. I didn't have time to think. That was a police inspector named De Angelis. It seems the colonel was staying in an apartment hotel, and somebody claims to have found him there last night, dead. . . ."

"Claims? The inspector doesn't know if it's true or not?"

"It sounds strange, but apparently he doesn't. They found my name and yesterday's appointment in a notebook. I believe we're the only clue. What can I say? Let's go."

We called a taxi. During the ride Belbo gripped my arm. "Listen, Casaubon, this may be just a coincidence. Maybe my mind is warped. But where I come from there's a saying: 'Whatever you do, don't name names.' When I was a boy, I used to go see this Nativity play performed in dialect. A pious farce, with shepherds who didn't know whether they were in Bethlehem or on the banks of the Tanaro, farther up the Po valley. The Magi arrive and ask a shepherd's boy what his master's name is. The boy answers: Gelindo. When Gelindo finds out, he beats the daylights out of the boy. 'Never give away a man's name,' he says. Anyway, if it's all right with you, the colonel never mentioned Ingolf or the Provins message."

"We don't want to meet Ingolf's mysterious end," I said, trying to smile.

"As I said, it's all nonsense. But there are some things it's better to keep out of."

I promised I would go along with him on this, but I was nervous. After all, I was a student who participated in demonstrations. The police made me uneasy. We arrived at the hotel—not one of the best—in an outlying neighborhood. They sent us right up to what they called Colonel Ardenti's apartment. Police on the stairs. They let us into number 27—two plus seven is nine, I thought. A bedroom, vestibule with a little table, closet-kitchen, bathroom with shower, no curtain. Through the half-open door I couldn't see if there was a bidet, though in a place like this it was probably the only convenience the guests demanded. Drab furnishings, not many personal effects, but what there was, in great disorder. Someone had hastily gone through the closets and suitcases. Maybe the police; there were about a dozen of them, including plainclothesmen.

A fairly young man with fairly long hair came over to us. "I'm De Angelis. Dr. Belbo? Dr. Casaubon?"

"I'm not a doctor yet. Still working toward my degree."

"Good for you. Keep at it. Without a degree you won't be able to take the police exams, and you don't know what you're missing." He seemed irritated. "Excuse me, but let's get the preliminaries out of the way. This is the passport that belonged to the man who rented this room. He registered as Colonel Ardenti. Recognize him?"

"That's Ardenti," Belbo said. "But can you tell us what's going on here? From what you said on the phone, I didn't quite understand if he's dead or—"

"I'd be delighted if you could tell *me* that," De Angelis said with a frown. "But all right, you gentlemen are probably entitled to know a bit more. Signor Ardenti—or Colonel Ardenti—checked in four days ago. As you may have noticed, this place isn't the Grand. The one desk clerk goes to bed at eleven, because the guests have a key to the front door. There are a couple of maids who come in every morning to do the rooms, and an old alcoholic who acts as porter and takes liquor up to the rooms if the customers ring. Not only alcoholic, but arteriosclerotic, too. It was hell getting anything out of him. The desk clerk says the old man sees spooks and sometimes scares the guests. Last night the clerk saw Ardenti come in around ten and go up to his room with two men. In this place they don't bat an eye if somebody takes a whole troop of transvestites upstairs. The men looked normal, though according to the clerk they had foreign accents. At ten-thirty Ardenti called the old alcoholic and asked him to bring up a bottle of whiskey, mineral water, and three glasses. At about one or one-thirty the old man heard someone ringing erratically from room 27. Judging by the way he looked this morning, though, he must have put away quite a few glasses by then, rotgut for sure. Anyway, the old man came up and knocked. No answer. He opened the door with his passkey. Found everything all messed up the way it is now. The colonel was lying on the bed with a length of wire wound tight around his neck, his eyes staring. The old man ran downstairs, woke the desk clerk, but neither of them felt like coming back up. They tried to use the phone, but the line seemed to be dead. It was working perfectly this morning, but we'll take their word for it. The clerk ran out to call the police from the pay phone on the corner, while the old man hobbled across the square to a doctor's house. To make a long story short, they were gone for twenty minutes. When they got back, they waited downstairs, still frightened. Meanwhile, the doctor got dressed and arrived almost at the same time as the squad car. They went up to twenty-seven, and there was no one on the bed."

"What do you mean, no one?" Belbo asked.

"No corpse. The doctor went home, and the police found only what you see here. They questioned the old alcoholic and the clerk, and got the story I just told you. What of the two gentlemen who came in with Ardenti at ten o'clock? They could have left anytime between eleven and one, and nobody would have noticed. Were they still in the room when the old man came in? Who knows? He stayed only a second, didn't look into the kitchen or the bathroom. Could they have left while the clerk and the alcoholic were out calling for help? Did they take the body with them? Not impossible. There's an outside staircase to the courtyard, and from the courtyard they could just walk out the front door, which opens into a side street.

"More important, was there really a body? Or did the colonel go out with the two men—at midnight, say—and the old alcoholic dreamed the whole thing? The clerk says it wouldn't be the first time the old man saw things that weren't there. A few years ago he saw a naked female guest hanged in her room, but half an hour later the woman came in, fresh as a daisy, and on the old man's cot they found one of those S-M magazines. Who knows? Maybe he was peeping through the keyhole and saw a curtain stirring in the shadows. All we know for sure is that this room has been searched and Ardenti is missing.

"But I've already talked too much. Now it's your turn, Dr. Belbo. The only thing we found was a slip of paper on the floor by that little table. '2 P.M. Rakosky, Hotel Principe e Savoia; 4 P.M. Garamond, Dr. Belbo.' You say he did come to see you. Tell me what happened."

22

The knights of the Graal wanted to face no further questions.
— Wolfram von Eschenbach, *Parzival*, XVI, 819

Belbo was brief. He repeated what he had already said on the phone:
The colonel had told a hazy story about discovering evidence of a
treasure in some documents he had found in France, but he hadn't
said much more about it. He seemed to think he was in possession
of a dangerous secret, and he wanted to make it public so he wouldn't
be the only one who knew it. He mentioned the fact that others
who had discovered the secret before him had disappeared mysteriously. He would show us the documents only if we guaranteed him
a contract, but Belbo couldn't guarantee a contract without seeing
something first. They vaguely agreed to get together again. The colonel had spoken of a meeting with someone named Rakosky, describing him as the editor of *Les Cahiers du Mystère*. The colonel
wanted this Rakosky to write a preface for him, and apparently Rakosky had advised him to delay publication. The colonel hadn't told
this man about the appointment at Garamond. That was all.

"I see," De Angelis said. "What sort of impression did he make
on you?"

"He seemed an eccentric to us, and he spoke about his past in,
well, an unrepentant tone. It included a spell in the Foreign Legion."

"He told you the truth, though not the whole truth. We were
already keeping an eye on him, at least to some extent. We have so
many such cases. . . . First of all, Ardenti wasn't his real name,
but he had a legitimate French passport. He started reappearing in
Italy from time to time a few years ago, and was tentatively identified as a Captain Arcoveggi, sentenced to death in absentia in 1945.
Collaboration with the SS. He sent some people to Dachau. They
were keeping an eye on him in France, too. He was tried for fraud
there, and just managed to get off. We have an idea—but only an
idea, mind you—that Ardenti at one point was calling himself Fas-

sotti, that he's the Fassotti that a small industrialist in Peschiera Borromeo filed a complaint against last year. This Fassotti—or Ardenti—had convinced the industrialist that the treasure of Dongo, the legendary Fascist gold reserve, was still lying at the bottom of Lake Como. Fassotti claimed to have identified the spot, and said all he needed was a few tens of millions of lire for a couple of divers and a power boat. Once he had the money, he vanished. Now you confirm that he had a kind of mania about treasures."

"And this Rakosky?"

"We checked. A Vladimir Rakosky was registered at the Principe e Savoia. French passport. Distinguished-looking gentleman. It matches the description the clerk here gave us. Alitalia says his name appears on the passenger list for the first flight to Paris this morning. I've alerted Interpol. Annunziata, anything come in from Paris?"

"Nothing so far, sir."

"And that's it. So Colonel Ardenti, or whatever his name is, arrived in Milan four days ago. We don't know what he did the first three, but yesterday at two he presumably saw Rakosky at the hotel, didn't tell him about going to see you—which is interesting—then last night he came here, probably with the same Rakosky and another man, and after that your guess is as good as mine. Even if they didn't kill him, they certainly searched his room. What were they looking for? In his jacket . . . which reminds me, if he went out, it was in shirtsleeves, because the jacket with his passport in the pocket is still here. But that doesn't make things any easier, because the old man says the colonel was stretched out on the bed in his jacket, unless it was a different jacket. God, I feel like I'm in a loony bin. Anyway, where was I? Oh, yes, in his jacket we found plenty of money, too much money. So it wasn't money they were looking for. And you gentlemen have given me the only lead. You say the colonel had some documents. What did they look like?"

"He was carrying a brown briefcase," Belbo said.

"It looked more red to me," I said.

"Brown," Belbo insisted. "But I could be wrong."

"Red or brown," De Angelis said, "it's not here now. Last night's visitors must have taken it. The briefcase is what we have to concentrate on. If you ask me, Ardenti wasn't trying to publish a book at all. He had probably come up with something he could blackmail

Rakosky with, and talking about a publishing contract was a way of applying pressure. That would have been more his style. From there, any number of hypotheses are possible. The two men may have threatened him and left, and Ardenti was so scared that he fled into the night, leaving everything behind except the briefcase, which he clutched under his arm. But first, for some reason, he tried to make the old man think he was dead. It all sounds too much like a novel, and it doesn't account for the way the room was torn up. On the other hand, if the two men killed him and stole the briefcase, why would they also steal the corpse? Excuse me, but may I see your IDs?"

He looked at my student card, turning it over a few times. "Philosophy student, eh?"

"There are lots of us," I said.

"Far too many. And you're studying the Templars. Suppose I wanted to get some background on them—what should I read?"

I suggested two books, popular but fairly serious. I also told him he would find reliable information only up to the trial. After that it was all raving nonsense.

"I see," he said. "Now it's the Templars, too. One splinter group I haven't run into yet."

The policeman named Annunziata came in with a telegram: "The reply from Paris, sir."

De Angelis read it. "Great," he said. "No one in Paris has heard of Rakosky, and the passport number shows that it was stolen two years ago. Now we're really stuck. Monsieur Rakosky doesn't exist. You say he's the editor of a magazine—what was it called?" He made a note. "Well, we'll try, but I bet we find that the magazine doesn't exist either, or else it folded ages ago. All right, gentlemen, thanks for your help. I may trouble you again at some point. Oh, yes, one last question: Did Argenti indicate that he had connections with any political organization?"

"No," Belbo said. "He seemed to have given up politics for treasures."

"And confidence games." He turned to me. "You seem not to have liked him much."

"Not my style," I said. "But it wouldn't have occurred to me to strangle him with a length of wire. Except in theory."

"Naturally. Too much trouble. Relax, Signor Casaubon. I'm not one of those cops who think all students are criminals. Good luck, also, on your thesis."

"Excuse me," Belbo asked, "but just out of curiosity, are you homicide or political?"

"Good question. My opposite number from homicide was here last night. After they found a bit more on Ardenti in the records, he turned the case over to me. Yes, I'm from political. But I'm really not sure I'm the right man. Life isn't simple, the way it is in detective stories."

"I guess not," Belbo said, shaking his hand.

We left, but I was still troubled. Not because of De Angelis, who seemed nice enough, but because for the first time in my life I found myself involved in something shady. I had lied. And so had Belbo.

We parted at the door of the Garamond office, and we were both embarrassed.

"We didn't do anything wrong," Belbo said defensively. "It won't make any difference if the police don't learn about Ingolf and the Cathars. It was all raving anyway. Maybe Ardenti had to disappear for other reasons; there could be a thousand reasons. Maybe Rakosky was an Israeli secret-service agent settling old scores. Or maybe he was sent by some big shot the colonel had conned. Or maybe they were in the Foreign Legion together and there was some old grudge. Or maybe Rakosky was an Algerian assassin. And maybe this Templar-treasure story was only a minor episode in the life of our colonel. All right, the briefcase is missing, red or brown. By the way, it was good that you contradicted me: that made it clear we had only had a quick glimpse of it."

I said nothing, and Belbo didn't know how to conclude.

"You'll say I've run away again. Like Via Larga."

"Nonsense. We did the right thing. I'll see you."

I was sorry for him, because he felt like a coward. But I didn't. I had learned in school that when you deal with the police, you lie. As a matter of principle. But a guilty conscience can poison a friendship.

I didn't see Belbo for a long time after that. I was his remorse, and he was mine.

I worked for another year and produced two hundred and fifty typewritten pages on the trial of the Templars. It was then that I learned that a graduate student is less an object of suspicion than an undergraduate. Those were years when defending a thesis was considered evidence of respectful loyalty to the state, and you were treated with indulgence.

In the months that followed, some students started using guns. The days of mass demonstrations in the open air were drawing to a close.

I was short on ideals, but for that I had an alibi, because loving Amparo was like being in love with the Third World. Amparo was beautiful, Marxist, Brazilian, enthusiastic, disenchanted. She had a fellowship and splendidly mixed blood. All at the same time.

I met her at a party, and acted on impulse. "Excuse me," I said, "but I would like to make love to you."

"You're a filthy male chauvinist pig."

"Forget I said it."

"Never. I'm a filthy feminist."

She was going back to Brazil, and I didn't want to lose her. She put me in touch with the University of Rio, where the Italian department was looking for a lecturer. They offered me a two-year contract with an option to renew. I didn't feel at home in Italy anymore; I accepted.

Besides, I told myself, in the New World I wouldn't run into any Templars.

Wrong, I thought Saturday evening as I huddled in the periscope. Climbing the steps to the Garamond office had been like entering the Palace. Binah, Diotallevi used to say, is the palace Hokhmah builds as He spreads out from the primordial point. If Hokhmah is the source, Binah is the river that flows from it, separating into its various branches until they all empty into the great sea of the last Sefirah. But in Binah all forms are already formed.

158

HESED

23

I went to Brazil out of love for Amparo, I stayed out of love for the country. I never did understand how it was that Amparo, a descendant of Dutch settlers in Recife who intermarried with Indians and Sudanese blacks—with her Jamaican face and Parisian culture—had wound up with a Spanish name. For that matter, I never managed to figure out Brazilian names. They defy all onomastic dictionaries, and exist only in Brazil.

Amparo told me that in their hemisphere, when water drains down a sink, the little eddy swirls counterclockwise, whereas at home, ours swirls clockwise. Or maybe it's the other way around: I've never succeeded in checking the truth of it. Not only because nobody in our hemisphere has ever looked to see which way the water swirls, but also because, after various experiments in Brazil, I realized it's very hard to tell. The suction is too quick to be studied, and its direction probably depends partly on the force and angle of the jet and the shape of the sink or the tub. Besides, if this is true, what happens at the equator? Maybe the water drains straight down, with no swirling, or maybe it doesn't drain at all.

At that time I didn't agonize over the problem, but Saturday night in the periscope I was thinking how everything depended on telluric currents, and the Pendulum contained the secret.

Amparo was steadfast in her faith. "The particular empirical event doesn't matter," she said. "It's an ideal principle, which can be verified only under ideal conditions. Which means never. But it's still true."

In Milan, Amparo's disenchantment had been one of her most desirable traits. But in Brazil, reacting to the chemistry of her native land, she became elusive, a visionary capable of subterranean rationality. Stirred by ancient passions, she was careful to keep them in check; but the asceticism which made her reject their seduction was not convincing.

I measured her splendid contradictions when I watched her argue with her comrades. The meetings were held in shabby houses decorated with a few posters and a lot of folk art, portraits of Lenin and Amerindian fetishes, or terra-cotta figures glorifying the cangaceiros, outlaws of the Northeast. I hadn't arrived during one of the country's most lucid moments politically, and, after my experiences at home, I decided to steer clear of ideologies, especially in a place where I didn't understand them. The way Amparo's comrades talked made me even more uncertain, but they also roused a new curiosity in me. They were, naturally, all Marxists, and at first they seemed to talk more or less like European Marxists, but the subject somehow was always different. In the middle of an argument about the class struggle, they would suddenly mention "Brazilian cannibalism" or the revolutionary role of Afro-Brazilian religions.

Hearing them talk about these cults convinced me that at least ideological suction, down there, swirled in the opposite direction. They described a panorama of internal migrations back and forth, the disinherited of the north moving down toward the industrial south, where they became subproletarians in immense smog-choked metropolises, eventually returning in desperation to the north, only to repeat their flight southward in the next cycle. But many ran aground in the big cities during these oscillations, and they were absorbed by a plethora of indigenous churches; they worshiped spirits, evoked African divinities . . . And here Amparo's comrades were divided: some considered this a return to their roots, a way of opposing the white world; others thought these cults were the opiate with which the ruling class held an immense revolutionary potential in check; and still others maintained that the cults were a melting pot in which whites, Indians, and blacks could be blended—for what purpose, they were not clear. Amparo had made up her mind: religion was always the opiate of the people, and pseudo-tribal cults were even worse. But when I held her by the waist in the escolas de samba, joining in the snaking lines to the unbearable rhythm of the drums, I realized that she clung to that world with the muscles of her belly, her heart, her head, her nostrils. . . . Afterward, she was the first to offer a bitter, sarcastic analysis of the orgiastic character of people's religious devotion—week after week and month after month—to the rite of carnival. Exactly the same sort of tribal witchcraft, she would say with revolutionary contempt, as the soccer rituals in which the disinherited expended their combative energy and sense of revolt, practicing spells and enchantments to win from the gods of every possible world the death of the opposing halfback, completely unaware of the Establishment, which wanted to keep them in a state of ecstatic enthusiasm, condemned to unreality.

In time I lost any sense of contradiction, just as I gradually abandoned any attempt to distinguish the different races in that land of age-old, unbridled hybridization. I gave up trying to establish where progress lay, and where revolution, or to see the plot—as Amparo's comrades expressed it—of capitalism. How could I continue to think like a European once I learned that the hopes of the far left were kept alive by a Nordeste bishop suspected of having harbored Nazi sympathies in his youth but who now faithfully and fearlessly held high the torch of revolt, upsetting the wary Vatican and the barracudas of Wall Street, and joyfully inflaming the atheism of the proletarian mystics won over by the tender yet menacing banner of a Beautiful Lady who, pierced by seven sorrows, gazed down on the sufferings of her people?

One morning Amparo and I were driving along the coast after having attended a seminar on the class structure of the lumpenproletariat. I saw some votive offerings on the beach, little candles, white garlands. Amparo told me they were offerings to Yemanjá, goddess of the waters. We stopped, and she got out and walked demurely onto the sand, stood a few moments in silence. I asked her if she believed in this. She retorted angrily: How could I think such a thing? Then she added, "My grandmother used to bring me to the beach here, and she would pray to the goddess to make me grow up beautiful and good and happy. Who was that Italian philosopher who made that comment about black cats and coral horns? 'It's not true, but I believe in it'? Well, I don't believe in it, but it's true." That was the day I decided to save some money to venture a trip to Bahia.

It was also the day I began to let myself be lulled by feelings of resemblance: the notion that everything might be mysteriously related to everything else.

Later, when I returned to Europe, I converted this metaphysics into mechanics—and thus fell into the trap in which I now lie. But back then I was living in a twilight that blurred all distinctions. Like a racist, I believed that a strong man could regard the faiths of others as an opportunity for harmless daydreaming and no more.

I learned some rhythms, ways of letting go with body and mind. Recalling them the other evening in the periscope, to fight off growing numbness I moved my limbs as if I were once again striking the agogô. You see? I said to myself. To escape the power of the unknown, to prove to yourself that you don't believe in it, you accept its spells. Like an avowed atheist who sees the Devil at night, you reason: He certainly doesn't exist; this is therefore an illusion, perhaps a result of indigestion. But the Devil is sure that he exists, and believes in his upside-down theology. What, then, will frighten him? You make the sign of the cross, and he vanishes in a puff of brimstone.

What happened to me was like what might happen to a pedantic ethnologist who has spent years studying cannibalism. He challenges the smugness of the whites by assuring everybody that actually human flesh is delicious. Then one day a doubter decides to see for himself and performs the experiment—on him. As the ethnologist is devoured piece by piece, he hopes, for he will never know who was right, that at least he is delicious, which will justify the ritual and his death. The other evening I had to believe the Plan was true, because if it wasn't, then I had spent the past two years as the omnipotent architect of an evil dream. Better reality than a dream: if something is real, then it's real and you're not to blame.

24

Sauvez la faible Aischa des vertiges de Nahash, sauvez la plaintive
Héva des mirages de la sensibilité, et que les Khérubs me gardent.
—Joséphin Péladan, *Comment on devient Fée*, Paris,
Chamuel, 1893, p. XIII

As I was advancing into the forest of resemblances, I received Belbo's letter.

Dear Casaubon,

I didn't know until the other day that you were in Brazil. I lost touch completely, not even knowing that you had graduated (congratulations). Anyway, someone at Pilade's gave me your coordinates, and I thought it would be a good idea to bring you up to date on some developments in that unfortunate Colonel Ardenti business. It's been more than two years now, I know, and again I must apologize: I was the one who got you into trouble that morning, though I didn't mean to.

I had almost forgotten the whole nasty story, but two weeks ago I was driving around in the Montefeltro area and happened upon the fortress of San Leo. In the eighteenth century, it seems, the region was under papal rule, and the pope imprisoned Cagliostro there, in a cell with no real door (you entered it, for the first and last time, through a trapdoor in the ceiling) and with one little window from which the prisoner could see only the two churches of the village. I saw a bunch of roses on the shelf where Cagliostro had slept and died, and I was told that many devotees still make the pilgrimage to the place of his martyrdom. Among the most assiduous pilgrims are the members of Picatrix, a group of Milanese students of the occult. It publishes a magazine entitled—with great imagination—*Picatrix.*

You know how curious I am about these oddities. So back in Milan I got hold of a copy of *Picatrix*, from which I learned that an evocation of the spirit of Cagliostro was to be held in a few days. I went.

The walls were draped with banners covered with cabalistic signs, an abundance of owls of all kinds, scarabs and ibises, and Oriental divinities of uncertain origin. Near the rear wall was a dais, a proscenium of burning torches held up by rough logs, and in the background an altar with a triangular altarpiece and statuettes of Isis and Osiris. The room was ringed by an amphitheater of figures of Anubis, and there was a portrait of Cagliostro (it could hardly have been of anyone else, could it?), a gilded mummy in Cheops format, two five-armed candelabra, a gong suspended from two rampant snakes, on a podium a lectern covered by calico printed with hieroglyphics, and two crowns, two tripods, a little portable sarcophagus, a throne, a fake seventeenth-century fauteuil, four unmatched chairs suitable for a banquet with the sheriff of Nottingham, and candles, tapers, votive lights, all flickering very spiritually.

Anyway, to go on with the story: seven altar boys entered in red cassocks and carrying torches, followed by the celebrant, apparently the head of Picatrix—he rejoiced in the commonplace name of Brambilla—in pink-and-olive vestments. He was, in turn, followed by the neophyte, or medium, and six acolytes in white, who all looked like Bing Crosby, but with infulas, the god's, if you recall our poets.

Brambilla put on a triple crown with a half-moon, picked up a ritual sword, drew magic symbols on the dais, and summoned various angelic spirits with names ending in "el." At this point I was vaguely reminded of those pseudo-Semitic incantations in Ingolf's message, but only for a moment, because I was immediately distracted by something unusual. The microphones on the dais were connected to a tuner that was supposed to pick up random waves in space, but the operator must have made a mistake, because first we heard a burst of disco music and then Radio Moscow came on. Brambilla opened the sarcophagus, took out a book of magic spells, swung a thurible, and cried, "O Lord, Thy kingdom come." This seemed to achieve something, because Radio Moscow fell silent, but then, at the most magical moment, it came on again, with a drunken Cossack song, the kind they dance to with their behinds scraping the ground. Brambilla invoked the Clavicula Salomonis, risked self-immolation by burning a parchment on a tripod, summoned several divinities of the temple of Karnak, testily asked to be placed on the cubic stone of Yesod, and insistently called out for "Familiar 39," who must have been familiar enough to the audience, since a shiver ran through the hall. One woman sank into a trance, her eyes rolling back until only the whites were visible. People called for a doctor, but Brambilla invoked the Power of the Pentacles, and the neophyte, who had meanwhile sat down on the fake fauteuil, began to writhe and groan. Brambilla hovered over her, anxiously asking questions of her, or, rather, of Familiar 39, who, I suddenly realized, was Cagliostro himself.

And now came the disturbing part, because the pathetic girl seemed to be in real pain: she trembled, sweated, bellowed, and began to speak in broken phrases of a temple and a door that must be opened. She said a vortex of power was being created, and we had to ascend to the Great Pyramid. Brambilla, up on the dais, became agitated; he banged the gong and called Isis in a loud voice. I was enjoying the performance until I heard the girl, still sighing and moaning, say something about six seals, a one-hundred-and-twenty-year wait, and thirty-six invisibles. Now, there could be no doubt: she was talking about the message of Provins. I waited to hear more, but the girl slumped back, exhausted. Brambilla stroked her brow, blessed the audience with his thurible, and proclaimed the rite over.

I was slightly awed, and also eager to understand. I tried to move closer to the girl, who in the meantime had come to her senses, slipped into a scruffy overcoat, and was on her way out through the rear exit. I was about to touch her on the shoulder, when I felt someone grasp my arm. I turned and it was Inspector De Angelis, who told me to let her go: he knew where to find her. He invited me out for coffee. I went, as if he had caught me doing something wrong, which in a sense he had. At the café he asked me what I was doing there and why I had tried to approach the girl. This irritated me. We aren't living in a dictatorship, I said. I can approach anyone I choose. He apologized and explained that, although the Ardenti investigation had no priority, they had tried to reconstruct the two days he had spent in Milan before his meeting at Garamond and with the mysterious Rakosky. A year after Ardenti's disappearance, the police had found out, by sheer luck, that someone had seen him leaving the Picatrix offices in the company of the psychic girl, who, incidentally, was of interest to De Angelis because she lived with an individual not unknown to the narcotics squad.

I told him I was there by chance, and I had been struck by the fact that the girl had spoken a phrase about six seals, which I had heard from the colonel. He remarked how strange it was that I could remember so clearly what the colonel said two years ago, yet, at the time, I had spoken only of some vague talk about the treasure of the Templars. I replied that the colonel had indeed said that the treasure was protected by six seals of some kind, but I hadn't considered this an important detail because all treasures are protected by seals, usually seven, and by gold bugs. He observed that if all treasures were protected by gold bugs, he couldn't see why I should have been struck by what the girl had said. I asked him to stop treating me like a suspect, and he laughed and changed his tone. He said he didn't find it strange that the girl had said what she did, because Ardenti must have talked to her about his fantasies, perhaps trying to use her to establish some astral contact, as they say in those circles. A psychic, he went on, was like a sponge, a photographic plate with an unconscious that must look like an amusement park. The Picatrix bunch probably give her a brainwashing all year round, so it was not unlikely that once in a trance—because the girl was in earnest, wasn't faking, and there was something wrong with her head—she would see images that had been impressed on her long ago.

But two days later De Angelis dropped in at the office to say that, curiously enough, when he went to see the girl the day after the ceremony, she was gone. The neighbors said nobody had seen her since the afternoon before the evening of the ceremony. His suspicions were aroused, so he entered the apartment and found it torn to pieces: sheets on the floor, pillows in one corner, trampled newspapers, emptied drawers. No sign of her. Or of her boyfriend, or roommate or whatever you wanted to call him.

He told me that if I knew anything more, I'd be wise to talk, because it was strange how the girl had disappeared into thin air, and he could think of only two reasons: either somebody realized that De Angelis had her under surveillance, or it was noticed that one Jacopo Belbo had tried to talk to her. The things she had said in the trance might therefore have concerned something serious, some unfinished business. They—whoever they were—hadn't realized she knew so much. "Now suppose some colleague of mine gets it into his head that you killed her," De Angelis added with a beautiful smile. "You can see we have every interest in working together." I almost lost my temper, and God knows I don't do that often. I asked him why a person who's not home is assumed to have been murdered, and he asked if I remembered what happened to the colonel. Then I told him that if she had been killed, or kidnapped, it must have happened that evening, when I was with him. He asked how I could be so sure of that, since we had said good-bye around midnight and he had no way of knowing what had happened after that. I asked him if he was serious, and he said what, hadn't I ever read a detective story? Didn't I know that the prime suspect was always the one who didn't have an alibi as radiant as Hiroshima? He said he would donate his head to an organ bank if I had an alibi for the time between one A.M. and the next morning.

What can I say, Casaubon? Maybe I should have told him the truth, but where I come from, men are stubborn and never back down.

I'm writing you because if I found your address, then De Angelis can find it, too. If he gets in touch with you, at least you know the line I've taken. But since it doesn't seem a very straight line to me, go ahead and tell him everything if you want to. I'm embarrassed, I apologize. I feel like some kind of accomplice. Try as I might, I can't seem to find any noble justification for myself. Must be my peasant origins; in our part of the country, we're a mean bunch.

The whole thing is—as the Germans say—unheimlich.

Yours,
Jacopo Belbo

25

. . . of these mysterious initiates—now become numerous, bold, conspiring—all was born: Jesuitism, magnetism, Martinism, philosopher's stone, somnambulism, eclecticism.
—C.-L. Cadet-Gassicourt, *Le tombeau de Jacques de Molay,*
Paris, Desenne, 1797, p. 91

The letter upset me. Not that I was afraid of being tracked down by De Angelis—we were in different hemispheres, after all—but for less definable reasons. At the time, I thought I was upset because a world I had left behind had bounced back at me. But today I realize that what bothered me was yet another strand of resemblance, the suspicion of an analogy. I was annoyed, too, at having to deal with Belbo again, Belbo and his eternal guilty conscience. I decided not to mention the letter to Amparo.

A reassuring second letter arrived from Belbo two days later.

The story of the psychic had had a reasonable ending. A police informer reported that the girl's lover had been involved in a settling of scores over a drug shipment, which he had sold retail instead of delivering it to the honest wholesaler who had already paid. They frown on that sort of behavior in those circles, and he vanished to save his neck. Obviously he took the woman with him. Rummaging then among the newspapers left in their apartment, De Angelis found some magazines on the order of *Picatrix,* with a series of articles heavily underlined in red. One was about the treasure of the Templars, another about Rosicrucians who lived in a castle, cave, or some damn place where "post CXX annos patebo" was written and they called themselves the thirty-six invisibles. So for De Angelis it was all clear. The psychic, consuming the same sort of literature that the colonel had, regurgitated it when she was in a trance. The matter was closed, passed on to the narcotics squad.

Belbo's letter exuded relief. De Angelis's explanation seemed the most economical.

The other evening in the periscope, I told myself that the facts might have been quite different. Granted, the psychic quoted something she had heard from Ardenti, but it was something her magazines never mentioned, something no one was supposed to know. Whoever had got rid of the colonel was in the Picatrix group, and this someone noticed that Belbo was about to question the psychic, so he eliminated her. To throw the investigators off the track, he also eliminated her lover, then instructed a police informer to say that the couple had fled.

Simple enough, if there was really a plan. But how could there have been? Since we invented "the Plan" ourselves, and only much later was it possible for reality not only to catch up with fiction but actually to precede it, or, rather, to rush ahead of it and repair the damage that it would cause.

At the time, though, in Brazil, these were not my thoughts on receiving Belbo's second letter. Instead, I felt once more that something was resembling something else. I had been thinking about my trip to Bahia and had spent an afternoon visiting bookstores and shops that sold cult objects, places I had ignored till then. I went to out-of-the-way little emporiums crammed with statues and idols. I purchased perfumadores of Yemanjá, pungently scented mystical smoke sticks, incense, sweetish spray cans labeled "Sacred Heart of Jesus," cheap amulets. I also found many books, some for devotees, others for people studying devotees, a mixture of exorcism manuals like *Como adivinhar o futuro na bola de cristal* and anthropology textbooks. And a monograph on the Rosicrucians.

Suddenly it all seemed to come together: satanic and Moorish rites in the Temple of Jerusalem, African witchcraft for the subproletarians of the Brazilian Northeast, the message of Provins with its hundred and twenty years, and the hundred and twenty years of the Rosicrucians.

I felt like a walking blender mixing strange concoctions of different liquors. Or maybe I had caused some kind of short circuit, tripping over a varicolored tangle of wires that had been entwining themselves for a long, long time. I bought the book on the Rosicrucians, thinking that if I spent a few hours in these bookstores, I would meet at least a dozen colonel Ardentis and brainwashed psychics.

I went home and officially informed Amparo that the world was full of unnatural characters. She promised me solace, and we ended the day naturally.

That was late 1975. I decided to put resemblances aside and concentrate on my work. After all, I was supposed to be teaching Italian culture, not the Rosicrucians.

I devoted myself to Renaissance philosophers and I discovered that the men of secular modernity, once they had emerged from the darkness of the Middle Ages, had found nothing better to do than devote themselves to cabala and magic.

After two years spent with Neoplatonists who chanted formulas designed to convince nature to do things she had no intention of doing, I received news from Italy. It seems my old classmates—or some of them, at least—were now shooting people who didn't agree with them, to convince the stubborn to do things they had no intention of doing.

I couldn't understand it. Now part of the Third World, I made up my mind to visit Bahia. I set off with a history of Renaissance culture and the book on the Rosicrucians, which had remained on a shelf, its pages uncut.

26

All the traditions of the earth must be seen as deriving from a fundamental mother-tradition that, from the beginning, was entrusted to sinful man and to his first offspring.
—Louis-Claude de Saint-Martin, *De l'esprit des choses*, Paris, Laran, 1800, II, "De l'esprit des traditions en général"

And I saw Salvador: Salvador da Bahia de Todos os Santos, the "black Rome," with three hundred and sixty-five churches, which stand out against the line of hills or nestle along the bay, churches where the gods of the African pantheon are honored.

Amparo knew a primitive artist who painted big wooden panels crammed with Biblical and apocalyptic visions, dazzling as a medieval miniature, with Coptic and Byzantine elements. Naturally he was a Marxist; he talked about the coming revolution, but he spent his days dreaming in the sacristies of the sanctuary of Nosso Senhor do Bomfim: a triumph of horror vacui, scaly with ex-votos that hung from the ceiling and encrusted the walls, a mystical assemblage of silver hearts, wooden arms and legs, images of wondrous rescues from glittering storms, waterspouts, maelstroms. He took us to the sacristy of another church, which was full of great furnishings redolent of jacaranda. "Who is that a painting of?" Amparo asked the sacristan. "Saint George?"

The sacristan gave us a knowing look. "They call him Saint George," he said, "and if you don't call him that, the pastor gets angry. But he's Oxossi."

For two days the painter led us through naves and cloisters hidden behind decorated façades like silver plates now blackened and worn. Wrinkled, limping famuli accompanied us. The sacristies were sick with gold and pewter, heavy chests, precious frames. Along the walls, in crystal cases, life-size images of saints towered, dripping blood, their open wounds spattered with ruby droplets; Christs writhed in pain, their legs red. In a glow of late-Baroque gold, I saw angels with Etruscan faces, Romanesque griffins, and Oriental sirens peeping out from the capitals.

I moved along ancient streets, enchanted by names that sounded like songs: Rua da Agonia, Avenida dos Amores, Travessa de Chico Diabo. Our visit to Salvador took place during a period when the local government, or someone acting in its name, was trying to renew the old city, and was closing down the thousands of brothels. But the project was only at midpoint. At the feet of those deserted and leprous churches embarrassed by their own evil-smelling alleys, fifteen-year-old black prostitutes still swarmed, ancient women selling African sweets crouched along the sidewalks with their steaming pots, and hordes of pimps danced amid trickles of sewage to the sound of transistor radios in nearby bars. The ancient palaces of the Portuguese settlers, surmounted by coats of arms now illegible, had become houses of ill-repute.

On the third day, our guide took us to the bar of a hotel in a renovated part of the upper city, on a street full of luxury antique shops. He was to meet an Italian gentleman, he told us, who wanted to buy—and for the asking price—a painting of his, three meters by two, in which teeming angelic hosts waged the final battle against the opposing legions.

And so we met Signor Agliè. Impeccably dressed in a double-breasted pin-striped suit despite the heat, he wore gold-rimmed eyeglasses and had a rosy complexion, silver hair. He kissed Amparo's hand as if he knew of no other way to greet a lady, and he ordered champagne. When the painter had to leave, Agliè handed him a pack of traveler's checks and said to send the picture to his hotel. We stayed on to chat. Agliè spoke Portuguese correctly, but it sounded as if he had learned it in Lisbon. This accent made him seem even more like a gentleman of bygone days. He asked about us, commented on the possible Genevan origin of my name, and expressed curiosity about Amparo's family history, though somehow he had already guessed that the main branch was from Recife. About his own origins he was vague. "I'm like many people here," he said. "Countless races are represented in my genes. . . . The name is Italian, from the ancient estate of an ancestor. Perhaps a nobleman, but who cares these days? It was curiosity that brought me to Brazil. All forms of tradition fascinate me."

He told us he had a fine library of religious sciences in Milan, where he had been living for some years. "Come and see me when you get back. I have a number of interesting things, from Afro-Brazilian rites to the Isis cults of the late Roman Empire."

"I adore the Isis cults," Amparo said, who often, out of pride, pretended to be silly. "You must know everything there is to know about them."

Agliè replied modestly: "Only what little I've seen of them."

Amparo tried again: "But wasn't it two thousand years ago?"

"I'm not as young as you are." Agliè smiled.

"Like Cagliostro," I joked. "Wasn't he the one who was heard to murmur to his attendant as they passed a crucifix, 'I told that Jew to be careful that evening, but he just wouldn't listen'?"

Agliè stiffened. Afraid I had offended him, I started to apologize, but our host stopped me with an indulgent smile. "Cagliostro was a humbug. It's common knowledge when and where he was born, and he didn't even manage to live very long. A braggart."

"I don't doubt it."

"Cagliostro was a humbug," Agliè repeated, "but that does not mean that there have not been—and still are—privileged persons who have lived many lives. Modern science knows so little about the aging process. It's quite possible that mortality is simply the result of poor education. Cagliostro was a humbug, but the Comte de Saint-Germain was not. He may not have been boasting when he claimed to have learned some of his chemical secrets from the ancient Egyptians. Nobody believed him, so out of politeness to his listeners he pretended to be joking."

"And now you pretend to be joking in order to convince us you're telling the truth," Amparo said.

"You are not only beautiful, but extraordinarily perceptive too," Agliè said. "But I beseech you, do not believe me. Were I to appear before you in the dusty splendor of my many centuries, your own beauty would wither, and I could never forgive myself."

Amparo was conquered, and I felt a twinge of jealousy. I changed the subject to churches, and to the Saint George–Oxossi we had seen. Agliè said we absolutely had to attend a candomblé. "Not one where they charge admission. They let you into the real ones without asking anything of you. You don't even have to be a believer. You must observe respectfully, of course, showing the same tolerance of all faiths as they do in accepting your unbelief. At first sight a pai or mãe-de-santo might seem to be straight out of *Uncle Tom's Cabin,* but they have as much culture as a Vatican theologian."

Amparo put her hand on his. "Take us!" she said. "I went to one many years ago, in a tenda de umbanda, but I can't recall much about it. All I remember is great turmoil."

The physical contact embarrassed Agliè, but he didn't take his hand away. He did something I later saw him do in moments of reflection: reaching into his vest with his other hand, he took out a little gold-and-silver box with an agate on the lid. It looked like a snuffbox or a pillbox. There was a small wax light burning on the table, and Agliè, as if by chance, held the box near it. When exposed to heat, the agate's color could no longer be discerned, and in its place appeared a miniature, very fine, in green, blue, and gold, depicting a shepherdess with a basket of flowers. He turned it in his fingers with absent-minded devotion, as if telling a rosary. When he noticed my interest, he smiled and put the object away.

"Turmoil? I hope, my sweet lady, that, although you are so perceptive, you are not excessively sensitive. An exquisite quality, of course, when it accompanies grace and intelligence, but dangerous if you go to certain places without knowing what to look for or what you will find. Moreover, the umbanda must not be confused with the candomblé. The latter is completely indigenous—Afro-Brazilian, as they say—whereas the former is a much later development born of a fusion of native rites and esoteric European culture, and with a mystique I would call Templar. . . ."

The Templars had found me again. I told Agliè I had studied them. He regarded me with interest. "A most curious circumstance, my young friend, to find a young Templar here, under the Southern Cross."

"I wouldn't want you to consider me an adept—"

"Please, Signor Casaubon. If you knew how much nonsense there is in this field."

"I do know."

"Good. But we'll see one another soon." In fact, we arranged to meet the next day: all of us wanted to explore the little covered market along the port.

We met there the next morning, and it was a fish market, an Arab souk, a saint's-day fair that had proliferated with cancerous virulence, like a Lourdes overrun by the forces of evil, wizard rainmakers side by side with ecstatic and stigmatized Capuchins. There were little propitiatory sacks with prayers sewn into the lining, little hands in semiprecious stones, the middle finger extended, coral horns, crucifixes, Stars of David, sexual symbols of pre-Judaic religions, hammocks, rugs, purses, sphinxes, sacred hearts, Bororo quivers, shell necklaces. The degenerate mystique of the European conquistadors was owed to the occult knowledge of the slaves, just as the skin of every passerby told a similar story of lost genealogies.

"This," Agliè said, "is the very image of what the ethnology textbooks call Brazilian syncretism. An ugly word, in the official view. But in its loftiest sense syncretism is the acknowledgment that a single Tradition runs through and nurtures all religion, all learning, all philosophy. The wise man does not discriminate; he gathers together all the shreds of light, from wherever they may come. . . . These slaves, or descendants of slaves, are therefore wiser than the ethnologists of the Sorbonne. At least you understand me, do you not, lovely lady?"

"In my mind, no," Amparo said. "But in my womb, yes. Sorry, I don't imagine the Comte de Saint-Germain ever expressed himself in such terms. What I mean is: I was born in this country, and even things I don't understand somehow speak to me from somewhere. . . . Here, I believe." And she touched her breast.

"What was it Cardinal Lambertini once said to a lady wearing a splendid diamond cross on her décolletage? 'What joy it would be to die on that Calvary!' Well, how I would love to listen to those voices! But now it is I who must beg your forgiveness, both of you. I am from an age when one would have accepted damnation to pay homage to beauty. You two must want to be alone. Let's keep in touch."

"He's old enough to be your father," I said to Amparo as I dragged her through the stalls.

"Even my great-great-grandfather. He implied that he's at least a thousand years old. Are you jealous of a pharaoh's mummy?"

"I'm jealous of anyone who makes a light bulb flash on in your head."

"How wonderful. That's love."

27

One day, saying that he had known Pontius Pilate in Jerusalem, he described minutely the governor's house and listed the dishes served at supper. Cardinal de Rohan, believing these were fantasies, turned to the Comte de Saint-Germain's valet, an old man with white hair and an honest expression. "My friend," he said to the servant, "I find it hard to believe what your master is telling us. Granted that he may be a ventriloquist; and even that he can make gold. But that he is two thousand years old and saw Pontius Pilate? That is too much. Were you there?" "Oh, no, Monsignore," the valet answered ingenuously, "I have been in M. le Comte's service only four hundred years."
— Collin de Plancy, *Dictionnaire infernal*, Paris, Mellier,
1844, p. 434

In the days that followed, Salvador absorbed me completely. I spent little time in the hotel. But as I was leafing through the index of the book on the Rosicrucians, I came across a reference to the Comte de Saint-Germain. Well, well, I said to myself, tout se tient.

Voltaire wrote of him, "C'est un homme qui ne meurt jamais et qui sait tout," but Frederick the Great wrote back, "C'est un comte pour rire." Horace Walpole described him as an Italian or Spaniard or Pole who had made a fortune in Mexico and then fled to Constantinople with his wife's jewels. The most reliable information about him comes from the memoirs of Madame du Hausset, la Pompadour's femme de chambre (some authority, the intolerant Amparo said). He had gone by various names: Surmont in Brussels, Welldone in Leipzig, the Marquis of Aymar or Bedmar or Belmar, Count Soltikoff. In 1745 he was arrested in London, where he excelled as a musician, giving violin and harpsichord recitals in drawing rooms. Three years later he offered his services as an expert in dyeing to Louis XV in Paris, in exchange for a residence in the château of Chambord. The king sent him on diplomatic missions to Holland, where he got into some sort of trouble and fled to London again. In 1762 he turned up in Russia, then again in Belgium, where he encountered Casanova, who tells us how the count turned a coin into gold. In 1776 he appeared at the court of Frederick the Great, to whom he proposed various projects having to do with chemistry. Eight years later he died in Schleswig, at the court of the landgrave of Hesse, where he was putting the finishing touches on a manufactory for paints.

Nothing exceptional, the typical career of an eighteenth-century adventurer; not as many loves as Casanova and frauds less theatrical than Cagliostro's. Apart from the odd incident here and there, he enjoyed some credibility with those in authority, to whom he promised the wonders of alchemy, though with an industrial slant. The only unusual feature was the rumor of his immortality, which he undoubtedly instigated himself. In drawing rooms he would casually mention remote events as if he had been an eyewitness, and he cultivated his legend gracefully, en sourdine.

The book also quoted a passage from Giovanni Papini's *Gog,* describing a nighttime encounter with the Comte de Saint-Germain on the deck of an ocean liner. The count, oppressed by his millennial past and by the memories crowding his brain, spoke in despairing tones reminiscent of Funes, "el memorioso" of Borges, except that Papini's story dates from 1930. "You must not imagine our lot is deserving of envy," the count says to Gog. "After a couple of centuries an incurable ennui takes possession of the wretched immortals. The world is monotonous, men learn nothing, and, with every generation, they fall into the same errors and nightmares, events are not repeated but they resemble one another . . . novelties end, surprises, revelations. I can confess to you now that only the Red Sea is listening to us: my immortality bores me. Earth holds no more secrets for me and I have no hope anymore in my fellows."

"Curious character," I remarked. "Obviously our friend Agliè is playing at impersonating him. A gentleman getting on in years, a bit dotty, with money to spend, free time for travel, and an interest in the supernatural."

"A consistent reactionary, with the courage to be decadent," Amparo said. "Actually, I prefer him to bourgeois democrats."

"Sisterhood is powerful, but let a man kiss your hand and you're ecstatic."

"That's how you've trained us, for centuries. Let us free ourselves gradually. I didn't say I wanted to marry him."

"That's good."

The following week Agliè telephoned me. That evening, he said, we would be allowed to visit a terreiro de candomblé. We wouldn't be admitted to the actual rite, because the ialorixá was suspicious of tourists, but she would welcome us herself and would show us around before it started.

He picked us up by car and drove through the favelas beyond the hill. The building where we stopped had a humble look, like a big garage, but on the threshold an old black man met us and purified us with a fumigant. Up ahead was a bare little garden with an immense corbeil of palm fronds, on which some tribal delicacies, the comidas de santo, were laid out.

Inside, we found a large hall, the walls covered with paintings, especially ex-votos, and African masks. Agliè explained the arrangement of furniture: the benches in the rear were for the uninitiated, the little dais for the instruments, and the chairs for the Ogã. "They are people of some standing, not necessarily believers, but respectful of the cult. Here in Bahia the great Jorge Amado is an Ogã in one terreiro. He was selected by Iansã, mistress of war and winds. . . ."

"But where do these divinities come from?" I asked.

"It's complicated. First of all, there's a Sudanese branch, dominant here in the north from the early days of slavery. The candomblé of the orixás—in other words, the African divinities—come from this branch. In the southern states you find the influence of the Bantu groups, and this is where all the intermingling starts. The northern cults remain faithful to the original African religions, but in the south the primitive macumba develops toward the umbanda, which is influenced by Catholicism, Kardecism, and European occultism. . . ."

"So no Templars tonight?"

"That was meant to be a metaphor, but no, no Templars tonight. Syncretism, however, is a very subtle process. Did you notice, outside, near the comidas de santo, a little iron statue, a sort of devil with a pitchfork, and with votive offerings at his feet? That's Exu, very powerful in the umbanda, but not in the candomblé. Still, the candomblé also honors him as a kind of degenerate Mercury. In the umbanda, they are possessed by Exu, but not here. However, he's treated affectionately. But you never can tell. You see that wall over there?" He was pointing at the polychrome statues of a naked Indio and an old black slave, seated, dressed in white, and smoking a pipe. "They are a caboclo and a preto velho, spirits of the departed. Very important in umbanda rites. What are they doing here? Receiving homage. They are not used, because the candomblé entertains relations only with the African orixás, but they are not cast out on that account."

"What do all these churches have in common, then?"

"Well, during the rite in all Afro-Brazilian cults the initiates go into a trance and are possessed by higher beings. In the candomblé these beings are the orixás; in the umbanda they are spirits of the departed."

"I forgot my own country and my own race," Amparo said. "My God, a bit of Europe and a bit of historical materialism, and I forgot everything, the stories I used to hear from my grandmother . . ."

"Historical materialism?" Agliè smiled. "Oh, yes, I believe I've heard of it. An apocalyptic cult that came out of the Trier region. Am I right?"

I squeezed Amparo's arm. "No pasarán, darling."

"God," she murmured.

Agliè watched our brief whispered dialogue in silence. "Infinite are the powers of syncretism, my dear. Shall I tell you a political version of this whole story? Legally, the slaves were freed in the nineteenth century, but all the archives of the slave trade were burned in an effort to wipe out the stigmata of slavery. Formally, slaves were free, but their past was gone. In the absence of any family identity, they tried to reconstruct a collective past. It was their way of opposing what you young people call the Establishment."

"But you just said those European sects were also part of it."

"My dear, purity is a luxury, and slaves take what they can get. But they have their revenge. By now they have captured more whites than you think. The original African cults possessed the weakness of all religions: they were local, ethnic, short-sighted. But when they met the myths of the conquerors, they reproduced an ancient miracle, breathing new life into the mystery cults that arose around the Mediterranean during the second and third centuries of our era, when Rome in decline was exposed to ferment that had originated in Persia, Egypt, and pre-Judaic Palestine. . . . In the centuries of the late empire, Africa received the influences of all the religions of the Mediterranean and condensed them into a package. Europe was corrupted by Christianity as a state religion, but Africa preserved the treasures of knowledge, just as it had preserved and spread them in the days of the Egyptians, passing them on to the Greeks, who wreaked such great havoc with them."

28

> There is a body that enfolds the whole of the world; imagine it in
> the form of a circle, for this is the form of the Whole. . . . Imagine
> now that under the circle of this body are the 36 decans, midway
> between the total circle and the circle of the zodiac, separating these
> two circles and, so to speak, delimiting the zodiac, transported along
> it with the planets. . . . The changing of kings, the rising up of
> cities, famine, plague, the tides of the sea, earthquakes: none of
> these takes place without the influence of the decans. . . .
>
> —*Corpus Hermeticus,* Stobaeus, excerptum VI

"What treasures of knowledge?"

"Do you realize how great the second and third centuries after
Christ were? Not because of the pomp of the empire in its sunset,
but because of what was burgeoning in the Mediterranean basin then.
In Rome, the Praetorians were slaughtering their emperors, but in
the Mediterranean area, there flourished the epoch of Apuleius, the
mysteries of Isis, and that great return to spirituality: Neoplatonism, gnosis. Blissful times, before the Christians seized power and
began to put heretics to death. A splendid epoch, in which dwelled
the nous, a time dazzled by ecstasies and peopled with presences,
emanations, demons, and angelic hosts. The knowledge I am talking
about is diffuse and disjointed; it is as ancient as the world itself,
reaching back beyond Pythagoras, to the Brahmans of India, the
Hebrews, the mages, the gymnosophists, and even the barbarians of
the far north, the Druids of Gaul and the British Isles. The Greeks
called the barbarians by that name because to overeducated Greek
ears, their languages sounded like barking, and the Greeks therefore
assumed that they were unable to express themselves. In fact, the
barbarians knew much more than the Hellenes at the time, precisely
because their language was impenetrable. Do you believe the people
who will dance tonight know the meaning of all the chants and magic
names they will utter? Fortunately, they do not, and each unknown
name will be a kind of breathing exercise, a mystical vocalization.

"The age of the Antonines . . . The world was full of marvelous correspondences, subtle resemblances; the only way to penetrate them—and to be penetrated by them—was through dreams, oracles, magic, which allow us to act on nature and her forces, moving like with like. Knowledge is elusive and volatile; it escapes measurement. That's why the conquering god of that era was Hermes, inventor of all trickery, god of crossroads and thieves. He was also the creator of writing, which is the art of evasion and dissimulation and a navigation that carries us to the end of all boundaries, where everything dissolves into the horizon, where cranes lift stones from the ground and weapons transform life into death, and water pumps make heavy matter float, and philosophy deludes and deceives. . . . And do you know where Hermes is today? Right here. You passed him when you came through the door. They call him Exu, messenger of the gods, go-between, trader, who is ignorant of the difference between good and evil."

He looked at us with amused distrust. "You believe that I am as hasty in distributing gods as Hermes is in distributing merchandise. But look at this book, which I bought this morning in a little shop in Pelourinho. Magic and mystery of Saint Cyprian, recipes for spells to win love or cause your enemy's death, invocations to the angels and to the Virgin. Popular literature for these mystics whose skin is black. But this is Saint Cyprian of Antioch, about whom there is an immense literature dating from the silver age. His parents wanted him to learn all there was to know about the earth—land, sea, and air—so they sent him to the most distant realms, that he might acquire all mysteries, including the generation and corruption of herbs and the virtues of plants and of animals: the secrets not of natural history but of occult science, those buried in the depths of distant and archaic traditions. At Delphi, Cyprian dedicated himself to Apollo and to the dramaturgy of the serpent; he studied the mysteries of Mithra; on Mount Olympus at fifteen, guided by fifteen hierophants, he attended the rites that summon the Prince of This World, in order to master his intrigues; in Argos he was initiated into the mysteries of Hera; in Phrygia he learned hepatoscopic fortunetelling. At last there was nothing left of land, sea, or air that he did not know, no ghost, no object, no artifice of any kind, not even the art of altering writing through sorcery. In the underground temples of Memphis he had learned how demons communicate with earthly things and places, what they loathe and love, how they dwell in darkness and how they mount resistance in certain domains, how they are able to possess souls and bodies, the feats of higher knowledge they can perform, of memory, terror, and illusion, and the art of causing turmoil in the earth, influencing underground currents. . . . Then, alas, he was converted, but something of his knowledge remained and was passed on, and we find it here, in the mouths and minds of these ragged people you call idolaters. My lovely friend, a little while ago you looked at me as if I were a ci-devant. Who among us is living in the past? You, who would bestow the horrors of the toiling industrial age upon this country, or I, who wish that our poor Europe might recover the naturalness and faith of these children of slaves?"

"Jesus," Amparo said in a nasty hiss. "You know as well as I do that it's just another way of keeping them quiet. . . ."

"Not quiet. Capable of expectation. Without a sense of expectation, there can be no paradise; isn't that what you Europeans have taught us?"

"I'm a European?"

"The important thing is not skin color but faith in Tradition. Granted, these children of slaves pay a price in returning a sense of expectation to a West paralyzed by well-being; perhaps they even suffer, but still they know the language of the spirits of nature, of the air, the waters, and the winds. . . ."

"You people are exploiting us again."

"Again?"

"Yes. You should have learned your lesson in '89, Count. We get fed up, and then . . ." Smiling like an angel, she drew her beautiful hand straight across her throat. For me, even Amparo's teeth aroused desire.

"How dramatic!" Agliè said, taking his snuffbox from his pocket and stroking it with his fingers. "So you've recognized me. But it wasn't the slaves who made heads roll in '89; it was the upstanding bourgeoisie, whom you should hate. Besides, the Comte de Saint-Germain has seen many a head roll in all his centuries, and many a head reattached. But wait, here comes the mãe-de-santo, the ialo-rixá."

Our meeting with the abbess of the terreiro was calm, cordial, civilized, and rich in folklore. She was a big black woman with a dazzling smile. At first you would have said she was a housewife, but when we began talking, I understood how women like this could rule the cultural life of Salvador.

"Are the orixás people or forces?" I asked her. The mãe-de-santo answered that they were forces, obviously: water, wind, leaves, rainbows. But how did she prevent ordinary people from seeing them as warriors, women, saints of the Catholic Church? "Do you yourselves not also worship a cosmic force in the form of virgins?" she replied. The important thing is to venerate the force. The aspect of the force must fit each man's ability to comprehend.

She invited us to visit the chapels in the garden before the rite began. In the garden were the houses of the orixás. A swarm of black girls in Bahian dress was cheerfully gathered there, making the final preparations.

The houses of the orixás were arranged around the garden like the chapels of a sacred mount. Outside each one was displayed the image of the corresponding saint. Inside, the garish colors of flowers clashed with those of the statues and the just-cooked foods offered to the gods. White for Oxalá, blue and pink for Yemanjá, red and white for Xangō, yellow and gold for Ogun . . . Initiates kneeled and kissed the threshold, touching themselves on the forehead and behind the ear.

"But is Yemanjá Our Lady of the Conception or not?" I asked. "Is Xangō Saint Jerome or not?"

"Don't ask embarrassing questions," Agliè advised. "It's even more complicated in an umbanda. Saint Anthony and Saints Cosmas and Damian are part of the Oxalá line. Sirens, water nymphs, caboclas of the sea and the rivers, sailors, and guiding stars are part of the Yemanjá line. The line of the Orient includes Hindus, doctors, scientists, Arabs and Moroccans, Japanese, Chinese, Mongols, Egyptians, Aztecs, Incas, Caribs, and Romans. To the Oxossi line belong the sun, the moon, the caboclo of waterfalls, and the caboclo of the blacks. In the Ogun line we come upon Ogun Beira-Mar, Rompe-Mato, Iara, Megé, Narueé . . . In other words, it all depends."

"Jesus," Amparo said again.

"Oxalá, you mean," I murmured to her, my lips brushing her ear. "Calm down. No pasarán."

The ialorixá showed us a series of masks that some acolytes were bringing into the temple. These were big straw dominoes, or hoods, which the mediums would put on as they went into a trance, falling prey to the divinity. This was a form of modesty, she explained. In some terreiros the chosen danced with their faces bare, letting on-lookers see their passion. But the initiates should be shielded, re-spected, removed from the curiosity of the profane or anyone who cannot understand the inner jubilation and grace. That was the cus-tom in this terreiro, she said, and that was why outsiders were not readily admitted. Maybe someday, she remarked, who knows? We might well meet again.

But she didn't want us to leave without sampling some of the comidas de santo—not from the corbeils, which had to remain in-tact until the end of the rite, but from her own kitchen. She took us to the back of the terreiro, where there was a multicolored ban-quet of manioc, pimento, coco, amendoim, gengibre, moqueca de siri-mole, vatapá, efó, caruru, black beans with farofa, amid a lan-guid odor of African spices, sweet and strong tropical flavors, which we tasted dutifully, knowing that we were sharing the food of the ancient Sudanese gods. And rightly so, the ialorixá told us, because each of us, whether he knew it or not, was the child of an orixá, and often it was possible to tell which one. I boldly asked whose son I was. The ialorixá demurred at first, saying she couldn't be sure, but then she agreed to examine the palm of my hand. She looked into my eyes and said: "You are a son of Oxalá."

I was proud. Amparo, now relaxed, suggested we find out whose son Agliè was, but he said he preferred not to know.

When we were home again, Amparo said to me: "Did you see his hand? Instead of the life line, he has a series of broken lines. Like a stream that comes to a stone, parts, and flows together again a meter farther on. The line of a man who must have died many times."

"World champion of the metempsychosis relay."

"No pasarán," Amparo said, laughing.

29

Diotallevi used to say that Hesed was the Sefirah of grace and love, white fire, south wind. The other evening in the periscope, I thought that those last days with Amparo in Bahia belonged under that sign.

You remember so much while you wait for hours and hours in the darkness. I remembered especially one of the last evenings. We had walked through so many alleys and squares that our feet ached, and we went to bed early, but we didn't feel like sleeping. Ampāro, huddled against the pillow in the fetal position, was pretending to read one of my little pamphlets on the umbanda, propping it on her knees. From time to time she would roll lazily onto her back, legs spread, the book balanced on her belly, listening to me read from the book on the Rosicrucians. I was trying to involve her in my discoveries. It was a mild evening; as Belbo, exhausted with literature, might have put it in one of his files, there was nought but a lovely sighing of the wind. We had splurged on a good hotel; there was a view of the sea from the window, and the still-lighted closet kitchen offered the comforting sight of the basket of tropical fruit we had bought at four that morning.

"It says that in 1614 an anonymous work appeared in Germany entitled *Allgemeine und general Reformation*, or *General and common Reform of the entire Universe, followed by Fama Fraternitatis of the Honorable Confraternity of the Rosy-Cross, addressed to all learned Men and Sovereigns of Europe, together with a brief Reply by Herr Haselmeyer, who for this Reason was cast into Prison by the Jesuits and then placed in Irons on a Galley. Now printed and made known to all the sincere of Heart. Published in Cassel by Wilhelm Wessel.*"

"A little long, isn't it?"

"Apparently all titles were like that in the seventeenth century. Lina Wertmuller wrote them, too. Anyway, this was a satirical work, a fairy tale about a general reform of mankind, partly plagiarized from Traiano Boccalini's *Ragguagli di Parnaso*. But it contained a manifesto of about a dozen pages—the *Fama Fraternitatis*—which was republished separately a year later, at the same time as another manifesto, this one in Latin: *Confessio fraternitatis Roseae Crucis, ad eruditos Europae*. Both present the Confraternity of the Rosy Cross and talk about its founder, a mysterious C.R. Only later—and from other sources—was it learned, or presumed, that C.R. was one Christian Rosencreutz."

"Why didn't they use the full name?"

"The whole thing's full of initials; they didn't use anybody's full name. They're all G.G.M.P.I.; one is called P.D., an affectionate nickname. Anyway, the pamphlet tells of the formative years of C.R., who first visited the Holy Sepulcher, then set off for Damascus, moved on to Egypt, and from there went to Fez, which must have been one of the sanctuaries of Moslem wisdom at the time. There, our Christian, who already knew Greek and Latin, learned Oriental languages, physics, mathematics, and the sciences of nature, accumulating all the millennial wisdom of the Arabs and Africans, as well as cabala and magic. He also translated a mysterious *Liber M* into Latin, and thus came to know all the secrets of the macrocosm and the microcosm. For two centuries, everything Oriental had been fashionable, especially if it was incomprehensible."

"They always go for that. Hungry? Frustrated? Exploited? Mystery cocktail coming up. Here . . ." She passed me a joint. "This is good stuff."

"See? You also seek to lose yourself."

"Except that I know it's only chemical. No mystery at all. It works even if you don't know Hebrew. Come here."

"Wait. Next Rosencreutz went to Spain, where he picked up more occult doctrines, claiming that he was drawing closer to the center of all knowledge. In the course of these travels—which for an intellectual of the time was a sort of total-wisdom trip—he realized that what was needed in Europe was an association that would guide rulers along the paths of wisdom and good."

"Very original. Well worth it, all that studying. I want some cold mamaia."

"In the fridge. Do me a favor. You go. I'm working."

"If you're working, that makes you the ant. So be a good ant and get some provisions."

"Mamaia is pleasure, so the grasshopper should go. Otherwise I'll go, and you read."

"No. Jesus, I hate the white man's culture. I'll go."

Amparo went to the little kitchen, and I enjoyed seeing her against the light. Meanwhile, C.R. was on his way back from Germany, but instead of devoting himself to the transmutation of metals, of which his now immense knowledge made him capable, he decided to dedicate himself to spiritual reformation. He therefore founded the confraternity, inventing a language and magic writing that would be the foundation of the wisdom of generations of brothers to come.

"No, I'll spill it on the book. Put it in my mouth. Come on, no tricks, silly. That's right . . . God, how good mamaia is, rosen-creutzlische Mutti-ja-ja . . . Anyway, what the first Rosicrucians wrote in the first few years could have enlightened the world."

"Why? What did they write?"

"There's the rub. The manifesto doesn't say; it leaves you with your mouth watering. But it was important; so important, it had to remain secret."

"The bastards."

"No! Hey, cut that out! Well, as the Rosicrucians gained more and more members, they decided to spread to the four corners of the earth, vowing to heal the sick without charging, to dress according to the customs of each country (never wearing clothes that would identify them), to meet once a year, and to remain secret for a hundred years."

"Tell me: what kind of reformation were they after? I mean, hadn't there just been one? What was Luther then? Shit?"

"No, you're wrong. This was before the Protestant Reformation. There's a note here; it says that a thorough reading of the *Fama* and the *Confessio* evinces—"

"Evinces?"

"Evinces. Shows, makes evident. Stop that, I'm trying to talk about the Rosy Cross. It's serious."

"It evinces."

"Rosencreutz was born in 1378 and died in 1484, at the ripe old age of a hundred and six. And it's not hard to guess that the secret confraternity made a considerable contribution to the Reformation that celebrated its centenary in 1615. In fact, Luther's coat of arms includes a rose and a cross."

"Some imagination."

"You expect Luther to use a burning giraffe or a limp watch? We're all children of our own time. I've found out whose child I am, so shut up and let me go on. Around 1604 the brethren of the Rosy Cross were rebuilding a part of their palace or secret castle, and they came across a plaque with a big nail driven into it. When they pulled out the nail, part of the wall collapsed, and they saw a door with something written on it in big letters: POST CXX ANNOS PATEBO . . ."

I had already learned this from Belbo's letter, but still couldn't help reacting. "My God . . ."

"What is it?"

"It's like a Templar document that . . . A story I never told you, about a colonel who—"

"What of it? The Templars must have copied from the Rosicrucians."

"But the Templars came first."

"Then the Rosicrucians copied from the Templars."

"What would I do without you, darling?"

"That Agliè's ruined you. You're looking everywhere for revelation."

"Me? I'm not looking for anything."

"And a good thing, too. Watch out for the opiate of the masses."

"El pueblo unido jamás será vencido."

"Go ahead, laugh. So what did those idiots say?"

"Those idiots learned everything they knew in Africa, weren't you listening?"

"And while they were in Africa, they started packing us up and sending us here."

"Thank God. Otherwise you might have been born in Pretoria." I kissed her. "Beyond the door," I went on, "they found a sepulcher with seven sides and seven corners, miraculously illuminated by an artificial sun. In the middle was a circular altar decorated with various mottoes or emblems, on the order of NEQUAQUAM VACUUM. . . ."

"Quack quack what? Signed, Donald Duck?"

"It's Latin. It means 'the void does not exist.' "

"That's good to know. Otherwise, think of the horror—"

"Do me a favor and turn on the fan, animula vagula blandula."

"But it's winter."

"Only for you people of the wrong hemisphere, darling. For me it's July. Please, the fan. It's not because you're a woman; just that it's on your side of the bed. Thanks. Anyway, under the altar they found Rosencreutz's body, intact. In his hand was a copy of *Book I*, crammed with infinite knowledge. Too bad the world can't read it—the manifesto says—otherwise, gulp, wow, brr, squisssh!"

"Ouch."

"As I was saying, the manifesto ends by promising that a huge treasure remains to be discovered, along with stupendous revelations about the ties between the macrocosm and the microcosm. And don't think that these were a bunch of tacky alchemists offering to show us how to make gold. No, that was small potatoes. They were aiming higher, in every sense of the word. The manifesto announced that the *Fama* was being distributed in five languages, and, soon to appear on this screen, the *Confessio*. The brothers awaited replies and reviews from learned and ignorant alike. Write, telephone, send in your names, and we'll see if you're worthy to share our secrets, of which we have given you only the faintest notion. Sub umbra alarum tuarum Iehova."

"Which means?"

"It's a formula of conclusion. Over and out. It sounds as if the Rosicrucians were dying to tell what they had learned, and were anxiously waiting for the right listener. But not one word about what it was they knew."

"Like that fellow whose picture was in the ad we saw on the plane: Send me ten dollars, and I'll tell you how to become a millionaire."

"And it's no lie. He *has* discovered the secret. And so have I."

"Listen, you better read on. You're acting as if we just met tonight."

"With you, it's always like the first time."

"Ah, but I don't get too familiar with the first one who comes along. Anyway, you have quite a collection now. First Templars, then Rosicrucians. You haven't read Plekhanov by any chance?"

"No. I'm waiting to discover his sepulcher a hundred and twenty years from now. Unless Stalin buried him with tractors."

"Idiot. I'm taking a bath."

30

And the famous confraternity of the Rosy Cross declares even now that throughout the universe delirious prophecies circulate. In fact, the moment the ghost appeared (though *Fama* and *Confessio* prove that this was a mere invention of idle minds), it produced a hope of universal reform, and generated things partly ridiculous and absurd, partly incredible. Thus upright and honest men of various countries exposed themselves to contempt and derision in order to lend open support, or to reveal themselves to these brothers . . . through the Mirror of Solomon or in some other occult way.

—Christoph von Besold (?), Appendix to Tommaso
Campanella, *Von der Spanischen Monarchy*, 1623

The best came later, and when Amparo returned, I was able to give her a foretaste of wondrous events. "It's an incredible story. The manifestoes appeared in an age teeming with texts of that sort. Everyone was seeking renewal, a golden century, a Cockaigne of the spirit. Some pored over magic texts, others labored at forges, melting metals, others sought to rule the stars, and still others invented secret alphabets and universal languages. In Prague, Rudolph II turned his court into an alchemistic laboratory, invited Comenius and John Dee, the English court astrologer who had revealed all the secrets of the cosmos in the few pages of his *Monas Ierogliphica*. Are you with me?"

"To the end of time."

"Rudolph's physician was a man named Michael Maier, who later wrote a book of visual and musical emblems, the *Atalanta Fugiens*, an orgy of philosopher's eggs, dragons biting their tails, sphinxes. Nothing was more luminous than a secret cipher; everything was the hieroglyph of something else. Think about it. Galileo was dropping stones from the Tower of Pisa, Richelieu played Monopoly with half of Europe, and in the meantime they all had their eyes peeled to read the signs of the world. Pull of gravity, indeed; something else lies beneath (or, rather, above) all this, something quite different. Would you like to know what? Abracadabra. Torricelli invented the barometer, but the rest of them were messing around with ballets, water games, and fireworks in the Hortus Palatinus in Heidelberg. And the Thirty Years' War was about to break out."

"Mutter Courage must have been delighted."

"But even for them it wasn't all fun and games. In 1619 the Palatine elector accepted the crown of Bohemia, probably because he was dying to rule Prague, the magic city. But the next year, the Hapsburgs nailed him to the White Mountain. In Prague the Protestants were slaughtered, Comenius's house and library were burned, and his wife and son were killed. He fled from court to court, harping on how great and full of hope the idea of the Rosy Cross was."

"Poor man, but what did you expect him to do? Console himself with the barometer? Wait a minute. Give a poor girl time to think. Who wrote these manifestoes?"

"That's the whole point: we don't know. Let's try to figure it out. . . . How about scratching my rosy cross . . . no, between the shoulder blades, higher, to the left, there. Yes, there. Now then, there were some incredible characters in this German environment. Like Simon Studion, author of *Naometria*, an occult treatise on the measurements of the Temple of Solomon; Heinrich Khunrath, who wrote *Amphitheatrum sapientiae aeternae*, full of allegories, with Hebrew alphabets and cabalistic labyrinths that must have inspired the authors of *Fama*, who were probably friends of one of the countless little utopian conventicles of Christian rebirth. One popular rumor is that the author was a man named Johann Valentin Andreae. A year later, he published *The Chemical Wedding of Christian Rosencreutz*, but he had written that in his youth, so he must have been kicking the idea of the Rosy Cross around for quite some time. There were other enthusiasts, in Tübingen, who dreamed of the republic of Christianopolis. Perhaps they all got together. But it sounds as if it was all in fun, a joke. They had no idea of the pandemonium they were unleashing. Andreae spent the rest of his life swearing he hadn't written the manifestoes, which he claimed were a lusus, a ludibrium, a prank. It cost him his academic reputation. He grew angry, said that the Rosicrucians, if indeed they existed, were all impostors. But that didn't help. Once the manifestoes appeared, it was as if people had been waiting for them. Learned men from all over Europe actually wrote to the Rosicrucians, and since there was no address, they sent open letters, pamphlets, printed volumes. In that same year Maier published *Arcana arcanissima*, in which the brethren of the Rosy Cross were not mentioned explicitly, but everyone was sure he was talking about them and that there was more to his book than met the eye. Some people boasted that they had read *Fama* in manuscript. It wasn't so easy to prepare a book for publication in those days, especially if it had engravings, but in 1616, Robert Fludd—who wrote in England but printed in Leyden, so you have to figure in the time to ship the proofs—circulated *Apologia compendiaria Fraternitatem de Rosea Cruce suspicionis et infamiis maculis aspersam, veritatem quasi Fluctibus abluens et abstergens,* to defend the brethren and free them from suspicion, from the 'slander' that had been their reward. In other words, a debate was raging in Bohemia, Germany, England, and Holland, alive with couriers on horseback and itinerant scholars."

"And the Rosicrucians themselves?"

"Deathly silence. Post CXX annos patebo, my ass. They watched, from the vacuum of their palace. I believe it was their silence that agitated everyone so much. The fact that they didn't answer was taken as proof of their existence. In 1617 Fludd wrote *Tractatus apologeticus integritatem societatis de Rosea Cruce defendens,* and somebody in a *De Naturae Secretis,* 1618, said that the time had come to reveal the secret of the Rosicrucians."

"And did they?"

"Anything but. They only complicated things, explaining that if you subtracted from 1618 the one hundred and eighty-eight years promised by the Rosicrucians, you got 1430, the year when the Order of the Golden Fleece, la Toison d'Or, was established."

"What's that got to do with anything?"

"I don't understand the one hundred and eighty-eight years. It seems to me it should have been one hundred and twenty, but mystical subtractions and additions always come out the way you want. As for la Toison d'Or, it's a reference to the Argonauts, who, an unimpeachable source once told me, had some connection with the Holy Grail and therefore with the Templars. But that's not all. Fludd, who seems to have been as prolific as Barbara Cartland, brought out four more books between 1617 and 1619, including *Utriusque cosmi historia,* brief remarks on the universe, illustrated with roses and crosses throughout. Maier then mustered all his courage and put out his *Silentium post clamores,* in which he claimed that the confraternity did indeed exist and was connected not only to la Toison d'Or but also to the Order of the Garter. Except that he was too lowly a person to be received into it. Imagine the reaction of the scholars of Europe! If the Rosicrucians didn't accept even Maier, the order must have been really exclusive. So now all the pseuds bent over backward to get in. In other words, everyone said the Rosicrucians existed, though no one admitted to having actually seen them. Everyone wrote as if trying to set up a meeting or wheedle an audience, but no one had the courage to say I'm one, and some, maybe only because they had never been approached, said the order didn't exist; others said the order existed precisely because they had been approached."

"And not a peep out of the Rosicrucians."

"Quiet as mice."

"Open your mouth. You need some mamaia."

"Yum. Meanwhile, the Thirty Years' War began, and Johann Valentin Andreae wrote *Turris Babel*, promising that the Antichrist would be defeated within the year, while one Ireneus Agnostus wrote *Tintinnabulum sophorum*—"

"Tintinnabulum! I love it."

"—not a word of which is comprehensible. But then Campanella, or someone acting on his behalf, declared in *Spanischen Monarchy* that the whole Rosy Cross business was a game of corrupt minds. . . . And that's it. Between 1621 and 1623 they all shut up."

"Just like that?"

"Just like that. They got tired of it. Like the Beatles. But only in Germany. Otherwise, it's the story of a toxic cloud. It shifted to France. One fine morning in 1623, Rosicrucian manifestoes appeared on the walls of Paris, informing the good citizens that the deputies of the confraternity's chief college had moved to their city and were ready to accept applications. But according to another version, the manifestoes came right out and said there were thirty-six invisibles scattered through the world in groups of six, and that they had the power to make their adepts invisible. Hey! The thirty-six again!"

"What thirty-six?"

"The ones in my Templar document."

"No imagination at all, these people. What next?"

"Collective madness broke out. Some defended the Rosicrucians, others wanted to meet them, still others accused them of devil worship, alchemy, and heresy, claiming that Ashtoreth had intervened to make them rich, powerful, capable of flying from place to place. The talk of the town, in other words."

"Smart, those brethren. Nothing like a Paris launching to make you fashionable."

"You're right. Listen to what happened next. Descartes—that's right, Descartes himself—had, several years before, gone looking for them in Germany, but he never found them, because, as his biographer says, they deliberately disguised themselves. By the time he got back to Paris, the manifestoes had appeared, and he learned that everybody considered him a Rosicrucian. Not a good thing to be, given the atmosphere at the time. It also irritated his friend Mersenne, who was already fulminating against the Rosicrucians, calling them wretches, subversives, mages, and cabalists bent on sowing perverted doctrines. So what does Descartes do? Simply appears in public as often as possible. Since everybody can undeniably see him, he must not be a Rosicrucian, because if he were, he'd be invisible."

"That's method for you!"

"Of course, denying it wouldn't have worked. The way things were, if somebody came up to you and said, 'Hi there, I'm a Rosicrucian,' that meant he wasn't. No self-respecting Rosicrucian would acknowledge it. On the contrary, he would deny it to his last breath."

"But you can't say that anyone who denies being a Rosicrucian is a Rosicrucian, because I say I'm not, and that doesn't make *me* one."

"But the denial is itself suspicious."

"No, it's not. What would a Rosicrucian do once he realized people weren't believing those who said they were, and that people suspected only those who said they weren't? He'd say he was, to make them think he wasn't."

"Damnation. So those who say they're Rosicrucians are lying, which means they really are! No, no, Amparo, we mustn't fall into their trap. Their spies are everywhere, even under this bed, so now they know that we know, and therefore they say they aren't."

"Darling, you're scaring me."

"Don't worry, I'm here, and I'm stupid, so when they say they aren't, I'll believe they are and unmask them at once. The Rosicrucian unmasked is harmless; you can shoo him out the window with a rolled-up newspaper."

"What about Agliè? He wants us to think he's the Comte de Saint-Germain. Obviously so we'll think he isn't. Therefore, he's a Rosicrucian. Or isn't he?"

"Listen, Amparo, let's get some sleep."

"Oh, no, now I want to hear the rest."

"The rest is a complete mess. Everybody's a Rosicrucian. In 1627 Francis Bacon's *New Atlantis* was published, and readers thought he was talking about the land of the Rosicrucians, even though he never mentioned them. Poor Johann Valentin Andreae died, still swearing up and down that he wasn't a Rosicrucian, or if he said he was, he had only been kidding, but by now it was too late. The Rosicrucians were everywhere, aided by the fact that they didn't exist."

"Like God."

"Now that you mention it, let's see. Matthew, Mark, Luke, and John are a bunch of practical jokers who meet somewhere and decide to have a contest. They invent a character, agree on a few basic facts, and then each one's free to take it and run with it. At the end, they'll see who's done the best job. The four stories are picked up by some friends who act as critics: Matthew is fairly realistic, but insists on that Messiah business too much; Mark isn't bad, just a little sloppy; Luke is elegant, no denying that; and John takes the philosophy a little too far. Actually, though, the books have an appeal, they circulate, and when the four realize what's happening, it's too late. Paul has already met Jesus on the road to Damascus, Pliny begins his investigation ordered by the worried emperor, and a legion of apocryphal writers pretends also to know plenty. . . . Toi, apocryphe lecteur, mon semblable, mon frère. It all goes to Peter's head; he takes himself seriously. John threatens to tell the truth, Peter and Paul have him chained up on the island of Patmos. Soon the poor man is seeing things: Help, there are locusts all over my bed, make those trumpets stop, where's all this blood coming from? The others say he's drunk, or maybe it's arteriosclerosis. . . . Who knows, maybe it really happened that way."

"It did happen that way. You should read some Feuerbach, instead of those junk books of yours."

"Amparo, the sun's coming up."

"We must be crazy."

"Rosy-fingered dawn gently caresses the waves . . ."

"Yes, go on. It's Yemanjá. Listen! She's coming."

"Show me your ludibria . . ."

"Oh, the Tintinnabulum!"

"You are my Atalanta Fugiens. . . ."

"Oh, my Turris Babel . . ."

"I want the Arcana Arcanissima, the Golden Fleece, pâle et rose comme un coquillage marin. . . ."

"Sssh . . . Silentium post clamores," she said.

It is probable that the majority of the supposed Rosy Crosses, generally so designated, were in reality only Rosicrucians. . . . Indeed, it is certain that they were in no way members, for the simple fact that they were members of such associations. This may seem paradoxical at first, and contradictory, but is nevertheless easily comprehensible. . . .

— René Guénon, *Aperçu sur l'initiation*, Paris, Editions
   Traditionelles, 1981, XXXVIII, p. 241

We returned to Rio, and I went back to work. One day I read in an illustrated magazine that there was an Order of the Ancient and Accepted Rosy Cross in the city. I suggested to Amparo that we go and take a look, and reluctantly she came along.

The office was in a side street; its plate-glass window contained plaster statuettes of Cheops, Nefertiti, the Sphinx.

There was a plenary session scheduled for that very afternoon: "The Rosy Cross and the Umbanda." The speaker was one Professor Bramanti, Referendary of the Order in Europe, Secret Knight of the Grand Priory in Partibus of Rhodes, Malta, and Thessalonica.

We decided to go in. The room, fairly shabby, was decorated with Tantric miniatures depicting the serpent Kundalini, the one the Templars wanted to reawaken with the kiss on the behind. All things considered, I thought, it had hardly been worth crossing the Atlantic to discover a new world: I could have found the same things at the Picatrix office.

Professor Bramanti sat behind a table covered with a red cloth, facing a rather sparse and sleepy audience. He was a corpulent gentleman who might have been described as a tapir if it hadn't been for his bulk. He was already talking when we came in. His style was pompous and oratorical. He couldn't have started long before, however, because he was still discussing the Rosicrucians during the eighteenth dynasty, under the reign of Ahmose I.

Four Veiled Masters, he said, kept watch over the race that twenty-five thousand years before the foundation of Thebes had originated the civilization of the Sahara. The pharaoh Ahmose, influenced by them, established the Great White Fraternity, guardian of the ante-diluvian wisdom the Egyptians still retained. Bramanti claimed to have documents (naturally, inaccessible to the profane) that dated back to the sages of the Temple of Karnak and their secret archives. The symbol of the rose and the cross had been conceived by the pharaoh Akhenaton. Someone has the papyrus, Bramanti said, but don't ask me who.

The Great White Fraternity was ultimately responsible for the education of: Hermes Trismegistus (who influenced the Italian Renaissance just as much as he later influenced Princeton gnosis), Homer, the Druids of Gaul, Solomon, Solon, Pythagoras, Plotinus, the Essenes, the Therapeutae, Joseph of Arimathea (who took the Grail to Europe), Alcuin, King Dagobert, Saint Thomas, Bacon, Shakespeare, Spinoza, Jakob Böhme, Debussy, Einstein. (Amparo whispered that he seemed to be missing only Nero, Cambronne, Geronimo, Pancho Villa, and Buster Keaton.)

As for the influence of the original Rosy Cross on Christianity, Bramanti pointed out, for those who hadn't got their bearings, that it was no accident that Jesus had died on a cross.

The sages of the Great White Fraternity were also the founders of the first Masonic lodge, back in the days of King Solomon. It was clear, from his works, that Dante had been a Rosicrucian and a Mason—as had Saint Thomas, incidentally. In cantos XXIV and XXV of the "Paradiso" one finds the triple kiss of Prince Rosicrux, the pelican, white tunics (the same as those worn by the old men of the Apocalypse), and the three theological virtues of Masonic chapters (Faith, Hope, and Charity). In fact, the symbolic flower of the Rosicrucians (the white rose of cantos XXX and XXXI) was adopted by the Church of Rome as symbol of the mother of the Savior. Hence the Rosa Mystica of the litanies.

It was equally clear that the Rosicrucians had lived on through the Middle Ages, a fact shown not only by their infiltration of the Templars, but also by far more explicit documents. Bramanti cited one Kiesewetter, who demonstrated in the late nineteenth century that the Rosicrucians had manufactured four quintals of gold for the Prince-Elector of Saxony in medieval times, clear proof being available on a certain page of the *Theatrum Chemicum*, published in Strasbourg in 1613. But few have remarked the Templar references in the legend of William Tell. Tell cuts his arrow from a branch of mistletoe, a plant of Aryan mythology, and he hits an apple, symbol of the third eye activated by the serpent Kundalini. And we know, of course, that the Aryans came from India, where the Rosicrucians took refuge after leaving Germany.

Of the various groupings that claimed descent from the Great White Fraternity—often childishly—Bramanti recognized just one as legitimate: the Rosicrucian Fellowship of Max Heindel, and that only because Alain Kardek had been educated in its circles. Kardek was the father of spiritualism, and it was his theosophy, which contemplated contact with the souls of the departed, that spiritually formed umbanda spirituality, the glory of our most noble Brazil. In this theosophy, Aum Banda, it seems, is a Sanskrit expression denoting the divine principle and source of life. ("They tricked us again," Amparo murmured. "Not even the word 'umbanda' is ours; the only African thing about it is the sound.")

The root is Aum or Um, which is the Buddhist Om and also the name of God in the language of Adam. If the syllable *um* is properly pronounced, it becomes a powerful mantra and produces fluid currents of harmony in the psyche through the siakra, or frontal plexus. ("What's the frontal plexus?" Amparo asked. "An incurable disease?")

Bramanti explained that there was a big difference between true brethren of the Rosy Cross—heirs of the Great White Fraternity, obviously secret, such as the Ancient and Accepted Order, whose unworthy representative he was, and the "Rosicrucians," who claimed attachment to the Rosy Cross mystique for opportunistic reasons, lacking any justification. He urged his audience to give no credence to any Rosicrucian who called himself a brother of the Rosy Cross. (Amparo remarked that one man's Rosy Cross was another man's Rosicrucian.)

One ill-advised member of the audience stood up and asked how Professor Bramanti's order could claim to be authentic, since it violated the law of silence observed by all true adepts of the Great White Fraternity.

Bramanti rose to reply. "I was unaware that we had been infiltrated by the paid provocateurs of atheistic materialism. Under these circumstances I have no more to say." And at that he walked out with a certain majesty.

That evening, Agliè telephoned to see how we were and to tell us that we had finally been invited to a rite, the next day. In the meantime, he suggested we have a drink. Amparo had a political meeting with her friends; I went to join Agliè by myself.

32

Aglié invited me to a place where some ageless men still made a batida in the traditional way. In just a few steps we left the civilization of Carmen Miranda, and I found myself in a dark room where some natives were smoking cigars thick as sausages. The tobacco, as broad, transparent leaves, was rolled into what looked like old hawser, worked with the fingertips, and wrapped in oily straw paper. It kept going out, but you could understand what it must have been like when Sir Walter Raleigh discovered it.

I told him about my afternoon adventure.

"So now it's the Rosicrucians as well? Your thirst for knowledge is insatiable, my friend. But pay no attention to those lunatics. They constantly talk about irrefutable documents that no one ever produces. I know that Bramanti. He lives in Milan, but he travels all over the world spreading his gospel. A harmless man, though he still believes in Kiesewetter. Hordes of Rosicrucians insist on that page of the *Theatrum Chemicum*. But if you actually take a look at it—and I might modestly add that I have a copy in my little Milanese library—there is no such quotation."

"Herr Kiesewetter's a clown, then."

"But much quoted. The trouble is that even the nineteenth-century occultists fell victim to the spirit of positivism: a thing is true only if it can be proved. Take the debate on the *Corpus Hermeticum*. When that document came to light in Europe in the fifteenth century, Pico della Mirandola, Ficino, and many other people of great wisdom immediately realized that it had to be a work of most ancient wisdom, antedating the Egyptians, antedating even Moses himself. It contained ideas that would later be expressed by Plato and by Jesus."

"What do you mean, later? That's the same argument Bramanti used to prove Dante was a Mason. If the *Corpus* repeats ideas of Plato and Jesus, it must have been written after them!"

"You see? You're doing it, too. That was exactly the reasoning of modern philologists, who also added wordy linguistic analyses intended to show that the *Corpus* was written in the second or third century of our era. It's like saying that Cassandra must have been born after Homer because she predicted the destruction of Troy. The belief that time is a linear, directed sequence running from A to B is a modern illusion. In fact, it can also go from B to A, the effect producing the cause. . . . What does 'coming before' mean, or 'coming after'? Does your beautiful Amparo come before or after her motley ancestors? She is too splendid—if you will allow a dispassionate opinion from a man old enough to be her father. She thus comes before. She is the mysterious origin of whatever went into her creation."

"But at this point . . ."

"It is the whole idea of 'point' that is mistaken. Ever since Parmenides, points have been posited by science in an attempt to establish whence and whither something moves. But in fact nothing moves, and there is only one point, the one from which all others are generated at the same instant. The occultists of the nineteenth century, like those of our own time, naïvely tried to prove the truth of a thing by resorting to the methods of scientific falsehood. You must reason not according to the logic of time but according to the logic of Tradition. One time symbolizes all others, and the invisible Temple of the Rosicrucians therefore exists and has always existed, regardless of the current of history—your history. The time of the final revelation is not time by the clock. Its bonds are rooted in the time of 'subtle history,' where the befores and afters of science are of scant importance."

"In other words, those who maintain that the Rosicrucians are eternal—"

"Are scientific fools, because they seek to prove that which must be known without proof. Do you think the worshipers we will see tomorrow night are capable of proving all the things that Kardec told them? Not at all. They simply know, because they are willing to know. If we had all retained this receptivity to secret knowledge, we would be dazzled by revelations. There is no need to wish; it's enough to be willing."

"But look—and forgive my banality—do the Rosicrucians exist or not?"

"What do you mean by exist?"

"You tell me."

"The Great White Fraternity—whether you call them Rosicrucians or the spiritual knighthood of which the Templars are a temporary incarnation—is a cohort of a few, a very few, elect wise men who journey through human history in order to preserve a core of eternal knowledge. History does not happen randomly. It is the work of the Masters of the World, whom nothing escapes. Naturally, the Masters of the World protect themselves through secrecy. And that is why anyone who says he is a master, a Rosicrucian, a Templar is lying. They must be sought elsewhere."

"Then the story goes on endlessly."

"Exactly. And it demonstrates the shrewdness of the Masters."

"But what do they want people to know?"

"Only that there's a secret. Otherwise, if everything is as it appears to be, why go on living?"

"And what is the secret?"

"What the revealed religions have been unable to reveal. The secret lies beyond."

33

The visions are white, blue, white, pale red. In the end they mingle and are all pale, the color of the flame of a white candle; you will see sparks, you will feel gooseflesh all over your body. This announces the beginning of the attraction exerted on the one who fulfills the mission.

—Papus, *Martines de Pasqually*, Paris, Chamuel, 1895, p. 92

The promised evening arrived. Agliè picked us up just as he had in Salvador. The tenda where the session, or gira, was to take place was in a fairly central district, if you can speak of a center in a city whose tongues of land stretch through hills and lick the sea. Seen from above, illuminated in the evening, the city looks like a head with patches of alopecia areata.

"Remember, this is an umbanda tonight, not a candomblé. The participants will be possessed not by orixás, but by the eguns, spirits of the departed. And by Exu, the African Hermes you saw in Bahia, and his companion, Pompa Gira. Exu is a Yoruba divinity, a demon inclined to mischief and joking, but there was a trickster god in Amerind mythology, too."

"And who are the departed?"

"Pretos velhos and caboclos. The pretos velhos are old African wise men who guided their people at the time of deportation, like Rei Congo and Pai Agostinho. . . . They are the memory of a milder phase of slavery, when the blacks, no longer animals, became family friends, uncles, grandfathers. The caboclos, on the other hand, are Indian spirits, virgin forces representing the purity of original nature. In the umbanda the African orixás stay in the background, completely syncretized with Catholic saints, and these beings alone intervene. They are the ones who produce the trance. At a certain point in the dance, the medium, the cavalo, is penetrated by a higher being and loses all awareness of self. He continues to dance until the divine being has left him, and he emerges feeling better. Clean, purified."

"Lucky mediums," Amparo said.

"Lucky indeed," Agliè said. "They attain contact with mother earth. These worshipers have been uprooted, flung into the horrible melting pot of the city, and, as Spengler said, at a time of crisis the mercantile West turns once more to the world of the earth."

We arrived. The tenda looked like an ordinary building from the outside. Here, too, you entered through a little garden, more modest than the one in Bahia, and at the door of the barracão, a kind of storehouse, was a little statue of Exu, already surrounded by propitiatory offerings.

Amparo drew me aside as we went in. "I've figured it out," she said. "That tapir at the lecture talked about the Aryan age, remember? And this one talks about the decline of the West. Blut und Boden, blood and earth. It's pure Nazism."

"It's not that simple, darling. This is a different continent."

"Thanks for the news. The Great White Fraternity! You eat your God for dinner."

"It's the Catholics who do that. It's not the same thing."

"It is too. Weren't you listening? Pythagoras, Dante, the Virgin Mary, and the Masons. Always out to screw us. Make umbanda, not love."

"You're the one who's syncretized. Come on, let's have a look. This, too, is culture."

"There's only one culture: strangle the last priest with the entrails of the last Rosicrucian."

Agliè signaled us to go in. If the outside was seedy, the inside was a blaze of violent colors. It was a quadrangular hall, with one area set aside for the dancing of the cavalos. The altar was at the far end, protected by a railing, against which stood the platform for the drums, the atabaques. The ritual space was still empty, but on our side of the railing a heterogeneous crowd was already stirring: believers and the merely curious, blacks and whites, all mixed, some barefoot, others wearing tennis shoes. I was immediately struck by the figures around the altar: pretos velhos, caboclos in multicolored feathers, saints who would have seemed to be marzipan were it not for their Pantagruelian dimensions, Saint George in a shining breastplate and scarlet cloak, saints Cosmas and Damian, a Virgin pierced by swords, and a shamelessly hyperrealist Christ, his arms outstretched like the redeemer of Corcovado, but in color. There were no orixás, but you could sense their presence in the faces of the crowd and in the sweetish odor of cane and cooked foods, in the stench of sweat caused by the heat and by the excitement of the imminent gira.

The pai-de-santo went forward and took a seat near the altar, where he received the faithful, scenting them with dense exhalations of his cigar, blessing them, and offering them a cup of liquor as if in a rapid Eucharistic rite. I knelt and drank with my companions, noticing, as I watched a cambone pour the liquid from a bottle, that it was Dubonnet. No matter. I savored it as if it were an elixir from the Fountain of Youth. On the platform the atabaques were already beating, to brisk blows, as the initiates chanted a propitiatory song to Exu and to Pompa Gira: Seu Tranca Ruas é Mojuba! É Mojuba, é Mojuba! Sete Encruzilhadas é Mojuba! É Mojuba, é Mojuba! Seu Marabōe é Mojuba! Seu Tiriri é Mojuba! Exu Veludo, é Mojuba! A Pompa Gira é Mojuba!

The pai-de-santo began to swing his thurible, releasing a heavy odor of Indian incense, and to chant special orations to Oxalá and Nossa Senhora.

The atabaques beat faster, and the cavalos invaded the space before the altar, beginning to fall under the spell of the pontos. Most were women, and Amparo made sarcastic asides about the sensitivity of her sex.

Among the women were some Europeans. Agliè pointed out a blonde, a German psychologist who had been participating in the rites for years. She had tried everything, but if you are not chosen, it's hopeless: for her, the trance never came, was beyond achieving. Her eyes seemed lost in the void as she danced, and the atabaques gave neither her nerves nor ours any relief. Pungent fumes filled the hall and dazed both worshipers and observers, somehow hitting everybody—me included—in the stomach. But the same thing had happened to me at the escolas de samba in Rio. I knew the psychological power of music and noise, the way they produced Saturday night fevers in discos. The German woman's eyes were wide, and every movement of her hysterical limbs begged for oblivion. The other daughters of the saint went into ecstasy, flung their heads back, wriggled fluidly, navigating a sea of forgetfulness. The German tensed, distraught and almost in tears, like someone desperately struggling to reach orgasm, wriggling and straining, but finding no release.

However much she tried to lose control, she constantly regained it. Poor Teuton, sick from too many well-tempered clavichords.

The elect, meanwhile, were making their leap into the vacuum, their gaze dulled, their limbs stiffened. Their movements became more and more automatic, but not haphazard, because they revealed the nature of the beings taking possession of them: some of the elect seemed soft, their hands moving sideways, palms down, in a swimming motion; others were bent over and moved slowly, and the cambones used white linen cloths to shield them from the crowd's view, for these had been touched by an excellent spirit.

Some of the cavalos shook violently, and those possessed by pretos velhos emitted hollow sounds—hum hum hum—as they moved with their bodies tilted forward, like old men leaning on canes, jaws jutting out in haggard, toothless faces. But those possessed by the caboclos let out shrill warrior cries—hiahou!—and the cambones rushed to assist the ones unable to bear the violence of the gift.

The drums beat, the pontos rose in the air thick with fumes. I was holding Amparo's arm when all of a sudden her hands were sweating, her body trembled, and her lips parted. "I don't feel well," she said. "I want to go."

Agliè noticed what had happened and helped me take her outside. The night air brought her around. "I'm all right," she said. "It must have been something I ate. And the smells, the heat . . ."

"No," said the pai-de-santo, who had followed us. "You have the qualities of a medium. You reacted well to the pontos. I was watching you."

"Stop!" Amparo cried, adding a few words in a language I didn't know. I saw the pai-de-santo turn pale—or gray, as they used to say in adventure stories, where men with black skin turned gray with fear. "That's enough. I got a little sick. I ate something I shouldn't have. . . . Please, go back inside. Just let me get some air. I'd rather be by myself; I'm not an invalid."

We did as she asked, but when I went back inside, after the break in the open air, the smells, the drums, the sweat that now covered every body acted like a shot of alcohol gulped down after a long abstinence. I ran a hand over my brow, and an old man offered me an agogô, a small gilded instrument like a triangle with bells, which you strike with a little bar. "Go up on the platform," he said. "Play. It'll do you good."

There was homeopathic wisdom in that advice. I struck the agogô, trying to fall in with the beat of the drums, and gradually I became part of the event, and, becoming part of it, I controlled it. I found relief by moving my legs and feet, I freed myself from what surrounded me, I challenged it, I embraced it. Later, Agliè was to talk to me about the difference between the man who knows and the man who undergoes.

As the mediums fell into trances, the cambones led them to the sides of the room, sat them down, offered them cigars and pipes. Those of the faithful who had been denied possession ran and knelt at their feet, whispered in their ears, listened to their advice, received their beneficent influence, poured out confessions, and drew comfort from them. Some hovered at the edges of trance, and the cambones gently encouraged them, leading them, now more relaxed, back among the crowd.

In the dancing area many aspirants to ecstasy were still moving. The German woman twitched unnaturally, waiting to be visited—in vain. Others had been taken over by Exu and were making wicked faces, sly, astute, as they moved in jerks.

It was then that I saw Amparo.

Now I know that Hesed is not only the Sefirah of grace and love. As Diotallevi said, it is also the moment of expansion of the divine substance, which spreads out to the edge of infinity. It is the care of the living for the dead, but someone also must have observed that it is the care of the dead for the living.

Striking the agogô, I no longer followed what was happening in the hall, focused as I was on my own control, letting myself be led by the music. Amparo must have come in at least ten minutes before, and surely she had felt the same effect I had experienced earlier. But no one had given her an agogô, and by now she probably wouldn't have wanted one. Called by deep voices, she had stripped herself of all defenses, of all will.

I saw her fling herself into the midst of the dancing, stop, her abnormally tense face looking upward, her neck rigid. Then, oblivious, she launched into a lewd saraband, her hands miming the offer of her own body. "A Pomba Gira, a Pomba Gira!" some shouted, delighted by the miracle, since until then the she-devil had not made her presence known. O seu manto é de veludo, rebordado todo em ouro, o seu garfo é de prata, muito grande é seu tesouri . . . Pomba Gira das Almas, vem toma cho cho . . .

I didn't dare intervene. I may have accelerated the strokes of my little bar, trying to join carnally with my woman, or with the indigenous spirit she now incarnated.

The cambones went to her, had her put on the ritual vestment, and held her up as she came out of her brief but intense trance. They led her to a chair. She was soaked with sweat and breathed with difficulty. She refused to welcome those who rushed over to beg for oracles. Instead, she started crying.

The gira was coming to an end. I left the platform and ran to Amparo. Agliè was already there, delicately massaging her temples.

"How embarrassing!" Amparo said. "I don't believe in it, I didn't want to. How could I have done this?"

"It happens," Agliè said softly, "it happens."

"But then there's no hope," Amparo cried. "I'm still a slave. Go away," she said to me angrily. "I'm a poor dirty black girl. Give me a master; I deserve it!"

"It happens to blond Achaeans, too," Agliè consoled her. "It's human nature. . . ."

Amparo asked the way to the toilet. The rite was ending. The German woman was still dancing, alone in the middle of the hall, ostentatious but now listless. She had followed Amparo's experience with envious eyes.

Amparo came back about ten minutes later, as we were taking our leave of the pai-de-santo, who congratulated us on the splendid success of our first contact with the world of the dead.

Agliè drove in silence through the night. When he stopped outside our house, Amparo said she wanted to go upstairs alone. "Why don't you take a little walk," she said to me. "Come back when I'm asleep. I'll take a pill. Excuse me, both of you. I really must have eaten something I shouldn't have. All those women tonight must have. I hate my country. Good night."

Agliè understood my uneasiness and suggested we go to an all-night bar in Copacabana.

At the bar I didn't speak. Agliè waited until I had started sipping my batida before he broke the silence.

"Race—or culture, if you prefer—is part of our unconscious mind. And in another part of that unconscious dwell archetypes, figures identical for all men and in all centuries. This evening, the atmosphere, the surroundings lulled our vigilance. It happened to all of us; you felt it yourself. Amparo discovered that the orixás, whom she has destroyed in her heart, still live in her womb. You must not think I consider this a positive thing. You have heard me speak respectfully of the supernatural energies that vibrate around us in this country. But I have no special fondness for the practices of possession. An initiate is not the same as a mystic. Being an initiate—having an intuitive comprehension of what reason cannot explain—is a very deep process; it is a slow transformation of the spirit and of the body, and it can lead to the exercise of superior abilities, even to immortality. But it is secret, intimate; it does not show itself externally; it is modest, lucid, detached. That is why the Masters of the World, initiates, do not indulge in mysticism. For them, a mystic is a slave, a site of the manifestation of the numinous, through which site the signs of a secret can be observed. The initiate encourages the mystic and uses him as you might use a telephone, to establish long-distance contact, or as a chemist might use litmus paper, to detect the action of a particular substance. The mystic is useful, because he is conspicuous. He broadcasts himself. Initiates, on the contrary, are recognizable only to one another. It is they who control the forces that mystics undergo. In this sense there is no difference between the possession experienced by the cavalos and the ecstasies of Saint Theresa of Avila or Saint John of the Cross. Mysticism is a degenerate form of contact with the divine, whereas initiation is the fruit of long askesis of mind and heart. Mysticism is a democratic, if not demagogic, phenomenon; initiation is aristocratic."

"It is mental as opposed to carnal?"

"In a sense. Your Amparo was guarding her mind tenaciously, but she was not on guard against her body. The lay person is weaker than we are."

It was late. Agliè informed me that he was leaving Brazil. He gave me his Milan address.

I went home and found Amparo asleep. I lay down beside her in silence, in the dark, and spent a sleepless night. It was as if there were an unknown being next to me.

In the morning Amparo told me that she was going to Petrópolis to visit a girlfriend. We said good-bye awkwardly.

She left with a canvas bag, a volume of political economy under her arm.

For two months she sent me no word, and I made no attempt to seek her out. Then she wrote me a brief, evasive letter, telling me she needed time to think. I didn't answer.

I felt no passion, no jealousy, no nostalgia. I was hollow, clear-headed, clean, and as emotionless as an aluminum pot.

I stayed in Brazil for another year, with the constant feeling that I was on the brink of departure. I didn't see Agliè again, I didn't see any of Amparo's friends. I spent long, long hours on the beach, sunbathing.

I flew kites, which down there are very beautiful.

GEVURAH

34

Beydelus, Demeymes, Adulex, Matucgayn, Atine, Ffex, Uquizuz, Gadix, Sol, Veni cito cum tuis spiritibus.
—*Picatrix*, Sloane Ms. 1305, 152, verso

The Breaking of the Vessels. Diotallevi was to talk to us often about the late cabalism of Isaac Luria, in which the orderly articulation of the Sefirot was lost. Creation, Luria held, was a process of divine inhalation and exhalation, like anxious breathing or the action of a bellows.

"God's asthma," Belbo glossed.

"You try creating from nothing. It's something you do once in your life. God blows the world as you would blow a glass bubble, and to do that He takes a deep breath, holds it, and emits the long luminous hiss of the ten Sefirot."

"A hiss of light?"

"God hissed, and there was light."

"Multimedia."

"But the lights of the Sefirot must be gathered in vessels that can contain their splendor without shattering. The vessels destined to receive Keter, Hokhmah, and Binah withstood their magnificence, but for the lower Sefirot, from Hesed to Yesod, light was exhaled too strongly in a single burst, and the vessels broke. Fragments of light were spilled into the universe, and gross matter was thus born."

The breaking of the vessels was a catastrophe, Diotallevi said. What could be more unbearable than an aborted world? There must have been some defect in the cosmos from the beginning, and not even the most learned rabbis had been able to explain it completely. Perhaps at the moment God exhaled and was emptied, a few drops of oil lay in the first receptacle, a material residue, the reshimu, thus adulterating God's essence. Or perhaps the seashells—the qelippot, the beginnings of ruin—were slyly waiting in ambush somewhere.

"Slippery folk, those qelippot," Belbo said. "Agents of the diabolical Dr. Fu Manchu. And then what happened?"

And then, Diotallevi patiently explained, in the light of Severe Judgment, or Gevurah—also known as Pachad, or Terror—the Sefirah in which, according to Isaac the Blind, Evil first shows itself, the seashells acquired a real existence.

"Then the seashells are in our midst," Belbo said.

"Just look around you," Diotallevi said.

"But is there no way out?"

"There's a way back in, actually," Diotallevi said. "All emanates from God, in the contraction of simsum. The problem is to bring about tikkun, the restoration of Adam Qadmon. Then we will rebuild everything in the balanced structure of the parzufim, the faces— or, rather, forms—that will take the place of the Sefirot. The ascension of the soul is like a cord of silk that enables devout intention, groping in the darkness, to find the path to the light. And so the world constantly strives, by combining the letters of the Torah, to regain its natural form, to emerge from its horrible confusion."

And this is what I am doing now, in the middle of the night, in the unnatural calm of these hills. The other evening in the periscope, however, I was still mired in the slime of the seashells I felt all around me, of the slugs trapped in the crystal cases of the Conservatoire, among the barometers and rusted clockworks, in deaf hibernation. I thought then that if there had been a breaking of the vessels, the first crack probably appeared that evening in Rio, during the rite, but it was on my return to my native country that the shattering occurred. It happened slowly, soundlessly, so that we all found ourselves caught in the morass of gross matter, where noxious vermin emerge by spontaneous generation.

When I returned from Brazil, I hardly knew who I was anymore. I was approaching thirty. At that age, my father was a father; he knew who he was and where he lived.

I had been too far from my country while prodigious things were happening. I had lived in a world swollen with the incredible, where events in Italy wore a halo of legend. Shortly before leaving the other hemisphere—it was near the end of my stay and I was treating myself to an airplane ride over the forests of Amazonia—I picked up a local newspaper during a stopover in Fortaleza. On the front page was a prominent photograph of someone I recognized: I had seen him sipping white wine at Pilade's for years. The caption read: "O homem que matou Moro."

When I got back, I found out that, of course, he wasn't the man who killed Moro. Handed a loaded pistol, he would have shot himself in the ear when checking to see if it worked. What had happened was simply that an antiterrorist squad had burst in on him and found three pistols and two packs of explosives hidden under the bed. He was lying on the bed, since it was the only piece of furniture in that one-room apartment, whose rent was shared by a group of survivors of '68 who used it as a place to satisfy the demands of the flesh. If its sole decoration hadn't been a poster of Che, the place could have been taken for any bachelor's pied-à-terre. But one of the tenants belonged to an armed group, and the others had no idea that they were financing the group's safe house. They all ended up in jail for a year.

I understood very little of what had happened in Italy over the past few years. The country had been on the brink of great changes when I left—left guiltily, feeling almost that I was running away at the moment of the settling of scores. Before I left, I could tell a man's ideology just by the tone of his voice. I was back and now could not figure out who was on whose side. No one was talking about revolution; the new thing was the unconscious. People who claimed to be leftists quoted Nietzsche and Céline, while right-wing magazines hailed revolution in the Third World.

I went back to Pilade's, but I felt I was on foreign soil. The billiard table was still there, and more or less the same painters, but the young fauna had changed. I learned that some of the old customers had opened schools of transcendental meditation or macrobiotic restaurants. Apparently nobody had thought of a tenda de umbanda yet. Maybe I was ahead of the times.

To appease the historic hard core, Pilade still had one of those old-fashioned pinball machines, the kind that now seemed copied from a Lichtenstein painting and were bought up wholesale by antique dealers. Next to it, however, the younger customers crowded around other machines, machines with fluorescent screens on which stylized hawks or kamikazes from Planet X hovered, or frogs jumped around grunting in Japanese. Pilade's was an arcade of sinister flashing lights, and couriers from the Red Brigades on recruiting missions may well have been taking their turn at the Space Invaders screen. But they couldn't play the pinball; you can't play pinball with a pistol stuck in your belt.

I realized this one night when I followed Belbo's gaze and saw Lorenza Pellegrini at the machine. Or, rather, when I later read one of his files. Lorenza isn't named, but it's obviously about her. She was the only one who played pinball like that.

FILENAME: Pinball

You don't play pinball with just your hands, you play it with the groin too. The pinball problem is not to stop the ball before it's swallowed by the mouth at the bottom, or to kick it back to midfield like a halfback. The problem is to make it stay up where the lighted targets are more numerous and have it bounce from one to another, wandering, confused, delirious, but still a free agent. And you achieve this not by jolting the ball but by transmitting vibrations to the case, the frame, but gently, so the machine won't catch on and say Tilt. You can only do it with the groin, or with a play of the hips that makes the groin not so much bump, as slither, keeping you on this side of an orgasm. And if the hips move according to nature, it's the buttocks that supply the forward thrust, but gracefully, so that when the thrust reaches the pelvic area, it is softened, as in homeopathy, where the more you shake a solution and the more the drug dissolves in the water added gradually, until the drug has almost entirely disappeared, the more medically effective and potent it is. Thus from the groin an infinitesimal pulse is transmitted to the case, and the machine obeys, the ball moves against nature, against inertia, against gravity, against the laws of dynamics, and against the cleverness of its constructor, who wanted it disobedient. The ball is intoxicated with vis movendi, remaining in play for memorable and immemorial lengths of time. But a female groin is required, one that interposes no spongy body between the ileum and the machine, and there must be no erectile matter in between, only skin, nerves, padded bone sheathed in a pair of jeans, and a sublimated erotic fury, a sly frigidity, a disinterested adaptability to the partner's response, a taste for arousing desire without suffering the excess of one's own: the Amazon must drive the pinball crazy and savor the thought that she will then abandon it.

That, I believe, was when Belbo fell in love with Lorenza Pellegrini: when he realized that she could promise him an unattainable happiness. But I also believe it was through her that he began to be aware of the erotic nature of automated universes, the machine as metaphor of the cosmic body, the mechanical game as talismanic evocation. He was already hooked on Abulafia and perhaps had entered, even then, into the spirit of Project Hermes. Certainly he had seen the Pendulum. Somehow, Lorenza Pellegrini held out the promise of the Pendulum.

I had trouble readjusting to Pilade's. Little by little, but not every evening, in the forest of alien faces, I was rediscovering familiar ones, the faces of survivors, though they were blurred by my effort of recognition. This one was a copywriter in an advertising agency; this one, a tax consultant; and this one sold books on the installment plan—in the old days he peddled the works of Che, but now he was offering herbals, Buddhism, astrology. They had gained a little weight and some gray in their hair, but I felt that the Scotch-on-the-rocks in their hands was the same one they had held ten years ago. They were sipping slowly, one drop every six months.

"What are you up to? Why don't you come by and see us?" one of them asked me.

"Who's *us* nowadays?"

He looked at me as if I'd been away for a century. "The Cultural Commission at City Hall, of course."

I had skipped too many beats.

I decided to invent a job for myself. I knew a lot of things, unconnected things, but I would be able to connect them after a few hours at a library. I once thought it was necessary to have a theory, and that my problem was that I didn't. But nowadays all you needed was information; everybody was greedy for information, especially if it was out of date. I dropped in at the university, to see if I could fit in somewhere. The lecture halls were quiet; the students glided along the corridors like ghosts, lending one another badly made bibliographies. I knew how to make a good bibliography.

One day, a doctoral candidate, mistaking me for faculty (the teachers now were the same age as the students, or vice versa), asked me what this Lord Chandos they were talking about in an economics course on cyclical crises had written. I told him Chandos was a character in Hofmannsthal, not an economist.

That same evening I was at a party with old friends and recognized a man who worked for a publisher. He had joined the staff after the firm had switched from novels by French collaborationists to Albanian political texts. They were still publishing political books, but with government backing. And they didn't reject an occasional good work in philosophy—provided it was in the classical line, he added.

"By the way," he said to me then, "since you're a philosopher—"

"Thanks, but unfortunately I'm not."

"Come on, in your day you knew everything. I was just looking over the translation of a book on the crisis of Marxism, and I came across a quotation from Anselm of Canterbury. Who's he? I couldn't even find him in the *Dictionary of Authors*." I told him it was Anselmo d'Aosta, and that only the English, who had to be different from everybody else, called him Anselm of Canterbury.

A sudden illumination: I had a trade after all. I would set up a cultural investigation agency, be a kind of private eye of learning.

Instead of sticking my nose into all-night dives and cathouses, I would skulk around bookshops, libraries, corridors of university departments. Then I'd sit in my office, my feet propped on the desk, drinking, from a Dixie cup, the whiskey I'd brought up from the corner store in a paper bag. The phone rings and a man says: "Listen, I'm translating this book and came across something or someone called Motakallimûn. What the hell is it?"

Give me two days, I tell him. Then I go to the library, flip through some card catalogs, give the man in the reference office a cigarette, and pick up a clue.

That evening I invite an instructor in Islamic studies out for a drink. I buy him a couple of beers and he drops his guard, gives me the lowdown for nothing. I call the client back. "All right, the Motakallimûn were radical Moslem theologians at the time of Avicenna. They said the world was a sort of dust cloud of accidents that formed particular shapes only by an instantaneous and temporary act of the divine will. If God was distracted for even a moment, the universe would fall to pieces, into a meaningless anarchy of atoms.

That enough for you? The job took me three days. Pay what you think is fair."

I was lucky enough to find two rooms and a little kitchen in an old building in the suburbs. It must have been a factory once, with a wing for offices. All the apartments that had been made from it opened onto one long corridor. I was between a real estate agent and a taxidermist's laboratory (A. Salon, the sign said). It was like being in an American skyscraper of the thirties; if I'd had a glass door, I'd have felt like Marlowe. I put a sofa bed in the back room and made the front one an office. In a pair of bookcases I arranged the atlases, encyclopedias, catalogs I acquired bit by bit. In the beginning, I had to turn a deaf ear to my conscience and write theses for desperate students. It wasn't hard: I just went and copied some from the previous decade. But then my friends in publishing began sending me manuscripts and foreign books to read—naturally, the least appealing and for little money.

Still, I was accumulating experience and information, and I never threw anything away. I kept files on everything. I didn't think to use a computer (they were coming on the market just then; Belbo was to be a pioneer). Instead, I had cross-referenced index cards. Nebulae, Laplace; Laplace, Kant; Kant, Königsberg, the seven bridges of Königsberg, theorems of topology . . . It was a little like that game where you have to go from sausage to Plato in five steps, by association of ideas. Let's see: sausage, pig bristle, paintbrush, Mannerism, Idea, Plato. Easy. Even the sloppiest manuscript would bring twenty new cards for my hoard. I had a strict rule, which I think secret services follow, too: No piece of information is superior to any other. Power lies in having them all on file and then finding the connections. There are always connections; you have only to want to find them.

After about two years in business, I was pleased with myself. I was having fun. Meanwhile I had met Lia.

35

Sappia qualunque il mio nome dimanda
ch'i' mi son Lia, e vo movendo intorno
le belle mani a farmi una ghirlanda.
                —Dante, *Purgatorio*, XXVII, 100–102

Lia. Now, I despair of seeing her again, but I might never have met her, and that would have been worse. I wish she were here, to hold my hand while I reconstruct the stages of my undoing. Because she told me so. But no, she must remain outside this business, she and the child. I hope they put off their return, that they come back when everything is finished, however it may finish.

It was July 16, 1981. Milan was emptying; the reference room of the library was almost deserted.

"Hey, I need volume 109 myself."

"Then why did you leave it here?"

"I just went back to my seat for a minute to check a note."

"That's no excuse."

She took the volume stubbornly and went to her table. I sat down across from her, trying to get a better look at her face.

"How can you read it like that, unless it's in Braille?" I asked.

She raised her head, and I really couldn't tell whether I was looking at her face or the nape of her neck. "What?" she asked. "Oh. I can see through it all right." But she lifted her hair as she spoke, and she had green eyes.

"You have green eyes."

"Of course I do. Is that bad?"

"No. There should be more eyes like that."

That's how it began.

"Eat. You're thin as a rail," she said to me at supper. At midnight we were still in the Greek restaurant near Pilade's, the candle guttering in the neck of the bottle as we told each other everything. We did almost the same work: she checked encyclopedia entries.

I felt I had to tell her. At twelve-thirty, when she pulled her hair aside to see me better, I aimed a forefinger at her, thumb raised, and went: "Pow."

"Me too," she said.

That night we became flesh of one flesh, and from then on she called me Pow.

We couldn't afford a new house. I slept at her place, and sometimes she stayed with me at the office, or went off investigating, because she was smarter than I when it came to following up clues. She was good, also, at suggesting connections.

"We seem to have a half-empty file on the Rosicrucians," she said.

"I should go back to it one of these days. They're notes I took in Brazil. . . ."

"Well, put in a cross reference to Yeats."

"What's Yeats got to do with it?"

"Plenty. I see here that he belonged to a Rosicrucian society that was called Stella Matutina."

"What would I do without you?"

I resumed going to Pilade's, because it was like a marketplace where I could find customers.

One evening I saw Belbo again. He must have been coming rarely in the past few years, but he showed up regularly after meeting Lorenza Pellegrini. He looked the same, maybe a bit grayer, maybe slightly thinner.

It was a cordial meeting, given the limits of his expansiveness: a few remarks about the old days, sober reticence about our complicity in that last event and its epistolary sequel. Inspector De Angelis hadn't been heard from again. Case closed? Who could say?

I told him about my work, and he seemed interested. "Just the kind of thing I'd like to do: the Sam Spade of culture. Twenty bucks a day and expenses."

"Except that no fascinating, mysterious women have dropped in on me, and nobody ever comes to talk about the Maltese falcon," I said.

"You never can tell. Are you enjoying yourself?"

"Enjoying myself?" I asked. I quoted him: "It's the only thing I seem to be able to do well."

"Bon pour vous," he said.

We saw each other again after that, and I told him about my Brazilian experience, but he seemed more absent than usual. When Lorenza Pellegrini wasn't there, he kept his eyes glued to the door, and when she was, he glanced nervously along the bar, following her every move. One night near closing time, he said, without looking at me, "Listen, we might be able to use your services, but not for a single consultation. Could you give us, say, a few afternoons each week?"

"We can discuss it. What does it involve?"

"A steel company has commissioned a book about metals. Something with a lot of illustrations. Serious, but for the mass market. You know the sort of thing: metals in history, from the Iron Age to spaceships. We need somebody who'll dig around in libraries and archives and find beautiful illustrations, old miniatures, engravings from nineteenth-century volumes on smelting, for instance, or lightning rods."

"All right. I'll drop by tomorrow."

Lorenza Pellegrini came over to him. "Would you take me home?"

"Why me?" Belbo asked.

"Because you're the man of my dreams."

He blushed, as only he could blush, and looked away. "There's a witness," he said. And to me: "I'm the man of her dreams. This is Lorenza."

"Ciao."

"Ciao."

He got up, whispered something in her ear.

She shook her head. "I asked for a ride home, that's all."

"Ah," he said. "Excuse me, Casaubon, I have to play chauffeur to the woman of someone else's dreams."

"Idiot," she said to him tenderly, and kissed him on the cheek.

36

Yet one caution let me give by the way to my present or future reader, who is actually melancholy—that he read not the symptomes or prognosticks of the following tract, lest, by applying that which he reads to himself, aggravating, appropriating things generally spoken, to his own person (as melancholy men for the most part do), he trouble or hurt himself, and get, in conclusion, more harm than good. I advise them therefore warily to peruse that tract.

—Robert Burton, *The Anatomy of Melancholy*, Oxford, 1621, Introduction

It was obvious that there was something between Belbo and Lorenza Pellegrini. I didn't know exactly what it was or how long it had been going on. Abulafia's files did not help me to reconstruct the story.

There is no date, for example, on the file about the dinner with Dr. Wagner. Belbo knew Dr. Wagner before my departure, and may well have been in contact with him after I started working at Garamond, which was when, in fact, I got to know him myself. So the dinner could have been before or after the evening I have in mind. If it was before, then I understand Belbo's embarrassment, his solemn desperation.

Dr. Wagner—an Austrian who for years had been practicing in Paris (hence the pronunciation "Vagnère" for those who wanted to boast of their familiarity with him)—had been coming to Milan regularly for about ten years, at the invitation of two revolutionary groups of the post-'68 period. They fought over him, and of course each group gave a radically different interpretation of his thought. How and why this famous man allowed himself to be sponsored by extremists, I never understood. Wagner's theories had no political color, so to speak, and, had he wanted, he could easily have been invited by the universities, the clinics, the academies. I believe he accepted the invitations because he was basically an epicurean and required regal expense accounts. The private hosts could raise more money than the institutions, and for Dr. Wagner this meant first-class tickets, luxury hotels, plus fees in keeping with his therapist rates, for the lectures and seminars.

Why the two groups found ideological inspiration in Wagner's theories was another story. But in those days Wagner's brand of psychoanalysis seemed sufficiently deconstructive, diagonal, libidinal, and non-Cartesian to provide some theoretical justification for revolutionary activity.

It proved difficult to get the workers to swallow it, so at a certain point the two groups had to choose between the workers and Wagner. They chose Wagner. Which gave rise to the theory that the new revolutionary protagonist was not the proletarian but the deviate.

"Instead of deviating the proletariat, they would do better to proletarianize the deviates, which would be more economical, considering Dr. Wagner's prices," Belbo said to me one day.

The Wagnerian revolution was the most expensive in history.

Garamond, subsidized by a university psychology department, had published a translation of Wagner's minor essays—very technical, nearly impossible to find, and therefore in great demand among the faithful. Wagner had come to Milan for a publicity launch, and that was when his acquaintance with Belbo began.

FILENAME: Doktor Wagner

The diabolical Doktor Wagner
Twenty-sixth installment

Who, on that gray morning of

During the discussion I raised an objection. The satanic old man must have been irritated, but he didn't let it show. On the contrary, he replied as if he wanted to seduce me.

Like Charlus with Jupien, bee and flower. A genius can't bear not being loved; he must immediately seduce the dissenter, make the dissenter love him. He succeeded. I loved him.

But he must not have forgiven me, because that evening of the divorce he dealt me a mortal blow. Unconsciously, instinctively, not thinking, he seduced me, and unconsciously, he punished me. Though it cost him deontologically, he psychoanalyzed me free. The unconscious bites even its handlers.

Story of the Marquis de Lantenac in *Quatre-vingt-treize*. The ship of the Vendéeiens is sailing through a storm off the Breton coast. Suddenly a cannon slips its moorings, and as the ship

230

pitches and rolls it begins a mad race from rail to rail, an immense beast smashing larboard and starboard. A cannoneer (alas, the very one whose negligence had left the cannon improperly secured) seizes a chain and with unparalleled courage flings himself at the monster, which nearly crushes him, but he stops it, bolts it fast, leads it back to its stall, saving the ship, the crew, the mission. With sublime liturgy, the fearsome Lantenac musters all the men on deck, praises the cannoneer's heroism, takes an impressive medal from around his own neck and puts it on the man, embraces him, and the crew makes the welkin ring with its hurrahs.

Then stern Lantenac, reminding the honored sailor that he was responsible for the danger in the first place, orders him to be shot.

Splendid, just Lantenac, man of virtue, above corruption. And this is what Dr. Wagner did for me: he honored me with his friendship, and executed me with the truth.

and executed me, revealing to me what I desired

revealing to me that the thing that I desired, I feared.

Begin the story in a bar. The need to fall in love.

Some things you can feel coming. You don't fall in love because you fall in love; you fall in love because of the need, desperate, to fall in love. When you feel that need, you have to watch your step: like having drunk a philter, the kind that makes you fall in love with the first thing you meet. It could be a duck-billed platypus.

Because at that time I felt the need. I had just given up drinking. Relationship between the liver and the heart. A new love is a good reason for going back to drink. Somebody to go to a bar with. Feel good with.

The bar is brief, furtive. It allows you a long, sweet expectation through the day, then you go and hide in the shadows among the leather chairs; at six in the evening there's nobody there, the sordid clientele comes later, with the piano man. Choose a louche American bar empty in the late afternoon. The waiter comes only if you call him three times, and he has the next martini ready.

It has to be a martini. Not whiskey, a martini. The liquid is clear. You raise your glass and you see her over the olive. The difference between looking at your beloved through a dry martini straight up, where the glass is small, thin, and looking at her through a martini on the rocks, through thick glass, and her face broken by the transparent cubism of the ice. The effect is doubled if you each press your glass to your forehead, feeling the chill, and lean close until the glasses touch. Forehead to forehead with two glasses in between. You can't do that with martini glasses.

The brief hour of the bar. Afterward, trembling, you await another day. Free of the blackmail of certainty.

He who falls in love in bars doesn't need a woman all his own. He can always find one on loan.

His role. He allowed her great freedom, he was always traveling. His suspect generosity: I could telephone even at midnight. He was there, you weren't. He said you were out. Actually, while I have you on the line, do you have any idea where she is? The only moments of jealousy. But still, in that way I was taking Cecilia from the sax player. To love, or believe you love, as an eternal priest of an ancient vengeance.

With Sandra, things were complicated. That time she decided I was too involved. Our life as a couple had become strained. Should we break up? Let's break up, then. No, wait, let's talk it over. No, we can't go on like this. The problem, in a nutshell, was Sandra.

When you hang out in bars, the drama of love isn't the women you find but the women you leave.

Then comes the dinner with Dr. Wagner. At the lecture he had just given a heckler a definition of psychoanalysis. La psychanalyse? C'est qu'entre l'homme et la femme . . . chers amis . . . ça ne colle pas.

There was discussion: the couple, divorce as a legal fiction. Taken up by my own problems, I participated intensely. We allowed ourselves to be drawn into dialectical exchanges, speaking while Wagner was silent, forgetting there was an oracle in our presence. And it was with a pensive

and it was with a sly expression

and it was with melancholy detachment

and it was as if he entered our conversation playfully, off the subject, he said (I remember his exact words; they are carved on my mind): In professional life not once have I had a patient made neurotic by his own divorce. The cause of the trouble was always the divorce of the Other.

Dr. Wagner always said Other with a capital O. I gave a start, as if bitten by an asp.

the viscount started, as if bitten by an asp

a cold sweat beaded his brow

the baron peered at him through the lazy whorls of smoke from
his thin Russian cigarette

Are you saying, I asked, that a person has a breakdown not
because he is divorced but on account of the divorce, which may
or may not happen, of the third party, that is, of the one who
created the crisis for the couple of which he is a member?

Wagner looked at me with the puzzlement of a layman who
encounters a mentally disturbed person for the first time. He
asked me what I meant. To tell the truth, whatever I meant, I
had expressed it badly. I tried to be more concrete. I took a
spoon from the table and put it next to a fork. Here, this is me,
Spoon, married to her, Fork. And here is another couple: she's
Fruit Knife, married to Steak Knife, alias Mackie Messer. Now
I, Spoon, believe I'm suffering because I have to leave Fork and
I don't want to; I love Fruit Knife, but it's all right with me if
she stays with Steak Knife. And now you're telling me, Dr.
Wagner, that the real reason I'm suffering is that Fruit Knife
won't leave Steak Knife. Is that it?

Wagner told someone else at the table that he had said nothing of the sort.

What do you mean, you didn't say it? You said that not once
had you come across anyone made neurotic by his own divorce,
it was always the divorce of the Other.

That may be, I don't remember, Wagner said then, bored.

If you did say it, did you mean what I understood you to
mean?

Wagner was silent for a few moments.

While the others waited, not even swallowing, Wagner signaled for his wineglass to be filled. He looked carefully at the
liquid against the light and finally spoke.

What you understood was what you wanted to understand.

Then he looked away, said it was hot, hummed an aria, moved
a breadstick as if he were conducting an orchestra, yawned, concentrated on a cake with whipped cream, and finally, after another silence, asked to be taken back to his hotel.

The others looked at me as if I had ruined a symposium from
which Words of Wisdom might have come.

The truth is that I had heard Truth speak.

I telephoned. You were at home, and with the Other. I spent
a sleepless night. It was all clear: I couldn't bear your being with
him. Sandra had nothing to do with it.

233

Six dramatic months followed, in which I clung to you, breathed down your neck, trying to undermine your couplehood, telling you I wanted you for myself, convincing you that you hated the Other. You began quarreling with him, and he grew jealous, demanding; he never went out in the evening, and when he was traveling he called twice a day, in the middle of the night, and one night he slapped you. You asked me for money so you could run away. I collected the little I had in the bank. You abandoned the conjugal bed, went off to the mountains with friends, no forwarding address. The Other telephoned me in despair, asked if I knew where you were; I didn't know, but it looked as if I were lying, because you had told him you were leaving him for me.

When you returned, you announced, radiant, that you had written him a letter of farewell. I wondered then what would happen with me and Sandra, but you didn't give me time to worry, you told me you had met this man with a scar on his cheek and a very gypsy apartment. You were going to live with him.

Don't you love me anymore?

Of course I do, you're the only man in my life, but after everything that's happened I need to have this experience, don't be childish, try to understand. After all, I left my husband for you. Let people follow their tempo.

Their tempo? You're telling me you're going off with another man.

You're an intellectual and a leftist. Don't act like a mafioso. I'll see you soon.

I owe everything to Dr. Wagner.

37

Whoever reflects on four things, it were better he had never been born: that which is above, that which is below, that which is before, and that which is after.
—Talmud, Hagigah 2.1

I showed up at Garamond the morning they were installing Abulafia, as Belbo and Diotallevi were lost in a diatribe about the names of God, and Gudrun suspiciously watched the men who were introducing this new, disturbing presence among the increasingly dusty piles of manuscripts.

"Sit down, Casaubon. Here are the plans for our history of metals." We were left alone, and Belbo showed me indexes, chapter outlines, suggested layouts. I was to read the texts and find illustrations. I mentioned several Milan libraries that seemed promising sources.

"That won't be enough," Belbo said. "You'll have to visit other places, too. The science museum in Munich, for instance, has a splendid photographic archive. In Paris there's the Conservatoire des Arts et Métiers. I'd go back there myself, if I had time."

"Interesting?"

"Disturbing. The triumph of the machine, housed in a Gothic church . . ." He hesitated, realigned some papers on his desk. Then, as if afraid of giving too much importance to the statement, he said, "And there's the Pendulum."

"What pendulum?"

"The Pendulum. Foucault's Pendulum."

And he described it to me, just as I saw it two days ago, Saturday. Maybe I saw it the way I saw it because Belbo had prepared me for the sight. But at that time I must not have shown much enthusiasm, because Belbo looked at me as if I were a man who, seeing the Sistine Chapel, asks: Is this all?

"It may be the atmosphere—that it's in a church—but, believe me, you feel a very strong sensation. The idea that everything else

is in motion and up above is the only fixed point in the universe
. . . For those who have no faith, it's a way of finding God again,
and without challenging their unbelief, because it is a null pole. It
can be very comforting for people of my generation, who ate disappointment for breakfast, lunch, and dinner."

"My generation ate even more disappointment."

"Don't brag. Anyway, you're wrong. For you it was just a phase.
You sang the 'Carmagnole,' and then you all met in the Vendée.
For us it was different. First there was Fascism, and even if we were
kids and saw it as an adventure story, our nation's immortal destiny
was a fixed point. The next fixed point was the Resistance, especially for people like me, who observed it from the outside and
turned it into a rite of passage, the return of spring—like an equi-
nox or a solstice; I always get them mixed up. . . . For some, the
next thing was God; for some, the working class; and for many,
both. Intellectuals felt good contemplating the handsome worker,
healthy, strong, ready to remake the world. And now, as you've
seen for yourself, workers exist, but not the working class. Perhaps
it was killed in Hungary. Then came your generation. For you personally, what happened was natural; it probably seemed like a hol-
iday. But not for those my age. For us, it was a settling of scores,
a time of remorse, repentance, regeneration. We had failed, and you
were arriving with your enthusiasm, courage, self-criticism. Bringing hope to us, who by then were thirty-five or forty, hope and
humiliation, but still hope. We had to be like you, even at the price
of starting over from the beginning. We stopped wearing ties, we
threw away our trench coats and bought secondhand duffle coats.
Some quit their jobs rather than serve the Establishment. . . ."

He lit a cigarette and pretended that he had only been pretending
bitterness. An apology for letting himself go.

"And then you gave it all up. We, with our penitential pilgrimages to Buchenwald, refused to write advertising copy for Coca-
Cola because we were antifascists. We were content to work for
peanuts at Garamond, because at least books were for the people.
But you, to avenge yourselves on the bourgeoisie you hadn't managed to overthrow, sold them videocassettes and fanzines, brainwashed them with Zen and the art of motorcycle maintenance. You've
made us buy, at a discount, your copies of the thoughts of Chairman Mao, and used the money to purchase fireworks for the cele-

bration of the new creativity. Shamelessly. While we spent our lives being ashamed. You tricked us, you didn't represent purity; it was only adolescent acne. You made us feel like worms because we lacked the courage to face the Bolivian militia, and you started shooting a few poor bastards in the back while they were walking down the street. Ten years ago, we had to lie to get you out of jail; you lied to send your friends *to* jail. That's why I like this machine: it's stupid, it doesn't believe, it doesn't make me believe, it just does what I tell it. Stupid me, stupid machine. An honest relationship."

"But I—"

"You're innocent, Casaubon. You ran away instead of throwing stones, you got your degree, you didn't shoot anybody. Yet a few years ago I felt you, too, were blackmailing me. Nothing personal, just generational cycles. And then last year, when I saw the Pendulum, I understood everything."

"Everything?"

"Almost everything. You see, Casaubon, even the Pendulum is a false prophet. You look at it, you think it's the only fixed point in the cosmos, but if you detach it from the ceiling of the Conservatoire and hang it in a brothel, it works just the same. And there are other pendulums: there's one in New York, in the UN building, there's one in the science museum in San Francisco, and God knows how many others. Wherever you put it, Foucault's Pendulum swings from a motionless point while the earth rotates beneath it. Every point of the universe is a fixed point: all you have to do is hang the Pendulum from it."

"God is everywhere?"

"In a sense, yes. That's why the Pendulum disturbs me. It promises the infinite, but where to put the infinite is left to me. So it isn't enough to worship the Pendulum; you still have to make a decision, you have to find the best point for it. And yet . . ."

"And yet?"

"And yet . . . You're not taking me seriously by any chance, are you, Casaubon? No, I can rest easy; we're not the type to take things seriously. . . . Well, as I was saying, the feeling you have is that you've spent a lifetime hanging the Pendulum in many places, and it's never worked, but there, in the Conservatoire, it works. . . . Do you think there are special places in the universe? On the ceiling of this room, for example? No, nobody would believe that.

You need atmosphere. I don't know, maybe we're always looking for the right place, maybe it's within reach, but we don't recognize it. Maybe, to recognize it, we have to believe in it. Well, let's go see Signor Garamond."

"To hang the Pendulum?"

"Ah, human folly! Now we have to be serious. If you're going to be paid, the boss must see you, touch you, sniff you, and say you'll do. Come and let the boss touch you; the boss's touch heals scrofula."

38

We walked along the corridor, climbed three steps, went through a frosted-glass door, and abruptly entered another universe. The rooms I had seen so far were dark, dusty, with peeling paint, but this looked like a VIP lounge at an airport. Soft music, a plush waiting room with designer furniture, pale-blue walls decorated with photographs showing gentlemen who looked like Members of Parliament presenting Winged Victories to gentlemen who looked like senators. On a coffee table, as in a dentist's office, were slick magazines, in casual disarray, with titles like *Literature and Wit*, *The Poetic Athanor*, *The Rose and the Thorn*, *The Italic Parnassus*, *Free Verse*. I had never seen any of them before, and I later found out why: they were distributed only to Manutius clients.

At first I thought these were the offices of the Garamond directors, but I soon learned otherwise. This was another publishing firm entirely. The Garamond lobby had a little glass case, dusty and clouded, displaying the latest publications, but the books were unassuming, with uncut pages and sober gray covers imitating French university publications. The paper was the kind that turned yellow in a few years, giving the impression that the author, no matter how young, had been publishing for a long time. But here the glass case, lighted inside, displayed Manutius books, some of them opened to reveal bright pages. They had gleaming white covers sheathed in elegant transparent plastic, with handsome rice paper and clean print.

Whereas the Garamond catalog contained such scholarly series as Humanist Studies and Philosophia, the Manutius series were delicately, poetically named: The Flower Unplucked (poetry), Terra Incognita (fiction), The Hour of the Oleander (including *Diary of a*

Young Girl's Illness), Easter Island (assorted nonfiction, I believe), New Atlantis (the most recent release being *Königsberg Revisited: Prolegomena to Any Future Metaphysics Presented as Both a Transcendental System and a Science of the Phenomenal Noumenon*). On every cover there was the firm's logo: a pelican under a palm tree, with the D'Annunzian motto "I have what I have given."

Belbo had been laconic: Signor Garamond owned two publishing houses. In the days that followed, I realized that the passageway between Garamond and Manutius was private and secret. The official entrance to Manutius Press was on Via Marchese Gualdi, the street in which the purulent world of Via Sincero Renato ceded to spotless façades, spacious sidewalks, lobbies with aluminum elevators. No one could have suspected that an apartment in an old Via Sincero Renato building might be joined, by a mere three steps, to a building on Via Marchese Gualdi. To obtain permission for this, Signor Garamond must have had to perform feats of persuasion. I believe he had help from one of his authors, an official in the City Planning Bureau.

We were received promptly by Signora Grazia, bland and matronly, her designer scarf and suit the exact color of the walls. With a guarded smile she showed us into an office that recalled Mussolini's.

The room was not so immense, but it suggested that hall in the Palazzo Venezia. Here, too, there was a globe near the door, and at the far end the mahogany desk of Signor Garamond, who seemed to be looking at us through reversed binoculars. He motioned us to approach, and I felt intimidated. Later, when De Gubernatis came in, Garamond got up and went to greet him, an act of cordiality that enhanced even more the publisher's importance. The visitor first watches him cross the room, then crosses it himself, arm in arm with his host, and as if by magic the space is doubled.

Garamond waved us to seats opposite his desk. He was brusque but friendly: "Dr. Belbo speaks highly of you, Dr. Casaubon. We need good men. You realize, of course, we're not putting you on the staff. Can't afford it. But you'll be well paid for your efforts. For your devotion, if I may say so, because I consider our work a mission."

He mentioned a flat fee based on estimated hours of work; it seemed reasonable for those times. I accepted.

"Excellent, Casaubon." Now that I was an employee, the title disappeared. "This history of metals," he went on, "must be splendid—more, a thing of beauty. Popular, but scholarly, too. It must catch the reader's imagination. An example. Here in the first draft there is mention of these spheres—what were they called? Yes, the Magdeburg hemispheres. Two hemispheres which, when put together and the air is pumped out, create a pneumatic vacuum inside. Teams of draft horses are hitched to them and they pull in opposite directions. The horses can't separate the hemispheres. This is scientific information. But it's special, it's picturesque. You must single it out from all the other information, then find the right image—a fresco, an oil, whatever—and we'll give it a full page, in color."

"There's an engraving I know of," I said.

"You see? Bravo! A whole page. Full color."

"Since it's an engraving, it'll have to be in black and white," I said.

"Really? Fine, black and white it is. Accuracy above all. But against a gold background. It has to strike the reader, make him feel he's there on the day the experiment was carried out. See what I mean? Science, realism, passion. With science you can grab the reader by the throat. What could be more dramatic than Madame Curie coming home one evening and seeing that phosphorescent glow in the dark? Oh, my goodness, whatever can that be? Hydrocarbon, golconda, phlogiston, whatever the hell they called it, and voilà, Marie Curie invents X rays. Dramatize! But with absolute respect for the truth."

"What connection do X rays have with metals?" I asked.

"Isn't radium a metal?"

"Yes."

"Well then. The entire body of knowledge can be viewed from the standpoint of metals. What did we decide to call the book, Belbo?"

"We were thinking of something sober, like *Metals*."

"Yes, it has to be sober. But with that extra hook, that little detail that tells the whole story. Let's see . . . *Metals: A World History*. Are there Chinese in it, too?"

"Yes."

"World, then. Not an advertising gimmick: it's the truth. Wait, I know: *The Wonderful Adventure of Metals*."

It was at that moment Signora Grazia announced the arrival of Commendatore De Gubernatis. Signor Garamond hesitated, gave me a dubious look. Belbo made a sign, as if to say that I could be trusted. Garamond ordered the guest to be shown in and went to greet him. De Gubernatis wore a double-breasted suit, a rosette in his lapel, a fountain pen in his breast pocket, a folded newspaper in his side pocket, a leatherette briefcase under his arm.

"Ah, my dear Commendatore," Garamond said, "come right in. Our dear friend De Ambrosiis told me all about you. A life spent in the service of the state. And a secret poetic vein, yes? Show me, show me the treasure you hold in your hands. . . . But first let me introduce two of my senior editors."

He seated the visitor in front of the desk, cluttered with manuscripts, while his hands, trembling with anticipation, caressed the cover of the work held out to him. "Not a word. I know everything. You come from Vitipeno, that great and noble city. You were in the customs service. And, secretly, night after night, you filled these pages, fired by the demon of poetry. Poetry . . . it consumed Sappho's young years, it nourished Goethe's old age. Drug, the Greeks called it, both poison and medicine. Naturally, we'll have to read this creation of yours. I always insist on at least three readers' reports, one in-house and two from consultants (who must remain anonymous; you'll forgive me, but they are quite prominent people). Manutius doesn't publish a book unless we're sure of its quality, and quality, as you know better than I, is an impalpable, it can be detected only with a sixth sense. A book may have imperfections, flaws—even Svevo sometimes wrote badly, as you know better than I—but, by God, you still feel the idea, rhythm, power. I know—don't say it. The moment I glanced at the incipit of your first page, I felt something, but I don't want to judge on my own, though time and again—ah, yes, often—when the readers' reports were lukewarm, I overruled them, because you can't judge an author without having grasped, so to speak, his rhythm, and here, for example, I open this work of yours at random and my eyes fall on a verse, 'As in autumn, the wan eyelid' . . . Well, I don't know how it continues, but I sense an inspiration, I see an image. There are times you start a work like this with a surge of ecstasy, carried away. Cela dit, my dear friend, ah, if only we could always do what we like! But publishing, too, is a business, perhaps the noblest of all, but still a business. Do you have any idea what printers charge these days? And the cost of paper? Just look at this morning's news: the rise of the prime rate on Wall Street. Doesn't affect us, you say? Ah, but it does. Do you know they tax even our inventory? And they tax returns, the books I don't sell. Yes, I pay even for failure—such is the calvary of genius unrecognized by the philistines. This onionskin—most refined of you, if I may say so, to type your text on such thin paper. It smacks of the poet. The typical clod would have used parchment to dazzle the eye and confuse the spirit, but here is poetry written with the heart—this onionskin might as well be paper money."

The phone rang. I later learned that Garamond had pressed a button under the desk, and Signora Grazia had sent through a fake call.

"My dear Maestro! What? Splendid! Great news! Ring out, wild bells! A new book from your pen is always an event. Why, of course! Manutius is proud, moved—more, thrilled—to number you among its authors. You saw what the papers wrote about your latest epic poem? Nobel material. Unfortunately, you're ahead of your time. We had trouble selling the three thousand copies. . . ."

Commendatore De Gubernatis blanched: three thousand copies was an achievement beyond his dreams.

"Sales didn't cover the production costs. Take a look through the glass doors and you'll see how many people I have in the editorial department. For a book to break even nowadays I have to sell at least ten thousand copies, and luckily I sell more than that in many cases, but those are writers with—how shall I put it?—a different vocation. Balzac was great, and his books sold like hotcakes; Proust was equally great, but he published at his own expense. You'll end up in school anthologies, but not on the stands in train stations. The same thing happened to Joyce, who, like Proust, published at his own expense. I can allow myself the privilege of bringing out a book like yours once every two or three years. Give me three years' time . . ." A long pause followed. An expression of pained embarrassment came over Garamond's face.

"What? At your own expense? No, no, it's not the amount. We can hold the costs down. . . . But as a rule Manutius doesn't . . . Of course, you're right, even Joyce and Proust . . . Of course, I understand. . . ."

Another pained pause. "Very well, we'll talk about it. I've been honest with you, and you're impatient. . . . Let's try what the Americans call a *joint venture*. They're always way ahead of us, the Yanks. Drop in tomorrow, and we'll do some figuring. . . . My respects and my admiration."

Garamond seemed to wake from a dream. He rubbed his eyes, then suddenly remembered the presence of his visitor. "Forgive me. That was a writer, a true writer, perhaps one of the Greats. And yet, for that very reason . . . Sometimes this job is humbling. If it weren't for the vocation . . . But where were we? Ah, yes, I think we've said everything there is to be said now. I'll write you, hmm, in about a month. Please leave your work here; it's in good hands."

Commendatore De Gubernatis went out, speechless. He had set foot in the forge of glory.

39

Manutius was a publishing house for SFAs.

An SFA, in Manutiuan jargon, was . . . But why do I use the past tense? SFAs still exist, after all. Back in Milan, all continues as if nothing has happened, and yet I cast everything into a tremendously remote past. What occurred two nights ago in the nave of Saint-Martin-des-Champs has made a rent in time, reversing the order of the centuries. Or perhaps it is simply that I have aged decades overnight, or that the fear that They will find me makes me speak as if I were now chronicling a collapsing empire as I lie in the balneum with my veins severed, waiting to drown in my own blood. . . .

An SFA is a self-financing author, and Manutius is a vanity press. Earnings high, overhead minuscule. A staff of four: Garamond, Signora Grazia, the bookkeeper in the cubbyhole in the back, and Luciano, the disabled shipping clerk in the vast storeroom in the half-basement.

"I've never figured out how Luciano manages to pack books with one arm," Belbo once said to me. "I believe he uses his teeth. However, he doesn't have all that much packing to do. Normal publishers ship to booksellers, but Luciano ships only to authors. Manutius isn't interested in readers. . . . The main thing, Signor Garamond says, is to make sure the authors remain loyal to us. We can get along fine without readers."

Belbo admired Signor Garamond. He felt the man possessed a strength that he himself lacked.

The Manutius system is very simple. A few ads are placed in local papers, professional magazines, provincial literary reviews, especially those that tend to survive for only a few issues. Medium-size announcements, with a photograph of the author and a few incisive lines: "A lofty voice in our nation's poetry," or "The latest narrative achievement by the author of *Floriana and Her Sisters*."

"At this point the net is cast," Belbo explained, "and the SFAs fall into it in clumps, if you can fall into a net in clumps."

"And then?"

"Well, take De Gubernatis for example. A month from now, as our retired customs official writhes with anxiety, a call from Signor Garamond will invite him to dinner with a few writers. They'll meet in the latest Arab restaurant: very exclusive, no sign outside, you ring the bell and give your name through a peephole. Deluxe interior, soft lights, exotic music. Garamond will shake the maître d's hand, call the waiters by name, and send back the first bottle of wine because the vintage isn't right. Or else he'll say, 'Excuse me, old friend, but this isn't couscous the way we eat it in Marrakesh.' De Gubernatis will be introduced to Inspector X; all the airport services are under his command, but his real claim to fame is that he is the inventor and apostle of Cosmoranto, the language of universal peace now being considered by UNESCO. There's also Professor Y, a remarkable storyteller, winner of the Petruzzellis della Gattina Prize in 1980, but also a leading figure in medical science. How many years did you teach, Professor? Ah, those were other times; education then was taken seriously. And finally, our charming poetess, the exquisite Odolinda Mezzofanti Sassabetti, author of *Chaste Throbs*, which you've surely read."

Belbo told me that he had long wondered why all female SFAs used a double surname: Lauretta Solimeni Calcanti, Dora Ardenzi Fiamma, Carolina Pastorelli Cefalù. Why was it that important women writers had just one surname (except for Ivy Compton-Burnett) and some (like Colette) had none at all, while an SFA felt the need to call herself Odolinda Mezzofanti Sassabetti? Perhaps because real writers wrote out of love of the work and didn't care whether they were known—they could even use a pseudonym, like Nerval—whereas an SFA wanted to be recognized by the family next door, by the people in her neighborhood, and in the neighborhood where she used to live. For a man, one surname is enough, but not for a woman, because there are some who knew her before her marriage and some who only met her afterward. Hence the need for two.

"Anyway," Belbo went on, "it is an evening rich in intellectual experiences. De Gubernatis will feel as if he's drained an LSD cocktail. He'll listen to the gossip of his fellow-guests, hear a tasty anecdote about a great poet who is notoriously impotent, and not worth that much as a poet either. He'll look, eyes glistening with emotion, at the latest edition of the *Encyclopedia of Illustrious Italians,* which Garamond will just happen to have on hand, to show Inspector X the appropriate page (You see, my dear friend, you, too, have entered the pantheon; ah, it is mere justice)."

Belbo showed me the encyclopedia. "Just an hour ago I was preaching at you, but nobody is innocent. The encyclopedia is compiled exclusively by Diotallevi and me. But I swear we don't do it just for the money. It's one of the most amusing jobs there is. Every year we have to prepare a new, updated edition. It works more or less this way: you include an entry on a famous writer and an entry on an SFA, making sure they're in alphabetical proximity. And you don't waste space on the famous name. See, for example, under L."

LAMPEDUSA, Giuseppe Tomasi di (1896–1957). Sicilian writer. Long ignored, achieved fame posthumously for his novel *The Leopard.*

LAMPUSTRI, Adeodato (1919–   ). Writer, educator, veteran (Bronze Star, East Africa), thinker, novelist, and poet. Looms large on the contemporary Italian literary scene. Lampustri's talent was revealed in 1959 with the publication of *The Carmassi Brothers,* volume one of a trailblazing trilogy. Narrated with unrelenting realism and noble poetic inspiration, the novel tells of a fisherman's family in Lucania. *The Carmassi Brothers* won the Petruzzellis della Gattina Prize in 1960 and was followed a few years later by *The Dismissed* and *Panther Without Eyelashes,* both of which, perhaps even more than the author's initial work, exhibit the epic sweep, the dazzling plastic invention, the lyrical flow that distinguish this incomparable artist. A diligent ministry official, Lampustri is esteemed by those who know him as a man of upright character, an exemplary father and husband, and a stunning public speaker.

"De Gubernatis," Belbo explained, "will want to appear in the encyclopedia. He's always said that the fame of the famous was a fraud, a conspiracy on the part of obliging critics. But, chiefly, he will want to join a family of writers who are also directors of state agencies, bank managers, aristocrats, magistrates. Appearing in the encyclopedia, he will expand his circle of acquaintances. If he needs to ask a favor, he'll know where to turn. Signor Garamond has the power to lift De Gubernatis out of the provinces and hurl him to the summit. Toward the end of the dinner, Garamond will whisper to him to drop by the office the next morning."

"And the next morning, he comes."

"You can bet on it. He'll spend a sleepless night, dreaming of the greatness of Adeodato Lampustri."

"And then?"

"Garamond will say to him: 'Yesterday, I didn't dare speak—it would have humiliated the others—but your work, it's sublime. Not only were the readers' reports enthusiastic—no, more, favorable—but I personally spent an entire night poring over these pages of yours. A book worthy of a literary prize. Great, really great.' Then Garamond will go back to his desk, slap the manuscript—now well worn by the loving attention of at least four readers (rumpling the manuscripts is Signora Grazia's job)—and stare at the SFA with a puzzled expression. 'What shall we do with it?' And 'What shall we do with it?' De Gubernatis will ask. Garamond will say that the work's value is beyond the slightest dispute. But clearly it is ahead of its time, and as for sales, it won't do more than two thousand copies, twenty-five hundred tops. Well, two thousand more than covers all the people De Gubernatis knows, and an SFA doesn't think in planetary terms—or, rather, his planet consists of familiar faces: schoolmates, bank managers, fellow teachers in the high school, retired colonels. The SFA wants to bring his poetry to all these people, even to those who couldn't care less, like the butcher or the prefect of police. Faced by the risk that Garamond might back off (and remember: everybody at home, in town and office, knows that De Gubernatis has submitted his manuscript to a big Milan publisher), he will make some quick calculations. He could empty his savings account, take out a loan against his pension, mortgage the house, cash in those few government bonds. Paris is well worth a mass. Shyly, he will offer to underwrite some of the costs. Garamond will look upset. 'That is not the usual practice of Manutius, but, well, all right, it's a deal, you've talked me into it, even Proust and Joyce had to bow to harsh necessity. The costs are so high, for the present we'll plan on two thousand copies, though the contract will provide for up to ten thousand. You'll receive two hundred author's copies, to send to anyone you like, another two hundred will be review copies, because we want to promote the book as if this were the new Stephen King. That leaves sixteen hundred for commercial distribution. On these, obviously, no royalties for you, but if the book catches on and we go into a second printing, you'll get twelve percent.' "

Later I saw the standard contract that De Gubernatis, now on his poetic trip, would sign without even reading, while Signor Garamond's bookkeeper loudly protested that the costs had been grossly underestimated. Ten pages of clauses in eight-point type: foreign rights, subsidiary rights, dramatizations, radio and television serialization, film rights, Braille editions, abridgments for *Reader's Digest*, guarantees against libel suits, all disputes to be settled by Milan courts. The SFA, lost in dreams of glory, would not notice the clause that specified a maximum print run of ten thousand but mentioned no minimum or the clause that said the amount to be paid by the author was independent of the print run (which was agreed upon only verbally), or the clause that said—most important of all—that the publisher had the right to pulp all unsold copies after one year unless the author wished to buy them at half the list price. Sign on the dotted line.

The launching would be lavish. Ten-page press releases, with biography and critical essays. No modesty; the newspaper editors would toss them out anyway. The actual printing: one thousand copies, of which only three hundred and fifty would be bound. Two hundred to the author, about fifty to minor or associated bookshops, fifty to provincial magazines, about thirty to the newspapers, just in case they needed to fill a couple of lines in the Books Received column. These copies would later be given as donations to hospitals or prisons—and you can see why the former don't heal and the latter don't redeem.

In summer the Petruzzellis della Gattina Prize, a Garamond creation, would be awarded. Total cost: two days' meals and lodging for the jury, plus a Nike of Samothrace, in vermeil, for the winner. Congratulatory telegrams from other Manutius authors.

Finally, the moment of truth. A year and a half later, Garamond writes: Dear friend, as I feared, you are fifty years ahead of your time. Rave reviews in the dozens, awards, critical acclaim, ça va sans dire. But few copies sold. The public is not ready. We are forced to make space in the warehouse, as stipulated in the contract (copy enclosed). Unless you exercise your right to buy the unsold copies at half the list price, we must pulp them.

De Gubernatis goes mad with grief. His relatives console him: People just don't understand you, of course if you belonged to the right clique, if you sent the requisite bribe, by now they'd have reviewed you in the *Corriere della Sera*, it's all Mafia, you have to hold out. Only five author's copies are left, and there are still so many important people to whom the work should go. You can't allow your writing to be pulped, recycled into toilet paper. Let's see how much we can scrape together, maybe we can buy back five hundred copies, and for the rest, sic transit gloria mundi.

Manutius still has six hundred and fifty copies in unbound sheets. Signor Garamond has five hundred of them bound and shipped, COD. The final balance: the author paid the production costs for two thousand copies, Manutius printed one thousand and bound eight hundred and fifty, of which five hundred were paid for a second time. About fifty authors a year, and Manutius always ends up well in the black.

And without remorse: Manutius is dispensing happiness.

40

Cowards die many times before their deaths.
—Shakespeare, *Julius Caesar*, II, 2

I was always aware of a conflict between Belbo's devotion in working with his respectable Garamond authors, his efforts to get from them books he could be proud of, and the piratical zeal with which he contributed to the swindling of the hapless Manutius authors, even referring to Via Marchese Gualdi those he considered unsuitable for Garamond, as I had seen him attempt to do with Colonel Ardenti.

Working with Belbo, I often wondered why he accepted this arrangement. I don't think it was the money. He knew his trade well enough to find a better-paying position.

For a long time I thought he did it because it enabled him to pursue his study of human folly from an ideal observation point. As he never tired of pointing out, he was fascinated by what he called stupidity—the impregnable paralogism, the insidious delirium hidden behind the impeccable argument. But that, too, was a mask. It was Diotallevi who did it for fun, or perhaps hoping that a Manutius book might someday offer an unprecedented combination of the Torah. And I, too, participated, for the amusement, the irony, out of curiosity, especially after Garamond launched Project Hermes.

For Belbo it was a different story. This became clear to me after I went into his files.

FILENAME: Vendetta

She simply arrives. Even if there are people in the office, she grabs me by my lapels, thrusts her face forward, and kisses me. How does that song go? "Anna stands on tiptoe to kiss me." She kisses me as if she were playing pinball.

She knows it embarrasses me. Puts me on the spot.

She never lies.

I love you, she says.

See you Sunday?

No. I'm spending the weekend with a friend. . . .

A girlfriend, naturally.

No, a man friend. You know him. He's the one who was at
the bar with me last week. I promised. You wouldn't want me
to break my promise?

Don't break your promise, but don't come here to make me
. . . Please, I have an author coming in.

A genius to launch?

A poor bastard to destroy.

. . . .

A poor bastard to destroy.

. . . .

I went to pick you up at Pilade's. You weren't there. I waited
a long time, then I went by myself; otherwise the gallery would
have been closed. Somebody there told me you had all gone on
to the restaurant. I pretended to look at the pictures, though
they tell me art's been dead since Hölderlin. It took me twenty
minutes to find the restaurant, because dealers always pick ones
that are going to become famous next month.

You were there, among the usual faces, and beside you was
the man with the scar. You weren't the least embarrassed. You
looked at me with complicity and—how do you manage both
at the same time?—defiance, as if to say: So what? The intruder
with the scar looked me up and down, as if I, not he, were the
intruder. The others, in on the story, waited. I should have found
an excuse to pick a fight. I'd have come out of it well, even if
he hit me. Everybody knew you were there with him to provoke me. My role was assigned. One way or the other, I was to
put on a show.

Since there had to be a show, I chose drawing-room comedy.
I joined the conversation, amiable, hoping someone would admire my control.

The only one who admired me was me.

You're a coward when you feel you're a coward.

The masked avenger. As Clark Kent I take care of misunderstood young geniuses; as Superman I punish justly misunderstood old geniuses. I collaborate in the exploitation of those who,
lacking my courage, have been unable to confine themselves to
the role of spectator.

Is this possible? To spend a life punishing people who will never know they have been punished? So you wanted to be a Homer, eh? Take that, wretch, and that!

I hate anyone who tries to see me as an illusion of passion.

41

In any case I wasn't supposed to concern myself with Manutius; my job was the wonderful adventure of metals. I began by exploring the Milan libraries. I started with textbooks, made a bibliography on file cards, and from there I went back to the original sources, old or new, looking for decent pictures. There's nothing worse than illustrating a chapter on space travel with a photograph of the latest American satellite. Signor Garamond had taught me that it needs, at the very least, an angel by Doré.

I reaped a harvest of curious reproductions, but they weren't enough. To choose the right picture for an illustrated book, you have to reject at least ten others.

I got permission to go to Paris for four days. Not much time to visit all the archives. Lia came with me. We arrived Thursday and had return reservations for the Monday-evening train, and I scheduled the Conservatoire for Monday, a mistake, because I found out the Conservatoire was closed Mondays. Too late. I left Paris crestfallen.

Belbo was vexed, but I had collected plenty of interesting things, and we went to show them to Signor Garamond. He leafed through the reproductions, many of them in color, then looked at the bill and let out a whistle. "My dear friend," he said, "our work is a mission, true, we toil in the fields of culture, ça va sans dire, but we're not the Red Cross—more, we're not UNICEF. Was it necessary to buy all this material? I mean, I see here a mustachioed gentleman in his underwear who looks like d'Artagnan, surrounded by abracadabras and capricorns. Who is he? Mandrake?"

"Primitive medicine. Influence of the zodiac on the different parts of the body, with the corresponding curative herbs. And minerals, including metals. The doctrine of the cosmic signatures. Those were times when the boundary between magic and science was rather ill-defined."

"Interesting. But what does this title page mean? *Philosophia Moysaica*. What's Moses got to do with it? Isn't that being a little too primitive?"

"It's the dispute over unguentum armarium, otherwise known as weapon salve. Illustrious physicians spent fifty years arguing whether this salve could heal wounds by being smeared on the weapon that had dealt the blow."

"Incredible. And that's science?"

"Not in today's sense of the word. But they considered this seriously, because they had just discovered the marvels of the magnet, the magic possibility of action at a distance. . . . These men were wrong, but later, Volta and Marconi were not. What are electricity and radio if not action at a distance?"

"Well, well. Bravo, Casaubon. Science and magic going arm in arm, eh? Great idea. Let's pursue this. Throw out some of those revolting generators and put in a few more Mandrakes. Perhaps a summoning of the Devil, say, on a gold background."

"I wouldn't want to go too far. This is the wonderful adventure of metals. Oddities work only when they're to the point."

"The wonderful adventure of metals must be, most of all, the story of science's mistakes. Stick in the catchy oddity, and in the caption say it's wrong. In the meantime, the reader's hooked, because he sees that even the greats had crazy ideas, just like him."

I told them about a strange thing I had seen in Paris, a bookshop near quai Saint-Michel. Its symmetrical windows advertised its own schizophrenia: on one side, books on computers and the electronics of the future; on the other, occult sciences. And it was the same inside: Apple and cabala.

"Unbelievable," Belbo said.

"Obvious," Diotallevi said. "Or, at least, you're the last person who should be surprised, Jacopo. The world of machines seeking to rediscover the secret of creation: letters and numbers."

Garamond said nothing. He had clasped his hands as if in prayer, and his eyes were turned heavenward. Then he smacked his hands together. "What you've said today confirms an idea of mine. For a while now I've . . . But all in good time; it needs more thought. Meanwhile, carry on. You've done well, Casaubon. We must look at your contract again; you're a valuable colleague. And, yes, put in plenty of cabala and computers. Computers are made with silicon, aren't they?"

"But silicon isn't a metal. It's a nonmetallic element."

"Metallic, nonmetallic, why split hairs? What is this, Rosa rosarum? Computers and cabala."

"Cabala isn't a metal either," I said.

He accompanied us to the door. At the threshold he said: "Casaubon, publishing is an art, not a science. Let's not think like revolutionaries, eh? Those days are past. Put in the cabala. Oh, yes, about your expenses: I've taken the liberty of disallowing the couchette. Not to be stingy, believe me. It's just that research requires—how shall I put it?—a Spartan spirit. Otherwise you lose your faith."

He summoned us again a few days later, telling Belbo there was a visitor in his office he wanted us to meet.

We went. Garamond was entertaining a fat gentleman with a face like a tapir's, no chin, a little blond mustache beneath a large, animal nose. I thought I recognized him; then I knew who it was: Professor Bramanti, the man I had gone to hear in Rio, the referendary or whatever of that Rosicrucian order.

"Professor Bramanti," Garamond said, "believes this is the right moment for a smart publisher, alert to the cultural climate of the time, to inaugurate a line of books on the occult sciences."

"For . . . Manutius," Belbo suggested.

"Why, naturally." Signor Garamond smiled shrewdly. "Professor Bramanti—who, by the way, was recommended to me by my dear friend Dr. De Amicis, the author of that splendid volume *Chronicles of the Zodiac*, which we brought out this year—has been lamenting the fact that the few works published on his subject—almost invariably by frivolous and unreliable houses—fail to do justice to the wealth, the profundity of this field of studies. . . ."

"Given the failure of the utopias of the modern world," Bramanti said, "the time is ripe for a reassessment of the culture of the forgotten past."

"What you say is the sacred truth, Professor. But you must forgive our—I don't like to say ignorance—our unfamiliarity with the subject. When you speak of occult sciences, what exactly do you have in mind? Spiritualism, astrology, black magic?"

Bramanti made a gesture of dismay. "Please! That's just the sort of nonsense that's foisted on the ingenuous. I'm talking about science, occult though it be. Of course, that may include astrology when appropriate, but not the kind that tells a typist that next Sunday she'll meet the man of her dreams. No. What I mean, to give an example, would be a serious study of the decans."

"Yes, I see. Scientific. It's in our line, to be sure; but could you be a little more specific?"

Bramanti settled into his chair and looked around the room, as if to seek astral inspiration. "I'd be happy to give you some examples, of course. I would say that the ideal reader of a collection of this sort would be a Rosicrucian adept, and therefore an expert in magiam, in necromantiam, in astrologiam, in geomantiam, in pyromantiam, in hydromantiam, in chaomantiam, in medicinam adeptam, to quote the book of Azoth, which, as the *Raptus philosophorum* explains, was given to Staurophorus by a mysterious maiden. But the knowledge of the adept embraces other fields, such as physiognosis, which deals with occult physics, the static, the dynamic, and the kinematic, or astrology and esoteric biology, the study of the spirits of nature, hermetic zoology. I could add cosmognosis, which studies the heavens from the astronomical, cosmological, physiological, and ontological points of view, and anthropognosis, which studies human anatomy, and the sciences of divination, psychurgy, social astrology, hermetic history. Then there is qualitative mathematics, arithmology . . . But the fundamentals are the cosmography of the invisible, magnetism, auras, fluids, psychometry, and clairvoyance, and in general the study of the five hyperphysical senses—not to mention horoscopic astrology (which, of course, becomes a mere mockery of learning when not conducted with the proper precautions), as well as physiognomics, mind reading, and the predictive arts (tarots, dream books), ranging to the highest levels, such as prophecy and ecstasy. Sufficient information would be required on alchemy, spagyrics, telepathy, exorcism, ceremonial and evocatory magic, basic theurgy. As for genuine occultism, I would advise exploration of the fields of early cabala, Brahmanism, gymnosophy, Memphis hieroglyphics—"

"Templar phenomenology," Belbo slipped in.

Bramanti glowed. "Absolutely. But I almost forgot: first, some idea of necromancy and sorcery among the other races, onomancy, prophetic furies, voluntary thaumaturgy, hypnotic suggestion, yoga, somnambulism, mercurial chemistry . . . For the mystical tendency, Wronski advises bearing in the mind the techniques of the possessed nuns of Loudon, the convulsives of Saint-Médard, the mystical beverages, the wine of Egypt, the elixir of life, and arsenic water. For the principle of evil—but I realize that here we come to the most delicate part of a possible series—I would say we need to acquaint the reader with the mysteries of Beelzebub as destruction proper, with Satan as dethroned prince, and with Eurynomius, Moloch, incubi and succubi. For the positive principle, the celestial mysteries of Saint Michael, Gabriel, Raphael, and the agathodemons. Then of course the mysteries of Isis, Mithra, Morpheus, Samothrace, and Eleusis, and the natural mysteries of the male sex, phallus, Wood of Life, Key of Science, Baphomet, mallet, then the natural mysteries of the female sex, Ceres, Cteis, Patera, Cybele, Astarte."

Signor Garamond leaned forward with an insinuating smile. "I wouldn't overlook the Gnostics . . ."

"Certainly not, although on that particular subject a great deal of rubbish is in circulation. In any case, every sound form of occultism is a gnosis."

"Just what I was going to say," said Garamond.

"And all this would be enough?" Belbo asked innocently.

Bramanti puffed out his cheeks, abruptly transforming himself from tapir to hamster. "Enough? To begin with, yes, but not for beginners, if you'll forgive the little joke. But with about fifty volumes you could enthrall an audience of thousands, readers who are only waiting for an authoritative word. . . . With an investment of perhaps a few hundred million lire—I've come to you personally, Dr. Garamond, because I know of your willingness to undertake such generous ventures—and with a modest royalty for myself, as editor in chief of the series . . ."

Bramanti had now gone too far; Garamond was losing interest. The visitor was dismissed hastily, with expansive promises. The usual committee of advisers would carefully weigh the proposal.

42

But you must know that we are all in agreement, whatever we say.
—*Turba Philosophorum*

After Bramanti had left, Belbo remarked that he should have pulled
his cork. Signor Garamond was unfamiliar with this expression, so
Belbo attempted a few polite paraphrases, but with little success.

"Let's not quibble," Garamond said. "Before that gentleman said
five words, I knew he wasn't for us. Not him. But the people he
was talking about, authors and readers alike—that's different. Professor Bramanti happened to confirm the very idea I've been pondering for some days now. Here, look at this," he said, theatrically
taking three books from his drawer.

"Here are three volumes that have come out in recent years, all
of them successful. The first is in English; I haven't read it, but the
author is a famous critic. What has he written? The subtitle calls it
a gnostic novel. Now look at this: a mystery, a best-seller. And
what's it about? A gnostic church near Turin. You gentlemen may
know who these Gnostics are. . . ." He paused, waved his hand.
"It doesn't matter. They're something demoniacal; that's all I need
to know. . . . Yes, maybe I'm being hasty, but I'm not trying to
talk like you, I'm trying to talk like Bramanti—that is, I'm speaking
as a publisher, not as a professor of comparative gnoseology or
whatever it is. Now, what was it that I found clear, promising,
inviting—no, more, intriguing—in Bramanti's talk? His extraordinary capacity for tying everything together. He didn't mention
Gnostics, but he easily could have, what with geomancy, maalox,
and mercurial Radames. And why do I insist on this point? Because
here is another book, by a famous journalist, who tells about incredible things that go on in Turin—Turin, mind you, the city of
the automobile. Sorceresses, black masses, consorting with the Devil—
and for paying customers, not for poor crazed peasants in the south.
Casaubon, Belbo tells me you were in Brazil and saw the savages

down there performing satanic rites. . . . Good, later you can tell me about it, but really, it's all the same. Brazil is right here, gentlemen. The other day I went personally into that bookshop—what's it called? Never mind; it doesn't matter—you know, the place where six or seven years ago they sold anarchist books, books about revolutionaries, Tupamaros, terrorists—no, more, Marxists . . . Well, the place has been recycled. They stock those things Bramanti was talking about. It's true today we live in an age of confusion. Go into a Catholic bookshop, where there used to be nothing but the catechism, and you find a reassessment of Luther, though at least they won't sell a book that says religion is all a fraud. But in the shops I'm talking about they sell the authors who believe and the authors who say it's all a fraud, provided the subject is—what do you call it?"

"Hermetic," Diotallevi prompted.

"Yes, I believe that's the right word. I saw at least a dozen books on Hermes. And that's what I want to talk to you about: Project Hermes. A new branch . . ."

"The golden branch," Belbo said.

"Exactly," Garamond said, missing the reference. "It's a gold mine, all right. I realized that these people will gobble up anything that's hermetic, as you put it, anything that says the opposite of what they read in their books at school. I see this also as a cultural duty: I'm no philanthropist, but in these dark times to offer someone a faith, a glimpse into the beyond . . . Yet Garamond also has a scholarly mission. . . ."

Belbo stiffened. "I thought you had Manutius in mind."

"Both. Listen, I rooted around in that shop, then went to another place, a very respectable place, but even it had an occult sciences section. There are university-level studies on these subjects sitting on the shelves alongside books written by people like Bramanti. Think a minute: Bramanti has probably never met any of the university authors, but he's read them, read them as if they were just like him. Whatever you say to such people, they think you're talking about their problem, like the story of the cat, where the couple was arguing about a divorce but the cat thought they were disagreeing about the giblets for its lunch. You must have noticed it, Belbo; you dropped that remark about the Templars and he nodded immediately. Sure, the Templars, too, and cabala, and the lottery, and tea leaves. They're omnivorous. Omnivorous. You saw Bramanti's face: a rodent. A huge audience, divided into two categories—I can see them lining up now, and they're legion. In primis: the ones who write about it, and Manutius will greet them with open arms. All we have to do to draw them is start a series that gets a little publicity. We could call it . . . let's see . . ."

"The Tabula Smaragdina," Diotallevi said.

"What? No. Too difficult. It doesn't say anything to me. No. What we want is something that suggests something else. . . ."

"Isis Unveiled," I said.

"Isis Unveiled! That's good. Bravo, Casaubon. It has Tutankhamen in it, the scarab of the pyramids. Isis Unveiled, with a slightly black-magical cover, but not overdone. Now let's continue. The second group: those who buy it. I know what you're thinking, my friends: Manutius isn't interested in the buyer. But there's no law to that effect. This time, we'll *sell* Manutius books. Progress, gentlemen!

"But there are also the scholarly studies, and that's where Garamond comes in. We'll look through the historical studies and the other university series and find ourselves an expert, a consultant. Then we'll publish three or four books a year. An academic series, with a title that's direct but not too picturesque . . ."

"Hermetica," Diotallevi said.

"Excellent. Classical, dignified. You ask me: Why spend money with Garamond when we can make money with Manutius? But the scholarly series will act as a lure, attracting intelligent people, who will make suggestions and point out new directions. And it will also attract the others, the Professor Bramantis, who will be rerouted to Manutius. It seems perfect to me: Project Hermes, a nice, clean, profitable operation that will strengthen the flow of ideas between the two firms. . . . To work, gentlemen. There are libraries to visit, bibliographies to compile, catalogs to request. And find out what's being done in other countries. . . . Who knows how many people have already slipped through our fingers, people bearing treasures, and we dismissed them as worthless. Casaubon, don't forget, in the history of metals, to put in a little alchemy. Gold's a metal, I believe. Hold your comments for later: you know I'm open to criticism, suggestions, objections, as all cultured people are. This project is in effect as of now.

"Signora Grazia, that gentleman's been waiting two hours. That's no way to treat an author! Show him in!" he shouted, to make himself heard as far as the reception room.

43

People who meet on the street . . . secretly dedicate themselves to operations of Black Magic, they bind or seek to bind themselves to the Spirits of Darkness, to satisfy their ambitions, their hates, their loves, to do—in a word—Evil.

—J. K. Huysmans, Preface to J. Bois, *Le satanisme et la magie*, 1895, pp. VIII–IX

I had thought that Project Hermes was the rough sketch of an idea, not a plan of action. But I didn't yet know Signor Garamond. In the days that followed, while I stayed late in libraries looking for illustrations about metals, at Manutius they were already at work.

Two months later in Belbo's office, I found, hot off the press, an issue of *The Italic Parnassus*, with a long article, "The Rebirth of Occultism," in which the well-known Hermeticist Dr. Moebius—Belbo's new pseudonym, and source of his first bonus from Project Hermes—talked about the miraculous renaissance of the occult sciences in the modern world and announced that Manutius intended to move in this direction with its new series "Isis Unveiled."

Meanwhile, Signor Garamond had written letters to various reviews of Hermeticism, astrology, tarot, UFOlogy, signing one name or another and requesting information about the new series announced by Manutius. Whereupon the editors of the reviews telephoned Manutius, requesting information, and Signor Garamond acted mysterious, saying he could not yet reveal the first ten titles, which were, however, in the works. In this way the world of the occultists, stirred by constant drumming of the tom-toms, was now alerted to Project Hermes.

"We disguise ourselves as a flower," Signor Garamond said, having summoned us to his office, "and the bees will come swarming."

That wasn't all. Garamond wanted to show us the flier (the dépliant, he called it): a simple affair, four pages, but on glossy paper. The first page reproduced what was to be the uniform cover of the books in the series: a kind of golden seal (the Pentacle of Solomon, Garamond explained) on a black ground; the page was framed by interwoven swastikas (but Asian swastikas, Garamond hastened to add, which went in the direction of the sun, not the Nazi kind, which went clockwise). At the top, where each volume's title would go, were the words "There are more things in heaven and earth . . ." The flier extolled the glories of Manutius in the service of culture, then stated, with some catchy phrases, that the contemporary world sought truths deeper and more luminous than those science could provide: "From Egypt, from Chaldea, from Tibet, a forgotten knowledge—for the spiritual rebirth of the West."

Belbo asked where the flier would go, and Garamond smiled like the evil genius of the rajah of Assam, as Belbo would have said. "From France I've ordered a directory of all the secret societies in the world today. It exists. Here it is. Editions Henry Veyrier, with addresses, postal codes, phone numbers. Take a look at it, Belbo, and eliminate those that don't apply, because I see it also includes the Jesuits, Opus Dei, the Carbonari, and Rotary. Find all the ones with occult tendencies. I've already underlined some."

He leafed through it. "Here you are: the Absolutists (who believe in metamorphosis), the Aetherius Society of California (telepathic relations with Mars), the Astara of Lausanne (oath of absolute secrecy), Atalanteans in Great Britain (search for lost happiness), Builders of the Adytum in California (alchemy, cabala, astrology), Cercle E. B. of Perpignan (dedicated to Hator, goddess of love and guardian of the Mountain of the Dead), Cercle Eliphas Levi of Maule (I don't know who this Levi is; perhaps that French anthropologist or whatever he was), Knights of the Templar Alliance of Toulouse, Druidic College of Gaul, Couvent Spiritualiste de Jericho, the Cosmic Church of Truth in Florida, Traditionalist Seminar of Ecône in Switzerland, the Mormons (I read about them in a detective story, too, but maybe they don't exist anymore), the Church of Mithra in London and Brussels, the Church of Satan in Los Angeles, the United Luciferan Church of France, the Apostolic Rosicrucian Church in Brussels, Children of Darkness and Green Order on the Ivory Coast (let's forget that one; God knows what language they write in), Escuela Hermetista Occidental of Montevideo, the National Institute of Cabala in Manhattan, the Central Ohio Temple of Hermetic Science, Tetra-Gnosis of Chicago, Ancient Brethren of the Rosie-Cross of Saint Cyr-sur-Mer, Johannite Fraternity for the Templar Resurrection in Kassel, International Fraternity of Isis in Grenoble, Ancient

Bavarian Illuminati of San Francisco, the Sanctuary of Gnosis of Sherman Oaks, the Grail Foundation of America, Sociedade do Graal do Brasil, Hermetic Brotherhood of Luxor, Lectorium Rosicrucianum in Holland, the Grail Movement of Strasbourg, Order of Anubis in New York, Temple of the Black Pentacle in Manchester, Odinist Fellowship in Florida, the Order of the Garter (even the Queen of England must be in that one), the Order of the Vril (neo-Nazi Masons, no address), Militia Templi in Montpellier, Sovereign Order of the Solar Temple in Monte Carlo, Rosy Cross of Harlem (you understand? Even the blacks now), Wicca (Luciferine association of Celtic obedience; they invoke the seventy-two geni of the cabala) . . . Need I go on?"

"Do all those really exist?" Belbo asked.

"Those and more. To work, gentlemen. Draw up a definitive list. Then we'll do our mailing. Include all those foreigners; news travels fast among them. One thing remains for us to do: we have to go around to the right shops and talk not only with the booksellers but also with the customers. Mention that such-and-such a series exists."

Diotallevi objected that we shouldn't expose ourselves in this way; we should find people to do it for us. Garamond told him to find some, "provided they're free."

"That's asking a lot," Belbo said when we were back in his office.

But the gods of the underworld were protecting us. At that very moment Lorenza Pellegrini came in, more solar than ever, making Belbo brighten. She saw the fliers and was curious.

When she heard about the project of the firm next door, she said: "Terrific! I have this fantastic friend, an ex-Tupamaro from Uruguay, who works for a magazine called *Picatrix*. He's always taking me to séances. There, I met a fantastic ectoplasm; he asks for me now every time he materializes!"

Belbo looked at Lorenza as if to ask her something, then changed his mind. Perhaps he was becoming accustomed to hearing about Lorenza's alarming friends and had decided to worry only about the ones that threatened his relationship with her (did they have a relationship?). In that reference to *Picatrix* he saw the threat not of the colonel but of the fantastic ex-Tupamaro. But Lorenza was now talking about something else, telling us that she visited many of those little shops that sold the kind of books Isis Unveiled wanted to publish.

"That's a real trip, you know," she was saying. "They tell all about medicinal herbs or list instructions for making a homunculus, remember what Faust did with Helen of Troy. Oh, Jacopo, let's! I'd love to have your homunculus, and then we could keep it like a dachshund. It's easy, the book says: you just have to collect a little human seed in a test tube. That wouldn't be hard for you—don't blush, silly. Then you mix it with hippomene, which is some liquid that is excreted—no, not excreted—what's the word?"

"Secreted," Diotallevi suggested.

"Really? Anyway, pregnant mares make it. I realize that's a bit harder to get. If I were a pregnant mare, I wouldn't like people coming to collect my hippomene, especially strangers, but I think you can buy it in packages, like joss sticks. Then you put it all in a pot and let it steep for forty days, and little by little you see a tiny form take shape, a fetus thing, which in another two months becomes a dear little homunculus, and he comes out and puts himself at your service. And they never die. Imagine: they'll even put flowers on your grave after you're dead!"

"What about the customers in those bookshops?"

"Fantastic people, people who talk with angels, people who make gold, and professional sorcerers with faces exactly like professional sorcerers . . ."

"What's the face of a professional sorcerer like?"

"An aquiline nose, Russian eyebrows, piercing eyes. The hair is long, like painters in the old days, and there's a beard, not thick, with bare patches between the chin and the cheeks, and the mustache droops forward and falls in clumps over their lips, but that's only natural, because their lips are thin, poor things, and their teeth stick out. They shouldn't smile, with those teeth, but they do, very sweetly, but the eyes—I said they were piercing, didn't I?—look at you in an unsettling way."

"Facies hermetica," Diotallevi remarked.

"Really? Well, you understand, then. When somebody comes in and asks for a book, say, of prayers against evil spirits, they immediately suggest the right title to the bookseller, and, of course, it's always a title he doesn't have in stock. But then, if you make friends and ask if the book works, they smile again, indulgently, as if they were talking to children, and they say that with this sort of thing you have to be quite careful. They tell you about cases of devils that did horrible things to friends of theirs, but when you get frightened, they say that often it's only hysteria. In other words, you never know whether they believe it or not. Sometimes the booksellers give me sticks of incense as presents; once one of them gave me a little ivory hand to ward off the evil eye."

"Then, if the occasion arises," Belbo said to her, "while you're browsing in those places, ask if they know anything about the new Manutius series, and show them our flier."

Lorenza went off with a dozen fliers. I guess she did a good job in the weeks that followed, but, even so, I wouldn't have believed things could move so fast. Within a few months, Signora Grazia simply couldn't keep up with the Diabolicals, as we had come to call the SFAs with occult interests. And, by their very nature, they were legion.

44

> Invoke the forces of the Tablet of Union by means of Supreme
> Ritual of Pentagram, with the Active and Passive Spirit, with Eheieh
> and Agla. Return to the Altar, and recite the following Enochian
> Spirit Invocation: Ol Sonuf Vaorsag Goho Iad Balt, Lonsh Calz
> Vonpho, Sobra Z-ol Ror I Ta Nazps, od Graa Ta Malprg . . . Ds
> Hol-q Qaa Nothoa Zimz, Od Commah Ta Nopbloh Zien . . .
> —Israel Regardie, *The Original Account of the Teachings,*
> *Rites and Ceremonies of the Hermetic Order of the Golden*
> *Dawn,* Ritual for Invisibility, St. Paul, Llewellyn
> Publications, 1986, p. 423

We were lucky; our first meeting was of the highest quality—at
least as far as our initiation was concerned.

For the occasion the trio was complete—Belbo, Diotallevi, and
I—and when our guest came in, we almost let out a cry of satisfaction. He had the facies hermetica described by Lorenza Pellegrini,
and, what's more, he was dressed in black.

He looked around circumspectly, then introduced himself: Professor Camestres. At the question "Professor of what?" he made a
vague gesture, as if urging us to exercise greater discretion. "Forgive
me," he said, "I don't know whether you gentlemen are interested
in the subject purely from a professional, commercial standpoint, or
whether you are connected with any mystical group . . ."

We reassured him on that point.

"Perhaps I am being excessively cautious," he said, "but I do not
wish to have anything to do with a member of the OTO." Seeing
our puzzlement, he added: "Ordo Templi Orientis, the conventicle
of the remaining self-styled followers of Aleister Crowley. . . . I
see that you are not connected. . . . All the better: there will be
no prejudices on your side." He agreed to sit down. "Because, you
understand, the work I would now like to show you takes a cou-
rageous stand against Crowley. All of us, myself included, are still
faithful to the revelations of the *Liber AL vel legis,* which, as you
probably know, was dictated to Crowley in Cairo in 1904 by a
higher intelligence named Aiwaz. This text is followed by the faithful

of the OTO even today. They draw on all four editions, the first of which preceded by nine months the outbreak of the war in the Balkans, the second by nine months the outbreak of the First World War, the third by nine months the Sino-Japanese War, and the fourth by nine months the massacres of the Spanish Civil War. . . ."

I couldn't help crossing my fingers. He noticed and said with a funereal smile, "I understand your apprehension. What I am bringing you is the fifth edition of that book. What, you ask, will happen in nine months' time? Nothing, gentlemen, rest assured. Because what I am proposing is an enlarged *Liber legis*, inasmuch as I have had the good fortune to be visited not by a mere higher intelligence but by Al himself, the supreme principle—namely, Hoor-paar-Kraat, who is the double or the mystical twin of Ra-Hoor-Khuit. My sole concern, also to ward off evil influences, is that my work be published before the winter solstice."

"I think that could be managed," Belbo said.

"I'm most pleased. The book will cause a stir in the circles of initiates, because, as you will understand, my mystical source is more serious and authenticated than Crowley's. I don't know how Crowley could have activated the Rituals of the Beast without bearing in mind the Liturgy of the Sword. Only by unsheathing the sword can the nature of Mahapralaya be understood, the Third Eye of Kundalini, in other words. And also in his arithmology, all based on the Number of the Beast, he failed to consider the New Numbers: 93, 118, 444, 868, and 1001.

"What do they mean?" asked Diotallevi, suddenly all ears.

"Ah," said Professor Camestres, "as was already stated in the first *Liber legis*, every number is infinite and therefore there is no real difference!"

"I understand," Belbo said. "But don't you think all this will be a bit obscure for the common reader?"

Camestres almost bounced in his chair. "Why, it's absolutely indispensable. Anyone who approached these secrets without the proper preparation would plunge headlong into the Abyss! Even by making them public in a veiled way, believe me, I am running risks. I work within the environment of the worship of the Beast, but more radically than Crowley: you will see, in my pages on the congressus cum daemone, the requirements for the furnishing of the temple and the carnal union with the Scarlet Woman and the Beast she rides.

Crowley stopped at so-called carnal congress against nature, while I carry the ritual beyond Evil as we conceive it. I touch the inconceivable, the absolute purity of goety, the extreme threshold of the Bas-Aumgn and the Sa-Ba-Ft. . . ."

The only thing left for Belbo to do was to sound out Camestres's financial capability. He did this with long, roundabout sentences, and finally it emerged that, like Bramanti before him, the professor had no thought of self-financing. Then the dismissal phase began, with a mild request of could we keep the manuscript for a week, we would have a look at it, and then we would see. But at this point Camestres clasped the manuscript to his bosom, said he had never been treated with such distrust, and went out, hinting that he had means, out of the ordinary, to make us regret the insult we had given him.

But before long we had dozens of manuscripts from eligible SFAs. A modicum of selectivity was necessary, since these books were also meant to be sold. Because it was impossible for us to read them all, we glanced at the contents, the indexes, some of the text, then traded discoveries.

45

And from this springs the extraordinary question: Did the Egyptians know about electricity?
—Peter Kolosimo, *Terra senza tempo*, Milan, Sugar,
1964, p. 111

"I have a text on vanished civilizations and mysterious lands," Belbo said. "It seems that originally there existed, somewhere around Australia, a continent of Mu, and from there the great currents of migration spread out. One went to Avalon, one to the Caucasus and the source of the Indus; then there were the Celts, and the founders of Egyptian civilization, and finally the founders of Atlantis. . . ."

"Old hat. If you're looking for books about Mu, I'll swamp your desk with them," I said.

"But this writer may pay. Besides, he has a beautiful chapter on Greek migrations into Yucatán, and tells about the bas-relief of a warrior at Chichén Itzá who is the spit and image of a Roman legionary. Two peas in a pod . . ."

"All the helmets in the world have either plumes or horse tails," Diotallevi said. "That's not evidence."

"Not for you, but for him. He finds serpent worship in all civilizations and concludes that there is a common origin. . . ."

"Who hasn't worshiped the serpent?" Diotallevi said. "Except, of course, the Chosen People."

"They worshiped calves."

"Only in a moment of weakness. I'd reject this one, even if he pays. Celtism and Aryanism, Kaly-yuga, the decline of the West, and SS spirituality. I may be paranoid, but he sounds like a Nazi to me."

"For Garamond, that isn't necessarily a drawback."

"No, but there's a limit to everything. Here's a book about gnomes, undines, salamanders, elves, sylphs, fairies, but it, too, brings in the origins of Aryan civilization. The SS, apparently, are descended from the Seven Dwarfs."

"Not the Seven Dwarfs, the Nibelungs."

"The dwarfs it mentions are the Little People of Ireland. The bad guys are the fairies, but the Little People are good, just mischievous."

"Put it aside. What about you, Casaubon? What have you found?"

"A text on Christopher Columbus: it analyzes his signature and finds in it a reference to the pyramids. Columbus's real aim was to reconstruct the Temple of Jerusalem, since he was grand master of the Templars-in-exile. Being a Portuguese Jew and therefore an expert cabalist, he used talismanic spells to calm storms and overcome scurvy. I didn't look at any texts on the cabala, because I assumed Diotallevi was checking them."

"The Hebrew letters are all wrong, photocopied from dream books."

"Remember, we're choosing texts for Isis Unveiled. Let's steer clear of philology. If the Diabolicals like to take their Hebrew letters from dream books, let them do it. The problem I have is all the submissions on the Masons. Signor Garamond told me to be very careful there; he doesn't want to get mixed up in polemics among the various rites. But I wouldn't neglect this manuscript about Masonic symbolism in the grotto of Lourdes. Or this one about a mysterious gentleman, probably the Comte de Saint-Germain, an intimate friend of Franklin and Lafayette, who appeared at the moment of the creation of the flag of the United States. It explains the meaning of the stars very well, but becomes confused on the subject of the stripes."

"The Comte de Saint-Germain!" I said. "Well, well!"

"You know him?

"If I said yes, you wouldn't believe me. Forget it. Now here, gentlemen, is a four-hundred-page monstrosity decrying the errors of modern science. The atom, a Jewish lie. The error of Einstein and the mystical secret of energy. The illusion of Galileo and the immaterial nature of the moon and the sun."

"In that line," Diotallevi said, "what I liked most is this review of Fortian sciences."

"What are they?"

"Named after Charles Hoy Fort, who gathered an immense collection of inexplicable bits of news. A rain of frogs in Birmingham, footprints of a fabulous animal in Devon, mysterious steps and sucker marks on the ridges of some mountains, irregularities in the precession of the equinoxes, inscriptions on meteorites, black snow, rains of blood, winged creatures at an altitude of eight thousand meters above Palermo, luminous wheels in the sea, fossils of giants, a shower of dead leaves in France, precipitations of living matter in Sumatra, and, naturally, all the signs marked on Machu Picchu and other peaks in South America that bear witness to the landing of powerful spacecraft in prehistoric times. We are not alone in the universe."

"Not bad," Belbo said. "But what particularly intrigues me are these five hundred pages on the pyramids. Did you know that the pyramid of Cheops sits right on the thirtieth parallel, which is the one that crosses the greatest stretch of land above sea level? That the geometric ratios found in the pyramid of Cheops are the same ones found at Pedra Pintada in Amazonia? That Egypt possessed two plumed serpents, one on the throne of Tutankhamen and the other on the pyramid of Saqqara, and the latter serpent points to Quetzalcoatl?"

"What does Quetzalcoatl have to do with Amazonia, if he's part of the Mexican pantheon?" I asked.

"Well, maybe I missed a connection. But for that matter, how do you explain the fact that the statues of Easter Island are megaliths exactly like the Celtic ones? Or that a Polynesian god called Ya is clearly the Yod of the Jews, as is the ancient Hungarian Io-v', the great and good god? Or that an ancient Mexican manuscript shows the earth as a square surrounded by sea, and in its center is a pyramid that has on its base the inscription Aztlán, which is close to Atlas and Atlantis? Why are pyramids found on both sides of the Atlantic?"

"Because it's easier to build pyramids than spheres. Because the wind produces dunes in the shape of pyramids and not in the shape of the Parthenon."

"I hate the spirit of the Enlightenment," Diotallevi said.

"Let me continue. The cult of Ra doesn't appear in Egyptian religion before the New Empire, and therefore it comes from the Celts. Remember Saint Nicholas and his sleigh? In prehistoric Egypt the ship of the Sun was a sleigh. Since there was no snow in Egypt, the sleigh's origin must have been Nordic. . . ."

I couldn't let that pass: "Before the invention of the wheel, sleighs were used also on sand."

"Don't interrupt. The book says that first you identify the analogies and then you find the reasons. And it says that, in the end, the reasons are scientific. The Egyptians knew electricity. Without electricity they wouldn't have been able to do what they did. A German engineer placed in charge of the sewers of Baghdad discovered electric batteries still operating that dated back to the Sassanids. In the excavations of Babylon, accumulators were found that had been made four thousand years ago. And, finally, the Ark of the Covenant (which contained the Tables of the Law, Aaron's rod, and a pot of manna from the desert) was a kind of electric strongbox capable of producing discharges on the order of five hundred volts."

"I saw that in a movie."

"So what? Where do you think scriptwriters get their ideas? The ark was made of acacia wood sheathed in gold inside and out—the same principle as electric condensers, two conductors separated by an insulator. It was encircled by a garland, also of gold, and set in a dry region where the magnetic field reached five hundred to six hundred volts per vertical meter. It's said that Porsena used electricity to free his realm from the presence of a frightful animal called Volt."

"Which is why Alessandro Volta chose that exotic pseudonym. Before, his name was simply Szmrszlyn Khraznapahwshkij."

"Be serious. Also, besides the manuscripts, I have letters that offer revelations on the connections between Joan of Arc and the Sibylline Books, between Lilith the Talmudic demon and the hermaphroditic Great Mother, between the genetic code and the Martian alphabet, between the secret intelligence of plants, cosmology, psychoanalysis, and Marx and Nietzsche in the perspective of a new angelology, between the Golden Number and the Grand Canyon, Kant and occultism, the Eleusian mysteries and jazz, Cagliostro and atomic energy, homosexuality and gnosis, the golem and the class struggle. In conclusion, a letter promising a work in eight volumes on the Grail and the Sacred Heart."

"What's its thesis? That the Grail is an allegory of the Sacred Heart or that the Sacred Heart is an allegory of the Grail?"

"He wants it both ways, I think. In short, gentlemen, I don't know what course to follow. We should sound out Signor Garamond."

So we sounded him out. He said that, as a matter of principle, nothing should be thrown out, and we should give everyone a hearing.

"But most of this stuff," I argued, "repeats things you can find on any station newsstand. Even published authors copy from one another, and cite one another as authorities, and all base their proofs on a sentence of Iamblicus, so to speak."

"Well," Garamond said, "would you try to sell readers something they knew nothing about? The Isis Unveiled books must deal with the exact same subjects as all the others. They confirm one another; therefore they're true. Never trust originality."

"Very well," Belbo said, "but we can't tell what's obvious and what isn't. We need a consultant."

"What sort of consultant?"

"I don't know. He must be less credulous than a Diabolical, but he must know their world. And then tell us what direction we should take in Hermetics. A serious student of Renaissance Hermeticism . . ."

"And the first time you hand him the Grail and the Sacred Heart," Diotallevi said, "he storms out, slamming the door."

"Not necessarily."

"I know someone who would be just right," I said. "He's certainly erudite; he takes these things fairly seriously, but with elegance, even irony, I'd say. I met him in Brazil, but he should be in Milan now. I must have his phone number somewhere."

"Contact him," Garamond said. "Tentatively. It depends on the cost. And try also to make use of him for the wonderful adventure of metals."

Agliè seemed happy to hear from me again. He inquired after the charming Amparo, and when I hinted that was over, he apologized and made some tactful remarks about how a young person could always begin, with ease, a new chapter in his life. I mentioned an editorial project. He showed interest, said he would be glad to meet us, and set a time, at his house.

From the birth of Project Hermes until that day, I had enjoyed myself heedlessly at the expense of many people. Now, They were preparing to present the bill. I was as much of a bee as the ones we wanted to attract; and, like them, I was being quickly lured to a flower, though I didn't yet know what that flower was.

46

During the day you will approach the frog several times and will utter words of worship. And you will ask it to work the miracles you wish. . . . Meanwhile you will cut a cross on which to sacrifice it.

—From a ritual of Aleister Crowley

Agliè lived in the Piazzale Susa area: a little secluded street, a turn-of-the-century building, soberly art nouveau. An elderly butler in a striped jacket opened the door and led us into a small sitting room, where he asked us to wait for the count.

"So he's a count," Belbo whispered.

"Didn't I tell you? He's Saint-Germain redivivus."

"He can't be redivivus if he's never died," Diotallevi said. "Sure he's not Ahasuerus, the wandering Jew?"

"According to some, the Comte de Saint-Germain had also been Ahasuerus."

"You see?"

Agliè came in, impeccable as always. He shook our hands and apologized: a tiresome meeting, quite unforeseen, forced him to remain in his study for another ten minutes or so. He told the butler to bring coffee and begged us to make ourselves at home. Then he went out, drawing aside a heavy curtain of old leather. It wasn't a door, and as we were having our coffee, we heard agitated voices coming from the next room. At first we spoke loudly among ourselves, in order not to listen; then Belbo remarked that perhaps we were disturbing the others. In a moment of silence, we heard a voice, and a sentence that aroused our curiosity.

Diotallevi got up and went over, as if he wanted to admire a seventeenth-century print on the wall by the curtain. It showed a mountain cave, to which some pilgrims were climbing by way of seven steps. Soon all three of us were pretending to study the print.

The man we had heard was surely Bramanti, and the sentence was: "See here, I don't send devils to people's houses!"

That day we realized Bramanti had not only a tapir's face but also a tapir's voice.

The other voice belonged to a stranger: a thick French accent and a shrill, almost hysterical tone. From time to time Agliè's voice, soft and conciliatory, intervened.

"Come, gentlemen," he was saying now, "you have appealed to my verdict, and I am honored, but you must therefore listen to me. Allow me, first of all, to say that you, dear Pierre, were imprudent, at the very least, in writing that letter. . . ."

"It's an extremely simple matter, Monsieur le Comte," the French voice replied. "This Signor Bramanti, he writes an article, in a publication we all respect, in which he indulges himself in some fairly strong irony about certain Luciferans, who, he says, make hosts fly though they don't even believe in the Real Presence, and they transmute silver, and so forth and so on. Bon, everyone knows that the only recognized Eglise Luciferienne is the one where I am the humble tauroboliaste and psychopompe, and it is also well known that my church does not indulge itself in vulgar Satanism and does not make ratatouille with hosts—things worthy of chanoine Docre at Saint-Sulpice. In my letter I said that we are not vieux jeu Satanists, worshipers of the Grand Tenancier du Mal, and that we do not have to ape the Church of Rome, with all those pyxes and those—comment dit-on?—chasubles. . . . We are, au contraire, Palladians, as all the world knows, and, for us, Luciferre is the principe of good. If anything, it is Adonai who is the principe of evil, because He created this world, whereas Luciferre tried to oppose . . ."

"All right," Bramanti said angrily. "I admit I may have been careless, but this doesn't entitle him to threaten me with sorcery!"

"Mais voyons! It was a metaphor! You are the one who, in return, caused me to have the envoûtement!"

"Oh, of course, my brothers and I have time to waste, sending little devils around! We practice Dogma and the Ritual of High Magic: we are not witch doctors!"

"Monsieur le Comte, I appeal to you. Signor Bramanti is notoriously in touch with the abbé Boutroux, and you well know that this priest is said to have the crucifix tattooed on the sole of his foot so that he may tread on Our Lord, or, rather, on his . . . Bon, I meet seven days ago this supposed abbé at the Du Sangreal Bookshop, you know; he smiles at me, very slimy, as is his custom, and he says to me, 'Well, we'll be hearing from each other one of these evenings.' What does it mean, one of these evenings? It means that, two evenings after, the visits begin. I am going to bed and I feel chocs strike my face, fluid chocs, you know; those emanations are easily recognized."

"You probably rubbed the soles of your slippers on the carpet."

"Yes, yes, then why were the bibelots flying? Why did one of my alembiques strike my head, and my plaster Baphomet, it falls to the floor, and that a memento of my late father, and on the wall three writings appear in red, ordures I cannot repeat, hein? You know well that no more than a year ago the late Monsieur Gros accused that abbé there of making the cataplasms with fecal matter, forgive the expression, and the abbé condemned him to death, and two weeks later the poor Monsieur Gros, he dies mysteriously. This Boutroux handles poisons, the jury d'honneur summoned by the Martinists of Lyon said so. . . ."

"Slander," Bramanti growled.

"Ah, that then! A trial in matters of this sort is always circumstantial. . . ."

"Yes, but nobody at the trial mentioned the fact that Monsieur Gros was an alcoholic in the last stages of cirrhosis."

"Do not be enfantine! Sorcelery proceeds by natural ways; if one has a cirrhosis, they strike one in the cirrhosis. That is the ABC of black magic. . . ."

"Then all those who die of cirrhosis have the good Boutroux to blame. Don't make me laugh!"

"Then tell me, please, what passed in Lyon in those two weeks. . . . Deconsecrated chapel, host with Tetragrammaton, your Boutroux with a great red robe with the cross upside down, and Madame Olcott, his personal voyante, among other things, with the trident that appears on her brow and the empty chalices that fill with blood by themselves, and the abbé who crached in the mouth of the faithful. . . . Is that true or is it not?"

"You've been reading too much Huysmans, my friend!" Bramanti laughed. "It was a cultural event, a pageant, like the celebrations of the school of Wicca and the Druid colleges!"

"Ouais, the carnival of Venise . . ."

We heard a scuffle, as if Bramanti was attempting to strike his adversary and Agliè was restraining him. "You see? You see?" the

Frenchman said in a falsetto. "But guard yourself, Bramanti, and ask your friend Boutroux what happened to *him*! You don't know yet, but he's in the hospital. Ask him who broke his figure! Even if I do not practice that goety of yours, I know a little of it myself, and when I realized that my house was inhabited, I drew on the parquet the circle of defense, and since I do not believe, but your diablotines do, I removed the Carmelite scapular and made the contresign, the envoûtement retourné, ah oui. Your abbé passed a mauvais moment!"

"You see? You see?" Bramanti was panting. "He's the one casting spells!"

"Gentlemen, that's enough," Agliè said politely but firmly. "Now listen to me. You know how highly I value, on a cognitive level, these reexaminations of obsolete rituals, and for me the Luciferine Church and the Order of Satan are equally to be respected above and beyond their demonological differences. You know my skepticism in this matter. But, in the end, we all belong to the same spiritual knighthood, and I urge you to show a minimum of solidarity. After all, gentlemen, to involve the Prince of Darkness in a personal spat! How very childish! Come, come, these are occultists' tales. You are behaving like vulgar Freemasons. To be frank, yes, Boutroux is a dissident, and perhaps, my dear Bramanti, you might suggest to him that he sell to some junk dealer all that paraphernalia of his, like the props for a production of Boito's *Mefistofele*. . . ."

"Ha, c'est bien dit, ça," the Frenchman snickered. "C'est de la brocanterie. . . ."

"Let's try to see this in perspective. There has been a debate on what we will call liturgical formalisms, tempers have flared, but we mustn't make mountains out of molehills. Mind you, my dear Pierre, I am not for one moment denying the presence in your house of alien entities; it's the most natural thing in the world, but with a little common sense it could all be explained as a poltergeist."

"Yes, I wouldn't exclude that possibility," Bramanti said. "The astral conjuncture at this time . . ."

"Well then! Come, shake hands, and a fraternal embrace."

We heard murmurs of reciprocal apologies. "You know yourself," Bramanti was saying, "sometimes to identify one who is truly awaiting initiation, it is necessary to indulge in a bit of folklore.

Even those merchants of the Great Orient, who believe in nothing, have a ceremony."

"Bien entendu, le rituel, ah ça . . ."

"But these are no longer the days of Crowley. Is that clear?" Agliè said. "I must leave you now. I have other guests."

We quickly went back to the sofa and waited for Agliè with composure and nonchalance.

47

Our exalted task then is to find order in these seven measures, a pattern that is distinct and will keep always the sense alert and the memory clear. . . . This exalted and incomparable configuration not only performs the function of preserving entrusted things, words, and arts . . . but in addition it gives us true knowledge. . . .
—Giulio Camillo Delminio, *L'idea del Theatro*, Florence, Torrentino, 1550, Introduction

A few minutes later, Agliè came in. "Do forgive me, dear friends, I had to deal with a dispute that was regrettable, to say the least. As my friend Casaubon knows, I consider myself a student of the history of religions, and for this reason people not infrequently come to me for illumination, relying perhaps more on my common sense than on my learning. It's odd how, among the adepts of sapiential studies, eccentric personalities are sometimes found. . . . I don't mean the usual seekers after transcendental consolation, I don't mean the melancholy spirits, but men of profound knowledge and great intellectual refinement who nevertheless indulge in nocturnal fantasies and lose the ability to distinguish between traditional truth and the archipelago of the prodigious. The people with whom I spoke just now were arguing about childish conjectures. Alas, it happens in the best families, as they say. But do come into my little study, please, where we can converse in more comfortable surroundings."

He raised the leather curtain and showed us into the next room. "Little study" is not how I would have described it; it was spacious, with walls of exquisite antique shelving crammed with handsomely bound books all of venerable age. What impressed me more than the books were some small glass cases filled with objects hard to identify—they looked like stones. And there were little animals, whether stuffed, mummified, or delicately reproduced I couldn't say. Everything was bathed in a diffuse crepuscular light that came from a large double-mullioned window at the end, with leaded diamond panes of transparent amber. The light from the window blended with that of a great lamp on a dark mahogany table covered with papers. It was one of those lamps sometimes found on reading tables in old libraries, with a dome of green glass that could cast a white oval on the page while leaving the surroundings in an opalescent penumbra. This play of two sources of light, both unnatural, somehow enlivened the polychrome of the ceiling. The ceiling was vaulted, supported on all four sides by a decorative fiction: little brick-red columns with tiny gilded capitals. The many trompe l'oeil images, divided into seven areas, enhanced the effect of depth, and the whole room had the feeling of a mortuary chapel, impalpably sinful, melancholy, sensual.

"My little theater," Agliè said, "in the style of those Renaissance fantasies where visual encyclopedias were laid out, sylloges of the universe. Not so much a dwelling as a memory machine. There is no image that, when combined with the others, does not embody a mystery of the world. You will notice that line of figures there, painted in imitation of those in the palace of Mantua: they are the thirty-six decans, the Masters of the Heavens. And respecting the tradition, after I found this splendid reconstruction—the work of an unknown artist—I went about acquiring the little objects in the glass cases, which correspond to the images on the ceiling. They represent the fundamental elements of the universe: air, water, earth, and fire. Hence the presence of this charming salamander, the masterwork of a taxidermist friend, and this delicate reproduction in miniature, a rather late piece, of the aeolipile of Hero, in which the air contained in the sphere, were I to activate this little alcohol stove, warming it, would escape from these lateral spouts and thereby cause rotation. A magic instrument. Egyptian priests used it in their shrines, as so many texts inform us. They exploited it to claim a miracle, which the masses venerated, while the true miracle is the golden law that governs this secret and simple mechanism of the elements earth and fire. Here is learning that our ancients possessed, as did the men of alchemy, but that the builders of cyclotrons have lost. And so I cast my gaze on my theater of memory, this child of so many vaster theaters that beguiled the great minds of the past, and I know. I know better than the so-called learned. As it is below, so it is above. And there is nothing more to know."

He offered us Cuban cigars, curiously shaped—not straight, but contorted, curled—though they were thick. We uttered cries of admiration. Diotallevi went over to the shelves.

"Oh," Agliè said, "a minimal library, as you see, barely two hundred volumes; I have more in my family home. But, if I may say so, all these have some merit, some value. And they are not arranged at random. The order of the subjects follows that of the images and the objects."

Diotallevi timidly reached out as if to touch a volume. "Help yourself," Agliè said. "That is the *Oedypus Aegyptiacus* of Athanasius Kircher. As you know, he was the first after Horapollon to try to interpret hieroglyphics. A fascinating man. I wish this study of mine were like his museum of wonders, now presumed lost, scattered, because one who knows not how to seek will never find. . . . A charming conversationalist. How proud he was the day he discovered that this hieroglyph meant 'The benefices of the divine Osiris are provided by sacred ceremonies and by the chain of spirits. . . .' Then that mountebank Champollion came along, a hateful man, believe me, childishly vain, and he insisted that the sign corresponded only to the name of a pharaoh. How ingenious the moderns are in debasing sacred symbols. The work is actually not all that rare: it costs less than a Mercedes. But look at this, a first edition, 1595, of the *Amphitheatrum sapientiae aeternae* of Khunrath. It is said there are only two copies in the world. This is the third. And this volume is a first edition of the *Telluris Theoria Sacra* of Burnetius. I cannot look at the illustrations in the evening without feeling a wave of mystical claustrophobia. The profundities of our globe . . . Unsuspected, are they not? I see that Dr. Diotallevi is fascinated by the Hebrew characters of Vigenère's *Traicté des Chiffres*. Then look at this: a first edition of the *Kabbala denudata* of Christian Knorr von Rosenroth. The book was translated into English— in part and badly—at the beginning of this century by that wretch McGregor Mathers. . . . You must know something of that scandalous conventicle that so fascinated the British esthetes, the Golden Dawn. Only from that band of counterfeiters of occult documents could such an endless series of debasements spring, from the Stella Matutina to the satanic churches of Aleister Crowley, who called up demons to win the favors of certain gentlemen devoted to the vice anglais. If you only knew, dear friends, the sort of people one has to rub elbows with in devoting oneself to such studies. You will see for yourselves if you undertake to publish in this field."

Belbo seized this opportunity to broach the subject. He explained that Garamond wished to bring out, each year, a few books of an esoteric nature.

"Ah, esoteric." Agliè smiled, and Belbo blushed.

"Should we say . . . hermetic?"

"Ah, hermetic." Agliè smiled.

"Well," Belbo said, "perhaps I am using the wrong word, but surely you know the genre."

Agliè smiled again. "It is not a genre. It is knowledge. What you wish to do is publish a survey of knowledge that has not been debased. For you it may be simply an editorial choice, but for me, if I am to concern myself with it, it will be a search for truth, a queste du Graal."

Belbo warned that just as the fisherman who casts his net could pull in empty shells and plastic bags, so Garamond Press might receive many manuscripts of dubious value, and that we were looking for a stern reader who would separate the wheat from the chaff, while also taking note of any curious by-products, because there was a friendly publishing firm that would be happy if we redirected less worthy authors to it. . . . Naturally, a suitable form of compensation would be worked out.

"Thank heavens I am what is called a man of means. Even a shrewd man of means. If, in the course of my explorations, I come upon another copy of Khunrath, or another handsome stuffed salamander, or a narwhal's horn (which I would be ashamed to display in my collection, though the Treasure of Vienna exhibits one as a unicorn's horn), with a brief and agreeable transaction I can earn more than you would pay me in ten years of consultancy. I will look at your manuscripts in the spirit of humility. I am convinced that even in the most commonplace text I will find a spark, if not of truth, at least of bizarre falsehood, and often the extremes meet. I will be bored only by the ordinary, and for that boredom you will compensate me. Depending on the boredom I have undergone, I will confine myself to sending you, at the end of the year, a little note, and I will keep my request within the confines of the symbolical. If you consider it excessive, you will just send me a case of fine wine."

Belbo was nonplussed. He was accustomed to dealing with consultants who were querulous and starving. He opened the briefcase he had brought with him and drew out a thick manuscript.

"I wouldn't want you to be overoptimistic. Look at this, for example. It seems to me typical."

Agliè took the manuscript: "The Secret Language of the Pyramids . . . Let's see the index. . . . Pyramidion . . . Death of Lord Carnarvon . . . Testimony of Herodotus . . ." He looked up. "You gentlemen have read it?"

"I skimmed through it," Belbo said.

Agliè returned the manuscript to him. "Now tell me if my summary is correct." He sat down behind the desk, reached into the pocket of his vest, drew out the pillbox I had seen in Brazil, and turned it in his thin, tapering fingers, which earlier had caressed his favorite books. He raised his eyes toward the figures on the ceiling and recited, as if from a text he had long known by heart:

"The author of this book no doubt reminds us that Piazzi Smyth discovered the sacred and esoteric measurements of the pyramids in 1864. Allow me to round off to whole numbers; at my age the memory begins to fail a bit. . . . Their base is a square; each side measures two hundred and thirty-two meters. Originally the height was one hundred and forty-eight meters. If we convert into sacred Egyptian cubits, we obtain a base of three hundred and sixty-six; in other words, the number of days in a leap year. For Piazzi Smyth, the height multiplied by ten to the ninth gives the distance between the earth and the sun: one hundred and forty-eight million kilometers. A good estimate at the time, since today the calculated distance is one hundred and forty-nine and a half million kilometers, and the moderns are not necessarily right. The base divided by the width of one of the stones is three hundred and sixty-five. The perimeter of the base is nine hundred and thirty-one meters. Divide by twice the height, and you get 3.14, the number π. Splendid, no?"

Belbo smiled and looked embarrassed. "Incredible! Tell me how you—"

"Let Dr. Agliè go on, Jacopo," Diotallevi said.

Agliè thanked him with a nod. His gaze wandered the ceiling as he spoke, but it seemed to me that the path his eyes followed was neither idle nor random, that they were reading, in those images, what he only pretended to be digging from his memory.

48

"I imagine your author holds that the height of the pyramid of Cheops is equal to the square root of the sum of the areas of all its sides. The measurements must be made in feet, the foot being closer to the Egyptian and Hebrew cubit, and not in meters, for the meter is an abstract length invented in modern times. The Egyptian cubit comes to 1.728 feet. If we do not know the precise height, we can use the pyramidion, which was the small pyramid set atop the Great Pyramid, to form its tip. It was of gold or some other metal that shone in the sun. Take the height of the pyramidion, multiply it by the height of the whole pyramid, multiply the total by ten to the fifth, and we obtain the circumference of the earth. What's more, if you multiply the perimeter of the base by twenty-four to the third divided by two, you get the earth's radius. Further, the area of the base of the pyramid multiplied by ninety-six times ten to the eighth gives us one hundred and ninety-six million eight hundred and ten thousand square miles, which is the surface area of the earth. Am I right?"

Belbo liked to convey amazement with an expression he had learned in the cinematheque, from the original-language version of *Yankee Doodle Dandy*, starring James Cagney: "I'm flabbergasted!" This is what he said now. Agliè also knew colloquial English, apparently, because he couldn't hide his satisfaction at this tribute to his vanity. "My friends," he said, "when a gentleman, whose name is unknown to me, pens a compilation on the mystery of the pyramids, he can say only what by now even children know. I would have been surprised if he had said anything new."

"So the writer is simply repeating established truths?"

"Truths?" Agliè laughed, and again opened for us the box of his deformed and delicious cigars. "Quid est veritas, as a friend of mine said many years ago. Most of it is nonsense. To begin with, if you divide the base of the pyramid by exactly twice the height, and do not round off, you don't get π, you get 3.1417254. A small difference, but essential. Further, a disciple of Piazzi Smyth, Flinders Petrie, who also measured Stonehenge, reports that one day he caught the master chipping at a granite wall of the royal antechamber, to make his sums work out. . . . Gossip, perhaps, but Piazzi Smyth was not a man to inspire trust; you had only to see the way he tied his cravat. Still, amid all the nonsense there are some unimpeachable truths. Gentlemen, would you follow me to the window?"

He threw open the shutters dramatically and pointed. At the corner of the narrow street and the broad avenue, stood a little wooden kiosk, where, presumably, lottery tickets were sold.

"Gentlemen," he said, "I invite you to go and measure that kiosk. You will see that the length of the counter is one hundred and forty-nine centimeters—in other words, one hundred-billionth of the distance between the earth and the sun. The height at the rear, one hundred and seventy-six centimeters, divided by the width of the window, fifty-six centimeters, is 3.14. The height at the front is nineteen decimeters, equal, in other words, to the number of years of the Greek lunar cycle. The sum of the heights of the two front corners and the two rear corners is one hundred and ninety times two plus one hundred and seventy-six times two, which equals seven hundred and thirty-two, the date of the victory at Poitiers. The thickness of the counter is 3.10 centimeters, and the width of the cornice of the window is 8.8 centimeters. Replacing the numbers before the decimals by the corresponding letters of the alphabet, we obtain C for ten and H for eight, or $C_{10}H_8$, which is the formula for naphthalene."

"Fantastic," I said. "You did all these measurements?"

"No," Agliè said. "They were done on another kiosk, by a certain Jean-Pierre Adam. But I would assume that all lottery kiosks have more or less the same dimensions. With numbers you can do anything you like. Suppose I have the sacred number 9 and I want to get the number 1314, date of the execution of Jacques de Molay—a date dear to anyone who, like me, professes devotion to the Templar tradition of knighthood. What do I do? I multiply nine by one hundred and forty-six, the fateful day of the destruction of Carthage. How did I arrive at this? I divided thirteen hundred and fourteen by two, by three, et cetera, until I found a satisfying date. I could also have divided thirteen hundred and fourteen by 6.28, the double of 3.14, and I would have got two hundred and nine. That is the year Attalus I, king of Pergamon, ascended the throne. You see?"

"Then you don't believe in numerologies of any kind," Diotallevi said, disappointed.

"On the contrary, I believe firmly. I believe the universe is a great symphony of numerical correspondences, I believe that numbers and their symbolisms provide a path to special knowledge. But if the world, below and above, is a system of correspondences where tout se tient, it's natural for the kiosk and the pyramid, both works of man, to reproduce in their structure, unconsciously, the harmonies of the cosmos. The so-called pyramidologists discover with their incredibly tortuous methods a straightforward truth, a truth far more ancient, and one already known. It is the logic of research and discovery that is tortuous, because it is the logic of science. Whereas the logic of knowledge needs no discovery, because it knows already. Why must it demonstrate that which could not be otherwise? If there is a secret, it is much more profound. These authors of yours remain simply on the surface. I imagine this one also repeats all the tales of how the Egyptians knew about electricity. . . ."

"I won't ask how you managed to guess."

"You see? They are content with electricity, like any old Marconi. The hypothesis of radioactivity would be less puerile. *There* is an interesting idea. Unlike the electricity hypothesis, it would explain the much vaunted curse of Tutankhamen. And how were the Egyptians able to lift the blocks of the pyramids? Can you lift boulders with electric shocks, can you make them fly with nuclear fission? No, the Egyptians found a way to eliminate the force of gravity; they possessed the secret of levitation. Another form of energy . . . It is known that the Chaldean priests operated sacred machines by sounds alone, and the priests of Karnak and Thebes could open the doors of a temple with only their voice—and what else could be the origin, if you think about it, of the legend of Open Sesame?"

"So?" Belbo asked.

"Now here's the point, my friend. Electricity, radioactivity, atomic energy—the true initiate knows that these are metaphors, masks, conventional lies, or, at most, pathetic surrogates, for an ancestral, forgotten force, a force the initiate seeks and one day will know. We should speak perhaps"—he hesitated a moment—"of telluric currents."

"What?" one of us asked, I forget who.

Agliè seemed disappointed. "You see? I was beginning to hope that among your prospective authors one had appeared who could tell me something more interesting. But it grows late. Very well, my friends, our pact is made; the rest was just the rambling of an elderly scholar."

As he held out his hand to us, the butler entered and murmured something in his ear. "Ah, the sweet friend," Agliè said, "I had forgotten. Ask her to wait a moment. . . . No, not in the living room, in the Turkish salon."

The sweet friend must have been familiar with the house, because she was already on the threshold of the study, and without even looking at us, in the gathering shadows of the day at its end, she proceeded confidently to Agliè, patted his cheek, and said: "Simon, you're not going to make me wait outside, are you?" It was Lorenza Pellegrini.

Agliè moved aside slightly, kissed her hand, and said, gesturing at us: "My sweet Sophia, you know you are always welcome, as you illuminate every house you enter. I was merely saying goodbye to these guests."

Lorenza turned, saw us, and made a cheerful wave of greeting—I don't believe I ever saw her discomposed or embarrassed. "Oh, how nice," she said; "you also know my friend! Hello, Jacopo."

Belbo turned pale. We said good-bye. Agliè expressed pleasure that we knew each other. "I consider our mutual acquaintance to be one of the most genuine creatures I ever had the good fortune to know. In her freshness she incarnates—allow an old man of learning this fancy—the Sophia, exiled on this earth. But, my sweet Sophia, I haven't had time to let you know: the promised evening has been postponed for a few weeks. I'm so sorry."

"It doesn't matter," Lorenza said. "I'll wait. Are you going to the bar?" she asked us—or, rather, commanded us. "Good. I'll stay here for a half hour or so. Simon's giving me one of his elixirs. You should try them. But he says they're only for the elect. Then I'll join you."

Agliè smiled with the air of an indulgent uncle; he had her take a seat, then accompanied us to the door.

Out in the street again, we headed for Pilade's, in my car. Belbo was silent. We didn't talk all the way there. But at the bar, the spell had to be broken.

"I hope I haven't delivered you into the hands of a lunatic," I said.

"No," Belbo said. "The man is keen, subtle. It's just that he lives in a world different from ours." Then he added grimly: "Or almost."

49

The *Traditio Templi* postulates, independently, the tradition of a *templar* knighthood, a spiritual knighthood of initiates . . .
  —Henry Corbin, *Temple et contemplation*, Paris,
  Flammarion, 1980

"I believe I've got your Agliè figured out, Casaubon," Diotallevi said, having ordered a sparkling white wine from Pilade, making all of us fear for his moral health. "He's a scholar, curious about the secret sciences, suspicious of dilettantes, of those who learn by ear. Yet, as we ourselves learned today, by our eavesdropping, he may scorn them but he listens to them, he may criticize them but he doesn't dissociate himself from them."

"Signor or Count or Margrave Agliè, or whatever the hell he is, said something very revealing today," Belbo added. "He used the expression 'spiritual knighthood.' He feels joined to them by a bond of spiritual knighthood. I think I understand him."

"Joined, in what sense?" we asked.

Belbo was now on his third martini (whiskey in the evening, he claimed, because it was calming and induced reverie; martinis in the afternoon, because they stimulated and fortified). He began talking about his childhood in ***, as he had already done once with me.

"It was between 1943 and 1945, that is, the period of transition from Fascism to democracy and then to the dictatorship of the Salò republic, with the partisan war going on in the mountains. At the beginning of this story I was eleven, and staying in my uncle Carlo's house. My family normally lived in the city, but in 1943 the air raids were increasing and my mother had decided to evacuate.

"Uncle Carlo and Aunt Caterina lived in ***. Uncle Carlo came from a farming family and had inherited the *** house, with some land, which was cultivated by a tenant farmer named Adelino Canepa. The tenant planted, harvested the grain, made the wine, and gave half of everything to the owner. A tense situation, obviously: the tenant considered himself exploited, and so did the owner, who received only half the produce of his land. The landowners hated the tenants and the tenants hated the landowners. But in Uncle Carlo's case they lived side by side.

"In 1914 Uncle Carlo had enlisted in the Alpine troops. A bluff Piedmontese, all duty and Fatherland, he became a lieutenant, then a captain. One day, in a battle on the Carso, he found himself beside an idiot soldier who let a grenade explode in his hands—why else call them hand grenades? Uncle Carlo was about to be thrown into a common grave when an orderly realized he was still alive. They took him to a field hospital, removed the eye that was hanging out of its socket, cut off one arm, and, according to Aunt Caterina, they also put a metal plate in his head, because he had lost some of his skull. In other words, a masterpiece of surgery on the one hand and a hero on the other. Silver medal, cavalier of the Crown of Italy, and after the war a good steady job in public administration. Uncle Carlo ended up head of the tax office in ***, where, after inheriting the family property, he went to live in the ancestral home with Adelino Canepa and family.

"As head of the tax office, Uncle Carlo was a local bigwig, and as a mutilated veteran and cavalier of the Crown of Italy, he was naturally on the side of the government, which happened to be the Fascist dictatorship. Was Uncle Carlo a Fascist?

"In those days, Fascism had given veterans status, had rewarded them with decorations and promotions; so let's say Uncle Carlo was moderately Fascist. Fascist enough to earn the hatred of Adelino Canepa, who was ardently anti-Fascist, for obvious reasons. Canepa had to go to Uncle Carlo every year to make his income declaration. He would arrive in the office with a bold expression of complicity, having tried to corrupt Aunt Caterina with a few dozen eggs. And he would find himself up against Uncle Carlo, who, being a hero, was not only incorruptible, but also knew better than anyone how much Canepa had stolen from him in the course of the year, and who wouldn't forgive him one cent. Adelino Canepa, considering himself a victim of the dictatorship, began spreading slanderous rumors about Uncle Carlo. One lived on the ground floor, the other on the floor above; they met every morning and night, but no longer exchanged greetings. Communication was maintained through Aunt Caterina and, after our arrival, through my mother—to whom Adelino Canepa expressed much sympathy and understanding, since she was the sister-in-law of a monster. My uncle, in his gray double-breasted suit and bowler, would come home every evening at six with his copy of *La Stampa* still to be read. He walked erect, like an Alpine soldier, his gray eye on the peak to be stormed. He passed by Adelino Canepa, who at that hour was enjoying the cool air on a bench in the garden, and it was as if my uncle did not see him. Then he would encounter Signora Canepa at the downstairs door and ceremoniously doff his hat. And so it went, every evening, year after year."

It was eight o'clock; Lorenza wasn't coming, as she had promised. Belbo was on his fifth martini.

"Then came 1943. One morning Uncle Carlo came into our room, waked me with a kiss, and said, 'My boy, you want to hear the biggest news of the year? They've kicked out Mussolini.' I never figured out whether or not Uncle Carlo suffered over it. He was a citizen of total integrity and a servant of the state. If he did suffer, he said nothing about it, and he went on running the tax office for the Badoglio government. Then came September 8, and the area in which we lived fell under the control of the Fascists' Social Republic, and Uncle Carlo again adjusted. He collected taxes for the Social Republic.

"Adelino Canepa, meanwhile, boasted of his contacts with the partisan groups forming in the mountains, and he promised vengeance, the making of examples. We kids didn't yet know who the partisans were. There were great tales about them, but so far nobody had seen them. There was talk about a Badoglian leader known as Mongo—a nickname, naturally, as was the custom then; many said he had taken it from *Flash Gordon*. Mongo was a former Carabinieri sergeant major who had lost a leg in the first fighting against the Fascists and the SS and now commanded all the brigades in the hills around ***.

"And then came the disaster: one day the partisans showed up in town. They had descended from the hills, they were running wild in the streets, still without uniforms, just blue kerchiefs, and firing rounds into the air to make their presence known. The news spread; all the people locked themselves in their houses. It wasn't yet clear what sort of men these partisans were. Aunt Caterina was only mildly concerned: after all, those partisans were friends of Adelino Canepa, or at least Adelino Canepa claimed to be a friend of theirs, so they wouldn't do anything bad to Uncle, would they? They would. We were informed that around eleven o'clock a squad of partisans with automatic rifles aimed had entered the tax office, arrested Uncle Carlo, and carried him off, destination unknown. Aunt Caterina lay down on her bed, and whitish foam began to dribble from her lips. She declared that Uncle Carlo would be killed. A blow with a rifle butt would be enough: with the metal plate in his head, he would die on the spot.

"Drawn by my aunt's moans, Adelino Canepa arrived with his wife and children. My aunt cried that he was a Judas, that he had reported Uncle to the partisans because Uncle collected taxes for the Social Republic. Adelino Canepa swore by everything sacred that this was not true, but obviously he felt responsible, because he had talked too much in town. My aunt sent him away. Adelino Canepa wept, appealed to my mother, reminded her of all the times he had sold her a rabbit or a chicken at a ridiculously low price, but my mother maintained a dignified silence, Aunt Caterina continued to dribble whitish foam, I cried. Finally, after two hours of agony, we heard shouts, and Uncle Carlo appeared on a bicycle, steering it with his one arm and looking as if he were returning from a picnic. Seeing a disturbance in the garden, he asked what had happened. Uncle hated dramas, like everyone in our parts. He went upstairs, approached the bed of pain of Aunt Caterina, who was still kicking her scrawny legs, and inquired why she was so agitated."

"What had happened?"

"What had happened was this. Mongo's partisans, probably hearing some of Adelino Canepa's mutterings, had identified Uncle Carlo as one of the local representatives of the regime, so they arrested him to teach the whole town a lesson. He was taken outside the town in a truck and found himself before Mongo. Mongo, his war medals shining, stood with a gun in his right hand and his left holding a crutch. Uncle Carlo—but I really don't think he was being clever; I think it was instinct, or the ritual of chivalry—snapped to attention, introduced himself: Major Carlo Covasso, Alpine Division, disabled veteran, silver medal. And Mongo also snapped to attention and introduced himself: Sergeant Major Rebaudengo, Royal Carabineers, commander of the Badoglian brigade Bettino Ricasoli, bronze medal. 'Where?' Uncle Carlo asked. And Mongo, impressed, said: 'Pordoi, Major, hill 327.' 'By God,' said Uncle Carlo,

'I was at hill 328, third regiment, Sasso di Stria!' The battle of the solstice? Battle of the solstice it was. And the cannon on Five-Finger Mountain? Dammit to hell, do I remember! And the bayonet attack on Saint Crispin's Eve? Yessir! That sort of thing. Then, the one without an arm, the other without a leg, on the same impulse they took a step forward and embraced. Mongo said then, 'You see, Cavalier, it's this way, Major: we were informed that you collect taxes for the Fascist government that toadies to the invaders.' 'You see, Commander,' Uncle Carlo said, 'it's this way: I have a family and receive a salary from the government, and the government is what it is; I didn't choose it, and what would you have done in my place?' 'My dear Major,' Mongo replied, 'in your place, I'd have done what you did, but try at least to collect the taxes slowly; take your time.' 'I'll see what I can do,' Uncle Carlo said. 'I have nothing against you men; you, too, are sons of Italy and valiant fighters.' They understood each other, because they both thought of Fatherland with a capital F. Mongo ordered his men to give the major a bicycle, and Uncle Carlo went home. Adelino Canepa didn't show his face for several months.

"There, I don't know if this qualifies as spiritual knighthood, but I'm certain there are bonds that endure above factions and parties."

50

For I am the first and the last. I am the honored and the hated. I
am the saint and the prostitute.
  —Fragment of *Nag Hammadi* 6, 2

Lorenza Pellegrini entered. Belbo looked up at the ceiling and ordered a final martini. There was tension in the air, and I got up to
leave, but Lorenza stopped me. "No. All of you come with me.
Tonight's the opening of Riccardo's show; he's inaugurating a new
style! He's great! You know him, Jacopo."

I knew who Riccardo was; he was always hanging around Pilade's. But at that moment I didn't understand why Belbo's eyes
were fixed so intensely on the ceiling. Having read the files, I realize
now that Riccardo was the man with the scar, the man with whom
Belbo had lacked the courage to start a fight.

The gallery wasn't far from Pilade's, Lorenza insisted. They had
organized a real party—or, rather, an orgy. Diotallevi became nervous at this and immediately said he had to go home. I hesitated,
but it was obvious Lorenza wanted me along, and this, too, made
Belbo suffer, since he saw the possibility of a tête-à-tête slipping
farther and farther away. But I couldn't refuse; so we set out.

I didn't care that much for Riccardo. In the early sixties he turned
out very boring paintings, small canvases in blacks and grays, very
geometric, slightly optical, the sort of stuff that made your eyes
swim. They bore titles like *Composition 15*, *Parallax 17*, *Euclid X*.
But in 1968 he started showing in squats, he changed his palette;
now there were only violent blacks and whites, no grays, the strokes
were bolder, and the titles were like *Ce n'est qu'un début*, *Molotov*,
A Hundred Flowers. When I got back to Milan, I saw a show of his
in a club where Dr. Wagner was worshiped. Riccardo had eliminated black, was working in white only, the contrasts provided
by the texture and relief of the paint on porous Fabriano paper,
so that the pictures—as he explained—would reveal different figures

in different lightings. Their titles were *In Praise of Ambiguity*, *A/Travers, Ça, Bergstrasse,* and *Denegation 15*.

That evening, as soon as we entered the new gallery, I saw that Riccardo's poetics had undergone a profound change. The show was entitled *Megale Apophasis*. Riccardo had turned figurative with a dazzling palette. He played with quotations, and, since I don't believe he knew how to draw, I guess he worked by projecting onto the canvas the slide of a famous painting. His choices hovered between the turn-of-the-century pompiers and the early-twentieth-century Symbolists. Over the projected image he worked with a pointillist technique, using infinitesimal gradations of color, covering the whole spectrum dot by dot, so that he always began from a blindingly bright nucleus and ended at absolute black, or vice versa, depending on the mystical or cosmological concept he wanted to express. There were mountains that shot rays of light, which were broken up into a fine powder of pale spheres, and there were concentric skies with hints of angels with transparent wings, something like the Paradise of Doré. The titles were *Beatrix, Mystica Rosa, Dante Gabriele 33, Fedeli d'Amore, Atanòr, Homunculus 666*. This is the source of Lorenza's passion for homunculi, I said to myself. The largest picture was entitled *Sophia*, and it showed a rain of black angels, which faded at the ground and created a white creature caressed by great livid hands, the creature a copy of the one you see held up against the sky in *Guernica*. The juxtaposition was dubious, and, seen close up, the execution proved crude, but at a distance of two or three meters the effect was quite lyrical.

"I'm a realist of the old school," Belbo whispered to me. "I understand only Mondrian. What does a nongeometric picture say?"

"He was geometric before," I said.

"That wasn't geometry, that was bathroom tiles."

Meanwhile, Lorenza rushed to embrace Riccardo. He and Belbo exchanged a nod of greeting. There was a crowd; the gallery was trying to look like a New York loft, all white, with heating or water pipes exposed on the ceiling. God knows what it had cost them to backdate the place like that. In one corner, a sound system was deafening those present with Asian music—sitar music, if I recall rightly, the kind where you can't pick out a tune. Everybody walked absently past the pictures to crowd around the tables at the end and grab paper cups. We had arrived well into the evening: the air was thick with smoke, some girls from time to time hinted at dance movements in the center of the room, but everybody was still busy conversing, busy consuming the plentiful buffet. I sat on a sofa, and at my feet lay a great glass bowl half-filled with fruit salad. I was about to take a little, because I hadn't had any supper, but then I saw in it a footprint, which had crushed the little cubes of fruit in the center, reducing them to a homogeneous pavé. This was not that surprising, because the floor was now spattered in many places with white wine, and some of the guests were already staggering.

Belbo had captured a paper cup and was proceeding lazily, without any apparent goal, occasionally slapping someone on the shoulder. He was trying to find Lorenza.

But few people remained motionless; the crowd was intent on a kind of circular movement, like bees hunting for a hidden flower. Though I wasn't looking for anything myself, I stood up and moved, shifted in response to the impulses transmitted to me by the group, and not far from me I saw Lorenza. She was wandering, miming the impassioned recognition of this man, of that: head high, eyes deliberately myopic-wide, back straight, breasts steady, and her steps haphazard, like a giraffe's.

At a certain point the human flow trapped me in a corner behind a table, where Lorenza and Belbo had their backs to me, having finally met, perhaps by chance, and they were also trapped. I don't know if they were aware of my presence, but the noise was so great that nobody could hear what others were saying at any distance. Lorenza and Belbo therefore considered themselves isolated, and I was forced to hear their conversation.

"Well," Belbo said, "where did you meet your Agliè?"

"My Agliè? Yours, too, from what I saw. You can know Simon, but I can't. Fine."

"Why do you call him Simon? Why does he call you Sophia?"

"Oh, it's a game. I met him at a friend's place—all right? And I find him fascinating. He kisses my hand as if I were a princess. He could be my father."

"He could be the father of your son, if you aren't careful."

It sounded like me, in Bahia, talking to Amparo. Lorenza was right. Agliè knew how to kiss the hand of a young lady unfamiliar with that ritual.

"Why Simon and Sophia?" Belbo insisted. "Is his name Simon?"

"It's a wonderful story. Did you know that our universe is the result of an error and that it's partly my fault? Sophia was the female part of God, because God then was more female than male; it was you men who later put a beard on him and started calling him He. I was his good half. Simon says I tried to create the world without asking permission—I, the Sophia, who is also called—wait a minute—the Ennoia. But my male part didn't want to create; maybe he lacked the courage or was impotent. So instead of uniting with him, I decided to make the world by myself. I couldn't resist; it was through an excess of love. Which is true; I adore this whole mixed-up universe. And that's why I'm the soul of this world, according to Simon."

"How nice! Does he give that line to all the girls?"

"No, stupid, just to me, because he understands me better than you do. He doesn't try to create me in his image. He understands I have to be allowed to live my life in my own way. And that's what Sophia did; she flung herself into making the world. She came up against primordial matter, which was disgusting, probably because it didn't use a deodorant. And then, I think, she accidentally created the Demi—how do you say it?"

"You mean the Demiurge?"

"That's him, yes. Or maybe it wasn't Sophia who made this Demiurge; maybe he was already around and she egged him on: Get moving, silly, make the world, and then we'll have real fun. The Demiurge must have been a real screwup, because he didn't know how to make the world properly. In fact, he shouldn't even have tried it, because matter is bad, and he wasn't authorized to touch the stuff. Anyway, he made this awful mess, and Sophia was caught inside. Prisoner of the world."

Lorenza was drinking a lot. A number of people had started dancing sleepily in the center of the room, their eyes closed, and Riccardo came by every few minutes and filled her cup. Belbo tried to stop him, saying she had already had too much to drink, but Riccardo laughed and shook his head, and she said indignantly that she could hold her alcohol better than Jacopo because she was younger.

"All right," Belbo said, "don't listen to Granddad, listen to Simon. What else did he tell you?"

"What I said: I'm prisoner of the world, or, rather, of the bad angels . . . because in this story the angels are bad and they helped the Demiurge make all this mess. . . . The bad angels, anyhow, are holding me; they don't want me to get away, and they make me suffer. But every now and then in the world of men there is someone who recognizes me. Like Simon. He says it happened to him once before, a thousand years ago—I forgot to tell you Simon's practically immortal; you can't imagine all the things he's seen. . . ."

"Of course . . . but don't drink anymore now."

"Sssh . . . Simon found me once when I was a prostitute in a brothel in Tyre and my name was Helen. . . ."

"He tells you that? And you're overjoyed. Pray let me kiss your hand, whore of my screwed-up universe. . . . Some gentleman."

"If anything, that Helen was the whore. And besides, in those days, when they said prostitute, they meant a woman who was free, without ties, an intellectual who didn't want to be a housewife. She might hold a salon. Today she'd be in public relations. Would you call a PR woman a whore or a hooker, who lights bonfires along the highway for truck drivers?"

At that point Riccardo came and took her by the arm. "Come and dance," he said.

In the middle of the room, they made faint, dreamy movements, as if beating a drum. But from time to time Riccardo drew her to him, put a hand possessively on the back of her neck, and she would follow him with closed eyes, her face flushed, head thrown back, hair hanging free, vertically. Belbo lit one cigarette after another.

Then Lorenza grabbed Riccardo by the waist and slowly pulled him until they were only a step from Belbo. Still dancing, she took the paper cup from Belbo's hand. Holding Riccardo with her left hand, the cup with her right, she turned her moist eyes on Belbo. It was almost as if she had been crying, but she smiled and said: "It wasn't the only time, either."

"The only time, what?" Belbo asked.

"That he met Sophia. Centuries after that, Simon was also Guillaume Postel."

"A letter carrier?"

"Idiot. He was a Renaissance scholar who read Jewish—"

"Hebrew."

"Same difference. He read it the way kids read *Superman*. Without a dictionary. Anyhow, in a hospital in Venice he meets an old illiterate maidservant, Joanna. He looks at her and says, 'You are the new incarnation of Sophia, the Ennoia, the Great Mother descended into our midst to redeem the whole world, which has a female soul.' And so Postel takes Joanna with him; everybody says he's crazy, but he pays no attention; he adores her, wants to free her from the angels' imprisonment, and when she dies, he sits and stares at the sun for an hour and goes for days without drinking or eating, inhabited by Joanna, who no longer exists but it's as if she did, because she's still there, she inhabits the world, and every now and then she resurfaces, that is, she's reincarnated. . . . Isn't that a story to make you cry?"

"I'm dissolved in tears. Are you so pleased to be Sophia?"

"But I'm Sophia for you, too, darling. You know that before you met me you wore the most dreadful ghastly ties and had dandruff on your shoulders."

Riccardo was holding her neck again. "May I join in the conversation?" he said.

"You keep quiet and dance. You're the instrument of my lust."

"Suits me."

Belbo went on as if the other man didn't exist. "So you're his prostitute, his feminist who does public relations, and he's your Simon."

"My name's not Simon," Riccardo said, his tongue thick.

"We're not talking about you," Belbo said.

His behavior had been making me uneasy for some while now. He, as a rule so guarded about his feelings, was having a lovers' quarrel in front of a witness, in front of a rival, even. But this last remark made me realize that with his baring of himself before the other man—the true rival being yet another—Belbo was reasserting, in the only way he could, his possession of Lorenza.

Meanwhile, holding out her cup for more drink, Lorenza answered: "But it's a game. I love you."

"Thank God you don't hate me. Listen, I'd like to go home, I have a stomachache. I'm still a prisoner of base matter. Simon hasn't done me any good. Will you come with me?"

"Let's stay a little longer. It's so nice. Aren't you having fun? Besides, I still haven't looked at the pictures. Did you see? Riccardo made one on me."

"There are other things I'd like to do on you," Riccardo said.

"You're vulgar. Stop it. I'm talking about Jacopo. My God, Jacopo, are you the only one who can make intellectual jokes with your friends? Who treats me like a prostitute from Tyre? You do."

"I might have known. Me. I'm the one pushing you into the arms of old gentlemen."

"He's never tried to take me in his arms. He isn't a satyr. You're cross because he doesn't want to take me to bed but considers me an intellectual partner."

"Allumeuse."

"You really shouldn't have said that. Riccardo, get me something to drink."

"No, wait," Belbo said. "Now, I want you to tell me if you take him seriously. Stop drinking, dammit! Tell me if you take him seriously!"

"But, darling, it's our game, a game between him and me. And besides, the best part of the story is that when Sophia realizes who she is and frees herself from the tyranny of the angels, she frees herself from sin. . . ."

"You've given up sinning?"

"Think it over first," Riccardo said, kissing her chastely on the forehead.

"I don't have to," she replied—to Belbo, ignoring the painter. "Those things aren't sins anymore; I can do anything I like. Once you've freed yourself from the flesh, you're beyond good and evil."

She pushed Riccardo away. "I'm Sophia, and to free myself from the angels I have to perpet . . . per-pet-rate all sins, even the most marvelous!"

Staggering a little, she went to a corner where a girl was seated, dressed in black, her eyes heavily mascaraed, her complexion pale. Lorenza led the girl into the center of the room and began to sway with her. They were belly to belly, arms limp at their sides. "I can love you, too," Lorenza said, and kissed the girl on the mouth.

The others gathered around, mildly aroused. Belbo sat down and looked at the scene with an impenetrable face, like a producer watching a screen test. He was sweating, and there was a tic by his left eye, which I had never noticed before. Lorenza danced for at least five minutes, with movements increasingly suggestive. Then suddenly he said: "Now you come here."

Lorenza stopped, spread her legs, held her arms straight out, and cried: "I am the saint and the prostitute!"

"You are the pain in the ass." Belbo got up, went straight to her, grabbed her by the wrist, and dragged her toward the door.

"Stop it!" she shouted. "Don't you dare . . ." Then she burst into tears and flung her arms around his neck. "But darling, I'm your Sophia; you can't get mad. . . ."

Belbo tenderly put an arm around her shoulders, kissed her on the temple, smoothed her hair, then said to everybody: "Excuse her; she isn't used to drinking like this."

I heard some snickers from those present, and I believe Belbo heard them, too. He saw me on the threshold, and did something—whether for me, for the others, or for himself, I've never figured out. It was a whisper, when everybody else had turned away from the couple, losing interest.

Still holding Lorenza by the shoulders, he addressed the room, softly, in the tone of a man stating the obvious: "Cock-a-doodle-doo."

5 1

The illustrations I found in Milan and Paris weren't enough. Signor Garamond authorized me to spend a few days at the Deutsches Museum in Munich.

I spent my evenings in the bars of Schwabing—or in the immense crypts where elderly mustached gentlemen in lederhosen played music and lovers smiled at each other through a thick cloud of pork steam over full-liter beer steins—and in the afternoons I went through card catalogs of reproductions. Now and then I would leave the archive and stroll through the museum, where every human invention had been reconstructed. You pushed a button, and dioramas of oil exploration came to life with working drills, you stepped inside a real submarine, you made the planets revolve, you played at producing acids and chain reactions. A less Gothic Conservatoire, totally of the future, peopled by unruly school groups being taught to idealize engineers.

In the Deutsches Museum you also learned everything about mines: you went down a ladder and found yourself in a mine complete with tunnels, elevators for men and horses, narrow passages where scrawny exploited children (made of wax, I hoped) were crawling. You went along endless dark corridors, you stopped at the edge of bottomless pits, you felt chilled to the bone, and you could almost catch a whiff of firedamp. Everything life-size.

I was wandering in a tunnel, despairing of ever seeing the light of day again, when I came upon a man looking down over the railing, someone I seemed to recognize. The face was wrinkled and pale, the hair white, the look owlish. But the clothes were not right—I had seen that face before, above some uniform. It was like meeting, after many years, a priest now in civilian clothes, or a Capuchin without a beard. The man looked back at me, also hesitating. As usually happens in such situations, there was some fencing of furtive glances before he took the initiative and greeted me in Italian. Suddenly I could picture him in his usual dress: if he had been wearing a long yellow smock, he would have been Signor Salon: A. Salon, taxidermist. His laboratory was next door to my office on the corridor of the former factory building where I was the Marlowe of culture. I had encountered him at times on the stairs, and we had nodded to each other.

"Strange," he said, holding out his hand. "We have been fellow-tenants for so long, and we introduce ourselves in the bowels of the earth a thousand miles away."

We exchanged a few polite remarks. I got the impression that he knew exactly what I did, which was an achievement of sorts, since I wasn't sure myself. "How do you happen to be in a technological museum? I thought your publishing firm was concerned with more spiritual things."

"How did you know that?"

"Oh"—he gestured vaguely—"people talk, I have many customers. . . ."

"What sort of people go to a taxidermist?"

"You are thinking, like everyone else, that it's not an ordinary profession. But I do not lack for customers, and I have all kinds: museums, private collectors."

"I don't often see stuffed animals in people's homes," I said.

"No? It depends on the homes you visit. . . . Or the cellars."

"Stuffed animals are kept in cellars?"

"Some people keep them in cellars. Not all crèches are in the light of the sun or the moon. I'm suspicious of such customers, but you know how it is: a job is a job. . . . I'm suspicious of everything underground."

"Then why are you strolling in tunnels?"

"I'm checking. I distrust the underground world, but I want to understand it. There aren't many opportunities. The Roman catacombs, you'll say. No mystery there, too many tourists, and everything is under the control of the Church. And then there are the sewers of Paris. . . . Have you been? They can be visited on Monday, Wednesday, and the last Saturday of every month. But that's another tourist attraction. Naturally, there are catacombs in Paris, too, and caves. Not to mention the Métro. Have you ever been to 145 rue Lafayette?"

"I must confess I haven't."

"It's a bit out of the way, between Gare de l'Est and Gare du Nord. An unremarkable building at first sight. But if you look at it more closely, you realize that though the door looks wooden, it is actually painted iron, and the windows appear to belong to rooms unoccupied for centuries. People walk past and don't know the truth."

"What is the truth?"

"That the house is fake. It's a façade, an enclosure with no room, no interior. It is really a chimney, a ventilation flue that serves to release the vapors of the regional Métro. And once you know this, you feel you are standing at the mouth of the underworld: if you could penetrate those walls, you would have access to subterranean Paris. I have had occasion to spend hours and hours in front of that door that conceals the door of doors, the point of departure for the journey to the center of the earth. Why do you think they made it?"

"To ventilate the Métro, as you said."

"A few ducts would have been enough for that. No, when I see those subterranean passages, my suspicions are aroused. Do you know why?"

As he spoke of darkness, he seemed to give off light. I asked him why his suspicions were aroused.

"Because if the Masters of the World exist, they can only be underground: this is a truth that all sense but few dare utter. Perhaps the only man bold enough to say it in print was Saint-Yves d'Alveydre. You know him?"

I may have heard the name mentioned by one of our Diabolicals, but I wasn't sure.

"He is the one who told us about Agarttha, the underground headquarters of the King of the World, the occult center of the Synarchy," the taxidermist said. "He had no fear; he felt sure of himself. But all those who spoke out after him were eliminated, because they knew too much."

As we walked along the tunnel, Signor Salon cast nervous glances at the mouths of new passageways, as if in those shadows he was seeking confirmation of his suspicions.

"Have you ever wondered why in the last century all the great metropolises hastened to build subways?"

"To solve traffic problems?"

"Before there were automobiles, when there were only horse-drawn carriages? From a man of your intelligence I would have expected a more perceptive explanation."

"You have one?"

"Perhaps," Signor Salon said, and he looked pensive, absent. The conversation died. Then he said that he had to be running along. But, after shaking my hand, he lingered another few seconds, as if struck by a thought. "Apropos, that colonel—what was his name?— the one who came to Garamond some time ago to talk to you about a Templar treasure . . . have you had any news of him?"

It was like a slap in the face, this brutal and indiscreet display of knowledge about something I considered private and buried. I wanted to ask him how he knew, but I was afraid. I confined myself to saying, in an indifferent tone, "Oh, that old story. I'd forgotten all about it. But apropos: why did you say apropos?"

"Did I say that? Ah, yes, well, it seemed to me he had discovered something, underground. . . ."

"How do you know?"

"I really can't say. I can't remember who spoke to me about it. A customer, perhaps. But my curiosity is always aroused when the underground world is involved. The little manias of old age. Good evening."

He went off, and I stood there, to ponder the meaning of this encounter.

52

In certain regions of the Himalayas, among the twenty-two temples that represent the twenty-two Arcana of Hermes and the twenty-two letters of some sacred alphabets, Agarttha forms the mystic Zero, which cannot be found. . . . A colossal chessboard that extends beneath the earth, through almost all the regions of the Globe.
—Saint-Yves d'Alveydre, *Mission de l'Inde en Europe*, Paris, Calmann Lévy, 1886, pp. 54 and 65

When I got back, I told the story to Belbo and Diotallevi, and we ventured various hypotheses. Perhaps Salon, a gossiping eccentric who dabbled in mysteries, had happened to meet Ardenti, and that was the whole story. Unless Salon knew something about Ardenti's disappearance and was working for the ones who had caused him to disappear. Another hypothesis: Salon was a police informer. . . .

Then, as our Diabolicals came and went, the memory of Salon faded, was lost among his similars.

One day, Agliè came to the office to report on some manuscripts Belbo had sent him. His opinions were precise, severe, comprehensive. Agliè was clever; it didn't take him long to figure out the Garamond-Manutius double game, and we now talked openly in front of him. He understood: he would destroy a text with a few sharp observations, then remark with smooth cynicism that it would be fine for Manutius.

I asked him what he could tell me about Agarttha and Saint-Yves d'Alveydre.

"Saint-Yves d'Alveydre . . ." he said. "A bizarre man, beyond any doubt. From his youth he spent time with the followers of Fabre d'Olivet. He became a humble clerk in the Ministry of the Interior, but ambitious . . . We naturally took a dim view of his marriage to Marie-Victoire. . . ."

Agliè couldn't resist shifting to the first person, as if he were reminiscing.

"Who was Marie-Victoire? I love gossip," Belbo said.

"Marie-Victoire de Risnitch, very beautiful when she was the intimate of the empress Eugénie. But by the time she met Saint-Yves, she was over fifty. And he was in his early thirties. For her, a més-alliance, of course. What's more, to give him a title, she bought some property—I can't remember where—that had belonged to a certain Marquis d'Alveydre. So, while our unscrupulous character boasted of his title, in Paris they sang songs about the gigolo. Since he could now live off his income, he devoted himself to his dream, which was to find a political formula that would lead to a harmo-nious society. Synarchy, as opposed to anarchy. A European soci-ety governed by three councils, representing economic power, judicial power, and spiritual power—the Church and the scientists, in other words. An enlightened oligarchy that would eliminate class con-flicts. We've heard worse."

"What about Agarttha?"

"Saint-Yves claimed to have been visited one day by a mysterious Afghan, a man named Hadji Scharipf, who can't have been an Af-ghan, because the name is clearly Albanian. . . . This man revealed to him the secret dwelling place of the King of the World, though Saint-Yves himself never used that expression: he called it Agarttha, the place that cannot be found."

"Where did he write this?"

"In his *Mission de l'Inde en Europe*, a work that, incidentally, has influenced a great deal of contemporary political thought. In Agarttha there are underground cities, and below them, closer to the center, live the five thousand sages that govern it. The number five thousand suggests, of course, the hermetic roots of the Vedic language, as you gentlemen know. And each root is a magic hiero-gram connected to a celestial power and sanctioned by an infernal power. The central dome of Agarttha is lighted from above by something like mirrors, which allow the light from the planet's sur-face to arrive only through the enharmonic spectrum of colors, as opposed to the solar spectrum of our physics books, which is merely diatonic. The wise ones of Agarttha study all holy languages in or-der to arrive at the universal language, which is Vattan. When they come upon mysteries too profound, they levitate, and would crack their skulls against the vault of the dome if their brothers did not restrain them. They forge the lightning bolts, they guide the cyclic currents of the interpolar and intertropical fluids, the interferential extensions in the different zones of the earth's latitude and longitude. They select species and have created small animals with extraordinary psychic powers, animals which have a tortoise shell with a yellow cross, a single eye, and a mouth at either end. And polypod animals which can move in all directions. Agarttha is probably where the Templars found refuge after their dispersion, and where they perform custodial duties. Anything else?"

"But . . . was he serious?" I asked.

"I believe he was. At first, we considered him a fanatic, but then we realized that he was referring, perhaps in a visionary, figurative way, to an occult direction of history. Isn't it said that history is a bloodstained and senseless riddle? No, impossible; there must be a Design. There must be a Mind. That is why over the centuries men far from ignorant have thought of the Masters or the King of the World not as physical beings but as a collective symbol, as the successive, temporary incarnation of a Fixed Intention. An Intention with which the great priestly orders and the vanished chivalries were in touch."

"Do you believe this?" Belbo asked.

"Persons more balanced than d'Alveydre seek the Unknown Superiors."

"And do they find them?"

Agliè laughed, as if to himself. "What sort of Unknown Superiors would they be if they allowed the first person who comes along to know them? Gentlemen, we have work to do. There is one more manuscript here and—what a coincidence!—it's a treatise on secret societies."

"Any good?" Belbo asked.

"Perish the thought. But it could do for Manutius."

53

Unable to control destinies on earth openly because governments would resist, this mystic alliance can act only through secret societies. . . . These, gradually created as the need for them arises, are divided into distinct groups, groups seemingly in opposition, sometimes advocating the most contradictory policies in religion, politics, economics, and literature; but they are all connected, all directed by the invisible center that hides its power as it thus seeks to move all the scepters of the earth.

—J. M. Hoene-Wronski, quoted by P. Sédir, *Histoire et doctrine des Rose-Croix,* Bibliothèque des Hermétistes, Paris, 1910

One day I saw Signor Salon at the door of his laboratory. Suddenly, for no reason, I expected him to hoot like an owl. He greeted me as if I were an old friend and asked how things were going at work. I made a noncommittal gesture, smiled at him, and hurried on.

I was struck again by the thought of Agarttha. Saint-Yves's ideas, as Agliè had explained them, might be fascinating to a Diabolical— but certainly not alarming. And yet in Salon's words and in his face, when we met in Munich, there had been alarm.

So, as I went out, I decided to drop in at the library and look for *La Mission de l'Inde en Europe.*

There was the usual mob in the catalog room and at the call desk. With some shoving I got hold of the drawer I needed, found the call number, filled out a slip, and handed it to the clerk. He informed me that the book had been checked out—and, as usual in libraries, he seemed to enjoy giving me this news. But at that very moment a voice behind me said, "Actually, it is available. I just returned it." I looked around and saw Inspector De Angelis.

And he recognized me—too quickly, I thought, since I had seen him in circumstances that for me were exceptional, whereas he had met me in the course of a routine inquiry. Also, in the Ardenti days I had had a wispy beard and longer hair. What a sharp eye!

Had he been keeping me under surveillance since my return to

Italy? Or was he simply good at faces? Policemen had to master the science of observation, memorize features, names . . .

"Signor Casaubon! We're reading the same books!"

I held out my hand. "It's Dr. Casaubon now. Has been for a while. Maybe I'll take the police entrance exam, as you advised me that morning. Then I'll be able to get the books first."

"All you have to do is be here first," he said. "But the book's returned now, and you can collect it. Let me buy you a coffee meanwhile."

The invitation made me uncomfortable, but I couldn't say no. We sat in a neighborhood café. He asked me how I happened to be interested in the mission of India, and I was tempted to ask him how *he* happened to be interested in it, but I decided first to deflect his suspicion. I told him that in my spare time I was continuing my study of the Templars. According to Eschenbach, the Templars left Europe and went to India, some believe to the kingdom of Agarttha. Now it was his turn. "But tell me," I asked, "why did you take out the book?"

"Oh, you know how these things go," he replied. "Ever since you suggested that book on the Templars to me, I've been reading up on the subject. I don't have to tell *you* that after the Templars, the next logical step is Agarttha." Touché. Then he said: "I was joking. I took out the book because . . ." He hesitated. "The fact is, when I'm off duty, I like to browse in libraries. It keeps me from turning into a robot, a mechanical cop. You could probably express the idea more elegantly. . . . But tell me about yourself."

I gave a performance: an autobiographical summary, down to the wonderful adventure of metals.

He asked me: "In that publishing firm, and in the one next door, aren't you doing books on the occult sciences?"

How did he know about Manutius? From information gathered years before, when he was keeping an eye on Belbo? Or was he still on the Ardenti case?

"With characters like Colonel Ardenti turning up constantly at Garamond, and with Manutius there to handle them," I said, "Signor Garamond decided that was rich soil, worth tilling. If you look for such types, you can find them by the carload."

"But Ardenti disappeared. I hope the others don't."

"They haven't yet, though I almost wish they would. However, satisfy my curiosity, Inspector. I imagine in your job people disappear, or worse, every day. Do you devote so much time to all of them?"

He looked at me with amusement. "What makes you think I'm still devoting time to Colonel Ardenti?"

All right, he was gambling, had raised the ante, and it was up to me now to call his bluff if I had the courage, make him show his cards. What was there to lose? "Come, Inspector," I said, "you know everything about Garamond and Manutius, and you were looking for a book on Agarttha. . . ."

"You mean Ardenti spoke to you about Agarttha?"

Touché again. Yes, Ardenti had spoken to us about Agarttha, too, as far as I could remember. But I parried: "No, only about the Templars."

"I see," he said. Then he added: "You mustn't think we follow a case until it's solved. That only happens on television. Being a cop is like being a dentist: a patient comes in, you give him a little of the old drill, prescribe something, he comes back in two weeks, and in the meantime you deal with a hundred other patients. A case like the colonel's can remain in the active file maybe for ten years, and then, while you're in the middle of a different case, taking some confession, there's a hint, a clue, and, wham!, a short circuit in the brain, you get an idea—or else you don't, and that's it."

"And what did you find recently that brought on a short circuit?"

"An indiscreet question, don't you think? But there are no mysteries, believe me. The colonel came up again by chance. We were keeping an eye on a character, for quite different reasons, and found he was spending time at the Picatrix Club. You've heard of it? . . ."

"I know the magazine, not the club. What goes on there?"

"Nothing, nothing at all. People a bit loony, maybe, but well behaved. Then I remembered that Ardenti used to go there—a cop's talent consists entirely of remembering things, a name, a face, even after ten years have gone by. And so I began wondering what was happening at Garamond. That's all."

"What does the Picatrix Club have to do with your political squad?"

"Perhaps it's the impertinence of a clear conscience, but you seem tremendously curious."

"You're the one who invited me for coffee."

"True, and both of us are off duty. See here: if you look at the world in a certain way, everything is connected to everything else." A nice hermetic philosopheme, I thought. He immediately added: "I'm not saying that those people are connected with politics, but . . . There was a time when we went looking for the Red Brigades in squats and the Black Brigades in martial arts clubs; nowadays the opposite could be true. We live in a strange world. My job, I assure you, was easier ten years ago. Today, even among ideologies, there's no consistency. There are times when I think of switching to narcotics. There, at least you can rely on a heroin pusher to push heroin."

There was a pause—he was hesitating, I think. Then, from his pocket, he produced a notebook the size of a missal. "Look, Casaubon, you see some strange people as part of your job. You go to the library and look up even stranger books. Help me. What do you know about synarchy?"

"Now you're embarrassing me. Almost nothing. I heard it mentioned in connection with Saint-Yves; that's all."

"What are they saying about it, around?"

"If they're saying anything, I haven't heard. To be frank, it sounds like fascism to me."

"Actually, many of its theses were picked up by Action Française. If that were the whole story, I'd be okay. I find a group that talks about synarchy and I can give it a political color. But in my reading, I've learned that in 1929 a certain Vivian Postel du Mas and Jeanne Canudo founded a group called Polaris, which was inspired by the myth of the King of the World. They proposed a synarchic project: social service opposed to capitalist profit, the elimination of the class struggle through cooperatives. . . . It sounds like a kind of Fabian socialism, a libertarian and communitarian movement. Note that both Polaris and the Irish Fabians were accused of being involved in a synarchic plot led by the Jews. And who accused them? The *Revue internationale des sociétés secrètes*, which talks about a Jewish-Masonic-Bolshevik plot. Many of its contributors belonged to a secret right-wing organization called La Sapinière. And *they* say that all these revolutionary groups are only the front for a diabolical plot hatched by an occultist cénacle. Now you'll say: All right, Saint-Yves ended up inspiring reformist groups, but these days the right lumps everything together and sees it all as a demo-pluto-social-Judaic conspiracy. Mussolini did the same thing. But why accuse them of being controlled by an occultist cénacle? According to the little I know—take Picatrix, for example—those occultism people couldn't care less about the workers' movement."

"So it seems also to me, O Socrates. So?"

"Thanks for the Socrates. But now we're coming to the good part. The more I read on the subject, the more I get confused. In the forties various self-styled synarchic groups sprang up; they talked about a new European order led by a government of wise men, above party lines. And where did these groups meet? In Vichy collaborationist circles. Then, you say, we got it wrong; synarchy is right-wing. But hold on! Having read this far, I begin to see that there is one theme that finds them all in agreement: Synarchy exists and secretly rules the world. But here comes the 'but'. . ."

"But?"

"But on January 24, 1937, Dmitri Navachine, Mason and Martinist (I don't know what Martinist means, but I think it's one of those sects), economic adviser of the Front Populaire, after having been director of a Moscow bank, was assassinated by the Organisation secrète d'action révolutionnaire et nationale, better known as La Cagoule, financed by Mussolini. It was said then that La Cagoule was guided by a secret synarchy and that Navachine was killed because he had discovered its mysteries. A document originating from left-wing circles during the Occupation denounced a synarchic Pact of the Empire, which was responsible for the French defeat, a pact that was a manifestation of Portuguese-style fascism. But then it turned out that the pact was drawn up by Du Mas and Canudo and contained ideas they had published and publicized everywhere. Nothing secret about it. But these ideas were revealed as secret, extremely secret, in 1946 by one Husson, who denounced a revolutionary synarchic pact of the left, as he wrote in his *Synarchie, panorama de 25 années d'activité occulte*, which he signed . . . wait, let me find it . . . Geoffroy de Charnay."

"Fine!" I said. "Charnay was a companion of Molay, the grand master of the Templars. They died together at the stake. Here we have a neo-Templar attacking synarchy from the right. But synarchy is born at Agarttha, which is the refuge of the Templars!"

"What did I tell you? You see, you've given me an additional

316

clue. Unfortunately, it only increases the confusion. So, on the right, a synarchic pact of the left is denounced as socialist and secret, though it's not really secret; it's the same synarchic pact, as you saw, that was denounced by the left. And now we come to new revelations: synarchy is a Jesuit plot to undermine the Third Republic. A thesis expounded by Roger Mennevée, leftist. To allow me to sleep nights, my reading then tells me that in 1943 in certain Vichy military circles—Pétainist, yes, but anti-German—documents circulated that prove synarchy was a Nazi plot: Hitler was a Rosicrucian influenced by the Masons, who now have moved from hatching a Judeo-Bolshevik plot to making an imperial German one."

"So everything is settled."

"If only that were all. Yet another revelation: Synarchy is a plot of the international technocrats. This was asserted in 1960 by one Villemarest, *Le 14ᵉ complot du 13 mai.* The techno-synarchic plot wants to destabilize governments and, to do it, provokes wars, backs coups d'état, foments schisms in political parties, promotes internecine hatreds. . . . Do you recognize these synarchists?"

"My God, it's the IMS, the Imperialist Multinational State—what the Red Brigades were talking about a few years ago!"

"The answer is correct. And now what does Inspector De Angelis do if he finds a reference to synarchy somewhere? He asks the advice of Dr. Casaubon, the Templar expert."

"My answer: There exists a secret society with branches throughout the world, and its plot is to spread the rumor that a universal plot exists."

"You're joking, but I—"

"I'm not joking. Come and read the manuscripts that turn up at Manutius. But if you want a more down-to-earth explanation, it's like the story of the man with a bad stammer who complains that the radio station wouldn't hire him as an announcer because he didn't carry a party card. We always have to blame our failures on somebody else, and dictatorships always need an external enemy to bind their followers together. As the man said, for every complex problem there's a simple solution, and it's wrong."

"And if, on a train, I find a bomb wrapped in a flier that talks about synarchy, is it enough for me to say that this is a simple solution to a complex problem?"

"Why? Have you found bombs on trains that . . . No, excuse

me. That's really not my business. But why did you say that to me, then?"

"Because I was hoping you'd know more than I do. Because perhaps I'm relieved to see you can't make head or tail of it either. You say you have to read lunatics by the carload and you consider it a waste of time. I don't. For me, the works of your lunatics—by 'your' I'm referring to you normal people—are important texts. What a lunatic writes may explain the thinking of the man who puts the bomb on the train. Or are you afraid of becoming a police informer?"

"No, not at all. Besides, looking for things in card catalogs is my business. If the right piece of information turns up, I'll keep you in mind."

As he rose from his chair, De Angelis dropped the last question: "Among your manuscripts . . . have you ever found any reference to the Tres?"

"What's that?"

"I don't know. An organization, maybe. I don't even know if it exists. I've heard it mentioned, and it occurred to me in connection with your lunatics. Say hello to your friend Belbo for me. Tell him I'm not keeping tabs on any of you. The fact is, I have a dirty job, and my misfortune is that I enjoy it."

As I went home, I asked myself who had come out ahead. He had told me a number of things; I'd told him nothing. If I wanted to be suspicious, I could think perhaps that he had got something out of me without my being aware or it. But if you're too suspicious, you fall into the psychosis of synarchic plots.

When I told Lia about this episode, she said: "If you ask me, he was sincere. He really did want to get it all off his chest. You think he can find anyone at police headquarters who will listen to him wonder whether Jeanne Canudo was right-wing or left? He only wanted to find out if it's his fault he can't understand it or if the whole thing is too difficult. And you weren't able to give him the one true answer."

"The one true answer?"

"Of course. That there's nothing to understand. Synarchy is God."

"God?"

"Yes. Mankind can't endure the thought that the world was born

318

by chance, by mistake, just because four brainless atoms bumped into one another on a slippery highway. So a cosmic plot has to be found—God, angels, devils. Synarchy performs the same function on a lesser scale."

"Then I should have told him that people put bombs on trains because they're looking for God?"

"Why not?"

54

It was autumn. One morning I went to Via Marchese Gualdi, because I had to get Signor Garamond's authorization to order some color photographs from abroad. I glimpsed Agliè in Signora Grazia's office, bent over the file of Manutius authors, but I didn't disturb him, because I was late for my meeting.

When our business was over, I asked Signor Garamond what Agliè was doing in the secretary's office.

"The man's a genius," Garamond said. "An extraordinary mind, keen, learned. The other evening, I took him to dinner with some of our authors, and he made me look great. What conversation! What style! A gentleman of the old school, an aristocrat; they've thrown away the mold. What knowledge, what culture—no, more, what information! He told delightful anecdotes about characters of a century ago, and I swear it was as if he had known them personally. Do you want to hear the idea he gave me as we were going home? He said we shouldn't just sit and wait for Isis Unveiled authors to turn up on their own. It's a waste of time and effort to read when you don't even know whether the authors are willing to underwrite the expenses. Instead, we have a gold mine at our disposal: the list of all the Manutius authors of the last twenty years! You understand? We write to our old, glorious authors, or at least the ones who bought up their remainders, and we say to them: Dear sir, are you aware that we have inaugurated a series of works of erudition, tradition, and the highest spirituality? Would you, as an author of distinction and refinement, be interested in venturing into this terra incognita, et cetera, et cetera? A genius, I tell you. I believe he wants us all to join him Sunday evening. Plans to take us to a castle, a fortress—no, more, a villa in the Turin area. It seems that extraordinary things are to happen there, a rite, a sabbath, where someone will make gold or quicksilver. It's a whole world to be discovered, my dear Casaubon, even if, as you know, I have the greatest respect for science, the science to which you are devoting yourself with such passion. Indeed, I am very, very pleased with your work, and yes, there's that little financial adjustment you mentioned; I haven't forgotten it, and in due course we'll talk about it. Agliè told me the lady will also be there, the beautiful lady—or perhaps not beautiful, but attractive; there's something about her eyes—that friend of Belbo's—what's her name—?"

"Lorenza Pellegrini."

"Yes. There's something—no?—between her and our Belbo."

"I believe they're good friends."

"Ah! A gentleman's answer. Bravo, Casaubon. But I do not inquire out of idle curiosity; the fact is that I feel like a father to all of you and . . . glissons, à la guerre comme à la guerre. . . . Goodbye, dear boy."

We really did have an appointment with Agliè in the hills near Turin, Belbo told me. A double appointment. The early hours of the evening would be a party in the castle of a very well-to-do Rosicrucian. Then Agliè would take us a few kilometers away, to a place where—at midnight, naturally—some kind of druidic rite, Belbo wasn't sure what, would be held.

"I was also thinking," Belbo added, "that we should sit down somewhere and give some thought to our history of metals, because here we keep being interrupted. Why don't we leave Saturday and spend a couple of days in my old house in ***? It's a beautiful spot; you'll see, the hills are worth it. Diotallevi is coming, and maybe Lorenza will, too. Of course you can bring along anyone you want."

He didn't know Lia, but he knew I had a companion. I said I'd come alone. Lia and I had quarreled two days before. Nothing serious; it would be forgotten in a few days, but meanwhile I wanted to get away from Milan.

So we all went to ***, the Garamond trio and Lorenza Pellegrini. At our departure, a tense moment. When it came time to get into the car, Lorenza said, "Maybe I'll stay behind, so you three can work in peace. I'll join you later with Simon."

Belbo, both hands on the wheel, locked his elbows, stared straight ahead, and said in a low voice, "Get in." Lorenza got in, and all through the trip, sitting up front, she kept her hand on the back of Belbo's neck as he drove in silence.

*** was still the town Belbo had known during the war. But new houses were few, he told us, agriculture was in decline, because the young people had migrated to the city. He pointed to hills, now pasture, that had once been yellow with grain. The town appeared suddenly, after a curve at the foot of the low hill where Belbo's house was. We got a view, beyond it, of the Monferrato plain, covered with a light, luminous mist. As the car climbed, Belbo directed our attention to the hill opposite, almost completely bare: at the top of it, a chapel flanked by two pines. "It's called the Bricco," he said, then added: "It doesn't matter if it has no effect on you. We used to go there for the Angel's lunch on Easter Monday. Now you can reach it in the car in five minutes, but then we went on foot, and it was a pilgrimage."

55

I call a theatre [a place in which] all actions, all words, all particular
subjects are shown *as in a public theatre, where comedies and trag-
edies are acted.*
— Robert Fludd, *Utriusque Cosmi Historia*, Tomi Secundi
Tractatus Primi Sectio Secunda, Oppenheim (?), 1620 (?),
p. 55

We arrived at the villa. Villa—actually, a large farmhouse, with great
cellars on the ground floor, where Adelino Canepa—the quarrel-
some tenant who had denounced Uncle Carlo to the partisans—
once made wine from the vineyards of the Covasso land. It had long
been unoccupied.

In a little peasant house nearby Adelino Canepa's aunt still lived—
a very old woman, Belbo told us, who tended a little vegetable garden, kept a few hens and a pig. The others were now long dead,
uncle and aunt, the Canepas; only this centenarian remained. The
land had been sold years before to pay the inheritance taxes and
other debts. Belbo knocked at the door of the little house. The old
woman appeared on the threshold, took a while to recognize the
visitor, then made a great show of deference, inviting us in, but
Belbo, after having embraced and calmed her, cut the meeting short.

We entered the villa, and Lorenza gave cries of joy as she discovered stairways, corridors, shadowy rooms with old furniture. As
usual, Belbo played everything down, remarking only that each of
us has the Tara he deserves, but he was clearly moved. He continued to visit the house, from time to time, he told us, but not often.

"It's a good place to work: cool in summer, and in winter the
thick walls protect you against the cold, and there are stoves everywhere. Naturally, when I was a child, an evacuee, we lived only in
two side rooms at the end of the main corridor. Now I've taken
possession of my uncle and aunt's wing. I work here, in Uncle Carlo's study." There was a secretaire with little space for a sheet of
paper but plenty of small drawers, both visible and concealed. "I
couldn't put Abulafia here," Belbo said. "But the rare times I come,

323

I like to write by hand, as I did then." He showed us a majestic cupboard. "When I'm dead, remember this contains all my juvenilia, the poems I wrote when I was sixteen, the sketches for sagas in six volumes made at eighteen, and so on. . . ."

"Let's see! Let's see!" Lorenza cried, clapping her hands and advancing with exaggerated feline tread toward the cupboard.

"Stop right where you are," Belbo said. "There's nothing to see. I don't even look at it myself anymore. And, in any case, when I'm dead, I'll come back and burn everything."

"This place has ghosts, I hope," Lorenza said.

"It does now. In Uncle Carlo's day, no; it was lots of fun then. Georgic. That's why I come. It's wonderful working at night while the dogs bark in the valley."

He showed us the rooms where we would be sleeping: mine, Diotallevi's, Lorenza's. Lorenza looked at her room, touched the old bed and its great white counterpane, sniffed the sheets, said it was like being in one of her grandmother's stories, because everything smelled of lavender. Belbo said it wasn't lavender, it was mildew. Lorenza said it didn't matter, and then, leaning against the wall, her hips thrust forward as if she were at the pinball machine, she asked, "Am I sleeping here by myself?"

Belbo looked away, then at us, then away again. He made as if to leave and said: "We'll talk about it later. In any case, if you want it, you have a refuge all your own." Diotallevi and I moved off, but we heard Lorenza ask Belbo if he was ashamed of her. He said that if he hadn't offered her the room, she would have asked him where she was supposed to sleep. "I made the first move, so you have a choice," he said. "The wily Turk," she said. "In that case, I'll sleep here in my darling little room." "Sleep where you want," Belbo said, irritated. "But the others are here to work. Let's go out on the terrace."

So we set to work on the broad terrace, where a pergola stood, supplied with cold drinks and plenty of coffee. Alcohol forbidden till evening.

From the terrace we could see the Bricco, and below it a large plain building with a yard and a soccer field—all inhabited by multicolored little figures, children, it seemed to me. "It's the Salesian parish hall," Belbo explained. "That's where Don Tico taught me to play. In the band."

I remembered the trumpet Belbo had denied himself after the dream. I asked: "Trumpet or clarinet?"

He had a moment's panic. "How did you . . . Ah, yes, I told you about the dream, the trumpet. Don Tico taught me the trumpet, but in the band I played the bombardon."

"What's a bombardon?"

"Oh, that's all kid stuff. Back to work now."

But as we worked, I noticed that he often glanced at that hall. I had the impression that he talked about other things as an excuse to look at it. For example, he would interrupt our discussion and say:

"Just down there was some of the heaviest shooting at the end of the war. Here in *** there was a kind of tacit agreement between the Fascists and the partisans. Two years in a row the partisans came down from the hills in spring and occupied the town, and the Fascists kept their distance and didn't make trouble. The Fascists weren't from around here; the partisans were all local boys. In the event of a fight, they could move easily; they knew every cornfield and the woods and hedgerows. The Fascists mostly stayed holed up in the town and ventured out only for raids. In winter it was harder for the partisans to stay down in the plain: there was no place to hide, and in the snow they could be seen from a distance and picked off by a machine gun even a kilometer away. So they climbed up into the higher hills. There, too, they knew the passes, the caves, the shelters. The Fascists returned to control the plain. But that spring we were on the eve of liberation, the Fascists were still here, and they were dubious about going back to the city, sensing that the final blow would be delivered there, as it in fact was, around April 25. I believe there was communication between the Fascists and the partisans. The latter held off, wanting to avoid a clash, sure that something would happen soon. At night Radio London gave more and more reassuring news, the special messages for the Franchi brigade became more frequent: Tomorrow it will rain again; Uncle Pietro has brought the bread—that sort of thing. Maybe you heard them, Diotallevi . . . Anyway, there must have been a misunderstanding, because the partisans came down and the Fascists hadn't left.

"One day my sister was here on the terrace, and she came inside and told us there were two men playing tag with guns. We weren't surprised: they were kids, on both sides, whiling away the time with their weapons. Once—it was only in fun—two of them really did shoot, and a bullet hit the trunk of a tree in the driveway. My sister was leaning on the tree; she didn't even notice, but the neighbors did, and after that she was told that when she saw men playing with guns, she must go inside. 'They're playing again,' she said, coming in, to show how obedient she was. And at that point we heard the first volley. Then a second, a third, and then the rounds came thick and fast. You could hear the bark of the shotguns, the ratatat of the automatic rifles, and a duller sound, maybe hand grenades. Finally, the machine guns. We realized they weren't playing any longer, but we didn't have time to discuss it, because by then we couldn't hear our own voices. Bang, wham, ratatat! We crouched under the sink—me, my sister, and Mama. Then Uncle Carlo arrived, along the corridor, on all fours, to tell us that we were too exposed, we should come over to their wing. We did, and Aunt Caterina was crying because Grandmother was out. . . ."

"Is that when your grandmother found herself facedown in a field, in the cross fire?"

"How did you know about that?"

"You told me in '73, after the demonstration that day."

"My God, what a memory! A man has to be careful what he says around you. . . . Yes. But my father was also out. As we learned later, he had taken shelter in a doorway in town, and couldn't leave it because of all the shooting back and forth in the street, and from the tower of the town hall a Black Brigade squad was raking the square with a machine gun. The former mayor of the city, a Fascist, was standing in the same doorway. At a certain point, he said he was going to run for it: to get home, all he had to do was reach the corner. He waited for a quiet moment, then flung himself out of the doorway, reached the corner, and was mowed down. But the instinctive reaction of my father, who had also gone through the First World War, was: Stay in the doorway."

"This is a place full of sweet memories," Diotallevi remarked.

"You won't believe it," Belbo said, "but they *are* sweet. They're the only real things I remember."

The others didn't understand, and I was only beginning to. Now

I know for sure. In those months especially, when he was navigating the sea of falsehoods of the Diabolicals, and after years of wrapping his disillusion in the falsehoods of fiction, Belbo remembered his days in *** as a time of clarity: a bullet was a bullet, you ducked or got it, and the two opposing sides were distinct, marked by their colors, red or black, without ambiguities—or at least it had seemed that way to him. A corpse was a corpse was a corpse was a corpse. Not like Colonel Ardenti, with his slippery disappearance. I thought that perhaps I should tell Belbo about synarchy, which in those years was already making inroads. Hadn't the encounter between Uncle Carlo and Mongo been synarchic, really, since both men, on opposing sides, were inspired by the same ideal of chivalry? But why should I deprive Belbo of his Combray? The memories were sweet because they spoke to him of the one truth he had known; doubt would begin only afterward. Though, as he had hinted to me, even in the days of truth he had been a spectator, watching the birth of other men's memories, the birth of History, or of many histories: all stories that he would not be the one to write.

Or had there been, for him, too, a moment of glory and of choice? Because now he said, "And also, that day I performed the one heroic deed of my life."

"My John Wayne," Lorenza said. "Tell me."

"Oh, it was nothing. After crawling to my uncle's part of the house, I stubbornly insisted on standing up in the corridor. The window was at the end, we were on the upper floor, nobody could hit me, I argued. I felt like a captain standing erect in the center of the battle while the bullets whistle around him. Uncle Carlo became angry, roughly pulled me into the room; I almost started crying because the fun was over, and at that moment we heard three shots, glass shattering, and a kind of ricochet, as if someone were bouncing a tennis ball in the corridor. A bullet had come through the window, glanced off a water pipe, and buried itself in the floor at the very spot where I had been standing. If I had stayed there, I would have been wounded. Maybe."

"My God, I wouldn't want you a cripple," Lorenza said.

"Maybe today I'd be happier," Belbo said.

But the fact was that even in this case he hadn't chosen. He had let his uncle pull him away.

About an hour later, he was again distracted. "Then Adelino Canepa came upstairs. He said we'd all be safer in the cellar. He and my uncle hadn't spoken for years, as I told you. But in this tragic moment, Adelino Canepa had become a human being again, and Uncle even shook his hand. So we spent an hour in the darkness among the barrels, with the smell of countless vintages, which made your head swim a little, not to mention the shooting outside. Then the gunfire died down, became muffled. We realized one side was retreating, but we didn't know which, until, from a window above our heads, which overlooked a little path, we heard a voice, in dialect: 'Monssu, i'è d'la repubblica bele si?' "

"What does that mean?" Lorenza asked.

"Roughly: Sir, would you be so kind as to inform me if there are still any sustainers of the Italian Social Republic in these parts? Republic, at that time, was a bad word. The voice was a partisan's, asking a passerby or someone at a window, and that meant the Fascists had gone. It was growing dark. After a little while both Papa and Grandmother arrived, and told of their adventures. Mama and Aunt prepared something to eat, while Uncle and Adelino Canepa ceremoniously stopped speaking to each other again. For the rest of the evening we heard shooting in the distance, toward the hills. The partisans were after the fugitives. We had won."

Lorenza kissed Belbo on the head, and he wrinkled his nose. He knew he had won, though with some help from the Fascists. In reality it had been like watching a movie. For a moment, risking the ricocheting bullet, he had entered the action on the screen, but only for a moment, on the run, as in *Hellzapoppin*, where the reels get mixed up and an Indian on horseback rides into a ballroom and asks which way did they go. Somebody says, "That way," and the Indian gallops off into another story.

56

He began playing his shining trumpet with such power that the
whole mountain rang.
    —Johann Valentin Andreae, *Die Chymische Hochzeit des*
    Christian Rosencreutz, Strassburg, Zetzner, 1616, 1, p. 4

We had reached the chapter on the wonders of hydraulic pipes, and
a sixteenth-century engraving from the *Spiritalia* of Heron depicted
a kind of altar with a steam-driven apparatus that played a trumpet.

I brought Belbo back to his reminiscing. "How did it go, then,
the story of that Don Tycho Brahe, or whatever his name was—the
man who taught you to play the trumpet?"

"Don Tico. I never found out if Tico was a nickname or his last
name. I've never gone back to the parish hall. The first time I went
there, it was by chance: Mass, catechism, all sorts of games, and if
you won, he gave you a little holy card of Blessed Domenico Savio,
that adolescent with the wrinkled canvas pants, always hanging on
to Don Bosco in the statues, his eyes raised to heaven, not listening
to the other boys, who are telling dirty jokes. I learned that Don
Tico had formed a band, boys between ten and fourteen. The little
ones played toy clarinets, fifes, soprano sax, and the bigger ones
carried the tubas and the bass drum. They had uniforms, khaki tunics and blue trousers, and visored caps. A dream, and I wanted to
be part of it. Don Tico said he needed a bombardon."

He gave us a superior look, and said, as if repeating familiar information: "A bombardon is a kind of tuba, a bass horn in E flat.
It's the stupidest instrument in the whole band. Most of the time it
just goes oompah-oompah-oompah, or—when the beat changes—
pa-pah, pa-pah, pa-pah. It's easy to learn, though. Belonging to the
brass family, it works more or less like the trumpet. The trumpet
demands more breath, and you need an embouchure—you know,
that kind of callus on the upper lip, like Louis Armstrong. . . .
Then you get a clear, clean sound, and you don't hear the blowing.
The important thing is not to puff out your cheeks: that only happens in movies, cartoons, or New Orleans brothels."

"What about the trumpet?"

"The trumpet I learned on my own, during those summer afternoons when there was nobody at the parish hall, and I would hide in the seats of the little theater. . . . But I studied the trumpet for erotic reasons. You see that little villa over there, a kilometer from the hall? That's where Cecilia lived, the daughter of the Salesians' great patroness. So every time the band performed, on holy days of obligation, after the procession, in the yard of the parish hall, and especially in the theater before performances of the amateur dramatic society, Cecilia and her mama were always in the front row, in the place of honor, next to the provost of the cathedral. In the theater the band would begin with a march that was called 'A Good Start.' It opened with trumpets, the trumpets in B flat, gold and silver, carefully polished for the occasion. The trumpets stood up, played by themselves. Then they sat down, and the band began. Playing the trumpet was the only way for me to attract Cecilia's attention."

"The only way?" Lorenza asked, moved.

"There was no other way. First, I was thirteen and she was thirteen and a half, and a girl thirteen and a half is already a woman; a boy at thirteen is a snot-nose kid. Besides, she loved an alto sax, a certain Papi, a mangy horror, he seemed to me, but she only had eyes for him, as he bleated lasciviously, because the saxophone, when it isn't Ornette Coleman's and it's part of a band—and played by the horrendous Papi—is a goatish, guttural instrument, with the voice of, say, a fashion model who's taken to drink and turning tricks. . . ."

"What do *you* know about models who turn tricks?"

"Anyway, Cecilia didn't even know I existed. Of course, in the evening, when I struggled up the hill to fetch the milk from a farm above us, I invented splendid stories in which she was kidnapped by the Black Brigades and I rushed to save her as the bullets whistled around my head and went chack-chack as they hit the sheaves of wheat. I revealed to her what she couldn't have known: that in my secret identity I headed the Resistance in the whole Monferrato region, and she confessed to me that this was what she had always hoped, and at that point I would feel a guilty flood of honey in my veins—I swear, not even my foreskin got wet; it was something else, something much more awesome and grand—and on coming home, I would go and confess. . . . I believe all sin, love, glory are this: when you slide down the knotted sheets, escaping from Gestapo headquarters, and she hugs you, there, suspended, and she whispers that she's always dreamed of you. The rest is just sex, copulation, the perpetuation of the vile species. In short, if I were switched to the trumpet, Cecilia would be unable to ignore me: on my feet, gleaming, while the saxophone sits miserably on his chair. The trumpet is warlike, angelic, apocalyptic, victorious; it sounds the charge. The saxophone plays so that young punks in the slums, their hair slicked down with brilliantine, can dance cheek to cheek with sweating girls. I studied the trumpet like a madman, then went to Don Tico and said: Listen to this. And I was Oscar Levant when he had his first tryout on Broadway with Gene Kelly. Don Tico said: You're a trumpet, all right, but . . .''

"How dramatic this is," Lorenza said. "Go on. Don't keep us on pins and needles."

"But I had to find somebody to take my place on the bombardon. Work out something, Don Tico said. So I worked out something. Now I must tell you, dear children, that in those days there lived in *** a couple of wretches, classmates of mine, though they were two years older than I, and this fact tells you something about their mental ability. These two brutes were named Annibale Cantalamessa and Pio Bo. Asterisk: Historical fact."

"What?" Lorenza asked.

I explained, smugly: "When Salgari, in his adventure stories, includes a true event, or something he thinks is true—let's say that, after Little Big Horn, Sitting Bull eats General Custer's heart—he always puts an asterisk and a footnote that says: Historical fact."

"Yes, and it's a historical fact that Annibale Cantalamessa and Pio Bo really had those names, but the names were the least of it. A real pair of sneaks: they stole comic books from the newsstand, shell cases from other boys' collections. And they would think nothing of parking their greasy salami sandwich on your prized Christmas book, a deluxe volume of tales of the high seas. Cantalamessa called himself a Communist, Bo, a Fascist, but they were both ready to sell themselves to the enemy for a slingshot. They told stories about their sexual prowess, with erroneous anatomical information, and argued over who had masturbated more the night before. Here were two villains ready for anything; why not the bombardon? So

I decided to seduce them. I sang the praises of the band uniform, I took them to public performances, I held out hopes of amatory triumphs with the Daughters of Mary. . . . They fell for it. I spent my days in the theater with a long stick, as I had seen in illustrated pamphlets about missionaries; I rapped them on the knuckles when they missed a note. The bombardon has only three keys, but it's the embouchure that matters, as I said. I won't bore you any further, my little listeners. The day came, after long sleepless afternoons, when I could introduce to Don Tico two bombardons—I won't say perfect, but at least acceptable. Don Tico was convinced; he put them in uniform and moved me to the trumpet. Within the space of a week, for the feast of Our Lady Help of Christians, for the opening of the theatrical season with *They Had to See Paris*, there before the curtain, in the presence of the authorities, I was standing to play the opening bars of 'Good Start.' "

"Oh, joyous moment," Lorenza said, making a face of tender jealousy. "And Cecilia?"

"She wasn't there. Maybe she was sick. I don't know. But she wasn't there."

He raised his eyes and surveyed the audience, and at that moment he was bard—or jester. He calculated the pause. "Two days later, Don Tico sent for me and told me that Annibale Cantalamessa and Pio Bo had ruined the evening. They wouldn't keep time, their minds wandered when they weren't playing, they joked and never came in at the right place. 'The bombardon,' Don Tico said to me, 'is the backbone of the band, its rhythmic conscience, its soul. The band, it is a flock; the instruments are the sheep, the bandmaster the shepherd, but the bombardon is the faithful snarling dog that keeps the flock together. The bandmaster looks first to the bombardon, for if the bombardon follows him, the sheep will follow. Jacopo, my boy, I must ask of you a great sacrifice: to go back to the bombardon. You have a good sense of rhythm, you will keep those other two in time for me. I promise, as soon as they can play on their own, I'll let you play the trumpet.' I owed everything to Don Tico. I said yes. And on the next holy day the trumpets rose to their feet and played the opening of 'Good Start' in front of Cecilia, once more in the first row. But I was in the darkness, a bombardon among bombardons. As for those two wretches, they never were able to play on their own, and I never went back to the trumpet. The war ended,

I returned to the city, abandoned music, the brass family, and never even learned Cecilia's last name."

"Poor boy," Lorenza said, hugging him from behind. "But you still have me."

"I thought you liked saxophones," Belbo said. Then he turned and kissed her hand. "But, to work," he said, serious again. "We're here to create a story of the future, not a remembrance of things past."

That evening, the lifting of the ban on alcohol was much celebrated. Jacopo seemed to have forgotten his elegiac mood and competed with Diotallevi in imagining absurd machines—only to discover, each time, that the machines had already been invented. At midnight, after a full day, we all decided it was time to experience what it was like sleeping in the hills.

On my bed the sheets were even damper than they had been in the afternoon. Jacopo had insisted that we use a "priest": an oval frame that kept the covers raised and had a place for a little brazier with embers—he wanted to make sure we tasted all the pleasures of rural life. But when dampness is inherent, a bedwarmer encourages it: you feel welcome warmth, but the sheets remain humid. Oh, well. I lit a lamp, the kind with a fringed shade, where the mayflies flutter until they die, as the poet says, and I tried to make myself sleepy by reading the newspaper.

For an hour or two I heard footsteps in the corridor, an opening and closing of doors, and the last closing was a violent slam. Lorenza Pellegrini putting Belbo's nerves to the test.

I was half-asleep when I heard a scratching at the door, my door. I couldn't tell whether it was an animal or not (I had seen neither dogs nor cats in the house), but I had the impression that it was an invitation, a request, a trap. Maybe Lorenza was doing it because she knew Belbo was spying on her. Maybe not. Until then, I had considered Lorenza Belbo's property—at least as far as I was concerned—and besides, now that I was living with Lia, other women didn't interest me. The sly glances, often conspiratorial, that Lorenza gave me in the office or in a bar when she was teasing Belbo, as if seeking an ally or a witness, were part—I had always thought—of the game she played. Without a doubt, Lorenza had a talent for looking at any man as if challenging his sexual capacity. But it was a curious challenge, as if she were saying: "I want you, but only to show how afraid you really are. . . ." That night, however, hearing her fingernails scrape my door, I felt something different. It was desire: I desired Lorenza.

I stuck my head under the pillow and thought of Lia. I want to have a child with Lia, I said to myself. And I'll make him (or her) learn the trumpet as soon as he (or she) has enough breath.

57

On every third tree a lantern had been hung, and a splendid virgin, also dressed in blue, lighted them with a marvelous torch, and I lingered, longer than necessary, to admire the sight, which was of an ineffable beauty.
— Johann Valentin Andreae, *Die Chymische Hochzeit des Christian Rosencreutz*, Strassburg, Zetzner, 1616, 2, p. 21

Toward noon Lorenza joined us on the terrace, smiling, and announced that she had found a terrific train that stopped at *** at twelve-thirty, and with only one change she could get back to Milan in the afternoon. Would we drive her, she asked, to the station?

Belbo continued leafing through some notes. "I thought Agliè was expecting you, too," he said. "In fact, it seemed to me he organized the whole expedition just for you."

"That's his problem," Lorenza said. "Who's driving me?"

Belbo stood up and said to us, "It'll only take a moment; I'll be right back. Then we can stay here another couple of hours. Lorenza, you had a bag?"

I don't know if they said anything to each other during the trip to the station. Belbo was back in about twenty minutes and resumed working without referring to the incident.

At two o'clock we found a comfortable restaurant in the market square, and the choosing of food and wine gave Belbo further opportunity to recall his childhood. But he spoke as if he were quoting from someone else's biography. He had lost the narrative felicity of the day before. In midafternoon we set off to join Agliè and Garamond.

Belbo drove southwest, and the landscape changed gradually, kilometer by kilometer. The hills of ***, even in late autumn, were gentle, domestic, but as we went on, the horizons became more vast, at every curve the peaks grew, some crowned by little villages; we glimpsed endless vistas. Like Darién, Diotallevi remarked,

335

verbalizing these discoveries. We climbed in third gear toward great expanses and the outline of mountains, which at the end of the plateau was already fading into a wintry haze. Though we were already in the mountains, it seemed to be a plain modulated by dunes. As if the hand of a clumsy demiurge had compressed heights that seemed to him excessive, transforming them into a lumpy dough that extended all the way to the sea or—who knows?—to the slopes of harsher and more determined chains.

We reached the specified village and met Agliè and Garamond, as arranged, at the café in the main square. If Agliè was displeased to hear that Lorenza wasn't coming, he gave no indication of it. "Our exquisite friend does not wish to take part, in the presence of others, in the mysteries that define her. A singular modesty, which I appreciate," he said. And that was all.

We continued, Garamond's Mercedes in the lead and Belbo's Renault behind, until, as the sunlight was dying, we came within sight of a strange yellow edifice on a hill, a kind of eighteenth-century castle, from which extended terraces with flowers and trees, flourishing despite the season.

As we reached the foot of the hill, we found ourselves in an open space where many cars were parked. "We stop here," Agliè said, "and continue on foot."

Dusk was now becoming night. The path up was illuminated for us by a host of torches that burned along the slope.

It's odd, but of everything that happened, from that moment until late at night, I have memories at once clear and confused. I reviewed them the other evening in the periscope and sensed a family resemblance between the two experiences. Yes, I said to myself, now you are here, in an unnatural situation, groggy from the smell of old wood, imagining yourself in a tomb or in the belly of a ship as a transformation is taking place. You have only to peer outside the cabin, and you will see objects in the gloom that earlier today were motionless, but now they stir like Eleusinian shadows among the fumes of a spell. And so it had been that evening at the castle: the lights, the surprises of the route, the words I heard, and then the incense; everything conspired to make me feel I was dreaming, but dreaming the way you dream when you are on the verge of waking, when you dream that you are dreaming.

I should remember nothing, yet, on the contrary, I remember everything, not as if I had lived it, but as if it had been told to me by someone else.

I do not know if what I remember, with such anomalous clarity, is what happened or is only what I wished had happened, but it was definitely on that evening that the Plan first stirred in our minds, stirred as a desire to give shape to shapelessness, to transform into fantasized reality that fantasy that others wanted to be real.

"The route itself is ritual," Agliè was telling us as we climbed the hill. "These are hanging gardens, just like—or almost—the ones Salomon de Caus devised for Heidelberg, that is, for the Palatine elector Frederick V, in the great Rosicrucian century. The light is poor, and so it should be, because it is better to sense than to see: our host has not reproduced the Salomon de Caus design literally; he has concentrated it in a narrower space. The gardens of Heidelberg imitated the macrocosm, but the person who reconstructed them here has imitated only the microcosm. Look at that rocaille grotto. . . . Decorative, no doubt. But Caus had in mind the emblem of the *Atalanta Fugiens* of Michael Maier, where coral is the philosopher's stone. Caus knew that the heavenly bodies can be influenced by the form of a garden, because there are patterns whose configuration mimes the harmony of the universe. . . ."

"Fantastic," Garamond said. "But how does a garden influence the planets?"

"There are signs that attract one another, that look at one another, embrace, and enforce love. But they do not have—they must not have—a certain and definite form. A man will try out given forces according to the dictates of his passion or the impulse of his spirit; this happened with the hieroglyphics of the Egyptians. For there can be no relationship between us and divine beings except through seals, figures, characters, and ceremonies. Thus the divinities speak to us through dreams and oracles. And that is what these gardens are. Every aspect of this terrace reproduces a mystery of the alchemist's art, but unfortunately we can no longer read it, not even our host can. An unusual devotion to secrecy, you will agree, in this man who spends what he has saved over the years in order to design ideograms whose meaning he has lost."

As we climbed from terrace to terrace, the gardens changed. Some were in the form of a labyrinth, others in the form of an emblem, but each terrace could be viewed in its entirety only from a higher one. Looking down, I saw the outline of a crown, and other patterns I had been unable to embrace as I was passing through them. But even from above, I could not decipher them. Each terrace, seen as one moved among its hedges, presented some images, but the perspective from above revealed new, even contradictory images, as if every step of that stairway spoke two different languages at once.

As we moved higher, we noticed some small structures. A fountain of phallic shape stood beneath a kind of arch or portico, and there was a Neptune trampling a dolphin, a door with vaguely Assyrian columns, an arch of imprecise form, as if polygons had been set upon other polygons, and each construction was surmounted by the statue of an animal: an elk, a monkey, a lion . . .

"And all this means something?" Garamond asked.

"Unquestionably! Just read the *Mundus Symbolicus* of Picinelli, which, incidentally, Alciati foresaw with extraordinary prophetic power. The whole garden may be read as a book, or as a spell, which is, after all, the same thing. If you knew the words, you could speak what the garden says and you would then be able to control one of the countless forces that act in the sublunar world. This garden is an instrument for ruling the universe."

He showed us a grotto. A growth of algae; the skeletons of marine animals, whether natural or not, I couldn't say; perhaps they were in plaster, or stone . . . A naiad could be discerned embracing a bull with the scaly tail of some great Biblical fish; it lay in a stream of water that flowed from the shell a Triton held like an amphora.

"I will tell you the deeper significance of this, which otherwise might seem a banal hydraulic joke. Caus knew that if one fills a vessel with water and seals it at the top, the water, even if one then opens a hole in the bottom, will not come out. But if one opens a hole at the top also, the water spurts out below."

"Isn't that obvious?" I said. "Air enters at the top and presses the water down."

"A typical scientific explanation, in which the cause is mistaken for the effect, or vice versa. The question is not why the water comes out in the second case, but why it refuses to come out in the first case."

"And why does it refuse?" Garamond asked eagerly.

"Because, if it came out, it would leave a vacuum in the vessel, and nature abhors a vacuum. Nequaquam vacui was a Rosicrucian principle, which modern science has forgotten."

"Very impressive," Garamond said. "Casaubon, this has to be put in our wonderful adventure of metals, these things must be highlighted: remember that. And don't tell me water's not a metal. You must use your imagination."

"Excuse me," Belbo said to Agliè, "but your argument is simply post hoc ergo ante hoc. What follows causes what came before."

"You must not think linearly. The water in these fountains doesn't. Nature doesn't; nature knows nothing of time. Time is an invention of the West."

As we climbed, we encountered other guests. Belbo nudged Diotallevi, who said in a whisper: "Ah, yes, facies hermetica."

And among the pilgrims with the facies hermetica, a little off to one side, a stiff smile of condescension on his lips, was Signor Salon. I nodded, he nodded.

"You know Salon?" Agliè asked me.

"You mean you know him?" I asked. "I do, of course. We live in the same building. What do you think of him?"

"I know him slightly. Some friends, whose word I trust, tell me he's a police informer."

That's why Salon knew about Garamond and Ardenti. What was the connection, exactly, between Salon and De Angelis? But I confined myself to asking Agliè: "What is a police informer doing at a party like this?"

"Police informers," Agliè said, "go everywhere. They can use any experience for inventing their confidential reports. For the police, the more things you know, or pretend to know, the more powerful you are. It doesn't matter if the things are true. What counts, remember, is to possess a secret."

"But why was Salon invited?" I asked.

"My friend," Agliè replied, "probably because our host respects the golden rule of sapiental thought, which says that any error can be the unrecognized bearer of truth. True esotericism does not fear contradiction."

"You're telling me that, finally, all contradictions agree."

"Quod ubique, quod ab omnibus et quod semper. Initiation is the discovery of the underlying and perennial philosophy."

With all this philosophizing, we had reached the top terrace and were on a path through a broad garden that led to the entrance of the castle or villa. In the light of a torch larger than the others and set upon a column, we saw a girl wrapped in a blue garment spangled with golden stars. In her hand she held a trumpet, the kind heralds blow in operas. As in one of those holy plays where the angels are adorned with tissue-paper feathers, the girl wore on her shoulders two large white wings decorated with almond-shaped figures, each with a dot in the center, looking almost like an eye.

Professor Camestres was there, one of the first Diabolicals to visit us at Garamond, the adversary of the Ordo Templi Orientis. We had difficulty recognizing him, because he was costumed most singularly, though Agliè said it was appropriate to the occasion: a white linen toga, loins girt by a red ribbon that also crisscrossed both chest and back, and a seventeenth-century hat to which were pinned four red roses. He knelt before the girl with the trumpet and uttered some words.

"It's true," Garamond murmured, "there are more things in heaven and earth . . ."

We went through a storied doorway, which reminded me of the Genoa cemetery. Above it, an intricate neoclassical allegory and the carved words: CONDOLEO ET CONGRATULATOR.

Inside, the guests were many and lively, crowding around a buffet in a spacious hall from which two staircases rose to upper floors. I saw other faces not unknown to me, among them Bramanti and—to my surprise—Commendatore De Gubernatis, an SFA already exploited by Garamond, but perhaps not yet made to face the terrible prospect of having all the copies of his masterpiece pulped, because he approached my boss with a show of obsequious gratitude. Agliè was in turn approached obsequiously by a tiny man with wild eyes, whose thick French accent told us that this was the Pierre we had heard accusing Bramanti of sorcery through the curtain of Agliè's study.

I went to the buffet. There were pitchers with colored liquids I couldn't identify. I poured myself a yellow beverage that resembled wine; it wasn't bad, tasting like an old-fashioned cordial, and it was definitely alcoholic. Perhaps there was a drug in it as well: my head began to swim. Around me facies hermeticae swarmed, the stern countenances of retired prefects, fragments of conversation. . . .

"In the first stage you must renounce all communication with other minds; in the second you project thoughts and images into beings, infuse places with emotional auras, gain control over the animal kingdom, and in the third stage you project your double—bilocation—like the yogis, and you can appear in different places simultaneously and in different forms. Beyond that, it's a question of passing to hypersensitive knowledge of vegetable essences. Then, you achieve dissociation, you assume telluric form, dissolving in one place, reappearing in another, but intact, not just as a double. The final stage is the extension of physical life. . . ."

"Not immortality . . ."

"Not at once."

"What about you?"

"It takes concentration, it's hard work, and, you know, I'm not twenty anymore. . . ."

I found my group again. They were just entering a room with white walls, curved corners. In the rear, as in a musée Grévin—but the image that came into my mind that evening was the altar I had seen in Rio, in the tenda de umbanda—were two wax statues, almost life-size, clad in material that glittered like sequins, pure thrift shop. One statue was of a lady on a throne, with an immaculate (or almost immaculate) garment studded with rhinestones. Above her, from wires, hung creatures of indefinite form, made, I thought, out of Lenci felt. In one corner, a loudspeaker: a distant sound of trumpets, music of good quality, perhaps Gabrieli. The sound effects showed better taste than the visuals. To the right, a second female figure, dressed in crimson velvet with a white girdle, and on her head a crown of laurel. She held gilded scales. Agliè explained to us the various symbols, but I was not paying attention; I was interested in the expressions of many of the guests, who moved from image to image with an air of reverence and emotion.

"They're no different from those who go to the sanctuary to see the Black Madonna in an embroidered dress covered with silver hearts," I said to Belbo. "Do the pilgrims think it's the mother of Christ in flesh and blood? No, but they don't think the opposite, either. They delight in the similarity, seeing the spectacle as a vision and the vision as a reality."

"Yes," Belbo said, "but the question isn't whether these people here are better or worse than Christians who go to shrines. I was asking myself: Who do we think we are? We for whom Hamlet is more real than our janitor? Do I have any right to judge—I who keep searching for my own Madame Bovary so we can have a big scene?"

Diotallevi shook his head and said to me in a low voice that it was wrong to make images of divine things, that these were all epiphanies of the Golden Calf. But he was enjoying himself.

58

Alchemy, however, is a chaste prostitute, who has many lovers but disappoints all and grants her favors to none. She transforms the haughty into fools, the rich into paupers, the philosophers into dolts, and the deceived into loquacious deceivers. . . .
　—Trithemius, *Annalium Hirsaugensium Tomi II*, S. Gallo, 1690, 141

Suddenly the room was plunged into darkness and the walls lighted up. I realized that three-quarters of the wall space was a semicircular screen on which pictures were about to be projected. When these appeared, I became aware that a part of the ceiling and of the floor was made of reflecting material, as were some of the objects that had first struck me as cheap because of the tawdry way they sparkled: the sequins, the scales, a shield, some copper vases. We were immersed in a subaqueous world where images were multiplied, fragmented, fused with the shadows of those present. The floor reflected the ceiling, the ceiling the floor, and together they mirrored the figures that appeared on the screen. Along with the music, subtle odors spread through the room: first Indian incense, then others, less distinct, and sometimes disagreeable.

At first the penumbra about us fell into absolute night. Then a grumbling was heard, a churning of lava, and we were in a crater, where dark and slimy matter bubbled up in the fitful light of yellow and bluish flames.

Oily vapors rose, to descend again, condensing as dew or rain, and an odor of fetid earth drifted up, a stench of decay. I inhaled sepulcher, tartar, darkness; a poisonous liquid oozed around me, snaking between tongues of dung, humus, coal dust, mud, smoke, lead, scum, naphtha, a black blacker than black, which now paled to allow two reptiles to appear—one light blue, the other reddish—entwined in an embrace, each biting the other's tail, to form a single circle.

It was as if I had drunk too much alcohol: I could no longer see my companions, who were lost in the shadows, I could not recognize the forms gliding past me, hazy, fluid outlines. . . . Then I felt my hand grasped. I didn't turn, not wanting to discover that I had deceived myself, because I caught Lorenza's perfume, and only then did I realize how great was my desire for her. It must have been Lorenza; she had come to resume the dialogue of fingernails scraping on my door, to finish what she had left unfinished the night before. Sulfur and mercury joined in a wet warmth that made my groin throb, but without urgency.

I was expecting the Rebis, the androgynous youth, the philosopher's salt, the coronation of the Work of the White. I seemed to know everything. All my reading of the past few months was, perhaps, now resurfacing in my mind, or perhaps Lorenza was transmitting the knowledge to me through the touch of her hand. Her palm was moist with sweat.

I surprised myself by murmuring obscure names, names that the philosophers, I knew, had given to the White. With them, perhaps, I was calling Lorenza to me, or perhaps I was only repeating them to myself, in a propitiatory litany: White Copper, Immaculate Lamb, Aibathest, Alborach, Blessed Water, Purified Mercury, Orpiment, Azoch, Baurach, Cambar, Caspa, Cherry, Wax, Chaia, Comerisson, Electron, Euphrates, Eve, Fada, Favonius, Foundation of the Art, Precious Stone of Givinis, Diamond, Zibach, Ziva, Veil, Narcissus, Lily, Hermaphrodite, Hae, Hypostasis, Hyle, Virgin's Milk, Unique Stone, Full Moon, Mother, Living Oil, Legume, Egg, Phlegm, Point, Root, Salt of Nature, Leafy Earth, Tevos, Tincar, Steam, Evening Star, Wind, Virago, Pharaoh's Glass, Baby's Urine, Vulture, Placenta, Menstruum, Fugitive Slave, Left Hand, Sperm of Metals, Spirit, Tin, Juice, Oil of Sulfur . . .

In the pitch, now grayish, dark, an outline of rocks and withered trees, a black sun setting. Then an almost blinding light, and sparkling figures reflected everywhere, creating a kaleidoscopic effect. Now the smell was liturgical, churchly; my head ached; there was a weight on my brow, I saw a sumptuous hall lined with golden tapestries, perhaps a nuptial banquet, with a princely bridegroom and a bride in white, then an elderly king and queen enthroned, beside them a warrior, and another king with dark skin. Before the dark king, a little altar on which a book was set, covered with black velvet, and a lighted candle in an ivory candlestick. Next to the candlestick, a rotating globe and a clock surmounted by a tiny crystal fountain from which a liquid flowed, blood-red. Above the fountain was a skull; from an eye socket slid a white serpent. . . .

Lorenza was breathing words into my ear. But I couldn't hear her voice.

The serpent moved to the rhythm of slow, sad music. The king and queen now wore black, and before them were six closed coffins. After a few measures of grim bass tuba, a man in a black hood appeared. At first, in a hieratic performance, as if in slow motion, the king submitted with mournful joy, bowing his meek head. The hooded man raised an ax, and then the rapid slash of a pendulum, the blade multiplied in every reflecting surface, and the heads that rolled were a thousand. After this, the images succeeded one another, but I had difficulty following the story. I believe that all the characters in turn, including the dark king, were decapitated and laid in the coffins. The whole room was transformed into the shore of a sea or a lake, and we saw six vessels land, and the biers were carried aboard them; then the vessels departed across the water, faded into the night. All this took place while the incense curled, almost palpable, in dense fumes, and for a moment I feared I was among the condemned. Around me many murmured, "The wedding, the wedding . . ."

Lorenza was gone. I turned to look for her among the shadows.

The room now was a crypt or sumptuous tomb, its vault illuminated by a carbuncle of extraordinary size.

In every corner women appeared in virginal dress. They gathered around a cauldron two stories high, in a framework with a stone base and a portico like an oven. From twin towers emerged two alembics emptying into an egg-shaped bowl; a third, central, tower ended in a fountain. . . .

Inside the base of the framework the bodies of the decapitated were visible. One of the virginal women carried a box and drew from it a round object, which she placed in a niche of the central tower, and immediately the fountain at the top began to spurt. I had time to recognize the object: it was the head of the Moorish king, which now burned like a log, making the water of the fountain boil. Fumes, puffs of steam, gurgling . . .

Lorenza this time put her hand on the back of my neck, caressing it as I had seen her caress Jacopo in the car.

The woman brought a golden sphere, turned on a tap in the oven, and caused a thick red liquid to flow into the sphere. Then the sphere was opened, and, in place of the red liquid, it contained an egg, large, beautiful, white as snow. The woman took the egg out and set it on the ground in a pile of yellow sand. The egg opened, and a bird came out, still unformed and bloody. But, watered with the blood of the decapitated, it grew before our eyes, became handsome and radiant.

They decapitated the bird and reduced it to ashes on a little altar. Some kneaded the ash into a paste, poured the thin paste into two molds, and set them in the oven to bake, blowing on the fire with some pipes. In the end, the molds were opened, and two pretty figures appeared, pale, almost transparent, a youth and a maiden, no more than four spans high, as soft and fleshy as living creatures but with eyes still glassy, mineral. They were set on two cushions, and an old man poured drops of blood into their mouths. . . .

Other women arrived, with golden trumpets decorated with green garlands. They handed a trumpet to the old man, who put it to the lips of the two creatures still suspended in their vegetable lethargy, their sweet animal sleep, and he began to insufflate soul into their bodies. . . . The room filled with light; the light dimmed to a half-light, then to a darkness broken by orange flashes. There was an immense dawn while the trumpets sounded, loud and ringing, and all was a dazzle of ruby. At that point I again lost Lorenza and realized I would never find her.

Everything turned a flaming red, which slowly dulled to indigo and violet, and the screen went blank. The pain in my forehead became intolerable.

"Mysterium Magnum," Agliè said calmly at my side. "The rebirth of the new man through death and passion. A good performance, I must say, even if the taste for allegory perhaps marred the precision of the phases. What you saw was only a performance, but it spoke of a Thing. And our host claims to have produced this Thing. Come, let us go and see the miracle achieved."

59

And if such monsters are generated, we must believe them the work of nature, even if they be different from man.
—Paracelsus, *De Homunculis*, in *Operum Volumen Secundum*, Genevae, De Tournes, 1658, p. 465

He led us out into the garden, and I felt better at once. I didn't dare ask the others if Lorenza had come after all. Probably I had dreamed it. After a few steps we entered a greenhouse; the stifling heat dazed me. Among tropical plants were six glass ampules in the shape of pears—or tears—hermetically sealed, filled with a pale-blue liquid. Inside each vessel floated a creature about twenty centimeters high: we recognized the gray-haired king, the queen, the Moor, the warrior, and the two adolescents crowned with laurel, one blue and one pink. . . . They swayed with a graceful swimming motion, as if water were their element.

It was hard to determine whether they were models made of plastic or wax, or whether they were living beings, and the slight opacity of the liquid made it impossible to tell if the faint pulse that animated them was an optical illusion or reality.

"They seem to grow every day," Agliè said. "Each morning, the vessels are buried in fresh horse manure—still warm—which provides the heat necessary for growth. In Paracelsus there are prescriptions that say homunculi must be grown at the internal temperature of a horse. According to our host, these homunculi speak to him, tell him secrets, utter prophecies. Some revealed to him the true measurements of the Temple of Solomon, others told him how to exorcise demons. . . . I must confess that I have never heard them speak."

They had very mobile faces. The king looked at the queen tenderly.

"Our host told me that one morning he found the blue youth, who had escaped somehow from his prison, attempting to break the seal of the maiden's vessel. . . . But he was out of his element,

347

could not breathe, and they saved him just in time, returning him to his liquid."

"Terrible," Diotallevi said. "I wouldn't want such a responsibility. You'd have to take the vessels with you everywhere and find all that manure wherever you went. And then what would you do in the summer, on vacation? Leave them with the doorman?"

"But perhaps," Agliè concluded, "they are only Cartesian imps. Or automata."

"The devil!" Garamond said. "Dr. Agliè, you're opening a whole new universe to me. We should all be more humble, my dear friends. There are more things in heaven and earth . . . But, after all, à la guerre comme à la guerre . . ."

Garamond was awestruck; Diotallevi maintained an expression of cynical curiosity; Belbo showed no feeling at all.

To dispel my doubt, I said to him, "Too bad Lorenza didn't come; she would have loved this."

"Mm, yes," he replied absently.

So Lorenza hadn't come.

And I was the way Amparo had been in Rio. I was ill. I felt somehow cheated. They hadn't brought me the agogô.

I left the group and went back into the building, picking my way through the crowd. I passed the buffet, drank something cool, though I was afraid it might contain a philter. I looked for a bathroom, to splash cold water on my temples and neck. This accomplished, I again felt better. But as I came out, I saw a circular staircase and, suddenly curious, I was unable to resist the new adventure. Perhaps, even though I thought I had recovered, I was still looking for Lorenza.

60

Descending, I came to a room below the ground, dimly lighted, with walls in rocaille like those of fountains in a park. In one corner I saw an opening like the bell of a trumpet. I heard sounds coming from it. When I approached, the sounds became more distinct, until I could catch sentences, as clear and precise as if they were being uttered at my side. An Ear of Dionysius!

Evidently the ear communicated with one of the upper rooms, picking up the conversation of those who stood near its aperture.

"Signora, I'll tell you something I've never told anyone else. I'm tired. . . . I've worked with cinnabar, with mercury, I sublimated spirits, did distillations with salts of iron, fermentations, and still I haven't found the Stone. I prepared strong waters, corrosive waters, burning waters, all in vain. I used eggshells, sulfur, vitriol, arsenic, sal ammoniac, quartz, alkalis, oxides of rock, saltpeter, soda, salt of tartar, and potash alum. Believe me, do not trust them, avoid the imperfect metals; otherwise you will be deceived, as I was deceived. I tried everything: blood, hair, the soul of Saturn, marcasites, aes ustum, saffron of Mars, tincture of iron, litharge, antimony. To no avail. I extracted water from silver, calcified silver both with and without salt, and using aqua vitae I extracted corrosive oils. I employed milk, wine, curds, the sperm of the stars which falls to earth, chelidon, placentas, ashes, even . . ."

"Even . . . ?"

"Signora, there's nothing in this world that demands more caution than the truth. To tell the truth is like leeching one's own heart. . . ."

"Enough, enough! You've got me all excited."

"I dare confess my secret only to you. I am of no place and no era. Beyond time and space, I live my eternal existence. There are beings who no longer have guardian angels: I am one of them. . . ."

"But why have you brought me here?"

Another voice: "My dear Balsamo! Playing with the myth of immortality, eh?"

"Idiot! Immortality is not a myth. It's a fact."

I was about to leave, bored by this chatter, when I heard Salon. He was speaking in a whisper, tensely, as if gripping someone by the arm. I also recognized the voice of Pierre.

"Come now," Salon was saying, "don't tell me that you too are here for this alchemical foolishness. And don't tell me you came to enjoy the cool air of the gardens. Did you know that after Heidelberg, Caus accepted an invitation from the king of France to supervise the cleaning of Paris?"

"Les façades?"

"He wasn't Malraux. It must have been the sewers. Curious, isn't it? The man invented symbolic orange groves and apple orchards for emperors, but what really interested him were the underground passages of Paris. In the Paris of those days there wasn't an actual network of sewers; it was a combination of canals on the surface and, below, conduits, about which little was known. The Romans, from the time of the republic, knew everything about their Cloaca Maxima, yet fifteen hundred years later, in Paris, people were ignorant of what went on beneath their feet. Caus accepted the king's invitation because he wanted to find out. What did he find out?

"After Caus, Colbert sent prisoners down to clean the conduits— that was the pretext, and bear in mind that this was also the period of the Man in the Iron Mask—but they escaped through the excrement, followed the current to the Seine, and sailed off in a boat, because nobody had the courage to confront those wretches covered with stinking slime and swarms of flies. . . . Then Colbert stationed gendarmes outside the various openings of the sewer, and the prisoners, forced to stay in the passages, died. In three centuries the city engineers managed to map only three kilometers of sewers. But in the eighteenth century there were twenty-six kilometers of sewers, and on the very eve of the Revolution. Does that suggest anything to you?"

"Ah, you know, this—"

"New people were coming to power, and they knew something their predecessors didn't. Napoleon sent teams of men down into the darkness, through the detritus of the capital. Those who had the courage to work there found many things: gold, necklaces, jewels, rings, and God knows what else that had fallen into those passages. Some bravely swallowed what they found, then came out, took a laxative, and became rich. It was discovered that many houses had cellar trapdoors that led directly to the sewer."

"Ça alors . . ."

"In a period when people emptied chamber pots out the window? And why did they have sewers with sidewalks along them, and iron rings set in the wall, to hang on to? These passages were the equivalent of those tapis francs where the lowlife gathered—the pègre, as it was called then—and if the police arrived, they could escape and resurface somewhere else."

"Légendes . . ."

"You think so? Whom are you trying to protect? Under Napoleon III, Baron Haussmann required all the houses of Paris, by law, to construct an independent cesspool, then an underground corridor leading to the sewer system. . . . A tunnel two meters thirty centimeters high and a meter and a half wide. You understand? Every house in Paris was to be connected by an underground corridor to the sewers. And you know the extent of the sewers of Paris today? Two thousand kilometers, and on various levels. And it all began with the man who designed those gardens in Heidelberg. . . ."

"So?"

"I see you do not wish to talk. You know something, but you won't tell me."

"Please, leave me. It's late. I am expected at a meeting." A sound of footsteps.

———

I didn't understand what Salon was getting at. Pressed against the rocaille by the ear, I looked around and felt that I was underground myself, and it seemed to me that the mouth of that phonurgic channel was but the beginning of a descent into dark tunnels that went to the center of the earth, tunnels alive with Nibelungs. I felt cold. I was about to leave when I heard another voice: "Come. We're ready to begin. In the secret chamber. Call the others."

61

The Golden Fleece is guarded by a three-headed Dragon, whose first Head derives from the Waters, whose second Head derives from the Earth, and whose third Head derives from the Air. It is necessary that these three Heads belong to a single and very powerful Dragon, who will devour all other Dragons.

—Jean d'Espagnet, *Arcanum Hermeticae Philosophiae Opus*, 1623, 138

I found my group again, and told Agliè I had overheard something about a meeting.

"Aha," Agliè said, "what curiosity! But I understand. Having ventured into the hermetic mysteries, you want to find out all about them. Well, as far as I know, this evening there is the initiation of a new member of the Ancient and Accepted Order of the Rosy Cross."

"Can we watch?" Garamond asked.

"You can't. You mustn't. You shouldn't. But we'll act like those characters in the Greek myth who gazed upon what was forbidden them to see, and we'll risk the wrath of the gods. I'll allow you one peek."

He led us up a narrow stairway to a dark corridor, drew aside a curtain, and through a sealed window we could glance into the room below, which was lighted by burning braziers. The walls were covered with lilies embroidered on damask, and at the far end stood a throne under a gilded canopy. On one side of the throne was a sun, on the other a moon, both set on tripods and cut out of cardboard or some plastic material, crudely executed, covered with tinfoil or some metal leaf, gold and silver, of course, but effective, because each luminary spun, set in motion by the flames of a brazier. Above the canopy an enormous star hung from the ceiling, shining with precious stones—or bits of glass. The ceiling was covered with blue damask spangled with great silver stars.

Before the throne was a long table decorated with palms. A sword had been placed on it, and between throne and table stood a stuffed lion, its jaws wide. Someone must have put a red light bulb inside the head, because the eyes shone, incandescent, and flames seemed to come from the throat. This, I thought, must be the work of Signor Salon, remembering the odd customers he had referred to that day in the Munich coal mine.

At the table was Bramanti, decked out in a scarlet tunic and embroidered green vestments, a white cape with gold fringe, a sparkling cross on his chest, and a hat vaguely resembling a miter, decorated with a red-and-white plume. Before him, hieratically deployed, were about twenty men, also in scarlet tunics but without vestments. On their chests they all wore a gold medal that I thought I recognized: I remembered a Renaissance portrait, the big Hapsburg nose, and the curious lamb with legs dangling, hanging by the waist. They had adorned themselves with imitations, not bad, of the Order of the Golden Fleece.

Bramanti was speaking, his arms upraised, as if uttering a litany, and the others responded from time to time. Then Bramanti raised the sword, and from their tunics the others drew stilettos or paper knives and held them high. At this point Agliè lowered the curtain. We had seen too much.

We stole away with the tread of the Pink Panther (as Diotallevi put it; he was remarkably abreast of the perversions of popular culture) and found ourselves back in the garden, slightly breathless.

Garamond was overwhelmed. "But are they . . . Masons?"

"And what," Agliè replied, "does Mason mean? They are the adepts of a chivalric order inspired by the Rosicrucians, and indirectly by the Templars."

"But what does that have to do with the Masons?" Garamond asked again.

"If what you saw has anything in common with the Masons, it's the fact that Bramanti's rite is also a pastime for provincial politicians and professional men. It was thus from the beginning: Freemasonry was a weak exploitation of the Templar legend. And this is the caricature of a caricature. Except that those gentlemen take it extremely seriously. Alas! The world is teeming with Rosicrucians and Templars like the ones you saw this evening. You mustn't expect any revelation from them, though among their number occasionally you can come across an initiate worthy of trust."

"But you, after all," Belbo said, without irony, as if the matter concerned him personally, "spend time with them. Which ones do you believe in? Or did you once believe in?"

"None, of course. Do I look like a credulous individual? I consider them with the cold objectivity, the understanding, the interest with which a theologian might observe a Naples crowd shouting in anticipation of the miracle of San Gennaro. The crowd bears witness to a faith, a deep need, and the theologian wanders among the sweating, drooling people because he might encounter there an unknown saint, the bearer of a higher truth, a man capable of casting new light on the mystery of the most Holy Trinity. But the Holy Trinity is one thing, San Gennaro is another."

He could not be pinned down. I didn't know how to define it— hermetic skepticism? liturgical cynicism?—this higher disbelief that led him to acknowledge the dignity of all the superstitions he scorned.

"It's simple," he was saying to Belbo. "If the Templars, the real Templars, did leave a secret and did establish some kind of continuity, then it is necessary to seek them out, and to seek them in the places where they could most easily camouflage themselves, perhaps by inventing rites and myths in order to move unobserved, like fish in water. What do the police do when they seek the archvillain, the evil mastermind? They dig into the lower depths, the notorious dives filled with petty crooks who will never conceive the grandiose crimes of the dark genius the police are after. What does the terrorist leader do to recruit new acolytes? Where does he look for them and find them? He circulates in the haunts of the pseudosubversives, the fellow-travelers who would never have the courage to be the real thing, but who openly ape the attitudes of their idols. Concealed light is best sought in fires, or in the brush where, after the blaze, the flames go on brooding under twigs, under trampled muck. What better hiding place for the true Templar than in the crowd of his caricatures?"

62

We consider societies druidic if they are druidic in their titles or
their aims, or if their initiations are inspired by druidism.
—M. Raoult, *Les druides. Les sociétés initiatiques celtes
contemporaines*, Paris, Rocher, 1983, p. 18

Midnight was approaching, and according to Agliè's program the
second surprise of the evening awaited us. Leaving the Palatine gardens, we resumed our journey through the hills.

After we had driven three-quarters of an hour, Agliè made us
park the two cars at the edge of a wood. We had to cross some
underbrush, he said, to arrive at a clearing, and there were neither
roads nor trails.

We proceeded, picking our way through shrubs and vines, our
shoes slipping on rotted leaves and slimy roots. From time to time
Agliè switched on a flashlight to find a path, but only for a second,
because, he said, we should not announce our presence to the celebrants. Diotallevi made a remark—I don't recall it exactly, something about Little Red Riding-Hood—and Agliè, with tension in
his voice, asked him to be quiet.

As we were about to come to the end of the brush, we heard
voices. We had reached the edge of the clearing, which was illuminated by a glow from remote torches—or perhaps votive lights,
flickering at ground level, faint and silvery, as if a gas were burning
with chemical coldness in bubbles drifting over the grass. Agliè told
us to stop where we were, still shielded by bushes, and wait.

"In a little while the priestesses will come. The Druidesses, that
is. This is an invocation of the great cosmic virgin Mikil. Saint Michael is a popular Christian adaptation, and it's no accident that he
is an angel, hence androgynous, hence able to take the place of a
female divinity. . . ."

"Where do they come from?" Diotallevi whispered.

"From many places: Normandy, Norway, Ireland . . . It is a
very special event, and this is a propitious place for the rite."

356

"Why?" Garamond asked.

"Certain places have more magic than others."

"But who are they—in real life?"

"People. Secretaries, insurance agents, poets. People you might run into tomorrow and not recognize."

Now we could see a small group preparing to enter the clearing. The phosphorescent light, I realized, came from little lamps the priestesses held up in their hands. They had seemed, earlier, to be at ground level because the clearing was on the top of a hill; the Druidesses had climbed up from below and were approaching the flat, open hilltop. They were dressed in white tunics, which fluttered in the slight breeze. They formed a circle; in the center, three celebrants stood.

"Those are the three hallouines of Lisieux, Clonmacnoise, and Pino Torinese," Agliè said. Belbo asked why those three in particular. Agliè shrugged and said: "No more. We must wait now in silence. I can't summarize for you in a few words the whole ritual and hierarchy of Nordic magic. Be satisfied with what I can tell you. If I do not tell you more, it is because I do not know . . . or am not allowed to tell. I must respect certain vows of privacy."

In the center of the clearing I noticed a pile of rocks, which suggested a dolmen. Perhaps the clearing had been chosen because of the presence of those boulders. One of the celebrants climbed up on the dolmen and blew a trumpet. Even more than the trumpet we had seen a few hours earlier, this looked like something out of the triumphal march in *Aïda*. But a muffled and nocturnal sound came from it, as if from far away. Belbo touched my arm: "It's the ramsing, the horn of the Thugs around the sacred banyan. . . ."

My reply was cruel, because I didn't realize he was joking precisely to repress other associations, and it must have twisted the knife in the wound. "It would no doubt be less magical with the bombardon," I said.

Belbo nodded. "Yes, they're here precisely because they don't want a bombardon," he said.

Was it on that evening he began to see a connection between his private dreams and what had been happening to him in those months?

Agliè hadn't followed our words, but heard us whispering. "It's not a warning or a summons," he explained, "but a kind of ultrasound, to establish contact with the subterranean currents. You see, now the Druidesses are all holding hands, in a circle. They are creating a kind of living accumulator, to collect and concentrate the telluric vibrations. Now the cloud should appear. . . ."

"What cloud?" I whispered.

"Tradition calls it the green cloud. Wait . . ."

I didn't really expect a green cloud. Almost immediately, however, a soft mist rose from the ground—a fog, I would have said, if it had been thicker, more homogeneous. But it was composed of flakes, denser in some places than in others. The wind stirred it, raised it in puffs, like spun sugar. Then it moved with the air to another part of the clearing, where it gathered. A singular effect. For a moment, you could see the trees in the background, then they would be hidden in a whitish steam, while the turf in the center of the clearing would smoke and further obscure our view of whatever was going on, as the moonlight shone around the concealed area. The flake cloud shifted, suddenly, unexpectedly, as if obeying the whims of a capricious wind.

A chemical trick, I thought, but then I reflected: we were at an altitude of about six hundred meters, and it was possible that this was an actual cloud. Foretold by the rite? Summoned? Or was it just that the celebrants knew that on that hilltop, under favorable conditions, those erratic banks of vapor formed just above the ground?

It was difficult to resist the fascination of the scene. The celebrants' tunics blended with the white of the cloud, and their forms entered and emerged from that milky obscurity as if it had spawned them.

There was a moment when the cloud filled the entire center of the little meadow. Some wisps, rising, separating, almost hid the moon, but the clearing was still bright at its edges. We saw a Druidess come from the cloud and run toward the wood, crying out, her arms in front of her. I thought she had discovered us and was hurling curses. But she stopped within a few meters of us, changed direction, and began running in a circle around the cloud, disappearing in the whiteness to the left, only to reappear after a few minutes from the right. Again she was very close to us, and I could see her face.

She was a sibyl with a great, Dantean nose over a mouth thin as a cicatrix, which opened like a submarine flower, toothless but for two incisors and one skewed canine. The eyes were shifty, hawklike, piercing. I heard, or thought I heard—or think now that I remember hearing, but I may be superimposing other memories—a series of Gaelic words mixed with evocations in a kind of Latin, something on the order of "O pegnia (oh, e oh!) et eee uluma!!!" Suddenly the fog lifted, disappeared, the clearing became bright again, and I saw that it had been invaded by a troop of pigs, their short necks encircled by garlands of green apples. The Druidess who had blown the trumpet, still atop the dolmen, now brandished a knife.

"We go now," Agliè said sharply. "It's over."

I realized, as I heard him, that the cloud was above us and around us, and I could barely make out my companions.

"What do you mean, over?" Garamond said. "Looks to me like the real stuff is just beginning!"

"What you were permitted to see is over. Now it is not permitted. We must respect the rite. Come."

He reentered the wood, was promptly swallowed up by the mist that enfolded us. We shivered as we moved, slipping on dead leaves, panting, in disarray, like a fleeing army, and regrouped at the road. We could be in Milan in less than two hours. Before getting back into Garamond's car, Agliè said good-bye to us: "You must forgive me for interrupting the show for you. I wanted you to learn something, to see the people for whom you are now working. But it was not possible to stay. When I was informed of this event, I had to promise I wouldn't disturb the ceremony. Our continued presence would have had a negative effect on what follows."

"And the pigs? What happens to them?" Belbo asked.

"What I could tell you, I have told you."

63

"What does the fish remind you of?"
"Other fish."
"And what do other fish remind you of?"
"Other fish."
—Joseph Heller, *Catch 22*, New York, Simon & Schuster,
1961, xxvii

I came back from Piedmont with much guilt. But as soon as I saw Lia again, I forgot the desires that had grazed me.

Still, our expedition left other marks on me, and now it troubles me that at the time I wasn't troubled by them. I was putting in final order, chapter by chapter, the illustrations for the wonderful adventure of metals, but once again I could not elude the demon of resemblance, any more than I had been able to in Rio. How was this Réaumur cylindrical stove, 1750, different from this incubation chamber for eggs, or from this seventeenth-century athanor, maternal womb, dark uterus for the creation of God knows what mystic metals? It was as if they had installed the Deutsches Museum in the Piedmont castle I had visited the week before.

It was becoming harder for me to keep apart the world of magic and what today we call the world of facts. Men I had studied in school as bearers of mathematical and physical enlightenment now turned up amid the murk of superstition, for I discovered they had worked with one foot in cabala and the other in the laboratory. Or was I rereading all history through the eyes of our Diabolicals? But then I would find texts above all suspicion that told me how in the time of positivism physicists barely out of the university dabbled in séances and astrological cénacles, and how Newton had arrived at the law of gravity because he believed in the existence of occult forces, which recalled his investigations into Rosicrucian cosmology.

I had always thought that doubting was a scientific duty, but now I came to distrust the very masters who had taught me to doubt.

I said to myself: I'm like Amparo; I don't believe in it, yet I surrender to it. Yes, I caught myself marveling over the fact that the height of the Great Pyramid really was one-billionth of the distance between the earth and the sun, and that you really *could* draw striking parallels between Celtic and Amerind mythologies. And I began to question everything around me: the houses, the shop signs, the clouds in the sky, and the engravings in the library, asking them to tell me not their superficial story but another, deeper story, which they surely were hiding—but finally would reveal thanks to the principle of mystic resemblances.

Lia saved me, at least temporarily.

I told her everything—or almost—about the trip to Piedmont, and evening after evening I came home with curious new bits of information to add to my file of cross references. She said, "Eat. You're thin as a rail." One evening, she sat beside me at the desk. With her hair parted in the middle of her brow, she could now look straight into my eyes. She had her hands in her lap: a housewifely pose. I had never seen her sit like that before, her legs wide, skirt taut from knee to knee. An inelegant position, I thought. But then I saw her face: radiant, slightly flushed. I listened to her—though I didn't yet know why—with respect.

"Pow," she said, "I don't like what's happening to you with this Manutius business. First you collected facts the way people collect seashells. Now it's as if you were marking down lottery numbers."

"I just enjoy myself more, with the Diabolicals."

"It's not enjoyment; it's passion. There's a difference. Be careful: they'll make you sick."

"Now, don't exaggerate. They're the sick ones, not I. You don't go crazy because you work in an asylum."

"That remains to be seen."

"You know, I've always been suspicious of analogies. But now I find myself at a great feast of analogies, a Coney Island, a Moscow May Day, a Jubilee Year of analogies, and I'm beginning to wonder if by any chance there isn't a reason."

"I've seen your files, Pow," Lia said to me, "because I have to keep them in order. Whatever your Diabolicals have discovered is already here: take a good look." And she patted her belly, her thighs, her forehead; with her spread legs drawing her skirt tight, she sat like a wet nurse, solid and healthy—she so slim and supple—with a serene wisdom that illuminated her and gave her a matriarchal authority.

"Pow, archetypes don't exist; the body exists. The belly inside is beautiful, because the baby grows there, because your sweet cock, all bright and jolly, thrusts there, and good, tasty food descends there, and for this reason the cavern, the grotto, the tunnel are beautiful and important, and the labyrinth, too, which is made in the image of our wonderful intestines. When somebody wants to invent something beautiful and important, it has to come from there, because you also came from there the day you were born, because fertility always comes from inside a cavity, where first something rots and then, lo and behold, there's a little man, a date, a baobab.

"And high is better than low, because if you have your head down, the blood goes to your brain, because feet stink and hair doesn't stink as much, because it's better to climb a tree and pick fruit than end up underground, food for worms, and because you rarely hurt yourself hitting something above—you really have to be in an attic—while you often hurt yourself falling. That's why up is angelic and down devilish.

"But because what I said before, about my belly, is also true, both things are true, down and inside are beautiful, and up and outside are beautiful, and the spirit of Mercury and Manicheanism have nothing to do with it. Fire keeps you warm and cold gives you bronchial pneumonia, especially if you're a scholar four thousand years ago, and therefore fire has mysterious virtues besides its ability to cook your chicken. But cold preserves that same chicken, and fire, if you touch it, gives you a blister this big; therefore, if you think of something preserved for millennia, like wisdom, you have to think of it on a mountain, up, high (and high is good), but also in a cavern (which is good, too) and in the eternal cold of the Tibetan snows (best of all). And if you then want to know why wisdom comes from the Orient and not from the Swiss Alps, it's because the body of your ancestors in the morning, when it woke and there was still darkness, looked to the east hoping the sun would rise and there wouldn't be rain."

"Yes, Mama."

"Yes indeed, my child. The sun is good because it does the body good, and because it has the sense to reappear every day; therefore, whatever returns is good, not what passes and is done with. easiest way to return from where you've been without retracing y steps is to walk in a circle. The animal that coils in a circle is u serpent; that's why so many cults and myths of the serpent exist, because it's hard to represent the return of the sun by the coiling of a hippopotamus. Furthermore, if you have to make a ceremony to invoke the sun, it's best to move in a circle, because if you go in a straight line, you move away from home, which means the ceremony will have to be kept short. The circle is the most convenient arrangement for any rite, even the fire-eaters in the marketplace know this, because in a circle everybody can see the one who's in the center, whereas if a whole tribe formed a straight line, like a squad of soldiers, the people at the ends wouldn't see. And that's why the circle and rotary motion and cyclic return are fundamental to every cult and every rite."

"Yes, Mama."

"We move on to the magic numbers your authors are so fond of. You are one and not two, your cock is one and my cunt is one, and we have one nose and one heart; so you see how many important things come in ones. But we have two eyes, two ears, two nostrils, my breasts, your balls, legs, arms, buttocks. Three is the most magical of all, because our body doesn't know that number; we don't have three of anything, and it should be a very mysterious number that we attribute to God, wherever we live. But if you think about it, I have one cunt and you have one cock—shut up and don't joke— and if we put these two together, a new thing is made, and we become three. So you don't have to be a university professor or use a computer to discover that all cultures on earth have ternary structures, trinities.

"But two arms and two legs make four, and four is a beautiful number when you consider that animals have four legs and little children go on all fours, as the Sphinx knew. We hardly have to discuss five, the fingers of the hand, and then with both hands you get that other sacred number, ten. There have to be ten commandments because, if there were twelve, when the priest counts one, two, three, holding up his fingers, and comes to the last two, he'd have to borrow a hand from the sacristan.

"Now, if you take the body and count all the things that grow from the trunk, arms, legs, head, and cock, you get six; but for women it's seven. For this reason, it seems to me that among your authors six is never taken seriously, except as the double of three, because it's familiar to the males, who don't have any seven. So when the males rule, they prefer to see seven as the mysterious sacred number, forgetting about women's tits, but what the hell.

"Eight . . . eight . . . give me a minute. . . . If arms and legs don't count as one apiece but two, because of elbows and knees, you have eight parts that move; add the torso and you have nine, add the head and you have ten. Just sticking with the body, you can get all the numbers you want. The orifices, for example."

"The orifices?"

"Yes. How many holes does the body have?"

I counted. "Eyes, nostrils, ears, mouth, ass: eight."

"You see? Another reason eight is a beautiful number. But I have nine! And with that ninth I bring you into the world, therefore nine is holier than eight! Or, if you like, take the anatomy of your menhir, which your authors are always talking about. Standing up during the day, lying down at night—your thing, too. No, don't tell me what it does at night. The fact is that erect it works and prone it rests. So the vertical position is life, pointing sunward, and obelisks stand as trees stand, while the horizontal position and night are sleep, death. All cultures worship menhirs, monoliths, pyramids, columns, but nobody bows down to balconies and railings. Did you ever hear of an archaic cult of the sacred banister? You see? And another point: if you worship a vertical stone, even if there are a lot of you, you can all see it; but if you worship, instead, a horizontal stone, only those in the front row can see it, and the others start pushing, me too, me too, which is not a fitting sight for a magical ceremony. . . ."

"But rivers . . ."

"Rivers are worshiped not because they're horizontal, but because there's water in them, and you don't need me to explain to you the relation between water and the body. . . . Anyway, that's how we're put together, all of us, and that's why we work out the same symbols millions of kilometers apart, and naturally they all resemble one another. Thus you see that people with a brain in their head, if they're shown an alchemist's oven, all shut up and warm inside, think of the belly of the mama making a baby, and only your Diabolicals think that the Madonna about to have the Child is a reference to the alchemist's oven. They spent thousands of years looking for a message, and it was there all the time: they just had to look at themselves in the mirror."

"You always tell me the truth. You are my Mirrored Me, my Self seen by You. I want to discover all the secret archetypes of the body." That evening we inaugurated the expression "discovering archetypes" to indicate our moments of greatest intimacy.

I was half-asleep when Lia touched my shoulder. "I almost forgot," she said. "I'm pregnant."

I should have listened to Lia. She spoke with the wisdom of life and birth. Venturing into the underground passages of Agarttha, into the pyramid of Isis Unveiled, we had entered Gevurah, the Sefirah of fear, the moment in which wrath manifests itself in the world. I had let myself be seduced by the thought of Sophia. Moses Cordovero says that the Female is to the left, and all her attributes point to Gevurah . . . unless the Male, using these attributes, adorns his Bride, and causes her to move to the right, toward good. Every desire must remain within its limits. Otherwise Gevurah becomes Judgment, the dark appearance, the universe of demons.

To discipline desire . . . This I had done in the tenda de umbanda. I had played the agogô, I had taken an active part in the spectacle, and I had escaped the trance. I had done the same with Lia: I had regulated desire out of homage to the Bride, and I had been rewarded in the depths of my loins; my seed had been blessed.

But I was not to persevere. I was to be seduced by the beauty of Tiferet.

TIFERET

64

To dream of living in a new and unknown city means imminent
death. In fact, the dead live elsewhere, nor is it known where.
—Gerolamo Cardano, *Somniorum Synesiorum*, Basel,
1562, 1, 58

While Gevurah is the Sefirah of awe and evil, Tiferet is the Sefirah
of beauty and harmony. As Diotallevi said: It is the light of understanding, the tree of life; it is pleasure, hale appearance. It is the
concord of Law and Freedom.

And that year was for us the year of pleasure, of the joyful sub-
version of the great text of the universe, in which we celebrated the
nuptials of Tradition and the Electronic Machine. We created, and
we delighted in our creation. It was the year in which we invented
the Plan.

For me at least, it was truly a happy year. Lia's pregnancy proceeded tranquilly, and between Garamond and my agency I was
beginning to make a comfortable living. I kept my office in the old
factory building, but we remodeled Lia's apartment.

The wonderful adventure of metals was now in the hands of the
compositors and proofreaders. That was when Signor Garamond had
his brainstorm: "An illustrated history of magic and the hermetic
sciences. With the material that comes in from the Diabolicals, with
the expertise you three have acquired, with the advice of that incredible man Agliè, we can put together a big volume, four hundred
pages, dazzling full-color plates, in less than a year. Reusing some
of the graphics from the history of metals."

"But the subject matter is so different," I said. "What can I do
with a photograph of a cyclotron?"

"What can you do with it? Imagination, Casaubon, use your
imagination! What happens in those atomic machines, in those me-
gatronic positrons or whatever they're called? Matter is broken down;
you put in Swiss cheese and out come quarks, black holes, churned
uranium! It's magic made flesh, Hermes and Hermès. Here on the

left, the engraving of Paracelsus, old Abracadabra with his alembics, against a gold background, and on the right, quasars, the Cuisinart of heavy water, gravitational galactic antimatter, et cetera. Don't you see? The real magician isn't the bleary-eyed guy who doesn't understand a thing; it's the scientist who has grasped the hidden secrets of the universe. Discover the miraculous all around us! Hint that at Mount Palomar they know more than they're letting on. . . ."

To encourage me, he gave me a raise, almost perceptible. I concentrated on the miniatures of the *Liber Solis* of Trismosin, the *Mutus Liber* of Pseudo-Lullus; I filled folders with pentacles, sefirotic trees, decans, talismans; I combed the loneliest rooms of libraries; I bought dozens of volumes from booksellers who in the old days had peddled the cultural revolution.

Among the Diabolicals, I moved with the ease of a psychiatrist who becomes fond of his patients, enjoying the balmy breezes that waft from the ancient park of his private clinic. After a while he begins to write pages on delirium, then pages of delirium, unaware that his sick people have seduced him. He thinks he has become an artist. And so the idea of the Plan was born.

Diotallevi went along with the game because, for him, it was a form of prayer. As for Jacopo Belbo, I thought he was having as much fun as I was. I realize only now that he derived no real pleasure from it. He took part in it nervously, anxiously biting his nails.

Or, rather, he played along, in the hope of finding at least one of the unknown addresses, the stage without footlights, which he mentions in the file named Dream. A surrogate theology for an angel that will never appear.

FILENAME: Dream

I don't remember if I dreamed one dream within another, or if they followed one another in the course of the same night, or if they alternated night by night.

I am looking for a woman, a woman I know, I have had an intense relationship with her, but cannot figure out why I let it cool, it was my fault, not keeping in touch. Inconceivable, that I could have allowed so much time to go by. I am looking for her—or for them, there is more than one woman, there are many, I lost them all in the same way, through neglect—and I am seized by uncertainty, because even just one would be enough for me, because I know this: in losing them, I have lost much. As a rule, in my dream, I cannot find, no longer possess, am unable to bring myself to open the address book where the phone number is written, and even if I do open it, it's as if I were farsighted, I can't read the names.

I know where she is, or, rather, I don't know where the place is, but I know what it's like. I have the distinct memory of a stairway, a lobby, a landing. I don't rush about the city looking for the place; instead, I am frozen, blocked by anguish, I keep racking my brain for the reason I permitted—or wanted—the relationship to cool, the reason I failed to show up at our last meeting. She's waiting for a call from me, I'm sure. If only I knew her name. I know perfectly well who she is, I just can't reconstruct her features.

Sometimes, in the half-waking doze that follows, I argue with the dream. You remember everything, I say, you've settled all your scores, there's no unfinished business. There is no place you remember whose location you don't know. There is nothing to the dream.

But the suspicion remains that I have forgotten something, left something among the folds of my eagerness, the way you forget a bank note or a paper with an important fact in some small marsupial pouch of your trousers or old jacket, and it's only later that you realize it was the most important thing of all, crucial, unique.

Of the city I have a clearer image. It's Paris. I'm on the Left Bank. And when I cross the river, I find myself in a square that could be Place des Vosges . . . no, more open, because at the end stands a kind of Madeleine. Passing the square, moving behind the temple, I come to a street—there's a secondhand bookshop on the corner—that curves to the right, through a series of alleys that are unquestionably the Barrio Gótico of Barcelona. It could turn into a very broad avenue full of lights, and it's on this avenue—and I remember it with the clarity of a photograph—that I see, to the right, at the end of a blind alley, the Theater.

I'm not sure what happens in that place of pleasure, no doubt something entertaining and slightly louche, like a striptease. For this reason I don't dare make inquiries, but I know enough to want to return, full of excitement. In vain: toward Chatham Road the streets become confused.

I wake with the taste of failure, an encounter missed. I cannot resign myself to not knowing what I've lost.

Sometimes I'm in a country house. It's big, I know there's

another wing, but I've forgotten how to reach it, as if the passage has been walled up. In that other wing there are rooms and rooms. I saw them once, and in detail, thoroughly—it's impossible that I dreamed them in another dream—with old furniture and faded engravings, brackets supporting little nineteenth-century toy theaters made of punched cardboard, sofas with embroidered coverlets, and shelves filled with books, a complete set of the *Illustrated Journal of Travel* and of *Adventures on Land and Sea*. It's not true that they came apart from being read so often and that Mama gave them to the trash man. I wonder who got the corridors and stairs mixed up, because that is where I would have liked to build my buen retiro, in that odor of precious junk.

....

Why can't I dream of college entrance exams like everybody else?

. . . the frame . . . was twenty foot square, placed in the middle of the room. The superficies was composed of several bits of wood, about the bigness of a die, but some larger than others. They were all linked together by slender wires. These bits of wood were covered on every square with paper pasted on them, and on these papers were written all the words of their language, in their several moods, tenses, and declensions, but without any order. . . . The pupils at his command took each of them hold of an iron handle, whereof there were forty fixed round the edges of the frame, and giving them a sudden turn, the whole disposition of the words was entirely changed. He then commanded six and thirty of the lads to read the several lines softly as they appeared upon the frame; and where they found three or four words together that might make part of a sentence, they dictated to the four remaining boys. . . .
—Jonathan Swift, *Gulliver's Travels*, III, 5

I believe that in embellishing his dream, Belbo returned once again to the idea of lost opportunity and his vow of renunciation, to his life's failure to seize—if it ever existed—the Moment. The Plan began because Belbo had now resigned himself to creating private, fictitious moments.

I asked him for some text or other, and he rummaged through the papers on his desk, where there was a heap of manuscripts perilously piled one on top of the other, with no concern for weight or size. He found the one he was looking for and tried to slip it out, thus causing the others to spill to the floor. Folders came open; pages escaped their flimsy containers.

"Couldn't you have moved the top half first?" I asked. Wasting my breath: this was how he always did it.

He replied, as he always did: "Gudrun will pick them up this evening. She has to have a mission in life; otherwise she loses her identity."

But this time I had a personal stake in the safety of the manuscripts, because I was now part of the firm. "Gudrun won't be able to put them back together," I said. "She'll put the wrong pages in the wrong folders."

"If Diotallevi heard you, he'd rejoice. A way of producing different books, eclectic, random books. It's part of the logic of the Diabolicals."

"But we'd find ourselves in the situation of the cabalists: taking millennia to discover the right combination. You're simply using Gudrun in place of the monkey that spends an eternity at the typewriter. As far as evolution goes, we've made no progress. Unless there's some program in Abulafia to do this work."

Meanwhile Diotallevi had come in.

"Of course there is," Belbo said, "and in theory you could have up to two thousand entries. All that's needed is the data and the desire. Take, for example, poetry. The program asks you how many lines you want in the poem, and you decide: ten, twenty, a hundred. Then the program randomizes the line numbers. In other words, a new arrangement each time. With ten lines you can make thousands and thousands of random poems. Yesterday I entered such lines as 'And the linden trees quiver,' 'Thou sinister albatross,' 'The rubber plant is free,' 'I offer thee my life,' and so on. Here are some of my better efforts."

I count the nights, the sistrum sounds . . .
Death, thy victory,
Death, thy victory . . .
The rubber plant is free.

From the heart of dawn
Thou sinister albatross.
(The rubber plant is free. . . .)
Death, thy victory.

And the linden trees quiver,
I count the nights, the sistrum sounds,
The hoopoe awaits me,
And the linden trees quiver.

"It's repetitive, yes, but repetitions can make poetic sense."

"Interesting," Diotallevi said. "This reconciles me to your machine. So if we fed it the entire Torah and told it—what's the term?—to randomize, it would perform some authentic temurah, recombining the verses of the Book?"

"Yes, but it's a question of time. That would take centuries."

I said: "What if, instead, you fed it a few dozen notions taken from the works of the Diabolicals—for example, the Templars fled to Scotland, or the Corpus Hermeticum arrived in Florence in 1460—and threw in a few connective phrases like 'It's obvious that' and 'This proves that'? We might end up with something revelatory. Then we fill in the gaps, call the repetitions prophecies, and—voilà—a hitherto unpublished chapter of the history of magic, at the very least!"

"An idea of genius," Belbo said. "Let's start right away."

"No. It's seven o'clock. Tomorrow."

"I'm starting tonight. Help me, just for a minute. Pick up, say, twenty of those pages on the floor, at random, glance at the first sentence of each, and that will be an entry."

I bent over, picked up, and read: "Joseph of Arimathea carries the Grail into France."

"Excellent. . . . I've written it. Go on."

"According to the Templar Tradition, Godefroy de Bouillon founded the Grand Priory of Zion in Jerusalem."

And "Debussy was a Rosicrucian."

"Excuse me," Diotallevi said, "but you also have to include some neutral data—for example, the koala lives in Australia, or Papin invented the pressure cooker."

"Minnie Mouse is Mickey's fiancée."

"We mustn't overdo it."

"No, we must overdo it. If we admit that in the whole universe there is even a single fact that does not reveal a mystery, then we violate hermetic thought."

"That's true. Minnie's in. And, if you'll allow me, I'll add a fundamental axiom: The Templars have something to do with everything."

"That goes without saying," Diotallevi agreed.

We went on for a while, but then it was really late. Belbo told us not to worry, he'd continue on his own. When Gudrun came in and told us she was locking up, he said he'd be staying to do some work and asked her to pick up the papers on the floor. Gudrun made sounds that could have belonged either to Latin sine flexione or to Chermish but that clearly expressed indignation and dismay, which demonstrated the universal kinship of all languages, descendants branched from a single, Adamic root. She obeyed, randomizing better than any computer.

The next morning, Belbo was radiant. "It works," he said. "It works beyond anything we could have hoped for." He handed us the printout.

The Templars have something to do with everything
What follows is not true
Jesus was crucified under Pontius Pilate
The sage Omus founded the Rosy Cross in Egypt
There are cabalists in Provence
Who was married at the feast of Cana?
Minnie Mouse is Mickey's fiancée
It logically follows that
If
The Druids venerated black virgins
Then
Simon Magus identifies Sophia as a prostitute of Tyre
Who was married at the feast of Cana?
The Merovingians proclaim themselves kings by divine right
The Templars have something to do with everything

"A bit obscure," Diotallevi said.

"Because you don't see the connections. And you don't give due importance to the question that recurs twice: Who was married at the feast of Cana? Repetitions are magic keys. Of course, I've compiled; but compiling the truth is the initiate's right. Here is my interpretation: Jesus was not crucified, and for that reason the Templars denied the Crucifix. The legend of Joseph of Arimathea covers a deeper truth: Jesus, not the Grail, landed in France, among the cabalists of Provence. Jesus is the metaphor of the King of the World, the true founder of the Rosicrucians. And who landed with Jesus? His wife. In the Gospels why aren't we told who was married at Cana? It was the wedding of Jesus, and it was a wedding that could not be discussed, because the bride was a public sinner, Mary Magdalene. That's why, ever since, all the Illuminati from Simon Magus to Postel seek the principle of the eternal feminine in a brothel. And Jesus, meanwhile, was the founder of the royal line of France."

66

If our hypothesis is correct, the Holy Grail . . . was the breed and descendant of Jesus, the "Sang real" of which the Templars were the guardians. . . . At the same time, the Holy Grail must have been, literally, the vessel that had received and contained the blood of Jesus. In other words it must have been the womb of the Magdalene.

— M. Baigent, R. Leigh, H. Lincoln, *The Holy Blood and the Holy Grail*, 1982, London, Cape, xiv

"Nobody would take that seriously," Diotallevi said.

"On the contrary, it would sell a few hundred thousand copies," I said grimly. "The story has already been written, with slight variations, in a book on the mystery of the Grail and the secrets of Rennes-le-Château. Instead of reading only manuscripts, you should look at what other publishers are printing."

"Ye Holy Seraphim!" Diotallevi said. "Then this machine says only what we already know." And he went out, dejected.

Belbo was piqued. "What is he saying—that my idea is an idea others have had? So what? It's called literary polygenesis. Signor Garamond would say that means I'm telling the truth. It must have taken years for the others to come up with it, whereas the machine and I solved the problem in one evening."

"I'm with you. The machine's useful. But I believe we should feed in more statements that don't come from the Diabolicals. The challenge isn't to find occult links between Debussy and the Templars. Everybody does that. The problem is to find occult links between, for example, cabala and the spark plugs of a car."

I was speaking off the top of my head, but I had given Belbo an idea. He talked to me about it a few mornings later.

"You were right. Any fact becomes important when it's connected to another. The connection changes the perspective; it leads you to think that every detail of the world, every voice, every word written or spoken has more than its literal meaning, that it tells us of a Secret. The rule is simple: Suspect, only suspect. You can read subtexts even in a traffic sign that says 'No littering.' "

"Of course. Catharist moralism. The horror of fornication."

"Last night I happened to come across a driver's manual. Maybe it was the semidarkness, or what you had said to me, but I began to imagine that those pages were saying Something Else. Suppose the automobile existed only to serve as metaphor of creation? And we mustn't confine ourselves to the exterior, or to the surface reality of the dashboard; we must learn to see what only the Maker sees, what lies beneath. What lies beneath and what lies above. It is the Tree of the Sefirot."

"You don't say."

"I am not the one who says; it is the thing itself that says. The drive shaft is the trunk of the tree. Count the parts: engine, two front wheels, clutch, transmission, two axles, differential, and two rear wheels. Ten parts, ten Sefirot."

"But the positions don't coincide."

"Who says they don't? Diotallevi's explained to us that in certain versions Tiferet isn't the sixth Sefirah, but the eighth, below Nezah and Hod. My axle-tree is the tree of Belboth."

"Fiat."

"But let's pursue the dialectic of the tree. At the summit is the engine, Omnia Movens, of which more later: this is the Creative Source. The engine communicates its creative energy to the two front or higher wheels: the Wheel of Intelligence and the Wheel of Knowledge."

"If the car has front-wheel drive."

"The good thing about the Belboth tree is that it allows metaphysical alternatives. So we have the image of a spiritual cosmos with front-wheel drive, where the engine, in front, transmits its wishes to the higher wheels, whereas in the materialistic version we have a degenerate cosmos in which motion is imparted by the engine to the two lower wheels: from the depths, the cosmic emanation releases the base forces of matter."

"What about an engine in back, rear-wheel drive?"

"Satanic. Higher and lower coincide. God is identified with the motion of crude matter. God as an eternally frustrated aspiration to divinity. The result of the Breaking of the Vessels."

"Not the Breaking of the Muffler?"

"That occurs in aborted universes, where the noxious breath of the Archons spreads through the ether. But we mustn't digress. After the engine and two wheels comes the clutch, the Sefirah of grace that establishes or interrupts the flow of love that binds the rest of the tree to the Supernal Energy. A disk, a mandala that caresses another mandala. Then the coffer of change—the gear box, or transmission, as the positivists call it, which is the principle of Evil, because it allows human will to speed up or slow down the constant process of emanation. For this reason, an automatic transmission costs more, for there it is the tree itself that decides, in accordance with its own Sovereign Equilibrium. Then comes the universal joint, the axle, the drive shaft, the differential—note the opposition/repetition of the quaternion of cylinders in the engine, because the differential (Minor Keter) transmits motion to the earthly wheels. Here the function of the Sefirah of difference is obvious, as, with a majestic sense of beauty, it distributes the cosmic forces to the Wheel of Glory and the Wheel of Victory, which in an unaborted universe (front-wheel drive) are subordinate to the motion imparted by the higher wheels."

"A coherent exegesis. And the heart of the engine, seat of the One, the Crown?"

"You have but to look with the eyes of an initiate. The supreme engine lives by an alternation of intake and exhaust. A complex, divine respiration, a cycle initially based on two units called cylinders (an obvious geometrical archetype), which then generate a third, and finally gaze upon one another in mutual love and bring forth the glory of a fourth. In the cycle of the first cylinder (none is first hierarchically, but only through the miraculous alternation of position), the piston (etymology: Pistis Sophia) descends from the upper neutral position to the lower neutral position as the cylinder fills with energy in the pure state. I'm simplifying, because here angelic hierarchies come into play, the distributor caps, which, as my handbook says, 'allow the opening and closing of the apertures that link the interior of the cylinders to the induction pipes leading out of the carburetor.' The inner seat of the engine can communicate with the rest of the cosmos only through this mediation, and here I believe is revealed—I am reluctant to utter heresy—the original limit of the One, which, in order to create, somehow depends on the Great Eccentrics. A closer reading of the text may be required here.

The cylinder fills with energy, the piston returns to the upper neutral position and achieves maximum compression—the simsun. And lo, the glory of the Big Bang: combustion, expansion. A spark flies, the mixture of fuel flares and blazes, and this the handbook calls the active phase of the cycle. And woe, woe if in the mixture of fuel the Shells intrude, the qelippot, drops of impure matter like water or Coca-Cola. Then expansion does not take place or occurs in abortive starts. . . ."

"Then the meaning of Shell is qelippot? We'd better not use it anymore. From now on, only Virgin's Milk . . ."

"We'll check. It could be a trick of the Seven Sisters, lower emanations trying to control the process of creation. . . . In any case, after expansion, behold the great divine release, the exhaust. The piston rises again to the upper neutral position and expels the formless matter, now combusted. Only if this process of purification succeeds can the new cycle begin. Which, if you think about it, is also the Neoplatonic mechanism of Exodus and Parodos, miraculous dialectic of the Way Up and the Way Down."

"Quantum mortalia pectora ceacae noctis habent! And the sons of matter never realized it!"

"They never saw the connection between the philosopher's stone and Firestone."

"For tomorrow, I'll prepare a mystical interpretation of the phone book."

"Ever ambitious, our Casaubon. Mind you, there you'll have to solve the unfathomable problem of the One and the Many. Better succeed slowly. Start, instead, with the washing machine."

"That's too easy. The alchemistic transformation from black to whiter than white."

67

Da Rosa, nada digamos agora . . .
—Sampayo Bruno, *Os Cavalheiros do Amor*, Lisbon,
Guimarães, 1960, p. 155

When you assume an attitude of suspicion, you overlook no clue. After our fantasy on the power train and the Tree of the Sefirot, I was prepared to see symbols in every object I came upon.

I had kept in touch with my Brazilian friends, and in Portugal just then, at Coimbra, a conference was being held on Lusitanian culture. More out of a wish to see me again than out of respect for my expertise, my Rio friends managed to have me invited. Lia didn't go with me; she was in her seventh month, and though her pregnancy had changed her slender figure only slightly, transforming her into a Flemish madonna, she preferred to stay home.

I spent three merry evenings with my old comrades. As we were returning by bus to Lisbon, an argument developed about whether we should stop at Fátima or Tomar. Tomar was the castle to which the Portuguese Templars had withdrawn after the king and the pope saved them from trial and ruin by transforming them into the Order of the Knights of Christ. I couldn't miss a Templar castle, and luckily the rest of the party was not enthusiastic about Fátima.

If I could have invented a Templar castle, it would have been Tomar. You reach it by ascending a fortified road that flanks the outer bastions, which have cruciform slits, and you breathe Crusader air from the first moment. The Knights of Christ prospered for centuries in that place. Tradition has it that both Henry the Navigator and Christopher Columbus belonged to that order, and in fact it devoted itself to the conquest of the seas—making the fortune of Portugal. The knights' long and happy existence there had caused the castle to be rebuilt and extended through the centuries, so to its medieval part were joined Renaissance and Baroque wings. I was moved as I entered the church of the Templars, which had an octagonal rotunda reproducing that of the Holy Sepulcher, and I was surprised to see that the Templars' crosses had different forms, depending on their location. It was a problem I had encountered before, when I went through the confused iconography on the subject. Whereas the cross of the Knights of Malta had remained more or less the same, the Templar cross had been influenced by periods and local traditions. That's why Templar-hunters, finding any kind of cross in a place, immediately think they've discovered a trace of the knights.

Our guide took us to see the Manueline window, the janela par excellence, a filigree, a collage of marine and submarine troves, seaweeds, shells, anchors, capstans, and chains, celebrating the knights' achievements on the oceans. The window was framed by two towers, which were decorated with carvings of the insigne of the Garter. What was the symbol of an English order doing in a Portuguese fortified monastery? The guide couldn't say; but a little later, on another side, the northeast, I believe, he showed us the insigne of the Golden Fleece. I couldn't help thinking of the subtle game of alliances that had united the Garter to the Golden Fleece, the Fleece to the Argonauts, the Argonauts to the Grail, and the Grail to the Templars. Remembering Colonel Ardenti's narrative and a few pages from the Diabolicals' manuscripts, I started when our guide showed us into a side room whose ceiling was gripped by keystones. They were rosettes, but on some of them was carved a bearded caprine face: Baphomet. . . .

We went down into a crypt. After seven steps, a bare stone floor led to the apse, where an altar could stand, or the chair of the grand master. You reached it by passing beneath seven keystones, each in the form of a rose, one larger than the next, with the last set over a well. The Cross and the Rose, in a Templar monastery, and in a room surely built before the Rosicrucian manifestoes. . . . I put some questions to the guide. He smiled. "If you knew how many students of the occult sciences come here on pilgrimages . . . It's said that this was the initiation chamber."

Entering by chance a room not yet restored, which contained a few pieces of dusty furniture, I found the floor cluttered with great cardboard boxes. Rummaging at random, I uncovered some fragments of volumes in Hebrew, presumably from the seventeenth century. What were the Jews doing in Tomar? The guide told me that the knights had maintained friendly relations with the local Jewish community. He had me look out the window and showed me a little garden designed like an elegant French maze—the work, he told me, of an eighteenth-century Jewish architect: Samuel Schwarz.

The second appointment in Jerusalem . . . And the first at the Castle? Wasn't that how the message of Provins went? By God, the Castle of the Ordonation mentioned in Ingolf's document was not the Monsalvat of chivalric novels, the Avalon of the Hyperboreal. No. What castle would the Templars of Provins, more used to directing commanderies than to reading romances of the Round Table, have chosen for their first meeting place? Why, Tomar, the castle of the Knights of Christ, a place where survivors of the order enjoyed complete freedom, unchanged guarantees, and where they could be in contact with the agents of the second group!

I left Tomar and Portugal with my mind ablaze. No longer was I laughing at the message Ardenti had shown us. The Templars, when they became a secret order, worked out a Plan that was to last six hundred years and conclude in our century. The Templars were serious men. If they talked about a castle, they meant a real castle. The Plan began at Tomar. And what would the ideal route have been, the sequence of the other five meetings? Places where the Templars could count on friendship, protection, complicity. The colonel spoke of Stonehenge, Avalon, Agarttha. . . . Nonsense. The message had to be completely restudied.

Of course—I reminded myself on my way home—the idea is not to discover the Templars' secret, but to construct it.

Belbo seemed disturbed at the thought of going back to the document left by the colonel, and he found it only after digging reluctantly in a lower drawer. But, I saw, he had kept it. Together we reread the Provins message, after so many years.

It began with the message coded by the method of Trithemius: Les XXXVI inuisibles separez en six bandes. And then:

a la . . . Saint Jean
36 p charrete de fein
6 . . . entiers avec saiel
p . . . les blancs mantiax
r . . . s . . . . chevaliers de Pruins pour la . . . j.nc.

6 foiz 6 en 6 places
chascune foiz 20 a . . . 120 a . . .
iceste est l'ordonation
al donjon li premiers
it li secunz joste iceus qui . . . pans
it al refuge
it a Nostre Dame de l'altre part de l'iau
it a l'ostel des popelicans
it a la pierre
3 foiz 6 avant la feste . . . la Grant Pute.

"Thirty-six years after the hay wain, the night of Saint John of the year 1344, six sealed messages for the knights with the white cloaks, the relapsed knights of Provins, revenge. Six times six in six places, twenty years each time, for a total of one hundred and twenty years, this is the Plan. The first at the Castle, then with those who ate the bread, then at the Refuge, then at Our Lady Beyond the River, then at the House of the Popelicans, then at the Stone. You see, in 1344 the message says that the first must go to the Castle. And, in fact, the knights were established in Tomar in 1357. Now, we must ask ourselves where the second group went. Come on: imagine you are an escaping Templar, where would you go to form the second group?"

"H'm . . . If it's true that those in the wain fled to Scotland . . . But why should they have gone to Scotland in particular to eat the bread?"

I was becoming a master of chains of association. You could start anywhere. Scotland. Highlands. Druidic rites. Night of Saint John. Summer solstice. Saint John's Fire. Golden bough. Because I had read about Saint John's Fire in Frazer's *Golden Bough*.

I telephoned Lia. "Do me a favor. Get *The Golden Bough* and see what it says about Saint John's Fire."

Lia was terrific at this sort of thing. She found the chapter at once. "What do you want to know? It's a very ancient rite, practiced in almost all European countries. It's celebrated at the moment when the sun is at its peak. Saint John was added to make the thing Christian. . . ."

"Do they eat bread in Scotland?"

"Let me see. . . . I don't think so. . . . Ah, here it is: they don't eat bread for Saint John, but on the night of the first of May, the night of the Beltane fires, originally a Druid festival, they eat bread, especially in the Scottish highlands. . . ."

"We've got it! What kind?"

"They knead a cake of flour and oats and toast it on embers. . . . Then a rite follows that recalls ancient human sacrifices. . . . The bread's called bannock cakes. . . ."

"What? Spell it!" She did, and I thanked her, I told her she was my Beatrice, my Morgan le Fay, and other endearments.

I tried to remember my thesis. The secret group, according to the legend, took refuge in Scotland with King Robert the Bruce, and the Templars helped the king win the battle of Bannockburn. In reward, the king set them up as the new Order of the Knights of Saint Andrew of Scotland.

I took a big English dictionary down from the shelf and looked up bannock: bannok in Middle English, bannuc in Anglo-Saxon, bannach in Gaelic. A kind of cake, cooked on a grill or a slab, made of barley, oats, or other grain. Burn is a stream. You had only to translate Bannockburn as the French Templars would have done when they sent news from Scotland to their compatriots in Provins, and you get something like the stream of the cake, or of the loaf, or of the bread. Those who ate the bread were those who had won at the stream of the bread, and hence the Scottish group, which perhaps by that time had spread throughout the British Isles. Logical: from Portugal to England. That was a shorter route, much shorter than Ardenti's from Pole to Palestine.

68

Let your garments be white. . . . If it is dark, set many lights
burning. . . . Now begin combining letters, few, many, shift them
and combine them until your heart is warm. Pay attention to the
movement of the letters and to what you can produce by combining
them. And when your heart is warm, when you see that through
the combination of the letters you grasp things you could not have
known by yourself or with the aid of tradition, when you are ready
to receive the influence of the divine power that enters into you,
then use all the profundity of your thought to imagine in your heart
the Name and His higher angels, as if they were human beings beside you.
— Abulafia, *Sefer Haie Olam*

"It makes sense," Belbo said. "And in that case, where would the
Refuge be?"

"The six groups settle in six places, but only one place is called
the Refuge. Odd. This must mean that in the other places, like Portugal and Britain, the Templars can live undisturbed, although under another name, whereas in the Refuge they are completely hidden.
I would say it is where the Templars of Paris went after they left
the Temple. To me it seems economical for the route to go to England from France, but why not assume that the Templars took an
even more economical course and set up a refuge in a secret and
protected place in Paris itself? Being sound politicians, they reasoned that in two hundred years the situation would change and
they would be able to act in the light of day, or almost."

"Paris it is. And the fourth place?"

"The colonel was thinking of Chartres, but if we make Paris the
third place, we can't put down Chartres as the fourth, because obviously the Plan has to involve all the centers of Europe. Besides,
we're leaving the mystical trail to work out a political trail. The
pattern appears to be a sine wave, so we should go to the north of
Germany. 'Beyond the water,' that is, beyond the Rhine, there's a
city—not a church—of Our Lady. Near Danzig, there's a city of
the Virgin—in other words, Marienburg."

"Why meet at Marienburg?"

"Because it was the seat of the Teutonic Knights! Relations between the Templars and the Teutonics hadn't been poisoned like those between the Templars and the Hospitalers, who had waited like vultures for the suppression of the Temple in order to seize its wealth. The Teutonics were created in Palestine by German emperors as a counterbalance to the Templars, but they were soon called north to stem the invasion of Prussian barbarians. They succeeded so well that in the space of two centuries they became a state that spread out over all the Baltic lands. They moved between Poland, Lithuania, and Livonia. They founded Königsberg. They were defeated only once, by Aleksandr Nevski in Estonia. About the time the Templars were arrested in Paris, the Teutonics established the capital of their realm at Marienburg. If there was any spiritual-knighthood plan of world conquest, the Templars and the Teutonics had divided the spheres of influence between them."

"You know what?" Belbo said. "I'm with you. Now the fifth group. Where are these Popelicans?"

"I don't know," I said.

"You disappoint me, Casaubon. Maybe we should ask Abulafia."

"No. Abulafia can only connect facts, not create them. The Popelicans are a fact, not a connection, and facts are the province of Sam Spade. Give me a few days."

"I'll give you two weeks," Belbo said. "If, within two weeks, you don't hand the Popelicans over to me, you'll buy me a bottle of twelve-year-old Ballantine's."

Beyond my means. A week later I delivered the Popelicans to my greedy partners.

"It's all clear. Now follow me, because we must go back to the fourth century, to Byzantium, when various movements of Manichean inspiration have already spread throughout the Mediterranean. We begin with the Archontics, founded in Armenia by Peter of Capharbarucha—and you have to admit that's a pretty grand name. Anti-Semitic, the Archontics identify the Devil with Sabaoth, the god of the Jews, who lives in the seventh heaven. To reach the Great Mother of Light in the eighth heaven, it is necessary to reject both Sabaoth and baptism. All right?"

"Consider them rejected," Belbo said.

"But the Archontics are still nice kids at heart. In the fifth century the Massalians come along, and actually they survive until the eleventh century, in Thrace. The Massalians are not dualists but monarchians, and they have dealings with the infernal powers, and in fact some texts call them Borborites, from borboros, filth, because of the unspeakable things they do."

"What do they do?"

"The usual unspeakable things. Men and women hold in the palm of their hand, and raise to heaven, their own ignominy, namely, sperm or menstruum, then eat it, calling it the Body of Christ. And if by chance a woman is made pregnant, at the opportune moment they stick a hand into her womb, pull out the embryo, throw it into a mortar, mix in some honey and pepper, and gobble it up."

"How revolting, honey and pepper!" Diotallevi said.

"So those are the Massalians, also known as Stratiotics and Phibionites, or Barbelites, who are made up of Nasseans and Phemionites. But for other fathers of the church, the Barbelites were latter-day Gnostics, therefore dualists, who worshiped the Great Mother Barbelo, and their initiates in turn called the Borborites Hylics, or Children of Matter, as distinct from the Psychics, who were already a step up, and the Pneumatics, who were the truly elect, the Rotary Club of the whole business. But maybe the Stratiotics were only the Hylics of the Mithraists."

"Sounds a bit confused," Belbo said.

"Naturally. None of these people left records. The only things we know about them come to us from the gossip of their enemies. But no matter. I'm just trying to show you what a mess the Middle East was at the time. And to set the stage for the Paulicians. These are the followers of a certain Paul, joined by some iconoclasts expelled from Albania. From the eighth century on, the Paulicians grow rapidly, the sect becomes a community, the community a force, a political power, and the emperors of Byzantium, beginning to get worried, send the imperial armies against them. The Paulicians extend as far as the confines of the Arab world; they spread toward the Euphrates, and northward as far as the Black Sea. They establish colonies more or less everywhere, and we find them as late as the seventeenth century, when they are converted by the Jesuits, and some communities still exist today in the Balkans or thereabouts. Now, what do the Paulicians believe in? In God, One and Three, except that the Demiurge defiantly created the world, with the unfortunate results visible to all. The Paulicians reject the Old Testament, refuse the sacraments, despise the Cross, and don't honor the Virgin, because Christ was incarnated directly in heaven and passed through Mary as through a pipe. The Bogomils, who are partly derived from them, say that Christ went in one ear of Mary and came out the other, without her even noticing. The Paulicians are also accused of worshiping the sun and the Devil and of mixing children's blood in their bread and the Eucharistic wine."

"Like everybody else."

"Those were the days when, for a heretic, going to Mass was a torment. Might as well become Moslem. Anyway, that's the sort of people they were. And I'm telling you about them because, when the *dualist* heretics spread through Italy and Provence, they are called—to indicate that they're like the Paulicians—Popelicans, Publicans, Populicans, who gallice etiam dicuntur ab aliquis popelicant!"

"So there they are."

"Yes, finally. The Paulicians continue into the ninth century, driving the Byzantine emperors crazy until Emperor Basil vows that if he gets his hands on their leader, Chrysocheir, who invaded the church of Saint John of God at Ephesus and watered his horse at the holy-water fonts . . ."

"A familiar nasty habit," Belbo said.

". . . he'll shoot three arrows into his head. He sends the imperial army after Chrysocheir; they capture him, cut off his head, send it to the emperor, who places it on a table—or a trumeau, on a little porphyry column—and shoots three arrows, wham wham wham, into it, probably an arrow for each eye and the third for the mouth."

"Nice folks," Diotallevi said.

"They didn't do it to be mean," Belbo said. "It was a question of faith. Go on, Casaubon: our Diotallevi doesn't understand theological fine points."

"To conclude: the Crusaders encounter the Paulicians. They come upon them near Antioch in the course of the First Crusade, where the heretics are fighting alongside the Arabs, and they encounter them also at the siege of Constantinople, where the Paulician community of Philippopolis tries to hand the city over to the Bulgarian tsar Yoannitsa to spite the French, as Villehardouin tells us. Here's the connection with the Templars and the solution to our riddle. Legend has the Templars inspired by the Cathars, but it's really the other way around. The Templars, encountering the Paulician communities in the course of the Crusades, established mysterious relations with them, as they had before with the mystics and the Moslem heretics. Just follow the track of the Ordonation. It has to pass through the Balkans."

"Why?"

"Because, clearly, the sixth appointment is in Jerusalem. The message says to go to the stone. And where is there a stone, a rock, which the Moslems venerate, and for which, if we want to see it, we have to take off our shoes? Why, right in the center of the Mosque of Omar in Jerusalem, where once stood the Temple of the Templars. I don't know who was to wait in Jerusalem, perhaps a core group of surviving and disguised Templars, or else some cabalists connected with the Portuguese, but this much is certain: to reach Jerusalem from Germany the most logical route is through the Balkans, and there the fifth group, the Paulician one, was waiting. You see how straightforward and economical the Plan becomes?"

"I must say I'm persuaded," Belbo said. "But where in the Balkans were the Popelicans waiting?"

"If you ask me, the natural successors of the Paulicians were the Bulgarian Bogomils, but the Templars of Provins couldn't have known that a few years later Bulgaria would be invaded by the Turks and remain under their dominion for five centuries."

"Which would suggest that the Plan was interrupted at the link between Germany and Bulgaria. When was that to take place?"

"In 1824," Diotallevi said.

"Why's that?"

Diotallevi quickly sketched the following diagram:

PORTUGAL	ENGLAND	FRANCE	GERMANY	BULGARIA	JERUSALEM
1344	1464	1584	1704	1824	1944

"In 1344 the first grand masters of each group establish themselves in the six prescribed places. In the course of a hundred and twenty years, six grand masters succeed one another in each group, and in 1464 the sixth master of Tomar meets the sixth master of the

English group. In 1584 the twelfth English master meets the twelfth French master. The chain proceeds at this pace, so if the appointment with the Paulicians fails, it must fail in 1824."

"Let's assume it fails," I said. "But I don't understand why such shrewd men, when they had four-sixths of the message in their hands, weren't able to reconstruct it. Or why, if the appointment with the Bulgarians fell through, they didn't get in touch with the next group."

"Casaubon," Belbo said, "do you really think the lawmakers of Provins were fools? If they wanted the revelation to remain concealed for six hundred years, they must have taken precautions. Every master of a group knows where to find the master of the following group, but not where to find the others, and none of the later groups know where to find the masters of the preceding groups. If the Germans lose the Bulgarians, they'll never know where the Jerusalemites are, and the Jerusalemites won't know where anyone else is. As for reconstructing a message from incomplete pieces, that depends on how the message has been divided. Certainly not in logical sequence. So if only one piece is missing, the message is incomprehensible, and the one who has that missing piece can't make any use of it."

"Just think," Diotallevi said. "If the Bulgarian meeting didn't take place, Europe today is the theater of a secret ballet, with groups seeking and not finding one another, while each group knows that one small piece of information might be enough to make it master of the world. What's the name of that taxidermist you told us about, Casaubon? Maybe a Plot really exists, and history is simply the result of this battle to reconstruct a lost message. We don't see them, but, invisible, they act all around us."

The same idea then occurred to Belbo and to me; we both started talking, and we quickly worked out the right connection. In addition, we discovered that at least two expressions in the Provins message—the reference to thirty-six invisibles divided into six groups, and the hundred-and-twenty-year deadline—also appeared in the debate on the Rosicrucians.

"After all, they were Germans," I said. "I'll read the Rosicrucian manifestoes."

"But you said the manifestoes were fake," Belbo said.

"So? What we're putting together is fake."

"True," he said. "I was forgetting that."

69

Elles deviennent le Diable: débiles, timorées, vaillantes à des heures exceptionnelles, sanglantes sans cesse, lacrymantes, caressantes, avec des bras qui ignorent les lois . . . Fi! Fi! Elles ne valent rien, elles sont faites d'un côté, d'un os courbe, d'une dissimulation rentrée. . . . Elles baisent le serpent. . . .
  —Jules Bois, *Le satanisme et la magie*, Paris, Chailley, 1895, p. 12

He was forgetting that, yes. The following file, brief and dazed, surely belongs to this period.

FILENAME: Ennoia

You arrived at the house suddenly with your grass. I didn't want any, I won't allow any vegetable substance to interfere with the functioning of my brain (I'm lying, I smoke tobacco, drink distillations of grain). The few times, in the early sixties, when somebody forced me to share in the circulation of a joint, with that cheap slimy paper impregnated with saliva, and the last drag using a pin, I wanted to laugh.

But yesterday it was you offering it to me, and I thought that maybe this was your way of offering yourself, so I smoked, trusting. We danced close, the way nobody's danced for years, and—the shame of it—while Mahler's Fourth was playing. I felt as if in my arms an ancient creature were yeasting, with the sweet and wrinkled face of an old nanny goat, a serpent rising from the depths of my loins, and I worshiped you as a very old and universal aunt. Probably I went on holding my body close to yours, but I felt also that you were in flight, ascending, being transformed into gold, opening locked doors, moving objects through the air as I penetrated your dark belly, Megale Apophasis, Prisoner of the Angels.

Was it not you I sought all along? I am here, always waiting for you. Did I lose you, each time, because I didn't recognize you? Did I lose you, each time, because I did recognize you but was afraid? Lose you because each time, recognizing you, I knew I had to lose you?

But where did you end up last night? I woke this morning with a headache.

70

Let us remember well, however, the secret references to a period of
120 years that brother A . . . , the successor of D and last of the
second line of succession—who lived among many of us—addressed to us, we of the third line of succession. . . .
    —*Fama Fraternitatis*, in *Allgemeine und general Reformation*,
    Cassel, Wessel, 1614

First thing, I read through the two manifestoes of the Rosicrucians,
the *Fama* and the *Confessio*. I also took a look at the *Chemical
Wedding of Christian Rosencreutz* by Johann Valentin Andreae, because Andreae was the presumed author of the manifestoes.

The two manifestoes appeared in Germany between 1614 and 1615,
thus about thirty years after the 1584 meeting between the French
and English Templars and almost a century before the French were
to meet with the Germans.

I read, not to believe what the manifestoes said, but to look beyond them, as if the words meant something else. To help them
mean something else, I knew I should skip some passages and attach
more importance to some statements than to others. But this was
exactly what the Diabolicals and their masters were teaching us. If
you move in the refined time of revelation, do not follow the fussy,
philistine chains of logic and their monotonous sequentiality.

Taken literally, these two texts were a pile of absurdities, riddles,
contradictions. Therefore they could not be saying what they seemed
to be saying, and were neither a call to profound spiritual reformation nor the story of poor Christian Rosencreutz. They were a coded
message to be read by superimposing them on a grid, a grid that left
certain spaces free while covering others. Like the coded message of
Provins, where only the initial letters counted. Having no grid, I
had to assume the existence of one. I had to read with mistrust.

The manifestoes spoke of the Plan of Provins—there could be no
doubt about that. In the grave of C. R. (allegory of the Grange-
aux-Dîmes, the night of June 23, 1344) a treasure had been placed

for posterity to discover, a treasure "hidden . . . for one hundred and twenty years." It was not money; that much was clear. Not only was there a polemic against the unrestrained greed of the alchemists, but the text said openly that what had been promised was a great historical change. And if the reader failed to understand that, the second manifesto said that there could be no ignoring an offer that concerned the *miranda sextae aetatis* (the wonders of the sixth and final appointment!), and it repeated: "If only it had pleased God to bring down to us the light of his sixth Candelabrum . . . if only we could read everything in a single book and, reading it, understand and remember . . . How pleasant it would be if through song (the message read aloud!) we could transform rocks (lapis exillis!) into pearls and precious stones. . . ." And there was further talk of arcane secrets, and of a government that was to be established in Europe, and of a "great work" to be achieved. . . .

It was said that C. R. had gone to Spain (or Portugal?) and had shown the learned there "whence to draw the true indicia of future centuries," but in vain. Why in vain? Was it because a group of German Templars at the beginning of the seventeenth century made public a very closely guarded secret, forced to come out into the open on account of a halt in the process of the transmission of the message?

The manifestoes undeniably tried to reconstruct the phases of the Plan as Diotallevi had summarized them. The first brother whose death was mentioned was Brother I. O., who had "come to the end" in England. So someone had arrived triumphantly at the first appointment. And a second line of succession was mentioned, and a third. Thus far all was apparently in order: the second line, the English one, met the third line, the French one, in 1584. Those writing at the beginning of the seventeenth century spoke only of what had happened to the first three groups. In the *Chemical Wedding*, written by Andreae in his youth, hence before the manifestoes (even if they appeared as early as 1614), three majestic temples were mentioned, the three places that must already have been known.

Yet, reading, I realized that while the two manifestoes did indeed speak later in the same terms as the *Chemical Wedding*, it was as if something upsetting had happened meanwhile.

For example, why such insistence on the fact that the time had come, the moment had come, though the enemy had employed all his tricks to keep the occasion from materializing? What occasion? It was said that C. R.'s final goal was Jerusalem, but he hadn't been able to reach Jerusalem. Why not? The Arabs were praised because they exchanged messages, but in Germany the learned didn't know how to assist one another. What did that mean? And there was a reference to "a larger group that wants the pasture all for itself." Evidently some party, pursuing its private interests, was trying to upset the Plan, and evidently there had in fact been a serious setback.

The *Fama* said that at the beginning someone had worked out a magic writing (why of course, the message of Provins), but that the Clock of God struck every minute "whereas ours is unable to strike even the hours." Who had missed the strokes of the divine clock, who had failed to arrive at a certain place at the right moment? There was a reference to an original group of brothers who could have revealed a secret philosophy but had decided, instead, to disperse throughout the world.

The manifestoes breathed uneasiness, uncertainty, bewilderment. The brothers of the first lines of succession had each arranged to be replaced "by a worthy successor," but "they decided to keep secret . . . the place of their burial and even today we do not know where they are buried."

What did this really refer to? What sepulcher was without an address? It was becoming obvious to me that the manifestoes were written because some information had been lost. An appeal was being made to anyone who happened to possess that information: He should come forward.

The end of the *Fama* was unequivocal: "Again we ask all the learned of Europe . . . to consider with kindly disposition our offer . . . to let us know their reflections. . . . Because even if for the present we have not revealed our names . . . anyone who sends us his name will be able to confer with us personally, or—if some impediment exists—in writing."

This was exactly what the colonel had intended to do by publishing his story: force someone to emerge from his silence.

There had been a gap, a hiatus, an unraveling. In the tomb of C.R., there was written not only post 120 annos patebo, to recall the schedule of the appointments, but also Nequaquam vacuum; not

"The void does not exist," but "The void should not exist." A void had been created, and it had to be filled!

Once again I asked myself: Why were these things being said in Germany, where, if anything, the fourth line should simply wait with saintly patience for its own turn to come? The Germans couldn't complain—in 1614—of a failed appointment in Marienburg, because the Marienburg appointment would not take place until 1704.

Only one conclusion was possible: the Germans were complaining because the *preceding* appointment had not taken place.

This was the key! The Germans (the fourth line) were lamenting the fact that the English (the second line) had failed to reach the French (the third line). Of course. In the text you could find allegories that were almost childishly transparent: the tomb of C. R. is opened and in it are found the signatures of the brothers of the first and second circles, but not of the third. The Portuguese and the English are there, but where are the French?

In other words, the English had missed the French. Yet the English, according to what we had established, were the only ones who had any idea where to find the French, just as the French were the only ones who had any idea where to find the Germans. So, even if the French found the Germans in 1704, they would have shown up minus two-thirds of what they were supposed to deliver.

The Rosicrucians came out into the open, accepting the known risks, because that was the only way to save the Plan.

71

> We do not even know with certainty if the Brothers of the second
> line possessed the same knowledge as those of the first, or if they
> were given all the secrets.
> —*Fama Fraternitatis*, in *Allgemeine und general Reformation*,
>   Cassel, Wessel, 1614

I told Belbo and Diotallevi. They agreed that the secret meaning of
the manifestoes should be clear even to a Diabolical.

"Now it's all clear," Diotallevi said. "We were stuck on the notion that the Plan had been blocked at the passage from the Germans to the Paulicians, while in fact it had been blocked in 1584, at
the passage from England to France."

"But why?" Belbo asked. "What reason can there be that the
English were unable to keep their appointment with the French in
1584? The English knew where the Refuge was."

Seeking truth, he turned to Abulafia. As a test, he asked for two
random entries. The output was:

Minnie Mouse is Mickey's fiancée
Thirty days hath September April June and November

"Now, let's see," Belbo said. "Minnie has an appointment with
Mickey, but by mistake she makes it for the thirty-first of September, and Mickey . . ."

"Hold it, everybody!" I said. "Minnie could have made a mistake
only if her date with Mickey was for October 5, 1582!"

"Why?"

"The Gregorian reform of the calendar! Why, it's obvious. In
1582 the Gregorian reform went into effect, correcting the Julian
calendar; and to make things come out even, ten days in the month
of October were abolished, the fifth to the fourteenth!"

"But the appointment in France is for 1584, Saint John's Eve,
June 23."

"That's right. But as I recall, the reform didn't go into effect immediately everywhere." I consulted the perpetual calendar we had on the shelf. "Here we are. The reform was promulgated in 1582, and the days between October 5 and October 14 were abolished, but this applied only to the pope. France adopted the new calendar in 1583 and abolished the tenth to the nineteenth of December. In Germany there was a schism: the Catholic regions adopted the reform in 1584, with Bohemia, but the Protestant regions adopted it in 1775, almost two hundred years later, and Bulgaria—and this is a fact to bear in mind—adopted it only in 1917! Now, let's look at England. . . . It adopted the Gregorian calendar in 1752. That's to be expected: in their hatred of the papists, the Anglicans also held out for two centuries. So you see what happened. France abolished ten days at the end of 1583, and by June 1584 the French were all accustomed to it. But when it was June 23, 1584, in France, in England it was still June 13, and ask yourself whether a good Englishman, Templar though he may have been, would have taken this into account. They drive on the left even today, and ignored the decimal system for ages. . . . So, then, the English show up at the Refuge on what for them is June 23, except that for the French it's already July 3. We can assume the appointment wasn't to take place with fanfares; it would be a furtive meeting at a certain corner at a certain hour. The French go to the place on June 23; they wait a day, two days, three, seven, and then they leave, thinking that something has happened. Maybe they give up in despair on the very eve of July 3. The English arrive on the third and find nobody there. Maybe they also wait a week, and nobody shows. The two grand masters have missed each other."

"Sublime," Belbo said. "That's what happened. But why is it the German Rosicrucians who go public, and not the English?"

I asked for another day, searched my card files, and came back to the office glowing with pride. I had found a clue, an almost invisible clue, but that's how Sam Spade works. Nothing is trivial or insignificant to his eagle eye. Toward 1584, John Dee, mage and cabalist, astrologer to the queen of England, was assigned to study the reform of the Julian calendar.

"The English Templars meet the Portuguese in 1464. After that date, the British Isles seem to be struck by a cabalistic fervor. Anyway, the Templars work on what they have learned, preparing for the next encounter. John Dee is the leader of this magic and hermetic renaissance. He collects a personal library of four thousand volumes, a library in the spirit of the Templars of Provins. His *Monas Hieroglyphica* seems directly inspired by the *Tabula smaragdina*, the bible of the alchemists. And what does John Dee do from 1584 on? He reads the *Steganographia* of Trithemius! He reads it in manuscript, of course, because it appeared in print for the first time only in the early seventeenth century. Dee, the grand master of the English group that suffered the failure of the missed appointment, wants to discover what happened, where the error lay. Since he is also a good astronomer, he slaps himself on the brow and says, 'What an idiot I was!' He starts studying the Gregorian reform, after he obtains an appanage from Elizabeth, to see how to rectify the mistake. But he realizes it's too late. He doesn't know whom to get in touch with in France. He has contacts, however, in the Mitteleuropäische area. The Prague of Rudolf II is one big alchemist laboratory; so Dee goes to Prague and meets Khunrath, the author of *Amphitheatrum sapientiae aeternae*, whose allegorical plates later influenced both Andreae and the Rosicrucian manifestoes. What sort of relationships does Dee establish? I don't know. Shattered by remorse at having committed an irreparable error, he dies in 1608. Not to worry, though, because in London someone else is at work—a man who, everybody now agrees, was a Rosicrucian and who spoke of the Rosicrucians in his *New Atlantis*. I mean Francis Bacon."

"Did Bacon really talk about them?" Belbo asked.

"Strictly speaking, no, but a certain John Heydon rewrote the *New Atlantis* under the title *The Holy Land,* and he put the Rosicrucians in it. But for us that makes no difference. Bacon didn't mention them by name for obvious reasons of discretion, but it's as if he did."

"And a pox on doubters."

"Right. It's because of Bacon that attempts are made to strengthen relations between the English and German circles. In 1613 Elizabeth, daughter of James I, now reigning, marries Frederick V, Elector Palatine of the Rhine. After the death of Rudolf II, Prague is no longer the ideal location; Heidelberg is. The wedding of the elector and the princess is a triumph of Templar allegories. In the course of the London festivities, Bacon himself is the impresario, and an allegory of mystical knighthood is performed, with an appearance of the knights on the top of a hill. It is obvious that Bacon is now Dee's successor, grand master of the English Templar group. . . ."

"And since he is clearly the author of the plays of Shakespeare, we should also reread the complete works of the bard, which certainly talk about nothing else but the Plan," Belbo said. "Saint John's Eve, a midsummer night's dream."

"June 23 is not midsummer."

"Poetic license. I wonder why everybody overlooked these clues, these clear indications. It's all so unbearably obvious."

"We've been led astray by rationalist thought," Diotallevi said. "I keep telling you."

"Let Casaubon go on; it seems to me he's done an excellent job."

"Not much more to say. After the London festivities, the festivities begin in Heidelberg, where Salomon de Caus has built for the elector the hanging gardens of which we saw a dim reflection that night in Piedmont, as you'll recall. And in the course of these festivities, an allegorical float appears, celebrating the bridegroom as Jason, and from the two masts of the ship re-created on the float hang the symbols of the Golden Fleece and the Garter. I hope you haven't forgotten that the Golden Fleece and the Garter are also found on the columns of Tomar. . . . Everything fits. In the space of a year, the Rosicrucian manifestoes come out: the appeal that the English Templars, with the help of their German friends, are making to all Europe, to reunite the lines of the interrupted Plan."

"But what exactly are they after?"

72

Nos inuisibles pretendus sont (à ce que l'on dit) au nombre de 36, separez en six bandes.
—*Effroyables pactions faictes entre le diable & les pretendus Inuisibles*, Paris, 1623, p. 6

"Maybe the manifestoes have a double purpose: to send an appeal to the French, and at the same time to collect the scattered pieces of the German group in the aftermath of the Lutheran Reformation. Germany, in fact, is where the biggest mess occurs. From the appearance of the manifestoes until about 1621, the Rosicrucians receive too many replies. . . ."

I mentioned a few of the countless pamphlets that had appeared on the subject, the ones that had entertained me that night in Salvador with Amparo. "Possibly among all these there is one person who knows something, but he is lost in a sea of fanatics, enthusiasts, who take the manifestoes literally, perhaps also provocateurs, who want to block the operation, and impostors. . . . The English try to take part in the debate, to channel it. It's no accident that Robert Fludd, another English Templar, in the space of a single year writes three works that point to the correct interpretation of the manifestoes. . . . But the response is by now out of control, the Thirty Years' War has begun, the Elector Palatine has been defeated by the Spanish, the Palatinate and Heidelberg are sacked, Bohemia is in flames. . . . The English decide to return to France and try there. This is why in 1623 the Rosicrucians appear in Paris, giving the French more or less the same invitation they gave the Germans. And what do you read in one of the libels against the Rosicrucians in Paris, written by someone who distrusts them or wants to confuse things? That they are worshipers of the Devil, obviously, but since even in slander you can't entirely erase the truth, it is hinted that they hold their meetings in the Marais."

"So?"

"Don't you know Paris? The Marais is the quarter of the Temple and, it so happens, the Jewish ghetto! What's more, the libel says that the Rosicrucians are in contact with a sect of Iberian cabalists, the Alumbrados! But maybe the pamphlets against the Rosicrucians, under the guise of attacking the thirty-six invisibles, are actually trying to foster their identification. . . . Gabriel Naudé, Richelieu's librarian, writes some *Instructions à la France sur la vérité de l'histoire des Frères de la Rose-Croix.* What do these instructions say? Is Naudé a spokesman for the Templars of the third group, or is he an adventurer barging into a game that isn't his? On the one hand, he dismisses the Rosicrucians as lunatic diabolists; on the other, he insinuates that there are still three Rosicrucian colleges in existence. And this would be true: after the third group, there are still three more. Naudé gives some almost fairy-tale hints (one college is in India, on the floating islands), but he also says that one of them is in the underground of Paris."

"And this explains the Thirty Years' War?" Belbo asked.

"Beyond any doubt," I said. "Richelieu receives privileged information from Naudé; he wants to have a finger in this pie, but he gets it all wrong, tries armed intervention, and makes matters even worse. There are two other events that shouldn't be overlooked. In 1619 a chapter of the Knights of Christ meets in Tomar, after forty-six years of silence. It had met in 1573, only eleven years before 1584, probably to prepare, along with the English, the Paris journey, but after the business of the Rosicrucian manifestoes it meets again, to decide what line to take, whether to join the English operation or try a different path."

"Yes," Belbo said, "these are now people lost in a maze: some choose one path, some another; some shout for help, and there's no telling if the replies they hear are other voices or the echo of their own. . . . They all are groping. And what are the Paulicians and the Jerusalemites doing in the meantime?"

"If we only knew," Diotallevi said. "But consider, too, that this is the period when Lurianic cabala spreads and the talk about the Breaking of the Vessels begins. . . . And the idea that the Torah is an incomplete message. There is a Polish Hasidic document that says: If another event takes place, other combinations of letters will be born. But remember this: the cabalists aren't happy that the Germans chose to jump the gun. The proper succession and order of the Torah have remained hidden, and they are known only by the Holy One, praised be He. But you make me talk nonsense. If cabala becomes involved in the Plan . . ."

"If the Plan exists, it must involve everything. Either it explains all or it explains nothing," Belbo said. "But Casaubon mentioned a clue."

"Yes. Actually, it's a series of clues. Even before the 1584 meeting fails, John Dee has begun devoting himself to the study of maps and the promotion of naval expeditions. And who is his associate? Pedro Nunes, the royal cosmographer of Portugal. . . . Dee has a hand in the voyages to discover the Northwest Passage to Cathay; he invests money in the expedition of a certain Frobisher, who ventures toward the Pole and returns with an Eskimo, whom everybody takes for a Mongol. Dee fires up Francis Drake and encourages him to make his voyage around the world. However, he wants the explorers to sail east, because the East is the source of all occult knowledge, and at the departure of one expedition—I forget which—he summons the angels."

"And what does this mean?"

"Dee, I think, isn't really interested so much in the actual discovery of places, as in their cartographic depiction, and for this reason he consults Mercator and Ortelius, the great cartographers. It's as if the fragments of the message in his possession have convinced him that the final whole will be a map, and he is attempting to discover it on his own. Indeed, I'll say more, like Signor Garamond. Is it really likely that a scholar of his standing would have missed the discrepancy between the calendars? Perhaps Dee wants to reconstruct the message himself, without the other groups. Perhaps he thinks the message can be reconstructed by magic or scientific means, instead of waiting for the Plan to be achieved. Impatience, greed. The bourgeois conqueror is born, and the principle of solidarity that sustained the spiritual knighthood is breaking down. If this was Dee's idea, you can imagine what Bacon thought. From Dee on, the English try to discover the message by using all the secrets of the new learning."

"And the Germans?"

"The Germans . . . We'd better have them stick to the path of Tradition. That way we can explain at least two centuries of their

404

history of philosophy. Anglo-Saxon empiricism versus romantic idealism . . ."

"Chapter by chapter, we are reconstructing the history of the world," Diotallevi said. "We are rewriting the Book. I like it, I really like it."

73

Another curious case of cryptography was presented to the public in 1917 by one of the best Bacon scholars, Dr. Alfred von Weber Ebenhoff of Vienna. Employing the same systems previously applied to the works of Shakespeare, he began to examine the works of Cervantes. . . . Pursuing the investigation, he discovered overwhelming material evidence: the first English translation of *Don Quixote* bears corrections in Bacon's hand. He concluded that this English version was the original of the novel and that Cervantes had published a Spanish translation of it.
—J. Duchaussoy, *Bacon, Shakespeare ou Saint-Germain?*,
    Paris, La Colombe, 1962, p. 122

It seemed obvious to me that in the days that followed Jacopo Belbo immersed himself in historical works on the Rosy Cross period. But when he reported his findings, he gave us only the bare outline of his fantasies, from which we drew valuable suggestions. I know now that in fact he was creating a far richer narrative on Abulafia, one in which a wild play of quotations mingled with his private myths. The opportunity of combining fragments of other stories spurred him to write his own. He never mentioned this to us. I still think he was, quite courageously, testing his talent in the realm of fiction. Or else he was defining himself in the Great Story he was distorting like any ordinary Diabolical.

FILENAME: The Cabinet of Dr. Dee

For a long time I forgot I was Talbot. From the time, at least, of my decision to call myself Kelley. All I had done, really, was to falsify some documents, like everybody else. The queen's men were merciless. To cover what's left of my poor severed ears I am forced to wear this pointed black cap, and people murmur that I am a sorcerer. So be it. Dr. Dee, with a similar reputation, flourishes.

    I went to see him in Mortlake. He was examining a map. He was evasive, the diabolical old man. Sinister glints in his shrewd eyes. His bony hand stroking his little goatee.

"It's a manuscript of Roger Bacon," he said to me, "and was lent me by the Emperor Rudolf. Do you know Prague? I advise you to visit it. You may find something there that will change your life. Tabula locorum rerum et thesaurorum absconditorum Menabani . . ."

Stealing a glance, I saw something written in a secret alphabet. But the doctor immediately hid the manuscript under a pile of other yellowed pages. How beautiful to live in a period where every page, even if it has just come from the papermaker's workshop, is yellowed.

I showed Dr. Dee some of my efforts, mainly my poems about the Dark Lady—radiant image of my childhood, dark because reclaimed by the shadow of time and snatched from my possession—and a tragic sketch, the story of Seven Seas Jim, who returns to England in the train of Sir Walter Ralegh and learns that his father has been murdered by his own incestuous brother. Henbane.

"You're gifted, Kelley," Dee said to me. "And you need money. There's a young man, the natural son of someone you couldn't dare imagine, and I want to help him climb the ladder of fame and honors. He has little talent. You will be his secret soul. Write, and live in the shadow of his glory. Only you and I, Kelley, will know that the glory is yours."

So for years I've been turning out work for the queen and for all England that goes under the name of this pale youth. If I have seen further, it is by standing on ye shoulders of a Dwarfe. I was thirty, and I will allow no man to say that thirty is the most beautiful time of life.

"William," I said to him, "let your hair grow down over your ears: it's becoming." I had a plan (to take his place?).

Can one live in hatred of this Spear-shaker, who in reality is oneself? That sweet thief which sourly robs from me. "Calm down, Kelley," Dee says to me. "To grow in the shadows is the privilege of those who prepare to conquer the world. Keepe a Lowe Profyle. William will be one of our covers." And he informed me—oh, only in part—of the Cosmic Plot. The secret of the Templars. "And the stakes?" I asked.

"Ye Globe."

For a long time I went to bed early, but one evening at midnight I rummaged in Dee's private strongbox and discovered some formulas and tried summoning angels as he does on nights of full moon. Dee found me sprawled, in the center of the circle of the Macrocosm, as if struck by a lash. On my brow, the Pentacle of Solomon. Now I must pull my cap even farther down, half over my eyes.

"You don't know how to do it yet," Dee said to me. "Watch yourself, or I'll have your nose cut off, too. I will show you fear in a handful of dust. . . ."

He raised a bony hand and uttered the terrible word: Garamond! I felt myself burn with an inner flame. I fled (into the night).

It was a year before Dee forgave me and dedicated to me his Fourth Book of Mysteries, "post reconciliationem kellianam."

That summer I was seized by abstract rages. Dee summoned me to Mortlake. There were William and I, Spenser, and a young aristocrat with shifty eyes, Francis Bacon. He had a delicate, lively, hazel Eie. Dr. Dee said it was the Eie of a Viper. Dee told us more about the Cosmic Plot. It was a matter of meeting the Frankish wing of the Templars in Paris and putting together two parts of the same map. Dee and Spenser were to go, accompanied by Pedro Nunes. To me and Bacon he entrusted some documents, which we swore to open only in the event that they failed to return.

They did return, exchanging floods of insults. "It's not possible," Dee said. "The Plan is mathematical; it has the astral perfection of my *Monas Hieroglyphica*. We were supposed to meet the Franks on Saint John's Eve."

Innocently I asked: "Saint John's Eve by their reckoning or by ours?"

Dee slapped himself on the brow, spewing out horrible curses. "O," he said, "from what power hast thou this powerful might?" The pale William made a note of the sentence, the cowardly plagiarist. Dee feverishly consulted lunar tables and almanacs. " 'Sblood! 'Swounds! How could I have been such a dolt?" He insulted Nunes and Spenser. "Do I have to think of everything? Cosmographer, my foot!" he screamed at Nunes. And then: "Amanasiel Zorobabel!" And Nunes was struck in the stomach as if by an invisible ram; he blanched, drew back a few steps, and slumped to the ground.

"Fool," Dee said to him.

Spenser was pale. He said, with some effort: "We can cast some bait. I am finishing a poem. An allegory about the queen of the fairies. What if I put in a knight of the Red Cross? The real Templars will recognize themselves, will understand that we know, will get in touch with us. . . ."

"I know you," Dee said. "Before you finish your poem and people find out about it, a lustrum will pass, maybe more. Still, the bait idea isn't bad."

"Why not communicate with them through your angels, Doctor?" I asked.

"Fool," he said to me. "Haven't you read Trithemius? The angels of the addressee intervene only to clarify a message if one is received. My angels are not couriers on horseback. The French are lost. But I have a plan. I know how to find some of the German line. I must go to Prague."

We heard a noise, a heavy damask curtain was raised, we glimpsed a diaphanous hand, then She appeared, the Haughty Virgin.

"Your Majesty," we said, kneeling.

"Dee," she said, "I know everything. Do not think my ancestors saved the knights in order to grant them dominion over the world. I demand, you hear me, I demand that the secret be the property of the Crown only."

"Your Majesty, I want the secret at all costs, and I want it for the Crown. But I must find the other possessors; it is the shortest way. When they have foolishly confided in me what they know, it will not be hard to eliminate them. Whether with a dagger or with arsenic water."

On the face of the Virgin Queen a ghastly smile appeared. "Very well then, my good Dee," she said. "I do not ask much, only Total Power. For you, if you succeed, the garter. For you, William"—and she addressed the little parasite with lewd sweetness—"another garter, and another golden fleece. Follow me."

I murmured into William's ear: "I perforce am thine, and all that is in me. . . ." William rewarded me with a look of unctuous gratitude and followed the queen, disappearing beyond the curtain. Je tiens la reine!

. . . .

I was with Dr. Dee in the Golden City. We went along narrow and evil-smelling passageways not far from the cemetery of the Jews, and Dee told me to be careful. "If the news of the failed encounter has spread," he said, "the other groups will even now be acting on their own. I fear the Jews; the Jerusalemites have too many agents here in Prague. . . ."

It was evening. The snow glistened, bluish. At the dark entrance to the Jewish quarter clustered the little stands of the Christmas market, and in their midst, decked in red cloth, was the obscene stage of a puppet theater lit by smoky torches. We passed beneath an arch of dressed stone, near a bronze fountain from whose grille long icicles hung, and there another passage opened. On old doors, gilded lion's heads sank their teeth into bronze rings. A slight shudder ran along the walls, inexplicable sounds came from the low roofs, rattlings from the drainpipes.

The houses betrayed a ghostly life of their own, a hidden life.
. . . An old usurer, wrapped in a worn coat, brushed us in
passing, and I thought I heard him murmur, "Beware Athana-
sius Pernath. . . ." Dee murmured back, "I fear quite another
Athanasius. . . ." And suddenly we were in the Alley of the
Goldsmiths.

There, in the gloom of another alley—and the ears I no longer
have, at this memory, quiver under my worn cap—a giant loomed
up before us, a horrible gray creature with a dull expression, his
body sheathed in bronze verdigris, leaning on a gnarled and
knobby stick of white wood. The apparition gave off an intense
odor of sandalwood. Mortal horror magically coalesced in that
being that confronted me, yet I could not take my eyes off the
nebulous globe that sat atop his shoulders, and in it discerned,
barely, the rapacious face of an Egyptian ibis, and behind that
face, more faces, incubi of my imagination and my memory.
The outlines of the ghost, in the darkness of that alley, dilated,
contracted, as in a slow, nonliving respiration . . . And—oh,
horror!—instead of feet, I saw, as I stared at him, on the snow
two shapeless stumps whose flesh, gray and bloodless, was rolled
up, as if in concentric swellings.

My voracious memories . . .

"The golem!" Dee cried, raising both arms to heaven. His
black coat with broad sleeves fell to the ground, as if to create a
cingulum, an umbilical cord between the aerial position of the
hands and the surface, or the depths, of the earth. "Jezebel,
Malkuth, Smoke Gets in Your Eyes!" he said. And suddenly
the golem dissolved like a sand castle struck by a gust of wind.
We were blinded by the particles of its clay body, which tore
through the air like atoms, until finally at our feet was a little
pile of ashes. Dee bent down, searched in the ashes with his
bony fingers, and drew out a scroll, which he hid in his bosom.

From the shadows then rose an old rabbi, with a greasy hat
that greatly resembled my cap. "Dr. Dee, I presume," he said.

"Here Comes Everybody," Dee replied humbly. "Rabbi Allevi, what a pleasant surprise . . ."

The man said, "Did you happen to see a creature roaming
these parts?"

"A creature?" Dee said, feigning amazement. "What sort of
creature?"

"Come off it, Dee," Rabbi Allevi said. "It was my golem."

"Your golem? I know nothing about a golem."

"Take care, Dr. Dee!" Rabbi Allevi said, livid. "You're playing a dangerous game, you're out of your league."

"I don't know what you're talking about, Rabbi Allevi," said

Dee. "We're here to make a few ounces of gold for the emperor. We're not a couple of cheap necromancers."

"Give me back the scroll, at least," Rabbi Allevi begged.

"What scroll?" Dee asked, with diabolical ingenuousness.

"Curse you, Dr. Dee," said the rabbi. "And verily I say unto thee, thou shalt not see the dawn of the new century." And he went off into the night, murmuring strange words without consonants. Oh, Language Diabolical and Holy.

Dee was huddled against the damp wall of the alley, his face ashen, his hair bristling on his head. "I know Rabbi Allevi," he said. "I will die on August 5, 1608, of the Gregorian calendar. So now, Kelley, you must help me to carry out my plan. You are the one who will have to bring it to fulfillment. Gilding pale streams with heavenly alchymy. Remember," he said. But I would remember in any case, and William with me. And against me.

. . . .

He said no more. The pale fog that rubs its back against the panes, the yellow smoke that rubs its back against the panes, licked with its tongue the street corners. We were now in another alley; whitish vapors came from the grilles at ground level, and through them you could glimpse squalid dens with tilting walls, defined by gradations of misty gray. I saw, as he came groping down a stairway (the steps oddly orthogonal), the figure of an old man in a worn frock coat and a top hat. And Dee saw him. "Caligari!" he exclaimed. "He's here, too, in the house of Madame Sosostris, the famous clairvoyante! We have to get moving."

Quickening our steps, we arrived at the door of a hovel in a poorly lit alley, sinister and Semitic.

We knocked, and the door opened as if by magic. We entered a spacious room: there were seven-branched candelabra, tetragrams in relief, Stars of David like monstrances. Old violins, the color of the veneer on certain old paintings, were piled in the entrance on a refectory table of anamorphic irregularity. A great crocodile hung, mummified, from the ceiling, swaying slightly in the dim glow of a single torch, or of many, or of none. In the rear, before a kind of curtain or canopy under which stood a tabernacle, kneeling in prayer, ceaselessly and blasphemously murmuring the seventy-two names of God, was an old man. I knew, by a sudden stroke of nous, that this was Heinrich Khunrath.

"Come to the point, Dee," he said, turning and breaking off his prayer. "What do you want?" He resembled a stuffed armadillo, an ageless iguana.

"Khunrath," Dee said, "the third encounter did not take place."

Khunrath exploded in a horrible curse: "Lapis exillis! Now what?"

"Khunrath," Dee said, "you could throw out some bait; you could put me in touch with the German line."

"Let me see," Khunrath said. "I could ask Maier, who is in touch with many people at the court. But you will tell me the secret of Virgin's Milk, the Most Secret Oven of the Philosophers."

Dee smiled. Oh the divine smile of that Sophos! He concentrated then as if in prayer, and said in a low voice: "When you wish to translate into water or Virgin's Milk a sublimate of Mercury, place the Thing duly pulverized over the lamina between the little weights and the goblet. Do not cover it but see that the hot air strikes the naked matter, administer it to the fire of three coals, and keep it alive for eight solar days, then remove it and pound it well on marble until it is a fine paste. This done, put it inside a glass alembic and distill it in a Balneum Mariae over a cauldron of water set in such a way that it does not touch the water below by the space of two fingers but remains suspended in air, and at the same time light the fire beneath the Balneum. Then, and only then, though the Silver does not touch the water, finding itself in this warm and moist womb, will it change to liquid."

"Master," said Khunrath, sinking to his knees and kissing the bony, diaphanous hand of Dr. Dee. "Master, so I will do. And you will have what you wish. Remember these words: the Rose and the Cross. You will hear talk of them."

Dee wrapped himself in his cloaklike coat, and only his eyes, glistening and malign, could be seen. "Come, Kelley," he said. "This man is now ours. And you, Khunrath, keep the golem well away from us until our return to London. And then, let all Prague burn as a sole pyre."

He started to go off. Crawling, Khunrath seized him by the hem of his coat. "One day, perhaps, a man will come to you. He will want to write about you. Be his friend."

"Give me the Power," Dee said with an unspeakable expression on his fleshless face, "and his fortune is assured."

We went out. Over the Atlantic a low-pressure air mass was advancing in an easterly direction toward Russia.

"Let's go to Moscow," I said to him.

"No," he said. "We're returning to London."

"To Moscow, to Moscow," I murmured crazily. You knew very well, Kelley, that you would never go there. The Tower awaited you.

Back in London, Dee said: "They're trying to reach the solution before we do. Kelley, you must write something for William . . . something diabolically insinuating about them."

Belly of the demon, I did it, but William ruined the text, shifting everything from Prague to Venice. Dee flew into a rage. But the pale, shifty William felt protected by his royal concubine. And still he wasn't satisfied. As I handed over to him, one by one, his finest sonnets, he asked me, with shameless eyes, about Her, about You, my Dark Lady. How horrible to hear your name on that mummer's lips! (I didn't know that he, his soul damned to duplicity and to the vicarious, was seeking her for Bacon.) "Enough," I said to him. "I'm tired of building your glory in the shadows. Write for yourself."

"I can't," he answered with the gaze of one who has seen a lemure. "He won't let me."

"Who? Dee?"

"No, Verulam. Don't you know he's now the one in charge? He's forcing me to write works that later he'll claim as his own. You understand, Kelley? I'm the true Bacon, and posterity will never know. Oh, parasite! How I hate that firebrand of hell!"

"Bacon's a pig, but he has talent," I said. "Why doesn't he write his own stuff?"

He didn't have the time. We realized this only years later, when Germany was invaded by the Rosy Cross madness. Then, from scattered references, certain phrases, putting two and two together, I saw that the author of the Rosicrucian manifestoes was really he. He wrote under the pseudonym of Johann Valentin Andreae!

Now, in the darkness of this cell where I languish, more clearheaded than Don Isidro Parodi, I know for whom Andreae was writing. I was told by Soapes, my companion in imprisonment, a former Portuguese Templar. Andreae was writing a novel of chivalry for a Spaniard, who was languishing meanwhile in another prison. I don't know why, but this project served the infamous Bacon, who wanted to go down in history as the secret author of the adventures of the knight of La Mancha. Bacon asked Andreae to pen for him, in secret, a novel whose hidden author he would then pretend to be, enjoying in the shadows (but why? why?) another man's triumph.

But I digress. I am cold in this dungeon and my thumb hurts. I am writing, in the dim light of a dying lamp, the last works that will pass under William's name.

Dr. Dee died, murmuring, "Light, more light!" and asking for a toothpick. Then he said: "Qualis Artifex Pereo!" It was Bacon who had him killed. Before the queen died, for years unhinged of mind and heart, Verulam managed to seduce her. Her features then were changed; she was reduced to the condition of a skeleton. Her food was limited to a little white roll and some soup of chicory greens. At her side she kept a sword, and in moments of wrath she would thrust it violently into the curtains and arras that covered the walls of her refuge. (And what if there were someone behind there, listening? How now! A rat? Good idea, old Kelley, must make a note of it.) With the poor woman in this condition, it was easy for Bacon to make her believe he was William, her bastard—presenting himself at her knees, she being now blind, covered in a sheep's skin. The Golden Fleece! They said he was aiming at the throne, but I knew he was after something quite different, control of the Plan. That was when he became Viscount St. Albans. His position strengthened, he eliminated Dee.

. . . .

The queen is dead, long live the king. . . . Now, I was an embarrassing witness. He led me into an ambush one night when at last the Dark Lady could be mine and was dancing in my arms with abandon under the influence of a grass capable of producing visions, she, the eternal Sophia, with her wrinkled face like an old nanny goat's. . . . He entered with a handful of armed men, made me cover my eyes with a cloth. I guessed at once: vitriol! And how he laughed. And she! How you laughed, Pinball Lady—and gilded honor shamefully misplaced and maiden virtue rudely strumpeted—while he touched her with his greedy hands and you called him Simon—and kissed his sinister scar . . .

"To the Tower, to the Tower." Verulam laughed. Since then, here I lie, with this human wraith who says he is Soapes, and the jailers know me only as Seven Seas Jim. I have studied thoroughly, and with ardent zeal, philosophy, jurisprudence, medicine, and, unfortunately, also theology. Here I am, poor madman, and I know as much as I did before.

. . . .

Through a slit of a window I witnessed the royal wedding, the knights with red crosses cantering to the sound of a trumpet. I should have been there playing the trumpet, for Cecilia, but once again the prize had been taken from me. It was William playing. I was writing in the shadows, for him.

414

"I'll tell you how to avenge yourself," Soapes whispered, and that day he revealed to me what he truly is: a Bonapartist abbé buried in this dungeon for centuries.

"Will you get out?" I asked him.

"If . . ." he began to reply, but then was silent. Striking his spoon on the wall, in a mysterious alphabet that, he confided in me, he had received from Trithemius, he began transmitting messages to the prisoner in the next cell. The count of Monsalvat.

. . . .

Years have gone by. Soapes never stops striking the wall. Now I know for whom and to what end. His name is Noffo Dei. This Dei (through what mysterious cabala do Dei and Dee sound so alike?), prompted by Soapes, has denounced Bacon. What he said, I do not know, but a few days ago Verulam was imprisoned. Accused of sodomy, because, they said (I tremble at the thought that it may be true), you, the Dark Lady, Black Virgin of Druids and of Templars, are none other . . . none other than the eternal androgyne created by the knowing hands of . . . of . . . ? Now, now I know . . . of your lover, the Comte de Saint-Germain! But who is Saint-Germain if not Bacon himself? (Soapes knows all sorts of things, this obscure Templar of many lives. . . .)

. . . .

Verulam has been released from prison, has regained through his magic arts the favor of the monarch. Now, William tells me, he spends his nights along the Thames, in Pilad's Pub, playing that strange machine invented for him by an Italian from Nola whom he then had burned at the stake in Rome. It is an astral device, which devours small mad spheres that race through infinite worlds in a sparkle of angelic light. Verulam gives obscene blows of triumphant bestiality with his groin against the frame, miming the events of the celestial orbs in the domain of the decans in order to understand the ultimate secrets of the Great Establishment and the secret of the New Atlantis itself, which he calls Gottlieb's, parodying the sacred language of the manifestoes attributed to Andreae. . . . Ah! I cry, now lucidly aware, but too late and in vain, as my heart beats conspicuously beneath the laces of my corset: this is why he took away my trumpet, amulet, talisman, cosmic bond that could command demons. What will he be plotting in the House of Solomon? It's late, I repeat to myself, by now he has been given too much power.

. . . .

They say Bacon is dead. Soapes assures me it is not true. No one has seen the body. He is living under a false name with the landgrave of Hesse; he is now initiated into the supreme mysteries and hence immortal, ready to continue his grim battle for the triumph of the Plan—in his name and under his control.

After this alleged death, William came to see me, with his hypocritical smile, which the bars could not hide from me. He asked me why I wrote, in Sonnet 111, about a certain dyer. He quoted the verse: "To what it works in, like the dyer's hand. . . ."

"I never wrote that," I told him. And it was true. . . . It's obvious: Bacon inserted those words before disappearing, to send some sign to those who will then welcome Saint-Germain in one court after another, as an expert in dyes. . . . I believe that in the future he will try to make people believe he wrote William's works himself. How clear everything becomes when you look from the darkness of a dungeon!

. . . .

Where art thou, Muse, that thou forget'st so long? I feel weary, sick. William is expecting new material from me for his crude clowneries at the Globe.

Soapes is writing. I look over his shoulder. An incomprehensible message: "riverrun, past Eve and Adam's . . ." He hides the page, looks at me, sees me paler than a ghost, reads Death in my eyes. He whispers to me, "Rest. Never fear. I'll write for you."

And so he is doing, mask behind a mask. I slowly fade, and he takes from me even the last light, that of obscurity.

74

Though his will be good, his spirit and his prophecies are illusions
of the Devil. . . . They are capable of deceiving many curious people and of causing great harm and scandal to the Church of Our
Lord God.
—Opinion on Guillaume Postel sent to Ignatius Loyola
by the Jesuit fathers Salmeron, Lhoost, and Ugoletto,
May 10, 1545

Belbo, detached, told us what he had concocted, but he didn't read
his pages to us and eliminated all personal references. Indeed, he led
us to believe that Abulafia had supplied him with the connections.
The idea that Bacon was the author of the Rosicrucian manifestoes
he had already come upon somewhere or other. But one thing in
particular struck me: that Bacon was Viscount St. Albans.

It buzzed in my head; it had something to do with my old thesis.
I spent that night digging in my card file.

"Gentlemen," I said to my accomplices with a certain solemnity
the next morning, "we don't have to invent connections. They exist.
When, in 1164, Saint Bernard launched the idea of a council at Troyes
to legitimize the Templars, among those charged to organize everything was the prior of Saint Albans. Saint Alban was the first English martyr, who evangelized the British Isles. He lived in
Verulamium, which became Bacon's property. He was a Celt and
unquestionably a Druid initiate, like Saint Bernard."

"That's not very much," Belbo said.

"Wait. This prior of Saint Albans was abbot of Saint-Martin-des-
Champs, the abbey where the Conservatoire des Arts et Métiers was
later installed!"

Belbo reacted. "My God!"

"And that's not all," I said. "The Conservatoire was conceived
as homage to Bacon. On 25 Brumaire of the year lll, the Convention authorized its Comité d'Instruction Publique to have the complete works of Bacon printed. And on 18 Vendémiaire of the same
year the same Convention had passed a law providing for the con-

struction of a house of arts and trades that would reproduce the House of Solomon as described by Bacon in his *New Atlantis,* a place where all the inventions of mankind are collected."

"And so?" Diotallevi asked.

"The Pendulum is in the Conservatoire," Belbo said. And from Diotallevi's reaction I realized that Belbo had told him about Foucault's Pendulum.

"Not so fast," I said. "The Pendulum was invented and installed only in the last century. We should skip it."

"Skip it?" Belbo said. "Haven't you ever seen the Monad Hieroglyph of John Dee, the talisman that is supposed to concentrate all the wisdom of the universe? Doesn't it look like a pendulum?"

"All right," I said, "let's suppose a connection can be established. But how do we go from Saint Albans to the Pendulum?"

I was to learn how in the space of a few days.

"So then, the prior of Saint Albans is the abbot of Saint-Martin-des-Champs, which therefore becomes a Templar center. Bacon, through his property, establishes a contact with the Druid followers of Saint Albans. Now listen carefully: as Bacon is beginning his career in England, Guillaume Postel in France is ending his."

An almost imperceptible twitch on Belbo's face. I recalled the dialog at Riccardo's show: Postel made Belbo think of the man who, in his mind, had robbed him of Lorenza. But it was the matter of an instant.

"Postel studies Hebrew, tries to demonstrate that it's the common matrix of all languages, translates the *Zohar* and the *Bahir,* has contacts with the cabalists, broaches a plan for universal peace similar to that of the German Rosicrucian groups, tries to convince the king of France to form an alliance with the sultan, visits Greece, Syria, Asia Minor, studies Arabic—in a word, he retraces the itinerary of Christian Rosencreutz. And it is no accident that he signs

418

some writings with the name of Rosispergius, 'he who scatters dew.' Gassendi in his *Examen Philosophiae Fluddanae* says that Rosencreutz does not derive from rosa but from ros, dew. In one of his manuscripts he speaks of a secret to be guarded until the time is ripe, and he says: 'That pearls may not be cast before swine.' Do you know where else this gospel quotation appears? On the title page of *The Chemical Wedding*. And Father Marin Mersenne, in denouncing the Rosicrucian Fludd, says he is made of the same stuff as atheus magnus Postel. Furthermore, it seems Dee and Postel met in 1550, but perhaps they didn't yet know that they were both grand masters of the Plan, scheduled to meet thirty years later, in 1584.

"Now, Postel declares—hear ye, hear ye—that, being a direct descendant of the oldest son of Noah, and since Noah is the founder of the Celtic race and therefore of the civilization of the Druids, the king of France is the only legitimate pretender to the title king of the world. That's right, he talks about the King of the World—but three centuries before d'Alveydre. We'll skip the fact that he falls in love with an old hag, Joanna, and considers her the divine Sophia; the man probably didn't have all his marbles. But powerful enemies he did have; they called him dog, execrable monster, cloaca of all heresies, a being possessed by a legion of demons. All the same, even with the Joanna scandal, the Inquisition doesn't consider him a heretic, only amens, a bit of a nut, let's say. The truth is, the Church doesn't dare destroy the man, because they know he's the spokesman of some fairly powerful group. I would point out to you, Diotallevi, that Postel travels also in the Orient and is a contemporary of Isaac Luria. Draw whatever conclusions you like. Well, in 1564, the year in which Dee writes his *Monas Hieroglyphica*, Postel retracts his heresies and retires to . . . guess where? The monastery of Saint-Martin-des-Champs! What's he waiting for? Obviously, he's waiting for 1584."

"Obviously," Diotallevi said.

I went on: "Are we agreed, then? Postel is grand master of the French group, awaiting the appointment with the English. But he dies in 1581, three years before it. Conclusions: first, the 1584 mishap took place because at that crucial moment a keen mind was missing, since Postel would have been able to figure out what was going on in the confusion of the calendars; second, Saint-Martin was a place where the Templars were safe, always at home, where the man responsible for the third meeting immured himself and waited. Saint-Martin-des-Champs was the Refuge!"

"It all fits, like a mosaic."

"Stick with me. At the time of the failed appointment Bacon is only twenty-three. But in 1621 he becomes viscount St. Albans. What does he find in the ancestral possessions? A mystery. Note that this is the year he is accused of corruption and imprisoned for a while. He had unearthed something that caused fear in someone. In whom? This is when Bacon understood that Saint-Martin should be watched; he conceived the idea of putting his House of Solomon there, the laboratory in which, through experimental means, the secret could be discovered."

"But," Diotallevi asked, "how do we find the link between Bacon's followers and the revolutionary groups of the late eighteenth century?"

"Could Freemasonry be the answer?" Belbo said.

"Splendid idea. Actually, Agliè suggested it to us that night at the castle."

"We should reconstruct the events. What exactly was going on then in those circles?"

75

The only ones who elude . . . the eternal sleep . . . are those who in life are able to orient their mind toward the higher way. The initiates, the Adepts, are at the edge of that path. Having achieved memory, anamnesis, in the expression of Plutarch, they become free, they proceed without bonds. Crowned, they celebrate the "mysteries" and see on earth the throng of those who are not initiated and are not "pure," those who are crushed and pushing one another in the mud and in the darkness.

> —Julius Evola, *La tradizione ermetica*, Rome, Edizioni
> Mediterranee, 1971, p. 111

Rashly I volunteered to do some quick research. I soon regretted it. I found myself in a morass of books, in which it was difficult to distinguish historical fact from hermetic gossip, and reliable information from flights of fancy. Working like a machine for a week, I drew up a bewildering list of sects, lodges, conventicles. I occasionally shuddered on encountering familiar names I didn't expect to come upon in such company, and there were chronological coincidences that I felt were curious enough to be noted down. I showed this document to my two accomplices.

1645 London: Ashmole founds Invisible College, Rosicrucian in inspiration.

1660 From the Invisible College is born the Royal Society; and from the Royal Society, as everyone knows, the Masons.

1666 Paris: founding of Académie Royal des Sciences.

1707 Birth of Claude-Louis de Saint-Germain, if he was really born.

1717 Creation of the Great Lodge in London.

1721 Anderson drafts the constitutions of English Masonry. Initiated in London, Peter the Great founds a lodge in Russia.

1730 Montesquieu, passing through London, is initiated.

1737 Ramsay asserts the Templar origin of Masonry. Origin of the Scottish rite, henceforth in conflict with the Great Lodge of London.

1738　Frederick, then crown prince of Prussia, is initiated. Later he is patron of Encyclopedists.

1740　Various lodges created in France around this year: Ecossais Fidèles of Toulouse, Souverain Conseil Sublime, Mère Loge Ecossaise du Grand Globe Français, Collège des Sublimes Princes du Royal Secret of Bordeaux, Cour des Souverains Commandeurs du Temple of Carcassonne, Philadelphes of Narbonnne, Chapitre des Rose-Croix of Montpellier, Sublimes Elus de la Vérité . . .

1743　First public appearance of Comte de Saint-Germain. In Lyon, the degree of chevalier kadosch originates, its task being to vindicate Templars.

1753　Willermoz founds lodge of Parfaite Amitié.

1754　Martínez Pasqualis founds Temple of the Elus Cohen (perhaps in 1760).

1756　Baron von Hund founds Templar Strict Observance, inspired, some say, by Frederick II of Prussia. For the first time there is talk of the Unknown Superiors. Some insinuate that the Unknown Superiors are Frederick and Voltaire.

1758　Saint-Germain arrives in Paris and offers his services to the king as chemist, an expert in dyes. He spends time with Madame Pompadour.

1759　Presumed formation of Conseil des Empereurs d'Orient et d'Occident, which three years later is said to have drawn up the Constitutions et Règlement de Bordeaux, from which Ancient and Accepted Scottish rite probably originates (though this does not appear officially until 1801).

1760　Saint-Germain on ambiguous diplomatic mission in Holland. Forced to flee, arrested in London, released. Dom J. Pernety founds Illuminati of Avignon. Martínez Pasqualis founds Chevaliers Maçons Elus de l'Univers.

1762　Saint-Germain in Russia.

1763　Casanova meets Saint-Germain, as Surmont, in Belgium. Latter turns coin into gold. Willermoz founds Souverain Chapitre des Chevaliers de l'Aigle Noire Rose-Croix.

1768　Willermoz joins Pasqualis's Elus Cohen. Apocryphal publication in Jerusalem of *Les plus secrets mystères des hauts grades de la maçonnerie devoilée, ou le vrai Rose-Croix:* it says that the lodge of the Rosicrucians is on Mount Heredon, sixty miles from Edinburgh. Pasqualis meets Louis Claude de Saint-Martin, later known as Le Philosophe Inconnu. Dom Pernety becomes librarian of king of Prussia.

1771   The Duc de Chartres, later known as Philippe-Egalité, becomes grand master of the Grand Orient (then, the Grand Orient de France) and tries to unify all the lodges. Scottish rite lodge resists.

1772   Pasqualis leaves for Santo Domingo, and Willermoz and Saint-Martin establish Tribunal Souverain, which becomes Grand Loge Ecossaise.

1774   Saint-Martin retires, to become Philosophe Inconnu, and as delegate of Templar Strict Observance goes to negotiate with Willermoz. A Scottish Directory of the Province of Auvergne is born. From this will be born the Rectified Scottish rite.

1776   Saint-Germain, under the name Count Welldone, presents chemical plans to Frederick II. Société des Philathètes is born, to unite all hermeticists. Lodge of the Neuf Soeurs has as members Guillotin and Cabanis, Voltaire and Franklin. Adam Weishaupt founds Illuminati of Bavaria. According to some, he is initiated by a Danish merchant, Kolmer, returning from Egypt, who is probably the mysterious Altotas, master of Cagliostro.

1778   Saint-Germain, in Berlin, meets Dom Pernety. Willermoz founds Ordre des Chevaliers Bienfaisants de la Cité Sainte. Templar Strict Observance and Grand Orient agree to accept the Rectified Scottish rite.

1782   Great conference of all the initiatory lodges at Wilhelmsbad.

1783   Marquis Thomé founds the Swedenborg rite.

1784   Saint-Germain presumably dies while in the service of the landgrave of Hesse, for whom he is completing a factory for making dyes.

1785   Cagliostro founds Memphis rite, which later becomes the Ancient and Primitive rite of Memphis-Misraim; it increases the number of high degrees to ninety. Scandal of the Affair of the Diamond Necklace, orchestrated by Cagliostro. Dumas describes it as Masonic plot to discredit

423

the monarchy. The Illuminati of Bavaria are suppressed, suspected of revolutionary plotting.

1786   Mirabeau is initiated by the Illuminati of Bavaria in Berlin. In London a Rosicrucian manifesto appears, attributed to Cagliostro. Mirabeau writes a letter to Cagliostro and to Lavater.

1787   There are about seven hundred lodges in France. Weishaupt publishes his *Nachtrag,* which describes the structure of a secret organization in which each adherent knows only his immediate superior.

1789   French Revolution begins. Crisis in the French lodges.

1794   On 8 Vendémiaire, Deputy Grégoire presents to the Convention the project for a Conservatoire des Arts et Métiers. It is installed in Saint-Martin-des-Champs in 1799, by the Council of Five Hundred. The Duke of Brunswick urges lodges to dissolve because a poisonous subversive sect has now corrupted them all.

1798   Arrest of Cagliostro in Rome.

1804   Announcement in Charleston of official foundation of Ancient and Accepted Scottish rite, with number of degrees increased to 33.

1824   Document from court of Vienna to French government denounces secret associations like the Absolutes, the Independents, the Alta Vendita Carbonara.

1835   The cabalist Oettinger claims to meet Saint-Germain in Paris.

1846   Viennese writer Franz Graffer publishes account of a meeting of his brother with Saint-Germain between 1788 and 1790. Saint-Germain received his visitor while leafing through a book by Paracelsus.

1865   Foundation of Societas Rosicruciana in Anglia (other sources give 1860, 1866, or 1867). Bulwer-Lytton, author of the Rosicrucian novel *Zanoni,* joins.

1868   Bakunin founds International Alliance of Socialist Democracy, inspired, some say, by the Illuminati of Bavaria.

1875   Elena Petrovna Blavatsky, with Henry Steel Olcott, founds Theosophical Society. Her *Isis Unveiled* appears. Baron Spedalieri proclaims himself a member of Grand Lodge of the Solitary Brothers of the Mountain, Frater Illuminatus of the Ancient and Restored Order of the Manicheans and of the Martinists.

1877 Madame Blavatsky speaks of the theosophical role of Saint-Germain. Among his incarnations are Roger and Francis Bacon, Rosencreutz, Proclus, Saint Alban. Grand Orient of France eliminates invocation to the Great Architect of the Universe and proclaims absolute freedom of conscience. Breaks ties with Grand Lodge of England and becomes firmly secular and radical.

1879 Foundation of Societas Rosicruciana in the USA.

1880 Beginning of Saint-Yves d'Alveydre's activity. Leopold Engler reorganizes the Illuminati of Bavaria.

1884 Leo XIII, with the encyclical *Humanum Genus,* condemns Freemasonry. Catholics desert it; rationalists flock to it.

1888 Stanislas de Guaita founds Ordre Kabbalistique de la Rose-Croix. Hermetic Order of the Golden Dawn founded in England, with eleven degrees, from neophyte to ipsissimus. Its imperator is McGregor Mathers, whose sister marries Bergson.

1890 Joseph Péladan, called Joséphin, leaves Guaita and founds the Rose-Croix Catholique du Temple et du Graal, proclaiming himself Sar Merodak. Conflict between Rosicrucians of Guaita's order and those of Péladan's is called the War of the Two Roses.

1891 Papus publishes his *Traité méthodique de science occulte.*

1898 Aleister Crowley initiated into Golden Dawn. Later founds Order of Thelema.

1907 From the Golden Dawn is born the Stella Matutina, which Yeats joins.

1909 In the United States, H. Spencer Lewis "reawakens" the Anticus Mysticus Ordo Rosae Crucis and in 1916, in a hotel, successfully transforms a piece of zinc into gold. Max Heindel founds the Rosicrucian Fellowship. At uncertain dates follow Lectorium Rosicrucianum, Frères Aînés de la Rose-Croix, Fraternitas Hermetica, Templum Rosae-Crucis.

1912 Annie Besant, disciple of Madame Blavatsky, founds, in London, Order of the Temple of the Rose-Cross.

1918 Thule Society is born in Germany.

1936   In France Le Grand Prieuré des Gaules is born. In the
        "Cahiers de la fraternité polaire," Enrico Contardi-Rhodio
        tells of a visit from Comte de Saint-Germain.

"What does all this mean?" Diotallevi said.

"Don't ask me. You wanted data? Help yourself. This is all I
know."

"We'll have to consult Agliè. I doubt that even he knows all these
organizations."

"Want to bet? They're his daily bread. But we can put him to the
test. Let's add a sect that doesn't exist. Founded recently."

I recalled the curious question of De Angelis, whether I had ever
heard of the Tres. And I said: "Tres."

"What's that?" Belbo asked.

"If it's an acrostic, there has to be a subtext," Diotallevi said.
"Otherwise my rabbis would not have been able to use the notarikon. Let's see . . . Templi Resurgentes Equites Synarchici. That
suit you?"

We liked the name, and put it at the bottom of the list.

"With all these conventicles, inventing one more was no mean
trick," Diotallevi said in a sudden fit of vanity.

76

If it were then a matter of defining in one word the dominant characteristic of French Freemasonry in the eighteenth century, only
one would do: dilettantism.
—René Le Forestier, *La Franc-Maçonnerie Templière et
Occultiste,* Paris, Aubier, 1970, 2

The next evening, we invited Agliè to Pilade's. Though the bar's
new customers had gone back to jackets and ties, the presence of
our guest, in blue chalk-stripe suit and snow-white shirt, tie fas-
tened with a gold pin, caused eyebrows to be raised. Luckily, at six
o'clock Pilade's was fairly empty.

Agliè confused Pilade by ordering a cognac by its brand name.
Pilade had it, of course, but the bottle had stood enthroned on the
shelf behind the zinc counter, untouched, for years.

Agliè studied the liquor in his glass against the light, then warmed
it with his hands, displaying gold cuff links that were vaguely Egyptian in style.

We showed him the list, telling him we had compiled it from the
manuscripts of the Diabolicals.

"The fact that the Templars were connected with the early lodges
of the master masons established during the construction of Solomon's Temple is certain," he said. "And it is equally certain that
these associates, on occasion, recalled the murder of the Temple's
architect, Hiram, a sacrificial victim. The masons vowed to avenge
him. After their persecution then, many knights of the Temple must
have joined those artisan confraternities, fusing the myth of avenging Hiram with the determination to avenge Jacques de Molay. In
the eighteenth century, in London, there were lodges of genuine
masons, and they were called operative lodges. Then, gradually, some
idle but thoroughly respectable gentlemen were determined to join
operative masonry, so it became symbolic, philosophical masonry.

"In this atmosphere a certain Desaguliers, popularizer of Newton, encouraged a Protestant pastor, Anderson, to draft the constitutions of a lodge of Mason brothers, deist in persuasion, and

Anderson began speaking of the Masonic confraternities as corporations dating back four thousand years, to the founders of the Temple of Solomon. These are the reasons for the Masonic masquerade: the apron, the trowel, the T square. Masonry became fashionable, attracting the aristocracy with the genealogical tables it hinted at, but it appealed even more to the bourgeoisie, who now not only could hobnob with the nobles but were actually permitted to wear a short sword. In the wretched modern world at its birth, the nobles need a place where they can come into contact with the new producers of capital, and the new producers of capital are looking to be ennobled."

"But the Templars seem to have emerged later."

"The one who first established a direct relation with the Templars, Ramsay, I'd prefer not to discuss. I suspect he was put up to it by the Jesuits. His preaching led to the birth of the Scottish wing of Masonry."

"Scottish?"

"The Scottish rite was a Franco-German invention. London Masonry had established three degrees: apprentice, fellow craft, and master. Scottish Masonry multiplied the degrees because doing so meant multiplying the levels of initiation and secrecy. The French, congenitally foolish, love secrecy. . . ."

"But what was the secret?"

"There was no secret, obviously. But if there had been one—or if they had possessed it—its complexity would have justified the number of degrees of initiation. Ramsay multiplied the degrees to make others believe he had a secret. You can imagine the thrill of those solid tradesmen now at last able to become princes of vengeance. . . ."

Agliè was prodigal with Masonic gossip. And in the course of his talk, as was his custom, he slipped gradually into first-person recollection.

"In those days, in France, they were already writing couplets about the new fashion, the Frimaçons. The lodges, multiplying, attracted monsignors, friars, barons, and shopkeepers, and the members of the royal family became grand masters. The Templar Strict Observance of that Hund character received Goethe, Lessing, Mozart, Voltaire. Lodges sprang up among the military; in the regimental mess they plotted to avenge Hiram and discussed the coming revolution. For others, Masonry was a société de plaisir, a club, a status symbol. You could find a bit of everything there: Cagliostro, Mesmer, Casanova, Baron d'Holbach, d'Alembert. . . . Encyclopedists and alchemists, libertines and hermetics. At the outbreak of the Revolution, members of the same lodge found themselves on opposite sides, and it seemed that the great brotherhood would never recover from this crisis. . . ."

"Wasn't there a conflict between the Grand Orient and the Scottish lodge?"

"Only verbally. For example: the lodge of the Neuf Soeurs welcomed Franklin, whose goals, naturally, were secular; he was interested only in supporting his American revolution. . . . But at the same time, one of its grand masters was the Comte de Milly, who was seeking the elixir of longevity. Since he was an imbecile, in the course of his experiments he poisoned himself and died. Or take Cagliostro: on the one hand, he invented Egyptian rites; on the other, he was implicated in the Affair of the Diamond Necklace, a scandal devised by the rising bourgeoisie to discredit the ancien régime. And Cagliostro was indeed involved! Just try to imagine the sort of people one had to live with. . . ."

"It must have been hard," Belbo said, with comprehension.

"But who," I asked, "are these barons von Hund who seek the Unknown Superiors . . . ?"

"New groups sprang up at the time of the necklace farce, altogether different in nature. To gain adepts, they identified themselves with the Masonic lodges, but actually they were pursuing more mystical ends. It was at this point that the debate about the Unknown Superiors took place. Hund, unfortunately, wasn't a serious person. At first he led his adepts to believe that the Unknown Superiors were the Stuarts. Then he said that the aim of the order was to rescue the original possessions of the Templars, and he scraped together funds from all sides. Unsatisfied with the proceeds, he fell into the hands of a man named Starck, who claimed to have learned the secret of making gold from the authentic Unknown Superiors, who were in Petersburg. Hund and Starck were surrounded by theosophists, cheap alchemists, last-minute Rosicrucians. All together, they elected as grand master a thoroughly upright man, the Duke of Brunswick. He immediately realized that he was in the worst possible company. One of the members of the Strict Observance, the landgrave of Hesse, summoned the Comte de Saint-Germain, believing this gentleman could produce gold for him. And why not? In those days the whims of the mighty had to be indulged. But the landgrave also believed himself to be Saint Peter. I assure you, gentlemen: once, when Lavater was the landgrave's guest, he had a dreadful time with the Duchess of Devonshire, who thought she was Mary Magdalene."

"But what about this Willermoz and this Martínez Pasqualis, who founded one sect after another?"

"Pasqualis was an old pirate. He practiced theurgical operations in a secret chamber, and angelic spirits appeared to him in the form of luminous trails and hieroglyphic characters. Willermoz took him seriously, because he himself was an enthusiast, honest but naïve. Fascinated by alchemy, Willermoz dreamed of a Great Work to which the elect should devote themselves: to discover the point of alliance of the six noble metals through studying the measurements comprised in the six letters of the original name of God, which Solomon had allowed his elect to know."

"And then?"

"Willermoz founded many orders and joined many lodges at the same time, as was the custom in those days, always seeking the definitive revelation, always fearing it was hidden elsewhere—which indeed is the case. That is, perhaps, the only truth. . . . So he joined the Elus Cohen of Pasqualis. But in '72 Pasqualis disappeared, sailed for Santo Domingo, and left everything up in the air. Why did he leave? I suspect he came into possession of a secret he didn't want to share. In any case, requiescat; he disappeared on that dark continent, into well-deserved darkness."

"And Willermoz?"

"In that year we had all been shaken by the death of Swedenborg, a man who could have taught many things to the ailing West, had the West listened to him. But now the century began its headlong race toward revolutionary madness, following the ambitions of the Third Estate. . . . It was then that Willermoz heard about Hund's rite of the Strict Observance and was fascinated by it. He was told that a Templar who reveals himself—by founding a public association, say—is not a Templar. But the eighteenth century was an era of great credulity. Willermoz created, with Hund, the various alliances that appear on your list, until Hund was unmasked—I mean, until they discovered he was the sort who runs off with the cash box—and the Duke of Brunswick expelled him from the organization."

Agliè cast another glance at the list. "Ah, yes, Weishaupt. I nearly forgot. The Illuminati of Bavaria: with a name like that, they attracted, at the beginning, a number of generous minds. But Weishaupt was an anarchist; today we'd call him a Communist, and if you gentlemen only knew the things they raved about in that ambience—coups d'état, dethroning sovereigns, bloodbaths . . . Mind you, I admired Weishaupt a great deal—not for his ideas, but for his extremely clearheaded view of how a secret society should function. It's possible to have a splendid organizational talent but quite confused ideas.

"In short, the Duke of Brunswick, seeing the confusion around him left by Hund, realized that at this juncture there were three conflicting currents in the German Masonic world: the sapiential-occultist camp, including some Rosicrucians; the rationalist camp; and the anarchist-revolutionary camp of the Illuminati of Bavaria. He proposed that the various orders and rites meet at Wilhelmsbad for a 'convent,' as they were called then, an Estates-General, you might say. The following questions had to be answered: Does the order truly originate from an ancient society, and if so, which? Are there really Unknown Superiors, keepers of the ancient Tradition, and if so, who are they? What are the true aims of the order? Is the chief aim to restore the order of the Templars? And so forth, including the problem of whether the order should concern itself with the occult sciences. Willermoz joined in, enthusiastic, hoping to find at last the answers to the questions he had been asking himself all his life. . . . And here the de Maistre affair began."

"Which de Maistre?" I asked. "Joseph or Xavier?"

"Joseph."

"The reactionary?"

"If he was reactionary, he wasn't reactionary enough. A curious man. Consider: this devout son of the Catholic Church, just when the first popes were beginning to issue bulls against Masonry, became a member of a lodge, assuming the name Josephus a Floribus. He approached Masonry in 1773, when a papal brief condemned the Jesuits. Of course it was the Scottish lodges that de Maistre approached, since he was not a bourgeois follower of the Enlightenment; he was an Illuminato."

Agliè sipped his cognac. From a cigarette case of almost white metal he took out some cigarillos of an unusual shape. "A tobacconist in London makes them for me," he said, "like the cigars you found at my house. Please . . . They're excellent. . . ." He spoke with his eyes lost in memory.

"De Maistre . . . a man of exquisite manners; to listen to him was a spiritual pleasure. He gained great authority in occult circles. And yet, at Wilhelmsbad he betrayed our expectations. He sent a letter to the duke, in which he firmly renounced any Templar affiliation, abjured the Unknown Superiors, and denied the utility of the esoteric sciences. He rejected it all out of loyalty to the Catholic Church, but he did so with the arguments of a bourgeois Encyclopedist. When the duke read the letter to a small circle of intimates, no one wanted to believe it. De Maistre now asserted that the order's aim was nothing but spiritual regeneration and that the ceremonials and the traditional rites served only to keep the mystical spirit alive. He praised all the new Masonic symbols, but said that an image that represented several things no longer represented anything. Which—you'll forgive me—runs counter to the whole hermetic tradition, for the more ambiguous and elusive a symbol is, the more it gains significance and power. Otherwise, what becomes of the spirit of Hermes, god of a thousand faces?

"Apropos of the Templars, de Maistre said that the order of the Temple had been created by greed, and greed had destroyed it, and that was that. The Savoyard could not forget, you see, that the order had been destroyed with the consent of the pope. Never trust Catholic legitimists, no matter how ardent their hermetic vocation. De Maistre's dismissal of the Unknown Superiors was also laughable: the proof that they do not exist is that we have no knowledge of them. We could not have knowledge of them, of course, or they would not be unknown. Odd, how a believer of such fiber could be impermeable to the sense of mystery. Then de Maistre made his final appeal: Let us return to the Gospels and abandon the follies of Memphis. He was simply restating the millennial line of the Church.

"You can understand the atmosphere in which the Wilhelmsbad meeting took place. With the defection of an authority like de Maistre,

432

Willermoz would be in the minority; at most, a compromise could be reached. The Templar rite was maintained; any conclusion about the origins of the order was postponed; in short, the convent was a failure. That was the moment the Scottish branch missed its opportunity; if things had gone differently, the history of the following century might have been different."

"And afterward?" I asked. "Was nothing patched together again?"

"What was there to patch—to use your word? . . . Three years later, an evangelical preacher who had joined the Illuminati of Bavaria, a certain Lanze, died in a wood, struck by lightning. Instructions of the order were found on him, the Bavarian government intervened, it was discovered that Weishaupt was plotting against the state, and the order was suppressed the following year. And further: Weishaupt's writings were published, containing the alleged projects of the Illuminati, and for a whole century they discredited all French and German neo-Templarism. . . . It's possible that Weishaupt's Illuminati were really on the side of Jacobin Masonry and had infiltrated the neo-Templar branch to destroy it. It was probably not by chance that this evil breed had attracted Mirabeau, the tribune of the Revolution, to its side. May I say something in confidence?"

"Please."

"Men like me, interested in joining together again the fragments of a lost Tradition, are bewildered by an event like Wilhelmsbad. Some guessed and remained silent; some knew and lied. And then it was too late: first the revolutionary whirlwind, then the uproar of nineteenth-century occultism. . . . Look at your list: a festival of bad faith and credulity, petty spite, reciprocal excommunications, secrets that circulated on every tongue. The theater of occultism."

"Occultists seem fickle, wouldn't you say?" Belbo remarked.

"You must be able to distinguish occultism from esotericism. Esotericism is the search for a learning transmitted only through symbols, closed to the profane. The occultism that spread in the nineteenth century was the tip of the iceberg, the little that surfaced of the esoteric secret. The Templars were initiates, and the proof of that is that when subjected to torture, they died to save their secret. It is the strength with which they concealed it that makes us sure of their initiation, and that makes us yearn to know what they knew. The occultist is an exhibitionist. As Péladan said, an initiatory secret revealed is of no use to anyone. Unfortunately, Péladan was not an initiate, but an occultist. The nineteenth century was the century of informers. Everybody rushed to publish the secrets of magic, theurgy, cabala, tarot. And perhaps they believed in it."

Agliè continued looking over our list, with an occasional snicker of commiseration. "Elena Petrovna. A good woman, at heart, but she never said a thing that hadn't already been written everywhere. . . . Guaita, a drug-addict bibliomane. Papus: What a character!" Then he stopped abruptly. "Tres . . . Where does this come from? Which manuscript?"

Good, I thought, he's noticed the interpolation. I answered vaguely: "Well, we put together the list from so many texts. Most of them have already been returned. They were plain rubbish. Do you recall, Belbo, where this Tres comes from?"

"I don't think I do. Diotallevi?"

"It was days ago . . . Is it important?"

"Not at all," Agliè said. "It's just that I never heard of it before. You really can't tell me who mentioned it?"

We were terribly sorry, we didn't remember.

Agliè took his watch from his vest. "Heavens, I have another engagement. You gentlemen will forgive me."

He left, and we stayed on, talking.

"It's all clear now. The English Templars put forth the Masonic proposal in order to make all the initiates of Europe rally around the Baconian plan."

"But the plan only half-succeeds. The idea of the Baconians is so fascinating that it produces results contrary to their expectations. The so-called Scottish line sees the new conventicle as a way to reestablish the succession, and it makes contact with the German Templars."

"To Agliè, what happened made no sense. But it's obvious—to us, now. The various national groups entered the lists, one against the other. I wouldn't be surprised if Martínez Pasqualis was an agent of the Tomar group. The English rejected the Scottish; then there were the French, obviously divided into two groups, pro-English and pro-German. Masonry was the cover, the pretext behind which all these agents of different groups—God knows where the Paulicians and the Jerusalemites were—met and clashed, each trying to tear a piece of the secret from the others."

"Masonry was like Rick's in Casablanca," Belbo said. "Which turns upside down the common view that it is a secret society."

"No, no, it's a free port, a Macao. A façade. The secret is elsewhere."

"Poor Masons."

"Progress demands its victims. But you must admit we are uncovering an immanent rationality of history."

"The rationality of history is the result of a good recombining of the Torah," Diotallevi said. "And that's what we're doing, and blessed be the name of the Most High."

"All right," Belbo said. "Now the Baconians have Saint-Martin-des-Champs, while the Franco-Roman neo-Templar line is breaking down into a hundred sects. . . . And we still haven't decided what this secret is all about."

"That's up to you two," Diotallevi said.

"Us two? All three of us are in this. If we don't come out honorably, we'll all look silly."

"Silly to whom?"

"Why, to history. Before the tribunal of Truth."

"Quid est veritas?" Belbo asked.

"Us," I said.

77

This herb is called Devilbane by the Philosophers. It has been demonstrated that only its seed can expel devils and their hallucinations. . . . When given to a young woman who was tormented by a devil during the night, this herb made him flee.
  —Johannes de Rupescissa, *Tractatus de Quinta Essentia*, 11

During the next few days, I neglected the Plan. Lia's pregnancy was coming to term, and whenever possible I stayed with her. I was anxious, but she calmed me, saying the time had not yet come. She was taking a course in painless childbirth, and I was trying to follow her exercises. Lia had rejected science's offer to tell us the baby's sex in advance. She wanted to be surprised. Accepting this eccentricity on her part, I touched her belly and did not ask myself what would come out. We called it the Thing.

I asked how I could take part in the birth. "It's mine, too, this Thing," I said. "I don't want to be one of those movie fathers, pacing up and down the corridor, chain-smoking."

"Pow, there's only so much you can do. The moment comes when it's all up to me. Besides, you don't smoke. Surely you're not going to start smoking just for this occasion."

"What'll I do, then?"

"You'll take part before and afterward. Afterward, if it's a boy, you'll teach him, guide him, give him a fine old Oedipus complex in the usual way, with a smile you'll play out the ritual parricide when the time comes—no fuss—and at some point you'll show him your squalid office, the card files, the page proofs of the wonderful adventure of metals, and you'll say to him, 'My son, one day all this will be yours.' "

"And if it's a girl?"

"You'll say to her, 'My daughter, one day all this will be your no-good husband's.' "

"And what do I do before?"

"During labor, between one wave of pain and the next, you have to count, because as the interval grows shorter, the moment approaches. We'll count together, and you'll set the rhythm for me, like rowers in a galley. It'll be as if you, too, were coaxing the Thing out from its dark lair. Poor little Thing . . . Feel it. Now it's so cozy there in the dark, sucking up humors like an octopus, all free, and then—wham—it pops out into the daylight, blinks, and says, Where the hell am I?"

"Poor little Thing. And it hasn't even met Signor Garamond. Come on, let's rehearse the counting part."

We counted in the darkness, holding hands. I daydreamed. The Thing, with its birth, would give reality and meaning to all the old wives' tales of the Diabolicals. Poor Diabolicals, who spent their nights enacting chemical weddings with the hope that eighteen-karat gold would result and wondering if the philosopher's stone was really the lapis exillis, a wretched terra-cotta grail—and my grail was in Lia's belly.

"Yes," Lia said, running her hand over her swelling, taut vessel, "here is where your good primal matter is steeping. Those people you saw at the castle, what did they think happened in the vessel?"

"Oh, they thought that melancholy was grumbling in it, sulfurous earth, black lead, oil of Saturn, a Styx of purifications, distillations, pulverizations, ablutions, liquefactions, submersions, terra foetida, stinking sepulcher . . ."

"What are they, impotent? Don't they know that in the vessel our Thing ripens, all white and pink and beautiful?"

"They know, but for them your dear little belly is also a metaphor, full of secrets. . . ."

"There are no secrets, Pow. We know exactly how the Thing is formed, its little nerves and muscles, its little eyes and spleens and pancreases . . ."

"Oh my God, more than one spleen? What is it, Rosemary's baby?"

"I was speaking in general. But of course we'll have to be ready to love it even if it has two heads."

"Of course! I'll teach it to play duets: trumpet and clarinet. . . . No, then it would need four hands, and that's too many. But, come to think about it, he'd make a great pianist. A concerto for two left hands? Nothing to it! Brr . . . But then, my Diabolicals also know that on that day, in the hospital, there will be born the Great Work, the White, the Rebis, the androgyne. . . ."

"That's all we need. Listen. We'll call him Giulio, or her Giulia, after my grandfather. What do you say?"

"I like it. Good."

If I had only stopped there. If I had only written a white book, a good grimoire, for all the adepts of Isis Unveiled, explaining to them that the secretum secretorum no longer needed to be sought, that the book of life contained no hidden meaning; it was all there, in the bellies of all the Lias of the world, in the hospital rooms, on straw pallets, on riverbanks, and that the stones in exile and the Holy Grail were nothing but screaming monkeys with their umbilical cord still dangling and the doctor giving them a slap on the ass. And that the Unknown Superiors, in the eyes of the Thing, were only me and Lia, and the Thing would immediately recognize us, without having to go ask that old fool de Maistre.

But no. We, the sardonic, insisted on playing games with the Diabolicals, on showing them that if there had to be a cosmic plot, we could invent the most cosmic of all.

Serves you right, I said to myself that other evening. Now here you are, waiting for what will happen under Foucault's Pendulum.

78

Surely this monstrous hybrid comes not from a mother's womb but
from an Ephialtes, an Incubus, or some other horrendous demon,
as though spawned in a putrid and venomous fungus, son of Fauns
and Nymphs, more devil than man.
—Athanasius Kircher, *Mundus Subterraneus*, Amsterdam,
Jansson, 1665, II, pp. 279–280

That day, I wanted to stay home—I had a presentiment—but Lia
told me to stop acting the prince consort and go to work. "There's
time, Pow; it won't be born yet. I have to go out, too. Run along."

I had almost reached my office when Signor Salon's door opened.
The old man appeared in his yellow apron. I couldn't avoid greeting
him, and he asked me to come inside. I had never seen his laboratory.

It must have been an apartment once, but Salon had had all the
dividing walls demolished, and what I saw was a cave, vast, hazy.
For some obscure architectural reason, this wing of the building had
a mansard roof, and the light entered obliquely. I don't know whether
the glass panes were dirty or frosted, or if Salon had installed shades
to keep out the direct sun, or if it was the heap of objects on all
sides proclaiming a fear of spaces left empty, but the light in the
cave was late dusk. The room was divided by old pharmacy shelves
in which arches opened to passages, junctions, perspectives. The
dominant color was brown: the objects, the shelves, the tables, the
diffuse blend of daylight and the patchy illumination from old lamps.
My first impression was of having entered an instrument maker's
atelier, abandoned from the time of Stradivarius, with years of accumulated dust on the striated bellies of the lutes.

Then, as my eyes gradually adjusted, I saw that I was in a petrified zoo. A bear cub with glassy eyes climbed an artificial bough; a
dazed and hieratic owl stood beside me; on the table in front of me
was a weasel—or marten or skunk; I couldn't tell. Behind it was a
prehistoric animal, feline, its bones showing. It might have been a
puma, a leopard, or a very big dog. Part of the skeleton had already

been covered with straw and paste, and it was all supported by an iron armature.

"The Great Dane of a rich lady with a soft heart," Salon said with a snicker, "who wants to remember it as it was in the days of their conjugal life. You see? You skin the animal, on the inside of the skin you smear arsenic soap, then you soak and bleach the bones. . . . Look at that shelf and you'll see a great collection of spinal columns and rib cages. A lovely ossuary, don't you think? You connect the bones with wire, reconstruct the skeleton, mount it on an armature. To stuff it, I use hay, papier-mâché, or plaster. Finally you fit the skin back on. I repair the damage done by death and corruption. This owl—doesn't it seem alive to you?"

From then on, every live owl would seem dead to me, consigned by Salon to a sclerotic eternity. I regarded the face of that embalmer of animal pharaohs, his bushy eyebrows, his gray cheeks, and I could not decide whether he was a living being or a masterpiece of his own art.

The better to look at him, I took a step backward, and felt something graze my nape. I turned with a shudder and saw I had set a pendulum in motion.

A great disemboweled bird swayed, following the movement of the lance that pierced it. The weapon had entered the head, and through the open breast you could see it pass where the heart and gizzard had once been, then branch out to form an upside-down trident. One, thicker prong went through the now-emptied belly and pointed toward the ground like a sword, while the two other prongs entered the feet and emerged symmetrically from the talons. The bird swung, and the three points cast their shadow on the floor, a mystic sign.

"A fine specimen of the golden eagle," Salon said. "But I still have a few days' work to do on it. I was just choosing the eyes." He showed me a box full of glass corneas and pupils, as if the executioner of Saint Lucy had collected the trophies of his entire career. "It's not always easy, as it is with insects, where all you need is a box and a pin. This, for example, has to be treated with formalin."

I smelled its morgue odor. "It must be an enthralling job," I said. And meanwhile I was thinking of the living creature that throbbed in Lia's belly. A chilling thought seized me. If the Thing dies, I said to myself, I want to bury it. I want it to feed the worms underground and enrich the earth. That's the only way I'll feel it's still alive. . . .

Salon was still talking. He took a strange specimen from one of the shelves. It was about thirty centimeters long. A dragon, a reptile with black membranous wings, a cock's crest, and gaping jaws that bristled with tiny sawlike teeth. "Handsome, isn't he? My own composition. I used a salamander, a bat, snake's scales. . . . A subterranean dragon. I was inspired by this. . . ." He showed me, on another table, a great folio volume, bound in ancient parchment, with leather ties. "It cost me a fortune. I'm not a bibliophile, but this was something I had to have. It's the *Mundus Subterraneus* of Athanasius Kircher, first edition, 1665. Here's the dragon. Identical, don't you think? It lives in the caves of volcanoes, that good Jesuit said, and he knew everything about the known, the unknown, and the nonexistent. . . ."

"You think always of the underground world," I said, recalling our conversation in Munich and the words I had overheard through the Ear of Dionysius.

He opened the volume to another page, to an image of the globe, which looked like an anatomical organ, swollen and black, covered by a spider web of luminescent, serpentine veins. "If Kircher was right, there are more paths in the heart of the earth than there are on the surface. Whatever takes place in nature derives from the heat and steam below . . ."

I thought of the Black Work, of Lia's belly, of the Thing that was struggling to break out of its sweet volcano.

". . . and whatever takes place in the world of men is planned below."

"Does Padre Kircher say that, too?"

"No. He concerns himself only with nature. . . . But it is odd that the second part of this book is on alchemy and the alchemists, and that precisely here, you see, there is an attack on the Rosicrucians. Why attack the Rosicrucians in a book on the underground world? Our Jesuit knew a thing or two; he knew that the last Templars had taken refuge in the underground kingdom of Agartha. . . ."

"And they're still there, it seems," I ventured.

"They're still there," Salon said. "Not in Agarttha, but in tunnels. Perhaps beneath us, right here. Milan, too, has a metro. Who decided on it? Who directed the excavations?"

"Expert engineers, I'd say."

"Yes, cover your eyes with your hands. And meanwhile, in that firm of yours, you publish such books . . . How many Jews are there among your authors?"

"We don't ask our authors to fill out racial forms," I replied stiffly.

"You mustn't think me an anti-Semite. No, some of my best friends . . . I have in mind a certain kind of Jew. . . ."

"What kind?"

"I know what kind. . . ."

79

He opened his coffer. In indescribable disorder it contained collars,
rubber bands, kitchen utensils, badges of different technical schools,
even the monogram of the Empress Alexandra Feodorovna and the
Cross of the Legion of Honor. On everything, in his madness, he
saw the seal of the Antichrist, in the form of two linked triangles.
—Alexandre Chayla, "Serge A. Nilus et les Protocoles," *La
Tribune Juive*, May 14, 1921, p. 3

"You see," Salon went on, "I was born in Moscow. And it was in
Russia, when I was a youth, that people discovered the secret Jewish documents that said, in so many words, that to control governments it was necessary to work underground. Listen." He picked
up a little notebook, in which he had copied out some quotations.
" 'Today's cities have metropolitan railroads and underground passages: from these we will blow up all the capitals of the world.'
Protocols of the Elders of Zion, Document Number Nine!"

It occurred to me that the collection of spinal columns, the box
with the eyes, the skins stretched over armatures came from some
extermination camp. But no, I was dealing with an elderly man nostalgic about the old days of Russian anti-Semitism. "If I follow you,
then, there's a conventicle of Jews—some Jews, not all—who are
plotting something. But why underground?"

"That's obvious! Any plotter must plot underground, not in the
light of day. This has been known from the beginning of time. Dominion over the world means dominion over what lies beneath it.
The subterranean currents."

I remembered a question of Agliè's in his study, and then the
Druidesses in Piedmont, who called on telluric currents.

"Why did the Celts dig sanctuaries in the heart of the earth, making tunnels that communicated with a sacred well?" Salon continued. "The well goes down into radioactive strata, as everyone knows.
How was Glastonbury built? And isn't the island of Avalon where
the myth of the Grail originated? And who invented the Grail if not
a Jew?"

443

The Grail again, my God. But what grail? There was only one grail: my Thing, in contact with the radioactive strata of Lia's womb, and perhaps now swimming happily toward the mouth of that well, perhaps now preparing to come out, and here I was among stuffed owls, among a hundred dead and one pretending to be alive.

"All Europe's cathedrals are built where the Celts had their menhirs. Why did the Celts set these stones in the ground, considering the effort it cost them?"

"Why did the Egyptians go to so much trouble to erect the pyramids?"

"There you are. Antennas, thermometers, probes, needles like the ones Chinese doctors use, stuck into the body's nodal points. At the center of the earth is a nucleus of fusion, something similar to the sun—indeed, an actual sun around which things revolve, describing different paths. Orbits of telluric currents. The Celts knew where they were, and how to control them. And Dante? What about Dante? What was he trying to tell us with the account of his descent into the depths? You understand me, dear friend?"

I didn't like being his dear friend, but I went on listening to him. Giulio/Giulia, my Rebis planted like Lucifer at the center of Lia's womb, but he/she, the Thing, would be upside down, would be struggling upward, and would somehow emerge. The Thing was created to emerge upward from the viscera, and not make its entrance with head bowed, in sticky secrecy.

Salon by now was lost in a monologue he seemed to repeat from memory. "You know what the English leys are? If you fly over England in a plane, you'll see that all the sacred places are joined by straight lines, a grid of lines interwoven across the whole country, still visible because they suggested the lines of later roads. . . ."

"The sacred places were connected by roads, and people simply tried to make roads as straight as possible."

"Indeed? Then why do birds migrate along these lines? Why do flying saucers follow them? It's a secret that was lost after the Roman invasion, but there are those who still know it. . . ."

"The Jews," I suggested.

"They also dig. The first alchemistic principle is VITRIOL: Visita Interiora Terrae, Rectificando Invenies Occultum Lapidem."

Lapis exillis. My Stone that was slowly coming out of exile, from the sweet oblivious hypnotic exile of Lia's vessel; my Stone, beautiful and white, not seeking further depths, but seeking the surface . . . I wanted to rush home to Lia, to wait with her, hour by hour, for the appearance of the Thing, the triumph of the surface regained. Salon's den had the musty smell of tunnels. Tunnels were the origin that had to be abandoned; they were not the destination. And yet I followed Salon, and new, malicious ideas for the Plan whirled in my head. While I awaited the one Truth of this sublunar world, I racked my brain to construct new falsehoods; blind as the animals underground.

I stirred. I had to get out of the tunnel. "I must go," I said. "Perhaps you can suggest some books on this subject."

"Ha! Everything they've written about it is false, false as the soul of Judas. What I know I learned from my father. . . ."

"A geologist?"

"Oh no," Salon said, laughing, "no, not at all. My father—nothing to be ashamed of; water under the bridge—worked for the Okhrana. Directly under the chief, the legendary Rachkovski."

Okhrana, Okhrana? Something like the KGB? The tsarist secret police, wasn't it? And who was Rachkovski? Wasn't there someone who had a similar name? By God, the colonel's mysterious visitor, Count Rakosky . . . No, enough of this. No more coincidences. I didn't stuff dead animals; I created living animals.

80

I mumbled some excuse, in haste. I believe I said, "My girlfriend's
having a baby tomorrow." Salon haltingly offered me congratulations, as if not sure who the father was. I ran home, to breathe some
clean air.

Lia wasn't in. On the kitchen table, a piece of paper: "Darling,
the waters have broken. Couldn't get you at the office. Taking a
taxi to the hospital. Come. I feel alone."

A moment of panic. I had to be there to count with Lia. I should
have been in the office, reachable. It was my fault: the Thing would
be born dead, Lia would die with it, Salon would stuff them both.

I entered the hospital on unsteady legs, asked directions of people
who didn't know anything, twice ended up in the wrong ward. I
shouted that they had to know where Lia was having the baby, and
they told me to calm down, because here everybody was having a
baby.

Finally—I don't know how—I found myself in a room. Lia was
pearly pale but smiling. Someone had lifted her hair and put it under
a white cap. For the first time I saw Lia's forehead in all its splendor. Next to her was the Thing.

"It's Giulio," she said.

My Rebis. I, too, had made him, and not with chunks of dead
bodies or arsenic soap. He was whole, all his fingers and toes were
in the right place.

I insisted on seeing all of him, his little cock, his big balls. Then

446

I kissed Lia on her naked brow: "The credit is yours, darling; it all depends on the vessel."

"Of course the credit is mine, you shit. I had to count all by myself."

"For me you are all that counts," I told her.

81

The subterranean people have reached the highest knowledge. . . .
If our mad humankind should begin a war against them, they would
be able to explode the whole surface of our planet. . . .
—Ferdinand Ossendowski, *Beasts, Men and Gods*, 1924, v

I stayed at home with Lia because, once she left the hospital and
had to change the baby's diapers, she cried and said she would never
be able to cope. Somebody explained to us that this was normal:
the excitement over the victory of birth is followed by a feeling of
helplessness in the face of the immensity of the job. During those
days, while I loafed around the house, useless and not qualified, of
course, for breast-feeding, I spent long hours reading everything I
had been able to find concerning telluric currents.

On my return, I sounded out Agliè on them. He made a gesture
of boredom. "Weak metaphors, referring to the secret of the serpent
Kundalini. Chinese geomancy also sought in the earth the traces of
the dragon. The telluric serpent simply stands for the occult serpent.
The goddess reposes, coiled, and sleeps her eternal sleep. Kundalini
throbs gently, binding heavy bodies to lighter bodies. Like a vortex
or a whirlpool, like the first half of the syllable om."

"But what secret does the serpent refer to?"

"To the telluric currents."

"What are the telluric currents?"

"A great cosmological metaphor, which refers to the serpent."

To hell with Agliè, I said to myself, I know more than that.

I read my notes to Belbo and Diotallevi, and we no longer had
any doubt. At last we were in a position to supply the Templars
with a decent secret. It was the most economical, the most elegant
solution to the problem, and all the pieces of our millennial puzzle
fit together.

So: the Celts knew about the telluric currents; they had learned
the secret from the Atlantides, when the survivors of the submerged
continent emigrated, some to Egypt, some to Brittany.

The Atlantides had learned it from those ancestors of ours who ventured forth from Avalon across the continent of Mu as far as the central desert of Australia—when all the continents were a single land mass, the wondrous Pangaea. If only we could still read (as the Aborigines can, but they remain silent) the mysterious alphabet carved on the great boulder Ayers Rock, we would have the Answer. Ayers Rock is the antipode of the great (unknown) mountain that is the Pole, the true, occult Pole, not the one that any bourgeois explorer can reach. As usual, and this should be obvious to anyone whose eyes have not been blinded by the false light of Western science, the Pole that we see is not the real Pole, for the real Pole is the one that cannot be seen, except by some adepts, whose lips are sealed.

The Celts, however, believed it was enough to discover the global configuration of the currents. That's why they erected megaliths. The menhirs had sensitive devices, like electric valves, planted at the points where the currents branched and changed direction. The leys marked the routes of currents already identified. The dolmens were chambers of accumulated energy, where the Druids, with geomantic tools, attempted to map, by extrapolation, the global design. The cromlechs and Stonehenge were micro-macrocosmic observatories from which they studied the pattern of the constellations in order to divine the pattern of the currents—because, as the *Tabula Smaragdina* tells us, what is above is isomorphic to what is below.

But there was more to the problem than that. The other branch of the Atlantidean emigration realized as much. The occult knowledge of the Egyptians passed from Hermes Trismegistus to Moses, who took care not to pass it on to his band of tatterdemalions, their craws still stuffed with manna; to them he offered the Ten Commandments, which was as much as they could comprehend. The higher truth is aristocratic; Moses encoded it in the Pentateuch. The cabalists understood this.

"Just think," I said, "everything was already written, an open book, in the measurements of the Temple of Solomon, and the keepers of the secret were the Rosicrucians, who formed the Great White Fraternity—the Essenes, in other words, who, as is well known, let Jesus in on their secrets. And there you have the real reason why Jesus was crucified. . . ."

"Of course, the Passion of Christ is an allegory, prefiguring the trial of the Templars."

"Right. And Joseph of Arimathea takes, or takes back, the secret of Jesus to the land of the Celts. But obviously the secret is still incomplete; the Christian Druids know only a fragment of it, and that is the esoteric meaning of the Grail: there is something missing, but we don't know what. The secret—what the Temple already said in full—is suspected only by a small group of rabbis who remained in Palestine. They entrust it to the occult Moslem sects, to the Sufis, the Ismailis, the Motakallimûn. And from them the Templars learn it."

"At last, the Templars! I was beginning to worry," Belbo said.

We were shaping the Plan, which, like soft clay, obeyed our thumbs, our narrative desires. The Templars had discovered the secret during those sleepless nights, embracing their saddle mates in the desert, where the implacable simoom was blowing. They had wrested it, bit by bit, from those who knew the powers of cosmic focus in the Black Stone of Mecca, the heritage of the Babylonian magi—for it was clear now that the Tower of Babel had been simply an attempt, however hasty and deservedly a failure because of the pride of its architects, to build the most powerful menhir of all. But the Babylonians got their calculations wrong. As Father Kircher has demonstrated, had the tower reached its peak, its excessive weight would have made the earth's axis rotate ninety degrees and maybe more, and our poor globe, instead of having an ithyphallic crown pointing upward, would have found itself with a sterile appendix, a limp mentula, a monkey tail flopping downward, a Shekhinah lost in the dizzying abyss of an antarctic Malkhut, a flaccid hieroglyph for penguins.

"So, in a word, what's the secret discovered by the Templars?"

"Don't rush me. We're getting there. It took seven days to make the world. And now *we'll* give it a try."

82

The earth is a magnetic body; in fact, as some scientists have found, it is one vast magnet, as Paracelsus affirmed some 300 years ago.
—H. P. Blavatsky, *Isis Unveiled*, New York, Boulton, 1877, I, p. xxiii

We gave it a try, and we succeeded.

The earth is a great magnet, and the force and direction of its currents are influenced by the celestial spheres, the cycle of the seasons, the precession of the equinoxes, the cosmic cycles. Thus the pattern of the currents changes. But it must change like hair, which, though it grows everywhere on the top and sides of the skull, nevertheless spirals out from a point toward the back, where it rebels most against the comb. When that point has been identified, when the most powerful station has been established there, it will be possible to control, direct, command all the telluric currents of the planet. The Templars realized that the secret lay not only in possessing the global map of the currents, but also in knowing the critical point, the Omphalos, the Umbilicus Telluris, the Navel of the World, the Source of Command.

All alchemistic talk—the chthonic descent of the Black Work, the electric charge of the White—is only a metaphor, a metaphor clear to the initiated, for this age-old auscultation whose final result will be the Red: global knowledge, brilliant dominion over the planetary system of currents. The secret, the real secret, of alchemy and Templars is the search for the Wellspring of that internal rhythm, as sweet, awesome, and regular as the throbbing of the serpent Kundalini, still unknown in many of its aspects, yet surely as precise as a clock, for it is the rhythm of the one true Stone that fell in exile from heaven, the Great Mother Earth.

This was what Philip the Fair wanted to know. Hence the inquisitors' sly insistence on the mysterious kiss in posteriori parte spine dorsi. They wanted the secret of Kundalini; who cares about sodomy.

"It's perfect," Diotallevi said. "But then, when you know how to direct the telluric currents, what do you do with them? Make beer?"

"Come on," I said. "Haven't you grasped the significance of this discovery? In the Telluric Navel you place the most powerful valve, which enables you to foresee rain and drought, to release hurricanes, tidal waves, earthquakes, to split continents, sink islands (no doubt Atlantis disappeared in some such reckless experiment), raise mountain chains . . . You realize the atomic bomb is nothing in comparison? Besides which, it also hurts the one who drops it. From your control tower you telephone, for example, the president of the United States, and you say to him: By tomorrow morning I want a dodecadillion dollars—or the independence of Latin America, or the state of Hawaii, or the destruction of your stockpile of nuclear weapons—or else the San Andreas Fault will crack definitively and Las Vegas will become a floating casino. . . ."

"But Las Vegas is in Nevada."

"Doesn't matter. When you control the telluric currents, you can snip off Nevada, too, and Colorado. Then you telephone the Supreme Soviet and you say: Comrades, by Monday I want all the caviar of the Volga, and I want Siberia as my frozen-food locker; otherwise I'll suck the Urals under, I'll make the Caspian overflow, I'll cut loose Lithuania and Estonia and sink them in the Philippine Trench."

"Yes," Diotallevi said. "The power would be immense. The earth could be rewritten like the Torah. Japan lands in the gulf of Panama."

"Panic on Wall Street."

"Forget about Star Wars. Forget about transforming base metal into gold. You aim the right current, stir up the bowels of the earth, and make them do in ten seconds what it used to take them billions of years to do, and the whole Ruhr becomes a diamond mine. Eliphas Lévi said the knowledge of the universe's tides and currents holds the secret of human omnipotence."

"That must be so," Belbo said. "It's like transforming the whole world into an orgone box. It's obvious. Reich was definitely a Templar."

"Everyone was, except us. Thank God we've caught on. Now we're a step ahead of them."

But what stopped the Templars, once they knew the secret? The problem was how to exploit it. Between knowing and know-how there was a gap. So, instructed by the diabolical Saint Bernard, the Templars replaced the menhirs, poor Celtic valves, with Gothic cathedrals, far more sensitive and powerful, their subterranean crypts containing black virgins, in direct contact with the radioactive strata; and they covered Europe with a network of receiver-transmitter stations communicating to one another the power and the direction, the flow and the tension, of the telluric currents.

"I say they located the silver mines in the New World, caused eruptions of silver there, and then, controlling the Gulf Stream, shifted that precious metal to the Portuguese coast. Tomar was the distribution center; the Forêt d'Orient, the chief storehouse. This was the origin of their wealth. But this was peanuts. They realized that to exploit their secret fully they would have to wait for a technological advance that would take at least six hundred years."

Thus the Templars organized the Plan in such a way that only their successors, at the moment when they would be able to make proper use of what they knew, would learn the location of the Umbilicus Telluris. But how did the Templars distribute the pieces of the revelation to the thirty-six scattered throughout the world? How could a straightforward message have that many parts? And why would they need such a complicated message just to say that the Umbilicus was, for example, in Baden-Baden, or Tralee, or Chattanooga?

A map? But a map would be marked with an X at the point of the Umbilicus. Whoever held the piece with the X would know everything and not need the other pieces. No; it had to be more involved. We racked our brains for several days, until Belbo decided to resort to Abulafia. And the reply was:

Guillaume Postel dies in 1581.
Bacon is Viscount St. Albans.
In the Conservatoire is Foucault's Pendulum.

The time had come to find a function for the Pendulum.

I was able, in few days, to suggest a rather elegant solution. A Diabolical had submitted to us a text on the hermetic secret of cathedrals. According to this author, the builders of Chartres one day left a plumb line hanging from the keystone of a vault, and from that had easily deduced the rotation of the earth. Hence the motive for the trial of Galileo, Diotallevi remarked: the Church had caught a whiff of Templar about him. No, Belbo said; the cardinals who condemned Galileo were Templar adepts infiltrating Rome. They wanted to shut up that damned Tuscan quickly, that traitor Templar who in his vanity was about to spill the beans four hundred years before the date of the Plan's fulfillment.

This explained why beneath the Pendulum those master masons had drawn a labyrinth, a stylized image of the system of subterranean currents. We sought an illustration of the labyrinth of Chartres: a solar clock, a compass card, a vein system, a sleepy sinusoidal trail of the Serpent. A global chart of the telluric tides.

"All right, let's assume the Templars used the Pendulum to indicate the Umbilicus. Instead of the labyrinth, which is, after all, an abstract scheme, on the floor you put a map of the world. The point marked by the tip of the Pendulum at a given hour is the point that marks the Umbilicus. But which Pendulum?"

"The place is beyond discussion: Saint-Martin-des-Champs, the Refuge."

"Yes," Belbo replied, "but let's suppose that at the stroke of midnight the Pendulum swings from Copenhagen to Capetown. Where is the Umbilicus? In Denmark or in South Africa?"

"A good observation," I said. "But our Diabolical tells us also that in Chartres there is a fissure in a stained-glass window of the choir, and at a given hour of the day a sunbeam enters through the crack and always hits the same place, always the same stone of the floor. I don't remember what conclusion he draws from this, but in any event it's a great secret. So here's the mechanism: in the choir of Saint-Martin there is a window that has an uncolored spot near the juncture of two lead cames. It was carefully calculated, and probably for six hundred years someone has always taken care to keep it as it is. At sunrise on a given day of the year . . ."

". . . which can only be the dawn of June 24, Saint John's day, feast of the summer solstice . . ."

". . . yes, on that day and at that hour, the first pure ray of sun that comes through the windows strikes the floor beneath the Pendulum, and the Pendulum's intersection of the ray at that instant is the precise point on the map where the Umbilicus is to be found!"

"Perfect," Belbo said. "But suppose it's overcast?"

"They wait until the following year."

"I'm sorry, but . . ." Belbo said. "The last meeting is to be in Jerusalem. Shouldn't the Pendulum be hanging from the top of the dome of the Mosque of Omar?"

"No," I said. "At certain places on the globe the Pendulum completes its circle in thirty-six hours; at the North Pole it takes twenty-four hours; at the Equator the cycle doesn't vary with the season. So the location matters. If the Templars made their discovery at Saint-Martin, their calculation is valid only in Paris; in Palestine, the Pendulum would mark a different curve."

"And how do we know they made the discovery at Saint-Martin?"

"The fact that they chose Saint-Martin as their Refuge, that from the prior of Saint Albans, to Postel, to the Convention they kept it under their control, that after Foucault's first experiments they installed the Pendulum there. Too many clues."

"But still, the last meeting is in Jerusalem."

"So? In Jerusalem they'll put the message together, and that's not a matter of a few minutes. Then they'll prepare for a year, and the following June 23 all six groups will meet in Paris, to learn finally where the Umbilicus is, and then they'll set to work to conquer the world."

"But," Belbo insisted, "there's still something I can't figure out. Although there's this final revelation about the Umbilicus, all thirty-six must have known that before. The Pendulum had been used in cathedrals; so it wasn't a secret. What would have prevented Bacon or Postel, or even Foucault—who must have been a Templar himself, seeing all the fuss he made over the Pendulum—from just putting a map of the world on the floor and orienting it by the cardinal points? We're off the track."

"No, we're not off the track," I said. "The message reveals something that none of them could know: what map to use!"

83

A map is not the territory.
—Alfred Korzybski, *Science and Sanity*, 1933; 4th ed., The
International Non-Aristotelian Library, 1958, II, 4, p. 58

"You're familiar with the situation of cartography at the time of the
Templars," I said. "In that century there were Arab maps that, among
other things, put Africa at the top and Europe at the bottom; navi-
gators' maps, fairly accurate, all things considered; and maps that
by then were already three or four hundred years old but were still
accepted in some schools. Mind you, to reveal the location of the
Umbilicus they didn't need an accurate map, in today's sense. It had
to be simply a map possessing this virtue: once oriented, it would
show the Umbilicus at the point where the arc of the Pendulum is
struck by the first ray of sun on June 24. Now listen carefully. Let's
suppose, purely as a hypothesis, that the Umbilicus is in Jerusalem.
Even with our modern maps, the position of Jerusalem depends on
the projection used. And God knows what kind of map the Templars had. But it doesn't matter. It's not the Pendulum that's calibrated according to the map; it's the map that's calibrated according
to the Pendulum. You follow me? It could be the craziest map in
the world, as long as, when placed beneath the Pendulum at the
crack of dawn on the twenty-fourth of June, it shows the one and
only spot that is Jerusalem."

"This doesn't solve our problem," Diotallevi said.

"Of course not, and it doesn't solve it for the invisible thirty-six
either. Because if you don't have the right map, forget it. Let's take
the case of a map oriented in the standard way, with east in the
direction of the apse and west toward the nave, since that's how
churches are built. Now let's say, at random, that on that fatal dawn
the Pendulum is near the boundary of the southeast quadrant. If it
were a clock, we'd say that the hour hand is at five-twenty-five. All
right? Now look."

I went to dig out a history of cartography.

"Here. Exhibit number 1: a twelfth-century map. It follows the T-structured maps: Asia is at the top with the Earthly Paradise; to the left, Europe; to the right, Africa; and here, beyond Africa, they've also put the Antipodes. Exhibit number 2: a map inspired by the *Somnium Scipionis* of Macrobius, and it survives in various versions into the sixteenth century. Africa's a bit narrow, but that's all right. Now look: orient the two maps in the same way, and you see that on the first map five-twenty-five corresponds to Arabia, and on the second map to New Zealand, since that's where the second map has the Antipodes. You may know everything about the Pendulum, but if you don't know what map to use, you're lost. So the message contained instructions, elaborately coded, on where to find the right map, which may have been specially drawn for the occasion. The message told where to look, in what manuscript, in what library, abbey, castle. It's even possible that Dee or Bacon or someone else reconstructed the message. Who knows? The message said the map was at X, but in the meantime, with everything that was going on in Europe, the abbey that housed the map burned down, or the map was stolen, hidden God knows where. Maybe someone has the map but doesn't know the use of it, or knows it's valuable but doesn't know why, and he's going around the world looking for a buyer. Imagine all the confusion of offers, false trails, messages that say other things but are understood to refer to the map, and messages that indeed refer to the map but are read as if hinting at, say, the production of gold. No doubt some people attempt to reconstruct the map purely on the basis of conjectures."

"What sorts of conjectures?"

"Well, for example, micro-macrocosmic correspondences. Here's another map. You know where it comes from? It appears in the second treatise of the *Utriusque Cosmi Historia* of Robert Fludd. Fludd is the Rosicrucians' man in London, don't forget. Now what does our man do, our Robertus de Fluctibus, as he liked to style himself? He offers what is no longer a map, but a strange projection of the entire globe from the point of view of the Pole, the mystic Pole, naturally, and therefore from the point of view of an ideal Pendulum suspended from an ideal keystone. This is a map specially conceived to be placed beneath a Pendulum! It's obvious, undeniable; I can't imagine why somebody hasn't already seen—"

"The fact is, the Diabolicals are very, very slow," Belbo said.

"The fact is, we are the only worthy heirs of the Templars. But, to continue. You recognize the design. It's a mobile rotula, like the ones Trithemius used for his coded messages. This isn't a map, then; it's a design for a machine to produce variations of maps, until the right map is found! And Fludd says as much in the caption: This is the sketch for an instrumentum, it still needs work."

"But wasn't Fludd the one who persisted in denying the rotation of the earth? How could he think of the Pendulum?"

"We're dealing with initiates. An initiate denies what he knows, denies knowing it, to conceal it."

"This," Belbo said, "would explain why Dee paid so much attention to those royal cartographers. It was not to discover the 'true' form of the earth, but to reconstruct, among all the mistaken maps, the one right map, the one of use to him."

"Not bad, not bad at all," Diotallevi said. "To arrive at the truth through the painstaking reconstruction of a false text."

84

The chief occupation of this Assembly—and, in my opinion, the most useful—should be to work on natural history following the plans of Verulam.
— Christian Huygens, Letter to Colbert, *Oeuvres Complètes*,
   La Haye, 1888–1950, vi, pp. 95–96

The vicissitudes of the six groups were not confined to the search for the map. In the first two pieces of the message, those in the hands of the Portuguese and the English, the Templars probably referred to a pendulum, but ideas about pendulums were still hazy. It's one thing to swing some lead on a length of cord and quite another to construct a mechanism precise enough to be hit by a ray of the sun at an exact time and place. This is why the Templars calculated for six centuries. The Baconian wing set immediately to work, and tried to draw to its side all the initiates, whom it made desperate efforts to reach.

It is no coincidence that Salomon de Caus, the Rosicrucians' man, writes for Richelieu a treatise on solar clocks. And afterward, from Galileo on, there is furious research devoted to pendulums. The pretext is to figure out how to use them for determining longitudes, but in 1681, when Huygens discovers that a pendulum accurate in Paris is slow in Cayenne, he immediately realizes that this discrepancy is due to the variation in centrifugal force caused by the rotation of the earth. And after he publishes his *Horologium Oscillatorium*, in which he elaborates on Galileo's intuitions about the pendulum, who summons him to Paris? Colbert, the same man who summons to Paris Salomon de Caus to work on the tunnels beneath the city!

In 1661, when the Accademia del Cimento foreshadows the conclusions of Foucault, Leopold of Tuscany dissolves it in the space of five years, and immediately afterward receives from Rome, as a secret reward, a cardinal's hat.

But there is more. In the centuries that follow, the hunt for the

Pendulum continues. In 1742 (a year before the first documented appearance of the Comte de Saint-Germain!), a certain Mairan presents a paper on pendulums at the Académie Royale des Sciences. In 1756 (the year the Templar Strict Observance originates in Germany!), a certain Bouguer writes *Sur la direction qu'affectent tous les fils à plomb*.

I found phantasmagorical titles, like that by Jean Baptiste Biot in 1821: *Recueil d'observations géodésiques, astronomiques et physiques, exécutées par ordre du Bureau des Longitudes de France, en Espagne, en France, en Angleterre et en Ecosse, pour déterminer la variation de la pésanteur et des degrès terrestres sur le prolongement du méridien de Paris*. In France, Spain, England, and Scotland! And referring to the meridian of Saint-Martin! And what about Sir Edward Sabine, who in 1823 publishes *An Account of Experiments to Determine the Figure of the Earth by Means of the Pendulum Vibrating Seconds in Different Latitudes*? And the mysterious Graf Feodor Petrovich Litke, who in 1836 publishes the results of his research into the behavior of the pendulum in the course of a voyage around the world? This under the auspices of the Imperial Academy of Sciences of St. Petersburg. The Russians, too?

And what if in the meantime a group, no doubt of Baconian descent, decides to discover the secret of the currents without map or pendulum, relying instead on the source, the respiration of the Serpent? Salon's hunch was right, for it was more or less at the time of Foucault that the industrial world, creature of the Baconian camp, began digging underground systems in the heart of the great cities of Europe.

"It's true," Belbo said, "the nineteenth century is obsessed with the underground—Jean Valjean, Fantomas and Javert, Rocambole, all that coming and going in sewers and tunnels. My God, now that I think of it, all of Verne is an occult revelation of the mysteries of the underground! The voyage to the center of the earth, twenty thousand leagues under the sea, the caverns of the Mysterious Island, the immense underground realm of the Black Indies! If we drew a diagram of his extraordinary travels, we would be sure to obtain, finally, a sketch of the coils of the Serpent, a chart of the leys drawn for each continent. Verne explores the network of the telluric currents from above and below."

I collaborated. "What's the name of the hero of the Black Indies? John Garral. Close to Grail."

"We're not ivory-tower eggheads; we're men with our feet on the ground. Verne gives even more explicit signals. Robur le Conquérant, R.C., Rosy Cross. And Robur read backward is Rubor, the red of the rose."

85

Phileas Fogg. A name that is also a signature: *Eas,* in Greek, has the sense of the global (it is therefore the equivalent of *pan,* of *poly,*) and Phileas is the same as Polyphile. As for Fogg, it is the English for brouillard . . . and no doubt Verne belonged to "Le Brouillard." He was even kind enough to indicate the relationship between this society and the Rose + Cross, because what, enfin, is our noble traveler Phileas Fogg if not a Rose + Cross? . . . And further, doesn't he belong to the Reform Club, whose initials, R.C., designate the reforming Rose + Cross? And this Reform Club stands in Pall Mall, suggesting once again the Dream of Polyphile.

    —Michel Lamy, *Jules Verne, initié et initiateur,* Paris, Payot,
      1984, pp. 237–238

The reconstruction took us days and days. We would interrupt our work to confide in one another the latest connection. We read everything we could lay our hands on—encyclopedias, newspapers, cartoon strips, publishers' catalogs—and read it squinting, seeking possible shortcuts. At every bookstall we stopped and rummaged; we sniffed newsstands, stole abundantly from the manuscripts of our Diabolicals, rushed triumphantly into the office, slamming the latest find on a desk. As I recall those weeks, everything seems to have taken place at a frenzied pace, as in a Keystone Kops film, all jerks and jumps, with doors opening and closing at supersonic speed, cream pies flying, dashes up flights of steps, up and down, back and forth, old cars crashing, shelves collapsing in grocery stores amid avalanches of cans, bottles, soft cheeses, spurting siphons, exploding flour sacks. Yet the intermissions, the idle moments—the rest of life going on around us—I remember as a story in slow motion, the Plan taking gradual shape with the discipline of gymnastics, or like the slow rotation of the discus thrower, the cautious sway of the shot-putter, the long tempos of golf, the senseless waits of baseball. But whatever the rhythm was, luck rewarded us, because, wanting connections, we found connections—always, everywhere, and between everything. The world exploded into a whirling network of kinships, where everything pointed to everything else, everything explained everything else. . . .

I said nothing about it to Lia, to avoid irritating her, and I even neglected Giulio. I would wake up in the middle of the night with the realization, for example, that René des Cartes could make R.C. and that he had been overenergetic in seeking and then denying having found the Rosicrucians. Why all that obsession with Method? Because it was through Method that you arrived at the solution to the mystery that was fascinating all the initiates of Europe. . . . And who had celebrated the enchantment of Gothic? René de Chateaubriand. And who, in Bacon's time, wrote *Steps to the Temple*? Richard Crashaw. And what about Ranieri de' Calzabigi, René Char, Raymond Chandler? And Rick of Casablanca?

86

This science, which was not lost, at least as far as its practice was concerned, was taught to the cathedral builders by the monks of Cîteaux. . . . They were known, in the last century, as Compagnons du Tour de France. It was to them that Eiffel turned to build his tower.
  —L. Charpentier, *Les mystères de la cathédrale de Chartres*,
    Paris, Laffont, 1966, pp. 55–56

Now we had the entire modern age filled with industrious moles tunneling through the earth, spying on the planet from below. But there had to be something else, another venture the Baconians had set in motion, whose results, whose stages were before everyone's eyes, though no one had noticed them. . . . The ground had been punctured and the deep strata tested, but the Celts and the Templars had not confined themselves to digging wells; they had planted their stations and aimed them straight at the heavens, to communicate from megalith to megalith, and to catch the influences of the stars.

The idea came to Belbo during a night of insomnia. He leaned out the window and saw in the distance, above the roofs of Milan, the lights of the steel tower of the Italian Radio, the great city antenna. A moderate, prudent Babel. And he understood.

"The Eiffel Tower," he said to us the next morning. "Why didn't we think of it before? The metal megalith, the menhir of the last Celts, the hollow spire taller than all Gothic spires. What need did Paris have of this useless monument? It's the celestial probe, the antenna that collects information from every hermetic valve stuck into the planet's crust: the statues of Easter Island; Machu Picchu; the Statue of Liberty, conceived first by the initiate Lafayette; the obelisk of Luxor; the highest tower of Tomar; the Colossus of Rhodes, which still transmits from the depths of a harbor that no one can find; the temples of the Brahman jungle; the turrets of the Great Wall; the top of Ayers Rock; the spires of Strasbourg, which so delighted the initiate Goethe; the faces of Mount Rushmore—how much the initiate Hitchcock understood!—and the TV antenna of the Empire State Building. And tell me to what empire this creation of American initiates refers if not the empire of Rudolf of Prague! The Eiffel Tower picks up signals from underground and compares them with what comes from the sky. And who is it who gave us the first, terrifying movie image of the Tour Eiffel? René Clair, in *Paris qui dort*. René Clair, R.C."

The entire history of science had to be reread. Even the space race became comprehensible, with those crazy satellites that did nothing but photograph the crust of the globe to localize invisible tensions, submarine tides, currents of warmer air. And speak among themselves, speak to the Tower, to Stonehenge . . .

87

When we traded the results of our fantasies, it seemed to us—and
rightly—that we had proceeded by unwarranted associations, by
shortcuts so extraordinary that, if anyone had accused us of really
believing them, we would have been ashamed. We consoled ourselves with the realization—unspoken, now, respecting the etiquette
of irony—that we were parodying the logic of our Diabolicals. But
during the long intervals in which each of us collected evidence to
produce at the plenary meetings, and with the clear conscience of
those who accumulate material for a medley of burlesques, our brains
grew accustomed to connecting, connecting, connecting everything
with everything else, until we did it automatically, out of habit. I
believe that you can reach the point where there is no longer any
difference between developing the habit of pretending to believe and
developing the habit of believing.

It's the old story of spies: they infiltrate the secret service of the
enemy, they develop the habit of thinking like the enemy, and if
they survive, it's because they've succeeded. And before long, pre-
dictably, they go over to the other side, because it has become theirs.
Or take those who live alone with a dog. They speak to him all day
long; first they try to understand the dog, then they swear the dog
understands them, he's shy, he's jealous, he's hypersensitive; next
they're teasing him, making scenes, until they're sure he's become
just like them, human, and they're proud of it, but the fact is that
they have become just like him: they have become canine.

Perhaps because I was in daily contact with Lia, and with the
baby, I was, of the three, the least affected by the game. I was
convinced I was its master; I felt as if I were again playing the agogô
during the rite in Brazil: you stay on the side of those who control

the emotions and not with those who are controlled by them. About Diotallevi, I didn't know then; I know now. He was training himself viscerally to think like a Diabolical. As for Belbo, he was identifying at a more conscious level. I was becoming addicted, Diotallevi was becoming corrupted, Belbo was becoming converted. But all of us were slowly losing that intellectual light that allows you always to tell the similar from the identical, the metaphorical from the real. We were losing that mysterious and bright and most beautiful ability to say that Signor A has grown bestial—without thinking for a moment that he now has fur and fangs. The sick man, however, thinking "bestial," immediately sees Signor A on all fours, barking or grunting.

In Diotallevi's case—as we would have realized if we hadn't been so excited ourselves—it began when he returned at the end of the summer. He seemed thinner, but it wasn't that healthy thinness of someone who has spent a few weeks hiking in the mountains. His delicate albino skin now had a yellowish cast. Perhaps we thought, if we noticed at all, that he had spent his vacation poring over rabbinic scrolls. But our minds were on other things.

In the days that followed, we were able to account also for the camps opposed to the Baconian.

For example, current Masonic studies believe that the Illuminati of Bavaria, who advocated the destruction of nations and the destabilization of the state, inspired not only the anarchism of Bakunin but also Marxism itself. Puerile. The Illuminati were provocateurs; they were Baconians who had infiltrated the Teutonics. Marx and Engels had something quite different in mind when they began their Manifesto of 1848 with the eloquent sentence "A specter is haunting Europe." Why this Gothic metaphor? *The Communist Manifesto* is alluding sarcastically to the secret hunt for the Plan, which has agitated the continent for centuries. The *Manifesto* suggests an alternative both to the Baconians and to the neo-Templars. Marx, a Jew, perhaps initially the spokesman for the rabbis of Gerona or Safed, tries to involve the entire Chosen People in the search. But then the project possesses him, and he identifies the Shekhinah—the exiled people in the Kingdom—with the proletariat, and thus, betraying the expectations of those who taught him, he turns all Messianic Judaism on its head. Templars of the world, unite! The map to the workers! Splendid! What better historical justification for Communism?

"Yes," Belbo said, "but the Baconians also run into trouble along the way; don't think they don't. Some of them set out for the superhighway of science and end up in a blind alley. At the end of the dynasty, the Einsteins and the Fermis, after hunting for the secret in the heart of the microcosm, stumble upon the wrong invention: instead of telluric energy—clean, natural, sapiential—they discover atomic energy—technological, unnatural, polluted. . . ."

"Space-time: the error of the West," Diotallevi said.

"It's the loss of the Center. Vaccine and penicillin as caricatures of the Elixir of Eternal Life," I added.

"Or like that other Templar, Freud," Belbo said, "who instead of probing the labyrinths of the physical underground, probed those of the psychic underground, as if everything about them hadn't already been said, and better, by the alchemists."

"But you're the one," Diotallevi objected, "who is trying to publish the books of Dr. Wagner. For me, psychoanalysis is for neurotics."

"Yes, and the penis is nothing but a phallic symbol," I concluded. "Come, gentlemen, let's not digress. And let's not waste time. We still don't know where to put the Paulicians and the Jerusalemites."

But before we were able to answer this question, we came upon another group, one that, not part of the thirty-six invisibles, had nevertheless entered the game at quite an early stage, somewhat upsetting its designs, causing confusion: the Jesuits.

88

The Baron Hundt, Chevalier Ramsay . . . and numerous others
who founded the grades in these rites, worked under instructions
from the general of the Jesuits. . . . Templarism is Jesuitism.
—Letter to Madame Blavatsky from Charles Southeran, 32 ∴
A and P.R. 94 ∴ Memphis, K.R. ✠, K. Kadosch, M.M.
104, Eng., etc. Initiate of the English Brotherhood of the
Rosicrucians and other secret societies, January 11, 1877;
from *Isis Unveiled*, 1877, vol. ii, p. 390

We had run into them too often, from the time of the first Rosicrucian manifestoes on. As early as 1620, in Germany, the *Rosa Jesuitica* appears, reminding us that the symbolism of the rose was Catholic and Marian before it was Rosicrucian, and the hint is made that the two orders are in league, that Rosicrucianism is only a reformulation of the Jesuit mystique for consumption in Reformation Germany.

I remembered what Salon had said about Father Kircher's rancorous attack on the Rosicrucians—right in the middle of his discourse on the depths of the terraqueous globe.

"Father Kircher," I said, "is a central character in this story. Why would this man, who so often showed a gift for observation and a taste for experiment, drown these few good ideas in thousands of pages overflowing with incredible hypotheses? He was in correspondence with the best English scientists. Each of his books deals with typical Rosicrucian subjects, ostensibly to contest them, actually to espouse them, offering his own Counter Reformation version. In the first edition of the *Fama*, Herr Haselmayer, condemned to the galleys by the Jesuits because of his reforming ideas, hastens to say that the Rosicrucians are the true Jesuits. Very well. Kircher writes his thirty-odd volumes to argue that the Jesuits are the true Rosicrucians. The Jesuits are trying to get their hands on the Plan. Kircher wants to study those pendulums himself, and he does, in his own way. He invents a planetary clock that will give the exact time in all the headquarters of the Society of Jesus scattered throughout the world."

"But how did the Jesuits know of the Plan, when the Templars let themselves be killed rather than reveal it?" Diotallevi asked.

It was no good answering that the Jesuits always know everything. We needed a more seductive explanation.

We quickly found one. Guillaume Postel again. Leafing through the history of the Jesuits by Crétineau-Joly (and how we chuckled over that unfortunate name), we learned that in 1554 Postel, in a fit of mystical fervor and thirst for spiritual regeneration, joined Ignatius Loyola in Rome. Ignatius welcomed him with open arms, but Postel was unable to part with his manias, his cabalism, his ecumenicalism, and the Jesuits couldn't accept these things, especially one mania that Postel absolutely refused to abandon: the idea that the King of the World was the king of France. Ignatius may have been a saint, but he was also Spanish.

So at last a rupture came about; Postel left the Jesuits—or the Jesuits kicked him out. But since he had been a Jesuit, even if only briefly, he had sworn obedience perinde ac cadaver to Saint Ignatius, and therefore must have revealed to him his mission. "Dear Ignatius," he must have said, "in receiving me you receive also the secret of the Templar Plan, whose unworthy representative I am in France, and indeed, while we are all awaiting the third centenary meeting in 1584, we might as well await it ad majorem Dei gloriam."

So the Jesuits, thanks to Postel's moment of weakness, come to know the secret of the Templars. This knowledge must be exploited. Saint Ignatius goes to his eternal reward, but his successors remain watchful. They keep an eye on Postel; they want to know whom he will meet in that fateful year 1584. But, alas, Postel dies before then. Nor is it any help that—as one of our sources tells us—an unknown Jesuit is present at his deathbed. The Jesuits do not learn who his successor is.

"I'm sorry, Casaubon," Belbo said, "but something here doesn't add up. If what you say is true, the Jesuits couldn't know that the meeting failed to come off in 1584."

"Don't forget that the Jesuits," Diotallevi remarked, "were men of iron, not easily fooled."

"Ah, as for that," Belbo said, "a Jesuit could eat two Templars for breakfast and another two for dinner. They also were disbanded, and more than once, and all the governments of Europe lent a hand, but they're still here."

We had to put ourselves in a Jesuit's shoes. What would a Jesuit do if Postel slipped from his grasp? I had an idea immediately, but it was so diabolical that not even our Diabolicals, I thought, would swallow it: The Rosicrucians were an invention of the Jesuits!

"After Postel's death," I argued, "the Jesuits—clever as they are—mathematically foresee the confusion of the calendars and decide to take the initiative. They set up this Rosicrucian red herring, calculating exactly what will happen. Among all the fanatics who swallow the bait, someone from one of the genuine groups, caught off guard, will come forward. Imagine the fury of Bacon: 'Fludd, you idiot, couldn't you have kept your mouth shut?' 'But, my lord, they seemed to be with us. . . .' 'Fool, weren't you taught never to trust papists? They should have burned you, not that poor wretch from Nola!'"

"But in that case," Belbo said, "when the Rosicrucians move to France, why do the Jesuits, or those polemicists in their hire, attack the newcomers as heretics possessed by devils?"

"Surely you don't expect the Jesuits to work in a straightforward way. What sort of Jesuits would they be then?"

We quarreled at length over my proposal and finally decided, unanimously, that the original hypothesis was better: The Rosicrucians were the bait cast, for the French, by the Baconians and the Germans. But the Jesuits, as soon as the manifestoes appeared, caught on. And they immediately joined in the game, to muddy the waters. Obviously, the Jesuits' aim was to prevent the English and German groups from meeting with the French; and to that end any trick would do, no matter how dirty.

Meanwhile, they recorded events, gathered information, and put it all—where? In Abulafia, Belbo joked. But Diotallevi, who had been gathering information himself, said it was no joke. Surely the Jesuits were constructing an immense, tremendously powerful computer that would draw a conclusion from this patiently accumulated, age-old brew of truth and falsehood.

"The Jesuits," Diotallevi said, "understood what neither the poor old Templars of Provins nor the Baconian camp had yet realized, namely, that the reconstruction of the map could be accomplished by ars combinatoria; in other words, with a method that foreshad-

EPILOGISMUS

Combinationis Lineʒris.

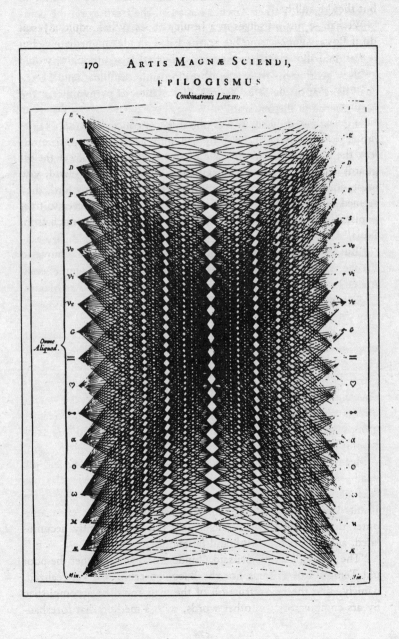

owed our modern electronic brains. The Jesuits were the first to invent Abulafia! Father Kircher reread all the treatises on the combinatorial art, from Lullus on, and you see what he published in his *Ars Magna Sciendi.* . . ."

"It looks like a crochet pattern to me," Belbo said.

"No, gentlemen, these are all the possible combinations. Factor analysis, that of the *Sefer Yesirah*. Calculation of permutations, the very essence of the temurah!"

This was certainly so. It was one thing to conceive Fludd's vague project of identifying the map by beginning with a polar projection; it was quite another to figure out how many trials would be required in order to arrive at the correct solution. And, again, it was one thing to create an abstract model of all the possible combinations, and another to invent a machine able to carry them out. So both Kircher and his disciple Schott built mechanical devices, mechanisms with perforated cards, computers ante litteram. Binary calculators. Cabala applied to modern technology.

IBM: Iesus Babbage Mundi, Iesum Binarium Magnificamur. AMDG: Ad Maiorem Dei Gloriam? Not on your life! Ars Magna, Digitale Gaudium! IHS: Iesus Hardware & Software!

89

In the bosom of the deepest darkness a society has been formed, a society of new beings, who know one another though they have never seen one another, who understand one another without explanations, who serve one another without friendship. . . . From the Jesuit rule this society adopts blind obedience; from the Masons it takes the trials and the ceremonies, and from the Templars the subterranean mysteries and the great audacity. Has the Comte de Saint-Germain simply imitated Guillaume Postel, who desperately wanted people to believe him older than he was?

—Marquis de Luchet, *Essai sur la secte des illuminés*, Paris, 1789, v and xii

The Jesuits knew that if you want to confound your enemies, the best technique is to create clandestine sects, wait for dangerous enthusiasms to precipitate, then arrest them all. In other words, if you fear a plot, organize one yourself; that way, all those who join it come under your control.

I remembered the reservation Agliè had expressed about Ramsay, the first to posit a direct connection between the Masons and the Templars; Agliè said that Ramsay had ties with Catholic circles. In fact, Voltaire had already denounced Ramsay as a tool of the Jesuits. Faced with the birth of English Freemasonry, the Jesuits in France responded with Scottish neo-Templarism.

Responding to this French plot, a certain Marquis de Luchet produced, in 1789, anonymously, *Essai sur la secte des illuminés*, in which he lashed out against the Illuminati of every stripe, Bavarian or otherwise, priest-baiting anarchists and mystical neo-Templars alike, and he threw on the heap (incredible, how all the pieces of our mosaic were fitting together!) even the Paulicians, even Postel and Saint-Germain. His complaint was that these forms of Templar mysticism were undermining the credibility of Masonry, which in contrast was a society of good and honest people.

The Baconians had invented Masonry to be like Rick's in Casablanca, Jesuit neo-Templarism had parried that move, and now Luchet was hired to bump off all the groups that weren't Baconian.

At this point, however, we were confronted with another problem, which was too much for poor Agliè to handle. Why had de Maistre, who was the Jesuits' man, gone to Wilhelmsbad to sow dissension among the neo-Templars a good seven years before the Marquis de Luchet appeared on the scene?

"Neo-Templarism was all right in the first half of the eighteenth century," Belbo said, "and it was all wrong at the end of the century; first because it had been taken over by revolutionaries, for whom anything served, the Goddess Reason, the Supreme Being, even Cagliostro, provided they could cut off the king's head, and second because the German princes were now putting their thumbs in the pie, especially Frederick of Prussia, and his aims surely didn't correspond to those of the Jesuits. When mystical neo-Templarism, whoever invented it, began producing things like *The Magic Flute*, Loyola's men naturally decided to wipe it out. It's like high finance: you buy a company, you sell off its assets, you declare bankruptcy, you close it down, and you reinvest its capital. The important thing is the overall strategy, not what happens to the janitor. Or it's like a used car: when it stops running, you send it to the junkyard."

90

In the true Masonic code no other god will be found save Mani. He is the god of the cabalist Masons, of the ancient Rosicrucians, of the Martinist Masons. . . . All the outrages attributed to the Templars are precisely those attributed, before them, to the Manicheans.
—Abbé Barruel, *Mémoires pour servir à l'histoire du jacobinisme*, Hamburg, 1798, 2, xiii

The Jesuits' strategy became clear to us when we discovered Father Barruel. Between 1797 and 1798, in response to the French Revolution, he writes his *Mémoires pour servir à l'histoire du jacobinisme*, a real dime novel that begins, surprise surprise, with the Templars. After the burning of Molay, they transform themselves into a secret society to destroy monarchy and papacy and to create a world republic. In the eighteenth century they take over Freemasonry and make it their instrument. In 1763 they create a literary academy consisting of Voltaire, Turgot, Condorcet, Diderot, and d'Alembert, which meets in the house of Baron d'Holbach and in 1776, plot after plot, they bring about the birth of the Jacobins. But they are mere marionettes, their strings pulled by the real bosses, the Illuminati of Bavaria—regicides by vocation.

Junkyard? After having split Masonry in two with the help of Ramsay, the Jesuits were putting it together again in order to fight it head-on.

Barruel's book had some influence; in fact, in the French National Archives there were at least two reports ordered by Napoleon on the clandestine sects. These reports were drawn up by a certain Charles de Berkheim, who—in the best tradition of secret police—obtained his information from sources already published; he copied freely, first from the book by the Marquis de Luchet and then from Barruel's.

Reading these horrifying descriptions of the Illuminati as well as the denunciation of a directorate of Unknown Superiors capable of ruling the world, Napoleon did not hesitate: he decided to join them.

He had his brother Joseph named grand master of the Great Orient, and he himself, according to many sources, made contact with the Masons and became a very high official in their ranks. It is not known, however, in which rite. Perhaps, prudently, in all of them.

We had no idea what Napoleon knew, but we weren't forgetting that he had spent time in Egypt, and God knows what sages he conversed with in the shadow of the pyramids (even a child could see that the famous forty centuries there looking down on him were a clear reference to the Hermetic Tradition).

Napoleon must have known something, because in 1806 he convoked an assembly of French Jews. The official reasons were banal: an attempt to reduce usury, to assure himself of the loyalty of the Jewish population, to find new financing. . . . None of which explains why he called that assembly the Grand Sanhedrin, a name suggesting a directorate of superiors more or less unknown. The truth is that the shrewd Corsican had identified the representatives of the Jerusalemite branch, and was trying to unite the various scattered Templar groups.

"It's no accident that in 1808 Maréchal Ney's troops are at Tomar. You see the connection?"

"We're here to see connections."

"Now Napoleon, about to defeat England, has almost all the European centers in his hand, and through the French Jews he has the Jerusalemites as well. What does he still lack?"

"The Paulicians."

"Exactly. And we haven't yet decided where they end up. But Napoleon provides us with a clue: he goes to look for them in Russia."

Living for centuries in Slavic regions, the Paulicians naturally reorganize under the labels of various Russian mystic groups. One of the most influential advisers of Alexander I is Prince Galitzin, connected with sects of Martinist inspiration. And who do we find in Russia, a good ten years before Napoleon, as plenipotentiary of the House of Savoy, tying bonds with the mystic cénacles of St. Petersburg? De Maistre.

At this point de Maistre distrusts any organization of Illuminati; for him, they are no different from the men of the Enlightenment responsible for the bloodbath of the Revolution. During this period, in fact, repeating Barruel almost word for word, he talks of a satanic sect that wants to conquer the world, and probably he has Napoleon in mind. If our great reactionary is aiming, then, to seduce the Martinist groups, it is because he suspects that they, though drawing their inspiration from the same sources as French and German neo-Templarism, are the heirs of the one group not yet corrupted by Western thought: the Paulicians.

But apparently de Maistre's plan does not succeed. In 1815 the Jesuits are expelled from St. Petersburg, and de Maistre returns to Turin.

"All right," Diotallevi said, "we've found the Paulicians again. Let's get rid of Napoleon, who obviously failed in his purpose—otherwise, on St. Helena, he could have made his enemies quake by merely snapping his fingers. What happens now among all these people? My head is splitting."

"At least you still have a head."

91

Oh, how well you have unmasked those infernal sects that are preparing the way for the Antichrist. . . . But there is still one sect
that you have touched only lightly.
—Letter from Captain Simonini to Barruel, published in
La civiltà cattolica, October 21, 1882

Napoleon's rapprochement with the Jews caused the Jesuits to alter
their course. Barruel's *Mémoires* had contained no reference to the
Jews. But in 1806 he received a letter from a certain Captain Simonini, who reminded him that Mani and the Old Man of the Mountain
were also Jews, that Masonry had been founded by the Jews, and
that the Jews had infiltrated all the existing secret societies.

Simonini's letter, shrewdly circulated in Paris, was an embarrassment for Napoleon, who had just got in touch with the Grand Sanhedrin. This move obviously alarmed the Paulicians too, because the
Holy Synod of the Russian Orthodox Church declared: "Napoleon
now proposes to unite all the Jews, whom the wrath of God has
scattered over the face of the earth, so that they will overturn the
church of Christ and proclaim Napoleon the true Messiah."

The good Barruel accepted the idea that the plot was not only
Masonic but also Judeo-Masonic. Further, this satanic element allowed him to attack a new enemy: the Alta Vendita Carbonara, and
later the anticlerical fathers of the Risorgimento, from Mazzini to
Garibaldi.

"But this all happens in the middle of the nineteenth century,"
Diotallevi said, "whereas the big anti-Semitic campaign gets under
way at the end of the century, with the publication of the *Protocols
of the Learned Elders of Zion*. And the Protocols appear in Russia.
So they are an initiative of the Paulicians."

"Naturally," Belbo said. "It's clear now that the Jerusalemite group
had broken up into three branches. The first branch, through the
Spanish and Provençal cabalists, went on to inspire the neo-Templar
camp; the second was taken over by the Baconian wing, and they
all became scientists and bankers. They're the ones the Jesuits op-

pose so fiercely. But there is a third branch, and it established itself in Russia. The Russian Jews are generally small tradesmen and moneylenders, and for that reason are hated by the impoverished peasants; but since Jewish culture is a culture of the Book, and all Jews know how to read and write, they eventually swell the ranks of the liberal and revolutionary intelligentsia. The Paulicians, in contrast, are mystics, reactionaries, hand in glove with the landowners, and they have also infiltrated the court. Obviously, between them and the Jerusalemites there can be no traffic. So they are bent on discrediting the Jews, and through the Jews—this they learned from the Jesuits—they cause trouble for their adversaries abroad, both the neo-Templars and the Baconians."

92

There can no longer be any doubt. With all the power and the terror of Satan, the reign of the triumphant King of Israel is approaching our unregenerate world; the King born from the blood of Zion, the Antichrist, approaches the throne of universal power.

—Sergei Nilus, *Epilogue to the Protocols*

The idea was acceptable. We had only to consider who had introduced the Protocols in Russia.

One of the most influential Martinists at the end of the century, Papus, dazzled Nicholas II during his visit to Paris, then went to Moscow, taking with him one Philippe Nizier Anselme Vachot. Possessed by the Devil at the age of six, healer at thirteen, magnetizer in Lyon, Philippe fascinated both Nicholas II and his hysterical wife. He was invited to court, named physician of the military academy of St. Petersburg, made a general and a councilor of state.

His enemies decided to diminish his influence by setting against him an equally charismatic figure. And Nilus was found.

Nilus was an itinerant monk who, in priestly habit, wandered in the forests (what else?) displaying a prophet's great beard, two wives, a little daughter, an assistant (or lover, perhaps), all hanging on his every word. Half guru, the kind that runs off with the collection plate, and half hermit, the kind that yells that the end is near, he was in fact obsessed by the Antichrist.

The plan of Nilus's supporters was to have him ordained, and then, after he married (what was another wife, more or less?) Elena Alexandrovna Ozerova, the tsarina's maid of honor, to have him become the confessor of the sovereigns.

"I'm anything but a bloodthirsty man," Belbo said, "but I begin to feel that the massacre of Tsarskoye Selo was perhaps a justifiable extermination of vermin."

Anyway, Philippe's supporters accused Nilus of leading a lewd life, and God knows they were right. Nilus had to leave the court, but at this point someone came to his aid, handing him the text of the Protocols. Since everybody got the Martinists (who derived from

Saint Martin) mixed up with the Martínezists (followers of Martínez Pasqualis, whom Agliè so dislikes), and since Pasqualis, according to a widespread rumor, was Jewish, by discrediting the Jews the Protocols also discredited the Martinists, and with the discrediting of the Martinists, Philippe was booted out.

Actually, a first, incomplete, version of the Protocols had already appeared in 1903, in *Znamia*, a St. Petersburg paper edited by a rabid anti-Semite named Kruscevan. In 1905, with the approval of the government censors, a complete text anonymously appeared, under the title *The Source of Our Evils*, edited by one Boutmi, who with Kruscevan had founded the Union of the Russian People, later known as the Black Hundreds, which enlisted common criminals to carry out pogroms and extremist right-wing acts of violence. Boutmi later published, under his own name, further editions of the work, with the title *The Enemies of the Human Race: Protocols from the Secret Archives of the Central Chancellery of Zion.*

But these were cheap booklets. An expanded version of the Protocols, the one that was to be translated all over the world, came out in 1905, in the third edition of Nilus's book, *The Great in the Small: The Antichrist Is an Imminent Political Possibility,* Tsarskoye Selo, under the aegis of a local chapter of the Red Cross. The scope was broader, the framework that of mystical reflection, and the book ended up in the hands of the tsar. The metropolitan of Moscow ordered it read aloud in all the churches of the city.

"But what," I asked, "is the connection between the Protocols and our Plan? We keep talking about these Protocols. Should we read them?"

"Nothing could be simpler," Diotallevi said. "There's always someone who reprints them. Publishers used to do it with a great show of indignation, purely out of a sense of duty to make available a historical document, then little by little they stopped apologizing and reprinted it with unrepentant pleasure."

"What genteel gentiles."

93

The only society known to us that is capable of rivaling us in these arts is that of the Jesuits. But we have succeeded in discrediting the Jesuits in the eyes of the stupid populace, because that society is an open organization, whereas we stay in the wings, maintaining secrecy.

—*Protocols*, v

The Protocols are a series of twenty-four declarations, a program of action, attributed to the Elders of Zion. To us, these Elders' intentions seemed somewhat contradictory. At one point they wanted to abolish freedom of the press, at another they seemed to encourage libertinage. They criticized liberalism, but supported the sort of thing today's leftist radicals attribute to the capitalist multinationals, including the use of sports and visual education to stultify the working class. They analyzed various methods of seizing world power; they praised the strength of gold; they advocated supporting revolution in every country, sowing discontent and confusion by proclaiming liberal ideas, but they also wanted to exacerbate inequality. They schemed to establish everywhere regimes of straw men they would control; they fomented war and urged the production of arms and (as Salon had said) the building of métros (the underground world!) in order to have a way of mining the big cities.

They said the end justified the means and were in favor of anti-Semitism both to control the population of Jewish poor and to soften the hearts of gentiles in the face of Jewish tragedy (an expensive ploy, Diotallevi said, but effective). They candidly declared, "We have unlimited ambition, an all-consuming greed, a merciless desire for revenge, and an intense hatred" (displaying an exquisite masochism by reinforcing, with gusto, the cliché of the evil Jew that was already in circulation in the anti-Semitic press, the stereotype that would adorn the cover of all the editions of their book). They called for abolishment of the study of the classics and of ancient history.

"In other words," Belbo said, "the Elders of Zion were a bunch of blockheads."

"Don't joke," Diotallevi said. "This book was taken very seriously. But there's something that strikes me as odd. While the Jewish plot was meant to seem centuries old, all the references in the Protocols are to petty fin-de-siècle French questions. The business about visual education stultifying the masses is a clear allusion to the educational program of Léon Bourgeois, who had five Masons in his government. Another passage advises electing people compromised in the Panama Scandal, and one of these was Emile Loubet, who in 1899 became president of the French republic. The Métro is mentioned because in those days the right-wing papers were complaining that the Compagnie du Métropolitain had too many Jewish shareholders. Hence the theory that the text was cobbled up in France in the last decade of the nineteenth century, at the time of the Dreyfus Affair, to weaken the liberal front."

"That isn't what impresses me," Belbo said. "It's the sense of déjà vu. The upshot is that these Elders are planning to conquer the world, and we've heard all that before. Take away the references to events and problems of the last century, replace the tunnels of the Métro with the tunnels of Provins, and everywhere it says Jews write Templars, and everywhere it says Elders of Zion write Thirty-six Invisibles divided into six. . . . My friends, this is the Ordonation of Provins!"

94

Voltaire lui-même est mort jésuite: en avoit-il le moindre soupçon?
—F. N. de Bonneville, *Les Jésuites chassés de la Maçonnerie
et leur poignard brisé par les Maçons*, Orient de Londres,
1788, 2, p. 74

All along it had been right in front of us, the whole thing, and we had failed to see it. Over six centuries, six groups fight to achieve the Plan of Provins, and each group takes the text of that Plan, simply changes the subject, and attributes it to its adversaries.

After the Rosicrucians turn up in France, the Jesuits reverse the Plan, replace it with its negative: discrediting the Baconians and the emerging English Masonry.

When the Jesuits invent neo-Templarism, the Marquis de Luchet attributes the Plan to the neo-Templars. The Jesuits, who by now are jettisoning the neo-Templars, copy Luchet, through Barruel, but they attribute the Plan to all Freemasons in general.

Then the Baconian counteroffensive. Digging into the texts of this liberal and secular polemic, we discovered that from Michelet and Quinet down to Garibaldi and Gioberti, the Ordonation was attributed to the Jesuits (perhaps that idea originated with the Templar Pascal and his friends). The subject was popularized by *Le Juif errant* of Eugène Sue and by his character, the evil Monsieur Rodin, quintessence of the Jesuit world conspiracy. But as we looked further into Sue, we found far more: a text that seemed copied—but half a century in advance—from the Protocols, almost word for word. This was the final chapter of *Les Mystères du peuple*, where the diabolical Jesuit plan is exposed down to the last criminal detail: in a document sent by the general of the Society, Father Roothaan (historical figure) to Monsieur Rodin (who appears in the earlier *Juif errant*). Rudolphe de Gerolstein (previously the hero of the *Mystères de Paris*) comes into possession of this document and reveals it to the other democracy-loving characters: "You see, my dear Lebrenn, how cunningly this infernal plot is ordered, and what frightful sorrows, what horrendous enslavement, what terrible despotism it would spell for Europe and the world, were it to succeed. . . ."

It seemed Nilus's preface to the Protocols. Sue also attributed to the Jesuits the motto (which will be found in the Protocols, attributed to the Jews), "The end justifies the means."

95

There is no need to multiply the evidence to prove that this degree of Rosy Cross was skillfully introduced by the leaders of Masonry. . . . The doctrine, its hatred, and its sacrilegious practices, exactly those of the Cabala, of the Gnostics, and of the Manicheans, reveals to us the identity of the authors, namely the Jewish Cabalists.

—Mons. Léon Meurin, S.J. *La Franc-Maçonnerie, Synagogue de Satan*, Paris, Retaux, 1893, p. 182

When *Les Mystères du peuple* appears and the Jesuits see that the Ordonation is attributed to them, they quickly adopt the one tactic not yet used by anyone. Exploiting Simonini's letter, they attribute the Ordonation to the Jews.

In 1869, Henri Gougenot de Mousseaux, famous for two books on magic, publishes *Les Juifs, le judaisme et la judaisation des peuples chrétiens*, which says that the Jews use the cabala and are worshipers of Satan, since a secret line of descent links Cain directly to the Gnostics, the Templars, and the Masons. Gougenot receives a special benediction from Pius IX.

But the Plan, novelized by Sue, is rehashed by others, who are not Jesuits. There's a nice story, almost a thriller, that takes place a bit later. In 1921—after the appearance of the Protocols, which it took very seriously—the *Times* of London learns that a Russian monarchist landowner who fled to Turkey has bought from a former officer of the Russian secret police, now a refugee in Constantinople, a number of old books, and among them is one without a cover. On its spine it has only "Joli," and there is a preface dated 1864. This is the source of the Protocols. The *Times* does some research in the British Museum and discovers the original book, by Maurice Joly, *Dialogue aux enfers entre Montesquieu et Machiavel*, Bruxelles (though it says Genève on the title page), 1864. Maurice Joly has no connection with Crétineau-Joly, but the similarity of the names must mean something.

Joly's book is a liberal pamphlet against Napoleon III, in which

Machiavelli, who represents the dictator's cynicism, argues with Montesquieu. Joly is arrested for this revolutionary venture, he serves fifteen years in prison, and in 1878 he kills himself. The Jewish plot enunciated in the Protocols is taken almost literally from the words Joly puts in Machiavelli's mouth (the end justifies the means); after Machiavelli, the words become Napoleon's. The *Times*, however, does not realize (but we do) that Joly had shamelessly copied Sue's document, which predates it by at least seven years.

An anti-Semite authoress, devotee of the plot theory and the Unknown Superiors, a certain Nesta Webster, faced by this development, which reduces the Protocols to the level of cheap plagiarism, provides us with a brilliant idea, the sort of idea that only a true initiate or initiate-hunter can have: Joly was an initiate, he knew the Plan of the Unknown Superiors, and attributed it to Napoleon III, whom he hated. But this does not mean that the Plan does not exist independently of Napoleon. Since the Plan outlined in the Protocols is a perfect description of the customary behavior of the Jews, then the Jews must have invented the Plan. We had only to reread Mrs. Webster in the light of her own logic: Since the Plan coincided exactly with what the Templars wanted, it was the Plan of the Templars.

Besides, we had the logic of facts on our side. We were particularly attracted by the episode in the Prague cemetery. This was the story of a certain Hermann Goedsche, an insignificant Prussian postal employee who published false documents to discredit the democrat Waldeck. The documents accused him of planning to assassinate the king of Prussia. Goedsche, after he was unmasked, became the editor of the organ of the big conservative landowners, *Die Preussische Kreuzzeitung*. Then, under the name Sir John Retcliffe, he began writing sensational novels, including *Biarritz*, 1868. In it he described an occultist scene in the Prague cemetery, very similar to the meeting of the Illuminati described by Dumas at the beginning of *Giuseppe Balsamo*, where Cagliostro, chief of the Unknown Superiors, among them Swedenborg, arranges the Affair of the Diamond Necklace. In the Prague cemetery the representatives of the twelve tribes of Israel gather, to expound their plans for the conquest of the world.

In 1876 a Russian pamphlet reprints the scene from *Biarritz*, but as if it were fact, not fiction. And in 1881, in France, *Le Contem-*

porain does the same thing, claiming that the news comes from an unimpeachable source: the English diplomat Sir John Readcliff. In 1896 one Bournand publishes a book, *Les Juifs, nos contemporains,* and repeats the scene of the Prague cemetery; he says that the subversive speech is made by the great rabbi John Readclif. A later version, however, reports that the real Readclif was taken to the fatal cemetery by Ferdinand Lassalle.

The plans revealed are more or less the same as described a few years earlier, in 1880, by the *Revue des Etudes Juives,* which publishes two letters attributed to Jews of the fifteenth century. The Jews of Arles ask the help of the Jews of Constantinople, because in France they are being persecuted, and the latter reply: "Well-beloved brothers in Moses, if the king of France forces you to become Christian, do so, because you cannot do otherwise, but preserve the law of Moses in your hearts. If they strip you of your possessions, raise your sons to be merchants, so that eventually they can strip Christians of their possessions. If they threaten your lives, raise your sons to be physicians and pharmacists, so that they can take the lives of Christians. If they destroy your synagogues, raise your sons to be canons and clerics, so that they can destroy the churches of the Christians. If they inflict other tribulations on you, raise your sons to be lawyers and notaries and have them mingle in the business of every state, so that putting the Christians under your yoke, you will rule the world and can then take your revenge."

It was, again, the Plan of the Jesuits and, before that, of the Ordonation of the Templars. Few variations, few changes: the Protocols were self-generating; a blueprint that migrated from one conspiracy to another.

And when we racked our brains to find the missing link that connected this whole fine story to Nilus, we encountered Rachkovsky, the head of the tsar's secret police, the terrible Okhrana.

96

A cover is always necessary. In concealment lies a great part of our strength. Hence we must always hide ourselves under the name of another society.
 —*Die neuesten Arbeiten des Spartacus und Philo in dem Illuminaten-Orden,* 1794, p. 165

At that same time, reading some pages of our Diabolicals, we found that the Comte de Saint-Germain, among his numerous disguises, had assumed the identity Rackoczi, at least according to the ambassador of Frederick II in Dresden. And the landgrave of Hesse, at whose residence Saint-Germain was supposed to have died, said that he was of Transylvanian origin and his name was Ragozki. We had also to consider that Comenius dedicated his *Pansophiae* (a work surely born in the odor of Rosicrucianism) to a landgrave (another landgrave) named Ragovsky. A final touch to the mosaic: browsing at a bookstall in Piazza Castello, I found a German work on Masonry, anonymous, in which an unknown hand had added, on the flyleaf, a note to the effect that the text was the work of one Karl Aug. Ragotgky. Bearing in mind that Rakosky was the name of the mysterious individual who had perhaps killed Colonel Ardenti, we now could include in the Plan our Comte de Saint-Germain.

"Aren't we giving that scoundrel too much power?" Diotallevi asked, concerned.

"No, no," Belbo replied, "we need him. Like soy sauce in Chinese dishes. If it's not there, it's not Chinese. Look at Agliè, who knows a thing or two: Did he take Cagliostro as his model? Or Willermoz? No. Saint-Germain is the quintessence of Homo Hermeticus."

Pierre Ivanovitch Rachkovsky: jovial, sly, feline, intelligent, and astute, a counterfeiter of genius. First a petty bureaucrat, later in contact with revolutionary groups, in 1879 he is arrested by the secret police and charged with having given refuge to terrorist companions after their attempted assassination of General Drentel. He becomes a police informer and (here we go!) joins the ranks of the

Black Hundreds. In 1890 he discovers in Paris an organization that makes bombs for demonstrations in Russia; he arranges the arrest, back home, of seventy-three terrorists. Ten years later, it is discovered that the bombs were made by his own men.

In 1887 he circulates a letter by a certain Ivanov, a repentant revolutionary, who declares that the majority of the terrorists are Jews; in 1890, a "confession par un veillard ancien révolutionnaire," in which the exiled revolutionaries in London are accused of being British agents; and in 1892, a bogus text of Plekhanov, which accuses the leaders of the Narodnaya Volya party of having had that confession published.

In 1902 he forms a Franco-Russian anti-Semitic league. To ensure its success he uses a technique similar to that of the Rosicrucians: he declares that the league exists, so that people will then create it. But he uses another tactic, too: he cleverly mixes truth with falsehood, the truth apparently damaging to him, so that nobody will doubt the falsehood. He circulates in Paris a mysterious appeal to support the Russian Patriotic League, headquarters in Kharkov. In the appeal he attacks himself as the man who wants to make the league fail, and he expresses the hope that he, Rachkovsky, will change his mind. He accuses himself of relying on discredited characters like Nilus, and this is true.

Why can the Protocols be attributed to Rachkovsky?

Rachkovsky's sponsor is Count Sergei Witte, a minister who desires to turn Russia into a modern country. Why the progressive Witte makes use of the reactionary Rachkovsky, God only knows; but at this point the three of us would have been surprised by nothing. Witte has a political opponent, Elie de Cyon, who has already attacked him publicly, making assertions that recall certain passages in the Protocols, except that in Cyon's writings there are no references to the Jews, since he is of Jewish origin himself. In 1897, at Witte's orders, Rachkovsky has Cyon's villa at Territat searched, and he finds a pamphlet by Cyon drawn from Joly's book (or Sue's), in which the ideas of Machiavelli–Napoleon III are attributed to Witte. With his genius for falsification, Rachkovsky substitutes the Jews for Witte and has the text circulated. The name Cyon is perfect, suggesting Zion, and now everybody sees that an eminent Jewish figure is denouncing a Jewish plot. This is how the Protocols are born. The text falls into the hands of Juliana or Justine Glinka, who in Paris frequents Madame Blavatsky's Parisian circle, and in her free time she spies on and denounces Russian revolutionaries in exile. This Glinka woman is undoubtedly an agent of the Paulicians, who are allied to the agrarians and therefore want to convince the tsar that Witte's programs are part of the international Jewish plot. Glinka sends the document to General Orgeievsky, and he, through the commander of the imperial guard, sees that it reaches the tsar. Witte is in trouble.

So Rachkovsky, driven by his anti-Semitism, contributes to the downfall of his sponsor. And probably to his own. Because from that moment on we lose all trace of him. But Saint-Germain perhaps donned new disguises, moved on to new reincarnations. Nevertheless, our story was plausible, rational, because it was backed by facts, it was true—as Belbo said, true as the Bible.

Which reminded me of what De Angelis had told me about the synarchy. The fine thing about the whole story—our story, and perhaps also History itself, as Belbo hinted, with feverish eyes, as he handed me his file cards—was that groups locked in mortal combat were slaughtering one another, each in turn using the other's weapons. "The first duty of a good spy," I remarked, "is to denounce as spies those whom he has infiltrated."

Belbo said: "I remember an incident in ***. At sunset, along a shady avenue, I always ran into this guy named Remo—or something like that—in a little black Balilla. Black mustache, curly black hair, black shirt, and black teeth, horribly rotten. And he would be kissing a girl. I was revolted by those black teeth kissing that beautiful blonde. I don't even remember what her face was like, but for me she was virgin and prostitute, the eternal feminine. And great was my revulsion." Instinctively he adopted a lofty tone to show irony, aware that he had allowed himself to be carried away by the innocent tenderness of the memory. "I asked myself why this Remo, who belonged to the Black Brigades, dared allow himself to be seen around like that, even in the periods when *** was not occupied by the Fascists. Someone whispered to me that he was a Fascist spy. However it was, one evening I saw him in the same black Balilla, with the same black teeth, kissing the same blonde, but now with a red kerchief around his neck and a khaki shirt. He had shifted to the Garibaldi Brigades. Everybody made a fuss over him, and he actually gave himself a nom de guerre: X9, like the Alex Raymond character whom I had read about in the *Avventuroso* comics. Bravo, X9, they said to him. . . . And I hated him more than ever, because he possessed the girl by popular consent. Those who said he was a Fascist spy among the partisans were probably men who wanted the girl themselves, so they cast suspicion on X9. . . ."

"And then what happened?"

"See here, Casaubon, why are you so interested in my life?"

"Because you make it sound like a folktale, and folktales are part of the collective imagination."

"Good point. One morning, X9 was driving along, out of his territory; maybe he had a date to meet the girl in the fields, to go beyond their kissing and pawing and show her that his prick was not as rotten as his teeth—I'm sorry, I still can't make myself love him. Anyway, the Fascists set a trap for him, captured him, took him into town, and at five o'clock the next morning, they shot him."

A pause. Belbo looked at his hands, which he had clasped, as if in prayer. Then he held them apart and said, "That was the proof that he wasn't a spy."

"The moral of the story?"

"Who said stories have to have a moral? But, now that I think about it, maybe the moral is that sometimes, to prove something, you have to die."

97

I am that I am.
　　—Exodus 3:14

Ego sum qui sum. An axiom of hermetic philosophy.
　　—Madame Blavatsky, *Isis Unveiled*, 1877, p. 1

　"Who are you?" three hundred voices asked as one, while
twenty swords flashed in the hands of the nearest ghosts. . . .
　"I am that I am," he said.
　　—Alexandre Dumas, *Giuseppe Balsamo*, ii

I saw Belbo the next morning. "Yesterday we sketched a splendid dime novel," I said to him. "But maybe, if we want to make a convincing Plan, we should stick closer to reality."

"What reality?" he asked me. "Maybe only cheap fiction gives us the true measure of reality. Maybe they've deceived us."

"How?"

"Making us believe that on one hand there is Great Art, which portrays typical characters in typical situations, and on the other hand you have the thriller, the romance, which portrays atypical characters in atypical situations. No true dandy, I thought, would have made love to Scarlett O'Hara or even to Constance Bonacieux or Princess Daisy. I played with the dime novel, in order to take a stroll outside of life. It comforted me, offering the unattainable. But I was wrong."

"Wrong?"

"Wrong. Proust was right: life is represented better by bad music than by a Missa solemnis. Great Art makes fun of us as it comforts us, because it shows us the world as the artists would like the world to be. The dime novel, however, pretends to joke, but then it shows us the world as it actually is—or at least the world as it will become. Women are a lot more like Milady than they are like Little Nell, Fu Manchu is more real than Nathan the Wise, and History is closer to what Sue narrates than to what Hegel projects. Shakespeare, Melville, Balzac, and Dostoyevski all wrote sensational fiction. What has taken place in the real world was predicted in penny dreadfuls."

"The fact is, it's easier for reality to imitate the dime novel than to imitate art. Being a Mona Lisa is hard work; becoming Milady follows our natural tendency to choose the easy way."

Diotallevi, silent until now, remarked: "Or our Agliè, for example. He finds it easier to imitate Saint-Germain than Voltaire."

"Yes," Belbo said, "and women find Saint-Germain more interesting than Voltaire."

Afterward, I found this file, in which Belbo translated our discussion into fictional form, amusing himself by reconstructing the story of Saint-Germain without adding anything of his own, only a few sentences here and there to provide transitions, in a furious collage of quotes, plagiarisms, borrowings, clichés. Once again, to escape the discomfort of History, Belbo wrote and reexamined life through a literary stand-in.

FILENAME: The Return of Saint-Germain

For five centuries now the avenging hand of the All-Powerful has driven me from deepest Asia all the way to this cold, damp land. I carry with me fear, despair, death. But no, I am the notary of the Plan, even if nobody else knows of it. I have seen things far more terrible; preparing the night of Saint Bartholomew was more irksome than the thing I am now preparing to do. Oh, why do my lips curl in this satanic smile? I am that I am. If only that wretch Cagliostro had not usurped from me even this last privilege.

But my triumph is near. Soapes, when I was Kelley, told me everything in the Tower of London. The secret is to become someone else.

By shrewd plotting I had Giuseppe Balsamo imprisoned in the fortress of San Leo, and I stole his secrets. Saint-Germain has vanished; now all believe I am the Conte di Cagliostro.

. . . .

Midnight is struck by all the clocks of the city. What unnatural peace. This silence does not persuade me. A beautiful evening, though cold; the high moon casts an icy glow over the

impenetrable alleys of old Paris. It is ten o'clock: the spire of
the abbey of the Black Friars has just tolled eight, slowly. The
wind with mournful creaks moves the iron weathercocks on the
desolate expanse of rooftops. A thick blanket of clouds covers
the sky.

Skipper, are we turning back? No. We're sinking! Damnation, the *Patna*'s going to the bottom. Jump, Seven Seas Jim,
jump! To be free of this anguish I'd give a diamond the size of
a walnut. Luff the mainsail, take the tiller, the topgallant, whatever you like, curse you, it's blowing up!

Horribly I clench the cloister of my teeth as a deathly pallor
flushes my green, waxen face.

How did I come here, I who am the very image of revenge?
The spirits of Hell will smile with contempt at the tears of the
creature whose menacing voice so often made them tremble even
in the womb of their fiery abyss.

Holla, lights!

How many steps did I come down to reach this den? Seven?
Thirty-six? There is no stone I grazed, no step taken that did
not hide a hieroglyph. When I have uncovered them all, the
Mystery will be revealed at last to my faithful followers. The
Message will be deciphered, its solution will be the Key, and to
the initiate, but only to the initiate, the Enigma will then be
revealed.

Between the Enigma and the deciphering of the Message, the
step is brief, and from it, radiant, the Hierogram will emerge,
upon which the Prayer of Interrogation will be defined. Then
the Arcanum will be drawn aside, the veil, the Egyptian tapestry
that covers the Pentacle. And thence to the light, to announce
the Occult Meaning of the Pentacle, the Cabalistic Question to
which only a few can reply, and to recite in a voice of thunder
the Impenetrable Sign. Bent over it, the Thirty-six Invisibles will
have to give the Answer, the uttering of the Rune whose Meaning is open only to the sons of Hermes. To them let the Mock-
ing Seal be given, the Mask behind which is outlined the
Countenance they seek to bare, the Mystic Rebus, the Sublime
Anagram. . . .

. . . .

"Sator Arepo!" I shout in a voice to make a specter tremble.
And Sator Arepo appears, abandoning the wheel he grips with
the clever hands of a murderer. At my command, he prostrates
himself. I recognize him, for I had already suspected his identity. He is Luciano, the handicapped shipping clerk, who the

Unknown Superiors have decreed will be the executor of my evil and bloody task.

"Sator Arepo," I ask mockingly, "do you know what is the Final Answer concealed behind the Sublime Anagram?"

"No, Count," the imprudent one replies. "I wait to learn it from your lips."

From my pale lips infernal laughter bursts and reechoes through the ancient vaults.

"Fool! Only the true initiate knows he does not know it!"

"Yes, master," the maimed clerk replies stupidly. "As you wish. I am ready."

We are in a squalid den in Clignancourt. This evening I must punish, first of all, you, who initiated me into the noble art of crime, who pretend to love me, and who, what is worse, believe you love me, along with the nameless enemies with whom you will spend the next weekend. Luciano, unwelcome witness of my humiliations, will lend me his arm—his one arm—then he, too, will die.

The room has a trapdoor over a ditch or chamber, a subterranean passage used since time immemorial for the storage of contraband goods, a place always dank because it is connected to the Paris sewers, that labyrinth of crime, and the ancient walls exude unspeakable miasmas, so that when with the help of Luciano, ever faithful in evil, I make a hole in the wall, water enters in spurts; it floods the cellar, the already rotting walls collapse, and the passage joins the sewers, and dead rats float past. The blackish surface that can be seen from above is now the vestibule to perdition: far, far off, the Seine, and then the sea. . . .

A ladder hangs down, fixed to the upper edge of the trap. On this, at water level, Luciano takes his place, with a knife: one hand gripping the bottom rung, the other holding the knife, the third ready to seize the victim. "Now wait in silence," I say to him, "and you will see."

I have convinced you to destroy all men with a scar. Come with me, be mine forever, let us do away with those importunate presences. I know well that you do not love them—you told me as much—but we two will remain, we and the subterranean currents.

Now you enter, haughty as a vestal, hoarse and numb as a witch. O vision of hell that stirs my age-old loins and grips my bosom in the clutch of desire, O splendid half-caste, instrument of my doom! With talonlike hands I rip the shirt of fine batiste that adorns my chest, and with my nails I stripe my flesh with bleeding furrows, while a horrible burning sears my lips as cold as the scales of the Serpent. A hollow roar erupts from the black

pit of my soul and bursts past the cloister of my fierce teeth—
I, centaur vomited by the Tartar. . . . But I suppress my cry
and approach you with a horrid smile.

"My beloved, my Sophia," I purr as only the secret chief of
the Okhrana can purr. "I have been waiting for you; come,
crouch with me in the shadows, and wait." And you laugh a
hoarse, slimy laugh, savoring in advance some inheritance, loot,
a manuscript of the Protocols to sell to the tsar. . . . How cleverly you conceal behind that angel face your demon nature, how
modestly you sheathe your body in androgynous blue jeans, and
your T-shirt, diaphanous, still hides the infamous lily branded
on your white flesh by the executioner of Lille!

. . . .

The first dolt arrives, drawn by me into the trap. I can barely
make out his features within the cloak that enfolds him, but he
shows me the sign of the Templars of Provins. It is Soapes, the
Tomar group's assassin.

"Count," he says to me, "the moment has come. For too
many years we have wandered, scattered over the world. You
have the final piece of the message. I have the one that appeared
at the beginning of the Great Game. But this is another story.
Let us join forces, and the others . . ."

I complete his sentence: "The others can go to hell. In the
center of the room, brother, you will find a coffer; in the coffer
is what you have been seeking for centuries. Do not fear the
darkness; it does not threaten, but protects us."

The dolt takes a few steps, groping. A thud, a splash. He has
fallen through the trapdoor, but Luciano grabs him, wields the
knife, the throat is quickly cut, the gurgle of blood mingles with
the churning of the chthonian muck.

. . . .

A knock at the door. "Is that you, Disraeli?"

"Yes," answers the stranger, in whom my readers will have
recognized the grand master of the English group, now risen to
the pomp of power, but still not satisfied. He speaks: "My lord,
it is useless to deny, because it is impossible to conceal that a
great part of Europe is covered with a network of these secret
societies, just as the superficies of the earth is now being covered
with railroads. . . ."

"You said that in the Commons, on July 14, 1856. Nothing
escapes me. Get to the point."

The Baconian Jew mutters a curse. He continues: "There are

too many. The Thirty-six Invisibles are now three hundred and sixty. Multiply that by two: seven hundred and twenty. Subtract the hundred and twenty years at the end of which the doors are opened, and you get six hundred, like the charge of Balaclava."

Devilish man, the secret science of numbers holds no secrets for him. "Well?"

"We have gold, you have the map. Let us unite. Together we will be invincible."

With a hieratic gesture, I point toward the spectral coffer that he, blinded by his desire, thinks he discerns in the shadows. He steps forward, he falls.

I hear the sinister flash of Luciano's blade, and in the darkness I see the death rattle that glistens in the Englishman's silent pupil. Justice is done.

. . . .

I await the third, the French Rosicrucians' man, Montfaucon de Villars, ready to betray the secrets of his sect.

"I am the Comte de Gabalis," he introduces himself, the lying ninny.

I have only to whisper a few words, and he is impelled toward his destiny. He falls, and Luciano, greedy for blood, performs his task.

You smile with me in the shadows, and you tell me you are mine, that your secret will be my secret. Deceive yourself, yes, sinister caricature of the Shekhinah. Yes, I am your Simon; but wait, you still do not know the best of it. When you do know, you will have ceased knowing.

. . . .

What to add? One by one, the others enter.

Padre Bresciani has informed me that, representing the German Illuminati, Babette d'Interlaken will come, the great-granddaughter of Weishaupt, the grand virgin of Helvetic Communism, who grew up amid roués, thieves, and murderers. Expert in stealing impenetrable secrets, in opening dispatches of state without breaking the seals, in administering poisons as her sect orders her.

She enters then, the young agathodemon of crime, enfolded in a polar-bear fur, her long blond hair flowing from beneath the bold busby; her eyes haughty, sarcastic. With the usual fraud, I direct her toward her destruction.

Ah, irony of language—this gift nature has given us to keep

silent the secrets of our spirit! The Daughter of Enlightenment falls victim to Darkness. I hear her spewing horrible curses, impenitent, as Luciano twists the knife three times in her heart. Déjà vu . . .

....

It is the turn of Nilus, who for a moment thought to possess both the tsarina and the map. Filthy lewd monk, you wanted the Antichrist? He stands before you, but you do not know him. I send him on, blind, amid a thousand mystical flatteries, to the evil trap awaiting him. Luciano rips open his breast with a wound in the form of a cross, and he sinks into eternal sleep.

....

I must overcome the ancestral distrust in the last, the Elder of Zion, who claims to be Ahasuerus, the Wandering Jew, immortal like me. He is suspicious as he smiles unctuously, his beard still steeped in the blood of the tender Christian creatures he habitually slaughters in the cemetery of Prague. But I will be as clever as a Rachkovsky, cleverer. I hint that the coffer contains not only the map but also uncut diamonds. I know the fascination uncut diamonds have for this deicide race. He approaches his destiny, dragged by his greed, and it is his own God, cruel and vengeful, that he curses as he dies, pierced like Hiram, but it is difficult for him to curse even now, because his God's name cannot be uttered.

....

In my delusion, I thought I had concluded the Great Work.

As if struck by a gust of wind, once again the door opens, and a figure appears, a livid face, numbed fingers devoutly held to the chest, a hooded gaze: he cannot conceal his identity, for he wears the black habit of his black Society. A son of Loyola!

"Crétineau!" I cry, misled.

He raises his hand in a hypocritical gesture of benediction. "I am not I am that I am," he says to me with a smile that contains nothing human.

It is true: this has always been the Jesuits' method. Sometimes they deny their own existence, and sometimes they proclaim the power of their order to intimidate the uninitiated.

"We are always other than what you think, sons of Belial," that seducer of sovereigns says now. "But you, O Saint-Germain . . ."

"How do you know who I really am?" I ask, alarmed.

He sneers. "We met in other times, when you tried to pull me away from the deathbed of Postel, when under the name of Abbé d'Herblay I led you to end one of your incarnations in the heart of the Bastille. (Oh, how I still feel on my face the iron mask to which the Society, with Colbert's help, had sentenced me!) We met when I spied on your secret talks with d'Holbach and Condorcet. . . ."

"Rodin!" I exclaim, thunderstruck.

"Yes, Rodin, the secret general of the Jesuits! Rodin, whom you will not trick into falling through the trapdoor, as you did with the others. Know this, O Saint-Germain: there is no crime, no evil machination that we did not invent before you, to the greater glory of that God of ours who justifies the means! How many crowned heads have we made tumble into the night that has no morning, or into snares more subtle, to achieve dominion over the world! And now, when we are within sight of the goal, you would prevent us from laying our rapacious hands on the secret that for five centuries has moved the history of the world?"

Rodin, speaking in this way, becomes fearsome. All the bloodthirsty ambition, all the execrable sacrilege that had smoldered in the breasts of the Renaissance popes, now appears on the brow of this son of Loyola. I see clearly: an insatiable thirst for power stirs his impure blood, a burning sweat soaks him, a nauseating vapor spreads around him.

How to strike this last enemy? To my aid comes an unexpected intuition . . . an intuition that can come only to one from whom the human soul, for centuries, has kept no inviolable secret place.

"Look at me," I say. "I, too, am a Tiger."

With one move I thrust you into the middle of the room, I rip from you your T-shirt, I tear the belt of the skin-tight armor that conceals the charms of your amber belly. Now, in the pale light of the moon that seeps through the half-open door, you stand erect, more beautiful than the serpent that seduced Adam, haughty and lascivious, virgin and prostitute, clad only in your carnal power, because a naked woman is an armed woman.

The Egyptian klaft descends over your thick hair, so black it seems blue; your breast throbs beneath the filmy muslin. The gold uraeus, arched and stubborn, with emerald eyes, flashes on your head its triple tongue of ruby. And oh, your tunic of black gauze with silver glints, your girdle embroidered in sinister rainbows, with black pearls! Your swelling pubis shaved so that for your lovers you are sleek as a statue! Your nipples gently touched by the brush of your Malabar slave girl, who has dipped it into the same carmine that bloodies your lips, inviting as a wound!

Rodin is now panting. The long abstinences of a life spent in a dream of power have only prepared him all the more for enslavement to uncontrollable desire. Faced by this queen, beautiful and shameless, her eyes black as the Devil's, her rounded shoulders, scented hair, white and tender skin, Rodin is seized by the possibility of unknown caresses, ineffable voluptuousness; his flesh yearns as a sylvan god yearns when gazing on a naked nymph mirrored in the water that has already doomed Narcissus. Against the light I see him stiffen, as one petrified by Medusa, sculpted by the desire of a repressed virility now at its sunset. The obsessive flame of lust surges through his body; he is like an arrow aimed at its target, a bow drawn to the breaking point.

Suddenly he falls to the floor and crawls before this apparition, his hand extended like a claw to implore a sip of balm.

"Oh, how beautiful you are," he groans, "with those little vixen teeth that gleam when you part your red and swollen lips . . . your great emerald eyes that flash, then fade. . . . Oh, demon of lust!"

He's not all that wrong, the wretch, as you now move your hips, sheathed in their blue denim, and thrust forward your groin to drive the pinball to its supreme folly.

"Vision," Rodin says, "be mine; for just one instant crown with pleasure a life spent in the hard service of a jealous divinity, assuage with one lubricious embrace the eternity of flame to which your sight now plunges me. I beseech you, brush my face with your lips, you Antinea, you Mary Magdalene, you whom I have desired in the presence of saints dazed in ecstasy, whom I have coveted during my hypocritical worship of virginity. O Lady, fair art thou as the sun, white as the moon; lo I deny both God and the saints, and the Roman pontiff himself—no, more, I deny Loyola and the criminal vow that binds me to my Society. A kiss, one kiss, then let me die!"

On numbed knees he crawls, his habit pulled up over his loins, his hand outstretched toward unattainable happiness. Suddenly he falls back, his eyes bulging, his features convulsed, like the unnatural shocks produced by Volta's pile on the face of a corpse. A bluish foam purples his lips; from his mouth comes a strangled hissing, like a hydrophobe's, for when it reaches its paroxysmal phase, as Charcot rightly puts it, this terrible disease, which is satyriasis, the punishment of lust, impresses the same stigmata as rabid madness.

It is the end. Rodin bursts into insane laughter, then crumples to the floor, lifeless, the living image of cadaveric rigor.

In a single moment he went mad and died in mortal sin.

I push the body toward the trapdoor, careful not to dirty my patent-leather boots on the greasy soutane of my last enemy.

There is no need for Luciano's dagger, but the assassin can no longer control his actions, his bestial compulsion to murder over and over. Laughing, he stabs a lifeless, dead cadaver.

. . . .

Now I move with you to the trap's rim, I stroke your throat as you lean forward to enjoy the scene, I say to you, "Are you pleased with your Rocambole, my inaccessible love?"

And as you nod lasciviously and sneer, drooling into the void, I slowly tighten my fingers.

"What are you doing, my love?"

"Nothing, Sophia. I am killing you. I am now Giuseppe Balsamo and have no further need of you."

The harlot of the Archons dies, drops to the water. With a thrust of his knife, Luciano seconds the verdict of my merciless hand, and I say to him: "Now you can climb up again, my trusty one, my black soul." As he climbs, his back to me, I insert between his shoulder blades a thin stiletto with a triangular blade that leaves hardly a mark. Down he plunges; I close the trapdoor: it is done. I abandon the sordid room as eight bodies float toward the Chatelet by conduits known only to me.

I return to my small apartment in the Faubourg Saint-Honoré, I look at myself in the mirror. There, I say to myself, I am the King of the World. From my hollow spire I rule the universe. My power makes my head spin. I am a master of energy. I am drunk with command.

. . . .

Alas, life's vengeance is not slow in coming. Months later, in the deepest crypt of the castle of Tomar, I—now master of the secret of the subterranean currents and lord of the six sacred places of those who had been the Thirty-six Invisibles, last of the last Templars and Unknown Superior of all Unknown Superiors—should win the hand of Cecilia, the androgyne with eyes of ice, from whom nothing now can separate me. I have found her again, after the centuries that intervened since she was stolen from me by the man with the saxophone. Now she walks on the back of the bench as on a tightrope, blue-eyed and blond; nor do I know what she is wearing beneath the filmy tulle that bedecks her.

The chapel has been hollowed from the rock; the altar is surmounted by a canvas depicting the torments of the damned in the bowels of Hell. Some hooded monks stand tenebrously at my side, but I am not disturbed, I am fascinated by the Iberian imagination. . . .

Then—O horror—the canvas is raised, and behind it, the admirable work of some Arcimboldo of caves, another chapel appears, exactly like this one. There before the other altar Cecilia is kneeling, and beside her—icy sweat beads my brow, my hair stands on end—whom do I see, mockingly displaying his scar? The Other, the real Giuseppe Balsamo. Someone has freed him from the dungeon of San Leo!

And I? It is at this point that the oldest of the monks raises his hood, and I recognize the ghastly smile of Luciano, who—God knows how—escaped my stiletto, the sewers, the bloody mire that should have dragged his corpse to the silent depths of the ocean. He has gone over to my enemies in his rightful thirst for revenge.

The monks slough off their habits; they are head to toe in armor, a flaming cross on their snow-white cloaks. The Templars of Provins!

They seize me, turn me around, toward an executioner standing between two deformed assistants. I am bent over, and with a searing brand I am made the eternal prey of the jailer as the evil smile of Baphomet is impressed forever on my shoulder. Now I understand: I am to replace Balsamo at San Leo—or, rather, to resume the place that was assigned to me for all eternity.

But they will recognize me, I tell myself, and somebody will surely come to my aid—my accomplices, at least—a prisoner cannot be replaced without anybody's noticing, these are no longer the days of the Iron Mask. . . . Fool! In a flash I understand, as the executioner forces my head over a copper basin from which greenish fumes are rising: vitriol!

A cloth is placed over my eyes, my face is thrust into the devouring liquid, a piercing unbearable pain, the skin of my cheeks shrivels, my nose, mouth, chin, a moment is all it takes, and as I am pulled up again by the hair, my face is unrecognizable—paralysis, pox, an indescribable absence of a face, a hymn to hideousness. I will go back to the dungeon like those fugitives who, to avoid recapture, had the courage to disfigure themselves.

Ah, I cry, defeated, and as the narrator says, one word escapes my shapeless lips, a sigh, an appeal: Redemption!

But Redemption from what, old Rocambole? You knew better than to try to be a protagonist! You have been punished, and with your own arts. You mocked the creators of illusion, and now—as you see—you write using the alibi of a machine, telling yourself you are a spectator, because you read yourself on the screen as if the words belonged to another, but you have fallen into the trap: you, too, are trying to leave footprints on the sands of time. You have dared to change the text of the romance of the world, and the romance of the world has taken you instead into its coils and involved you in its plot, a plot not of your making.

You would have done better to remain among your islands, Seven Seas Jim, and let her believe you were dead.

98

The National Socialist party did not tolerate secret societies, because it was itself a secret society, with its grand master, its racist
gnosis, its rites and initiations.
    —René Alleau, *Les sources occultes du nazisme*, Paris,
        Grasset, 1969, p. 214

It was around this time that Agliè slipped through our fingers. That
was the expression Belbo used, with a tone of excessive indifference.
I attributed the indifference once again to jealousy. Silently obsessed
by Agliè's power over Lorenza, aloud he wisecracked about the power
Agliè was gaining at Garamond.

Perhaps it was our own fault. Agliè had begun seducing Garamond almost a year earlier, from the time of the alchemistic party
in Piedmont. Soon after that, Garamond entrusted the SFA file to
him, for him to recruit new victims to flesh out the Isis Unveiled
catalog; by now, Garamond consulted him on every decision, and
no doubt gave him a monthly check. Gudrun, who carried out pe-
riodic expeditions to the end of the corridor and beyond the glass
door that gave access to the padded world of Manutius, told us from
time to time, in a worried voice, that Agliè had practically established himself in the office of Signora Grazia; he dictated letters to
her, escorted new visitors into Garamond's office, and, in short—
and here Gudrun's indignation robbed her of even more vowels—
acted as if he owned the place. We really should have wondered
why Agliè spent hours and hours on the Manutius address file. Selecting the SFAs to invite to join the list of authors for Isis Unveiled
should not have taken that much time. Yet he went on writing,
contacting, making appointments.

But we actually fostered his autonomy. The situation suited Belbo.
More Agliè in Via Marchese Gualdi meant less Agliè in Via Sincero
Renato. Thus, when Lorenza Pellegrini made one of her sudden
appearances, and Belbo, with unconcealed excitement, became pa-
thetically radiant, there was less likelihood that "Simon" would barge
in ruinously.

I wasn't displeased, either, since by now I had lost interest in Isis Unveiled and was more and more involved in my history of magic. Feeling I had learned from the Diabolicals everything there was to learn, I let Agliè handle the contacts (and contracts) with the new authors.

Nor did Diotallevi object. In general, the world seemed to matter less and less to him. Now that I think back, I realize that he continued losing weight in a troubling way. At times I would see him in his office bent over a manuscript, his eyes vacant, his pen about to drop from his hand. He wasn't asleep; he was exhausted.

There was another reason we accepted the increasing rarity of Agliè's appearances, and their brevity—for he would simply hand back to us the manuscripts he had rejected, then vanish into the corridor. The fact was, we didn't want him to hear our discussions. If anyone had asked us why, we would have said it was out of delicacy, or embarrassment, since we were parodying the metaphysics in which he somehow believed. But it was really distrust on our part; we were slowly assuming the natural reserve of those who possess a secret, we were putting Agliè in the role of the profane masses as we took more and more seriously the thing we had invented. Perhaps, too, as Diotallevi said in a moment of good humor, now that we had a real Saint-Germain, we didn't need an imitation.

Agliè didn't seem to take offense at our reserve. He would greet us, then leave us, with a politeness that bordered on hauteur.

One Monday morning I arrived at work late, and Belbo eagerly asked me to come to his office, calling Diotallevi, too. "Big news," he said. But before he could begin, Lorenza arrived. Belbo was torn between his joy at this visit and his impatience to tell what he had discovered. A moment later, there was a knock, and Agliè stuck his head in. "I don't want to disturb you. Please don't get up. I haven't the authority to intrude on such a consistory. I only wanted to tell our dearest Lorenza that I'm in Signor Garamond's office. And I hope I have at least the authority to summon her for a sherry at noon, in my office."

In his office! This time Belbo lost self-control. To the extent, that is, that he could lose it. He waited for Agliè to leave, then muttered through clenched teeth: "Ma gavte la nata."

Lorenza, still showing her pleasure at the invitation, asked Belbo what that meant.

"It's Turin dialect. It means, literally, 'Be so kind as to remove the cork.' A pompous, self-important, overweening individual is thought to hold himself the way he does because of a cork stuck in his sphincter ani, which prevents his vaporific dignity from being dispersed. The removal of the cork causes the individual to deflate, a process usually accompanied by a shrill whistle and the reduction of the outer envelope to a poor fleshless phantom of its former self."

"I didn't know you could be so vulgar."

"Now you know."

Lorenza went out, pretending to be annoyed. I knew this distressed Belbo all the more: real anger would have reassured him, but a pretense of irritation only confirmed his fear that, from Lorenza, the display of any passion was always staged, theatrical.

He said then, with grim determination, "To business." Meaning: Let's proceed with the Plan, seriously.

"I don't much want to," Diotallevi said. "I don't feel well. I have a pain here"—he touched his stomach—"I think it's gastritis."

"Ridiculous," Belbo said to him. "*I* don't have gastritis. . . . What could give you gastritis? Mineral water?"

"Could be," Diotallevi said with a wan smile. "Last night I overdid it. I'm accustomed to still Fiuggi, and I drank some fizzy San Pellegrino."

"You must be careful. Such excesses could kill you. But to business, gentlemen. I've been dying to tell you for two days now. . . . Finally, I know why the Thirty-six Invisibles were unable, for centuries, to work out the form of the map. John Dee got it wrong; the geography has to be done over. We live inside a hollow earth, enclosed by the terrestrial surface. Hitler realized this."

99

Nazism was the moment when the spirit of magic seized the helm
of material progress. Lenin said Communism was socialism plus
electricity. In a sense, Hitlerism was Guenonism plus armored di-
visions.

— Pauwels and Bergier, *Le matin des magiciens*, Paris,
Gallimard, 1960, 2, vii

Now Belbo had managed to work Hitler into the Plan. "It's all
there, black on white. The founders of Nazism were involved in
Teutonic neo-Templarism."

"An airtight case."

"I'm not inventing, Casaubon, for once I'm not inventing!"

"Take it easy. When did we ever invent anything? We've always
started with objective data, with information in the public domain."

"This time, too. In 1912 a Germanenorden group is formed, proposing the tenet of Aryan superiority. In 1918 a certain Baron von
Sebottendorf founds a related group, the Thule Gesellschaft, a secret
society, yet another variation on the Templar Strict Observance, but
with strong racist, pan-German, neo-Aryan tendencies. And in '33
Sebottendorf writes that he had sown what Hitler reaped. Furthermore, it is in Thule Gesellschaft circles that the hooked cross appears. And who was among the first to join the Thule? Rudolf Hess,
Hitler's evil genius! Then Rosenberg! Then Hitler himself! And note
that in his cell in Spandau even today, as you've surely read in the
papers, Hess studies the esoteric sciences. Sebottendorf in '24 writes
a pamphlet on alchemy, and remarks that the first experiments in
atomic fission demonstrate the truths of the Great Work. He also
writes a novel on the Rosicrucians! Later he edits an astrological
magazine, *Astrologische Rundschau*, and Trevor-Roper tells us that
the Nazi chiefs, Hitler first among them, never made a move without having a horoscope cast. In 1943 a group of psychics is consulted to discover where Mussolini is being held prisoner. In other
words, the whole Nazi leadership is connected with Teutonic neo-
occultism."

Belbo seemed to have got over the incident with Lorenza, and I built a fire under him to get on with his theory. "We can look at Hitler's power as a rabble-rouser also from this point of view," I said. "Physically, he was a toad, he had a shrill voice. How could such a man whip crowds into a frenzy? He must have possessed psychic powers. Perhaps, instructed by some Druid from his hometown, he knew how to establish contact with the subterranean currents. Perhaps he was a living valve, a biological menhir transmitting the currents to the faithful in the Nuremberg stadium. For a while it worked for him; then his batteries ran down."

100

To All the World: I declare the earth is hollow and habitable within; containing a number of solid, concentric spheres; one within the other, and that it is open at the poles twelve or sixteen degrees.
—J. Cleves Symmes of Ohio, late Captain of Infantry, April 10, 1818; quoted in Sprague de Camp and Ley, *Lands Beyond*, New York, Rinehart, 1952, x

"Congratulations, Casaubon. In your innocence you hit upon the truth. Hitler's one genuine obsession was the underground currents. He believed in the theory of the hollow earth, Hohlweltlehre."

"I'm leaving. I've got gastritis," Diotallevi said.

"Wait. We're getting to the best part. The earth is hollow: we don't live outside it, on the convex crust, but inside, on the concave surface. What we think is the sky is actually a gaseous mass, with points of brilliant light, which fills the interior of our globe. All astronomical measurements have to be reinterpreted. The sky is not infinite: it's circumscribed. The sun, if it really exists, is no bigger than it looks, a mere crumb having a diameter of thirty centimeters at the center of the earth. The Greeks had already suspected as much."

"You made this up," Diotallevi said wearily.

"I did not! Somebody had the idea at the beginning of the last century, an American, a man named Symmes. Then, at the end of the century, another American—name of Teed—revived the notion, supported by alchemistic experiments and a reading of Isaiah. After the First World War, the hollow-earth theory was perfected by a German—I forget his name—who founded the Hohlweltlehre movement. Hitler and his cronies discovered that Hohlweltlehre corresponded exactly to their principles, and they even, according to one report, misaimed some of the V-1s because they calculated their trajectories on the basis of a concave, not a convex, surface. Hitler at this point was convinced that the King of the World was himself and that the Nazi General Staff members were the Unknown Superiors. Where does the King of the World live? Beneath; not above.

"This hypothesis inspired Hitler to change the whole direction of German research toward the concept of the final map, the interpretation of the Pendulum! The six Templar groups had to be reassembled; everything had to be begun again from the beginning. Consider the logic of Hitler's conquests. . . . First, Danzig, to have under his control the classical places of the Teutonic group. Next he conquered Paris, to get his hands on the Pendulum and the Eiffel Tower, and he contacted the synarchic groups and put them into the Vichy government. Then he made sure of the neutrality—in effect, the cooperation—of the Portuguese group. His fourth objective was, of course, England; but we know that wasn't easy. Meanwhile, with the African campaigns, he tried to reach Palestine, but here again he failed. Then he aimed at the dominion of the Paulician territories, by invading the Balkans and Russia.

"When Hitler had four-sixths of the Plan in his hands, he sent Hess on a secret mission to England to propose an alliance. The Baconians, however, refused. He had another idea: those who were holding the most important part of the secret must be his eternal enemies the Jews. He didn't look for them in Jerusalem, where few were left. The Jerusalemite group's piece of the message wasn't in Palestine anyway; it was in the possession of a group of the Diaspora. And so the Holocaust is explained."

"How is that?"

"Just think for a moment. Suppose you wanted to commit genocide . . ."

"Excuse me," Diotallevi said, "but this is going too far. My stomach hurts. I'm going home."

"Wait, damn it. When the Templars were disemboweling the Saracens, you enjoyed yourself, because it was so long ago. Now you're being delicate, like a petty intellectual. We're remaking history; we can't be squeamish."

We let him continue, subdued by his vehemence.

"The striking thing about the genocide of the Jews is the lengthiness of the procedures. First they're kept in camps and starved, then they're stripped naked, then the showers, then the scrupulous piling up of the corpses, and the sorting and storing of clothes, the listing of personal effects. . . . None of this makes sense if it was just a question of killing them. It makes sense if it was a question of looking for something, for a message that one of those millions of people—the Jerusalemite representative of the Thirty-six Invisibles—was hiding in the hem of a garment, or in his mouth, or had tattooed on his body. . . . Only the Plan explains the inexplicable bureaucracy of the genocide! Hitler was searching the Jews for the clue that would allow him to determine, with the Pendulum, the exact point under the earth's concave vault where the telluric currents converged.

"And now you see the beauty of the idea. The telluric currents become equated with the celestial currents. The hollow-earth theory gives new life to the age-old hermetic intuition, namely, that what lies beneath is equal to what lies above! The Mystic Pole coincides with the Heart of the Earth. The secret pattern of the stars is nothing other than the secret pattern of the subterranean passages of Agarttha. There is no longer any difference between heaven and hell, and the Grail, the lapis exillis, is the lapis ex coelis, the philosopher's stone, the terminal, the limit, the chthonian uterus of the empyrean! And if Hitler can identify that point in the hollow center of the earth, which is also the exact center of the sky, he will be Master of the World, whose king he is by right of race. And that's why, to the very end, in the depths of his bunker, he thought he could still control the Mystic Pole."

"Stop," Diotallevi said. "Enough is enough. I'm sick."

"He's really sick. It's not an ideological protest," I said.

Belbo finally understood. Concerned, he went to Diotallevi, who was leaning against the desk, apparently on the verge of fainting. "Sorry, my friend. I got carried away. You're sure it's not anything I said? We've joked together for twenty years, you and I. Maybe you do have gastritis. Look, try a Merankol tablet and a hot-water bottle. Come, I'll drive you home. Then you'd better call a doctor, have yourself looked at."

Diotallevi said he could take a taxi home, he wasn't at death's door yet. He just had to lie down. Yes, he would call a doctor, he promised. And it wasn't the Holocaust business that had upset him; he had been feeling bad since the previous evening. Belbo, relieved, went with him to the taxi.

When he came back, he looked worried. "Now that I think about it, Diotallevi hasn't been himself for several weeks. Those circles under his eyes . . . It's not fair; I should have died of cirrhosis ten years ago, and here I am, the picture of health, whereas he lives like an ascetic and has gastritis or maybe worse. If you ask me, it's an ulcer. To hell with the Plan. We're not living right."

"A Merankol will fix him up," I said.

"Yes, and a hot-water bottle on his stomach. Let's hope he acts sensibly."

101

Qui operatur in Cabala . . . si errabit in opere aut non purificatus
accesserit, deuorabitur ab Azazale.
—Pico della Mirandola, *Conclusiones Magicae*

Diotallevi's condition took a decided turn for the worse in late November. He called the office to say he was going into the hospital.
The doctor had told him there was nothing to worry about, but it
would be a good idea to have some tests.

Belbo and I somehow connected Diotallevi's illness with the Plan,
which perhaps we had carried too far. It was irrational, but we felt
guilty. This was the second time I seemed to be Belbo's partner in
crime. Once, we had remained silent together, withholding information from De Angelis; and now we had talked too much. We
told each other this was silly, but we couldn't shake off our uneasiness. And so, for a month or more, we did not discuss the Plan.

Meanwhile, after he had been out for two weeks or so, Diotallevi
dropped by to tell us, in a nonchalant tone, that he had asked Garamond for sick leave. A treatment had been recommended to him.
He didn't go into details, but it involved his reporting to the hospital every two or three days, and it would leave him somewhat
weak. I didn't see how he could get much weaker; his face now was
as white as his hair.

"And forget about those stories," he said. "They're bad for the
health, as you'll see. It's the Rosicrucians' revenge."

"Don't worry," Belbo said to him, smiling. "We'll make life really
unpleasant for those Rosicrucians, and they'll leave you alone.
Nothing to it." And he snapped his fingers.

The treatment lasted until the beginning of the new year. I was
absorbed by my history of magic—the real thing, serious stuff, I
said to myself, not our nonsense. Garamond came by at least once
a day to ask for news of Diotallevi. "And please, gentlemen, let me
know if any need arises, any problem, any circumstance in which I,
the firm, can do something for our admirable friend. For me, he's

like a son—more, a brother—and thank heaven this is a civilized country, whatever people may say; we have a public health system we can be proud of."

Agliè expressed concern, asked for the name of the hospital, and telephoned its director, a dear friend (who, moreover, happened to be the brother of an SFA with whom Agliè was on excellent terms). Diotallevi would be treated with special consideration.

Lorenza showed up often to ask for news. This should have made Belbo happy, but he took it as another indication that his prognosis was not good. Lorenza was there, but still elusive, because she wasn't there for him.

Shortly before Christmas, I'd caught a snatch of their conversation. Lorenza was saying to him: "The snow is just right, and they have charming little rooms. You can do cross-country skiing, can't you?" I concluded that they would be spending New Year's Eve together. But one day after Epiphany, when Lorenza appeared in the corridor, Belbo said to her, "Happy New Year," and dodged her attempt to give him a hug.

102

Leaving this place, we came to a settlement known as Milestre . . .
where it is said that one known as the Old Man of the Mountain
dwelled. . . . And he built, over high mountains surrounding a
valley, a very thick and high wall, in a circuit of thirty miles, and
it was entered by two doors, and they were hidden, cut into the
mountain.
> —Odorico da Pordenone, *De rebus incognitis*, Impressus
> Esauri, 1513, xxi, p. 15

One day, at the end of January, as I was walking along Via Marchese Gualdi, where I had parked my car, I saw Salon coming out of Manutius. "A little chat with my friend Agliè," he said to me.

Friend? As I seemed to recall from the Piedmont party, Agliè was not fond of him. Was Salon snooping around Manutius, or was Agliè using him for some contact or other?

Salon didn't give me time to ponder this; he suggested a drink, and we ended up at Pilade's. I had never seen Salon in this part of town, but he greeted old Pilade as if they had known each other for years. We sat down. He asked me how my history of magic was progressing. So he knew about that, too. I prodded him about the hollow-earth theory and about Sebottendorf, the man Belbo had mentioned.

He laughed. "You people certainly draw your share of madmen. I'm not familiar with this business of the earth being hollow. As for Sebottendorf, now *there* was a character. . . . He gave Himmler and company some ideas that were suicidal for the German people."

"What ideas?

"Oriental fancies. That man, wary of the Jews, ended up worshiping the Arabs and the Turks. Did you know that on Himmler's desk, along with *Mein Kampf,* there was always the Koran? Sebottendorf, fascinated in his youth by an occult Turkish sect, began studying Islamic gnosis. He said Führer but thought Old Man of the Mountain. When they all got together and founded the SS, they had in mind an organization like the Assassins. . . . Ask yourself why Germany and Turkey, in the First World War, were allies."

"How do you know these things?"

"I told you, I think, that my poor father worked for the Okhrana. Well, I remember in those days how the tsarist police were concerned about the Assassins. Rachkovsky got wind of it first. . . . But they gave up that trail, because if the Assassins were involved, then the Jews couldn't be, and the Jews were the danger. As always. The Jews went back to Palestine and made those others leave their caves. But the whole thing is complicated, confused. Let's leave it at that."

He seemed to regret having said so much, and hastily took his leave. Then another thing happened. I'm now sure I didn't dream it, but that day I thought it was a hallucination: as I watched Salon walk away from the bar, I saw him meet a man at the corner, an Oriental.

In any case, Salon had said enough to start my imagination working again. The Old Man of the Mountain and the Assassins were no strangers to me: I had mentioned them in my thesis. The Templars were accused of being in collusion with them. How could we have overlooked this?

So I began exercising my mind again, and my fingertips, going through old card files, and an idea came to me, an idea so spectacular that I couldn't restrain myself.

The next morning I burst into Belbo's office. "They got it all wrong. We got it all wrong."

"Take it easy, Casaubon. What are you talking about? Oh, my God, the Plan." Then he hesitated. "You probably don't know. There's bad news about Diotallevi. He won't speak. I called the hospital, but they refuse to give me the particulars because I'm not a relative. The man doesn't have any relatives, so who is there to act on his behalf? I don't like this reticence. A benign growth, they say, but the therapy wasn't enough. He should go back into the hospital for a month or so, and minor surgery may be indicated. . . . In other words, those people aren't telling me the whole story, and I like this situation less and less."

I didn't know what to say. Embarrassed by my triumphal entry,

I started leafing through papers. But Belbo couldn't resist. He was like a gambler who's been shown a pack of cards. "What the hell," he said. "Life goes on, unfortunately. What did you find?"

"Well, Hitler goes to all that trouble with the Jews, but he accomplishes nothing. Occultists throughout the world, for centuries, have studied Hebrew, rummaged in Hebrew texts, and at most they can draw a horoscope. Why?"

"H'm . . . Because the Jerusalemites' fragment of the message is still hidden somewhere. Though the Paulicians' fragment never turned up either, as far as we know. . . ."

"That's an answer worthy of Agliè, not of us. I have a better one. The Jews have nothing to do with it."

"What do you mean?"

"The Jews have nothing to do with the Plan. They can't. Picture the situation of the Templars, first in Jerusalem, then in their commanderies in Europe. The French knights meet the Germans, the Portuguese, the Spanish, the Italians, the English: they all have contacts with the Byzantine area, and in particular they combat the Turk, an adversary with whom they fight but also maintain a gentlemanly relationship, a relationship of equals. Who were the Jews at that time, in Palestine? A religious and racial minority tolerated by the condescending Arabs but treated very badly by the Christians. We must remember that in the course of the various Crusades the ghettos were sacked as a matter of course and there were massacres all around. Is it conceivable that the Templars, snobs that they were, would exchange mystical information with the Jews? Never. And in the European commanderies, the Jews were considered usurers, were despised, people to be exploited, not trusted. We're talking about an alliance of knights, about a spiritual knighthood: would the Templars of Provins allow second-class citizens to join that? Out of the question."

"But what about all that Renaissance magic, and the study of cabala . . . ?"

"That was only natural. By then we're close to the third meeting; they're champing at the bit, looking for shortcuts; Hebrew is a sacred and mysterious language; the cabalists have been busy on their own and to other ends. The Thirty-six scattered around the world get the idea that a mysterious language might conceal God knows what secrets. It was Pico della Mirandola who said that nulla nomina, ut significativa et in quantum nomina sunt, in magico opere virtutem habere non possunt, nisi sint Hebraica. Pico della Mirandola was a cretin."

"Bravo! Now you're talking!"

"Furthermore, as an Italian, he was excluded from the Plan. What did he know? So much the worse for Agrippa, Reuchlin, and their pals, who fell for that red herring. I'm reconstructing the story of a red herring, a false trail: is that clear? We let ourselves be influenced by Diotallevi, who was always cabalizing. He cabalized, so we put the Jews in the Plan. If he had been a scholar of Chinese culture, would we have put the Chinese in the Plan?"

"Maybe we would have."

"Anyway, let's not rend our garments; we were led astray by everyone. They all, from Postel on, probably, made this mistake. Two hundred years after Provins, they were convinced that the sixth group was the Jerusalemites. It wasn't."

"Look, Casaubon, we were the ones who revised Ardenti's theory, we were the ones who said that the appointment at the rock didn't mean Stonehenge but the Rock in the Mosque of Omar."

"And we were wrong. There are other rocks. We should have thought of a place founded on rock, on a mountain, a stone, a spur, a cliff. . . . The sixth group waits in the fortress of Alamut."

103

And Kairos appeared, holding in his hand a scepter that signified
royalty, and he gave it to the first created God, and he took it and
said: "Your secret name shall have 36 letters."
—Ḥasan as-Sabbāḥ, *Sargozasht is-Sayyidna*

A bravura performance, but now explanations were in order. I provided them in the days that followed: long explanations, detailed,
documented. On a table at Pilade's I showed Belbo proof after proof,
which he followed with increasingly glazed eyes while he chain-
smoked and every five minutes held out his empty glass, the ghost
of an ice cube at the bottom, and Pilade would hasten to refill it,
without waiting to be told.

My first sources were the same ones in which the earliest accounts
of the Templars appeared, from Gerard of Strasbourg to Joinville.
The Templars had come into contact—into conflict, sometimes, but
more often into mysterious alliance—with the Assassins of the Old
Man of the Mountain.

The story was complicated and began after the death of Mahomet,
with the schism between the followers of the ordinary law, the Sun-
nis, and the supporters of Ali, the Prophet's son-in-law, Fatima's
husband, who saw the succession taken from him. It was the enthusiasts of Ali, the group of adepts called the Shiites, who created the
heretic branch of Islam, the Shī'ah. An occult doctrine, which saw
the continuity of the Revelation not in traditional meditation upon
the words of the Prophet but in the very person of the Imam, lord,
leader, epiphany of the divine, theophanic reality, King of the World.

Now, what happened to this heretic Islamic branch, which was
gradually infiltrated by all the esoteric doctrines of the Mediterranean basin, from Manicheanism to gnosticism, from Neoplatonism
to Iranian mysticism, by all those impulses whose shifts and development in the West we had followed for years? It was a long story,
impossible to unravel, partly because the various Arab authors and
protagonists had extremely long names, the texts were transcribed

with a forest of diacritical marks, and as the evening wore on we could no longer distinguish between Abū ʿAbd Allāh Muḥammad ibn ʿAlī ibn Razzām al-Ṭāʾī al-Kūfī, Abū Muḥammad ʿUbayd Allāh, and Abū Muʿīnī ʿAbd Dīn Nāṣir ibn Khusraw Marvāzī Qubādiyānī. But an Arab, I imagine, would have the same difficulty with Aristoteles, Aristoxenus, Aristarchus, Aristides, Aristagoras, Anaximander, Anaximenes, Anacreon, and Anacharsis.

But one thing was certain: Shiism in turn split into two branches, one called the Twelvers, who await a lost and future imam, and the other, the Ismailis, born in the realm of the Fatimids, in Cairo, who subsequently gave rise to reformed Ismailism in Persia through a fascinating figure, the mystical and ferocious Ḥasan as-Sabbāḥ. Sabbāḥ set up his headquarters to the southwest of the Caspian, in the impregnable fortress of Alamut, the Nest of the Raptor.

There Sabbāḥ surrounded himself with his devotees, the fidāʾīyīn or fedayeen, those faithful unto death; and he used them to carry out his political assassinations, to be instruments of the jihād hafī, the secret holy war. The fedayeen later gained an unfortunate reputation under the name Assassins—not a lovely word now, but for them it was splendid, the emblem of a race of warrior monks who greatly resembled the Templars; a spiritual knighthood.

The fortress or castle of Alamut: the Rock. Built on an airy crest four hundred meters long and in places only a few meters wide, thirty at most. From the distance, to one arriving along the Azerbaijan road, it looked like a natural wall, dazzling white in the sun, bluish in the purple dusk, bloody at dawn; on some days it blended with the clouds or flashed with lightning. Along its upper ridge you could just make out what seemed a row of flint swords that shot upward for hundreds of meters. The most accessible side was a treacherous slope of gravel, which archeologists even today are unable to scale. The fortress was reached by a secret stairway bitten out of the rock, like the spiral peel of a stone apple, and a single archer could defend it. Dizzying, a world elsewhere. Alamut could be reached only astride eagles.

Here Sabbāḥ ruled, and his successors after him, each to be known as the Old Man of the Mountain. First of them was the sulfurous Sinān.

Sabbāḥ had invented a method of dominion over his men, and to his adversaries he declared that if they did not submit to him, they would die. There was no escaping the Assassins. Nizām al-Mulk, prime minister of the sultan when the Crusaders were still exerting themselves to conquer Jerusalem, was stabbed to death, as he was being carried on his litter to the quarters of his women. The killer had approached him disguised as a dervish. And the atabeg of Hims, guarded by a squad of men armed to the teeth, as he came down from his castle to go to Friday prayers, was slain by the Old Man's killers.

Sinān decided to murder the Marquis Corrado di Montefeltro, a Christian, and readied two of his men, who introduced themselves among the infidels able to mimic their customs and language after much preparation. They had disguised themselves as monks and, while the bishop of Tyre was entertaining the hapless marquis at a banquet, leaped upon the victim and stabbed him. One Assassin was immediately killed by the bodyguards; the other took refuge in a church, waited until the wounded man was brought there, attacked him again, finishing him off, then died blissfully.

Blissfully because, as the Arab historiographers of the Sunni line and then the Christian chroniclers from Oderic of Pordenone to Marco Polo wrote, the Old Man had discovered a way to make his knights faithful even to the supreme sacrifice, to make them invincible, horrible war machines. He took them as youths, asleep, to the summit of the mountain, where he stupefied them with pleasures—wine, women, flowers, delectable banquets, and hashish—which gave the sect its name. When they could no longer do without the perverse delights of that invented paradise, he dragged them out of their sleep and set before them a choice: Go, kill, and if you succeed, this paradise you leave will again be yours, and forever; but if you fail, you will plunge back into the Gehenna of the everyday.

Dazed by the drug, helpless before his demands, they sacrificed themselves in sacrificing others; they were killers destined to be killed, victims condemned to make victims.

How they were feared! What tales the Crusaders told about them on moonless nights as the simoom howled over the desert! How the Templars admired, envied those splendid animals; how awed they were by the clear will to martyrdom! The Templars agreed to pay their tolls, asking, in exchange, formal tributes, in a game of reciprocal concessions, complicity, brotherhood of arms, disemboweling one another in the open field but embracing one another in secret, exchanging murmured words of mystical visions, magic formulas, alchemic subtleties. . . .

From the Assassins, the Templars learned occult rites. It was cowardice and ignorance that kept King Philip's inquisitors from seeing that the spitting on the cross, the kiss on the anus, the black cat, and the worship of Baphomet were simply a repetition of other ceremonies, ceremonies performed under the influence of the first secret the Templars learned in the Orient: the use of hashish.

So it was obvious that the Plan was born—had to be born—there. From the men of Alamut, the Templars learned of the subterranean currents. They met the men of Alamut in Provins and established the secret plot of the Thirty-six Invisibles, and that is why Christian Rosencreutz journeyed to Fez and other places in the Orient, and that is why it was to the Orient that Postel turned, and why it was from Egypt, home of the Fatimid Ismailis, that the mages of the Renaissance imported the eponymous divinity of the Plan, Hermes, Hermes-Teuth or Toth, and why Egyptian figures were used by the mountebank Cagliostro for his rituals. And the Jesuits, less narrow than we had thought, with the good Father Kircher, lost no time in throwing themselves into hieroglyphics, Coptic, and the other Oriental languages, and Hebrew was only a cover, a nod to the fashion of the period.

104

These texts are not addressed to common mortals. . . . Gnostic
perception is a path reserved for an elite. . . . For, in the words of
the Bible: Do not cast your pearls before swine.
   —Kamal Jumblatt, Interview in *Le Jour*, March 31, 1967

Arcana publicata vilescunt: et gratiam prophanata amittunt. Ergo:
ne margaritas obijce porcis, seu asinus substerne rosas.
   —Johann Valentin Andreae, *Die Chymische Hochzeit des
   Christian Rosencreutz*, Strassburg, Zetzner, 1616,
   frontispiece

For that matter, where else could you find someone able to wait on
the rock for six centuries, someone who had actually waited on the
rock? True, Alamut eventually fell, under the pressure of the Mongols, but the Ismaili sect survived throughout the East: it mingled
with non-Shiite Sufism, it generated the terrible sect of the Druzes,
and it survived finally among the Indian Khojas, the followers of
the Aga Khan, not far from the site of Agarttha.

But I had discovered more. Under the Fatimid dynasty, through
the Academy of Heliopolis, the hermetic notions of the ancient
Egyptians were rediscovered in Cairo, and a house of sciences was
established there. House of sciences! Was it from this that Bacon
drew the inspiration for his House of Solomon, which in turn was
the model for the Conservatoire?

"That's it, that's it, there's no doubt about it," Belbo said, intoxicated. "But now how do the cabalists fit in?"

"That's only a parallel story. The rabbis of Jerusalem sense that
something happened between the Templars and the Assassins, and
the rabbis of Spain, snooping around under the pretense of lending
money at interest to the European commanderies, get a whiff of
something. They have been excluded and, spurred by national pride,
they decide to figure it out on their own. What?! We, the Chosen
People, are kept in the dark about the Secret of Secrets? And, bang,
the cabalistic tradition begins: a heroic attempt of the dispersed, the

outsiders, to show up the masters, the ones in power, by claiming to know all."

"But, doing that, they give the Christians the impression that they really do know all."

"And at a certain point somebody makes the supreme goof, confusing Ismail with Israel."

"For God's sake, don't tell me that Barruel and the Protocols and all the rest were simply the result of a misspelling. Casaubon, we're reducing a tragic chapter in history to a mistake of Pico della Mirandola."

"No, maybe there's another reason. The Chosen People had taken on the duty of interpreting the Book. People are afraid of those who make them look squarely at the Law. But the Assassins? Why didn't they turn up sooner?"

"Belbo! Think what a depressed area that was after the battle of Lepanto. Sebottendorf knows that there is something to be learned from the Turk dervishes, but Alamut is no more; those Turks are holed up God knows where. They wait. And finally their moment comes; on the tide of Islamic irredentism they stick their heads out again. Putting Hitler in the Plan, we found a good reason for the Second World War. Now, putting in the Assassins of Alamut, we explain what has been happening for years in the Persian Gulf. And this is where we find a place for our Tres, Templi Resurgentes Equites Synarchici. A society whose aim is to heal the rift, at last, between the spiritual knighthoods of different faiths."

"Or else to stimulate conflict and take advantage of the confusion. Once again we've done our job and set History straight. Can it be that at the supreme moment the Pendulum will reveal that the Umbilicus Mundi is at Alamut?"

"Let's not go too far. I'd leave that last point hanging."

"Like the Pendulum."

"If you like. We can't just say whatever enters our heads."

"No, no. Strict scholarship, above all."

That evening I congratulated myself on having invented a great tale. I was an aesthete who used the flesh and blood of the world to make Beauty. But Belbo by now was an adept, and, like other adepts, not through enlightenment, but faute de mieux.

105

Claudicat ingenium, delirat lingua, labat mens.
—Lucretius, *De Rerum Natura*, iii, 453

It must have been about then that Belbo tried to take stock of what was happening to him. But the most severe self-analysis could not free him now from the sickness to which he had grown accustomed.

FILENAME: And what if it's true?

To invent a Plan. The Plan justifies you to such a degree that you can no longer be held accountable, not even for the Plan itself. Just throw the stone and hide your hand. If there really were a Plan, there would be no failure.

You never had Cecilia because the Archons made Annibale Cantalamessa and Pio Bo unskilled even with the friendliest of the brass instruments. You fled the Canal gang because the Decans wanted to spare you for another holocaust. And the man with the scar has a talisman more powerful than yours.

A Plan, a guilty party. The dream of our species. An Deus sit. If He exists, it's His fault.

The thing whose address I lost is not the End, it's the Beginning. Not the object to be possessed but the subject that possesses me. Misery loves company. Misery, company, too many dactyls.

Nothing can dispel from my mind the most reassuring thought that this world is the creation of a shadowy god whose shadow I prolong. Faith leads to Absolute Optimism.

I have committed fornication, true (or not true), but God is the one unable to solve the problem of Evil. Come, let us pound the fetus in the mortar with honey and pepper. Dieu le veult.

If belief is absolutely necessary, let it be in a religion that doesn't make you feel guilty. A religion out of joint, fuming, subterranean, without an end. Like a novel, not like a theology.

Five paths to a single destination. What a waste. Better a labyrinth that leads everywhere and nowhere. To die with style, live in the Baroque.

Only a bad Demiurge makes us feel good.

But if there is no cosmic Plan? What a mockery, to live in exile when no one sent you there. Exile from a place, moreover, that does not exist.

And what if there is a Plan, but it has eluded you—and will elude you for all eternity?

When religion fails, art provides. You invent the Plan, metaphor of the Unknowable One. Even a human plot can fill the void. They didn't publish my *Hearts in Exstasy* because I don't belong to the Templar clique.

To live as if there were a Plan: the philosopher's stone.

If you can't beat them, join them. If there's a Plan, adjust to it.

Lorenza puts me to the test. Humility. If I had the humility to appeal to the Angels, even without believing in them, and to draw the right circle, I would have peace. Maybe.

Believe there is a secret and you will feel like an initiate. It costs nothing.

To create an immense hope that can never be uprooted, because it has no root. Ancestors who do not exist will never appear and say that you have betrayed. A religion you can keep while betraying it infinitely.

Like Andreae: to create, in jest, the greatest revelation of history and, while others are destroyed by it, swear for the rest of your life that you had nothing to do with it.

. . . .

To create a truth with a hazy outline: when somebody tries to clarify it, you excommunicate him. Accept only those hazier than yourself. Jamais d'ennemis à droite.

Why write novels? Rewrite history. The history that then comes true.

Why not set it in Denmark, Mr. William S.? Seven Seas Jim Johann Valentin Andreae Luke-Matthew roams the archipelago of the Sunda between Patmos and Avalon, from the White Mountain to Mindanao, from Atlantis to Thessalonica to the Council of Nicaea. Origen cuts off his testicles and shows them, bleeding, to the fathers of the City of the Sun, and Hiram sneers filioque filioque while Constantine digs his greedy nails into the hollow eye sockets of Robert Fludd, death death to the Jews of the ghetto of Antioch, Dieu et mon droit, wave the Beauceant, lay on, down with the Ophites and the Borborites, the snakes. Trumpets blare, and here come the Chevaliers Bienfaisants de la Cité Sainte with the Moor's head bristling on their pike. The

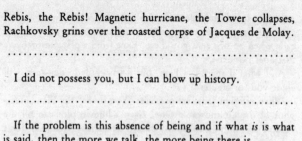

Rebis, the Rebis! Magnetic hurricane, the Tower collapses, Rachkovsky grins over the roasted corpse of Jacques de Molay.

. . . .

I did not possess you, but I can blow up history.

. . . .

If the problem is this absence of being and if what *is* is what is said, then the more we talk, the more being there is.

The dream of science is that there be little being, that it be concentrated and sayable, $E = mc^2$. Wrong. To be saved at the very beginning, for all eternity, it is necessary for that being to be tangled. Like a serpent tied into knots by a drunken sailor: impossible to untie.

. . . .

Invent, invent wildly, paying no attention to connections, till it becomes impossible to summarize. A simple relay race among symbols, one says the name of the next, without rest. To dismantle the world into a saraband of anagrams, endless. And then believe in what cannot be expressed. Is this not the true reading of the Torah? Truth is the anagram of an anagram. Anagrams = ars magna.

That must have been how it happened. Belbo decided to take the universe of the Diabolicals seriously, not because of an abundance of faith, but because of a total lack of it.

Humiliated by his incapacity to create (and all his life he had dined out on his frustrated desires and his unwritten pages, the former a metaphor of the latter and vice versa, all full of his alleged, impalpable cowardice), he came to realize that by inventing the Plan he had actually created. He fell in love with his golem, found it a source of consolation. Life—his life, mankind's—as art, and art as falsehood. Le monde est fait pour aboutir à un livre (faux). But now he wanted to believe in this false book, because, as he had also written, if there was a Plan, then he would no longer be defeated, diffident, a coward.

And this is what finally happened: he used the Plan, which he knew was unreal, to defeat a rival he believed real. And then, aware that the Plan was mastering him as if it existed, or as if he, Belbo, and the Plan, were made of the same stuff, he went to Paris, toward a revelation, a liberation.

Tormented by the daily remorse that for years and years he had lived only with ghosts of his own making, he was now finding solace in ghosts that were becoming objective, since they were known also to others, even though he was the Enemy. Should he fling himself into the lion's maw? Yes, because the lion taking shape was more real than Seven Seas Jim, more real than Cecilia, more real perhaps than Lorenza Pellegrini herself.

Belbo, sick from so many missed appointments, now felt able to make a real appointment. An appointment he could not evade from cowardice, because now his back was to the wall. Fear forced him to be brave. Inventing, he had created the principle of reality.

106

List No. 5
    6 undershirts
    6 shorts
    6 handkerchiefs
has always puzzled scholars, principally because of the total absence of socks.
    —Woody Allen, "The Metterling List," *Getting Even*, New
        York, Random House, 1966, p. 8

It was during those days, no more than a month ago, that Lia decided a vacation would do me good. "You look tired," she said. Maybe the Plan had worn me out. For that matter, the baby, as its grandparents said, needed clean air. Some friends lent us a house in the mountains.

We didn't leave at once. There were things to attend to in Milan, and Lia said that nothing was more restful than taking a little vacation in the city when you knew you'd soon be going off on your real vacation.

Now, for the first time, I talked to Lia about the Plan. Until then she had been too busy with the baby. She knew vaguely that Belbo, Diotallevi, and I were working on some puzzle, and that it occupied whole days and nights, but I hadn't said anything to her about it, not since the day she preached me that sermon about the psychosis of resemblances. Maybe I was ashamed.

I described the whole Plan to her, down to the smallest details, and told her about Diotallevi's illness, feeling guilty, as if I had done something wrong. I tried to present the Plan for what it was: a display of bravura.

Lia said: "Pow, I don't like your story."

"It isn't beautiful?"

"The sirens were beautiful, too. Listen, what do you know about your unconscious?"

"Nothing. I'm not even sure I have one."

"There. Imagine that a Viennese prankster, to amuse his friends, invented the whole business of the id and Oedipus, and made up dreams he had never dreamed and little Hanses he had never met. . . . And what happened? Millions of people were out there, all ready and waiting to become neurotic in earnest. And thousands more ready to make money treating them."

"Lia, you're paranoid."

"Me? You!"

"Maybe we're both paranoid, but you have to grant me this: we started with the Ingolf document. It's natural, when one comes across a message of the Templars, to want to decipher it. Maybe we exaggerated a little, to make fun of the decipherers of messages, but there was a message to begin with."

"All you know is what that Ardenti told you, and from your own description he's an out-and-out fraud. Anyway, I'd like to see this message for myself."

Nothing easier; I had it in my files.

Lia took the paper, looked at it front and back, wrinkled her nose, brushed the hair from her eyes to see the first, the coded, part better. She said: "Is that all?"

"Isn't it enough for you?"

"More than enough. Give me two days to think about it." When Lia asks for two days to think about something, she's determined to show me I'm stupid. I always accuse her of this, and she answers: "If I know you're stupid, that means I love you even if you're stupid. You should feel reassured."

For two days we didn't mention the subject again. Anyway, she was almost always out of the house. In the evening I watched her huddled in a corner, making notes, tearing up one sheet of paper after another.

When we got to the mountains, the baby scratched around all day in the grass, Lia fixed supper, and ordered me to eat, because I was thin as a rail. After supper, she asked me to fix her a double whiskey with lots of ice and only a splash of soda. She lit a cigarette, which she does only at important moments, told me to sit down, and then explained.

"Listen carefully, Pow, because I'm going to demonstrate to you that the simplest explanation is always the best. Colonel Ardenti told you Ingolf found a message in Provins. I don't doubt that at all. Yes, Ingolf went down into the well and really did find a case with this text in it," and she tapped the French lines with her finger. "We are not told that he found a case studded with diamonds. All the colonel said was that according to Ingolf's notes the case was sold. And why not? It was an antique; he may have made a little cash, but we are not told that he lived off the proceeds for the rest of his life. He must have had a small inheritance from his father."

"And why should the case be ordinary?"

"Because the message is ordinary. It's a laundry list. Come on, let's read it again."

> a la . . . Saint Jean
> 36 p charrete de fein
> 6 . . . entiers avec saiel
> p . . . les blancs mantiax
> r . . . s . . . chevaliers de Pruins pour la . . . j.nc
> 6 foiz 6 en 6 places
> chascune foiz 20 a . . . 120 a . . .
> iceste est l'ordonation
> al donjon li premiers
> it li secunz joste iceus qui . . . pans
> it al refuge
> it a Nostre Dame d l'altre part d l'iau
> it a l'ostel des popelicans
> it a la pierre
> 3 foiz 6 avant la feste . . . la Grant Pute.

"A laundry list?"

"For God's sake, didn't it ever occur to you to consult a tourist guide, a brief history of Provins? You discover immediately that the Grange-aux-Dîmes, where the message was found, was a gathering place for merchants. Provins was a center for fairs in Champagne. And the Grange is on rue St.-Jean. In Provins they bought and sold everything, but lengths of cloth were particularly popular, draps— or dras, as they wrote it then—and every length was marked by a guarantee, a kind of seal. The second most important product of Provins was roses, red roses that the Crusaders had brought from Syria. They were so famous that when Edmund of Lancaster married Blanche d'Artois and took the title Comte de Champagne, he added the red rose of Provins to his coat of arms. Hence, too, the war of the roses, because the House of York had a white rose as its symbol."

"Who told you all this?"

"A little book of two hundred pages published by the Tourist Bureau of Provins. I found it at the French Center. But that's not all. In Provins there's a fort known as the Donjon, which speaks for itself, and there is a Porte-aux-Pains, an Eglise du Refuge, various churches dedicated to Our Lady of this and that, a rue de la Pierre-Ronde, where there was a pierre de cens, a stone on which the count's subjects set the coins of their tithes. And then a rue des Blancs-Manteaux and a street called de la Grand-Pute-Muce, for reasons not hard to guess. It was a street of brothels."

"And what about the popelicans?"

"In Provins there had been some Cathars, who later were duly burned, and the grand inquisitor himself was a converted Cathar, Robert le Bougre. So it is hardly strange that a street or an area should be called the place of the Cathars even if the Cathars weren't there anymore."

"Still, in 1344 . . ."

"But who said this document dates from 1344? Your colonel read '36 years after the hay wain,' but in those days a p made in a certain way, with a tail, meant post, but a p without the tail meant pro. The author of this text is an ordinary merchant who made some notes on business transacted at the Grange, or, rather, on the rue St.-Jean—not on the night of Saint Jean—and he recorded a price of thirty-six sous, or crowns, or whatever denomination it was for one or each wagon of hay."

"And the hundred and twenty years?"

"Who said anything about years? Ingolf found something he transcribed as '120 a' . . . What is an 'a'? I checked a list of the abbreviations used in those days and found that for denier or dinarium odd signs were used; one looks like a delta, another looks like a theta, a circle broken on the left. If you write it carelessly and in haste, as a busy merchant might, a fanatic like Colonel Ardenti could take it for an a, having already read somewhere the story of the one hundred and twenty years. You know where better than I. He could have read it in any history of the Rosicrucians. The point is, he wanted to find something resembling 'post 120 annos patebo.' And then what does he do? He finds 'it' repeated several times and he reads it as *iterum*. But the abbreviation for *iterum* was *itm*, whereas 'it' means *item*, which means likewise, and is in fact used for repetitious lists. Our merchant is calculating how much he's going to make on the orders he's received, and he's listing the deliveries he has to make. He has to deliver some bouquets of roses of Provins, and that's the meaning of 'r . . . s . . . chevaliers de Pruins.' And where the colonel read 'vainjance' (because he had the kadosch knights on his mind), you should read 'jonchée.' The roses were used to make either hats or floral carpets on feast days. So here is how your Provins message should read:

> *"In Rue Saint Jean:*
> *36 sous for wagons of hay.*
> *Six new lengths of cloth with seal*
> *to rue des Blancs-Manteaux.*
> *Crusaders' roses to make a jonchée:*
> *six bunches of six in the six following places,*
> *each 20 deniers, making 120 deniers in all.*
> *Here is the order:*
> *the first to the Fort*
> *item the second to those in Porte-aux-Pains*
> *item to the Church of the Refuge*
> *item to the Church of Notre Dame, across the river*
> *item to the old building of the Cathars*
> *item to rue de la Pierre-Ronde.*
> *And three bunches of six before the feast, in the whores' street.*

"Because they, too, poor things, maybe wanted to celebrate the feast day by making themselves nice little hats of roses."

"My God," I said. "I think you're right."

"Of course I'm right. It's a laundry list, I tell you."

"Wait a minute. This may very well be a laundry list, but the first message really is in code, and it talks about thirty-six invisibles."

"True. The French text I polished off in an hour, but the other one kept me busy for two days. I had to examine Trithemius, at both the Ambrosiana and the Trivulziana, and you know what the librarians there are like: before they let you put your hands on an old book, they look at you as if you were planning to eat it. But the first message, too, is a simple matter. You should have discovered this yourself. To begin with, are you sure that 'Les 36 inuisibles separez en six bandes' is in the same French as our merchant's? Yes; this expression was used in a seventeenth-century pamphlet, when the Rosicrucians appeared in Paris. But then you reasoned the way your Diabolicals do: If the message is encoded according to the method of Trithemius, it means that Trithemius copied from the Templars, and since it quotes a sentence that was current in Rosicrucian circles, it means that the plan attributed to the Rosicrucians was none other than the plan of the Templars. Try reversing the argument, as any sensible person would: Since the message is written in Trithemius's code, it was written *after* Trithemius, and since it quotes an expression that circulated among the seventeenth-century Rosicrucians, it was written *after* the seventeenth century. So, at this point, what is the simplest hypothesis? Ingolf finds the Provins message. Since, like the colonel, he's an enthusiast of hermetic messages, he sees thirty-six and one hundred and twenty and thinks immediately of the Rosicrucians. And since he's also an enthusiast of cryptography, he amuses himself by putting the Provins message into code, as an exercise. So he translates his fine Rosicrucian sentence using a Trithemius cryptosystem."

"An ingenious explanation. But it's no more valid than the colonel's."

"So far, no. But suppose you make one conjecture, then a second and a third, and they all support one another. Already you're more confident that you're on the right track, aren't you? I began with the suspicion that the words used by Ingolf were not the ones taken from Trithemius. They're in the same cabalistic Assyro-Babylonian style, but they're not the same. Yet, if Ingolf had wanted words beginning with the letters that interested him, in Trithemius he could have found as many as he liked. Why didn't he use those words?"

"Well, why didn't he?"

"Maybe he needed specific letters also in the second, third, and fourth positions. Maybe our ingenious Ingolf wanted a multicoded message; maybe he wanted to be smarter than Trithemius. Trithemius suggests forty major cryptosystems: in one, only the initial letters count; in another, the first and third letters; in another, every other initial letter, and so on, until, with a little effort, you can

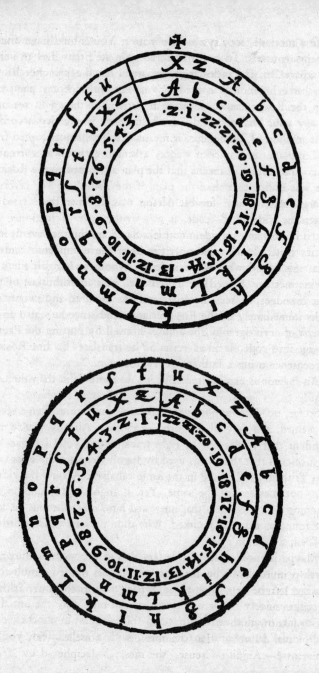

invent a hundred more systems on your own. As for the ten minor cryptosystems, the colonel considered only the first wheel, which is the easiest. But the following ones work on the principle of the second wheel. Here's a copy of it for you. Imagine that the inner circle is mobile and you can turn it so that the letter A coincides with any letter of the outer circle. You will have one system where A is written as X, another where A is U, and so on. . . . With twenty-two letters on each circle, you can produce not ten but twenty-one cryptosystems. The twenty-second is no good, because there A is A. . . ."

"Don't tell me that for each letter of each word you tried all twenty-one systems. . . ."

"I had brains on my side, and luck. Since the shortest words have six letters, it's obvious that only the first six are important and the rest are just for looks. Why six letters? Suppose Ingolf coded the first letter, then skipped one, then coded the third, then skipped two and coded the sixth. For the first letter I used wheel number 1, for the third letter I used wheel number 2, and got a sentence. Then I tried wheel number 3 for the sixth letter, and got a sentence again. I'm not saying Ingolf didn't use other letters, too, but three positive results are enough for me. If you want to, you can take it further."

"Don't keep me in suspense. What came out?"

"Look at the message again. I've underlined the letters that count.

Kuabris Defrabax Rexulon Ukkazaal Ukzaab Urpaefel
Taculbain Habrak Hacoruin Maquafel Tebrain Hmcatuin
Rokasor Himesor Argaabil Kaquaan Docrabax Reisaz
Reisabrax Decaiquan Oiquaquil Zaitabor Qaxaop Dugraq
Xaelobran Disaeda Magisuan Raitak Huidal Uscolda Arabaom
Zipreus Mecrim Cosmae Duquifas Rocarbis.

"Now, we know what the first message is: it's the one about the thirty-six invisibles. Now listen to what comes out if you substitute the third letters, using the second wheel: chambre des demoiselles, l'aiguille creuse."

"But I know that, it's—"

" 'En aval d'Etretat—La Chambre des Demoiselles—Sous le Fort du Fréfossé—Aiguille Creuse,' the message deciphered by Arsène

Lupin when he discovers the secret of the Hollow Peak! You remember: at Etretat, at the edge of the beach, stands the Aiguille Creuse, a natural castle, habitable inside, the secret weapon of Julius Caesar when he invaded Gaul, and later used by the kings of France. The source of Lupin's immense power. And you know how Lupinologists are crazy about this story; they make pilgrimages to Etretat, they look for secret passages, they make anagrams of every word of Leblanc. . . . Ingolf was no less a Lupinologist than he was a Rosicrucianologist, and so code after code. . . ."

"My Diabolicals could always argue that the Templars knew the secret of the peak, and therefore the message was written in Provins in the fourteenth century. . . ."

"Of course; I realize that. But now comes the third message. Third wheel applied to the sixth letter of each word. Listen: 'Merde j'en ai marre de cette steganographie.' And this is modern French; the Templars didn't talk like that. 'Shit, I'm sick of this hermetic writing.' That's how Ingolf talked, and having given himself a headache coding all this nonsense, he got a final kick cursing in code what he was doing. But he was not without shrewdness. Notice that each of these three messages has thirty-six letters. Poor Pow, Ingolf was having fun, just like the three of you, and that imbecile colonel took him seriously."

"Then why did Ingolf disappear?"

"Who says he was murdered? Ingolf got fed up living in Auxerre, seeing nobody but the pharmacist and a spinster daughter who whined all day. So maybe he went to Paris, pulled off a good deal selling one of his old books, found himself a buxom and willing widow, and started a new life. Like those men who go out to buy cigarettes, and the wives never see them again."

"And the colonel?"

"Didn't you tell me that not even that detective is sure they killed him? He got into some jam, his victims tracked him down, and he took to his heels. Maybe at this very moment he's selling the Eiffel Tower to an American tourist and going under the name Dupont."

I couldn't give in all along the line. "All right, we started out with a laundry list. Yet we were clever enough, inventive enough, to turn a laundry list into poetry."

"Your plan isn't poetic; it's grotesque. People don't get the idea of going back to burn Troy just because they read Homer. With Homer, the burning of Troy became something that it never was and never will be, and yet the *Iliad* endures, full of meaning, because it's all clear, limpid. Your Rosicrucian manifestoes are neither clear nor limpid; they're mud, hot air, and promises. This is why so many people have tried to make them come true, each finding in them what he wants to find. In Homer there's no secret, but your plan is full of secrets, full of contradictions. For that reason you could find thousands of insecure people ready to identify with it. Throw the whole thing out. Homer wasn't faking, but you three have been faking. Beware of faking: people will believe you. People believe those who sell lotions that make lost hair grow back. They sense instinctively that the salesman is putting together truths that don't go together, that he's not being logical, that he's not speaking in good faith. But they've been told that God is mysterious, unfathomable, so to them incoherence is the closest thing to God. The farfetched is the closest thing to a miracle. You've invented hair oil. I don't like it. It's a nasty joke."

This disagreement didn't spoil our weeks in the mountains. I took long walks, read serious books, became closer to the child than I'd ever been. But between me and Lia there was something left unsaid. On the one hand, she had put me in a tight corner, and was sorry to have humiliated me; on the other, she wasn't convinced that she had convinced me.

Indeed, I felt a pull to the Plan. I didn't want to abandon it, I had lived with it too long.

A few days ago I got up early to catch the one train for Milan, and in Milan I received Belbo's call from Paris, and I began this story, which for me is not yet finished.

Lia was right. We should have talked about it earlier. But I wouldn't have believed her, all the same. I had experienced the creation of the Plan like the moment of Tiferet, the heart of the sefirotic body, the harmony of Rule and Freedom. Diotallevi had told me that Moses Cordovero warned: "He who because of his Torah becomes proud over the ignorant, that is, over the whole people of Yahweh, leads Tiferet to grow proud over Malkhut." But what Malkhut is, the kingdom of this earth, in its dazzling simplicity, is something I understand only now—in time to grasp the truth; perhaps too late to survive the truth.

Lia, I don't know if I will see you again. If not, the last image I have of you is half-asleep, under the blankets, a few days ago. I kissed you that morning, and hesitated before I left.

NEZAH

107

Dost thou see yon black dog, ranging through shoot
  and stubble? . . .
Meseems he softly coileth magic meshes,
To be a sometime fetter round our feet . . .
The circle narrows, now he's near!
  —*Faust*, ii, Without the City-Gate

What had happened during my absence, particularly in the days just
before my return, I could deduce from Belbo's files. But only one
file, the last, was clear, containing ordered information; he had
probably written it before leaving for Paris, so that I, or someone
else, could read it. The other files, written for himself alone, as
usual, were not easy to interpret. But having entered the private
universe of his confidences to Abulafia, I was able to draw something from them.

It was early June. Belbo was upset. The doctors had finally accepted the idea that he and Gudrun were Diotallevi's only relatives,
and they talked. When the printers and proofreaders inquired about
Diotallevi, Gudrun now answered with pursed lips, uttering a bi-
syllable in such a way that no vowel escaped. Thus the taboo illness
was named.

Gudrun went to see Diotallevi every day. She must have disturbed him with those eyes of hers, glistening with pity. He knew,
but was embarrassed that others knew. He spoke with difficulty.
(Belbo wrote: "The face is all cheekbones.") He was losing his hair,
but that was from the therapy. (Belbo wrote: "The hands are all
fingers.")

In the course of one of their painful dialogues, Diotallevi gave
Belbo a hint of what he would say to him on the last day: that
identifying oneself with the Plan was bad, that it might be evil. Even
before this, perhaps to make the Plan objective and reduce it again
to its purely fictional dimension, Belbo had written it down, word
for word, as if it were the colonel's memoirs. He narrated it like an
initiate communicating the final secret. This, I believe, was to be a

cure: he was returning to literature, however second-rate, to that which was not life.

But on June 10, something bad must have happened. The notes are confused; all I have is conjectures.

Lorenza asked him to drive her to the Riviera, where she had to see a girlfriend and collect something or other, a document, a notarized deed, some nonsense that could just as well have been sent by mail. Belbo agreed, dazzled by the idea of spending a Sunday at the sea with her.

They went to the place—I haven't been able to figure out exactly where, perhaps near Portofino. Belbo's description was all emotion, tensions, dejections, moods; it contained no landscapes. Lorenza did her errand while Belbo waited in a café. Then she said they could go and eat fish in a place on a bluff high above the sea.

After this, the story becomes fragmentary. There are snatches of dialogue without quotation marks, as if transcribed at white heat lest a series of epiphanies fade. They drove as far as they could, then continued on foot, taking those toilsome Ligurian paths along the coast, surrounded by flowers, to the restaurant. When they were seated, they saw, on the table next to theirs, a card reserving it for Conte Agliè.

What a coincidence, Belbo must have said. A nasty coincidence, Lorenza replied; she didn't want Agliè to know she was there, and with Belbo. Why not, what was wrong with that? What gave Agliè the right to be jealous? Right? No, it was a matter of taste; Agliè had invited her out today and she'd told him she was busy. Belbo didn't want her to look like a liar, did he? She wouldn't look like a liar; she was in fact busy, she had a date with Belbo. Was that something to be ashamed of? Not ashamed of, but she had her own rules of tact, if Belbo didn't mind.

They left the restaurant, started back up the path, but Lorenza suddenly stopped; she saw some people arriving. Belbo didn't know them. Friends of Agliè, she said, and she didn't want them to see her. A humiliating situation: she leaned against the railing of a little bridge over a ravine full of olive trees, a newspaper in front of her face, as if she were consumed by a sudden interest in current events. Belbo stood ten paces away, smoking, as if he were just passing by.

A friend of Agliè walked past. Lorenza said that if they continued along the path, they were bound to run into Agliè himself. To hell with this, Belbo said. So what? Lorenza said he was insensitive. The solution: Get to the car without taking the path, cut across the slopes. A breathless flight over a series of sun-baked terraces, and Belbo lost the heel of a shoe. Lorenza said, You see how much more beautiful it is this way? Of course you're out of breath; you shouldn't smoke so much.

They reached the car, and Belbo said they might as well go back to Milan. No, Lorenza said, Agliè might be late, we might meet him on the highway, and he knows your car. It's such a lovely day, let's cut through the interior. It must be charming, and we'll get to the Autostrada del Sole and have supper along the Po somewhere, near Pavia.

Why there, and what do you mean, cut through the interior? There's only one solution; look at the map. We'd have to climb into the mountains after Uscio, then cross the Apennines, stop at Bobbio, and from there go on to Piacenza. You're crazy! Worse than Hannibal and the elephants. You have no sense of adventure, she said, and anyway, think of all the charming little restaurants we'll find in those hills. Before Uscio there's Manuelina's, which has at least twelve stars in the Michelin and all the fish you could want.

Manuelina's was full, with a line of customers eyeing the tables where coffee was being served. Never mind, Lorenza said, a few kilometers higher we'll find a hundred places better than this. They found a restaurant at two-thirty, in a wretched village that, according to Belbo, even the army maps were ashamed to record, and they ate overcooked pasta with a sauce made of canned meat. Belbo asked Lorenza what was behind all this, because it was no accident that she had made him take her to the very place where Agliè would be: she wanted to provoke someone, either Agliè or him, but he couldn't figure out which of the two it was. She asked him if he was paranoid.

After Uscio they tried a mountain pass and, as they were going through a village that looked like Sunday afternoon in Sicily during the reign of the Bourbons, a big black dog came to a stop in the middle of the road, as if it had never seen an automobile before. Belbo hit it. The impact did not seem great, but as soon as they got out, they saw that the poor animal's belly was red with blood, and some strange pink things (intestines?) were sticking out, and the dog was whimpering and drooling. Some villeins gathered, and soon it was like a town meeting. Belbo asked who the dog's owner was, he would pay. The dog had no owner. The dog represented perhaps ten percent of the population of that Godforsaken place, but they knew it only by sight. Some said they should fetch the carabiniere sergeant, who would fire a shot, and that would be that.

As they were looking for the sergeant, a lady arrived, declaring herself an animal lover. I have six cats, she said. This is a dog, not a cat, Belbo said, and he's dying, and I'm in a hurry. Cat or dog, you should have a heart, the lady said. No sergeant. Somebody must be brought from the SPCA, or from the hospital in the next town. Maybe the animal can be saved.

The sun was beating down on Belbo, on Lorenza, on the car, on the dog, and on the bystanders; it seemed to have no intention of setting. Belbo felt as if he were in his pajamas but unable to wake up; the lady was implacable, the sergeant couldn't be found, the dog went on bleeding and panting and making weak noises. He's whimpering, Belbo said, and then, with Eliotlike detachment: He's ending with a whimper. Of course he's whimpering, the lady said; he's suffering, poor darling, and why couldn't you look where you were going?

The village underwent a demographic boom; Belbo, Lorenza, and the dog had become the entertainment of that gloomy Sunday. A little girl with an ice-cream cone came over and asked if they were the people from the TV who were organizing the Miss Ligurian Apennine contest. Belbo told her to beat it or he'd do to her what he did to the dog. The girl started crying. The local doctor arrived, said the girl was his daughter, and Belbo didn't realize to whom he was talking. In a rapid exchange of apologies and introductions, it transpired that the physician had published a *Diary of a Village Doctor* with the famous Manutius Press in Milan. Belbo incautiously said that he was magna pars of that press. The doctor insisted that he and Lorenza stay for supper. Lorenza fumed, nudged Belbo: Now we'll end up in the papers, the diabolical lovers. Couldn't you keep your mouth shut?

The sun still beat down as the church bell rang compline. We're in Ultima Thule, Belbo muttered through clenched teeth: sun six months of the year, from midnight to midnight, and I'm out of cigarettes. The dog confined itself to suffering, and nobody paid it

548

any further attention. Lorenza said she was having an asthma attack. Belbo was sure by now that the cosmos was a practical joke of the Demiurge. Finally it occurred to him that they could take the car and look for help in the nearest town. The animal-loving lady agreed: they should go, they should hurry, she trusted a gentleman from a publishing house that published poetry, she herself was a great admirer of Khalil Gibran.

Belbo drove off and, when they reached the nearest town, cynically drove through it, as Lorenza cursed all the animals with which the Lord had befouled the earth from the first through the fifth day. Belbo agreed, and went so far as to curse the work of the sixth day, too, and perhaps also the rest on the seventh, because this was the most ill-starred Sunday he had ever lived through.

They began to cross the Apennines. On the map it looked easy, but it took them hours. They didn't stop at Bobbio, and toward evening they arrived at Piacenza. Belbo was tired, but at least he could have supper with Lorenza. He took a double room in the only available hotel, near the station. When they went upstairs, Lorenza said she wouldn't sleep in such a place. Belbo said they'd look for something else, if she would just give him time to go down to the bar and have a martini. He found nothing but cognac, domestic. When he went back up to the room, Lorenza wasn't there. At the front desk he found a message: "Darling, I've discovered a marvelous train for Milan. I'm leaving. See you next week."

Belbo rushed to the station: the track was empty. Just like a Western.

He had to spend the night in Piacenza. He looked for a paperback thriller, but the station newsstand was closed. All he could find in the hotel was a Touring Club magazine.

It had an article on Apennine passes like the one he had just crossed. In his memory—faded, as if the day's events had happened long ago—they were arid, sun-baked, dusty, scattered with mineral flotsam. But on the glossy pages of the magazine they were dream country, to return to even on foot, to be savored step by step. The Samoas of Seven Seas Jim.

How can a man rush to his own destruction simply because he runs over a dog? Yet that's how it was. That night in Piacenza,

Belbo decided to withdraw once more into the Plan, where he would suffer no more defeats, because there he was the one who decided who, how, and when.

That must also have been the night he decided to avenge himself on Agliè, even if he didn't have a clear reason. He would put him into the Plan without Agliè's knowing. It was typical of Belbo to seek revenges of which he would be the only witness. Not out of modesty, but because he distrusted the ability of others to appreciate them. Slipped into the Plan, Agliè would be annulled, would dissolve in smoke like the wick of a candle. Unreal as the Templars of Provins, the Rosicrucians: as unreal as Belbo himself.

It shouldn't be difficult, Belbo thought. We've cut Bacon and Napoleon down to size: why not Agliè? We'll send him out looking for the map, too. I freed myself of Ardenti and his memory by putting him into a fiction better than his own. The same will happen with Agliè.

I believe he really believed this; such is the power of frustrated desire. The file ended—it could not have been otherwise—with the quotation required of all those whom life has defeated: Bin ich ein Gott?

108

What is the hidden influence behind the press, behind all the subversive movements going on around us? Are there several Powers
at work? Or is there one Power, one invisible group directing all
the rest—the circle of the *real Initiates*?
—Nesta Webster, *Secret Societies and Subversive Movements*,
London, Boswell, 1924, p. 348

Maybe he would have forgotten his decision. Maybe it would have
been enough for him just to write it. Maybe, if he had seen Lorenza
again at once, he would have been caught up by desire, and desire
would have forced him to come to terms with life. But, instead,
that Monday afternoon, Agliè appeared in his office, wafting exotic
cologne, smiling as he handed over some manuscripts to be rejected,
saying he had read them during a splendid weekend at the seashore.
Belbo, seized once more by rancor, decided to taunt Agliè—by giving him a glimpse of the magic bloodstone.

Assuming the manner of Boccaccio's Buffamalcco, he said that for
more than ten years he had been burdened by an occult secret. A
manuscript, entrusted to him by a certain Colonel Ardenti, who
claimed to be in possession of the Plan of the Templars . . . The
colonel had been abducted or killed, and his papers had been taken.
Garamond Press had been left with a red-herring text, deliberately
erroneous, fantastic, even puerile, whose sole purpose was to let
others know that the colonel had seen the Provins message and Ingolf's final notes, the notes Ingolf's murderers were still looking
for. But there was also a very slim file, containing ten pages only,
but those ten pages were the authentic text, the one really found
among Ingolf's papers. They had remained in Belbo's hands.

What a curious story—this was Agliè's reaction—do tell me more.
Belbo told him more. He told him the whole Plan, just as we had
conceived it, as if it were all contained in that remote manuscript.
He even told him, in an increasingly cautious and confidential tone,
that there was also a policeman, by the name of De Angelis, who
had arrived at the brink of the truth but had come up against the

hermetic—no other way to describe it—silence of Belbo himself, keeper of mankind's greatest secret: a secret that boiled down to the secret of the Map.

Here he paused, in a silence charged with unspoken meaning, like all great pauses. His reticence about the final truth guaranteed the truth of its premises. For those who really believed in a secret tradition, he calculated, nothing was louder than silence.

"How interesting, how extremely interesting!" Agliè said, taking the snuffbox from his vest, as if his thoughts were elsewhere. "And . . . and the map?"

Belbo thought: You old voyeur, you're getting aroused; serves you right. With all your Saint-Germain airs, you're just another petty charlatan living off the shell game, and then you buy the Brooklyn Bridge from the first charlatan who's a bigger charlatan than you are. Now I'll send you on a wild-goose chase looking for maps, so you'll vanish into the bowels of the earth, carried away by the telluric currents, until you crack your head against the transoceanic monolith of some Celtic valve.

And, very circumspectly, he replied: "In the manuscript, of course, there was also the map, or, rather, a precise description of the map, of the original. It's surprising; you can't imagine how simple the solution is. The map was within everyone's grasp, in full view; why, thousands of people have passed it every day, for centuries. And the method of orientation is so elementary that you just have to memorize the pattern and the map can be reproduced on the spot, anywhere. So simple and so unexpected . . . Imagine—this is just to give you an idea—it's as if the map were inscribed in the Pyramid of Cheops, its elements displayed for everyone to see, and for centuries people have read and reread and deciphered the pyramid, seeking other allusions, other calculations, completely overlooking its incredible, splendid simplicity. A masterpiece of innocence. And fiendish cunning. The Templars of Provins were wizards."

"You pique my curiosity. Would you allow me to see it?"

"I must confess I destroyed everything: the ten pages, the map. I was frightened. You understand, don't you?"

"You mean to tell me you destroyed a document of such importance? . . ."

"I destroyed it. But, as I said, the revelation was of an absolute simplicity. The map is here," and Belbo touched his forehead. "For over ten years I've carried it with me, for over ten years I've carried the secret here," and he touched his forehead again, "like an obsession, for I fear the power that would be mine if I put forth my hand and grasped the heritage of the Thirty-six Invisibles. Now you realize why I persuaded Garamond to publish Isis Unveiled and the *History of Magic*. I'm waiting for the right contact." Then, more and more carried away by the role he had taken on, and to put Agliè definitively to the test, he recited, word for word, Arsène Lupin's ardent speech at the conclusion of *L'Aiguille Creuse:* "There are moments when my power makes my head swim. I am drunk with dominion."

"Come now, dear friend," Agliè said. "What if you have given excessive credence to the daydreams of some fanatic? Are you sure the text was authentic? Why don't you trust my experience in these matters? If you only knew how many revelations of this sort I've heard in my life, and how many proved, with my help, to be unfounded. I can boast some expertise at least—modest, perhaps, but precise—in the field of historical cartography."

"Dr. Agliè," Belbo said, "you would be the first to remind me that, once revealed, a mystic secret is no longer of any use. I have been silent for years; I can go on being silent."

And he was silent. Agliè too, rogue or not, performed his role in earnest. He had spent his life amusing himself with impenetrable secrets, so he was quite convinced that Belbo's lips would be sealed forever.

At that point Gudrun came in and told Belbo that the Bologna meeting had been set for Wednesday at noon. "You can take the morning Intercity," she said.

"Delightful train, the Intercity," Agliè said. "But you should reserve a seat, especially at this season."

Belbo said that even if you boarded at the last moment, you could find something, perhaps in the dining car, where they served breakfast. "I wish you luck, then," Agliè said. "Bologna. Beautiful city, but so hot in June . . ."

"I'll be there only two or three hours. I have to discuss a text on ancient inscriptions. There are problems with the illustrations." Then he fired his big gun: "I haven't had my vacation yet. I'll take it around the summer solstice. I may make up my mind to . . . You understand me. And I rely on your discretion. I've spoken to you as a friend."

"I can keep silent even better than you. In any case, I thank you, most sincerely, for your trust." And Agliè left.

From this encounter Belbo emerged confident: total victory of his astral narrative over the wretchedness and shame of the sublunar world.

The next day, he received a phone call from Agliè. "You must forgive me, dear friend. I have encountered a small contretemps. You know that, in a modest way, I deal in antique books. This evening I am to receive, from Paris, a dozen bound volumes, eighteenth-century, of a certain value, and I absolutely must deliver them to a correspondent of mine in Florence tomorrow. I would take them myself, but another engagement detains me here. I thought of this solution: you are going to Bologna. I'll meet you at your train tomorrow, ten minutes before you leave, and hand you a small suitcase. You put it on the rack over your seat and leave it there when you arrive in Bologna. You might wait and get off last, to be sure no one takes it. In Florence, my correspondent will board the train while it's standing in the station and collect the suitcase. It's a nuisance for you, I know, but if you could render me this service, I'd be eternally grateful."

"Gladly," Belbo replied. "But how will your friend in Florence know where I've left the suitcase?"

"I have taken the liberty of reserving a seat for you, seat number 45, car 8. It's reserved as far as Rome, so no one else will occupy it in Bologna or in Florence. You see, in exchange for the inconvenience I'm causing you, I make sure that you will travel comfortably and not have to make do in the dining car. I didn't dare buy your ticket, of course, not wanting you to think I meant to discharge my indebtedness in such an indelicate fashion."

A real gentleman, Belbo thought. He'll send me a case of rare wine. To drink his health. Yesterday I wanted to dispatch him to the bowels of the earth and now I'm doing him a favor. Anyway, I could hardly refuse.

Wednesday morning, Belbo went to the station early, bought his ticket to Bologna, and found Agliè standing beside car 8 with the suitcase. It was fairly heavy but not bulky.

Belbo put the suitcase above seat number 45 and settled down with his bundle of newspapers. The news of the day was Berlinguer's funeral. A little later, a bearded gentleman came and occupied the seat next to his. Belbo thought he had seen the man before. (With hindsight, he thought it might have been at the party in Piedmont, but he wasn't sure.) When the train left, the compartment was full.

Belbo read his paper, but the bearded passenger tried to strike up conversations with everybody. He began with remarks about the heat, the inadequacy of the air-conditioning, the fact that in June you never knew whether to wear summer things or between-seasons clothing. He observed that the best was a light blazer, just like Belbo's, and he asked if it was English. Belbo said yes, it was English, from Burberry's, and resumed his reading. "They're the best," the gentleman said, "but yours is particularly nice, because it doesn't have those gold buttons that are so ostentatious. And, if I may say so, it goes very well with your maroon tie." Belbo thanked him and reopened his paper. The gentleman went on talking with the others about the difficulty of matching ties with jackets, and Belbo continued reading. I know, he thought, they all think me rude, but I don't take trains to establish human relationships. I have too much of that as it is.

Then the gentleman said to him, "What a lot of papers you read! And of every political tendency. You must be a judge or a politician." Belbo replied that he was neither, but worked for a publishing firm that specialized in books on Arab metaphysics. He said this in the hope of terrifying his adversary. And the man was obviously terrified.

Then the conductor arrived. He asked Belbo why he had a ticket for Bologna and a seat reserved to Rome. Belbo said he had changed his mind at the last moment. "How lucky you are," the bearded gentleman said, "to be able to make such decisions, according to how the wind blows, without having to count pennies. I envy you." Belbo smiled and looked away. There, he said, now they all think I'm either a spendthrift or a bank robber.

At Bologna, Belbo stood up and prepared to get off. "Don't forget your suitcase," his neighbor said.

"No. A friend will collect it in Florence," Belbo said. "For that matter, I'd be grateful if you'd keep an eye on it."

"I will," the bearded gentleman said. "Rest assured."

Belbo returned to Milan toward evening, shut himself in his apartment with two cans of meat and some crackers, and turned on the TV. More Berlinguer, naturally. The news item about the train appeared at the end, almost as a footnote.

Late that morning on the Intercity between Bologna and Florence, a bearded gentleman had voiced suspicions after a passenger got off in Bologna leaving a suitcase on the luggage rack. True, the passenger had said someone would pick it up in Florence, but wasn't that what terrorists always said? Furthermore, why had he reserved his seat to Rome when he was getting off in Bologna?

A heavy uneasiness spread among the other travelers in that compartment. Finally, the bearded passenger said he couldn't bear the tension. It was better to make a mistake than to die, and he alerted the chief conductor. The chief conductor stopped the train and called the Railway Police. The train was stopped in the mountains; the passengers milled anxiously along the tracks; the bomb squad arrived. . . . The experts opened the suitcase and found a timer and explosive, set for the hour of arrival in Florence. Enough to wipe out a few dozen people.

The police were unable to find the bearded gentleman. Perhaps he had changed cars and got off in Florence because he didn't want to end up in the newspapers. The police were appealing to him to get in touch with them.

The other passengers remembered, with unusual precision, the man who had left the suitcase. He must have looked suspicious at first sight. He was wearing a blue English jacket without gold buttons, a maroon necktie; he was taciturn, and seemed to want to avoid attracting attention at all costs. But he had let slip the information that he worked for a paper, or a publisher, or for something having to do (the witnesses' testimony varied) with physics, methane, or metempsychosis—but Arabs were definitely involved.

Police stations and carabiniere headquarters had been alerted. Anonymous phone calls were already coming in and being sifted by the investigators. Two Libyan citizens had been detained in Bologna. A police artist had made a sketch, which now occupied the whole screen. The drawing didn't resemble Belbo, but Belbo resembled the drawing.

Belbo, plainly, was the man with the suitcase. But the suitcase had contained Agliè's books. He called Agliè. There was no answer.

It was already late in the evening. He didn't dare leave the house, so he took a pill to get some sleep. The next morning, he called Agliè again. Silence. He went out to buy the papers. Luckily the front page was still occupied by the funeral; the story about the train and the copy of the police sketch must be somewhere inside. He skulked back to his apartment, his collar turned up, then realized he was still wearing the blazer. At least he didn't have on the maroon tie.

While he was trying once more to sort out what had happened, he received a call. A strange foreign voice, a slightly Balkan accent, mellifluous: a completely disinterested party acting out of pure kindness of heart. Poor Signor Belbo, the voice said, finding yourself compromised by such an unpleasant business. You should never agree to act as someone else's courier without first checking the contents of the package. How awful it would be if someone were to inform the police that Signor Belbo was the unidentified occupant of seat number 45.

Of course, that extreme step could be avoided, if Belbo would only agree to cooperate. If he were to say, for example, where the Templars' map was. And since Milan had become hot, because everyone knew the Intercity terrorist had boarded the train there, it would be prudent to deal with the matter in neutral territory: for example, Paris. Why not arrange to meet at the Librairie Sloane, 3 rue de la Manticore, in a week's time? But perhaps Belbo would be better advised to set off at once, before anybody identified him. Librairie Sloane, 3 rue de la Manticore. At noon on Wednesday, June 20, he would find there a familiar face, that bearded gentleman with whom he had conversed so cordially on the train. The bearded gentleman would tell Belbo where to find other friends, and then, gradually, in good company, in time for the summer solstice, Belbo would tell what he knew, and the business would be concluded without any trauma. Rue de la Manticore, number 3: easy to remember.

109

Saint-Germain . . . very polished and witty . . . said he possessed
every kind of secret. . . . He often employed, for his apparitions,
that famous magic mirror of his . . . and through its catoptric effects summoned up the usual, well-known shades. His contact with
the other world was unquestioned.
—Le Coulteux de Canteleu, *Les sectes et les sociétés secrètes*,
    Paris, Didier, 1863, pp. 170–171

Belbo was devastated. Everything was clear. Agliè believed his story,
he wanted the map, he had set a trap for him, and now Belbo was
in the man's power. Either Belbo went to Paris, to reveal what he
didn't know (but he was the only one who knew he didn't know it,
since I had gone off without leaving an address, and Diotallevi was
dying), or all the police forces of Italy would be after him.

But was it really possible that Agliè had stooped to such a sordid
trick? Belbo should take that old lunatic by the collar and drag him
to the police station; that was the only way to get out of this mess.

He hailed a taxi and went to the little house near Piazza Piola.
Windows closed; on the gate, a real estate agency's sign, FOR RENT
This was insane. Agliè was living here just last week; Belbo had
telephoned him. He rang the bell of the house next door. "Oh, that
gentleman? He moved out yesterday. I have no idea where he's gone,
I knew him only by sight, he was such a reserved person. Always
traveling, I suppose."

The only thing left was to inquire at the agency. They had never
heard of Agliè. The house had been rented by a French firm. The
rent was paid regularly through a bank. The lease was canceled
overnight; the firm forfeited the deposit. All their communications,
by letter, had been with a certain M. Ragotgky. That was all they
knew.

It was impossible. Rakosky or Ragotgky, the colonel's mysterious visitor, wanted by De Angelis and by Interpol, and here he was
going around renting houses. In our story, Ardenti's Rakosky was

a reincarnation of Rachkovsky of the Okhrana, in other words, the inevitable Saint-Germain. What did he have to do with Agliè?

Belbo went to the office, sneaking upstairs like a thief, and locked himself in his room. He had to try to think things through.

It was enough to drive a man crazy, and Belbo suspected he had finally gone mad. There was no one he could confide in. While he was wiping the sweat from his face, and mechanically—without thinking—leafing through some manuscripts that had come in the day before, at the top of a page he suddenly saw Agliè's name.

He looked at the title. A little work by some run-of-the-mill Diabolical, *The True Story of the Comte de Saint-Germain*. He read the page again. Quoting Charcornac's biography, it said that Claude-Louis de Saint-Germain had gone variously by the names of Monsieur de Surmont, Count Soltikoff, Mr. Welldone, Marchese di Belmar, Rackoczi or Ragozki, and so on, but the real family names were Saint-Martin and Marquis of Agliè, the latter from an ancestral estate in Piedmont.

Good. Belbo could rest easy. Not only was he wanted for terrorism, not only was the Plan true, not only had Agliè disappeared in the space of two days, but, into the bargain, the count was no mythomane but the true and immortal Saint-Germain. And he had never done anything to conceal that fact. But no, the only true thing, in this growing whirlwind of falsehoods, was his name. No, even his name was false. Agliè wasn't Agliè. But it didn't matter who he really was, because he was acting, had been acting for years, like a character in the story we were to invent only later.

There was nothing Belbo could do. With the disappearance of Agliè, he couldn't prove to the police that Agliè had given him the suitcase. And even if the police believed him, it would come out that he had received it from a man wanted for murder, a man he had been employing as a consultant for at least two years. Great alibi.

To grasp this whole story—melodramatic to begin with—and to make the police swallow it, another story had to be assumed, even more outlandish. Namely, that the Plan, which we had invented, corresponded in every detail, including the desperate final search for the map, to a real plan, which had already involved Agliè, Rakosky,

Rachkovsky, Ragotgky, the bearded gentleman, and the Tres, not to mention the Templars of Provins. Which story in turn was based on the assumption that the colonel was right. Except that he was right by being wrong, because our Plan, after all, was different from his, and if his was true, then ours couldn't be true, and vice versa, and therefore, if we were right, why had Rakosky, ten years ago, stolen a wrong document from the colonel?

Just reading, the other morning, what Belbo had confided to Abulafia, I felt like banging my head against the wall: to convince myself that the wall, at least the wall, was really there. I imagined how Belbo must have felt that day, and in the days that followed. But it wasn't over yet.

Needing someone to talk to, he telephoned Lorenza. She wasn't in. He was willing to bet he would never see her again. In a way, Lorenza was a creature invented by Agliè, and Agliè was a creature invented by Belbo, and Belbo no longer knew who had invented Belbo. He picked up the newspaper again. The one sure thing was that he was the man in the police drawing. To convince him further, at that moment the phone rang. For him again, in the office. The same Balkan accent, the same instructions. Meeting in Paris.

"Who are you, anyway?" Belbo shouted.

"We're the Tres," the voice replied, "and you know more about the Tres than we do."

Belbo took the bull by the horns and called De Angelis. At headquarters they made difficulties; the inspector, they said, was no longer working there. When Belbo insisted, they gave in and put him through to some office.

"Ah, Dr. Belbo, what a surprise!" De Angelis said in a tone that suggested sarcasm. "You're lucky you caught me. I'm packing my suitcases."

"Suitcases?" Was that a hint?

"I've been transferred to Sardinia. A peaceful assignment, apparently."

"Inspector De Angelis, I have to talk to you. It's urgent. It's about that business. . . ."

"Business? What business?"

"The colonel. And the other thing . . . Once, you asked Casaubon if he'd heard any mention of the Tres. Well, I have. And I have things to tell you, important things."

"I don't want to hear them. It's not my case anymore. And it's a little late in the day, don't you think?"

"Yes, I admit it. I kept something from you years ago. But now I want to talk."

"Not to me, Dr. Belbo. First of all, I should tell you that someone is surely listening to our conversation, and I want that someone to know that I refuse to hear anything and that I don't know anything. I have two children, small children. And I've been told something could happen to them. To show me it wasn't a joke, yesterday morning, when my wife started the car, the hood blew off. A very small charge, hardly more than a firecracker, but enough to convince me that if they want to, they can. I went to the chief, told him I've always done my duty, sometimes went beyond the call of duty, but I'm no hero. My life I'm willing to lay down, but not the lives of my wife and children. I asked for a transfer. Then I went and told everybody what a coward I am, and how I'm shitting in my pants. Now I'm saying it to you and to whoever's listening to us. I've ruined my career, I've lost my self-respect, I'm a man without honor, but I'm saving my loved ones. Sardinia is very beautiful, I'm told, and I won't even have to lay money aside to send the children to the beach in the summer. Good-bye."

"Wait, I'm in trouble. . . ."

"You're in trouble? Good. When I asked for your help, you wouldn't give it to me. Neither would your friend Casaubon. But now that you're in trouble . . . Well, I'm in trouble, too. You've come too late. The police, as they say in the movies, are at the service of the citizen. Is that what you're thinking? Then call the police, call my successor."

Belbo hung up. Wonderful: they had even prevented him from turning to the one policeman who might have believed him.

Then it occurred to him that Signor Garamond, with all his acquaintances—prefects, police chiefs, high officials—could lend a hand. He rushed to him.

Garamond listened to his story affably, interrupting him with polite exclamations like "You don't say," "Of all things," "Why, it sounds like a novel." Then he clasped his hands, looked at Belbo with profound understanding, and said: "My boy, allow me to call you that, because I could be your father—well, perhaps not your father, because I'm still a young man, more, a youthful man, but your older brother, yes, if you'll allow me. I'll speak to you from the heart. We've known each other for so many years. It seems to me that you're overexcited, at the end of your tether, nerves shot, more, tired. Don't think I don't appreciate it; I know you give body and soul to the Press, and one day this must be considered also in what I might call material terms, because that never does any harm. But, if I were you, I'd take a vacation.

"You say you find yourself in an embarrassing situation. To be frank, I might say—not to dramatize—but it would be unpleasant for Garamond Press, too, if one of its editors, its best editor, were involved in any kind of dubious business. You tell me that someone wants you to travel to Paris. It's not necessary to go into details; I believe you, naturally. So go to Paris. Isn't it best to clear things up at once? You say you find yourself—how shall I put it?—on conflictual terms with a gentleman like Count Agliè. I don't want to know the details, or what happened between the two of you, but I wouldn't brood too much on that similarity of names you mentioned. The world is full of people named German, or something similar. Don't you agree? If Agliè sends you word to come to Paris and we'll clear everything up, well then, go to Paris. It won't be the end of the world. In human relationships, it's always best to be straightforward, frank. Go to Paris, and if you have anything on your chest, don't hold it back. What's in your heart should be on your lips. What do all these secrets matter!

"Count Agliè, if I've understood correctly, complains because you don't want to tell him where some map is, some paper or message or whatever, something you have and are making no use of, whereas maybe our good friend Agliè needs it for some scholarly reason. We're in the service of culture, aren't we? Or am I wrong? Give it to him, this map, this atlas, this chart—I don't even want to know what it is. If it means so much to him, he must have his reasons, surely worthy of respect; a gentleman is always a gentleman. Go to Paris, shake hands, and it's done. All right? And don't worry more than necessary. You know I'm always here." Then he pressed the intercom: "Signora Grazia . . . ah, not there. She's never around when you need her. You have your troubles, my dear Belbo, but if you only knew mine. Good-bye now. If you see Signora Grazia in the corridor, send her to me. And get some rest: don't forget."

Belbo went out. Signora Grazia wasn't in her office, but on her desk he saw that the red light of Garamond's personal line was on: Garamond was calling someone. Belbo couldn't resist (I believe it was the first time in his life he committed such an indelicacy); he picked up the receiver and listened in on the conversation. Garamond was saying: "Don't worry. I think I've convinced him. He'll come to Paris. . . . Only my duty. We belong to the same spiritual knighthood, after all."

So Garamond, too, was part of the secret. What secret? The one that only he, Belbo, could reveal. The one that did not exist.

It was evening by then. He went to Pilade's, exchanged a few words with someone or other, drank too much. The next morning, he sought out the only friend he had left, Diotallevi. He went to ask the help of a dying man.

Their last conversation he reported feverishly on Abulafia. It's a summary. I was unable to tell how much was Diotallevi's and how much was Belbo's, because in both cases it was the murmuring of one who speaks the truth because he knows the time has passed for playing with illusion.

110

He had never seen his friend so white. Diotallevi had hardly any hair now on his head or eyebrows or lashes. He looked like a billiard ball.

"Forgive me," Belbo said. "Can we discuss my situation?"

"Go ahead. I don't have a situation. Only needs."

"I heard they have a new therapy. These things devour twenty-year-olds, but at fifty it's slower; there's time to find a cure."

"Speak for yourself. I'm not fifty yet. My body is still young. I have the privilege of dying more quickly. But it's hard for me to talk. Tell me what you have to say, so I can rest."

Obedient, respectful, Belbo told him the whole story.

Then Diotallevi, breathing like the Thing in the science-fiction movie, talked. He had, also, the transparency of the Thing, that absence of boundary between exterior and interior, between skin and flesh, between the light fuzz on his belly, discernible in the gap of his pajamas, and the mucilaginous tangle of viscera that only X rays or a disease in an advanced state can make visible.

"Jacopo, I'm stuck here in a bed. I can't decide whether what you're telling me is happening only inside your head, or whether it's happening outside. But it doesn't matter. Whether you've gone crazy or the world has makes no difference. In either case, someone has mixed and shuffled the words of the Book more than was right."

"What do you mean?"

"We've sinned against the Word, against that which created and sustains the world. Now you are punished for it, as I am punished for it. There's no difference between you and me."

A nurse came in and put water on his table. She told Belbo not to tire him, but Diotallevi waved her away: "Leave us alone. I have to tell him. The Truth. Do you know the Truth?"

"Who, me? What a question, sir . . ."

"Then go. I have to tell my friend something important. Now listen, Jacopo. Just as man's body has limbs and joints and organs, so does the Torah. And as the Torah, so a man's body. You follow me?"

"Yes."

"Rabbi Meir, when he was learning from Rabbi Akiba, mixed vitriol in the ink, and the master said nothing. But when Rabbi Meir asked Rabbi Ismahel if he was doing the right thing, the rabbi said to him: Son, be cautious in your work, because it is divine work, and if you omit one letter or write one letter too many, you destroy the whole world. . . . We tried to rewrite the Torah, but we paid no heed to whether there were too many letters or too few. . . ."

"We were joking. . . ."

"You don't joke with the Torah."

"We were joking with history, with other people's writings. . . ."

"Is there a writing that founds the world and is not the Book? Give me a little water. No, not the glass; wet that cloth. . . . Thanks. Now listen. Rearranging the letters of the Book means rearranging the world. There's no getting away from it. Any book, even a speller. People like your Dr. Wagner, don't they say that a man who plays with words and makes anagrams and violates the language has ugliness in his soul and hates his father?"

"But those are psychoanalysts. They say that to make money. They aren't your rabbis."

"They're all rabbis. They're all saying the same thing. Do you think the rabbis, when they spoke of the Torah, were talking about a scroll? They were talking about us, about remaking our body through language. Now, listen. To manipulate the letters of the Book takes great piety, and we didn't have it. But every book is interwoven with the name of God. And we anagrammatized all the books of history, and we did it without praying. Listen to me, damn it. He who concerns himself with the Torah keeps the world in motion, and he keeps in motion his own body as he reads, studies, rewrites, because there's no part of the body that doesn't have an equivalent in the world. Wet the cloth for me. . . . Thanks. If you alter the Book, you alter the world; if you alter the world, you alter the body. This is what we didn't understand.

"The Torah allows a word to come out of its coffer; the word appears for a moment, then hides immediately. It is revealed only for a moment and only to its lover. It's a beautiful woman who hides in a remote chamber of her palace. She waits for one whose existence nobody knows of. If another tries to take her, to put his dirty hands on her, she dismisses him. She knows her beloved; she opens the door just a little, shows herself, and immediately hides again. The word of the Torah reveals itself only to him who loves it. But we approached books without love, in mockery. . . ."

Belbo again moistened his friend's lips with the cloth. "And so?"

"So we attempted to do what was not allowed us, what we were not prepared for. Manipulating the words of the Book, we attempted to construct a golem."

"I don't understand. . . ."

"You can't understand. You're the prisoner of what you created. But your story in the outside world is still unfolding. I don't know how, but you can still escape it. For me it's different. I am experiencing in my body everything we did, as a joke, in the Plan."

"Don't talk nonsense. It's a matter of cells. . . ."

"And what are cells? For months, like devout rabbis, we uttered different combinations of the letters of the Book. GCC, CGC, GCG, CGG. What our lips said, our cells learned. What did my cells do? They invented a different Plan, and now they are proceeding on their own, creating a history, a unique, private history. My cells have learned that you can blaspheme by anagrammatizing the Book, and all the books of the world. And they have learned to do this now with my body. They invert, transpose, alternate, transform themselves into cells unheard of, new cells without meaning, or with meaning contrary to the right meaning. There must be a right meaning and a wrong meaning; otherwise you die. My cells joke, without faith, blindly.

"Jacopo, while I could still read, during these past months, I read dictionaries, I studied histories of words, to understand what was happening in my body. I studied like a rabbi. Have you ever reflected that the linguistic term 'metathesis' is similar to the oncological term 'metastasis'? What is metathesis? Instead of 'clasp' one

566

says 'claps.' Instead of 'beloved' one says 'bevoled.' It's the temu-rah. The dictionary says that metathesis means transposition or in-terchange, while metastasis indicates change and shifting. How stupid dictionaries are! The root is the same. Either it's the verb metati-themi or the verb methistemi. Metatithemi means I interpose, I shift, I transfer, I substitute, I abrogate a law, I change a meaning. And methistemi? It's the same thing: I move, I transform, I transpose, I switch clichés, I take leave of my senses. And as we sought secret meanings beyond the letter, we all took leave of our senses. And so did my cells, obediently, dutifully. That's why I'm dying, Jacopo, and you know it."

"You talk like this because you're ill. . . ."

"I talk like this because finally I understand everything about my body. I've studied it day after day, I know what's happening in it, but I can't intervene; the cells no longer obey. I'm dying because I convinced myself that there was no order, that you could do what-ever you liked with any text. I spent my life convincing myself of this, I, with my own brain. And my brain must have transmitted the message to them. Why should I expect them to be wiser than my brain? I'm dying because we were imaginative beyond bounds."

"Listen, what's happening to you has no connection with our Plan."

"It doesn't? Then explain what's happening to you. The world is behaving like my cells."

He sank back, exhausted. The doctor came in and whispered to Belbo that it was wrong to submit a dying man to such stress.

Belbo left, and that was the last time he saw Diotallevi.

Very well, he wrote, the police are after me for the same reason that Diotallevi has cancer. Poor friend, he's dying, and I, who don't have cancer, what am I doing? I'm going to Paris to find the prin-ciple of neoplasm.

But he didn't give in immediately. He stayed shut up in his apart-ment for four days, reviewed his files sentence by sentence, to find an explanation. Then he wrote out this account, a final testament, so to speak, telling it to himself, to Abulafia, to me, or to anyone else who was able to read it. And finally, Tuesday, he left.

I believe Belbo went to Paris to say to them there was no secret, that the real secret was to let the cells proceed according to their own instinctive wisdom, that seeking mysteries beneath the surface reduced the world to a foul cancer, and that of all the people in the world, the most foul, the most stupid person was Belbo himself, who knew nothing and had invented everything. Such a step must have cost him dear, but he had accepted for too long the premise that he was a coward, and De Angelis had certainly shown him that heroes were few.

In Paris, after the first meeting, Belbo must have realized They wouldn't believe him. His words were too undramatic, too simple. It was a revelation They wanted, on pain of death. Belbo had no revelation to give, and—his final cowardice—he feared death. So he tried to cover his tracks, and he called me. But They caught him.

III

C'est une leçon par la suite. Quand votre ennemi se reproduira, car il n'est pas à son dernier masque, congédiez-le brusquement, et surtout n'allez pas le chercher dans les grottes.

—Jacques Cazotte, *Le diable amoureux*, 1772, from a page suppressed in later editions

Now, in Belbo's apartment, as I finished reading his confessions, I asked myself: What should I do? No point going to Garamond. De Angelis had left. Diotallevi had said everything he had to say. Lia was far off, in a place without a telephone. It was six in the morning, Saturday, June 23, and if something was going to happen, it would happen tonight, in the Conservatoire. I had to decide quickly.

Why—I asked myself later, in the periscope—didn't you pretend nothing had happened? You had before you the texts of a madman, a madman who had talked with other madmen, including a last conversation with an overexcited (or overdepressed) dying friend. You weren't even sure Belbo had called you from Paris. Maybe he was talking from somewhere a few kilometers outside Milan, or maybe from the booth on the corner. Why involve yourself in a story that was imaginary and that didn't concern you anyway?

This was the question I set myself in the periscope, as my feet were growing numb and the light was fading, and I felt the unnatural yet very natural fear that anyone would feel at night, alone, in a deserted museum. But early that morning, I had felt no fear. Only curiosity. And, perhaps, duty, friendship.

I told myself that I, too, should go to Paris. I wasn't quite sure why, but I couldn't desert Belbo now. Maybe he was counting on me to slip, under cover of night, into the cave of the Thugs, and, as Suyodhana was about to plunge the sacrificial knife into his heart, to burst into the underground temple with my sepoys, their muskets loaded with grapeshot, and carry him to safety.

Luckily, I had a little money on me. In Paris I got into a taxi and told the driver to take me to rue de la Manticore. He grumbled, cursed; the street couldn't be found even in those guides they have. In fact, it turned out to be an alley no wider than the aisle of a train. It was in the neighborhood of the old Bièvre, behind Saint-Julien-le-Pauvre. The taxi couldn't even enter it; the driver left me at the corner.

Uneasily, I entered the alley. There were no doorways. At a certain point the street widened a little, and I came to a bookshop. Why it had the number 3 I don't know, since there was no number 1 or 2, or any other street number. It was a grimy little shop, lighted by a single bulb. Half of the double door served as a display case. Its sides held perhaps a few dozen books, indicating the shop's specialties. On a shelf, some pendulums, dusty boxes of incense sticks, little amulets, Oriental or South American, and tarot decks of diverse origin.

The interior was no more welcoming: a mass of books on the walls and on the floor, with a little table at the back, and a bookseller who seemed put there deliberately, so that a writer could write that the man was more decrepit than his books. This person, his nose in a big handwritten ledger, was taking no interest in his customers, of which at the moment there were only two, and they raised clouds of dust as they drew out old volumes, nearly all without bindings, from teetering shelves, and began reading them, giving no impression of wanting to buy.

The only space not cluttered with shelves was occupied by a poster. Garish colors, a series of oval portraits with double borders, as in the posters of the magician Houdini. "Le Petit Cirque de l'Incroyable. Madame Olcott et ses liens avec l'Invisible." An olive-skinned, mannish face, two bands of black hair gathered in a knot at the nape. I had seen that face before, I thought. "Les Derviches Hurleurs et leur danse sacrée. Les Freaks Mignons, ou Les Petits-fils de Fortunio Liceti." An assortment of pathetic, abominable little monsters. "Alex et Denys, les Géants d'Avalon. Theo, Leo et Geo Fox, les Enlumineurs de l'Ectoplasme . . ."

The Librairie Sloane truly supplied everything from the cradle to the grave; it even advertised healthy entertainment, a suitable place to take the children before grinding them up in the mortar. I heard a phone ring. The shopkeeper pushed aside a pile of papers until he found the receiver. "Oui, monsieur," he said, "c'est bien ça." He listened for a few minutes, nodded, then assumed a puzzled look, or at least it was the pretense of puzzlement, on account of those present, as if everybody could hear what he was hearing and he didn't want to assume responsibility for it. Then he took on that shocked expression of a Parisian shopkeeper when you ask for something he doesn't have in his shop, or a hotel clerk when there are no rooms available. "Ah, non, monsieur. Ah, ça . . . Non, non, monsieur, c'est pas notre boulot. Ici, vous savez, on vend des livres, on peut bien vous conseiller sur des catalogues, mais ça . . . Il s'agit de problèmes très personnels, et nous . . . Oh, alors, il y a—sais pas, moi—des curés, des . . . oui, si vous voulez, des exorcistes. D'accord, je le sais, on connaît des confrères qui si prêtent . . . Mais pas nous. Non, vraiment la description ne me suffit pas, et quand même . . . Desolé, monsieur. Comment? Oui . . . si vous voulez. C'est un endroit bien connu, mais ne demandez pas mon avis. C'est bien ça, vous savez, dans ces cas, la confiance c'est tout. A votre service, monsieur."

The other two customers left. I felt ill at ease but steeled myself and attracted the old man's attention with a cough. I told him I was looking for an acquaintance, a friend who, I thought, often stopped by here: Monsieur Agliè. Again the man had the shocked look he had had while on the telephone. Perhaps, I said, he didn't know him as Agliè, but as Rakosky or Soltikoff or . . . The bookseller looked at me again, narrowing his eyes, and remarked coldly that I had friends with curious names. I told him never mind, it was not important, I was merely inquiring. Wait, he said; my partner is arriving and he may know the person you are looking for. Have a seat, please; there's a chair in the back, there. I'll just make a call and check. He picked up the phone, dialed a number, and spoke in a low voice.

Casaubon, I said to myself, you're even stupider than Belbo. What are you waiting for? For Them to come and say, Oh, what a fine coincidence, Jacopo Belbo's friend as well; come, come along, yes, you too. . . .

I stood up abruptly, said good-bye, and left. In a minute I was out of rue de la Manticore, in another alley, then at the Seine. Fool! I said to myself. What did you expect? To walk in, find Agliè, take him by the lapels, and hear him apologize and say it was all a misunderstanding, here's your friend, we didn't touch a hair on his head. And now they know that you're here, too.

It was past noon, and that evening something would take place in the Conservatoire. What was I to do? I turned into rue Saint-Jacques, every now and then looking over my shoulder. An Arab seemed to be following me. But what made me think he was an Arab? The thing about Arabs is that they don't look like Arabs, or at least not in Paris. In Stockholm it would be different.

I passed a hotel, went in, asked for a room, got a key. As I was going upstairs, wooden stairs with a railing, from the second-floor landing the desk was still visible and I saw the presumed Arab enter. Then I noticed that in the corridor there were other people who could have been Arabs. Of course, that neighborhood was full of little hotels for Arabs. What did I expect?

I went into the room. It was decent; there was even a telephone. Too bad I didn't know anyone I could call.

I dozed fitfully until three. Then I washed my face and headed for the Conservatoire. Now there was nothing else for me to do but enter the museum, stay on after closing, and wait for midnight.

Which I did. And a few hours before midnight, I found myself in the periscope, waiting.

Nezah, for some interpreters, is the Sefirah of endurance, forbearance, constant patience. In fact, a test lay ahead of us. But for other interpreters, it is victory. Whose victory? Perhaps, in this story full of the defeated, of the Diabolicals mocked by Belbo, of Belbo mocked by the Diabolicals, of Diotallevi mocked by his cells, I was—for the moment—the only victorious one. Lying in wait in the periscope, I knew about the others, but the others didn't know about me. The first part of my scheme had gone according to plan.

And the second? Would it, too, go according to plan, or would it go according to the Plan, which now was no longer mine?

HOD

II2

I had stayed in the periscope too long. It must have been ten, ten-
thirty. If something was going to happen, it would happen in the
nave, before the Pendulum. I had to go down there and find a hiding place, an observation post. If I arrived too late, after They entered (from where?), They would notice me.

Go downstairs. Move . . . For hours I had waited for this, but
now that it was possible, even wise, to do it, I felt somehow paralyzed. I would have to cross the rooms at night, using my flashlight
only when necessary. The barest hint of a nocturnal glow filtered
through the big windows. I had imagined a museum made ghostly
by the moon's rays; I was wrong. The glass cases reflected vague
glints from outside; that was all. If I didn't move carefully, I could
go sprawling on the floor, could knock over something with a shat-
ter of glass, a clang of metal. Now and then I turned on the flashlight, turned it off. Proceeding, I felt as if I were at the Crazy Horse.
The sudden beam revealed a nakedness, not of flesh, but of screws,
clamps, rivets.

What if I were suddenly to reveal a living presence, the figure of
an envoy of the Masters echoing, mirroring my progress? Who would
be the first to shout? I listened. In vain. Gliding, I made no noise.
Neither did he.

That afternoon I had studied carefully the sequence of the rooms,
in order to be able to find the great staircase even in the darkness.
But instead I was wandering, groping. I had lost my bearings.

Perhaps I was going in circles, crossing some of the rooms for the second time; perhaps I would never get out of this place; perhaps this groping among meaningless machines was the rite.

The truth was, I didn't want to go down. I wanted to postpone the rendezvous.

I had emerged from the periscope after a long and merciless examination of conscience, I had reviewed our error of the last years and tried to understand why, without any reasonable reason, I was now here hunting for Belbo, who was here for reasons even less reasonable. But the moment I set foot outside the periscope, everything changed. As I advanced, I advanced with another man's head. I became Belbo. Like Belbo, now at the end of his long journey toward enlightenment, I knew that every earthly object, even the most squalid, must be read as the hieroglyph of something else, and that there is nothing, no object, as real as the Plan. How clever I was! A flash of light, a glance, was all it took, and I understood. I would not let myself be deceived.

. . . Froment's Motor: a vertical structure on a rhomboid base. It enclosed, like an anatomical figure exhibiting its ribs and viscera, a series of reels, batteries, circuit breakers—what the hell did the textbooks call them?—and the thing was driven by a transmission belt fed by a toothed wheel. . . . What could it have been used for? Answer: for measuring the telluric currents, of course.

Accumulators. What did they accumulate? I imagined the Thirty-six Invisibles as stubborn secretaries (keepers of the secret) tapping all night on their clavier-scribes to produce from this machine a sound, a spark, all of them intent on a dialog from coast to coast, from abyss to surface, from Machu Picchu to Avalon, come in, come in, hello hello hello, Pamersiel Pamersiel, we've caught a tremor, current Mu 36, the one the Brahmans worshiped as the breath of God, now I'll plug in the tap, the valve, all micro-macrocosmic circuits operational, all the mandrake roots shuddering beneath the crust of the globe, you hear the song of the Universal Sympathetic, over and out.

My God, armies slaughtered one another across the plains of Europe, popes hurled anathemas, emperors met, hemophiliac and incestuous, in the hunting lodge of the Palatine gardens, all to supply a cover, a sumptuous façade for the work of these wireless operators who in the House of Solomon were listening for pale echoes from the Umbilicus Mundi.

And as they operated these pseudothermic hexatetragrammatic electrocapillatories—that's how Garamond would have put it—every now and then someone would invent, say, a vaccine or an electric bulb, a triumph in the wonderful adventure of metals, but the real task was quite different: here they are, assembled at midnight, to spin this static-electricity machine of Ducretet, a transparent wheel that looks like a bandoleer, and, inside it, two little vibrating balls supported by arched sticks, and when they touch, sparks fly, and Dr. Frankenstein hopes to give life to his golem, but no, the signal has another purpose: Dig, dig, old mole. . . .

A sewing machine (what else? One of those engraving-advertisements, along with pills for developing one's bust, and the great eagle flying over the mountains with the restorative cordial in its talons, Robur le Conquérant, R. C.), but when you turn it on, it turns a wheel, and the wheel turns a coil, and the coil . . . What does the coil do? Who is listening to the coil? The label says, "Currents induced from the terrestrial field." Shameless! There to be read even by children on their afternoon visits! Mankind believed it was going in a different direction, believed everything was possible, believed in the supremacy of experiment, of mechanics. The Masters of the World have deceived us for centuries. Enfolded, swaddled, seduced by the Plan, we wrote poems in praise of the locomotive.

I passed by. I imagined myself dwindling, an ant-sized, dazed pedestrian in the streets of a mechanical city, metallic skyscrapers on every side. Cylinders, batteries, Leyden jars one above the other, merry-go-round centrifuges, tourniquet électrique à attraction et repulsion, a talisman to stimulate the sympathetic currents, colonnade étincelante formée de neuf tubes, électroaimant, a guillotine, and in the center—it looked like a printing press—hooks hung from chains, the kind you might see in a stable. A press in which you could crush a hand, a head. A glass bell with a pneumatic pump, two-cylinder, a kind of alembic, with a cup underneath and, to the right, a copper sphere. In it Saint-Germain concocted his dyes for the landgrave of Hesse.

A pipe rack with two rows of little hourglasses, ten to a row, their necks elongated like the neck of a Modigliani woman, some unspecified material inside, and the upper bulge of each expanded to a different size, like balloons about to take off. This, an apparatus for the production of the Rebis, where anyone could see it.

Then the glassworks section. I had retraced my steps. Little green bottles: a sadist host offering me poisons in quintessence. Iron machines for making bottles, opened and closed by two cranks. What if, instead of a bottle, someone put a wrist in there? Whack! And it would be the same with those great pincers, those immense scissors, those curved scalpels that could be inserted into sphincters or ears, into the uterus to extract the still-living fetus, which would be ground with honey and pepper to sate the appetite of Astarte. . . . The room I was now crossing had broad cases, and buttons to set in motion corkscrews that would advance inexorably toward the victim's eye, the Pit and the Pendulum. We were close to caricature now, to the ridiculous contraptions of Rube Goldberg, the torture racks on which Big Pete bound Mickey Mouse, the engrenage extérieur à trois pignons, triumph of Renaissance mechanics, Branca, Ramelli, Zonca. I knew these gears, I had put them in the wonderful adventure of metals, but they had been added here later, in the last century, and were ready to restrain the unruly after the conquest of the world; the Templars had learned from the Assassins how to shut up Noffo Dei when the time of his capture came; the swastika of Sebottendorf would twist, in the direction of the sun, the twitching limbs of the enemies of the Masters of the World. All ready, these instruments awaited a sign, everything in full view, the Plan was public, but nobody could have guessed it, the creaking mechanical maws would sing their hymn of conquest, great orgy of mouths, all teeth that locked and meshed exactly, mouths singing in tick-tock spasms.

Finally I came to the émetteur à étincelles soufflées designed for the Eiffel Tower, for the emission of time signals between France, Tunisia, and Russia, the Templars of Provins, the Paulicians, the Assassins of Fez. (Fez isn't in Tunisia, and the Assassins, anyway, were in Persia, but you can't split hairs when you live in the coils of Transcendent Time.) I had seen it before, this immense machine, taller than I, its walls perforated by a series of portholes, air ducts. The sign said it was a radio apparatus, but I knew better, I had passed it that same afternoon. The Beaubourg!

For all to see. And, for that matter, what was the real purpose of that enormous box in the center of Lutetia (Lutetia, the air duct in a subterranean sea of mud), where once there was the Belly of Paris, with those prehensile proboscises of vents, that insanity of pipes, conduits, that Ear of Dionysius open to the sky to capture sounds, messages, signals, and send them to the very center of the globe, and then to return them, vomiting out information from hell? First the Conservatoire, a laboratory, then the Tower, a probe, and finally the Beaubourg, a global transmitter and receiver. Had they set up that huge suction cup just to entertain a handful of hairy, smelly students, who went there to listen to the latest record with a Japanese headset? For all to see. The Beaubourg, gate to the underground kingdom of Agarttha, the monument of the Resurgentes Equites Synarchici. And the rest—two, three, four billion of them—were unaware of this, or forced themselves to look the other way. Idiots and hylics. While the pneumatics headed straight for their goal, through six centuries.

Unexpectedly, I found the staircase. I went down, with increasing caution. Midnight was approaching. I had to hide in my observation post before They arrived.

It was about eleven. I crossed the Lavoisier hall without turning on the flashlight, remembering the hallucinations of that afternoon. I crossed the corridor with the model trains.

There were already people in the nave: dim lights moving, the sound of shuffling, of objects being dragged.

Would I have time to make it to the sentry box? I slipped along the cases with the model trains and was soon close to the statue of Gramme, in the transept. On a wooden pedestal, cubic in form (the cubic stone of Yesod!), it stood as if to guard the entrance to the choir. My Statue of Liberty was almost directly behind it.

The front panel of the pedestal had been lowered, a kind of gangplank allowing people to enter the nave from some concealed passage. In fact, an individual emerged from there with a lantern—a gas lantern, with colored glass, which illuminated his face in red patches. I pressed myself into a corner, and he didn't see me. A second man joined him from the choir. "Vite," he said. "Hurry. In an hour they'll be here."

So this was the vanguard, preparing something for the rite. If there weren't too many of them, I could still reach Liberty before

They arrived—God knows from where, and in what numbers—by the same route. For a long while I crouched low, following the glints of the lanterns in the church, the regular alternation of the lights between greater and lesser intensity. I calculated how far they moved away from Liberty and how much of it remained in shadow. Then, at a certain moment, I risked it, squeezed past the left side of Gramme, a tight fit, painful, even sucking in my stomach. Luckily, I was thin as a rail. Lia . . . I made a dash, slipped into the sentry box, where I sank to the floor and curled up in a fetal position. My heart raced; my teeth chattered.

I had to relax. I breathed through my nose rhythmically, my breaths gradually deeper and deeper. This is how, under torture, you can make yourself lose consciousness and escape the pain. And, in fact, I sank slowly into the embrace of the Subterranean World.

113

Slowly, I regained consciousness, heard sounds; the light, now stronger, made me blink. My feet were numb. When I tried to get up, making no noise, I felt I was standing on a bed of spiny sea urchins. The Little Mermaid. Silently I stood on tiptoe, then bent my knees, and the pain lessened. Peering out cautiously, left and right, I saw that the sentry box was still pretty much in the shadows. Only then did I take in the scene.

The nave was illuminated on all sides. There were now dozens and dozens of lanterns, carried by new arrivals, who were entering from the passage behind me. They moved by on my left, into the choir, or lined up in the nave. My God, I said to myself, a Night on Bald Mountain, Walt Disney version.

They didn't raise their voices; they whispered, together creating a noise like a crowd scene in a play: rhubarb rhubarb.

To the left, the lanterns were set on the floor in a semicircle, completing, with a flattened arc, the eastern curve of the choir, and touching, at the southernmost point, the statue of Pascal. A burning brazier had been placed there, and on it someone was throwing herbs, essences. The smoke reached me in the box, parched my throat, gave me a feeling of dazed excitement.

In the center of the choir, in the flickering of the lanterns, something stirred, a slender shadow.

The Pendulum! The Pendulum no longer swayed in its familiar place in the center of the transept. A larger version of it had been hung from the keystone in the center of the choir. The sphere was larger; the wire much thicker, like a hawser, I thought, or a cable of braided metal strands. The Pendulum, now enormous, must have appeared this way in the Panthéon. It was like beholding the moon through a telescope.

They had re-created the pendulum that the Templars first experimented with, half a millennium before Foucault. To allow it to sway freely, they had removed some ribs and supporting beams, turning the amphitheater of the choir into a crude symmetrical antistrophe marked out by the lanterns.

I asked myself how the Pendulum could maintain its constant oscillation, since the magnetic regulator could not be beneath it now, in the floor. Then I understood. At the edge of the choir, near the diesel engines, stood an individual ready to dart like a cat to follow the plane of oscillation. He gave the sphere a little push each time it came toward him, a precise light tap of the hand or the fingertips.

He was in tails, like Mandrake. Later, seeing his companions, I realized that he was indeed a magician, a prestidigitator from Le Petit Cirque of Madame Olcott; he was a professional, able to gauge pressures and distances, possessing a steady wrist skilled in working within the infinitesimal margins necessary in legerdemain. Perhaps through the thin soles of his gleaming shoes he could sense the vibrations of the currents, and move his hands according to the logic of both the sphere and the earth that governed it.

His companions—now I could see them as well. They moved among the automobiles in the nave, they scurried past the draisiennes and the motorcycles, almost tumbling in the shadows. Some carried a stool and a table covered with red cloth in the vast ambulatory in the rear, and some placed other lanterns. Tiny, nocturnal, twittering, they were like rachitic children, and as one went past me I saw mongoloid features and a bald head. Madame Olcott's Freaks Mignons, the horrible little monsters I had seen on the poster in the Librairie Sloane.

The circus was there in full force: the staff, guards, choreographers of the rite. I saw Alex and Denys, les Génts d'Avalon, sheathed in armor of studded leather. They were giants indeed, blond, leaning against the great bulk of the Obeissante, their arms folded as they waited.

I didn't have time to ask myself more questions. Someone had entered with solemnity, a hand extended to impose silence. I recognized Bramanti only because he was wearing the scarlet tunic, the white cape, and the miter I had seen on him that evening in Piedmont. He approached the brazier, threw something on it, a flame shot up, then thick, white smoke rose and slowly spread through the room. As in Rio, I thought, at the alchemistic party. And I didn't have an agogô. I held my handkerchief to my nose and mouth, as a filter. Even so, I seemed to see two Bramantis, and the Pendulum swayed before me in several directions at once, like a merry-go-round.

Bramanti began chanting: "Alef bet gimel dalet he vav zain het tet yod kaf lamed mem mun samek ayin pe sade qof resh shin tau!"

The crowd responded, praying: "Pamersiel, Padiel, Camuel, Aseliel, Barmiel, Gediel, Asyriel, Maseriel, Dorchtiel, Usiel, Cabariel, Raysiel, Symiel, Armadiel . . ."

Bramanti made a sign, and someone stepped from the crowd and knelt at his feet. For just an instant I saw the face. It was Riccardo, the man with the scar, the painter.

Bramanti questioned him, and Riccardo answered, reciting from memory the formulas of the ritual.

"Who are you?

"I am an adept, not yet admitted to the higher mysteries of the Tres. I have prepared myself in silence and meditation upon the mystery of the Baphomet, in the knowledge that the Great Work revolves around six intact seals, and only at the end will we know the secret of the seventh."

"How were you received?"

"Through the perpendicular of the Pendulum."

"Who received you?"

"A Mystical Envoy."

"Would you recognize him?"

"No, for he was masked. I know only the knight of the rank higher than mine, and he knows only the naometer of the rank higher than his, and each knows only one other. And so I wish it to be."

"Quid facit Sator Arepo?"

"Tenet Opera Rotas."

"Quid facit Satan Adama?"

"Tabat Amata Natas. Mandabas Data Amata, Nata Sata."

"Have you brought the woman?"

"Yes, she is here. I have delivered her to the person, as I was ordered. She is ready."

"Go, but remain ready."

The dialog proceeded in bad French, on both sides. Then Bramanti said: "Brothers, we are gathered here in the name of the One

Order, the Unknown Order, to which Order, until yesterday, you did not know that you belonged, and yet you have always belonged to it! Let us swear. Anathema on all profaners of the Secret. Anathema on all sycophants of the occult. Anathema on all those who have made a spectacle of the Rites and Mysteries!"

"Anathema!"

"Anathema on the Invisible College, on the bastard children of Hiram and the Widow, on the operative and speculative masters of the lie of the Orient and the Occident, Ancient, Accepted, or Revised, on Mizraim and Memphis, on the Philalethes and the Nine Sisters, on the Strict Observance and on the Ordo Templi Orientis, on the Illuminati of Bavaria and of Avignon, on the Kadosh Knights, on the Elus Cohen, on the Perfect Friendship, on the Knights of the Black Eagle and of the Holy City, on the Rosicrucians of Anglia, on the cabalists of the Rose + Cross of Gold, on the Golden Dawn, on the Catholic Rosy Cross of the Temple and of the Grail, on the Stella Matutina, on the Astrum Argentinum and Thelema, on Vril and Thule, on every ancient and mystical usurper of the name of the Great White Fraternity, on the Guardians of the Temple, on every college and priory of Zion and of Gaul!"

"Anathema!"

"Whoever out of ingenuity, submission, conversion, calculation, or bad faith has been initiated into any lodge, college, priory, chapter, or order that illicitly refers to obedience to the Unknown Superiors or to the Masters of the World, must this night abjure that initiation and implore total restoration in spirit and body to the one and true observance, the Tres, Templi Resurgentes Equites Synarchici, the triune and trinosophic mystical and most secret order of the Synarchic Knights of Templar Rebirth!"

"Sub umbra alarum tuarum!"

"Now enter the dignitaries of the thirty-six highest and most secret degrees."

As Bramanti called the elect, they appeared in liturgical vestments, wearing the insigne of the Golden Fleece on their chest.

"Knight of the Baphomet, Knight of the Six Intact Seals, Knight of the Seventh Seal, Knight of the Tetragrammaton, Knight Executioner of Florian and Dei, Knight of the Athanor . . . Venerable Naometer of the Turris Babel, Venerable Naometer of the Great Pyramid, Venerable Naometer of the Cathedrals, Venerable Naometer of the Temple of Solomon, Venerable Naometer of the Hortus Palatinus, Venerable Naometer of the Temple of Heliopolis . . ."

As Bramanti recited the titles, those named entered in groups, so I was unable to assign to each his individual dignity, but among the first twelve I saw De Gubernatis, the old man from the Librairie Sloane, Professor Camestres, and others I had met that evening in Piedmont. And I saw Signor Garamond, I believe as Knight of the Tetragrammaton, composed and hieratic, very much absorbed in his new role, with hands that trembled as they touched the Fleece on his chest. Meanwhile, Bramanti went on: "Mystical Legate of Karnak, Mystical Legate of Bavaria, Mystical Legate of the Barbelognostics, Mystical Legate of Camelot, Mystical Legate of Montsegur, Mystical Legate of the Hidden Imam . . . Supreme Patriarch of Tomar, Supreme Patriarch of Kilwinning, Supreme Patriarch of Saint-Martin-des-Champs, Supreme Patriarch of Marienbad, Supreme Patriarch of the Invisible Okhrana, Supreme Patriarch in partibus of the Rock of Alamut . . ."

The patriarch of the Invisible Okhrana was Salon, still gray-faced but, without his smock, now resplendent in a yellow tunic edged in red. He was followed by Pierre, the psychopomp of the Eglise Luciferienne, who wore on his chest, instead of the Golden Fleece, a dagger in a gilded sheath. Meanwhile, Bramanti went on: "Sublime Hierogam of the Chemical Wedding, Sublime Rodostauric Psychopomp, Sublime Referendarium of the Most Arcane Arcana, Sublime Steganograph of the Hieroglyphic Monad, Sublime Astral Connector Utriusque Cosmi, Sublime Keeper of the Tomb of Rosencreutz . . . Imponderable Archon of the Currents, Imponderable Archon of the Hollow Earth, Imponderable Archon of the Mystic Pole, Imponderable Archon of the Labyrinths, Imponderable Archon of the Pendulum of Pendula . . ." Bramanti paused, and it seemed to me that he uttered the last formula with reluctance: "And the Imponderable Archon of Imponderable Archons, the Servant of Servants, Most Humble Secretary of the Egyptian Oedipus, Lowest Messenger of the Masters of the World and Porter of Agarttha, Last Thurifer of the Pendulum, Claude-Louis, Comte de Saint-Germain, Prince Rackoczi, Comte de Saint-Martin, and Marchese di Agliè, Monsieur de Surmont, Mr. Welldone, Marchese di Monferrato, of Aymar, and of Belmar, Count Soltikoff, Knight Schoening, Count of Tzarogy!"

As the others of the elect took their places in the ambulatory facing the Pendulum, and the faithful stood in the nave, Agliè entered, pale and drawn, wearing a blue pinstripe suit. He led by the hand, as if escorting a soul along the path of Hades, Lorenza Pellegrini, also pale, and dazed, as if drugged; she was dressed only in a white, semitransparent tunic, and her hair fell loose over her shoulders. I saw her in profile as she went by, as pure and languid as a Pre-Raphaelite adulteress. Too diaphanous not to stir, once again, my desire.

Agliè led Lorenza to the brazier, near the statue of Pascal; he caressed her vacant face and made a sign to the Géants d'Avalon, who came and stood on either side of her, supporting her. Then he went and sat at the table, facing the faithful, and I could see him very well as he drew his snuffbox from his vest and stroked it in silence before speaking.

"Brothers, knights. You are here because in these past few days the Mystic Legates have informed you of the news, and therefore you all know the reason for our meeting. We should have met on the night of June 23, 1945. Some of you were not even born then— at least not in your present form. We are here because after six hundred years of the most painful error we have found one who knows. How he came to know—and to know more than we—is a disturbing mystery. But I trust that among us there is one . . . You could not fail to be here, could you, mystical friend already too curious on one occasion?. . . I trust, as I said, that in our presence there is one who can shed light on this matter. Ardenti!"

Colonel Ardenti—yes, it was he, raven-haired as before, though now doddering—made his way among the others and stepped forward before what seemed to be turning into a tribunal, but he was kept at a distance by the Pendulum, which marked a space that could not be crossed.

"We have not seen each other for some time, brother." Agliè was smiling. "I knew that you would be unable to resist coming. Well? You have been informed what the prisoner said, and he says he learned it from you. So you knew and you kept silent."

"Count," Ardenti said, "the prisoner is lying. It is humiliating for me to say this—but honor above all. The story I confided to him is not the story the Mystic Legates told me. The interpretation of the message—it's true, I came into possession of a message, but

I didn't hide that from you, years ago, in Milan—the interpretation is different. . . . I wouldn't have been capable of reading it as the prisoner has read it, and so, at that time, I sought help. And, I must say, I received no encouragement, only distrust, defiance, and threats. . . ." Perhaps he was going to say more, but as he stared at Agliè, he stared also at the Pendulum, which was acting on him like a spell. As if hypnotized, he sank to his knees and said only, "Forgive me, because I do not know."

"You are forgiven, because you know you do not know," Agliè said. "And so, brothers, the prisoner has knowledge that none of us has. He knows even who we are; in fact, we learned who we are through him. We must proceed: it will soon be dawn. While you remain here in meditation, I will withdraw once more, to wrest the revelation from him."

"Ah non, monsieur le comte!" Pierre stepped into the hemicycle, his pupils dilated. "For two days you have talked with him, tête-à-tête, and he has seen nothing, said nothing, heard nothing, like the three monkeys. What more do you wish to demand, this night? No, no. Let it be here. Here, before all of us!"

"Calm yourself, my dear Pierre. I have had brought here, this night, a woman I consider the most exquisite incarnation of the Sophia, the mystic bond between the world of error and the Superior Ogdoad. Do not ask me how or why, but in her presence the man will speak. Tell them who you are, Sophia."

And Lorenza, like a somnambulist, as if it were an effort to utter the words, said: "I am . . . the saint and the prostitute."

"Ah, that is to laugh," Pierre said. "We have here the crème de l'initiation and we call in a pute. No; the man must be brought immediately before the Pendule!"

"Let's not be childish," Agliè said. "Give me an hour. What makes you think he would speak here, before the Pendulum?"

"He will speak as he is undone. Le sacrifice humain!" Pierre shouted to the nave. And the nave, in a loud voice, repeated: "Le sacrifice humain!"

Salon stepped forward. "Count, our brother is not childish. He is right. We are not the police. . . ."

"You of all people say this," Agliè quipped.

"We are not the police," Salon said, "and it is not fitting for us to proceed with ordinary methods of inquiry. On the other hand, I do not believe that sacrifices to the forces of the underground will be efficacious either. If they had wanted to give us a sign, they would have done so long ago. Another one knows, besides the prisoner, but he has disappeared. This evening, we have the possibility of confronting the prisoner with those who knew . . ." He smiled, staring at Agliè, his eyes narrowing beneath their bushy brows. "And to make them also confront us . . ."

"What do you mean, Salon?" Agliè asked, in a voice that showed uncertainty.

"If Monsieur le Comte permits, I will explain," a woman said. It was Madame Olcott: I recognized her from the poster. Livid, in an olive garment, her hair, black with oil, tied at the nape. The hoarse voice of a man. In the Librairie Sloane I had recognized that face, and now I remembered: she was the Druidess who had run toward us in the clearing that night in Piedmont. "Alex, Denys, bring the prisoner here."

She spoke in an imperious tone. The murmuring in the nave expressed approval. The two giants obeyed, trusting Lorenza to two Freaks Mignons. Agliè's hands gripped the arms of his throne; he had been outvoted.

Madame Olcott signaled to her little monsters, and between the statue of Pascal and the Obeissante three armchairs were placed. On them three individuals were seated. The three were dark-skinned, small of stature, nervous, with large white eyes. "The Fox triplets. You know them well, Count. Theo, Leo, Geo, ready yourselves."

At that moment the giants of Avalon reappeared, holding Jacopo Belbo by the arms, though he barely came up to their shoulders. My poor friend was ashen, with several days' growth of beard; his hands were bound behind his back and his shirt was open. Entering the smoky arena, he blinked. He didn't seem surprised by the collection of hierophants he saw before him; after the past few days, he was probably prepared for anything.

He was surprised, though, to see the Pendulum in its new position. The giants dragged him to face Agliè's seat. The only sound was the swish of the Pendulum as it grazed his back.

Briefly, Belbo turned, and he saw Lorenza. Overwhelmed, he started to call her, and tried to free himself. But Lorenza, though she stared at him dully, seemed not to recognize him.

From the far end of the nave, near the ticket desk and the bookstall, a roll of drums was heard, and the shrill notes of some flutes. Suddenly, the doors of four automobiles opened, and four creatures emerged. I had seen them before, too, on the poster for Le.Petit Cirque.

Wearing fezlike felt hats and ample black cloaks buttoned to the neck, Les Derviches Hurleurs stepped from the automobiles like the dead rising from the grave, and they squatted at the edge of the magic circle. In the background a flute now played sweet music, and the four gently put their hands on the floor and bowed their heads.

From the fuselage of Bréguet's plane, a fifth Derviche leaned out like a muezzin from a minaret and began to chant in an unknown tongue, moaning and lamenting as the drums began again, increasing in intensity.

Crouched behind the Brothers Fox, Madame Olcott whispered words of encouragement to them. The three were slumped in their chairs, their hands clutching the arms, their eyes closed. They began to sweat, and all the muscles of their faces twitched.

Madame Olcott addressed the assembly of dignitaries. "My excellent little brothers will now bring into our midst three people who knew." She paused, then said: "Edward Kelley, Heinrich Khunrath, and . . ." Another pause. "Comte de Saint-Germain."

For the first time, I saw Agliè make a wrong move. Out of control, he sprang from his seat, flung himself toward the woman, narrowly avoiding the trajectory of the Pendulum, as he cried: "Viper, liar, you know that cannot be. . . ." Then, to the nave: "It's an imposture! A lie! Stop her!"

But no one moved except Pierre, who went up and sat on the throne. "Proceed, madame," he said.

Agliè, recovering his sangfroid, stood aside, mingling with the others. "Very well," he challenged. "Let's see, then."

Madame Olcott moved her arm as if signaling the start of a race. The music grew shrill, dissonant; the drumbeats lost their steady rhythm; the dancers, who had already begun swaying back and forth, right and left, as they squatted, got up now, threw off their cloaks, and held out their arms wide, rigid, as if they were about to take flight. A moment of immobility, and they began to spin in place, using the left foot as a pivot, faces upraised, concentrated, vacant, and their pleated tunics belled out as they pirouetted, making them look like flowers caught in a hurricane.

Meanwhile, the mediums, breathing hoarsely, seemed to knot up, their faces distorted, as if they were straining, unsuccessfully, to defecate. The light of the brazier dimmed. Madame Olcott's acolytes turned off the lanterns on the floor, and now the church was illuminated only by the glow from the nave.

And the miracle began to take place. From Theo Fox's lips a whitish foam trickled, a foam that seemed to thicken. A similar substance issued from the lips of his brothers.

"Come, brothers," Madame Olcott murmured, coaxed, "come, come. That's right, yes. . . ."

The dancers sang brokenly, hysterically, they shook and bobbed their heads, they shouted, then made convulsive noises, like death rattles.

The stuff emitted by the mediums took on body, grew more substantial; it was like a lava of albumin, which slowly expanded and descended, slid over their shoulders, their chests, their legs with the sinuous movement of a reptile. I could not tell now if it came from the pores of their skin or their mouths, ears, and eyes. The crowd pressed forward, pushing closer and closer to the mediums and the dancers. I lost all fear: confident that I would not be noticed among them, I stepped from the sentry box, exposing myself still more to the fumes that spread and curled beneath the vaults.

Around the mediums, a milky luminescence. The foam began to detach itself from them, to assume ameboid shape. From the mass that came from one of the mediums, a tip broke free, turned, and moved up along his body, like an animal that intended to strike him with its beak. At the end of it, two mobile knobs formed, like the horns of a giant snail. . . .

The dancers, eyes closed, mouths frothing, did not cease their spinning, and they began to revolve, as much as the space allowed, around the Pendulum, miraculously doing this without crossing its trajectory. Whirling faster and faster, they flung off their fezes, let their long black hair stream out, and it seemed their heads were flying from their necks. They shouted, like the dancers that evening in Rio: Houu houu houuuuu . . .

The white forms acquired definition: one of them grew vaguely human in appearance, another went from phallus to ampule to alembic, and the third was clearly taking on the aspect of a bird, an owl with great eyeglasses and erect ears, the hooked beak of an old schoolmistress, a teacher of natural sciences.

Madame Olcott questioned the first form: "Kelley, is that you?"

From the form a voice came. It was definitely not Theo Fox speaking. The voice, distant, said in halting English: "Now . . . I do reveale a . . . a mighty Secret, if ye marke it well . . ."

"Yes, yes," Madame Olcott insisted.

The voice went on: "This very place is call'd by many names. . . . Earth . . . Earth is the lowest element of all. . . . When thrice ye have turned this Wheele about . . . thus my greate Secret I have revealed. . . ."

Theo Fox made a gesture with his hand, as if to beg mercy. "No, hold on to it," Madame Olcott said to him. Then she addressed the owl shape: "I recognize you, Khunrath. What have you to tell us?"

The owl spoke: "Hallelu . . . 'aah . . . Hallelu . . . 'aah . . . Hallelu . . . 'aah . . . Was . . ."

"Was?"

"Was helfen Fackeln Licht . . . oder Briln . . . so die Leut . . . nicht sehen . . . wollen . . ."

"We do wish," Madame Olcott said. "Tell us what you know."

"Symbolon kósmou . . . tâ ántra . . . kaì tân enkosmiôn dunámeôn eríthento . . . oi theológoi . . ."

Leo Fox was also exhausted. The owl's voice weakened, Leo's head slumped, the effort to sustain the shape was too great. But the implacable Madame Olcott told him to persevere and addressed the last shape, which now had also taken on anthropomorphic features. "Saint-Germain, Saint-Germain, is that you? What do you know?"

The shape began to hum a tune. Madame Olcott called for silence. The musicians stopped, and the dancers no longer howled, but they continued spinning, though with increasing fatigue.

The shape was singing: "Gentle love, this hour befriends me . . ."

"It's you; I recognize you," Madame Olcott said invitingly. "Speak, tell us where, what . . ."

The shape said: "Il était nuit. . . . La tête couverte du voile de lin . . . j'arrive, je trouve un autel de fer, j'y place le rameau mystérieux. . . . Oh, je crus descendre dans un abîme . . . des galeries

composées de quartiers de pierre noire . . . mon voyage souter-
rain . . ."

"He's a fraud, a fraud!" Agliè cried. "Brothers, you all know
these words. They're from the *Très Sainte Trinosophie*, I wrote it
myself; anyone can read it for sixty francs!" He ran to Geo Fox
and began shaking him by the arm.

"Stop, you imposter!" Madame Olcott screamed. "You'll kill him!"

"And what if I do?" Agliè shouted, pulling the medium off the
chair.

Geo tried to support himself by clinging to the form he had secreted, but it fell with him and dissolved on the floor. Geo slumped
in the sticky matter that he continued to vomit, until he stiffened,
lifeless.

"Stop, madman," Madame Olcott screamed, seizing Agliè. And
then, to the other brothers: "Stand fast, my little ones. They must
speak still. Khunrath, Khunrath, tell him you are real!"

Leo Fox, to survive, was trying to reabsorb the owl. Madame
Olcott went around behind him and pressed her fingers to his temples, to bend him to her will. The owl, realizing it was about to
disappear, turned toward its creator: "Phy, Phy Diabolos," it muttered, trying to peck his eyes. Leo gave a gurgle, as if his jugular
had been severed, and sank to his knees. The owl disappeared in a
revolting muck ("Phiii, phiii," it went), and into it, choking, the
medium also fell, and was still. Madame Olcott, furious, turned to
Theo, who was doing his best to hold on: "Speak, Kelley! You
hear me?"

But Kelley did not speak. He was trying to detach himself from
the medium, who now yelled as if his bowels were being torn. The
medium struggled to take back what he had produced, clawing the
air. "Kelley, earless Kelley, don't cheat again," Madame Olcott cried.
Kelley, unable to separate himself from the medium, was now trying
to smother him, turning into a kind of chewing gum, from which
the last Fox brother was unable to extricate himself. Theo, too, sank
to his knees, choking, entangled in the parasite blob that was devouring him; he rolled and writhed as if enveloped in flame. The
thing that had been Kelley covered him like a shroud, then melted,
liquefied, leaving Theo on the floor, the drained, gutted mummy of
a child embalmed by Salon. At that same moment, the four dancers
stopped as one, flailed their arms—drowning men, sinking like

stones—then crouched, whined like puppies, and covered their heads with their hands.

Agliè had returned to the ambulatory. He wiped the sweat from his brow with the little handkerchief that adorned his breast pocket, took two deep breaths, and put a white pill in his mouth. Then he called for silence.

"Brother knights. You have seen the cheap tricks this woman inflicts on us. Let us regain our composure and return to my proposal. Give me one hour with the prisoner in private."

Madame Olcott, oblivious, bent over her mediums, was stricken with an almost human grief. But Pierre, who had followed everything and was still seated on the throne, resumed control of the situation. "Non," he said. "There is only one means: le sacrifice humain! Give to me the prisoner."

Galvanized by his energy, the giants of Avalon grabbed Belbo, who had watched the scene in a daze, and thrust him before Pierre, who, with the agility of an acrobat, jumped up, put the chair on the table, and pushed both giants to the center of the choir. He grabbed the wire of the Pendulum as it went by and stopped the sphere, staggering under the recoil. It took barely an instant. As if the thing had been prearranged—and perhaps, during the confusion, some signals had been exchanged—the giants climbed up on the table and hoisted Belbo onto the chair. One giant wrapped the wire of the Pendulum twice around Belbo's neck, and the other held the sphere, then set it at the edge of the table.

Bramanti rushed to this makeshift gallows, flashing with majesty in his scarlet cloak, and chanted: "Exorcizo igitur te per Pentagrammaton, et in nomine Tetragrammaton, per Alfa et Omega qui sunt in spiritu Azoth. Saddai, Adonai, Jotchavah, Eieazereie! Michael, Gabriel, Raphael, Anael. Fluat Udor per spiritum Eloim! Maneat Terra per Adam Iot-Cavah! Per Samael Zebaoth et in nomine Eloim Gibor, veni Adramelech! Vade retro Lilith!"

Belbo stood straight on the chair, the wire around his neck. The giants no longer had to restrain him. If he took one step in any direction, he would fall from that shaky perch, and the noose, tightening, would strangle him.

"Fools!" Agliè shouted. "How will we put it back on its axis now?" He was concerned for the safety of the Pendulum.

Bramanti smiled. "Do not worry, Count. We are not mixing your dyes here. This is the Pendulum, as They conceived it. It will know where to go. And to convince a Force to act, there is nothing better than a human sacrifice."

Until that moment, Belbo had trembled. But now I saw him relax. He looked at the audience, I will not say with confidence, but with curiosity. I believe that, hearing the argument between the two adversaries, seeing before him the contorted bodies of the mediums, the dervishes still jerking and moaning to the side, the rumpled vestments of the dignitaries, Belbo recovered his most genuine gift: his sense of the ridiculous.

I believe that at that moment he decided not to allow himself to be frightened anymore. Perhaps his elevated position gave him a sense of superiority, as if he were watching, from a stage, that gathering of lunatics locked in a Grand Guignol feud, and at the sides, almost to the entrance, the little monsters, now uninterested in the action, nudging each other and giggling, like Annibale Cantalamessa and Pio Bo.

He only turned an anxious eye toward Lorenza, as the giants again grasped her arms. Jolted, she came to her senses. She began crying.

Perhaps Belbo was reluctant to let her witness his emotion, or perhaps he decided instead that this was the only way he could show his contempt for that crowd, but he held himself erect, head high, chest bared, hands bound behind his back, like a man who had never known fear.

Calmed by Belbo's calm, resigned to the interruption of the Pendulum, but still eager to know the secret after a lifetime's search (or many lifetimes), and also in order to regain control over his followers, Agliè addressed him again: "Come, Belbo, make up your mind. As you can see, you are in a situation that, to say the least, is awkward. Stop this playacting."

Belbo didn't answer. He looked away, as if politely to avoid overhearing a conversation he had chanced upon.

Agliè insisted, conciliatory, paternal: "I understand your irritation, your reserve. How it must revolt you to confide an intimate and precious secret to a rabble that has just offered such an unedifying spectacle! Very well, you may confide your secret to me alone, whispering it in my ear. Now I will have you taken down, and I know you will tell me a word, a single word."

Belbo said: "You think so?"

Then Agliè changed his tone. I saw him imperious as never before, sacerdotal, hieratic. He spoke as if he had on one of the Egyptian vestments worn by his colleagues. But the note was false; he seemed to be parodying those whom he had always treated with indulgent commiseration. At the same time, he spoke with the full assumption of his authority. For some purpose of his own—because this couldn't have been unintentional—he was introducing an element of melodrama. If he was acting, he acted well: Belbo seemed unaware of any deception, listening to Agliè as if he had expected nothing else from him.

"Now you will speak," Agliè said. "You will speak, and you will join this great game. If you remain silent, you are lost. If you speak, you will share in the victory. For truly I say this to you: this night you and I and all of us are in Hod, the Sefirah of splendor, majesty, and glory; Hod, which governs ritual and ceremonial magic; Hod, the moment when the curtain of eternity is parted. I have dreamed of this moment for centuries. You will speak, and you will join the only ones who will be entitled, after your revelation, to declare themselves Masters of the World. Humble yourself, and you will be exalted. You will speak because I order you to speak, and my words efficiunt quod figurant!"

And Belbo, now invincible, said, "Ma gavte la nata . . ."

Agliè, even if he was expecting a refusal, blanched at the insult.

"What did he say?" Pierre asked, hysterical.

"He will not speak," Agliè roughly translated. He lifted his arms in a gesture of surrender, of obedience, and said to Bramanti: "He is yours."

And Pierre said, transported: "Assez, assez, le sacrifice humain, le sacrifice humain!"

"Yes, let him die. We'll find the answer anyway," cried Madame Olcott, equally carried away, as she now returned to the scene, rushing toward Belbo.

At the same time, Lorenza moved. She freed herself from the giants' grasp and stood before Belbo, at the foot of the gallows, her arms opened wide, as if to stop an invading army. In tears, she exclaimed: "Are you all crazy? You can't do this!"

Agliè, who was withdrawing, stood rooted to the spot for a moment, then ran to her, to restrain her.

What happened next took only seconds. Madame Olcott's knot of hair came undone; all rancor and flames, like a Medusa, she bared her talons, scratched at Agliè's face, shoved him aside with the force of the momentum of her leap. Agliè fell back, stumbled over a leg of the brazier, spun around like a dervish, and banged his head against a machine; he sank to the ground, his face covered with blood. Pierre, meanwhile, flung himself on Lorenza, drawing the dagger from the sheath on his chest as he moved, but he blocked my view, so I didn't see what happened. Then I saw Lorenza slumped at Belbo's feet, her face waxen, and Pierre, holding up the red blade, shouted: "Enfin, le sacrifice humain!" Turning toward the nave, he said in a loud voice: "I'a Cthulhu! I'a S'ha-t'n!"

In a body, the horde in the nave moved forward: some fell and were swept aside; others, pushing, threatened to topple Cugnot's car. I heard—I must have heard it, I can't have imagined such a grotesque detail—the voice of Garamond saying: "Gentlemen, please! Manners! . . ." Bramanti, in ecstasy, was kneeling by Lorenza's body, declaiming: "Asar, Asar! Who is clutching me by the throat? Who is pinning me to the ground? Who is stabbing my heart? I am unworthy to cross the threshold of the house of Maat!"

Perhaps no one intended it, perhaps the sacrifice of Lorenza was to have sufficed, but the acolytes were now pressing inside the magic circle, which was made accessible by the immobility of the Pendulum, and someone—Ardenti, I think—was hurled by the others against the table, which literally disappeared from beneath Belbo's feet. It skidded away, and, thanks to the same push, the Pendulum began a rapid, violent swing, taking its victim with it. The wire, pulled by the weight of the sphere, tightened around the neck of my poor friend, yanked him into the air, and he swung above and with the Pendulum, swung toward the eastern extremity of the choir, then returned, I hoped without life, in my direction.

Trampling one another, the crowd drew back, retreated to the edges of the semicircle, to allow room for the wonder. The man in charge of the oscillation, intoxicated by the rebirth of the Pendulum, supplied pushes directly on the hanged man's body. The axis of motion made a diagonal from my eyes to one of the windows, no doubt the window with the colorless spot through which, in a few hours, the first ray of the rising sun would fall. Therefore, I did not see Belbo swing in front of me, but this, I believe, was the pattern he drew in space . . .

His head seemed a second sphere, trapped in the loops of the wire that stretched from the center of the keystone; and when the metal sphere tilted to the right, Belbo's head tilted to the left, and vice versa. For most of the long swing, the two spheres tended in opposite directions, one on either side of the wire, so what cleaved the air was no longer a single line, but a kind of triangular structure. And, while Belbo's head followed the pull of the wire, his body— at first in its final spasms, then with the disarticulated agility of a wooden marionette, arm here, leg there—described other arcs in the void, arcs independent of the head, the wire, and the sphere beneath. I had the thought that if someone were to photograph the scene using Muybridge's system—fixing on the plate every moment as a succession of positions, recording the two extreme points the head reached in each period, the two rest points of the sphere, the points of intersection of the wire with time, independent of both head and sphere, and the intermediary points marked by the plane of oscillation of the trunk and legs—Belbo hanged from the Pendulum would have drawn, in space, the tree of the Sefirot, summing up in his final moment the vicissitude of all universes, fixing forever in his motion the ten stages of the mortal exhalation and defecation of the divine in the world.

Then, as the Mandrake in tails continued to encourage that funereal swing, Belbo's body, through a grisly addition and cancellation of vectors, a migration of energies, suddenly became immobile, and the wire and the sphere moved, but only from his body down; the rest—which connected Belbo with the vault—now remained perpendicular. Thus Belbo had escaped the error of the world and its movements, had now become, himself, the point of suspension, the Fixed Pin, the Place from which the vault of the world is hung, while beneath his feet the wire and the sphere went on swinging, from pole to pole, without peace, the earth slipping away under them, showing always a new continent. The sphere could not point out, nor would it ever know, the location of the World's Navel.

As the pack of Diabolicals, dazed for a moment in the face of this portent, began to yowl again, I told myself that the story was now finished. If Hod is the Sefirah of glory, Belbo had had glory. A single fearless act had reconciled him with the Absolute.

114

The ideal pendulum consists of a very thin wire, which will not hinder flexion and torsion, of length L, with the weight attached to its barycenter. For a sphere, the barycenter is the center; for the human body, it is a point 0.65 of the height, measuring from the feet. If the hanged man is 1.70m tall, his barycenter is located 1.10m from his feet, and the length L includes this distance. In other words, if the distance from the man's head to neck is 0.60m, the barycenter is 1.70 − 1.10 = 0.60m from his head, and 0.60 − 0.30 = 0.30m from his neck.

The period of the pendulum, discovered by Huygens, is given by:

$$T \text{ (seconds)} = \frac{2\pi}{\sqrt{g}} \sqrt{L} \tag{1}$$

where L is the length in meters, $\pi = 3.1415927 \ldots$, and $g = 9.8\text{m}/\text{sec}^2$. Thus (1) gives:

$$T = \frac{2 \times 3.1415927}{\sqrt{9.8}} \sqrt{L} = 2.00709 \sqrt{L}$$

or, more or less:

$$T = 2\sqrt{L} \tag{2}$$

Note: T is independent of the weight of the hanged man. (In God's eyes all men are equal. . . .)

As for a double pendulum, one with two weights attached to the same wire . . . If you shift A, A oscillates; then after a while it stops and B will oscillate. If the paired weights are different or if their lengths are different, the energy passes from one to the other, but the periods of these oscillations will not be equal. . . . This eccentricity of movement also occurs if, instead of beginning to make A oscillate freely by setting it in motion, you apply a force to the system already in motion. That is to say, if the wind blows in gusts on the hanged man in asynchronous fashion. After a while, the hanged man will become motionless and his gallows will oscillate as if its fulcrum were the hanged man.
— From a private letter of Mario Salvadori, Columbia University, 1984

Having nothing more to learn in that place, I took advantage of the melee to reach the statue of Gramme.

The pedestal was still open. I entered, went down a narrow ladder, and found myself on a small landing illuminated by a light bulb, where a spiral stone staircase began. At the end of this, I came to a dim passage with a higher, vaulted ceiling. At first I didn't realize where I was, and couldn't identify the source of the rippling sound I heard. Then my eyes adjusted: I was in a sewer, with a handrail that kept me from falling into the water but not from inhaling an awesome stink, half chemical, half organic. At least something in our story was true: the sewers of Paris, of Colbert, Fantomas, Caus.

I followed the biggest conduit, deciding against the darker ones that branched off, and hoped that some sign would tell me where to end my subterranean flight. In any case, I was escaping, far from the Conservatoire, and compared to that kingdom of darkness the Paris sewers were relief, freedom, clean air, light.

I carried with me a single image, the hieroglyph traced in the choir by Belbo's corpse. What was that symbol? To what other symbol did it correspond? I couldn't figure it out. I know now it was a law of physics, but this knowledge only makes the phenomenon more symbolic. Here, now, in Belbo's country house, among his many notes, I found a letter from someone who, replying to a question of his, told him how a pendulum works, and how it would behave if a second weight were hung elsewhere along the length of its wire. So Belbo—God knows for how long—had been thinking of the Pendulum as both a Sinai and a Calvary. He hadn't died as the victim of a Plan of recent manufacture; he had prepared his death much earlier, in his imagination, unaware that his imagination, more creative than he, was planning the reality of that death.

Somehow, losing, Belbo had won. Or does he who devotes himself to this single way of winning then lose all? He loses all if he does not understand that the victory is a different victory. But on that Saturday evening I hadn't yet discovered this.

I went along the tunnel, mindless, like Postel, perhaps lost in the same darkness, and suddenly I saw the sign. A brighter lamp, attached to the wall, showed me another ladder, temporary, leading to a wooden trapdoor. I tried it, and I found myself in a basement filled with empty bottles, then a corridor with two toilets, a little man on one door, a little woman on the other. I was in the world of the living.

I stopped, breathless. Only then did I remember Lorenza. Now I was crying. But she was slipping away, leaving my bloodstream, as if she had never existed. I couldn't even see her face. In that world of the dead, she was the most dead.

At the end of the corridor I came to another stairway, a door. I entered a smoky, evil-smelling place, a tavern, a bistro, an Oriental bar, black waiters, sweating customers, greasy skewers, and mugs of beer. I appeared, like an ordinary customer who had gone to urinate and returned. Nobody noticed me. Perhaps the man at the cash desk, seeing me arrive from the back, gave me an almost imperceptible signal, narrowing his eyes as if to say: Yes, I understand, go ahead, I haven't seen a thing.

115

If the eye could see the demons that people the universe, existence
would be impossible.
　—Talmud, Berakhot, 6

Leaving the bar, I find myself among the lights of Porte Saint-
Martin. The bar is Arab, and the shops around it, still open, are Arab,
too. A composite odor of couscous and falafel, and crowd. Clumps
of young people, thin, many with sleeping bags. I ask a boy what
is going on. The march, he says. Tomorrow there will be a big
march against the Savary law. Marchers are arriving by the busload.

A Turk—a Druze, an Ismaili in disguise—invites me in bad French
to go into some kind of club. Never. Flee Alamut. You do not
know who is in the service of whom. Trust no one.

I cross the intersection. Now I hear only the sound of my footsteps. The advantage of a big city: move on a few meters, and you
find solitude again.

Suddenly, after a few blocks, on my left, the Conservatoire, pale
in the night. From the outside, perfect peace, a monument sleeping
the sleep of the just. I continue southward, toward the Seine. I have
a destination, but I'm not sure what it is. I want to ask someone
what has happened.

Belbo dead? The sky is serene. I encounter a group of students.
They are silent, influenced by the genius loci. On the left, the hulk
of Saint-Nicolas-des-Champs.

I continue along rue Saint-Martin, I cross rue aux Ours, broad, a
boulevard, almost; I'm afraid of losing my way, but what way? Where
am I going? I don't know. I look around, and on my right, at the
corner, I see two display windows of Editions Rosicruciennes. They're
dark, but in the light of the street lamp and with the help of my
flashlight I manage to make out their contents. Books, objects. Histoire des juifs, Comte de St.-Germain, alchemy, monde caché, les
maisons secrètes de la Rose-Croix, the message of the builders of
the cathedrals, the Cathars, The New Atlantis, Egyptian medicine,

the temple of Karnak, the Bhagavad-Gita, reincarnation, Rosicrucian crosses and candelabra, busts of Isis and Osiris, incense in boxes and tablets, tarots. A dagger, a tin letter opener with a round hilt bearing the seal of the Rosicrucians. What are they doing, making fun of me?

I pass the façade of the Beaubourg. During the day the place is a village fair; now the plaza is almost deserted. A few silent groups, sleeping, a few lights from the brasseries opposite. It's all true. Giant air ducts that absorb energy from the earth. Perhaps the crowds that come during the day serve to supply them with vibrations; perhaps the hermetic machine is fed on fresh meat.

The church of Saint-Merri. Opposite, the Librairie la Vouivre, three-quarters occultist. I must not give in to hysteria. I take rue des Lombards, to avoid an army of Scandinavian girls coming out of a bistro laughing. Shut up; Lorenza is dead.

But is she? What if I am the one who is dead? Rue des Lombards intersects, at right angles, rue Nicolas-Flamel, and at the end of that you can see, white, the Tour Saint-Jacques. At the corner, the Librairie Arcane 22, tarots and pendulums. Nicolas Flamel the alchemist, an alchemistic bookshop, and then the Tour Saint-Jacques, with those great white lions at the base, a useless late-Gothic tower near the Seine, after which an esoteric review was named. Pascal conducted experiments there on the weight of air, and even today, at a height of fifty-two meters, the tower has a station for meteorological research. Maybe They began with the Tour Saint-Jacques, before erecting the Eiffel Tower. There are special locations. And no one notices.

I go back toward Saint-Merri. More girls' laughter. I don't want to see people. I skirt the church. Along rue du Cloître-Saint-Merri, a transept door, old, of rough wood. At the foot of the street, a square extends, the end of the Beaubourg area, here brilliantly lit. In the open space, machines by Tinguely, and other multicolored artifacts that float on the surface of a pool, a small artificial lake, their cogged wheels clanking insinuatingly. In the background I see again the scaffolding of Dalmine pipes, the Beaubourg with its gaping mouths—like an abandoned *Titanic* near a wall devoured by ivy, a shipwreck in a crater of the moon. Where the cathedrals failed, the great transatlantic ducts whisper, in contact with the Black Virgins. They are discovered only by one who knows how to circumnavigate Saint-Merri. And so I must go on; I have a clue, I must expose Their plot in the very center of the Ville Lumière, the plot of the Dark Ones.

I find myself at the façade of Saint-Merri. Something impels me to train my flashlight on the portal. Flamboyant Gothic, arches in accolade.

And suddenly, finding what I didn't expect to find, on the archivolt of the portal I see it.

The Baphomet. Where two curves join. At the summit of the first, a dove of the Holy Spirit with a glory of stone rays, but on the second, besieged by praying angels, there he is, the Baphomet, with his awful wings. On the façade of a church. Shameless.

Why here? Because we aren't far from the Temple. Where is the Temple, or what's left of it? I retrace my steps, north, and find myself at the corner of rue de Montmorency. At number 51, the house of Nicolas Flamel. Between the Baphomet and the Temple. The shrewd spagyric knew well with whom he was dealing. Poubelles full of foul rubbish opposite a house of undefined period, Taverne Nicolas Flamel. The house is old, restored for the tourists, for Diabolicals of the lowest order, hylics. Next door, an American shop with an Apple poster: "Secouez-vous les puces." Microsoft-Hermes. Directory, temurah.

Now I'm in rue du Temple, I walk along it and come to the corner of rue de Bretagne, and the Square du Temple, a garden blanched as a cemetery, the necropolis of the martyred knights.

Rue de Bretagne to rue Vieille du Temple. Rue Vieille du Temple, after rue Barbette, has novelty shops: electric bulbs in odd shapes, like ducks or ivy leaves. Too blatantly modern. They don't fool me.

Rue des Francs-Bourgeois: I'm in the Marais, I know, and soon the old kosher butcher shops will appear. What do the Jews have to do with the Templars, now that we gave their place in the Plan to the Assassins of Alamut? Why am I here? Is it an answer I am looking for? Perhaps I'm only trying to get away from the Conservatoire. Unless I do have a destination, a place I'm going to. But it can't be here. I rack my brain to remember where it is, as Belbo hunted in a dream for a lost address.

An obscene group approaches. Laughing nastily, they march in open order, forcing me to step off the sidewalk. For a moment I fear they are agents of the Old Man of the Mountain, that they have come for me. Not so; they vanish into the night, but they speak a foreign language, a sibilant Shiite, Talmudic, Coptic, like a serpent of the desert.

Androgynous figures loom, in long cloaks. Rosicrucian cloaks. They pass, turn into rue de Sévigné. It is late, very late. I fled the Conservatoire to find again the city of all, but now I realize that the city of all is a catacomb with special paths for the initiated.

A drunk. But he may be pretending. Trust no one, no one. I pass a still-open bar; the waiters, in aprons down to their ankles, are putting chairs on tables. I manage to enter just in time. I order a beer, drain it, ask for another. "A healthy thirst, eh?" one of them says. But without cordiality, suspicious. Of course I'm thirsty; I've had nothing to drink since five yesterday afternoon. A man can be thirsty without having spent the night under a pendulum. Fools. I pay and leave before they can commit my features to memory.

I'm at the corner of Place des Vosges. I walk along the arcades. What was that old movie in which the solitary footsteps of Mathias, the mad killer, echoed at night in Place des Vosges? I stop. Do I hear footsteps behind me? But I wouldn't, of course; the killer has stopped, too. These arcades—all they need is a few glass cases, and they could be rooms in the Conservatoire.

Low sixteenth-century ceilings, round-headed arches, galleries selling prints, antiques, furniture. Place des Vosges, with its old doorways, cracked and worn and leprous. The people here haven't moved for hundreds of years. Men with yellow cloaks. A square inhabited exclusively by taxidermists. They appear only at night. They know the movable slab, the manhole through which you penetrate the Mundus Subterraneus. In full view.

The Union de Recouvrement des Cotisation de Sécurité sociale et D'allocations familiales de la Patellerie, number 75, apartment 1. A new door—rich people must live there—but right next to it is an old door, peeling, like a door on Via Sincero Renato. Then, at number 3, a door recently restored. Hylics alternating with pneumatics. The Masters and their slaves. Then, planks nailed across what must have been an arch. It's obvious; there was an occultist bookshop here and now it's gone. A whole block has been emptied. Evacuated overnight. Like Agliè. They know someone knows; they are beginning to cover their tracks.

At the corner of rue de Birague, I see the line of arcades, infinite, without a living soul. I want darkness, not these yellow street lamps. I could cry out, but no one would hear me. Behind all the closed windows, through which not a thread of light escapes, the taxidermists in their yellow smocks will snicker.

But no; between the arcades and the garden in the center are parked cars, and an occasional shadow passes. A big Belgian shepherd crosses my path. A black dog alone in the night. Where is Faust? Did he send the faithful Wagner out for a piss?

Wagner. That's the word that was churning in my mind without surfacing. Dr. Wagner: he's the one I need. He will be able to tell me that I'm raving, that I've given flesh to ghosts, that none of it's true, Belbo's alive, and the Tres don't exist. What a relief it would be to learn that I'm sick.

I abandon the square, almost running. I'm followed by a car. But maybe it's only looking for a parking place. I trip on a plastic garbage bag. The car parks. It didn't want me. I'm on rue Saint-Antoine. I look for a taxi. As if invoked, one passes.

I say to the driver: "Sept, Avenue Elisée-Reclus."

116

Je voudrais être la tour, pendre à la Tour Eiffel.
—Blaise Cendrars

I didn't know where 7, Avenue Elisée-Reclus was, and I didn't dare ask the driver, because anyone who takes a taxi at that hour either is heading for his own home or is a murderer at the very least. The man was grumbling that the center of the city was still full of those damn students, buses parked everywhere, it was a scandal, if he was in charge, they'd all be lined up against a wall, and the best thing was to go the long way round. He practically circled Paris, leaving me finally at number 7 of a lonely street.

There was no Dr. Wagner at that address. Was it seventeen, then? Or twenty-seven? I walked, looked at two or three houses, then came to my senses. Even if I found the house, was I thinking of dragging Dr. Wagner out of bed at this time of night to tell him my story? I had ended up here for the same reason that I had roamed from Porte Saint-Martin to Place des Vosges: I was fleeing. I didn't need a psychoanalyst, I needed a straitjacket. Or the cure of sleep. Or Lia. To have her hold my head, press it between her breast and armpit, and whisper soothingly to me.

Was it Dr. Wagner I wanted or Avenue Elisée-Reclus? Because—now I remembered—I had come across that name in the course of my reading for the Plan. Elisée Reclus was someone in the last century who wrote a book about the earth, the underground, volcanoes; under the pretext of academic geography he stuck his nose into the Mundus Subterraneus. One of Them, in other words. I ran from Them, yet kept finding Them around me. Little by little, in the space of a few hundred years, They had occupied all of Paris. And the rest of the world.

I should go back to the hotel. Would I find another taxi? This was probably an out-of-the-way suburb. I headed in the direction where the night sky was brighter, more open. The Seine?

When I reached the corner, I saw it.

On my left. I should have known it would be there, in ambush, because in this city the street names wrote unmistakable messages; they gave you warnings. It was my own fault that I hadn't been paying attention.

There it was, foul metal spider, the symbol and instrument of their power. I should have run, but I felt drawn to that web, craning my neck, then looking downward, because from where I stood the thing could not be encompassed in one glance. I was swallowed by it, slashed by its thousand edges, bombarded by metal curtains that fell on every side. With the slightest move it could have crushed me with one of those Meccano paws.

La Tour. I was at the one place in the city where you don't see it in the distance, in profile, benevolent above the ocean of roofs, light-hearted as a Dufy painting. It was on top of me, it sailed at me. I could glimpse the tip, but I moved inward, between its legs, and saw its haunches, underside, genitalia, sensed the vertiginous intestine that climbed to join the esophagus of that polytechnical giraffe's neck. Perforated, it yet had the power to douse the light around it, and as I moved, it offered me, from different perspectives, different cavernous niches that framed sudden zooms into darkness.

To its right, in the northeast, still low on the horizon, a sickle moon. At times, the Tower framed it; and to me it looked like an optical illusion, the fluorescence of one of those skewed screens the Tower's structure formed; but if I walked on a little, the screens assumed new forms, the moon vanished, tangled in the metal ribs; the spider crushed it, digested it, and it went into another dimension.

Tesseract. Four-dimensional cube. Through an arch I saw a flashing light—no, two, one red, one white—surely a plane looking for Roissy or Orly. The next moment—I had moved, or the plane, or the Tower—the lights hid behind a rib; I waited for them to reappear in the next frame, but they were gone for good. The Tower had a hundred windows, all mobile, and each gave onto a different segment of space-time. Its ribs didn't form Euclidean curves, they ripped the very fabric of the cosmos, they overturned realities, they leafed through pages of parallel worlds.

Who was it who said that this spire of Notre Dame de la Brocante served "à suspendre Paris au plafond de l'univers"? On the contrary, it suspended the universe from its spire. It was thus the substitute for the Pendulum.

What had they called it? Lone suppository, hollow obelisk, Magnificat of wire, apotheosis of the battery, aerial altar of an idolatrous cult, bee in the heart of the rose of the winds, piteous ruin, hideous night-colored colossus, misshapen emblem of useless strength, absurd wonder, meaningless pyramid, guitar, inkwell, telescope, prolix as a cabinet minister's speech, ancient god, modern beast . . . It was all this and more. And, had I had the sixth sense of the Masters of the World, now that I stood within its bundle of vocal cords encrusted with rivet polyps, I would have heard the Tower hoarsely whisper the music of the spheres as it sucked waves from the heart of our hollow planet and transmitted them to all the menhirs of the world. Rhizome of junctures, cervical arthrosis, prothesis of protheses. The horror of it! To dash my brains out, from where I was, They would have to launch me toward the peak. Surely I was coming out of a journey through the center of the earth, I was dizzy, antigravitational, in the antipodes.

No, we had not been daydreaming: here was the looming proof of the Plan. But soon the Tower would realize that I was the spy, the enemy, the grain of sand in the gear system it served, soon it would imperceptibly dilate a diamond window in that lace of lead and swallow me, grab me in a fold of its hyperspace, and put me Elsewhere.

If I remained a little longer under its tracery, its great talons would clench, curve like claws, draw me in, and then the animal would slyly assume its former position. Criminal, sinister pencil sharpener!

Another plane: this one came from nowhere; the Tower itself had generated it between two of its plucked-mastodon vertebrae. I looked up. The Tower was endless, like the Plan for which it had been born. If I could remain there without being devoured, I would be able to follow the shifts, the slow revolutions, the infinitesimal decompositions and recompositions in the chill of the currents. Perhaps the Masters of the World knew how to interpret it as a geomantic design, perhaps in its metamorphoses they knew how to read their instructions, their unconfessable mandates. The Tower spun above my head, screwdriver of the Mystic Pole. Or else it was immobile, like a magnetized pin, and it made the heavenly vault rotate. The vertigo was the same.

609

How well the Tower defends itself! I said silently. From the distance it winks affectionately, but should you approach, should you attempt to penetrate its mystery, it will kill you, it will freeze your bones, simply by revealing the meaningless horror of which it is made. Now I know that Belbo is dead, and the Plan is real, because the Tower is real. If I don't get away now, fleeing once again, I won't be able to tell anyone. I must sound the alarm.

A noise. Stop, return to reality. A taxi bearing down. With a leap I managed to tear myself from the magic girdle, I waved my arms, and was almost run over, because the driver braked only at the last moment, stopping as if with great reluctance. During the ride he explained that he, too, when he passed beneath it at night, found the Tower frightening, so he speeded up. "Why?" I asked him. "Parce que . . . parce que ça fait peur, c'est tout."

At my hotel, I had to ring and ring before the sleepy night porter came. I said to myself: You have to sleep now. The rest, tomorrow. I took some pills, enough to poison myself. Then I don't remember.

117

Madness has an enormous pavilion
Where it receives folk from every region,
Especially if they have gold in profusion.
—Sebastian Brant, *Das Narrenschiff*, 1494, 46

I woke at two in the afternoon, dazed, catatonic. I remembered everything clearly, but didn't know if what I remembered was true. My first thought was to run downstairs and buy the newspapers; then I told myself that even if a company of spahis had stormed the Conservatoire immediately after the event, the news wouldn't have had time to appear in the morning papers.

Besides, Paris had other things on its mind that day. The desk clerk informed me as soon as I went down to look for some coffee. The city was in an uproar. Many Métro stations were closed; in some places the police were using force to disperse the crowds; the students were too numerous, they were going too far.

I found Dr. Wagner's number in the telephone book. I tried calling, but his office was obviously closed on Sunday. Anyway, I had to go and check at the Conservatoire. It was open on Sunday afternoons.

In the Latin Quarter groups of people were shouting and waving flags. On the Ile de la Cité I saw a police barricade. Shots could be heard in the distance. This is how it must have been in '68. At Sainte-Chapelle there must have been a confrontation, I caught a whiff of tear gas. I heard people charging, I didn't know if they were students or policemen; everybody around me was running. Some of us took refuge inside a fence behind a cordon of police, while there was some scuffling in the street. The shame of it: here I was with the aging bourgeoisie, waiting for the revolution to subside.

Then the way was clear, and I took back streets around the old Halles, until I was again in rue Saint-Martin. The Conservatoire was open, with its white forecourt, the plaque on the façade: "Conservatoire des Arts et Métiers, established by decree of the Convention on 19 Vendémiaire, Year III . . . in the former priory of Saint-Martin-des-Champs, founded in the eleventh century." Everything normal, with a little Sunday crowd ignoring the students' kermesse.

I went inside—Sundays free—and everything was as it had been at five o'clock yesterday afternoon. The guards, the visitors, the Pendulum in its usual place . . . I looked for signs of what had happened, but if it had happened, someone had done a thorough cleaning. If it had happened.

I don't recall how I spent the rest of the afternoon. Nor do I recall what I saw, wandering the streets, forced every now and then to turn into an alley to avoid a scuffle. I called Milan, just to see, dialed Belbo's number, then Lorenza's. Then Garamond Press, which would of course be closed.

As I sit here tonight, all this happened yesterday. But between the day before yesterday and this night an eternity has passed.

Toward evening I realized that I hadn't eaten anything. I wanted quiet, and a little comfort. Near the Forum des Halles I entered a restaurant that promised fish. There was too much fish. My table was directly opposite an aquarium. A universe sufficiently surreal to plunge me again into paranoia. Nothing is accidental. That fish seems an asthmatic Hesychast that is losing its faith and accusing God of having lessened the meaning of the cosmos. Sabaoth, Sabaoth, how can you be so wicked as to make me believe you don't exist? The flesh is covering the world like gangrene. . . . That other fish looks like Minnie; she bats her long lashes and purses her lips into a heart shape. Minnie Mouse is Mickey's fiancée. I eat a salade folle with a haddock tender as a baby's flesh. With honey and pepper. The Paulicians are here. That one glides among the coral like Bréguet's airplane, a leisurely lepidopteral fluttering of wings; a hundred to one he saw his homunculus abandoned at the bottom of an athanor, now with a hole in it, thrown into the garbage opposite Flamel's house. And now a Templar fish, all armored in black, looking for Noffo Dei. He grazes the asthmatic Hesychast, who navigates pensively, frowning, toward the Unspeakable. I look away. Across the street I glimpse the sign of another restaurant, Chez R . . .

612

Rosie Cross? Reuchlin? Rosispergius? Rachkovskyragotgkyzarogi? Signatures, signatures . . .

Let's see. The only way to discomfit the Devil is to make him believe you don't believe in him. There's no mystery in your night-time flight across Paris, in your vision of the Tower. To come out of the Conservatoire after what you saw, or believe you saw, and to experience the city as a nightmare—that is normal. But what did I see in the Conservatoire?

I absolutely had to talk to Dr. Wagner. I don't know why, but I had to. Talking was the panacea. The therapy of the word.

How did I pass the time till this morning? I went into a movie theater where they were showing *The Lady from Shanghai* by Orson Welles. When the scene with the mirrors came, it was too much for me, and I left. But maybe that's not true, maybe I imagined the whole thing.

This morning I called Dr. Wagner at nine. The name Garamond enabled me to get past the secretary; the doctor seemed to remember me, and, impressed by the urgency in my voice, he said to come at once, at nine-thirty, before his regular appointments. He seemed cordial, sympathetic.

Did I dream the visit to Dr. Wagner, too? The secretary asked for my vital statistics, prepared a card, had me pay in advance. Luckily I had my return ticket.

An office of modest size, with no couch. Windows overlooking the Seine. To the left, the shadow of the Tower. Dr. Wagner received me with professional affability. I was not his publisher now, I was his patient. With a wide gesture he had me sit opposite him, at his desk, like a government clerk called on the carpet. "Et alors?" He said this, and gave his rotating chair a push, turning his back to me. He sat with his head bowed and hands clasped. There was nothing left but for me to speak.

I spoke, and it was like a dam bursting; everything came out, from beginning to end: what I thought two years ago, what I thought last year, what I thought Belbo had thought, and Diotallevi. Above all, what had happened on Saint John's Eve.

Wagner did not interrupt once, did not nod or show disapproval. For all the response he made, he could have been fast asleep. But that must have been his technique. I talked and talked. The therapy of the word.

Then I waited for the word, his word, that would save me.

Wagner stood up very, very slowly. Without turning to me, he came around his desk and went to the window. He looked out, his hands folded behind his back, absorbed in thought.

In silence, for ten, fifteen minutes.

Then, still with his back to me, in a colorless voice, calm, reassuring: "Monsieur, vous êtes fou."

He did not move, and neither did I. After another five minutes, I realized that he wasn't going to add anything. That was it. End of session.

I left without saying good-bye. The secretary gave me a bright smile, and I found myself once more in Avenue Elisée-Reclus.

It was eleven. I picked up my things at the hotel and rushed to the airport. I had to wait two hours. In the meantime, I called Garamond Press, collect, because I didn't have a cent left. Gudrun answered. She seemed more obtuse than usual, I had to shout three times for her to say Sì, oui, yes, that she would accept the call.

She was crying: Diotallevi had died Saturday night at midnight.

"And nobody, not one of his friends was at the funeral this morning. The shame of it! Not even Signor Garamond! They say he's out of the country. There was only me, Grazia, Luciano, and a gentleman all in black, with a beard, side curls, and a big hat: he looked like an undertaker. God knows where he came from. But where were you, Casaubon? And where was Belbo? What's going on?"

I muttered something in the way of an explanation and hung up. My flight was called, and I boarded the plane.

YESOD

118

> The conspiracy theory of society . . . comes from abandoning God
> and then asking: "Who is in his place?"
> —Karl Popper, *Conjectures and Refutations*, London,
>   Routledge, 1969, iv, p. 123

The flight did me good. I not only left Paris behind, I left the underground, the ground itself, the terrestrial crust. Sky and mountains still white with snow. Solitude at ten thousand meters, and that sense of intoxication always produced by flying, the pressurization, the passage through slight turbulence. It was only up here, I thought, that I was finally putting my feet on solid ground. Time to draw conclusions, to list points in my notebook, then close my eyes and think.

I decided to list, first of all, the incontestable facts.

There is no doubt that Diotallevi is dead. Gudrun told me so. Gudrun was never part of our story—she wouldn't have understood it—so she is the only one left who tells the truth. Also, Garamond is not in Milan. He could be anywhere, of course, but the fact that he's not there and hasn't been there the past few days suggests he was indeed in Paris, where I saw him.

Similarly, Belbo is not there.

Now, let's assume that what I saw Saturday night in Saint-Martin-des-Champs really happened. Perhaps not the way I saw it, befuddled as I was by the music and the incense; but something did happen. It's like that time with Amparo. Afterward, she didn't believe she had been possessed by Pomba Gira, but she knew that in the tenda de umbanda something had possessed her.

Finally, what Lia told me in the mountains is true. Her interpretation is completely convincing: the Provins message is a laundry list. There were never any Templars' meetings at the Grange-aux-Dîmes. There was no Plan and there was no message.

The laundry list, for us, had been a crossword puzzle with the squares empty and no definitions. The squares had to be filled in such a way that everything would fit. But perhaps that metaphor isn't precise. In a crossword puzzle the words, intersecting, have to have letters in common. In our game we crossed not words but concepts, events, so the rules were different. Basically there were three rules.

Rule One: Concepts are connected by analogy. There is no way to decide at once whether an analogy is good or bad, because to some degree everything is connected to everything else. For example, potato crosses with apple, because both are vegetable and round in shape. From apple to snake, by Biblical association. From snake to doughnut, by formal likeness. From doughnut to life preserver, and from life preserver to bathing suit, then bathing to sea, sea to ship, ship to shit, shit to toilet paper, toilet to cologne, cologne to alcohol, alcohol to drugs, drugs to syringe, syringe to hole, hole to ground, ground to potato.

Rule Two says that if *tout se tient* in the end, the connecting works. From potato to potato, *tout se tient*. So it's right.

Rule Three: The connections must not be original. They must have been made before, and the more often the better, by others. Only then do the crossings seem true, because they are obvious.

This, after all, was Signor Garamond's idea. The books of the Diabolicals must not innovate; they must repeat what has already been said. Otherwise what becomes of the authority of Tradition?

And this is what we did. We didn't invent anything; we only arranged the pieces. Colonel Ardenti hadn't invented anything either, but his arrangement of the pieces was clumsy. Furthermore, he was much less educated than we, so he had fewer pieces.

They had all the pieces, but They didn't know the design of the crossword. We—once again—were smarter.

I remembered something Lia said to me in the mountains, when she was scolding me for having played the nasty game that was our Plan: "People are starved for plans. If you offer them one, they fall on it like a pack of wolves. You invent, and they'll believe. It's wrong to add to the inventings that already exist."

This is what always happens. A young Herostratus broods because he doesn't know how to become famous. Then he sees a movie in which a frail young man shoots a country music star and becomes the center of attention. Herostratus has found the formula; he goes out and shoots John Lennon.

It's the same with the SFAs. How can I become a published poet whose name appears in an encyclopedia? Garamond explains: It's simple, you pay. The SFA never thought of that before, but since the Manutius plan exists, he identifies with it, is convinced he's been waiting for Manutius all his life; he just didn't know it was there.

We invented a nonexistent Plan, and They not only believed it was real but convinced themselves that They had been part of it for ages, or, rather, They identified the fragments of their muddled mythology as moments of our Plan, moments joined in a logical, irrefutable web of analogy, semblance, suspicion.

But if you invent a plan and others carry it out, it's as if the Plan exists. At that point it does exist.

Hereafter, hordes of Diabolicals will swarm through the world in search of the map.

We offered a map to people who were trying to overcome a deep, private frustration. What frustration? Belbo's last file suggested it to me: There can be no failure if there really is a Plan. Defeated you may be, but never through any fault of your own. To bow to a cosmic will is no shame. You are not a coward; you are a martyr.

You don't complain about being mortal, prey to a thousand microorganisms you can't control; you aren't responsible for the fact that your feet are not very prehensile, that you have no tail, that your hair and teeth don't grow back when you lose them, that your arteries harden with time. It's because of the Envious Angels.

The same applies to everyday life. Take stock-market crashes. They happen because each individual makes a wrong move, and all the wrong moves put together create panic. Then whoever lacks steady nerves asks himself: Who's behind this plot, who's benefiting? He has to find an enemy, a plotter, or it will be, God forbid, his fault.

If you feel guilty, you invent a plot, many plots. And to counter them, you have to organize your own plot. But the more you invent enemy plots, to exonerate your lack of understanding, the more you fall in love with them, and you pattern your own on their model. Which is what happened when Jesuits and Baconians, Paulicians and neo-Templars each complained of the other's plan. Diotallevi's remark was: "Of course, you attribute to the others what you're doing

619

yourself, and since what you're doing yourself is hateful, the others become hateful. But since the others, as a rule, would like to do the same hateful thing that you're doing, they collaborate with you, hinting that—yes—what you attribute to them is actually what they have always desired. God blinds those He wishes to destroy; you just have to lend Him a helping hand."

A plot, if there is to be one, must be a secret. A secret that, if we only knew it, would dispel our frustration, lead us to salvation; or else the knowing of it in itself would be salvation. Does such a luminous secret exist?

Yes, provided it is never known. Known, it will only disappoint us. Hadn't Agliè spoken of the yearning for mystery that stirred the age of the Antonines? Yet someone had just arrived and declared himself the Son of God, the Son of God made flesh, to redeem the sins of the world. Was that a run-of-the-mill mystery? And he promised salvation to all: you only had to love your neighbor. Was that a trivial secret? And he bequeathed the idea that whoever uttered the right words at the right time could turn a chunk of bread and a half-glass of wine into the body and blood of the Son of God, and be nourished by it. Was that a paltry riddle? And then he led the Church fathers to ponder and proclaim that God was One and Triune and that the Spirit proceeded from the Father and the Son, but that the Son did not proceed from the Father and the Spirit. Was that some easy formula for hylics? And yet they, who now had salvation within their grasp—do-it-yourself salvation—turned deaf ears. Is that all there is to it? How trite. And they kept on scouring the Mediterranean in their boats, looking for a lost knowledge, of which those thirty-denarii dogmas were but the superficial veil, the parable for the poor in spirit, the allusive hieroglyph, the wink of the eye at the pneumatics. The mystery of the Trinity? Too simple: there had to be more to it.

Someone—Rubinstein, maybe—once said, when asked if he believed in God: "Oh, no, I believe . . . in something much bigger." And someone else—was it Chesterton?—said that when men stop believing in God, it isn't that they then believe in nothing: they believe in everything.

But everything is not a bigger secret. There are no "bigger secrets," because the moment a secret is revealed, it seems little. There is only an empty secret. A secret that keeps slipping through your fingers. The secret of the orchid is that it signifies and affects the testicles. But the testicles signify a sign of the zodiac, which in turn signifies an angelic hierarchy, which then signifies a musical scale, and the scale signifies a relationship among the humors. And so on. Initiation is learning never to stop. The universe is peeled like an onion, and an onion is all peel. Let us imagine an infinite onion, which has its center everywhere and its circumference nowhere. Initiation travels an endless Möbius strip.

The true initiate is he who knows that the most powerful secret is a secret without content, because no enemy will be able to make him confess it, no rival devotee will be able to take it from him.

Now I found more logical and consequential the dynamic of that nocturnal rite before the Pendulum. Belbo had claimed to possess a secret, and because of this he had gained power over Them. Their first impulse, even in a man as clever as Agliè, who had immediately beat the tom-tom to summon all the others, had been to wrest it from him. And the more Belbo refused to reveal it, the bigger They believed the secret to be; the more he vowed he didn't possess it, the more convinced They were that he did possess it, and that it was a true secret, because if it were false, he would have revealed it.

Through the centuries the search for this secret had been the glue holding Them all together, despite excommunications, internecine fighting, coups de main. Now They were on the verge of knowing it. But They were assailed by two fears: that the secret would be a disappointment, and that once it was known to all, there would be no secret left. Which would be the end of Them.

Agliè then thought: If Belbo spoke, all would know, and he, Agliè, would lose the mysterious aura that granted him charisma and power. But if Belbo confided in him alone, Agliè could go on being Saint-Germain, the immortal. The deferment of Agliè's death coincided with the deferment of the secret. He tried to persuade Belbo to whisper it in his ear, and when he realized that wouldn't be possible, he provoked him by predicting his surrender and, further, by putting on a display of pompous melodrama. Oh, the old count knew very well that for people from Piedmont stubbornness and a sense of the ridiculous could defeat even the fear of death. Thus he forced Belbo to raise the tone of his refusal and to say no definitively.

The others, out of the same fear, preferred to kill him. They might be losing the map—they would have centuries to continue the search for it—but they were preserving the vigor of their base, slobbering desire.

I remembered a story Amparo told me. Before coming to Italy, she had spent some months in New York City, living in a neighborhood of the kind where even on quiet days you could shoot a TV series featuring the homicide squad. She used to come home alone at two in the morning. When I asked if she wasn't afraid of sexual maniacs, she told me her method. When a sexual maniac approached, threatening, she would take his arm and say, "Come on, let's do it." And he would go away, bewildered.

If you're a sexual maniac, you don't want sex; you want the excitement of its theft, you want the victim's resistance and despair. If sex is handed to you on a platter, here it is, go to it, naturally you're not interested, otherwise what sort of sexual maniac would you be?

We had awakened their lust, offering them a secret that couldn't have been emptier, because not only did we not know it ourselves, but, even better, we knew that it was false.

The plane was flying over Mont Blanc, and the passengers all rushed to the same side so as not to miss the view of that blunt bubo that had grown there thanks to a fluke in the telluric currents. If what I was thinking was correct, then the currents didn't exist any more than the Provins message existed. But the story of the deciphering of the Plan, as we had reconstructed it, that was History.

My memory went back to Belbo's last file. But if existence is so empty and fragile that it can be endured only by the illusion of a search for its secret, then—as Amparo said that evening in the tenda, after her defeat—there's no redemption; we are all slaves, give us a master, that's what we deserve. . . .

No. Lia taught me there is more, and I have the proof: his name is Giulio, and at this moment he is playing in a valley, pulling a goat's tail. No, because Belbo twice said no.

The first no he said to Abulafia, and to those who would try to steal its secret. "Do you have the password?" was the question. And the answer, the key to knowledge, was "No." Not only does the magic word not exist, but we do not know that it does not exist. Those who admit their ignorance, therefore, can learn something, at least what I was able to learn.

The second no he said on Saturday night, when he refused the salvation held out to him. He could have invented a map, or used one of the maps I had shown him. In any event, with the Pendulum hung as it was, incorrectly, that bunch of lunatics would never have found the X marking the Umbilicus Mundi, and even if they did, it would have been several more decades before they realized this wasn't the one. But Belbo refused to bow, he preferred to die.

It wasn't that he refused to bow to the lust for power; he refused to bow to nonmeaning. He somehow knew that, fragile as our existence may be, however ineffectual our interrogation of the world, there is nevertheless something that has more meaning than the rest.

What had Belbo sensed, perhaps only at that moment, which allowed him to contradict his last, desperate file, and not surrender his destiny to someone who guaranteed him a mere Plan? What had he understood—at last—that allowed him to sacrifice his life, as if he had learned everything there was to learn without realizing it, and as if compared to this one, true, absolute secret of his, everything that took place in the Conservatoire was irreparably stupid— and it was stupid, now, stubbornly to go on living?

There was still something, a link missing in the chain. I had all of Belbo's feats before me now, from life to death, except one.

On arrival, as I was looking for my passport, I found in one of my pockets the key to this house. I had taken it last Thursday, along with the key to Belbo's apartment. I remembered that day when Belbo showed us the old cupboard that contained, he said, his opera omnia or, rather, his juvenilia. Perhaps Belbo had written something there that couldn't be found in Abulafia, perhaps it was buried somewhere in ***.

There was nothing reasonable about this conjecture of mine. All the more reason to consider it good. At this point.

I collected my car, and I came here.

I didn't find the old relative of the Canepas, the caretaker, or whatever she was. Maybe she, too, had died in the meantime. There was no one. I went through the various rooms. A strong smell of mildew. I considered lighting the bedwarmer in one of the bedrooms, but it made no sense to warm the bed in June. Once the windows were opened, the warm evening air would enter.

After sunset, there was no moon. As in Paris, Saturday night. The moon rose late, I saw less of it now than in Paris, as it slowly climbed above the lower hills, in a dip between the Bricco and another yellowish hump, perhaps already harvested.

I arrived around six in the evening. It was still light. But I had brought nothing with me to eat. Roaming the house, I found a salami in the kitchen, hanging from a beam. My supper was salami and fresh water: going on ten o'clock, I think. Now I'm thirsty. I've brought a big pitcher of water to Uncle Carlo's study and drink a glass every ten minutes. Then I go down, refill the pitcher, and start again.

It must be at least three in the morning. I have the light off and can hardly read my watch. I look out the window. On the flanks of the hills, what seem to be fireflies, shooting stars: the headlights of occasional cars going down into the valley or climbing toward the villages on the hilltops. When Belbo was a boy, this sight did not exist. There were no cars then, no roads. At night there was the curfew.

As soon as I arrived, I opened the cupboard of juvenilia. Shelves and shelves of paper, from elementary-school exercises to bundles of adolescent poems and prose. Everyone has written poems in adolescence; true poets destroy them, bad poets publish them. Belbo, too cynical to save them, too weak to chuck them out, stuck them in Uncle Carlo's cupboard.

I read for hours. And for hours, up to this moment, I meditated on the last text, which I found just when I was about to give up.

I don't know when Belbo wrote it. There are pages where different handwritings, insertions, are interwoven, or else it's the same hand in different years. As if he wrote it very early, at the age of sixteen or seventeen, then put it away, then went back to it at twenty, again at thirty, and maybe later. Until he gave up the idea of writing altogether—only to begin again with Abulafia, but not having the heart to recover these lines and subject them to electronic humiliation.

Reading them, I followed a familiar story: the events of *** between 1943 and 1945, Uncle Carlo, the partisans, the parish hall, Cecilia, the trumpet. These were the obsessive themes of the romantic Belbo, disappointed, grieving, drunk. The literature of memory: he knew himself that it was the last refuge of scoundrels.

But I'm no literary critic. I'm Sam Spade again, looking for the final clue.

And so I found the Key Text. It must represent the last chapter of the story of Belbo in ***. For, after it, nothing more could have happened.

119

The garland of the trumpet was set afire, and then I saw the aperture of the dome open and a splendid arrow of fire shoot down through the tube of the trumpet and enter the lifeless body. The aperture then was closed again, and the trumpet, too, was put away.
—Johann Valentin Andreae, *Die Chymische Hochzeit des Christian Rosencreutz*, Strassburg, Zetzner, 1616, pp. 125–126

Belbo's text has some gaps, some overlappings, some lines crossed out. I am not so much rereading it as reconstructing, reliving it.

It must have been toward the end of April of 1945. The German armies were already routed, the Fascists were scattering, and *** was firmly in the hands of the partisans.

After the last battle, the one Belbo narrated to us in this very house almost two years ago, various partisan brigades gathered in ***, in order to head for the city. They were awaiting a signal from Radio London; they would depart when Milan was ready for the insurrection.

The Garibaldi Brigades also arrived, commanded by Ras, a giant with a black beard, very popular in the town. They were dressed in invented uniforms, each one different except for the kerchiefs and the star on the chest, red in both cases, and they were armed in makeshift fashion, some with old shotguns, some with submachine guns taken from the enemy. A marked contrast to the Badoglio Brigades, with their blue kerchiefs, khaki uniforms similar to the British, and brand-new Sten guns. The Allies assisted the Badoglio forces with generous nighttime parachute drops, after the passage, every evening at eleven for the past two years, of the mysterious Pippetto, a British reconnaissance plane. Nobody could figure out what it reconnoitered, since not a light was visible on the ground for kilometers and kilometers.

There was tension between the Garibaldini and the Badogliani. It was said that on the evening of the battle the Badogliani had flung themselves at the enemy, shouting "Forward, Savoy!" Well, but that was out of habit, some said. What else could you shout when you attacked? It didn't necessarily mean they were monarchists; they, too, knew that the king had grave things to answer for. The Garibaldini sneered: You could cry Savoy if you attacked with fixed bayonets in the open field, but not darting around a corner with a Sten. The fact was, the Badogliani had sold out to the British.

The two forces arrived, nevertheless, at a modus vivendi; a joint command under one head was needed for the assault on the city. The choice fell on Mongo; he led the best-equipped brigade, was the oldest, had fought in the First World War, was a hero, and enjoyed the trust of the Allied command.

In the days that followed, sometime before the Milan insurrection, I believe, they set out to take the city. Good news arrived: the operation had succeeded, the brigades were returning victorious to ***. There had been some casualties, however. Rumor had it that Ras had fallen in battle, and Mongo was wounded.

Then one afternoon the sound of vehicles was heard, songs of victory, and people rushed into the main square. From the highway the first units were arriving, clenched fists upraised, flags and weapons brandished from the windows of the cars and the running boards of the trucks. The men had already been strewn with flowers along the way.

Suddenly some people shouted, "Ras, Ras!" and Ras was there, seated on the front fender of a Dodge, his beard tangled and his sweaty, black, hairy chest visible through his open shirt. He waved to the crowd, laughing.

Beside Ras, Rampini also climbed down from the Dodge. He was a nearsighted boy who played in the band, a little older than the others; he had disappeared three months earlier, and it was said he'd joined the partisans. And there he was, with a red kerchief around his neck, a khaki tunic, a pair of blue trousers—the uniform of Don Tico's band—but now he had a big belt with a holster and a pistol. Through the thick eyeglasses that had earned him so much teasing from his old companions at the parish hall, he now looked at the girls who crowded around him, as if he were Flash Gordon. Jacopo asked himself if Cecilia was there, among the people.

In half an hour the whole square was full of colorful partisans, and the people called in loud voices for Mongo; they wanted a speech. On a balcony of the town hall, Mongo appeared, leaning on his crutch, pale, and with one hand he tried to calm the crowd. Jacopo waited for the speech, because his whole childhood, like that of others his age, had been marked by the great historic speeches of il Duce, whose most significant passages were memorized in school. Actually, the students memorized whole speeches, because every sentence was a significant declaration.

Silence. Mongo spoke in a hoarse voice, barely audible. He said: "Citizens, friends. After so many painful sacrifices . . . here we are. Glory to those who have fallen for freedom."

And that was it. He went back inside.

The crowd yelled, and the partisans raised their submachine guns, their Stens, their shotguns, their '91s, and fired festive volleys. With shell cases falling on all sides, the kids slipped between the legs of the armed men and civilians, because they'd never be able to add to their collections like this again, not with the war looking like it would end in a month, worst luck.

But there had been some casualties: two men killed. By a grim coincidence, both were from San Davide, a little village above ***, and the families asked permission to bury the victims in the local cemetery.

The partisan command decided that there should be a solemn funeral: companies in formation, decorated hearses, the village band, the provost of the cathedral—and the parish hall band.

Don Tico accepted immediately. Because, he said, he had always harbored anti-Fascist sentiments. And because, as the musicians murmured, for a year he had been making them practice two funeral marches, and he had to have them performed sooner or later. Also because, the sharp tongues of the village said, he wanted to make up for "Giovinezza."

The "Giovinezza" story went like this:

Months earlier, before the arrival of the partisans, Don Tico's band had gone out for some saint's feast or other, and they were stopped by the Black Brigades. "Play 'Giovinezza,' Reverend," the captain ordered, drumming his fingers on the barrel of his submachine gun. What could Don Tico do? He said, "Boys, let's try it; you only have one skin." He beat time with his pitch pipe, and horrible clattering cacophony drifted over ***. Only someone desperate to save his skin would have agreed that the sounds heard were "Giovinezza." Shameful for everyone. Shameful for having consented, Don Tico said afterward, but even more shameful for having played like dogs. Priest he was, and anti-Fascist, but, above all, damn it, he was an artist.

Jacopo had been absent on that day. He had tonsillitis. On the bombardons there were only Annibale Cantalamessa and Pio Bo, and their presence, without Jacopo, must have made a crucial contribution to the collapse of Nazism-Fascism. But this was not what troubled Belbo, at least at the time he was writing. He had missed another opportunity to find out if he would have had the courage to say no. Perhaps that is why he died on the gallows of the Pendulum.

The funeral, anyway, was scheduled for Sunday morning. In the cathedral square everyone was present: Mongo with his troops, Uncle Carlo and other municipal dignitaries, with their Great War decorations—and it didn't matter who had been a Fascist and who had not, it was a question of honoring heroes. The clergy were there, the town band in dark suits, and the hearses with the horses decked in trappings of cream, black, and gold. The Automedon was dressed like one of Napoleon's marshals, cocked hat, short cape, and great cloak, in the same colors as the horses' trappings. And there was the parish hall band, their visored caps, khaki tunics, and blue trousers, brasses shining, woodwinds severe black, cymbals and drums sparkling.

Between *** and San Davide were five or six kilometers of uphill curves. This road was taken, on Sunday afternoons, by the retired men; they would walk, playing bowls as they walked, take a rest, have some wine, play a second game, and so on until they reached the sanctuary at the top.

A few uphill kilometers are nothing for men who play bowls, and perhaps it's nothing to cover them in formation, rifle on your shoulder, eyes staring straight ahead, lungs inhaling the cool spring air. But try climbing them while playing an instrument, cheeks swollen, sweat trickling, breath short. The town band had done nothing else for a lifetime, but for the boys of the parish hall it was torture. They held out like heroes. Don Tico beat his pitch pipe in the air, the clarinets whined with exhaustion, the saxophones gave strangled bleats, the bombardons and the trumpets let out squeals of agony, but they made it, all the way to the village, to the foot of the steep path that led to the cemetery. For some time Annibale Cantalamessa and Pio Bo had only pretended to play, but Jacopo stuck to his role of sheepdog, under Don Tico's benedictive eye. Compared to the town band, they made not a bad showing, and Mongo himself and the other brigade commanders said as much: Good for you, boys. It was magnificent.

A commander with a blue kerchief and a rainbow of ribbons from both world wars said: "Reverend, let the boys rest here in the town; they're worn out. Climb up later, at the end. There'll be a truck to take you back to ***."

They rushed to the tavern. The men of the town band, veterans toughened by countless funerals, showed no restraint in grabbing the tables and ordering tripe and all the wine they could drink. They would stay there having a spree until evening. Don Tico's boys, meanwhile, crowded at the counter, where the host was serving mint ices as green as a chemistry experiment. The ice, sliding down the throat, gave you a pain in the middle of your forehead, like sinusitis.

Then they struggled up to the cemetery, where a pickup truck was waiting. They climbed in, yelling, and were all packed together, all standing, jostling one another with the instruments, when the commander who had spoken before came out and said: "Reverend, for the final ceremony we need a trumpet. You know, for the usual bugle calls. It's a matter of five minutes."

"Trumpet," Don Tico said, very professional. And the hapless holder of that title, now sticky with green mint ice and yearning for the family meal, a treacherous peasant insensitive to aesthetic impulses and higher ideals, began to complain: It was late, he wanted to go home, he didn't have any saliva left, and so on, mortifying Don Tico in the presence of the commander.

Then Jacopo, seeing in the glory of noon the sweet image of Cecilia, said: "If he'll give me the trumpet, I'll go."

A gleam of gratitude in the eyes of Don Tico; the sweaty relief of the miserable titular trumpet. An exchange of instruments, like two guards.

Jacopo proceeded to the cemetery, led by the psychopomp with the Addis Ababa ribbons. Everything around them was white: the wall struck by the sun, the graves, the blossoming trees along the borders, the surplice of the provost ready to impart benediction. The only brown was the faded photographs on the tombstones. And a big patch of color was created by the ranks lined up beside the two graves.

"Boy," the commander said, "you stand here, beside me, and at my order play Assembly. Then, again at my order, Taps. That's easy, isn't it?"

Very easy. Except that Jacopo had never played Assembly or Taps.

He held the trumpet with his right arm bent, against his ribs, the horn at a slight angle, as if it were a carbine, and he waited, head erect, belly in, chest out.

Mongo was delivering a brief speech, with very short sentences. Jacopo thought that to emit the blast he would have to lift his eyes to heaven, and the sun would blind him. But that was the trumpeter's death, and since you only died once, you might as well do it right.

The commander murmured to him: "Now." He ordered Assembly. Jacopo played only do mi sol do. For those rough men of war, that seemed to suffice. The final do was played after a deep breath, so he could hold it, give it time—Belbo wrote—to reach the sun.

The partisans stood stiffly at attention. The living as still as the dead.

Only the gravediggers moved. The sound of the coffins being lowered could be heard, the creak of the ropes, their scraping against the wood. But there was little motion, no more than the flickering glint on a sphere, when a slight variation of light serves only to emphasize the sphere's invariability.

Then, the dry sound of Present Arms. The provost murmured the formulas of the aspersion; the commanders approached the graves and flung, each of them, a fistful of earth. A sudden order unleashed a volley toward the sky, *rat-tat-tat-a-boom*, and the birds rose up, squawking, from the trees in blossom. But all that, too, was not really motion. It was as if the same instant kept presenting itself from different perspectives. Looking at one instant forever doesn't mean that, as you look at it, time passes.

For this reason, Jacopo stood fast, ignoring even the fall of the shell cases now rolling at his feet; nor did he put his trumpet back at his side, but kept it to his lips, fingers on the valves, rigid at attention, the instrument aimed diagonally upward. He played on.

His long final note had never broken off: inaudible to those present, it still issued from the bell of the trumpet, like a light breath, a gust of air that he kept sending into the mouthpiece, holding his tongue between barely parted lips, without pressing them to the metal. The instrument, not resting on his face, remained suspended by the tension alone in his elbows and shoulders.

He continued holding that virtual note, because he felt he was playing out a string that kept the sun in place. The planet had been arrested in its course, had become fixed in a noon that could last an eternity. And it all depended on Jacopo, because if he broke that contact, dropped that string, the sun would fly off like a balloon, and with it this day and the event of this day, this action without transition, this sequence without before and after, which was unfolding, motionless, only because it was in his power to will it thus.

If he stopped, stopped to attack a new note, a rent would have been heard, far louder than the volleys that had deafened him, and the clocks would all resume their tachycardial palpitation.

Jacopo wished with his whole soul that this man beside him would not order Taps. I could refuse, he said to himself, and stay like this forever.

He had entered that trance state that overwhelms the diver when he tries not to surface, wanting to prolong the inertia that allows him to glide along the ocean floor. Trying to express what he felt then, Belbo, in the notebook I was now reading, resorted to broken, twisted, unsyntactical sentences, mutilated by rows of dots. But it was clear to me that in that moment—though he didn't come out and say it—in that moment he was possessing Cecilia.

The fact is that Jacopo Belbo did not understand, not then and not later, when he was writing of his unconscious self, that at that moment he was celebrating once and for all his chemical wedding—with Cecilia, with Lorenza, with Sophia, with the earth and with the sky. Alone among mortals, he was bringing to a conclusion the Great Work.

No one had yet told him that the Grail is a chalice but also a spear, and his trumpet raised like a chalice was at the same time a weapon, an instrument of the sweetest dominion, which shot toward the sky and linked the earth with the Mystic Pole. With the only Fixed Point in the universe. With what he created, for that one instant, with his breath.

Diotallevi had not yet told him how you can dwell in Yesod, the Sefirah of foundation, the sign of the superior bow drawn to send arrows to Malkhut, its target. Yesod is the drop that springs from the arrow to produce the tree and the fruit, it is the anima mundi, the moment in which virile force, procreating, binds all the states of being together.

Knowing how to spin this Cingulum Veneris means knowing how to repair the error of the Demiurge.

You spend a life seeking the Opportunity, without realizing that the decisive moment, the moment that justifies birth and death, has already passed. It will not return, but it was—full, dazzling, generous as every revelation.

That day, Jacopo Belbo stared into the eyes of Truth. The only truth that was to be granted him. Because—he would learn—truth is brief (afterward, it is all commentary). So he tried to arrest the rush of time.

He didn't understand. Not as a child. Not as an adolescent when he was writing about it. Not as a man who decided to give up writing about it.

I understood it this evening: the author has to die in order for the reader to become aware of his truth.

The Pendulum, which haunted Jacopo Belbo all his adult life, had been—like the lost addresses of his dream—the symbol of that other moment, recorded and then repressed, when he truly touched the ceiling of the world. But that moment, in which he froze space and time, shooting his Zeno's arrow, had been no symbol, no sign, symptom, allusion, metaphor, or enigma: it was what it was. It did not stand for anything else. At that moment there was no longer any deferment, and the score was settled.

Jacopo Belbo didn't understand that he had had his moment and that it would have to be enough for him, for all his life. Not recognizing it, he spent the rest of his days seeking something else, until he damned himself. But perhaps he suspected this. Otherwise he wouldn't have returned so often to the memory of the trumpet. But he remembered it as a thing lost, not as a thing possessed.

I believe, I hope, I pray that as he was dying, swaying with the Pendulum, Jacopo Belbo finally understood this, and found peace.

Then Taps was ordered. But Jacopo would have stopped in any case, because his breath was failing. He broke the contact, then blared a single note, high, with a decrescendo, tenderly, to prepare the world for the melancholy that lay in store.

The commander said, "Bravo, young fellow. Run along now. Handsome trumpet."

The provost slipped away, the partisans made for a rear gateway where their vehicles awaited them, the gravediggers went off after filling the graves. Jacopo was the last to go. He couldn't bring himself to leave that place of happiness.

In the yard below, the pickup truck of the parish hall was gone.

Jacopo asked himself why Don Tico had abandoned him like this. From a distance in time, the most probable answer is that there had been a misunderstanding; someone had told Don Tico that the partisans would bring the boy back down. But Jacopo at that moment thought—and not without reason—that between Assembly and Taps too many centuries had passed. The boys had waited until their hair turned white, until death, until their dust scattered to form the haze that now was turning the expanse of hills blue before his eyes.

He was alone. Behind him, an empty cemetery. In his hands, the trumpet. Before him, the hills fading, bluer and bluer, one behind the other, into an infinity of humps. And, vindictive, over his head, the liberated sun.

He decided to cry.

But suddenly the hearse appeared, with its Automedon decorated like a general of the emperor, all cream and silver and black, the horses decked with barbaric masks that left only their eyes visible, caparisoned like coffins, the little twisted columns that supported the Assyro-Greco-Egyptian tympanum all white and gold. The man with the cocked hat stopped a moment by the solitary trumpeter, and Jacopo asked: "Will you take me home?"

The man smiled. Jacopo climbed up beside him on the box, and so it was on a hearse that he began his return to the world of the living. That off-duty Charon, taciturn, urged his funereal chargers down the slopes, as Jacopo sat erect and hieratic, the trumpet clutched under his arm, his visor shining, absorbed in his new, unhoped-for role.

They descended, and at every curve a new view opened up, of vines blue with verdigris in dazzling light, and after an incalculable time they arrived in ***. They crossed the big square, all arcades, deserted as only Monferrato squares can be deserted at two o'clock on a Sunday afternoon. A schoolmate at the corner saw Jacopo on the hearse, the trumpet under his arm, eyes fixed on infinity, and gave him an admiring wave.

Jacopo went home, wouldn't eat anything, wouldn't tell anything. He huddled on the terrace and began playing the trumpet as if it had a mute, blowing softly so as not to disturb the silence of the siesta.

His father joined him and, guilelessly, with the serenity of one who knows the laws of life, said: "In a month, if all goes as it should, we'll be going home. You can't play the trumpet in the city. Our landlord would evict us. So you'll have to forget that. If you really like music, we'll have you take piano lessons." And then, seeing the boy with moist eyes, he added: "Come now, silly. Don't you realize the bad days are over?"

The next day, Jacopo returned the trumpet to Don Tico. Two weeks later, the family left ***, to rejoin the future.

MALKHUT

I20

I should be at peace. I have understood. Don't some say that peace
comes when you understand? I have understood. I should be at
peace. Who said that peace derives from the contemplation of order,
order understood, enjoyed, realized without residuum, in joy and
triumph, the end of effort? All is clear, limpid; the eye rests on the
whole and on the parts and sees how the parts have conspired to
make the whole; it perceives the center where the lymph flows, the
breath, the root of the whys. . . .

I should be at peace. From the window of Uncle Carlo's study I
look at the hill, and the little slice of rising moon. The Bricco's
broad hump, the more tempered ridges of the hills in the background tell the story of the slow and drowsy stirrings of Mother
Earth, who stretches and yawns, making and unmaking blue plains
in the dread flash of a hundred volcanoes. The Earth turned in her
sleep and traded one surface for another. Where ammonoids once
fed, diamonds. Where diamonds once grew, vineyards. The logic of
the moraine, of the landslip, of the avalanche. Dislodge one pebble,
by chance, it becomes restless, rolls down, in its descent leaves space
(ah, horror vacui!), another pebble falls on top of it, and there's

height. Surfaces. Surfaces upon surfaces. The wisdom of the Earth. And of Lia.

Why doesn't understanding give me peace? Why love Fate if Fate kills you just as dead as Providence or the Plot of the Archons? Perhaps I haven't understood, after all; perhaps I am missing one piece of the puzzle, one space.

Where have I read that at the end, when life, surface upon surface, has become completely encrusted with experience, you know everything, the secret, the power, and the glory, why you were born, why you are dying, and how it all could have been different? You are wise. But the greatest wisdom, at that moment, is knowing that your wisdom is too late. You understand everything when there is no longer anything to understand.

Now I know what the Law of the Kingdom is, of poor, desperate, tattered Malkhut, where Wisdom has gone into exile, groping to recover its former lucidity. The truth of Malkhut, the only truth that shines in the night of the Sefirot, is that Wisdom is revealed naked in Malkhut, and its mystery lies not in existence but in the leaving of existence. Afterward, the Others begin again.

And, with the others, the Diabolicals, seeking abysses where the secret of their madness lies hidden.

Along the Bricco's slopes are rows and rows of vines. I know them, I have seen similar rows in my day. No doctrine of numbers can say if they are in ascending or descending order. In the midst of the rows—but you have to walk barefoot, with your heels callused, from childhood—there are peach trees. Yellow peaches that grow only between rows of vines. You can split a peach with the pressure of your thumb; the pit comes out almost whole, as clean as if it had been chemically treated, except for an occasional bit of pulp, white, tiny, clinging there like a worm. When you eat the peach, the velvet of the skin makes shudders run from your tongue to your groin. Dinosaurs once grazed here. Then another surface covered theirs. And yet, like Belbo when he played the trumpet, when I bit into the peach I understood the Kingdom and was one with it. The rest is only cleverness. Invent; invent the Plan, Casaubon. That's what everyone has done, to explain the dinosaurs and the peaches.

I have understood. And the certainty that there is nothing to understand should be my peace, my triumph. But I am here, and They are looking for me, thinking I possess the revelation They sordidly desire. It isn't enough to have understood, if others refuse and continue to interrogate. They are looking for me, They must have picked up my trail in Paris, They know I am here now, They still want the Map. And when I tell Them that there is no Map, They will want it all the more. Belbo was right. Fuck you, fool! You want to kill me? Kill me, then, but I won't tell you there's no Map. If you can't figure it out for yourself, tough shit.

It hurts me to think I won't see Lia again, and the baby, the Thing, Giulio, my philosopher's stone. But stones survive on their own. Maybe even now he is experiencing his Opportunity. He's found a ball, an ant, a blade of grass, and in it he sees paradise and the abyss. He, too, will know it too late. He will be good; never mind, let him spend his day like this, alone.

Damn. It hurts all the same. Patience. When I'm dead, it won't hurt.

It's very late. I left Paris this morning, I left too many clues. They've had time to guess where I am. In a little while, They'll be here. I would have liked to write down everything I thought today. But if They were to read it, They would only derive another dark theory and spend another eternity trying to decipher the secret message hidden behind my words. It's impossible, They would say; he can't only have been making fun of us. No. Perhaps, without his realizing it, Being was sending us a message through its oblivion.

It makes no difference whether I write or not. They will look for other meanings, even in my silence. That's how They are. Blind to revelation. Malkhut is Malkhut, and that's that.

But try telling Them. They of little faith.

So I might as well stay here, wait, and look at the hill.

It's so beautiful.

www.randomhouse.co.uk/vintage